A LOVE WINDS ACROSS TIME . . .

Out of the greatest of passions, the magnificent union of Leah and Baptiste Fontaine, comes one of the richest romantic legacies of all time. Now Barbara Ferry Johnson weaves her most enthralling tapestry, a story of the men and women who will inherit a world with everything to live for: romance, power, lust, ambition, wealth, fame, glamor, revenge, sorrow, beauty . . . and love.

Together their glittering destinies will stretch across decades and continents, capturing the heart, in a novel of unbounded passion—and unconquerable love!

Other Avon books by
Barbara Ferry Johnson

BARBARA FERRY JOHNSON
THE HEIRS OF LOVE

AVON
PUBLISHERS OF BARD, CAMELOT AND DISCUS BOOKS

THE HEIRS OF LOVE is an original publication of Avon Books. This work has never before appeared in book form.

AVON BOOKS
A division of
The Hearst Corporation
959 Eighth Avenue
New York, New York 10019

First Avon Printing, August, 1980

Printed in the U.S.A.

For
Newell and Elsa
and
Buzz and Audrey

Chapter One

IT WAS A STRANGE COMPULSION, this need to go for a long walk. Not through the château gardens, not in the fields of wildflowers beyond, not even along the mint-scented bank of the river. Those were the places where Leah strolled leisurely every day.

This was an insatiable urge to keep walking with no thought of turning back. Something was stirring inside her that made her want to break into a run, to force herself to the outer limits of her energies, to see how much she could endure without collapsing. She wanted to share with all the elements of nature the awareness that she was as vitally alive as they were.

Leah moved along the well-trodden path beside the river at a fast, steady pace for at least half a mile before she allowed herself to pause and look across the water at the trees bordering the opposite bank. The gray-green cypresses formed a shield against the still-bright setting sun. It would be hot again tomorrow. Resuming her walk, she turned from the river into the woods; through these woods ran the road to St. Denis. All around her, birds were settling in for the night, and the air was alive with their singing.

Like the roses and the larkspur and the lilies in her garden, Leah was in the full bloom of mature womanhood. At eighteen she had been a strikingly beautiful octoroon with a tall, slim figure, a delicate fawn complexion, long black hair, and dark, almond-shaped eyes that glinted with deep purple lights. At twenty-eight she had acquired the haunting beauty of one who had suffered greatly during years of death, war, and privation. By the time she was thirty-two, Leah's face had reflected the ageless beauty that comes with being cherished and loved. Now the fine lines etched into her face by the years of war and the weeks in prison were a little deeper, and there were streaks of gray in her glossy hair. But her body was still as slim and erect as ever, and she glowed with an inner contentment.

1

Yet she was not entirely at peace, and it was to quench a nagging thirst for reassurance that she had left the château and gone in search of an earlier self, the self that once had sailed fearlessly and enthusiastically from all that was familiar in America toward what was strange and unknown in France. More than that, the voyage had been taken with the sure knowledge that having decided to leave, she was foranbidden to return, that she would spend the rest of her life as an exile in France. But she had never regretted the decision. Behind her lay a homeland where she would forever bear the stigma of her heritage; in France she had finally found the acceptance she'd desired for so long.

Having tired at last from the exertion of walking faster than she was accustomed to, Leah sat down to rest beneath a tree. Now that she was at the midpoint of her life, she knew she must try to come to grips with what was disturbing her. No, admit it, she said to herself, I am on the far side of the midpoint. It was time to re-evaluate her situation and sweep away the hazy fear that kept her from seeing the future clearly.

In the past, when she'd been burdened with this heavy, immovable weight in the pit of her stomach, it was always at those times when she'd been challenged by having to make some momentous decision. Now it was not a decision she was facing, but a *fait accompli*. She did not have to make a choice, but had instead to cope with reality. Part of her problem now was the throbbing awareness of her own mortality. Not that there hadn't been moments in the past when she'd been conscious of the inevitability of death, but now that awareness was a more poignant, almost palpable intrusion into her life.

Overshadowing that, however, was an even deeper turmoil she had not wanted to acknowledge, even though it kept her both from dealing with the details of the present and from making plans for the future. She was homesick. She was homesick for Louisiana and the *Vieux Carré* in New Orleans. And there was no rational explanation for it.

Leah had hoped that this long walk through the countryside that had been her home for more than ten years would help. But it hadn't, and she was furious with herself. She knew herself to be a sane, rational person who could usually bring her emotions under control. Instead, she began to cry as she hadn't cried for years. Suddenly she wanted her mother. She couldn't believe it: A grown woman with five children of her own shouldn't be crying for her mother as if

2

she were a child of three. But there it was, and there was no help for it. She would give anything to have Clotilde beside her, advising and comforting her.

Strange, Leah thought. When young, she had resented her mother and their life in the *Vieux Carré*. She had loved Clotilde, but she had not understood or appreciated her until just before her death.

Recalling those horrible weeks in which the yellow fever epidemic had killed her infant son, René, as well as her mother, Leah leaned against the tree and allowed her memory to wander back to her childhood in the *Vieux Carré*. It was there that she had been born and reared in the house owned by her father, Jean-Paul Bonvivier, but visited by him only when he could get away from his legal, white family.

From the time she had known what it meant to be an octoroon, Leah had been inflamed with one desire—to go North, to "pass" as white, and to marry a white man. Technically a free woman of color, she had been reared a slave in the custom of *plaçage*, being the *placée*, or mistress, of a wealthy Creole. Her mother had trained her well for that position. Wasn't Clotilde the *placée* of Jean-Paul? There had been one abortive attempt to go North before Leah had become the *placée* of Baptiste Fontaine, a wealthy sugar planter and cotton broker. Sometimes her smoldering passion to be free of her past had been banked by the contentment she'd felt from being loved by Baptiste. At other times, especially when forced to endure silently the indignities suffered by all free people of color, the flames of that passion had raged almost out of control.

In spite of the growing love she'd felt for Baptiste through long years of joy and sorrow, through the yellow fever epidemic that had taken their son, the desperate years of the Civil War, the Federal occupation of New Orleans, and their struggle to regain Baptiste's plantation, she had always yearned to create a new identity for herself as the wife of a white man. When she met James Andrews, a lawyer from Indiana, she was offered that opportunity. That had been the most difficult decision of her life: whether to remain with Baptiste whom she loved but could never marry, or to go North as wife to James whom she respected but did not love. She had chosen to go North.

Leah would always remember her marriage to James as a time of peaceful contentment if not overwhelming joy. After his untimely death, she had returned to New Orleans and to

3

Baptiste, as she had always known she would. She'd felt then that she would know real happiness only with Baptiste, as his mistress if not as his wife. And eventually, with his decision to open an export office in France, where there were no miscegenation laws, their marriage became possible.

Even before leaving for France, Leah and Baptiste had clearly imagined where and how they wanted to live—not in Paris proper but near enough for Baptiste to drive to his office in the morning and return at night. They would look for a château, set within a domain of several acres alongside a river. Even a small river, Leah had thought, would help to assuage homesickness for the Mississippi.

They'd found exactly the château they wanted, and Leah had gloried in the surrounding gardens and lawns. After spending most of her life in the close confines of the *Vieux Carré*, she suddenly realized how she'd been longing for space. Now that she would be free of the strictures of being a woman of color, she wanted the freedom of space as well.

And so they had lived here for more than ten years, a time when she was happier than she'd ever thought it possible to be. So why this disturbing restlessness? Why this yearning to return to a place that had harbored death from plague and war, impoverishment, the relentless tyranny of the Northern troops during the occupation, and, above all, the humiliation of being an octoroon in a white-dominated world?

The elusive answer finally revealed itself. During those early days in New Orleans, she'd still had an unquenchable youthful optimism. The years in France had still been ahead of her. But what did the future hold for her now?

I won't think about it any more, Leah told herself sternly. *I'll think only of today and live for what I have today. It's more than I ever dreamed of having—and if I'm meant to lose it, so be it.*

With that, she stood up and began walking back to the château. She was finally able to smile as she thought about what was probably taking place there. Under the guidance of Baptiste, the children would be decorating the dining room for her birthday supper. What would be the motif this time? A *fête* with ribbons and streamers, or a garden party with bouquets adorning the table and sideboard? And there certainly would be packages, which would be accompanied by the giggles of the donors, as she opened and exclaimed over them.

Leah tried to remember when the tradition of making

4

something special of her birthday had begun. She thought it had been the first year they were in France, when Baptiste was trying to rescue her from the wave of homesickness that had smitten her when she thought of her birthday celebrations in New Orleans.

She began running along the riverbank. The restlessness and worry had not disappeared completely, but she felt able to force to the back of her mind the pernicious threat that had been haunting her every waking hour. Now, at least she could face her family with a smile. If nothing else, the long walk had shown her she could live with the thought that whatever must come, will come. She was ready to accept whatever the future held, if for no other reason than there was nothing she could do to change or prevent it.

Chapter Two

"WHERE HAVE YOU BEEN, chérie?" Baptiste rolled his comfortably padded, wicker wheelchair nearer the steps that led from the terrace to the garden.

"Just walking," Leah answered, smiling at the concern on his face.

"This late in the day? The children are frantic that you won't have time to open the packages, and Blanchette keeps threatening that the soufflé is about to fall."

"Well, let's go in then." Leah put her hands on the back of the chair and began pushing it toward the double doors. "We certainly mustn't upset Blanchette. Good cooks are too hard to find."

Baptiste reached out to hold the door as Leah maneuvered the chair through it. "Any special reason for the walk?"

"Just a little restless, I think. It was very beautiful along the river, and the wildflowers have taken over the woods."

"Papa," called a boyish voice from the dining room. "Has Mama returned yet?"

"She's here now, Henri. We'll be right in."

Pausing just inside the dining room, Leah "oohed" and

"aahed" in mock surprise over the multicolored ribbons draped extravagantly across the ceiling and over the doorways. Ribbons also ran the length of the damask-covered table, on which were scattered dozens of fresh flowers in delightfully haphazard array. The napkins at each place were tied with more ribbons and embellished with a fresh flower.

"Oh, it is beautiful!" Leah cried. "And such work you have put into it."

"You were surprised, weren't you, Mama?" This from six-year-old Nicole.

"Indeed I was. I'd forgotten what day this is." A little white lie, but one that was sure to be forgiven.

"I hung the ribbons," Jean said.

"And I held the ladder for him," Henri piped up. "He told me he couldn't have done it if I hadn't."

"I put the ribbons and flowers on the table," Lisette announced grandly. "The perfect touch, don't you think?"

"Oh, indeed I do," Leah agreed.

"But I carried the flowers in," Nicole said, "and handed them to her. And see, I pricked my finger. Henri forgot to get all the thorns off the roses. See?" She held up her finger for her mother's kiss.

"There," Leah said, "does that feel better?"

"Thank you, Mama. It's stopped hurting already."

"And what did you do?" Leah looked at Denise. "I know you had a hand in it somewhere."

"Oh, I supervised the whole thing."

I'm sure you did, Leah thought.

Blanchette appeared in the doorway. Braced on her stocky legs, arms akimbo, she shook her head disapprovingly at one and all.

"Five more minutes, Blanchette?" Leah asked. "I can't wait until after supper to open these exciting packages."

"Five minutes, but no longer. Or pouf! and the soufflé is no more." She threw up her hands in dismay and waddled out.

"Happy birthday, Mama." As the eldest, Jean presented his gift first.

"Thank you, Jean." Leah opened the box, reached into the voluminous nest of tissue paper, and pulled out an exquisite gold and blue enamel music box. On its lid were Limoges figurines, two ballet dancers caught magically in the middle of a *pas de deux*. "Oh, son, this is magnificent!"

"I'm glad you like it, Mama. Papa let me earn the money for it by working in the warehouse."

"Old enough to work but not too old to kiss," she said and pulled his reddening face down to hers.

"Happy birthday, Mama." Lisette handed her a slim box.

"Oh, Lisette, just what I needed," Leah said as she lifted out a pale apricot chiffon scarf, fringed with fine silk threads at both ends.

"Papa gave me the material, but I made it myself," Lisette said proudly.

"And how beautifully you did it, too. It will be perfect with my new dinner gown when we go to the theatre next week."

"Now mine, Mama," Henri insisted. "Oh, happy birthday," he added and gave her a quick kiss.

Leah noted with a smile how the paper wrinkled around the awkwardly shaped object. It was obvious that his childish hands had wrapped and rewrapped it many times before he'd been able to get the paper to stay put.

"Whatever can it be?" Leah said as if to herself but loud enough for Henri to hear.

"Try to guess, Mama. I'll give you a hint. I made it myself."

"Well, it feels like wood." Henri grinned. "And it has a most unusual shape. Let's see. Do I use it in the living room?"

Henri shook his head.

"In the dining room? No? Then I guess I'd better unwrap it and see." She withdrew a small square tray with hand-carved, two-inch molding glued around all four sides.

"It's for your dressing table, Mama. To keep all those fancy bottles of perfume from sliding off."

"Just the thing! I should have guessed. Thank you, darling. I'll put the bottles on it right after supper."

"Happy birthday, Mama." Denise handed her a large box gaily decorated with ribbons and flowers.

"My," Leah said, "I hate to open this. It's so pretty just as it is."

"Hand me the ribbons," Denise said matter-of-factly, "and I'll roll them up so we can use them again. But you can put the flowers in your hair."

"And I shall." Leah tucked one over each ear. "And now to see what's inside." She opened the box and brought out a linen apron with a cross-stitch embroidery of fruits and flowers. "My, isn't this elegant!"

7

"It took me nearly three months, Mama, but I didn't have to pull out a single stitch. Aren't you proud of me?"

"Indeed I am."

"It's for parties, of course," Denise said seriously. "Not just for everyday."

"Oh, I wouldn't think of wearing it for everyday. But for parties it will be perfect."

Nicole walked up and gave a deep sigh as she handed a flat package to her mother.

"Did you think your turn would never come, little one?" Leah asked, hugging her youngest. "It's hard being the last, isn't it?"

"Oh, no, because then you can spend more time looking at mine. You won't have to hurry."

Such wisdom from a six-year-old, Leah thought. Her surprise was genuine when she unwrapped a painting depicting the garden with the summer house in the middle.

"Papa helped me sketch it," Nicole said, "but I painted it with my watercolors."

Leah looked over at Baptiste, who nodded in acknowledgment.

"It's very beautiful, Nicole. And the colors—the colors are perfect." Indeed, the way in which the various hues were blended was amazing for a child her age. "I'll have it framed the very next time I go into the city, and you can tell me where it should be hung."

With a sigh of resignation that meant: If this soufflé isn't as good as it should be, you have only yourself to blame, Blanchette brought in the main course, and the children's interest turned from the gifts to their plates.

Leah looked down the table toward Baptiste sitting at the other end. The curly black hair and smooth moustache of his young manhood were now steel gray, yet he was still as handsome as he'd been the day she'd become his mistress. Time and suffering had added strength to his finely honed, classic features. He was laughing at something Nicole had whispered to him, and Leah felt her whole body glow with love for the man who, after years of travail and separation, had finally become her husband.

Then she looked at the children sitting between them. These were the inheritors. In them ran bloodlines with sources in Africa, Polynesia, France, England, and America. Rich sources that had endowed previous generations with strength, determination, pride, and a fervor for life.

8

Baptiste's mother was Virginia-born, her ancestors among the earliest to emigrate from England after Sir Walter Raleigh had praised the new land as a latter-day Eden. Baptiste's father was born in Louisiana on the land his great-grandfather had acquired on his arrival from France. He'd come there with gold in his pocket and an ambition to establish the finest line of blooded thoroughbred racehorses in all of the Louisiana territory. Subsequently, that desire had been eclipsed when Baptiste's great-grandfather took one look at the land and envisioned the wealth to be gained from planting it with sugar cane. In the succeeding years, there were always fine horses in the Fontaine stables, but the Fontaine wealth came from the fields.

Then Leah thought about her own heritage. Her maternal great-grandmother had also emigrated to the new land, not with gold in her pocket but with chains around her ankles. Captured in Africa by black slave traders in the pay of nefarious ship captains, she was dragged away from her family, marched to the coast, put aboard a ship, and finally sold in New Orleans. Leah knew nothing more about her, not even her name, for the woman's daughter, Leah's grandmother, had been taken away and sold when she was still a child. The pure, black African heritage of this great-grandmother had been diluted by the white blood of males like Leah's father in succeeding generations. He was the son of a French sea captain who had settled with his Polynesian wife on the island of Martinique and begun a flourishing import business.

As Leah glanced from one to another of her children, she could see clearly the disparate racial and ethnic elements in each of them.

At fourteen, Jean was the image of his father, but he was already exhibiting the business acumen of Leah's father, Jean-Paul Bonvivier, for whom he was named. She was not surprised that Jean's gift to her had come from the import firm's stock, or that he had worked to earn the money. Jean considered it a special privilege to work with his father in the Paris office of the Bonvivier-Fontaine Import Company. He could spend hours opening boxes of silks from China, paper-thin porcelain from Japan, brass bowls from India, leather goods from Morocco, carved ivory from Africa, furs from Scandinavia, laces from Belgium, and enamelware filigree from Italy—all of which would be transshipped to the office in New Orleans. He was equally fascinated with the account books, and he did not hesitate to point out to his father mistakes in addition or subtraction.

Jean had almost never known his father. He had been conceived while Leah was still Baptiste's mistress, but was born after she became the wife of James Andrews. But James' death, Leah's return to New Orleans, and Baptiste's insistence that they leave America to live in France made it possible for Jean to learn that Baptiste, not James, was his real father.

Leah's glance rested next on Lisette, Baptiste's daughter but not hers. During her stay in Indiana, Baptiste had endured a disastrous marriage with Catherine DeLisle Fouché. However, their daughter, Lisette, although a beautiful blonde like her mother, had the sweet disposition of her father. At thirteen, she was beginning to develop physically and exhibit the instincts of a natural-born flirt. Leah loved Lisette, who had come into her care as a baby, as much as she loved her own children. And since Lisette had never known her own mother, the love was reciprocated.,

Ten-year-old Henri was a quiet, hard-to-fathom child. He was unquestionably the son of Baptiste and herself, but he didn't look particularly like either of them. Henri was never a problem in any way, but Leah was concerned that his constant, even-tempered obedience was based more on a desire to please his parents than to satisfy himself. Leah often felt there was a tempestuous volcano inside of him just waiting to erupt.

Amazingly adept with his hands, Henri delighted in taking apart mechanical objects and putting them back together, inventing little machines, and carving models of ships and carriages. On the table now was his latest invention, a wind-up combination of miniature train and relish tray whose little cars, bearing condiments and garnishes, ran around a track in the center of the table. His earlier creations included a small elevator that went up into a tree house he had built. Yes, Henri might well be hiding a restlessness that could find release only in some sort of challenge. They would have to watch him closely to understand how best to guide him.

Although only eight, Denise was already the little mother bustling around the house—pestering Blanchette to be allowed to cook, rearranging the furniture, and announcing to all the world that when she married she wanted at least a hundred children. Leah smiled; it was Denise who would have planned this dinner, supervised each detail, and told

10

everyone, including Baptiste, how and what to do. Although only two and a half when Nicole was born, Denise had immediately taken the baby under her wing and was more of a mother to her than Leah was. Even now she was urging her little sister to clean up her plate and fold her napkin neatly beside it. Nicole did as she was told without question, and then looked to Denise with adoring eyes for approval.

Those two are inseparable, Leah thought. *I doubt that anything will ever come between them. Someday, when they marry, it had better be to men who live near each other and who will understand this very rare and beautiful relationship.*

Nicole. Leah's gaze remained lovingly on the six-year-old, a miniature of herself with her long, straight black hair and almond-shaped eyes. Also like Leah, Nicole was her own person, willfully independent though fiercely attached to Denise, much more so than to either of her parents. She could spend hours alone and then emerge from her reclusive solitude as gay and cheerful as a butterfly. It was as if her system craved those moments by herself to regenerate her spirit. How well Leah could understand this need that she, too, had had all her life.

"And now," announced Denise in a motherly but autocratic tone, "if everyone is finished it's time for the entertainment." What she meant was that everyone had better be finished because according to her timetable, dinner was over.

"May we have our coffee and brandy in the salon?" Baptiste asked, his tone expressing both mock humility and genuine respect.

"Of course you may, silly," Denise giggled. "You always do." Then realizing she'd allowed her aplomb to slip for a moment, she again became the serious moderator of the evening. "And now, Lisette, you may take over."

Baptiste and Leah were excused to go into the salon where Blanchette served them coffee and brandy. Leah rearranged the chair cushions to ease the nagging pain in the small of her back, and Baptiste lit up his cigar.

"What's on the program for tonight?" he asked.

"I don't know. They've been whispering and giggling all week. And Lisette's pulled out I don't know how many books, especially ones with pictures." Denise might be the planner, but it was Lisette who had the imagination.

In a minute Lisette came in wrapped in a blanket, obviously attempting to hide what she was wearing underneath.

"Ladies and gentlemen," she said with such seriousness

that Leah and Baptiste dared not laugh. "The Fontaine company of actors will now present a series of tableaux entitled 'Peace at Last.' Will you please direct your attention to the front windows." With that, she scurried out of the room.

As usual, the draperies had been drawn for the night, but Leah now noticed them fluttering. The floor-to-ceiling casement windows, which looked onto the front verandah, were open. In another minute, Nicole came through them and pulled back the draperies. The other four children stepped through.

"My God!" Baptiste exclaimed. "My old uniform."

Indeed, there stood Jean wearing the Confederate major's gray uniform that Baptiste had dared to wear when he drove through New Orleans during the Federal occupation, an act which had almost cost him his life. In one hand Jean held Baptiste's old saber and in the other he held a staff bearing a replica of the Confederate battle flag. Lisette, wearing one of Leah's old crinolines covered with what looked suspiciously like Denise's bedroom curtains, stood on tiptoe to kiss Jean on the cheek. Clinging to both of them were Henri and Denise, pretending to wipe tears from their eyes. Each of them carried smaller flags. All four remained absolutely still until Lisette twitched a finger at Nicole to pull the curtains.

The second tableau had Jean and Lisette in Confederate uniforms fighting Henri, Denise, and Nicole in Federal blues. Lisette confided later that only a combination of threats and bribes had forced the three younger ones into the blue uniforms.

In the third tableau, Jean, still in uniform and lying on a table, was covered with an inordinant amount of gauze and a viscous red liquid. "Good Lord, I hope it's not paint," Leah whispered. Beside him stood Henri in one of Baptiste's white shirts, buttoned in back. Henri or Lisette obviously thought that was what a doctor should wear. He was holding a rather vicious-looking carving knife in his hand.

"My God, is that what they used on me?" Baptiste murmured.

"Something like that, yes. Blanchette will be furious if she finds her favorite knife missing."

Beside Jean, who was lying very still with his eyes closed, was Lisette, also in a white shirt, buttoned in back and tied with an apron for a skirt. She was bending over Jean and

12

wiping blood from his face. Denise stood by in similar attire with a second knife in her hand.

"Certainly going to make sure the cutting gets done," Baptiste mumbled.

Jean and Henri appeared in the fourth tableau in the blue uniforms of the Federal occupiers; they were harassing and beating the three girls who were wearing ragged dresses and piteously holding out dolls that obviously represented starving babies. At one point, Jean pretended to spit on the small flag Denise was holding.

"My word, Leah, what did you tell them about the occupation?" Baptiste asked when the curtain was drawn again.

"Exactly what it was like. They should never forget the indignities we suffered."

"No 'let-bygones-be-bygones'?"

"Never! They must never forget why you lost your legs or what we suffered those four years under the occupation."

"How about what you went through?" he asked.

"That's not as important."

But Leah was wrong. The next tableau had all but Nicole dressed in blue uniforms. They stood over her, pointing their fingers, as she, still dressed in rags, mopped the floor at their feet.

"So you did tell them how you slaved in a Federal office," Baptiste said.

"Well, Lisette asked me once what I had done during the war, and I guess I mentioned it."

The final tableau took longer to stage, and Leah was at a complete loss as to why so much of the furniture had to be rearranged. This tableau featured only three of the children. Jean and Lisette, in their own clothes, stood with their arms around each other in what was meant to be the prow of a ship. Wearing one of Henri's suits, Nicole stood beside them. In Lisette's arms was a doll wrapped in one of her own baby shawls that Leah had saved. In Jean's hand was a replica of the French flag. Leah wanted to weep. It was their flight to France.

At the conclusion, all five came out to take their bows, while Baptiste and Leah clapped until their hands were sore.

"*Magnifique!*" Baptiste shouted.

"Thank you, Papa," Lisette said. "We did do it beautifully, didn't we?"

"I had no idea I'd saved so many of our things," Leah murmured. "We're regular pack rats, aren't we?"

"That's what gave us the idea," Lisette said, while Nicole

13

scrambled into Leah's lap for further praise and the boys ran off to the kitchen to tell Blanchette they were ready for their hot chocolate.

"Yes," Denise added, "we were playing in the attic and found all those things in the trunks. You must have been very handsome in your uniform, Papa."

"Oh, I was. Hasn't your mama told you that?"

"For shame, Baptiste, you have no humility at all," Leah laughed.

"None. Because I also married the most beautiful woman in the world, and what man would she have except the handsomest?"

"Enough of that," Leah said. She slid Nicole off her lap. "It was a wonderful surprise. The whole evening has been beautiful. Thank you. Now, run along and get your hot chocolate and then to bed. Come back and kiss us goodnight."

It had been a wonderful evening. If the restlessness of the earlier hours had not disappeared completely, it at least had been subdued. For the time being, that was enough.

Chapter Three

"You've been very quiet most of the evening, Leah," Baptiste said as he sat on the edge of the bed and loosened his tie. "You feeling all right?"

"Just a little tired perhaps."

"I wondered. It's so unlike you. Especially on your birthday." Several times during the evening he'd noticed her staring straight ahead into space, and it worried him. Leah was usually the gayest person at a party. "The children tried so hard to make it something special for you."

"I'm sorry, Baptiste. I wouldn't want to disappoint them after all they did."

"I don't think they noticed. You were more than effusive in your appreciation of the dinner and the presents. And they were busy with their own games after the tableaux, but usually you do more than just smile at their antics."

14

Instead of replying, Leah turned her back while she unbuttoned her gown and slipped out of it. She had to get herself under control before she let Baptiste see her face. Her petticoat fell to the floor, and she picked it up, folded it, and placed it on a chair. To stop the shaking in her hands, she slowly reached into a drawer for a clean nightgown. Then, in spite of herself, she began to cry.

"What is it, chérie?" *Damn*, he thought, *if only I could stand up and walk over to her and put my arms around her.* Instead, he willed her to turn around and held out his arms in a silent invitation to sit beside him on the bed. "Something pretty serious to bring the tears like that."

Still clutching the nightgown, Leah turned only her head, but then, like a child seeking to be consoled after a fall, she ran across the room and into Baptiste's comforting arms.

"I'm frightened, Baptiste. I'm forty years old and I'm scared."

"My poor Leah," Baptiste said, half consoling, half jesting. "She thinks life is almost over because she is now forty. A little wrinkle here, a bit of gray there, and her youth has fled forever."

"Please, Baptiste, don't tease. I'm really frightened." This was it. This was the moment she dreaded, when voicing the truth made it become real, when she must accept what she could no longer deny. "I'm not old, but I'm too old to—to be pregnant again." And again she dissolved into tears.

"Really, chérie!" Immediately, elation had replaced the genuine concern he'd had for her and for whatever was upsetting her. "Are you sure? It's been six years."

"I know," she said, sitting up and curling her legs under her. "And quit grinning like an old fool. I'll start laughing and then feel ashamed for having cried."

Six years, she thought. *Two miscarriages within a year after Nicole's birth and then nothing. So why now?*

"But it's wonderful, chérie. The children will be thrilled." Then, in spite of her mild protests, he gathered her into his arms again.

"Don't tell them. Not yet."

"You're not sure? Or you think it's too long for them to wait?"

"No, it's not that." She looked up directly into his eyes, those eyes that had reassured her so many times before. "I'm either pregnant or—or I have a tumor." There, she'd said it, voiced the vicious fear that had been eating at her with its own malignancy.

"You wouldn't know the difference?" Although really worried now, Baptiste was trying to keep fear out of his voice. Leah had to be pregnant. She was not too old. Many women had babies after they were forty. *God help us,* he thought, *it can't be cancer. I couldn't live without her.*

"Some of the symptoms could be the same," she said. "And there are some I've never had before."

"So—we go to the city tomorrow and see Dr. Boucher. How far along do you think you are?" He refused even to speak the word "if." He tried to remember something, any little thing, about Leah's looks or behavior during her earlier pregnancies—something he could cling to for assurance until they saw the doctor. But she'd always been so healthy, or at least she'd never voiced a complaint to him. In spite of being a most passionate and satisfying lover, she had an innate modesty about her body that made him reluctant to ask intimate questions.

"At least three and a half months," she said.

"And it's not the change of life?"

"No, it's not the change." She did not elaborate.

Whatever was taking place inside her, he thought, it was still her secret and he would not probe.

"Then Dr. Boucher should be able to tell," he said tersely. "And when he says you're pregnant, we'll celebrate at Chez Madeleine with champagne and dancing."

"And if I'm not? If it is a tumor?" Once she'd acknowledged a possibility, Leah was never one to pretend it no longer existed. She always preferred to meet an obstacle head on and conquer it or accept what could not be defeated.

"Surgical techniques are much more advanced than when I lost my legs twenty years ago, and I'm still alive. But for tonight we'll think about the baby, a baby that will soon be kicking his mama. Remember how Henri actually kicked a plate off your lap when you were eight months along?"

"And Nicole. Never would get frisky until I was ready to go to sleep." She'd picked up the cue from Baptiste. Tomorrow was time enough to worry. In less than twenty-four hours, she'd know for certain, and there was no point in wasting those hours if they might be the last truly happy ones she'd ever know. "What do you mean, *his!* Maybe it's a her," she said.

"Has to be a boy," he replied, "to even out the family."

Boy, girl, or whatever, this thing inside her had to mean the beginning of a new life, not the destruction of her own.

"Hold me tight, Baptiste, and tell me everything's going to

be all right." She curled inside his arms and rested her head against his shoulder.

"It is, chérie, and by tomorrow night we'll know for sure." He kissed away the trace of a tear on her cheek. "You look tired. It won't take me long to finish undressing, and then we'll turn out the light so you can go right to sleep."

She reached over and began unbuttoning his shirt. "I'm not that tired. Are you?"

"No, but I thought—"

"I need you tonight, Baptiste. More than I ever have."

As he looked at her beside him, his whole body was consumed with love for her. There had never been a time when she hadn't responded to him, and often she had initiated their lovemaking. She would embrace him passionately and eagerly await the touching and caressing that he knew pleased her most. But never before had she said she needed him, and he was keenly aware that this time it was not a bodily hunger craving satisfaction. It was a desperate need to be reassured that at forty she was still a desirable woman. More than that, it was a need to share an act, which, at its most elemental level, was the creation of life.

Murmuring age-old but ever-meaningful endearments, he gathered her to him with a gentle passion. Soon, with lips touching and fingers caressing, they were swept up into a throbbing, raw-nerved joining of body to body, body within body, and they remained together even after the last convulsive movements had left them limp and dozing.

"I thought the dinner party was Friday night," Lisette said the next morning when she saw her mother come from her room dressed to go into the city.

"It is, but Papa wants to go in today to check something at the office, and I thought I'd go along and do some shopping. Anything you need?"

"What a question, Mama. You know I never have enough of anything."

"I know. Only a wardrobe brimming over and drawers so full you can hardly get them closed. More to the point, what do you want?"

"A long skirt?" Lisette suggested. "Could I, please?"

"Well, I had intended one as a surprise for your fourteenth birthday, but maybe—"

"Oh, Mama, I do love you so." There were times, infrequent to be sure, when Lisette thought about her own mother, the beautiful Catherine, whose picture, at Leah's

17

insistence, was kept on her dresser. Lisette knew Catherine had died in a tragic boating accident when Lisette was still a baby. Also, when questioned, Baptiste spoke of Catherine in only the most complimentary terms. But Lisette also knew that Leah had been her father's mistress before he married Catherine, and that Jean was his child even though he'd been born after Leah married James Andrews in Indiana. It was not something that often worried or puzzled Lisette, because she loved Leah as dearly as if Leah were her own mother, but still she wondered. She was unaware that such wondering was fertile soil for the seeds of rebellion that would blossom within a few years.

"Now, where are the others?" Leah called, and soon had all the children gathered around her. "Be good, and I'll bring each of you a surprise from the city."

"I thought Papa said I could go in with him this week," Jean said, frowning.

Leah grasped the chin of her eldest in her palm. How tall he was becoming. It wouldn't be long before he was a man. "Next time. There's something I need to tend to. Now, no problems for Blanchette. Promise?" All five heads nodded.

"Will you spend the night at the apartment?" Lisette asked.

"I think so. So don't worry if we're not back." Baptiste had promised a celebration if she were pregnant—and if not, she'd need time to settle her nerves and collect her thoughts before returning home.

"Kiss me 'bye, Mama." Nicole turned up her face and pursed her lips.

" 'Bye, sweetie."

"Could my surprise be a new doll?" Nicole whispered. "I washed Fifi's hair and it all fell out."

"Oh my, that's a real tragedy. Maybe Fifi would like a new wig, too."

"Ready, Leah?" Baptiste was maneuvering his crutches through the hall.

"Ready. Henri, do you think you can manage the portmanteau? And Jean, help Papa with the steps. The rain last night might have left them slippery. Denise, would you like to plan supper for tonight? Tell Blanchette I said you could help."

Not until she was seated beside Baptiste in the landau and they were on the road that ran through St. Denis to Paris did Leah notice how badly her hands were shaking. And

18

judging from the way Baptiste was mutilating his long, black cigar, he wasn't feeling any too calm, either.

"How many cigars did you bring along?" she asked.

"About half a dozen. Why?"

"Because you're going to have that one completely chewed up before it's half smoked. I don't suppose you have one to spare."

"A cigar?" Baptiste's eyebrows shot up.

"I thought one might help me as much as they do you."

"If I thought you'd really smoke it, I'd light it for you," he laughed.

"Try me and see," she answered, half joking, half serious.

"Oh, no, I'm not going to let you acquire that habit. It's too expensive. Anyway, next thing you'd be wanting to wear trousers like that George Sand you were reading the other night." He reached over and took her hand. "Don't worry, chérie. Dr. Boucher will put your fears to rest."

"I wish I were as confident as you," she said and released a deep sigh.

"It's just that I refuse to believe you are anything but a healthy mother-to-be," he said, attempting to relieve the fear gnawing inside him. There was no need to let her know how worried he really was.

Promptly at ten, Dr. Boucher's nurse led Leah into the examining room. Cursing the infirmity that prevented him from pacing up and down in the waiting room, Baptiste fell into a chair and lit up another cigar. In spite of the antimacassar-covered, overstuffed chairs, mahogany tables, and a spindle-legged étagère filled with an assortment of china souvenirs that might have made the waiting room resemble a family parlor, an overpoweringly cloying, antiseptic smell reminded one constantly that this was a doctor's office.

Dr. Boucher was one of the most modern medical men in Paris, a specialist in female physiology, and the patients who came to him had to be prepared to dispense with any false modesty. They had to remove all their clothing; he allowed no petticoats and underdrawers to hinder him in conducting a thorough examination. Leah, however, was familiar with his routine, having had him at the accouchement of both Denise and Nicole. She let the nurse help her off with her clothes and then wrap the long sheet around her.

"*Enceinte*, Madame Fontaine?" the nurse asked.

"I—I think so." She lay back on the table, crooking one

arm under her head for a pillow and resting the other across her chest. Within a minute Dr. Boucher came in.

"Good morning, Leah." He moved the sheet just enough to reveal her abdomen. "Still quite flat, I see. So what brings you here this early in your pregnancy? Not that I'm displeased, mind you. I wish more women would consult me throughout their term."

"I—I think I'm pregnant, but I want to make certain it's that and not—not something else."

"Your last period?"

"Four months ago." Strange how she could speak of it so casually to the doctor when it was a subject she and Baptiste acknowledged each month but never discussed.

"How old are you, Leah?"

"Forty. Yesterday." Could it have been only yesterday that fear had driven her out of the house and sent her on that long walk, that journey into the past? It seemed ages ago.

"A bit young for the change, but not out of the question. Any problems?"

"A few." And she detailed some of the symptoms.

"And so you are worried it is something other than a pregnancy."

She nodded, afraid she would cry if she spoke.

He moved aside more of the sheet and began palpating her abdomen, pressing gently but more firmly in her vital areas. "Any pain? Tenderness?"

"No."

"Very good. Let me check your breasts." Again his gentle hands moved lightly, professionally across her skin.

"I'm not going to do an internal examination this time for fear of inducing a miscarriage. Especially after the two you suffered. In another two or three months I will. Just to check a couple of things."

"Then . . . ? You mean . . . ?" Her mouth was so dry she could hardly get the words out.

"I mean that in about five and a half months you'll be calling me to deliver you of a healthy child."

"Are you quite sure? How do you know?" Leah wanted to hear the words over and over again, just to make certain she hadn't imagined them.

"My fingers tell me. I could give you the medical details, but just believe me. You feared a tumor, didn't you?"

"Yes. After six years, what else could I think?"

"You could think that you are a normal, healthy woman

20

who is made to have children and who simply happened not to get pregnant during those years."

With that, Leah broke into tears. "I'm sorry," she sobbed. "I didn't mean to give way like this."

"That's all right," Dr. Boucher said. "Better tears of relief than of fear. I've seen those, too."

"I guess you have, and I should be ashamed for crying when I feel so happy."

"Now, get dressed," he said, patting her on the shoulder, "and I'll go out and talk to Baptiste. Remember, I want to see you every month. Nothing wrong, just a wise precaution."

Baptiste slid forward in his chair when Dr. Boucher came through the door.

"Congratulations, Baptiste. I hope you have room in that house of yours for another one."

"Leah's pregnant? It's—it's not something else?"

"She is indeed, and seems very healthy. I've told her I want to see her once a month, however. Nothing wrong, I assure you, but it's wise to keep a check on a woman past forty. She may have some aches and pains she didn't experience before, but that's to be expected. If, however, she becomes ill, or overtired, or there is any swelling in her legs, I want to see her immediately. There are things I can do to combat the problems as long as we don't wait."

"Do you expect such problems?"

"No, I don't, but that doesn't mean they might not occur. Now, go buy her something pretty and then take her out to dinner. I think she's endured a rough few weeks of fearing the worst."

"She has." Baptiste exhaled a long breath. The pain left his chest, but his hands were still shaking. "She didn't tell me until last night, or we would have been here sooner. And I've already promised her dinner and champagne to celebrate."

After shopping for a long skirt for Lisette, a short, bright red velvet cape for Denise, a doll for Nicole *and* a wig for Fifi, Leah met Baptiste at the office. He was taking back woodworking tools for Henri and imported leather boots for Jean.

"Am I too early?" Leah asked. "If I am, I can walk to the apartment and rest before we go out to dinner."

"Only if you're too tired for another shopping spree."

"I can't think of anything else I need to buy."

"I'm buying this time," he smiled. "Dr. Boucher said to

21

find you something pretty, and that's just what I intend to do."

"But I don't need anything, Baptiste. And I'll soon have to see the dressmaker about a new wardrobe."

"What I have in mind will fit you now and for years to come." And with that, he reached for his hat and called for the landau to be brought around.

"To Cartier's, Nicolas," he said.

"Cartier's!" Leah gasped.

"Yes, and not another word from you," he said, grinning.

Meekly, Leah lapsed into silence, and Baptiste said nothing more until they pulled up at the jeweler's, left the carriage, and walked through the door.

"I want to see something with six diamonds," Baptiste announced. "Six stones as perfectly matched as possible."

But he shook his head when the manager brought out necklaces and bracelets.

"No, I want something unique."

"Ah, I have just the thing. Wait here a minute." The man returned almost immediately, carrying a velvet cushion. On it lay a miniature lily-of-the-valley spray: six blossoms clustered within a green-enameled leaf. Nestled in the center of each blossom was a diamond.

"Lovely," Baptiste said, nodding, "but the stones are smaller than I had in mind."

"No, Baptiste," Leah said, putting her hand on his arm, "they're perfect. Just what I would like."

"Are you sure? I meant to get something really magnificent."

"I don't want anything magnificent, as you put it. I want this. I can wear it on a suit or an afternoon dress, as well as on an evening gown. I want to wear it often, in memory of this day." Six diamonds for their six children. What a sentimental sweetheart Baptiste was.

"It's your choice, darling."

"Then pin it on, and we'll go to the apartment. I think I would like to rest before dressing for dinner."

Sophie, a live-in housekeeper, kept the Paris apartment in constant readiness for their visits to the city. Although small, it was ideal for the nights Baptiste had to stay in town, or the times when they went to the theatre and it was too late to return to the country afterward. Situated in a fashionable section of the city, it was as richly and meticulously furnished as the château. The dining room seated only eight

22

comfortably, but invitations to the Fontaines' small, intimate dinners were eagerly sought. Rarely did Leah and Baptiste entertain at the château—they considered it their family sanctuary—but when they did, it was during the warm months when the doors of the large main center hall could be opened to the terrace, and guests could wander at their leisure from the living and dining rooms out into the garden.

Leah walked into the bedroom after asking Sophie to bring her a glass of wine. She looked into the wardrobe to decide which of the two dinner gowns she kept there she wanted to wear.

"Sophie, I think I'll wear the ivory silk." She thought how beautiful the new pin, with its emerald green leaf, would look against the wide ivory lace bertha. "Will you see if it needs a touch-up pressing? And then will you fill the tub? I think I'll bathe before I rest. I didn't realize how hot I'd gotten shopping."

"*Oui,* madame. You're dining out?"

"Yes. And I'd like you to help me with my hair. There'll be no need for you to wait up, but we would like breakfast early. Monsieur Fontaine wants to return directly to the country."

"It will be ready when you ring. And I'll see to your bath now before I press the gown."

"Thank you, Sophie." Leah looked at the new pin, sparkling in its velvet case. The sixth diamond seemed to represent the easing of the heavy, nagging weight she'd borne for so long. Its sparkle reassured her of the life she carried within her.

Baptiste reached for Leah's hand across the candlelit table at Chez Madeleine. In his other hand he held a glass of champagne.

"Did I tell you how beautiful you look tonight?" he asked.

"Yes, but say it again. I like the sound of it." Then she became quiet and lowered her head.

"What's troubling you now, chérie? I still haven't seen that smile you should be wearing."

"And—and when my time comes?" she asked hesitantly.

"You'll come through beautifully," he assured her, "just as you always have."

"I don't know. I have a feeling. Women can sense these things. I'm still frightened."

"You sense it, or have you been listening to too many old wives' tales?" He was constantly amazed at the way women frightened each other with the lurid details of their confinements.

"No. There are no voodoo packets under the bed or screech owls haunting my dreams this time." In New Orleans she'd been influenced by a supersitious belief in the power of voodoo and the efficacy of its charms, but no longer. "Things—things are different from before."

"And so you're a little older and you tire more easily. There are new aches and pains." He tried to smile away her fears. "Dr. Boucher didn't seem concerned." No point in telling her how the doctor had cautioned him about watching for signs of overtiredness or swelling in her legs.

"He didn't carry the other four either," she insisted.

"And each one of those was different. Now, drink your champagne, and then I'll take my old wife home and put her to bed." He grinned and squeezed her hand.

"Only if you come to bed with me. I'm not that old, damn it!"

"An invitation I never refuse, my love."

While they were undressing, Baptiste said, "Jean came into the library the other day and said he wanted to talk to me."

"About what?" Leah laid her new pin in its case and began removing her earrings. "Something bothering him?"

"About love. Only he used a somewhat more vulgar term for it."

"Yes," she nodded, "at fourteen, it's time he was curious."

"Seems he's been spending time with some of the boys in the village and listening to their crude stories."

"That's not surprising." Leah started brushing her hair.

"No, but what amazed me was how they were telling the same jokes here in France that I heard when I was a boy in New Orleans."

"So? Boys are boys the world over. And there are just so many ways of doing it. Why did he come to you?"

"Since the other boys are older, he thought they'd laugh at him if he asked questions. For one thing, he wanted to know the meaning of some of the words they used."

"Oh, yes, the vocabulary that titillates." Leah laughed.

"I'm not going to repeat the words. Let's just say they were the common, vulgar expressions for various parts of the male and female body and for the act itself."

"And you're not going to tell me? Just let me stew in my own curiosity? You are a prude, Baptiste!"

"When it comes to saying certain things to my wife, yes."

"Balls!" she exclaimed.

"What did you say?" He couldn't believe what he'd heard.

"I said 'balls.' Bull balls. Does that shock you?"

"Yes, yes it does." Baptiste looked properly horrified even as he tried to hide his grin at the vehemence with which Leah had spat out the word.

"Well, I probably know all the others, too. But never mind, I won't shock you anymore. What else did Jean want to know?"

"Various little details, straightening out some misconceptions. Such as: Do women go into heat the way a dog does, or into season like a cow?"

Leah fell across the bed laughing. "I don't believe it. But, oh, it would solve a lot of problems." She rolled over and lay on her back for a minute, gazing quietly at the ceiling. "Are you going to take him into the city the way—the way you were taken to Madame Broulé's in New Orleans?"

"Hell, no! I haven't been to one of those places since I met you." A small white lie to cover the few visits he had made while she was in Indiana. "Anyway, there are enough haylofts and willing partners around the château. That's where I first dipped my wick, as Benji called it. Madame Broulé's was just to teach me finesse, the finer points of pleasing a woman."

" 'Dip your wick.' Now that is a new one. I shall have to add it to my pornographic vocabulary." Leah got off the bed, finished undressing, and slipped into a sheer nightgown.

"Now that I like," Baptiste said. "And this bed is much softer than a hayloft."

"And I want some of that finesse you learned." She stretched out full length, pulling her gown teasingly to the top of her thighs. "I never tumbled in the hay, but I always thought it sounded like fun. Maybe when we get back to the country—"

"Leah! It's a good thing Jean came to me and not to you. You'd shock him to death. You should have seen the state he was in when I even hinted that old folks in their forties still made love. Haystacks. Madame Broulé's. What kind of a mother are you?"

"A very practical one who knows that sooner or later her children have to face the facts of life. And if it's going to be sooner, it should be from the right source, instead of garbled misinformation from dirty stories and filthy postcards. But I am glad it was you he came to and that you

25

spoke to him. Now, come to bed. All this discussion is getting me very excited."

Baptiste ran his hand along her thighs. "Leah, you're a most delightful wench, and I do love you."

This time there was no thought of why they made love. They simply came together with the exhilaration of two people still as much in love as they were when they first discovered each other.

Chapter Four

IN SPITE OF LEAH'S FEARS, her pregnancy went smoothly. The children were all delighted at the prospect of a new brother or sister, and couldn't do enough for her. After Baptiste told her about his talk with Jean, she was concerned over the boy's reaction, but he grinned and then whooped with joy.

"Well," Baptiste said, "either he's developed a new attitude, or he thinks there's still fire in the old man yet."

"Whichever," Leah said, "I'm glad he's pleased. I've seen children that age become very embarrassed and alienated."

It was Jean who brought pillows for her back when the family sat in the library after supper, and he refused to let her carry anything heavier than a coffee cup.

"I'm not an invalid, Jean," she insisted.

"I know, Mama, but—but at—" he stammered and then said no more.

"At my age, I must be careful. Is that it?"

"Something like that, yes. I really thought you'd be more comfortable with the pillows."

"And I am. Thank you for being so considerate."

Lisette immediately offered to help with the sewing for the baby. "I've been practicing several new embroidery stitches, Mama. And I'd be very careful."

"That's wonderful, Lisette. Would you like to go into the city with Papa and pick out the materials we need?"

"Just me? I mean, just he and I alone?"

"Yes, I think you'd enjoy a few days together." Although

the child gave no sign, Leah often wondered if Lisette felt separate from the others. It would do her good to spend some time alone with her father. She might have questions about Catherine that she hesitated to ask when Leah was present. It was important to Leah that Lisette should never feel she had to forget about Catherine.

Charmed with her new doll, promptly named Rosemarie, and the blond wig for Fifi, Nicole offered her best doll cradle for the baby.

"Thank you, honey," Leah said, hugging her youngest. "But I think if we make a trip to the storage shed in a few days, we'll find the cradle that you and Denise used when you were babies."

"Really!" Nicole's dark eyes grew larger and rounder.

"Yes, and we'll see what needs to be done to get it ready and then you can help me. Would you like that?"

"If you'll tell me all about what I was like as a baby."

Leah immediately pulled Nicole up on her lap and began reminiscing, interrupted occasionally by the girl's "Tell me again, Mama."

It was, however, Henri's and Denise's activities that most fascinated Leah. There were dozens of whispered conferences between the two and numerous trips to the tool shed that Henri had turned into a workshop. Finally, after nearly three weeks of whispered hints and hand-stifled giggles— which Leah pretended had her curiosity at fever pitch— Henri and Denise walked into the library carrying a large package between them.

With great solemnity Leah removed the wrappings—and then was truly astounded. Henri had sawed, nailed, and carved odds and ends of scrap lumber into a masterfully constructed footstool. Denise had scrounged enough remnants from her mother's sewing-room scrap bag to make a soft padding for the top. Over this, the child had stretched a larger piece of blue silk, amazingly similar to the dress she was wearing. Jean, the only one they'd let in on their secret, had sneaked away to St. Denis for the gold upholsterer's tacks with which it was fastened down.

Leah stared at it a minute. "I'm speechless," she said finally.

"You, Mama?" Lisette laughed. "I've never known you when you didn't have something to say."

"Well then, behold the miracle. Henri and Denise have done it with this magnificent footstool. And it's just what I

27

need." She lifted up her feet and they slipped it under. "The perfect height. Thank you, my darlings."

Some two months before the baby was due, Leah found herself tiring easily and spending a great part of the day lying on the bed or on the chaise longue that Baptiste had moved to the terrace as the weather warmed. Concerned by her tiredness, Baptiste refused to wait for the regular monthly visit to Dr. Boucher and insisted on taking her to the city immediately.

"I don't see any real problem here," Dr. Boucher assured them. "Let's admit it. Part of it is your age, and the fact that you're carrying around considerably more weight than you're used to. Anyone who puts on twenty-four pounds in seven months is going to tire more easily. Do you like to walk, Leah?"

"I used to love to take long, brisk walks along the river. But not lately."

"Well, forget about long, brisk walks, but try some leisurely strolls and sit down to rest along the way. I think that will help bring some of your strength back."

Leah tried to do as he suggested, but even a walk through the garden left her back aching and her legs painfully sore. To go as far as the river, which she tried once, required all the energy she could muster, and she'd feared she wasn't going to make it back to the house.

Then, some three weeks before the baby was due, her legs, arms, and face began to swell so suddenly and severely that she couldn't walk at all or even dress herself. With help, she could don a loose robe and then be carried by Jean and Nicolas, their manservant, to the chaise longue, where she lay in restless misery all day. This time, Dr. Boucher came out from Paris to see her.

"What's wrong, Dr. Boucher?" Baptiste asked after they'd left Leah and were sitting in the library.

"There's no easy way to explain it, Baptiste."

"But her condition is serious." Baptiste thought *"and fatal,"* but did not say it. If his fears weren't verbalized, they wouldn't be real.

"Yes, but not necessarily lethal. What has happened is this: Her pregnancy has poisoned her system. We don't know why it happens or what triggers it. One inexplicable fact we do know is that as soon as she delivers, the toxic condition will disappear."

"Until then?"

"We can only try to keep her comfortable. If there were a safe way to induce labor, I would, but we just have to wait. Then we'll deliver the baby as quickly as possible. The baby is still alive and its heartbeat is strong."

"You're equivocating, Dr. Boucher. 'Keeping her comfortable' sounds too simple. There is danger, isn't there?"

"Yes, for both of them, and I'll be specific in a minute. But one thing is reassuring. Some women develop this poisoning early in pregnancy, and with them it's much more serious and dangerous. Leah has three—maybe only two—more weeks to go. For the baby—we can only pray it won't be a stillbirth. For now, what we have to prevent are convulsions. We'll use laudanum for that. It contains just enough morphine to relax her. If she does convulse, a larger dose of laudanum will bring it under control." What Dr. Boucher didn't say was that there was greater danger of convulsions during labor, and that for some reason laudanum tended to induce hemorrhaging. But one worry at a time was enough for Baptiste now.

"So we just wait." Baptiste sagged in his chair.

"Yes, and keep her diet simple. Again, we don't know why, but it helps."

Worry, added to her physical discomfort, prevented Leah from sleeping well at night or resting during the day. In spite of Dr. Boucher's reassurances, she was not so naive as to think there was no danger for either her or the baby. As much as she hated drugs of any kind, she took the laudanum. Dr. Boucher had been vague when she asked if it would alleviate the swelling, and she suspected he'd prescribed it merely to help her sleep.

When Leah's contractions began, they were strong and rapid, which should have augured a quick delivery. Instead, there were two immediate complications: First, the baby had not yet descended into position, and second, Leah went into the first of a series of convulsions.

With the first convulsion, Dr. Boucher administered more laudanum, and the spasms ceased. When the second came soon after, Dr. Boucher wasted no time on nice explanations but ordered Baptiste to leave the room at once, because he had to deliver the baby as fast as possible.

"And Leah?" Baptiste was frantic.

"If we don't stop the convulsions, they're both dead." Saying that, Dr. Boucher reached into his bag and took out a

29

large apparatus. "Forceps to pull the head down. I can't take time to be gentle, and she's going to suffer a great deal more pain than usual, so I suggest you leave now." He didn't want to say that he might have to crush the child's head. If that should happen, he would simply tell Baptiste that the baby was born dead. Also, he wasn't at all sure just how much damage he would do to Leah, and that was something that Baptiste definitely should not see.

Under the strain, Baptiste's strength had given way, and he was forced to sit in his wheel-chair by the bedroom door. Worry over Leah and frustration at being unable to do so much as walk off his anxiety made him so despondent that he wanted to throw his crutches through the glass door onto the terrace. He'd done that once before, on the night Leah walked out on him, to go North with James Andrews. Was he going to lose her again. If so, the difference this time was that she would never return.

He could hear her shallow breathing through the door, and he knew she was fighting for her life. He felt that with every breath he inhaled, he was taking oxygen away from her, and that if he could only stop breathing, he would increase her chances for survival. It was foolish, he knew, like trying to make a pact with God. But he couldn't help it. He took out his watch and held his breath as long as he could, the equivalent of three, maybe four, exhalations. How many times did a normal man breathe in fifteen seconds? In thirty? It was that many that he gave her during those breathless intervals. Time, Dr. Boucher had said, was so important. Time was needed to bring the baby's head down; yet Leah didn't have that time if the convulsions continued. *Maybe I'm giving her that time*, Baptiste thought. *It's all I have, all I can do to save her life*.

Dr. Boucher worked rapidly, almost savagely, but all the movements of his hands, arms, and forceps were meticulously calculated to save both Leah and the baby.

Throughout her ordeal, Leah moved in and out of consciousness. Before now, she'd thought she'd endured all the many levels of pain at one time or another in her life, managing to steel herself against all but the most acute. But what she was suffering now seemed intolerable, beyond human endurance. She no longer knew where she was or why she was feeling this pain. There was no progression of time, no sense of the seconds passing into minutes. There was only a single extended moment of agony. With her eyes closed, she willed absolute blackness to descend over her. But inside her burning eyelids were darting lights and violent colors whirling around in kaleidoscopic fury.

If only she could lose all conscious awareness. But she had never fainted, not when she assisted at Baptiste's surgery, not when René and her mother died, not during the torture in prison. And she did not faint now; she only became very cold, even though the pain was like fire. It burned, but it did not consume. Like a fire being stoked, it swelled inside her body, becoming an engorged mass pressing on her chest and heart until she could no longer breathe.

This is death, she thought. *This is the never-ending tunnel that leads to eternity.*

Nor did Leah know how far she was traveling down that tunnel. There was one faltering heartbeat as Dr. Boucher pulled the baby's head through. The boy was still alive, crying lustily. For the moment he seemed completely out of danger.

Not so with Leah.

"I don't know whether I want to hear the truth about her condition," Baptiste said when Dr. Boucher came out to assure him he had a strong, healthy son. "Maybe I want you to keep telling me that everything is going to be all right regardless of how serious it is."

"I know," Dr. Boucher said. "Most people are like you. They say they want to know the truth. What they mean is they want the truth to be good news. They're sure that by asking for the truth, that's what they will hear. A kind of plea to fate or the gods: 'I am asking for the truth, therefore reward me by making it good news.'"

"So, what are you going to tell me?"

"I'm going to tell you the truth because there is some hope in it. Leah has sustained a tremendous loss of blood from hemorrhaging—"

"Can she survive that?" Through the open door he'd glimpsed her pale, waxen face on the pillow. She looked completely bereft of life, like a marble carving of some medieval queen on a tomb. His hands ached to rub her cheeks until they flushed with color again.

"She's weak," Dr. Boucher said, "and will be weak for a long time, but her condition is stable. More important, the bleeding relieved the pressure causing the toxemia and the convulsions. That's why I say there is hope. The bleeding has stopped now, and if it does not recur, she should be all right. She'll need to eat the proper foods to regain her strength. But," he paused, "there is something you should know. In

31

getting the baby out as fast as I could, Leah was badly torn inside. That, too, means weeks of slow recovery, and—"

"And—?"

"No more children," Dr. Boucher warned him.

"That won't disturb us. She was worried about having this one." Actually Baptiste was relieved for there'd be no more anxiety about her becoming pregnant again.

"I don't think you understand, Baptiste. I do not say she is incapable. I mean, she *must not* become pregnant again. Do you know now what I'm saying?"

Baptiste nodded his head slowly. "I know what you're saying." It would be hard. Their need to touch and become one was not the result of lust but of adoration and contentment and joy. Leah would find it as difficult as he.

"As badly damaged as Leah is," Dr. Boucher continued, "there can be no marital relations for several weeks, months even. But when Leah is ready, and she will know when she is, come to see me. There are ways, and you are both too young to become celibate."

"Can I see her now?" Baptiste barely heard the doctor's last words. All he knew was that Leah was alive and that she would need care. He was ready to devote all his time and energies to her.

"Not yet. I still have some work to do. But you can see your son. He's fine and healthy, no worries there. If his skin seems a bit yellowish, don't be concerned. He's slightly jaundiced, but that's not unusual. Good rich milk from a wet nurse—and I've already sent for one—and he'll be pink and rosy in a few days. Leah, of course, cannot nurse him."

"Then—then you think Leah is out of danger."

"No, Baptiste, I wish I could say that."

"But all that talk about no more children. And how healthy the baby is. Why? Why!" Baptiste pounded the arms of his chair at the unfairness of it. She'd suffered so much in order to live, to have the baby. She couldn't die now.

"To give you time to catch your breath, give you something to be thankful for. She is not out of danger, and we won't know for certain, one way or the other, for several days. All I said was—there is hope, and there is. It is not hopeless."

Chapter Five

LEAH SMILED AT BAPTISTE over her breakfast tray. "Did you see what Blanchette sent in this morning? An omelet that I know had three eggs in it. Hot rolls piled with butter and jam. Cocoa with whipped cream. Whatever happened to the simple breakfasts of croissants and coffee? If I keep eating like this, I'll be fatter than when I was pregnant. And puffier, too."

"You ate every bit of it, didn't you?" Baptiste grinned.

"I did, because Blanchette said she'd come in and force it down my throat if I didn't."

"She's right. You don't realize how much weight you've lost since having Robert. Or how much strength."

"I know," Leah said. "I can't wait, though, to get on my feet."

"How are you feeling?"

"Very well and very restless. The view from the windows is beautiful, but I would love to see it from another angle for a change."

"Well then, how about trying a short walk? Dr. Boucher said you could when you felt strong enough."

"Really!" Leah exclaimed. "He really said I could get out of bed?"

"That he did. If—and it's a big *if*—you feel up to it."

"How long a walk did you have in mind?" She couldn't believe it. She wiggled her legs under the covers. It had been so long since she'd walked that she wondered if her legs would hold her up.

"To the terrace," Baptiste said. "It's beautiful outside this morning. The chestnuts have burst into bloom just for you."

"Then I have to see them." Leah swung her legs over the side of the bed and tentatively put one foot, then the other, on the floor. Not for the world would she let Baptiste know of the pain that shot suddenly through her feet and up her legs. He'd insist she get right back into bed, but she knew it would get worse the longer she put off standing up. If Dr. Boucher said it was time, then she had to begin moving

33

around. While she waited for the pain to subside to an irritating tingle, she reached for her blue robe and let Baptiste help her put it on.

Clutching the tall post at the footboard, she stood up but almost fell back onto the bed as her legs gave way beneath her. Worst of all was the dizziness that made the room spin.

"You all right, Leah?" Baptiste saw immediately how pale her face and lips had become. Before he could urge her to sit down again, she nodded.

"Just weak. But this is how it will be whenever I start moving around, so it might as well be now. Maybe you'd better call Blanchette though. I'm not sure I can make it out of this room alone." All the muscles in her legs were aching, which she knew she could endure as long as they didn't cramp up and send her falling to the floor.

"That's why I'm here," Baptiste said. "Lean on me." He squared his shoulders and grasped his crutches more firmly.

"Can you? I mean—can we manage?" Baptiste had learned how to maneuver with his crutches under almost every conceivable situation, but he'd never had to help someone else at the same time.

"Chérie, for years you've given me your strength. Today I'm going to give you mine."

Leah saw the determination blazing in his eyes. She had to let him help her, even if she had to pretend she was leaning on him. The only trouble was, if she were to get to the terrace she really would need his support.

Then his face broke into the mischievous grin that always set her heart to fluttering. "Even if we both land in a heap on the floor," he said.

Resting her hand lightly on his shoulder, Leah felt his shoulder muscles tense and his spine stiffen. He would not fall. He would not let her down—or himself. This was his moment to prove he was still every bit the man he'd been the night that he'd ridden up along the Natchez Trace and rescued her from rape and sale into prostitution. Nor was she unaware of the effort it cost him to keep his strong arm and back muscles working to support her.

Oh, Baptiste, she wanted to say, *don't you know there are different kinds of strength. You've been my emotional bulwark through the worst turmoil any woman could endure. Thank you for your arm and shoulder today, but thank you even more for the will of iron I've depended on for more than twenty years.* But she didn't say it. Let him have his day.

Slowly, they progressed toward the terrace where Baptiste had already prepared the wicker chaise lounge with soft pillows and a downy light afghan.

"Thank you, darling," Leah said as she collapsed gratefully on the chaise, "you did that splendidly." She knew better than to overreact to his accomplishment. Ever since the moment he had awakened to discover that both his legs had been amputated after the explosion at Fort St. Philip, he had always—except for one occasion—maintained a light tone about his disability.

"Comfortable?" He arranged the pillows behind her.

"Very, and much more than the last time I lay here." She was remembering those days before Robert came, when she lay as helpless as a beached, bloated whale.

"It's over, chérie, and you're still with us. That's what matters." He leaned down and kissed her lovingly on the cheek. His desire to hold her in his arms was too strong for him to allow himself to touch her lips. After all these years, she was more beautiful, more alluring than when he first saw her at the quadroon balls and decided to have her as his *placée.* Now she'd been his wife for more than ten years, a dream he'd once thought would be impossible to realize.

"And you'll never go through it again," he vowed, tightening his lips. He placed his crutches carefully against the wall and sat down in the chair near her.

Leah could not deny she was haunted by the same fear. Never—never could she live in the same house with Baptiste —even if they moved to separate rooms—without sharing his love completely. Yet the eventual outcome could be another dangerous pregnancy. She had long weighed in her mind the idea of strict continence against her love for Baptiste, and always she came to the same decision: She would love Baptiste for the rest of her life. And it would be fate and nature that determined how long that life would be. She could never stop expressing her love for him in the one way that brought them together into a single, perfect being.

"I hope I won't have to, Baptiste, but I will not—"

"Leave that to me, chérie." He stopped her words gently. "I've talked to Dr. Boucher and there are ways. Believe me, darling, when you're strong enough, we'll make up for all the weeks you've had to sleep alone. But you'll never have to worry again."

35

"What did Dr. Boucher say? How?" If there were a way, it would be an answer to her prayers.

Leah knew, of course, that since time immemorial various methods of contraception had been practiced. She'd even seen some of the herbs and concoctions used by believers in voodoo, but she shied away from them, as she did from the drugs she thought Dr. Boucher might have in mind. She found it hard to believe that an ethical doctor would prescribe them.

"In the first place," Baptiste said, "after what you went through, you probably could not get pregnant again. But just to make sure, there are ways." He paused to extract a long, black cigar from his ever-present silver cigar case and then took a long time lighting it.

Why, I believe he's actually embarrassed to talk about it, Leah thought. "Are you going to tell me, or are you going to keep me guessing?" she asked finally.

Baptiste's cheeks began to flush. His hand went to his pocket and then stopped, as if paralyzed in midair. From the expression on his face, one would think he was mentally debating a momentous, earth-shaking issue. "I hadn't thought to show you this just yet, and certainly not in broad daylight." His hand moved again, and he pulled a small object from his pocket.

"What *is* that thing?" Leah was both curious and slightly repulsed.

"Section of a lamb's small intestine." He spread the gray, wrinkled tube of skin across his palm. One end was open; the other was twisted and tied with fine surgical thread. It looked to Leah like a particularly repulsive, deflated balloon.

"What is it, and what's it doing in your pocket?" she said, grimacing.

Baptiste grinned. "Take a look at the size and shape and see if you can guess."

Leah stared at the object, and a sudden flash of understanding struck her as she recalled a whispered conversation she'd overheard between would-be *placées* at a quadroon ball.

"Oh, no!"

"Do you understand?" Baptiste asked.

"All too well." Now Leah was blushing, too, and she laughed self-consciously.

Baptiste, however, became serious. "Don't laugh. Dr.

36

Boucher says they're almost foolproof. He's making them up for me. He asked how many I'd need."

"And what did you say?"

"Oh, I said I'd need a gross to begin with." There was no change of expression on Baptiste's face.

"A gross!" Leah broke into a real laugh. "Excuse me, but the word *gross* seems to apply in more than one way. And you ordered one hundred and forty-four of those gross-looking things?" She paused. "Is that right? One hundred and forty-four? I don't like to puncture your masculine ego, but are you planning to use them or—or export them?"

Now it was Baptiste's turn to laugh uproariously. "I was just teasing. Dr. Boucher is going to make up a few to see how—how well they work."

"You mean they might not?" How could she ever truly enjoy lovemaking again if there were the constant fear of pregnancy? No, she'd have to put that out of her mind. Nothing must ever be allowed to spoil those moments when with frolicking laughter or intense passion they shared the exquisite knowledge of each other's bodies. Baptiste's next words eased her fears somewhat.

"I mean if I—if we minded using them. But your remark about exporting them might turn out to be more than a joke. Using intestines of lamb and pig and God knows what else isn't new. Been around as long as there've been men and fancy ladies who had to keep from getting pregnant to continue earning money. I saw my first one at Madame Broulé's. But—they've never been accepted as something decent for married couples to use. They've never been made with an eye to general widespread distribution."

"Why not?" Now Leah was serious. There must be hundreds, thousands of other women who feared pregnancy as much as she did.

"Because of the association with brothels. They're not nice. No man would bring one into his wife's bedroom. That, and the feeling that copulation is dirty or nasty unless it's for procreation. So what's happened? You saw it in New Orleans. If a wife doesn't want a child every year, the husband acquires a mistress—if he's wealthy. If not, he goes to a whorehouse or picks a prostitute from the streets. And picks up some painful and undesirable side effects, too."

Leah found herself fascinated. "So what do you have in mind? How can you change people's attitudes?"

"I don't know. That may be the unanswerable question. But what do you think if we worked through other doctors?

37

They'd know who the women are—at least some of the women—who dare not get pregnant again but who don't want to lose their husbands' love. The doctors could approach the husbands, just as Dr. Boucher did with me."

"And the ones who simply don't want more children? What about them?" She was thinking about women who conceived year after year, with no hope of relief.

"No," Baptiste said, "I think we'd have to stick with the ones who were in danger. At least for a while."

"Even so, it's a very delicate subject, Baptiste. You're entering the forbidden area—the marital bed."

"I know, but do you think I'm wrong?"

"I don't know." Leah flexed her legs under the coverlet. Something that could save lives couldn't be all wrong, and yet—"I don't know how many other couples have as close, as understanding, a relationship as we have."

"We're not the world's only ideal lovers, chérie, though we may think there's never been a love to equal ours."

"Please, Baptiste, don't shatter my romantic illusions. Seriously, though, how many others can talk about something like this as freely as we do?"

"Well, we sure as hell can't go around asking them, but I'll wager a thousand-franc investment that enough do to make it a profitable venture."

"You're serious, aren't you?" she asked. "You've already figured—just while we've talked—how much to put into it?"

"I have. And I've more ideas. Dr. Boucher could supervise the manufacturing and make the contacts. Then I'd handle the actual distribution."

"And you'd make money?"

"Will you believe me, chérie, if I say I don't even care if I get my investment back? I've had to watch you suffer and nearly die because we love each other. Why should death result from two people loving each other and wanting to find fulfillment in each other's arms? No, if Dr. Boucher will agree, I'll handle the distribution at a loss. But I don't think I'll have to."

"Don't you—don't you think we should try it first?"

"Is that an invitation?"

"Not yet, darling. I wish I could say yes, but I'm just not ready."

"Pain?" Baptiste's worried look returned.

"No, just more of a feeling I'm not quite ready yet. Dr. Boucher said at least two months, and I think he's right.

Don't worry," she said, reaching for his hand, "I don't want to wait any longer than you do."

For the moment they were content to sit together quietly, hold hands, and feel the love flowing between them.

Madame Charpentier, the wet nurse, came out onto the terrace carrying Robert. "He's just finished eating," she said, smiling, "and now he wants to be held by his mama."

"And his mama wants to hold him," Leah said, reaching up and taking him into her arms. She unwrapped the light blanket and ran her fingers over his cheeks. "Look, Baptiste, he's getting a dimple in the same place as yours. And I think his hair is going to curl."

"Those few wisps! How can you tell?"

"See, right here." She pointed to a little swirl of hair near the crown of his head. Then she spoke to Madame Charpentier. "We'll keep him here with us a while. Where are the other children?"

"At lunch, ma'am. They've asked if they can come out here to have their dessert with you."

"They're eating lunch," Leah exclaimed, "and I've just finished breakfast. What a lazy person I'm getting to be."

"Not lazy, Leah," Baptiste insisted, "recuperating."

"Yes, tell them to come out. And have Blanchette bring me some dessert, too."

"Your sweet tooth is never satisfied, is it, chérie?" Baptiste laughed.

"Never! I hope it's something good and rich and gooey with lots of the whipped cream I had on my cocoa. Forget about my figure. Will you care if I get old and fat?"

"On you, chérie, anything will look good. You're not getting too tired to stay out here for a while longer?"

"Good heavens, no. This is more comfortable than sitting up in bed. Anyway, I want to be one of the family again." She began playing with Robert's fingers and toes. "I love you, Baptiste."

"I'm glad. But why did you say it now?"

"Because I feel that love every time I look at the baby—and the others. And I decided I don't say it often enough just—just to say it."

When the children came out, they all crowded around Leah until Blanchette brought dessert; then they scrambled away to find comfortable seats. Lisette, the proper young lady, sat at a small table. Jean pulled a chair up next to his father, while Henri and Nicole plopped down on the steps of the terrace. Denise remained close to Leah's chair and held one of Robert's tiny hands in hers.

"May I hold him, Mama? I'll be very careful."

"I don't know why not. Pull a chair close to me. Now, sit far back and keep him on your lap."

Denise sat without moving, completely enraptured by the tiny creature yawning and squirming in her lap. Even after the others wandered away to their own interests, she remained quiet and still.

"May I sleep in his room, Mama?"

"Oh, no. He needs to have Madame Charpentier sleep with him. She has to remain close so that when he wakes in the night, she can feed him."

"But I can do all of that, all but feed him. I could carry him into Madame's room. Or I could share the room with them. Please, Mama, I'm his sister. I won't get in the way, I promise. I just want to be near him all the time. He's so beautiful." She swirled one of the tiny tendrils of hair with the tip of her finger. "I love babies. I hope I have hundreds of them."

Leah looked over at Nicole, who had come back to the terrace and was standing shyly to one side. This was very unlike the vibrant Nicole, who was usually in the middle of things. She and Denise had shared a room almost since she was born, and Denise had been her confidante, comforter, and constant playmate all her life. If the truth were told, Denise was far more of a mother to Nicole than Leah had ever been. It was Denise to whom Nicole ran when she was hurt, and it was Denise's bed she crawled into when she was cold or frightened. What Leah saw now in the eyes of the one who had been the baby in the family for more than six years was not so much jealousy of Robert, but deep, unremitting hurt at Denise's rejection. It was what one sees in the eyes of a little puppy when the mother dog is ready to wean it and pushes it away.

"No, Denise, you may not move into Robert's room. But you may help me care for him every day. We'll bathe him together as soon as I feel strong enough."

"May I help Madame until then? Please."

"We'll see. I'll have to talk to her." Leah looked again at Nicole, who had not moved from her place by the pillar. "Would you like to hold Robert for a little bit?"

"No!" Nicole said, and Leah was struck by the defiance in her voice. "I don't like babies." She turned and ran into the garden.

There will be another day, Leah thought, *when I can get her alone with the baby. She'll learn to love him, too.*

Denise's great pleasure was to hold Robert as often as permitted. In the past, it had been Nicole she held every evening and read to, and at first Nicole thought that if she ignored Denise, her sister would come seeking her. But it hadn't worked out that way. Denise remained as absorbed in Robert as ever. So she tried another tack.

"Hold me, Denise."

"Please, Nicole, can't you see I'm holding Robert so he won't cry? He's always quiet when I hold him. He loves me."

I love you, too! Nicole wanted to scream. Instead, she began jumping up and down, saying, "Hold me, hold me," over and over in a singsong, mewing voice.

"Stop it, Nicole! You'll make him cry. I've just gotten him to sleep."

"I don't care. Give him to Mama. Then you can hold me. Papa brought me a new picture book today. We can read it together."

"Mama's asleep and Madame's eating her supper. That's why I'm holding Robert. Now go play. I'll read to you later."

But later would never come, at least not for Nicole. She looked at Denise cradling Robert in her arms. *I hate you,* she thought, not realizing that what she really meant was: *I love you, but you no longer love me enough to realize how much I need you.*

Chapter Six

"PAPA."

Baptiste felt Jean's hand on his arm. Baptiste and Leah were sitting on the terrace; they'd been talking until just moments before, when she'd fallen asleep.

"Sssh, Jean," Baptiste whispered. "I want your mama to sleep a bit. She's been up most of the morning, and she needs her rest."

"I know," Jean said quietly. "That's why I want you to

41

come with me. So we won't disturb her while I tell you something."

"Can't it wait? She may wake up if I move my chair."

"No, Papa. It's terribly important. I mean, it's really serious."

What could Jean want now? Baptiste turned and looked at his son's face. He was surprised to see fear there.

"Then whisper it to me. If it's as important as you say, I'll come with you."

Jean put his lips close to Baptiste's ear. "Nicole is missing."

"What!" The word exploded from him, and Leah opened her eyes.

"Anything wrong, Baptiste?" she asked.

"No, just something the children want me to see. Go back to sleep. I'll send Blanchette out to sit with you."

Jean rolled his father's chair from the terrace into the main hall, where Lisette, Henri, and Denise were waiting for them. It wasn't until the heavy doors were closed that Baptiste trusted himself to speak.

"What do you mean Nicole is missing?" Missing could mean so many things—hiding during a game, wandering away for a few minutes; or disappearing completely—lost. But Nicole couldn't get lost in the house; she'd lived in it all her life.

"Oh, Papa," Lisette sobbed, and wrung her hands, "we've looked all over for her."

"All through the house?"

"Yes and the garden and—"

"And even the sheds," Denise interrupted.

"How long has she been gone?" Baptiste tried not to reveal in his voice the fear gnawing at his heart.

"We don't know," Lisette said. "I saw her at breakfast, but when Blanchette called us for lunch, she didn't answer."

Baptiste pulled his watch from his pocket and saw that it was now past three. "Why didn't you tell me then?" Only God knew what might have happened to her during those hours.

"You were eating with Mama in her room," Jean answered, "and we didn't want to worry her. We were sure we'd find Nicole before now."

"Breakfast was the last time anyone saw her?" That was well over six hours ago. A little girl of seven could get hurt, lost, or stuck somewhere; by now, she'd be absolutely terrified and hysterical. "Why didn't you miss her earlier? Surely you were used to seeing her around at some point during the morning." He felt like whipping every one of them, but then he realized they couldn't be blamed for something their sister had done if they'd had no part in it.

"No, Papa," Jean said, becoming the spokesman for the others. "Nicole often goes off by herself. She says she wants to be alone. Sometimes she's gone all morning or afternoon. Sometimes she even has lunch in the kitchen with Blanchette."

"She did say she was going into the garden with her dolls," Henri offered.

"I—I offered to play with her," Denise said, "but she said something about wanting to have her babies all to herself."

The garden, Baptiste thought. That seemed safe enough. But the garden led to the fields and to the river. No, he mustn't think about the river. Nicole was old enough to know not to get too close to the water. She'd been warned often enough. But if she'd been playing on the bank, she might have slipped and been pulled under by her full skirts.

He thought about Catherine, Lisette's mother. She'd been found in the water, trapped under a log after her dress had caught on it. No, he'd think about the fields and how Nicole loved to watch the farmers working. Or perhaps she'd wandered into the nearby woods filled with the tempting splendor of wild flowers. It would be very easy for her to get lost there.

"Henri," Baptiste said.

"Yes, Papa."

"I want you to go to the village. Tell the schoolmaster what's happened and ask him to call all the men together for a search party. Ask them to meet me at the front of the house. If at all possible, I want to keep your mama from becoming alarmed."

"What do you think has happened to Nicole?" Jean's fifteen-year-old voice had suddenly assumed a more mature, more serious timbre.

"I think she's probably wandered a bit too far and got lost. She might not yet realize she's lost, but I want to find her before dark or she'll be a very frightened little girl. While Henri goes to the village, I want you to go to the Villemonts', the Jacquards', the Beaumonts', and Count Boileau's." These were friends who lived on nearby domains. "Ask the men for help. Move as fast as you can, but take time to make clear what's happened and why we don't want Mama to know."

"You—you don't think she's run away on purpose?" Jean asked hesitantly.

"No. Is there any reason she should?"

Jean shook his head, but he looked at Denise, who lowered her eyes without saying anything. "Yes, sir," he answered, "we'll go right now. Come on, Henri."

The two boys ran off, and Baptiste turned to the girls. "I want you to search the house again from top to bottom, garret to kitchen."

Lisette nodded. "Yes, Papa. Maybe she's returned since we stopped looking."

"Maybe. So look in closets and cupboards. She might have crawled into one and fallen asleep."

Clutching her beloved rag doll to her mud-splattered bodice, Nicole huddled against the damp, clammy stones. She'd forgotten how dark it could be. The last time she'd ventured in here she'd been with all the others, and Denise had held her hand the whole time. Nicole had always been teeth-chatteringly afraid of the dark. If only someone were with her. Anyone. No, anyone but Denise. She never wanted to see her again.

It was getting colder, and the darkness kept closing in. She found it harder to breathe. Her heart began pounding; she could hear it and feel it inside her chest. The stale, musty smell was making her sick. When she started shivering again, she wished she'd brought her hooded cape; yet, young as she was, she sensed that the shivering was more from fear than from cold. If she shifted a little, she could pull her wool skirt up around her shoulders. It helped a bit, but only for a few minutes. The damp from the stone floor seeped through her light flannel petticoat and linen bloomers, and she pulled the skirt back down under her.

Why had she come to this place anyway? There was only one answer: to get away from Denise. To be alone where no one would find her. At least until she figured out how she could run away for good. She'd gone first to the woods, where she'd picked a whole armful of flowers while she thought about running away. She'd heard Jean say there was a path through the woods to St. Denis, and she just knew someone there would like to have a little girl who was no longer loved at home. But she couldn't find the path, and she was afraid of getting lost. She would have to think of some other way to get there. Or someplace else to go.

Nicole didn't want to return home. Never again did she

44

want to see Denise or Robert. She'd miss Mama and Papa and maybe some of the others. But not Denise, who'd deserted her in favor of the new baby. Denise who'd shared her room all these years and whose bed she could crawl into whenever she awoke from a nightmare, or if she got cold when her covers slid to the floor. Or even when she'd had an accident and wet the bed. It was Denise who took care of her in the day, too, never laughed when she said stupid things, and defended her when Lisette and the boys teased her.

In her innermost heart, Nicole always called Denise *"ma petite maman."* She wished she'd never confided to Denise that she was her little mother. She sobbed now, remembering how, at the time, they'd snuggled deeper under the covers and Denise had said she wanted a dozen children just like her precious Nicole.

No, she didn't ever want to return home. At first, she hadn't known where to go. Then she'd remembered this place and the entrance to it that Henri had found when they were playing in the shrubbery. It was possible to get in here without having to go into the house.

She'd only meant to stay here until she'd figured out where to go. But she'd forgotten how dark it was. And last time she'd had Denise's hand to hold the whole time. She clutched Nissi, her rag doll, more tightly. Nissi, named after her early childish lisping of the name Denise. Somehow she had to find the courage to make her way back. She'd missed lunch and she was hungry. Maybe it wouldn't be too bad to go back to the house, at least for supper and the night. Let Denise spend all her time with Robert. Nicole would show her she didn't need her.

In spite of her resolve not to cry, tears welled up in Nicole's eyes and ran unchecked down her cheeks. She'd loved Denise so completely, and now she felt terribly, terribly alone. No one would ever take Denise's place. She wouldn't let them.

Now she curled up against the wall, finding a certain security in its protection, and she hugged Nissi tighter in her arms. Maybe she'd fall asleep; then, when she woke up, she'd think about returning home.

Waiting at the front entrance of the château, Baptiste was pleased to see the men from the village coming in response to his call for help in finding Nicole. But it was Count Boileau, with several of his laborers, who approached him first.

"What's this I hear, Baptiste, about Nicole being missing?"

"Afraid it's true, Simon. We've searched the house and the grounds. No sign of her."

"You think she wandered off or—" Count Boileau stopped here.

"You're saying she might have been taken? I haven't allowed myself to think about that. No, one or the other of the children have been outside all day, and they didn't see either Nicole or a stranger near the house."

"So we need a search party," the count concluded. "Where do you want me to start?"

"I see Jacquard and Beaumont coming with their workers," Baptiste said. "And the schoolmaster with the men from the village. Let's wait until they get here so we can plan it carefully."

Count Boileau turned to meet the others and explain the situation. At the same time, Jean ran up the steps to say that Monsieur Villemont wasn't home, but Madame Villemont would soon be there with several of her servants to see what she could do to help.

Soon there were more than forty men ready to begin the search. All of them were deeply concerned about their pretty little Nicole. She had won their hearts long ago when she'd walked through the fields with her older brother and talked with them while they worked.

"We'll find her, Monsieur Fontaine," vowed one of the farmers. "We love her almost as much as you do."

"You know her that well?" Baptiste was stunned.

"Yes, sir. She often comes to the fields with Jean, and she has almost as many questions about what we're doing as he does."

Baptiste raised his eyebrows at his oldest son. He had no idea that Jean was interested in farming; he'd talk with him about that later.

Aware of Baptiste's worry, Count Boileau assumed the role of leader of the group. Quickly, and with no wasted words, he organized the men into small groups and dispatched them to the woods, the adjoining fields, and the river.

"We've time to search carefully before dark," he said, "so don't overlook any hiding place—shrubs, sheds, barns, and so on. Also, places where she might have fallen and gotten hurt. We don't know how long she's been missing, so we can't know how far she's gone. We won't stop until we find her.

And remember—keep calling her name and then stop long enough to listen."

Like an army on the offensive, the men dispersed immediately in every direction. Count Boileau remained behind to join the Fontaine children for another search of the estate.

Almost immediately after they'd begun, the Villemont carriage turned into the drive and stopped in front of the house. Madame Villemont, in an elegant tea gown and with her white hair piled atop her head, stepped carefully down.

"I'm so sorry, Baptiste, but don't fret; the men will find Nicole."

"If only I could be sure of that. I feel so helpless—and yes, cowardly, standing here and letting others do what I should be doing."

"Nonsense, Baptiste." Madame Villemont was never one to mince words. "You can't and that's that. No use weeping over what can't be helped. Those men are your friends, and they're happy to help. Don't ever be afraid to take when you must; the time will come when you'll be the one to give."

"I guess you're right." Baptiste collapsed into the chair Jean had placed near him.

"Of course I am. Now, send for some wine, and I'll sit here with you while we wait. How's Leah?"

"Feeling somewhat better, but—she doesn't know about Nicole."

"Very wise. Is Blanchette with her?"

"Yes, but she'll soon begin to wonder where I am," Baptiste said.

"Then go back with her, but only if you can keep her from questioning you. You'll have to straighten up your face."

"I'll tell her the children have me doing something out here."

"No, you won't," Madame Villemont said imperiously. "You'll never make Leah believe it. Stay here while I go visit with her. I can lie much better than you. We'll talk woman talk about food and babies, and I'll bore her with all my stories about my grandchildren. Then I'll ask to see Robert. That will keep her occupied for a while."

"What about the wine you wanted me to send for?"

"You drink it. You look as if you need it. I'll wait until they find Nicole. Meanwhile, I'll suggest to Blanchette that she bring us cakes and coffee. If I know Blanchette, she'll be delighted."

Baptiste watched Madame Villemont walk away with the

assured stride of a true horsewoman and the proudly arched neck of a natural châtelaine. "To the manner born," thought Baptiste, quoting *Hamlet*.

She was right. He could never have hidden his fears from Leah. He'd never been able to conceal his feelings from her. She'd known he loved her long before he would admit it to himself. She had recognized that his unwillingness to make love after losing his legs was from the fear that he was impotent. It was she who had dared to take the initiative by making love to him, thereby restoring his confidence in himself. He would have gone the rest of his life avoiding her for fear he could not act rather than risk failure. No, nothing could be kept from Leah for long.

He could only pray Nicole would be found before Leah realized that something unusual was going on and asked where all the children were. Usually, when she was on the terrace, they would run to her constantly to ask how she was feeling and to tell her what they were doing.

Then he heard it. Echoing and re-echoing across the fields came the voices of the men calling Nicole's name. If he heard it, so could Leah. There would be no hiding the situation from her now. He turned his chair around, made his way through the wide doors and down the hall, and wheeled out onto the terrace.

"Baptiste, what's going on?" Leah demanded in her don't-try-to lie-to-me voice. She was sitting straight up on the chaise longue. "Madame Villemont and I were sitting here chatting. Then suddenly I heard voices calling for Nicole. She's missing, isn't she?"

Baptiste looked at Leah and knew he had to tell her the truth. She prided herself on her strength, yet he wondered if she were strong enough to accept that her favorite was missing. In one sense—the most important one—she loved her children equally, but everyone knew and understood the special feelings she had for Nicole, who was so much like her.

"We think she's wandered away—maybe into the woods or fields—and maybe gotten lost. But there are enough men looking for her to find her before dark."

"Oh, Baptiste, it's all my fault." Leah tried hard to hide her tears.

"No, no, chérie, it's not. Why ever would you think that?"

"Because I've given her so little attention since Robert came."

48

"You've been ill. You can't blame yourself. As to that, all of us have been guilty of making a fuss over Robert."

"Not all. Not Nicole. She won't even look at him. More than that, I think she's hurt because Denise spends so much time with him. I should have spoken to Denise when I realized what was happening." She paused. "Yes, it really is my fault if she's run away."

"If you saw that, I should have, too," Baptiste said.

"Stop berating yourselves," Madame Villemont said sternly. "What's done is done. I had nine children and there were plenty of times when one was jealous of another. But it always passed with a little extra love from me. As long as Nicole is assured of your love, she'll be all right."

"I hope so," Baptiste said. What he was really thinking was: *I pray she will be found so we can smother her with love.*

Count Boileau returned to the house shaking his head. His and the children's search of the grounds had been futile. Not even a clue of any kind to indicate that Nicole had been playing there—if indeed she had.

Baptiste drew the count aside. "How far did you go?"

"Not as far as the river if that's what you're thinking. Not with the children. But I have several men looking along there. We should hear from them soon."

Baptiste's head and shoulders drooped. He couldn't keep from his mind the sight of a little body floating atop the water or trapped beneath one of the overhanging trees.

Nicole woke up and thought for the briefest moment that she was in her own room and someone had turned out the light. She started to call for Denise. Then she remembered where she was, but she was not going to cry again.

"It's all right, Nissi. I'll hold you tight. There's nothing to fear. We're not going to be afraid, 'cause there's nothing to be scared of. Not even in the dark. You're my only Nissi now, and I won't leave you behind."

In the stillness she heard the fearsome, continual lapping of the river against the banks. She was nearer to the water than she'd realized. So close she might have fallen in. Papa had always forbidden her to go near the banks, and he would be angry if he knew she'd disobeyed him.

Now she imagined other sounds, too, haunting the blackness. Footsteps and voices. Coming nearer, then receding. She remembered the stories Papa had told them of wicked men in hoods and capes who chased frightened people as they fled toward the river. They couldn't be here now. They were all dead. But it could be their ghosts, and ghosts were more terrifying than real people, because they could walk through walls and float down from the ceiling. Henri loved to sneak into her room and turn off the light, then pretend to be a ghost to frighten her. Maybe this was where the ghosts lived when they weren't in the house.

Now there was no thought of going back, not if she had to pass the ghosts. She was really very tired and hungry. She'd long since eaten the apple and the cookies she'd taken from the kitchen. Now she was so hungry her stomach was hurting. In spite of her fear of the ghosts, she thought maybe she should go back toward the house after all.

"Come, Nissi, Mama and Papa will be glad to see us."

But which way to go? She'd been surrounded by darkness for so long that she'd forgotten which way she'd come. She listened for the sound of the river, but now it seemed to be lapping and rushing all around her.

"We'll go this way, Nissi," she said, but when she tried to stand after sitting for so long in the same position, her legs were cramped and her feet slipped in the muddy ooze.

At sunset, most of the searchers returned to the house.

"We'll need torches now, Baptiste," Monsieur Jacquard said, "and whatever lanterns we can round up."

"Then send the men to find them. And we'll have something here for them to eat before they set out again."

Blanchette set up buffet tables in the long hall, and some men ate while others went for the lanterns and torches. When they returned, the first group resumed the search while the second group ate. The children stood around and watched silently. They feared no less than their parents did that something dreadful had happened to Nicole. Blanchette kept urging them to eat something even as the tears coursed down her plump, heat-reddened cheeks. Nicole was a favorite of hers, too. Always stealing cookies behind her back and then smiling like the little angel she was. "Eat," Blanchette scolded the other children once again. "Your mama wouldn't want you to starve to death."

All but Denise obeyed without question. She felt sick to her stomach, and she knew it was from guilt. It was she who had sent Nicole away by paying so much attention to Robert. She'd made her sister feel unwanted and unloved.

"And who's been into my cookie jar today?" Blanchette

asked. "Don't lie to me. One of you was, and you left enough crumbs to bring every mouse from the fields into my kitchen."

All four shook their heads. "I haven't even been in the kitchen," Jean said. He turned to the others. "Have you?" Again they shook their heads in denial.

"What was that you said, Blanchette?" Baptiste had caught part of the conversation.

"I said someone got into my cookie jar and left crumbs all over the counter and the floor. It took the better part of the morning to clean it up. It's a wonder we aren't already besieged by mice."

"And none of you has been in there today?" Baptiste asked. "Answer me and don't lie about it."

"No, Papa." They spoke as one. Then, still in one voice, they shouted, "Nicole!"

"But you searched the kitchen, didn't you?"

"Yes, Papa," Lisette answered, "the kitchen and the pantries."

"The wine cellar," Baptiste said. "Did any of you think to go down there?"

"No, sir," Henri answered. "You've forbidden us to even open the door."

"But Nicole might have. Jean, run see if the door is still locked."

Why Nicole would go down into that dark, damp, chilly place Baptiste could not imagine, unless it was because she was not running away but merely seeking a place to be alone. Nicole was his and Leah's most sensitive child and if, as Leah had said, she'd been deeply hurt, she might react in the way of a wounded animal, crawling away to suffer its pain in peace. Well, he would find her and she wouldn't have to suffer anymore.

Jean came panting back into the hall. "It's unlocked, Papa. I called down the stairs, but she didn't answer. Should we go look?"

"Yes, but I'm coming with you. Hand me my crutches and go find us some lanterns."

The search through the wine cellar revealed neither Nicole nor any clue that she'd been there. Baptiste had been so certain he would find cookie crumbs leading to her hiding place. But there were none.

Baptiste leaned on his crutches for more than physical support. "I was so sure we'd find her here."

"How about the tunnel?" Lisette asked.

"I tried the door," Jean said, "and it's still locked."

A tunnel from the wine cellar to the river had been excavated during the religious persecutions of the sixteenth century. It had enabled the residents of the château to hide or to flee by way of the river. Whether the original owners had been Roman Catholics or Huguenots, Baptiste did not know, but there was ample evidence that the tunnel had been used frequently. The door leading into it from the wine cellar originally had been hidden by a cupboard that could be swung away by means of a concealed device. Baptiste had found the device when he tore down the decayed cupboard while restoring the cellar for his own use. But he'd put a strong lock on the door and, after taking the children through the tunnel just once, had strictly forbidden them to enter it again.

Knowing children, Baptiste realized they had probably disobeyed him more than once, but now was not the time to think about chastising them.

"How about the secret entrance?" Henri asked.

"What secret entrance?" Now it was Baptiste's turn to be surprised.

"The one behind the shrubbery around the tool shed," Lisette said.

A second entrance. Baptiste paused to consider it. Of course, there would be another entrance for anyone in the family caught outside if the persecutors arrived unexpectedly.

"When did you find it?" he asked.

"Oh, a long time ago," Jean said. "We were playing hide-and-seek, and when Henri leaned against the door, it broke open. It's a very small door, just big enough to crawl through. But it opens onto steps down to the tunnel. Nicole was with us when we went in it one time, so she knows about it."

Baptiste hobbled as fast as he could to the locked door from the wine cellar, reached to the ledge overhead for the key, and opened the lock.

"Bring the lanterns over here. Henri, you lead the way. Jean, I'll need your shoulder to lean on. Those steps and the rocky floor are slippery. You girls stay here."

"No, Papa," they pleaded in unison, "please let us go. We want to find Nicole, too."

"Please, Papa, I have to find her." Baptiste could see the tears in Denise's eyes.

"All right. You follow Henri while Jean and I bring up the rear. But slowly and carefully. We don't want any broken bones."

The tunnel was only wide enough for them to walk single file. Even with the lanterns, it was hard to keep an eye on the person ahead and on the slippery stones underfoot at the same time.

The nearer they got to the river, the more Baptiste feared that either Nicole had not come in here or that she had gone too far and fallen into the water where it washed the entrance to the tunnel. If she had, she would still be out of sight of the men searching for her. Pray God they would find her alive—or not at all.

Jean seemed to sense what was troubling his father. "Don't worry, Papa, we haven't come to the second entrance yet. It's still several feet along. And if she did enter that way, she'd probably be farther ahead."

They continued to move slowly, Henri leading with the largest lantern and calling Nicole's name from time to time.

"Here they are, Papa, the second steps," Jean said. "So it won't be long before we find her."

"Look," Henri said, lowering his lantern to the floor, "here's a cookie she dropped and then stepped on. She is in here!"

His voice was so elated that Baptiste felt the same excitement in his own heart. Knowing Nicole's fear of the dark, he realized she wouldn't have come in here unless she were deeply troubled. If—no, when—they found her, they must do everything possible to assure her of their love.

"Nicole! Nicole!" It was Jean who had rushed ahead and was shouting now. "I've found her. She's asleep, but I don't think she's hurt at all."

"Let me by," Denise pleaded. "Let me wake her up."

"Wait a minute," Jean said. "Don't shove. Wait till Papa gets here."

As well as he could while being supported by Jean, Baptiste bent down and gently shook Nicole as he called her name. She lay no more than three feet from where the river swirled in and washed the stone floor of the tunnel. But it was Denise who sat on the muddy floor and tried to take her sister into her arms.

Slowly Nicole awoke, but she was blinded for a moment by the bright light. And for just that moment she thought she'd been attacked by the ghosts of the persecutors.

"No! No!" she screamed. "Let me alone." When she finally recognized Denise, she screamed even louder. "Go away! I hate you!" Ferociously, like a trapped animal, she struck out at Denise and began clawing her face. "I hate you. I hate you. I won't go back with you."

Gradually her screams turned into sobs, and when Baptiste finally lowered himself to the floor, she allowed him to comfort her.

"Mama's very worried about you," he said gently. "We've all been worried. Won't you come back with us?" Leah had been right. Nicole had felt deserted because of all their attention to Robert, especially Denise's. Perhaps it had been natural for the children to expend all their love on the new baby, after their fear that their mother was going to die and then Leah's inability to care for them. But Nicole was much too young to understand. In a sense she had been deprived of two mothers.

"I—I guess so," she hiccupped between sobs.

Nicole allowed Jean to pick her up and carry her back through the tunnel, but only if Baptiste stayed between her and Denise. Nor would she listen to anything Denise tried to say to her. It was too late.

"Now we can have the wine," Baptiste suggested to Madame Villemont. Nicole, in her wet and muddy dress, had been sufficiently hugged and reassured of her mother's love and then taken away by Blanchette to be bathed and fed. Throughout it all, the other children had hovered close around her, refusing to let her out of their sight.

"And I presume you will be opening one of your best vintages," Madame Villemont said with a chuckle.

"Not just for us, either," Baptiste affirmed. "But for all the men. Jacquard, Beaumont, and Count Boileau are taking care of that for me, and they will be joining us in a few minutes."

While Baptiste sipped his wine and watched the color return to Leah's face, he knew it would be a long time before the knots in his heart would loosen and he could breathe easily again.

As for Leah, she knew her turn had come now to help her disturbed youngest daughter. Baptiste had told her how Nicole lashed out at Denise and refused to let her sister near her. Something had to be done or the breach between the two of them would become irreparable. Leah had long ago determined that she would find time every day to be alone with each of her children. Even when one or another was ill and demanded more of her time, she had managed to be

54

available to the others. Her own illness after the birth of Robert had made it difficult to keep that tacit promise to them, but now that she was recovering she would let them know she was able to see them whenever they needed her.

Right now it was Denise she must talk to. For the past two days she'd devoted most of her time to Nicole; she'd held her when the child wanted to remain quietly in her lap or listened when Nicole wanted to talk. But surprisingly, the girl had said nothing about her flight or her hours in the tunnel. Sometime—somehow—Leah would have to get her to talk about her experience, or it would eat away like a cancer in the dark recesses of Nicole's mind.

"And what have you been doing this morning?" Leah asked when Denise came into her room.

"Helped dress Robert and then talked to Madame Charpentier while she nursed him. He was awake and I held him in my lap while she put clean blankets in his cradle."

"You love Robert very much, don't you?"

"He's like my own baby, Mama, until I'm old enough to have my very own."

"And when you do have your own children," Leah said gently but firmly, "will you give them away when they reach six or seven? Or when a new one comes along?"

"Of course not, Mama. What a horrible idea."

"Isn't that what you've done with Nicole?"

"Oh, Mama, that's different. She's my sister."

"Is it so different, Denise? Is Nicole any less easily hurt because she is your sister rather than your daughter?"

Denise recalled with shame how Nicole had called her *"petite maman"* from the time she began to talk. Yet she knew she'd offered to play with Nicole whenever Robert was asleep. And wasn't it Nicole who had struck out at her and was now refusing to talk to her or share the dollhouse that Papa had made for both of them?

"I've tried, Mama, truly I have. It's not all my fault Nicole ran away and hid in the tunnel "

"No, dear, we've all paid too much attention to the baby."

"She could play with him, too, if she wanted to. She's not a baby anymore."

"That's the problem," Leah said. "She's no longer the baby of the family, and she feels the change in all of us. But you've always been someone special to her. Much more than Papa and I. So if we all try a little harder . . . ?"

"I will, Mama, but I can't do anything if she won't talk to me."

"Just give her a little more time and be very patient with her." The gentlest, most considerate, most loving of the children, Denise had, this time, been misguided by her own motherly instincts. But Leah trusted her to know how to restore Nicole's love and confidence.

"I promise, Mama," Denise said and leaned over for the kiss that always concluded these intimate chats.

But the damage had been done, and from that time on, Nicole would have nothing to do with Denise. The final break came when Nicole spent a whole day patiently and laboriously moving her things into the spare bedroom across the hall from the room she had always shared with Denise.

When Baptiste found she had pulled her mattress off the bed and was trying to lug it across to the new room, he asked Jean and Henri to help her. The boys moved her bed and other furniture, and she was not content until every single one of her possessions was in the room and she could close her own door on the rest of the world.

Chapter Seven

BAPTISTE'S ENTRY into the contraceptive business never quite became the unqualified success he and Dr. Boucher had worked so hard to achieve. There were immediate objections from most of Dr. Boucher's colleagues. Some doctors felt they would be tampering with God's will; others shook their heads and said the lamb skins would never move from the bordello to the boudoir. The more practical said that men wouldn't use them and women wouldn't allow any artificial substance into their bodies from revulsion and fear of infection. Privately, Dr. Boucher and Baptiste felt that these doctors were cowards and reactionaries, since many who came to this conclusion about contraceptives had never even talked to their patients about them.

A few doctors, however, said they would suggest using

contraceptives to the husbands of those patients who really should not get pregnant again. For them, Dr. Boucher manufactured a few dozen a month, which Baptiste distributed. The only really discouraging note was that the majority went to—of all places—bordellos in and around Paris. The owners were ecstatic at finding a ready supply.

A few of the skins went to Dr. Boucher's professional acquaintances in England, and Baptiste shipped them in boxes labeled "Medical Supplies." Eventually a customs officer opened one box, and then all hell broke loose in Victorian England. The export business came to an immediate end.

"Are you disappointed?" Leah asked, after Baptiste told her the news.

"Yes, dammit! Those narrow-minded, do-gooding busybodies have nothing better to do than condemn something that would save hundreds of lives and, according to Dr. Boucher, control the spread of disease. Instead, those men are piously wringing their hands and shaking their heads over the high rate of maternity deaths and the plight of the poor women who walk the streets to earn a living and then die from the foulest of diseases. I'll never understand the way men's minds work, Leah. But I'll try exporting again after all the furor calms down. I won't give up."

"I'll bet if the women in England were asked what they wanted," Leah said, "you'd be shipping hundreds every week."

"And when have women ever been asked, or been allowed to speak out, about anything concerning what's in their best interests?"

"My word, Baptiste, you sound like some of those independent women I've read about."

"Well, maybe it's time women were heard. Weren't there times when you wanted to shout out to all the world your feelings about your own humiliating and degrading situation in New Orleans before the war?"

"Yes, but I was younger then." Leah thought a moment. "Maybe it's the young ones who should do it now, and I think they will. Perhaps I was too passive—or maybe cowardly—but there was much to be afraid of then."

"Never a coward, Leah. You had the kind of quiet courage that always endures. So maybe the world needs both, the quiet ones who learn to endure and the outspoken ones who ultimately bring about change. But don't you change. I like you just the way you are."

"Thank you, darling. Have you thought about trying to

export them to the States through the New Orleans office?"

"Yes, but I gave it up. At least for the time being. No point in being slapped down again, but maybe sometime in the future."

As disappointed as he was over his failure to revolutionize the medical community's and the public's attitude toward contraceptive devices, Baptiste was soon deeply immersed in a new project. In 1880, Ferdinand de Lesseps, who had become a French hero with the building of the Suez Canal, organized the Panama Company to construct a canal through the Isthmus of Panama. Since then, Baptiste had read about the project from time to time, and he was becoming increasingly fascinated by the plans to open up a waterway between the Atlantic and Pacific oceans. As well, he was interested in making the kind of money the backers of the Suez had made.

So far he'd said nothing to Leah. Now he thought he'd like her opinion of his investing in the Panama Company.

"Isn't the export company doing well?" was her response to his suggestion.

"Very well. In fact we have surplus funds that should be invested someplace. I've continued to put most of our profits back into the company, but we have as many ships as we need, and I don't see opening any additional offices at this time. Ultimately, once the canal is completed, we could consider an office in San Francisco. Then we could really expand our Far Eastern business as far as the States are concerned."

"But you are doubtful about the future of the Panama Company?"

"Not at all. Look at the fantastic returns the investors in the Suez have received. And there's long been a need for a water passage bisecting Central America. Men have trekked across the Isthmus for years to get from one ocean to the other, from one end of the United States to the other, instead of rounding the Horn. So think what a tremendous boon this will be for shipping as well as travelers. Yes, a San Francisco office would definitely be in the picture then."

"I can understand all that," Leah said, not wanting to dampen his enthusiasm. "But isn't this something for large investors, like banks and the big money houses?" She asked the question both because she wanted to know all the aspects of the project and because she was wary of investing money in anything Baptiste did not control himself.

"No, that's just it. DeLesseps is seeking the small investors. He says that after the success of the Suez, he wants to give more people the chance to make money."

"But something's bothering you," she persisted, "or you wouldn't be asking my advice."

"Not really. I just wanted to let you know what I was planning to do. I don't like making decisions involving that much money without consulting you. After the success of the Suez Canal, there can be no question about the financial returns from the Panama project."

"Thank you, Baptiste," she said, smiling. "I like to be assured I'm still important to you."

"Important to me! It was your family that put me here. And I certainly would never have got the plantation back if it hadn't been for your advice and insistence on using the gold your father left you to pay the taxes."

"In other words, I'm a very good business asset." In spite of herself, there was a hurt tone in her voice. Was it even remotely possible that Baptiste had married her because he felt he owed it to her?

"No, chérie." He took her in his arms. "You are my dearest possession, the wife I love very much and could not live without."

"I like that better." She'd known it, yet it was wonderful to be reassured. "But I'm glad you wanted to tell me about investing in the canal."

"And now a surprise for you," he said. "You and I are going on a holiday."

"Why? Where?" For a moment she couldn't imagine what he had in mind. Then the thought of it delighted her. Except for an occasional evening in Paris, they'd never really had any time alone together since they'd been married.

"The 'why' is that even though you're much better—doing very well indeed—you're not really going to recover your strength as long as you must run the house and also be available to the children every time they want you. In other words, you need to get away. And I need you all to myself for a while. Children are very nice things to have, but they can get in the way. I sometimes feel I'm surrounded by five chaperones. And if I want to make love to you in the afternoon, well—"

Leah laughed. "I know what you mean." She, too, thought of the numerous times one or the other of the children had awakened from a bad dream or been ill and come wandering down to their bedroom at the most awkward of times.

59

Yet she always refused to lock the door, feeling that the children should never, at any time, think they could not come to her if they needed her.

"As to the 'where,'" Baptiste said, "that's my secret. Just ask Blanchette to pack enough things for at least a fortnight, because we're not coming home until we feel like it."

"And when are we leaving?" Leah was flushed with excitement.

"Day after tomorrow. I'll drive into Paris tomorrow to see about the Panama investment, and then we'll take off."

Leah sat on the tiny second-floor balcony of the *pension* in Isigny, a small fishing village on the Normandy coast. She looked at the small but busy harbor. As both she and Baptiste had hoped, the sea air and the calm, unhurried days were already hastening her recuperation. Every morning they rose in time to breakfast on this balcony and watch the fishing boats sail off into the sunrise. Sometimes they walked the few yards to the quay to wish *bon voyage* and *bonne chance* to the last of the departing boats. Always, in the evening, they were on the quay to greet them on their return. These were their only regular rituals during the quietly lazy days.

In the mornings, while Baptiste looked over the business letters and notations sent to him, Leah read. In the afternoons, they made love and then napped. Often, before their evening visit to the quay, they drove the carriage around the small town or out into the countryside, where the cultivated fields were a flourishing green and the roadsides were one massive bouquet of colorful wildflowers.

One day Baptiste was inside, at the desk in their room, reading over the latest mail from the office. Leah had already read the short, loving notes from the children, and the longer one dictated by Blanchette to Lisette, reaffirming that all was going well and that they need not hurry home. She was relieved and not yet impatient to return to the château. In a few days she might feel differently, but right now she was enjoying her respite from familial concerns. Her greatest relief had come from Lisette's personal note, which said that while Nicole continued to avoid Denise, she was otherwise her usual happy self. It was good to know that Lisette had taken Nicole under her wing until Leah's return.

A breeze from the harbor ruffled the letters in her hand, and Leah once again felt wonderment at being alive and watching her children grow up. The experience of being close to death had reminded her of her own mortality and revealed how very finite and limited man was. What a contrast was presented by the boundless reaches beyond the harbor. She knew there was a coast on the other side, but her eyes could not see it, and therefore it seemed as if all of the seas were spread out before her—infinite, eternal, and immortal. The sky had darkened along the horizon, and now the storm-borne waves were rolling and heaving against the man-made quay. The quay would eventually at some distant time, be weakened and destroyed by the pounding waters; the waters would outlive the quay by eons and eons of time.

How like the quay she was, vulnerable and defenseless. Had she died, there would have been no violent upheaval in nature. Did that mean that in the great scheme of things her life had no significance? Or was she so much a part of all eternal life that she would be fulfilling her place in nature?

Finite and *infinite*. Her mind played with the words. Finite was anything perceived by the senses. It was anything in life that was limited to birth, growth, erosion, and ultimate destruction. Then, if everything had its opposite, what was infinite could not be perceived, nor could it grow, alter, erode, or die. Was there any part of her that was infinite? Or would her immortality be only as she was remembered in her children's minds, as René and her mother were memories in her own?

Leah shook herself. There was no point in dwelling on all this. She was getting well. But she knew that her close acquaintance with death had caused her to speculate about what was beyond.

Baptiste called to ask if she'd like to go for a short drive.

"Yes, if we leave right now before the rain comes. I think we're in for a real storm."

"I'll ring for the brougham. It should be at the door by the time we get downstairs."

Leah stood to one side while Baptiste adjusted his crutches to his satisfaction, and then she preceded him down the stairs. He never argued with her when she casually followed behind as he climbed steps, or preceded him as he descended. Leah quietly admired his refusal to pity his condition and his willingness to accept tacitly that he needed someone nearby in case he should stumble.

While they rode through the dimming twilight, Leah watched the lamps being lighted in windows, and she thought how much more alive the houses looked at night. Perhaps it was because they were filled with life: the men returning from the sea or the fields; the children in from play; the women busy at the stoves.

Suddenly Leah was overcome with a longing to return home. She missed the children dreadfully.

"Baptiste, let's go back tomorrow."

"Why? Not enjoying yourself?"

"Yes, but I'm feeling much stronger, and—I'm homesick." Not for New Orleans as she'd been on her birthday, but for the home she and Baptiste had built together.

"So am I, chérie. It's been fun, but I miss the children. Chaperones they may be, but I can't get along without them."

Leah made no move to reach for the nightgown that lay folded carefully on the chair, but she did begin to pull up the sheet.

"No," Baptiste said, and drew the sheet out of her hand.

Leah shifted ever so slightly from a supine position into a more relaxed and comfortable one on her side. "Why did you do that?"

"Are you cold?" Baptiste asked.

"No, just feeling exposed." She felt neither shame nor modesty, just a bit uncomfortable. While they made love, it was natural to lie naked under Baptiste's gaze. Afterward, it seemed more appropriate to curl up under the covers.

"I want to look at you," he said. Then, both his gaze and his fingers moved from her shoulders, breasts, and abdomen toward her thighs, and Leah reached up and put her fingertips to his cheek.

"And what do you see?" she asked.

He knew what she thought he was seeing: legs more fully fleshed, no longer as taut and firm as when she was younger; a belly slightly mounded and scoriated with faint reminders of her many pregnancies; breasts still large and full but now more pendulous from having nursed four children. It was not the body Baptiste had seen the night she became his mistress, but it was the body he loved and had possessed during the ensuing years.

"I see a very beautiful woman who grows more desirable every time I look at her."

"Do you really, Baptiste?" There was nothing coy or compliment-seeking in her voice. Having been lovers for more than twenty years, they scorned such pretensions.

"I do. I love you, Leah, more than I ever thought I could when you first came to me." He reached down and pulled the covers over both of them. It was enough now just to hold her in his arms. Passion had been satisfied and was replaced with a need for quiet contentment. "Let's never get too old to be lovers." He nestled his head in the soft curve of her neck.

This was the happiness Leah had sought for so many years. Tomorrow they would return to the children. Tonight, it was only the two of them in their own wonderfully intimate world of love.

Chapter Eight

DURING THE NEXT FEW YEARS, the character of each child began to take more definite, unique form. Leah was fascinated to see how the ultimate patterns of their lives were beginning to be evident in their diverse personalities.

From the time her children were infants, Leah had assumed the natural, maternal responsibility of watching over them closely and making decisions for them. As the older ones reached adolescence, she recognized it was time to begin letting go, to allow them to make their own decisions and then bear the responsibility for their actions.

Gradually, a step at a time, she eased up on the invisible reins that tied them to her. She continued to guide, to be ready to give advice when asked, and to be available when any of them needed her for confidential, mother-and-child talks. She remembered all too well her own fearful adolescence, full of questions she wanted to ask. But she'd been allowed only to listen. Leah was determined there would be no distance between herself and her children, especially the girls. And she was happy that Jean felt comfortable about approaching Baptiste when he wanted to talk. Lately, however, Leah had begun to sense a growing distance between Lisette and herself. She loved Lisette as deeply as she did her own children, and until recently she'd sensed Lisette returned that love and felt as close to her as if Leah had been her own mother.

Outwardly, Lisette was fulfilling her earlier promise of growing into a beautiful young woman with the blonde hair and fair skin of her mother, Catherine. To the casual observer, she was still the same loving daughter and sister she'd always been. When Nicole felt deserted by Denise, it was Lisette who stepped into the breach and it was Lisette to whom Nicole turned for comfort. Nor was Lisette ever impatient with her little shadow. But something was troubling the older girl, and Leah was at a loss to discern what it could be.

At times, Leah felt that Lisette was going through a normal period of adolescent confusion, that time when every girl seeks her own identity as she arrives at the threshold of young womanhood. All too aware of her own problems during those years, Leah yearned to take Lisette into her arms and assure her that the confusion would end and that she'd find the path she wanted to take, that she would become the woman she wanted to be. But she said nothing, because Leah knew it was also a time when a girl wanted to keep secret her thoughts and feelings, to keep her fears and hopes hidden in her own mind behind a sign that read "Private—Keep Out."

At other times, Leah wondered if there were something Lisette really wanted, or wanted to do, and was hesitant about telling them because she feared they would think her foolish. Leah finally decided all she could do was watch and listen; maybe Lisette herself would provide the clue.

When it came, the answer was so obvious Leah wondered why she'd needed so long to see it—or rather hear it.

One evening, when she and Baptiste were sitting by the fire in the library, Leah decided to bring up the subject of what she had in mind for Lisette. The younger children were upstairs playing in the long hall; Jean had gone for a walk; and Lisette was practicing on the piano in the salon. The music gave Leah the opening she'd been waiting for.

"Lisette has real talent, hasn't she?" Leah asked.

Baptiste nodded and reached for his glass of after-dinner brandy.

"No, I mean it. We should really encourage her with her music. I was talking with her teacher the other day, and Madame Celestine says she far outshines the other pupils. She hopes Lisette will eventually study at the conservatory in Paris."

"Really?" Baptiste put down his brandy. "I enjoy listening to her play, but I had no idea she was that good."

"She is, and what's more important, she really loves her music. I think we should encourage her more."

"Are you saying she should go to the conservatory now? Isn't she too young?"

"She's almost fifteen, Baptiste. But, no, she's not quite ready for advanced study yet. There's something we could do, though. She has only that old spinet to play on. She needs a larger and better piano."

"Are you hinting we should buy her a concert grand?" Baptiste fell back in his chair.

"Maybe not that large, but certainly something better than what we have now."

"Well, I can afford the piano," he said, "but where do you suggest we put it? Anything larger than that spinet will scarcely fit into the salon."

"I'm—I'm coming to that," Leah said hesitantly. "I have it all figured out."

"I rather thought you did," Baptiste said, and grinned. "What do you have in mind?"

"Not just Lisette's music, although she does need a room of her own where she can practice whenever she wants to. I'm thinking of the other children, too. And us." She paused, sure that Baptiste would have some remark to make. When she saw he was waiting for her to go on, she breathed deeply and pulled some sketches from beneath the pillow at her back. For the moment she kept them clutched in her hand.

"We need a schoolroom for all of them," she said. "You know how it upsets you to have this room in use all morning and half the afternoon when the tutor is here. This was supposed to be your office, a place to retire to when you needed to attend to business, or where you could be secluded with your friends. How often do you come in here now?"

He nodded grimly. "At night after supper. More and more I'm going into the city to conduct business when I could do it out here. So what have you schemed up now?"

"An addition to the house. Just this main floor," she added, seeing him scowl. Then she continued quickly. "We can build a wing that will have a bedroom for us, an office for you, a sitting room for me, and dressing rooms. Then our room can once again be the music room it was originally, and this library can be what it is now—the schoolroom. The only other solution is to have Monsieur Balaine teach them in the dining room, and you know what that would do to Blanchette. And, of course, Lisette would have to continue with the spinet in the salon."

She was pretty certain she had convinced him with that last statement. Lisette adored her father, and he would do anything to please her. Leah had long since accepted that he would always feel guilty about not loving Catherine when he'd married her, in spite of the fact that Catherine herself had married for money rather than for love. But if it eased his conscience to have a special place in his heart for Lisette, Leah would not resent him for it. In no way did it subtract from his love and attention to the other children.

"And I suppose you have it all sketched out," he said teasingly.

"I have." She moved to sit next to him on the couch and spread out the sheets of paper over which she'd worked so diligently. "See, we can enclose the terrace with a wall of windows so it will be like a sunroom as well as a hall, and the new wing can open off to the south side from there. And here's the bedroom, the office and the sitting room." She pointed to each of them in turn.

"And what is this?" His finger touched a small square between the dressing rooms.

Leah fidgeted. She hadn't meant for him to see that just yet. "That's the bathroom with—with one of those new water closets that are so popular." She watched him frown. "Oh, they're all the rage now, Baptiste, and so much more elegant than chamber pots and privies."

"And we must be elegant!" he said sarcastically.

"They're a great deal more sanitary, too. There's no point in building if we don't include some modern conveniences."

"You've figured up how much all of this will cost, I suppose."

"No, I've left that all to you." She smiled and put her arm around his shoulder. "You're the financial expert in the family."

"Well, I suppose you're right," he said. "We haven't made any major improvements since we bought the place." He looked at her sketchy plans again and began to frown. "Only one problem. The house will look lopsided with just one wing. Maybe if we built toward the back instead of the side."

"That would ruin the garden and eliminate the sunroom. The wing will be large enough to give the house an

66

L shape, and I have a feeling we'll want to do something on the other side in the future."

Baptiste laughed. "You and your feelings. All right, have it built however you want."

"Thank you, Baptiste. I know you won't be sorry. How soon can we begin?"

"Whoa there! I'll have to find a builder and go over the plans with him."

"But you will start tomorrow, won't you?" she pleaded. "Now that I know we're going to do it, I can't wait to see how it will look."

"Yes, chérie, I will look into it tomorrow. Count Boileau added a wing to his place last year, so I'll ride over and talk to him in the morning. Now, let me study those plans in peace while I finish my cigar."

Leah smiled inwardly. She had no illusions that giving Lisette her own music room would automatically bridge the distance between them, but it might ease the strain Lisette had been under while she tried to concentrate on her playing as the whole family ran in and out of the salon. Lisette also needed to be shown that Leah no longer considered her a little girl but was quite aware she was growing up. Another idea was blossoming in Leah's mind, but that, however, had to wait for a few months before she could reveal it.

The building of the new wing progressed rapidly, and when it was finished, Baptiste was as delighted with the additional rooms as Leah had hoped. Lisette was ecstatic over having a place of her very own where she could practice without being disturbed. Leah and Baptiste had said nothing about the new piano, and on the day it was due to arrive, Leah found an excuse for her and Lisette to drive into St. Denis. When they returned, Baptiste suggested to Lisette that she play something for him before supper. When she saw the magnificent new instrument, she dissolved into tears.

"Here, here," Baptiste said while he hugged her, "we came in here to listen to you play, not to watch you cry."

"But Papa, it's so beautiful."

Baptiste reached in his pocket for a handkerchief while Leah watched and smiled. He'd always had to provide her with handkerchiefs when she needed them, and now it looked as if his daughter had the same tendency never to have one handy when the tears came.

"Now," he said, wiping her cheeks, "what are you going to play?"

Still crying, Lisette sat down at the piano and ran her fingers over the keyboard. Then, in a burst of ecstatic gaiety, she began to play Chopin's *Polonaise*, one of her father's favorites.

The other children were somewhat less thrilled about the schoolroom. After all, they already spent a large part of each day in what had been the library. The only difference now was that their father's desk and belongings had been moved out and regulation school desks had been moved in. Then Leah told them they could decorate the room themselves, in any way they chose. Jean and Henri immediately laid claim to the bookshelves for their various collections, while Denise insisted on adding such feminine touches as calico curtains and gingham-covered pillows for the straight chairs. Much to her parents' surprise, Nicole contributed several childish but quite well-executed drawings for the walls. From the time Nicole could scribble with a pencil, she'd ferreted out every piece of scrap paper in the house to use for the quick sketches of whatever held her fancy at the moment. Most of these were never seen by any eyes other than her own; a few she showed her parents, but none were ever destroyed.

"That's another talent we need to watch," Leah whispered to Baptiste while they quietly watched Nicole, whose tongue protruded from her mouth as she concentrated on placing each picture to her artistic satisfaction.

The children are growing up, Leah thought, *and we need to be more aware of their individual interests.* Nicole might be only nine, but already she needed to be encouraged if indeed she had real talent.

Some months later, it was time for Leah to execute her second idea for Lisette. On a shopping trip to Paris, Leah bought a length of blue silk, and that night she called Lisette to her room and showed it to her.

"Oh, Mama, it's beautiful. Where are you going to wear it when it's made up?"

"It's not for me, Lisette, it's for you."

"But this is for an evening gown." Lisette ran the material through her fingers, delighting in the touch of its luxurious softness against her skin. "An evening gown," she breathed. "And for me." It was as if she hesitated to say it too loudly for fear the beautiful material would disappear.

"Yes," Leah said. "Papa and I thought it would be nice to

have a supper dance for your sixteenth birthday. After all, you're getting to be quite a young lady, and it's time you thought of yourself that way."

Lisette herself had been thinking this very thing, but she'd been convinced that she was still considered a little girl by everyone else. If only she could talk to Leah as she had when she was little. She yearned to confide in her, to ask questions, and to be comforted when she was troubled, but she could not. Some of the very things she wanted to talk about, like her mother and her parents' marriage, were the reasons she could not.

"Thank you, Mama, for the material. And for thinking about a party. I'll look forward to it." Her formal tone and unsmiling face were those of a schoolgirl receiving rare and unexpected praise from her teacher.

"We'll start making some real plans in a week or so." It was all Leah could do to keep from reaching out and taking the girl into her arms. She wanted to cry at Lisette's calm, emotionless response to the suggestion of a supper dance. She knew that some part of Lisette wanted to react more enthusiastically, but another was insisting she remain cool and unmoved. "I'll check with the dressmaker tomorrow, and make an appointment for her to come with some patterns. You'll want to choose your own, I know."

Lisette merely put the material down and ran out of the room. Leah knew she had not reached the girl; worse, she had somehow further disturbed her. Why? What was it Lisette wanted that they had not given her—or could not give her?

Sobbing uncontrollably, Lisette sat at her dressing table, her face buried in her crossed arms. She didn't know how long she'd been sitting there, but she felt completely washed out from all the tears she'd shed since coming into her room and slamming the door behind her.

"Oh, Mama, why can't I love you the way I used to? Why can't I talk to you and let you know how I feel?" she moaned aloud.

She still loved Leah, but the way she loved her had changed since she'd understood the meaning of Leah's having been her father's mistress before he married Catherine. It meant he had always loved Leah, and there had been something wrong about his marriage to her own mother. Lisette could not find it in herself to hate Leah, but she had an ugly feeling that Leah had in some way contributed to

69

Catherine's death. The truth that hurt the most was that her father had not loved her mother.

Lisette looked from one to another of her mother's pictures. No one had to tell her she was developing into a perfect image of the beautiful Catherine. She had the same long, pale blonde hair and fair skin that had been painted with such delicate colors in the small oil portrait for which Catherine had sat soon after her marriage to Baptiste. The similarities were evident even in the faded sepia tintype taken when Catherine was eighteen.

Although she'd never known her mother, Lisette's imagination had created a gentle, sweet, kindly woman who was always ready to listen to her and whose arms were warm and enveloping. Over the past several months, she had fallen in love with the person she'd created, unaware that the qualities she bestowed on Catherine were the very ones that had first made her love Leah. But Catherine was her own flesh and blood, the one who had endowed her with her features and thus, most certainly, her personality. Catherine then, not Leah, would be the inspiration for her own life. Or rather, it would be the ideal Catherine she had formed in her imagination.

Lisette looked again at the oil portrait, at the slim face, the delicate features, the half-smile, the smooth white shoulders rising above the softly draped décolletage of the blue silk gown.

If only Leah hadn't chosen blue silk, Lisette thought, sobbing. In her confused state of mind, she was certain it was to remind her she was not Leah's daughter. Leah knew how much Lisette loved that portrait of her mother. The choice of the material was a mockery, of both Catherine's marriage to her father and of Lisette's former feelings for Leah. Well, Lisette thought, she'd continue to be a dutiful daughter, but only until she was old enough to leave home.

Gradually, her misery dissolved into thoughts about the supper dance. It would be fun. It was kind of Leah to think of it. And the new piano. That had probably been Leah's idea, too. Then a new truth occurred to Lisette. Leah loved her. She had chosen the blue silk purposely, yes, but she'd done it so that Lisette could look like the mother she adored. It was Leah who had looked through the trunks and found the pictures of Catherine for Lisette so she would never forget who her mother was.

Lisette wiped her eyes and took one last glance at Catherine's pictures. Then she ran downstairs to where

Leah was still in her room and where the blue silk lay spread out on the bed.

"Thank you for everything you're doing for me, Mama," Lisette sobbed. "I love you. I truly do."

Leah had no way of knowing what had passed through Lisette's mind while she'd been upstairs, but she felt certain the girl had come to a new understanding of herself and her feelings for herself, Leah. Leah was quite certain that that understanding also involved Lisette's feelings about her mother and father. Whatever, the outcome had been positive, and maybe the breach between them was on its way to being mended.

"I love you, too, Lisette. Now, let's think about what style you'd like for the dress."

"And who we're going to invite to the party?" Lisette asked with more elation than she'd shown in a long time.

"We'll start a list. Anyone special in mind?"

It would not be hard, Lisette thought, to confide in Leah again, but it was Catherine, the ideal, whom she wished to emulate.

Chapter Nine

FOR MORE THAN TWO YEARS, Nicole appeared to have recovered from the pain of being deserted by Denise, and seemed happy to attach herself to Lisette. It was true she acted as if Denise no longer existed, seldom speaking to her and preferring to play by herself when Lisette was busy. Nicole seemed content to lie on the floor of the salon—and later the music room—and draw while Lisette practiced her music. At other times she took her drawing pad into the garden, where she sketched by the hour.

Baptiste and Leah continued to be amazed at the artistic talent she displayed, and Leah asked Monsieur Balaine, the children's tutor and a fine amateur artist himself, to remain an extra afternoon a week to instruct her.

If Denise were upset at Nicole's attitude toward her, she gave little indication. She was now blissfully happy playing *"petite maman"* to Robert, who gleefully chased her from room to room and only cried when she had to leave him for the schoolroom. Leah had never completely recovered her strength from his birth, and she was grateful her baby had someone to play with whenever his natural energies wore her out.

Then, for no apparent reason, Nicole began running away again. Each time she was found—in the fields or the village—she listened stoically to her father's lecture but went to her room without making any promises. Leah and Baptiste agreed that she was merely bidding for attention, and as long as she never strayed too far from home, they felt they shouldn't make an issue of her flights.

Nor would they have if Nicole hadn't frightened them all by disappearing for several days. She was finally found living in St. Denis with Monsieur and Madame Schumann, a baker and his wife. She had elicited their sympathy by telling them she was an orphan. When Leah and Baptiste arrived to take her home, they found her playing happily with the Schumanns' seven children in the rooms over the bakery.

"My name is Michele," Nicole insisted, "and I'm an orphan. I want to stay with the Schumanns."

"Nicole," Baptiste said, so sternly that Leah was shocked, "this charade has gone on long enough. I don't know what you told these kind people, but you are coming home with us."

For a moment Nicole glanced at her father; then, since she was just as shocked as Leah at his tone, she broke down in tears. Papa had never spoken to her that way before. Where were the soft voice and comforting arms that had always awaited her before? Then she looked again, and she saw them in his eyes.

"Yes, Papa."

"Good. Now thank these nice people for taking care of you. And tell them you're sorry you lied to them."

"Thank you, Madame Schumann." She turned to Baptiste. "But I didn't lie. Truly I didn't. It was only make-believe."

"Then," Baptiste said, "you will confine your make-believe to the house from now on and not upset people anymore." He bent down and kissed her; when she put her hand on the brace of his crutch, he put his own hand over it.

"Nicole is not going to stop rebelling," Baptiste said later that evening.

"I know," Leah answered. "There will be a short respite, and she'll try something else."

"That business about being an orphan," he sighed. "She isn't happy here."

"I realize that, too. But I'm at a complete loss about what to do, how to handle her. She's gotten too far away from me."

"If she wants to leave us, I think she should go away for a while," Baptiste suggested.

"What are you trying to say?"

"I think she needs us more than she realizes, but she has to find that out for herself—by herself. That is, with strangers who will be good to her and perhaps can guide her better than we can."

"You have something in mind, don't you?" She'd be willing to agree to almost anything to help Nicole.

"A convent school. I know of several in Paris, but there's an especially fine one whose Mother Superior I've come to know. She has a brother in the exporting business in China, and has stopped by the office a number of times just to chat. She's a lovely, warm person. Nicole would be safe there. At least she wouldn't be wandering through the countryside."

Recalling her own days at a convent school in New Orleans, Leah thought about how much she had loved the nuns, especially Sister Angelique. "And she will be loved and well cared for. The nuns are kindness itself. I think you may be right, Baptiste. At least it's worth a try. They can let us know how she's doing, and we can see her when we go into the city."

"Then if you agree, I'll drive in tomorrow and make arrangements. I think you should stay out here with her."

"I can get her things ready. I don't think we should postpone carrying out the decision."

While Leah packed Nicole's trunk, she had to stop every minute or so to wipe her eyes or blow her nose. Her precious Nicole was leaving her. Or had she already left? No, now everything would be different—better. It had to be. She loved Nicole too much to lose her. She mustn't lose her. Loosen the strings, yes, but not let her go completely.

On Friday, Nicole rode to Paris between Baptiste and Leah in the ~arriage. It had been harder to explain why Nicole was leaving to the other children than to Nicole herself. She had become so docile and quiet, Leah was almost more frightened than when she rebelled or lost her temper. Either she was reconciled to going away to school or she was patiently biding her time and putting on an act. Leah prayed it was the former, that perhaps Nicole was genuinely relieved to be moving out of the house. The convent accepted orphans as well as girls with families, and it might be a revelation to Nicole to live among them and find out what it really meant to have no parents to return to.

There were no tears on either side when Leah and Baptiste left Nicole at the convent. Accompanied by one of the nuns, Nicole marched stoically down the hall from the Mother Superior's office without looking back. Leah would not allow herself to cry; this was the best thing for her youngest daughter. It had to be. Leah only hoped that when the time came for their first visit, Nicole would be ready to greet them more emotionally than she was bidding them farewell.

Nicole loved the nuns. She especially loved their soft voices and their kindly way of giving orders. Surprisingly, she also loved how they acted quickly and sternly when you disobeyed orders. When you made an innocent mistake, there was no lack of understanding, but when you deliberately disobeyed, a nun could become very severe. Nicole learned this all too well during her first few days at the convent, when she refused to bathe in cold water and later when she stayed in her room to draw instead of going to class.

The first time, Sister Joseph merely repeated the order to Nicole, in a less than gentle voice, to take off all her clothes and bathe with the sponge beside the basin. Worse than that, Sister Joseph stayed right with her the whole time, giving her no privacy at all. When it was over, the sister smiled and quietly led her down to breakfast. Two days later, Sister Theresa found Nicole in her room. Again, there was no smile until Nicole said she was sorry and picked up her school books. Somehow she sensed that these calm, unruffled women loved her as much when she was naughty as when she was good.

All the little girls who were near her age went together to the same classes and shared the same large dormitory room. It was the first time since Nicole had moved out of Denise's room that she was not sleeping alone, and she found a certain comfort in having someone close by on either side. Unlike home, there was no light left on, but she didn't need it anymore. She could look through the long window at the head of her bed and see the stars. Sometimes the moon rode overhead, and she was fascinated at the way its size and shape changed.

From the beginning, Nicole sought out and identified with the orphans near her own age, and on Sundays she always accompanied them on the walk from the convent school to the church. Weekdays, the priests conducted morning mass in the school's small chapel. But Sundays were special; Nicole would put on the new bonnet Mama had bought her and slip her hands into her first pair of white kid gloves. Her dress was an old one, but Mama had sewed new lace around the collar and cuffs. Nicole was overawed at the size of the church, at the distance between the slate floor and the high, vaulted ceiling. She'd always thought the parish church in the village was large, towering as it did over the houses, but this church was enormous. Not only had she moved to another city, but into another world.

For a while Nicole still thought of herself as an orphan. She liked it better that way. It meant she didn't have to think about—or, more important, talk about—the family at home. In fact, she revealed very little about herself. She was already learning it was better to be a private person if you didn't want to be badgered with questions or disturbed when you preferred being alone. But she listened, and she learned what it was like to be a real orphan, without any home to go back to if you wanted to. She also learned that most of the orphans planned to take the vows eventually and become nuns. As much as she loved the nuns, she had no desire to become one. She knew already she wanted to be an artist.

I'm glad I have a family, she said to herself, and then was shocked at her own thought. It was also a jolt to find herself missing them, missing them very much. Especially Mama and Papa.

She couldn't understand why at times she hated her family and at other times she loved them. Gradually, however, she came to realize they were an important part of her life. She needed to know they were there in case she should want to go back. She would not yet admit to herself that she needed them for the kind of comfort and security the convent couldn't offer, but she began to think of all of them with affection.

Leah awoke with intensely strange feelings about Nicole.

Seldom was the child absent from her mind during the day, and now she'd dreamed about her all night. The reports from the convent were all favorable: Nicole was a very sweet, obedient child, and she seemed to be making many friends. After one or two rebellious refusals to study, she had settled down to her books and was doing moderately well. The sisters expected her grades would improve with more application.

Leah sent her little surprises each week, but Mother Bernadette suggested they wait a bit before visiting her. While in the city, Baptiste stopped by to be sure all was well with Nicole, but he did not see her. Leah wanted desperately to see Nicole and had made up her mind to ride in with Baptiste the following Monday and go to the convent. She hoped Nicole would be glad to see her, but if not, Leah would at least be assured her daughter was happy in her new surroundings. She had sent them a picture she'd painted in her art class, which she'd signed "Love, Nicole." It had to be a beginning.

After breakfast, Leah walked through the garden. There was much to be done now that the spring flowering was almost over. The beds should be weeded and the dead blossoms cut off. The work would be good for her. With her hands in the dirt, pulling and pruning, maybe she could also work loose the cords that bound her to Nicole and drew tighter around her heart whenever she thought of her daughter, living apart and estranged from them in Paris.

Returning to the house, Leah put an old wrapper over her dress, checked with Baptiste in his office to see if he needed anything, and headed toward the shed where she kept the garden tools and baskets. The sun was hot, though the air was cool—a perfect day for working at least until noon.

She opened the door and stared into the shed. Someone had left one of the burlap bags in the middle of the floor. Musty-smelling and spattered with chunks of dried mud, it must have been left out in the rain after being used to carry leaves to the compost pile and then tossed in here to dry. She didn't want to touch it until she put her work gloves on. She started to kick it to one side but was stopped by a sudden memory of having been frightened half out of her wits once before. She'd moved a pile of manure bags and a whole family of rats had scurried out. She decided to go around to where Nicolas was working the the kitchen garden and get him to move it. A shaft of light filtering through the grimy window touched the bag, and Leah nearly fainted.

"Nicole! My God, how did you get here?" There was no thought now of rats or dirt as she fell to the floor, lifted the bag off Nicole, and took her into her arms. "Where did you come from?"

But Nicole was too exhausted or hurt to respond. Leah gently laid her down and ran to the door. "Jean! Henri! Someone come out here right away!" Then she remembered that both of the older boys were in the classroom at the front of the house and would not hear her. She'd have to run and get them. She knew she couldn't possibly carry Nicole, and she wasn't yet sure the child wasn't seriously hurt.

Leah ran as fast as she could to fetch the boys. It was Jean who picked Nicole up, carried her to the sunroom, and settled her on the chaise longue. Leah examined her daughter, from her torn and dirty dress and the once white pinafore, down to her feet. The soles of Nicole's soft leather slippers were worn through completely, as were her stockings, and her feet were covered with blisters. How far had the child walked? She couldn't have made it in one night, and if she'd been missing longer than that, the convent would have called.

Hearing the commotion, Baptiste wondered what in the world was happening. In less than a minute he was out of his desk chair and into his wheelchair and making his way to the sunroom.

"Good Lord, it's Nicole! What's happened to her?"

"We don't know yet," Leah said. "She's still fast asleep, but she doesn't seem to be hurt, except for these blisters and scratches."

"I'd better call Mother Bernadette," Baptiste said. "They must be frantic at the convent. I'm surprised they haven't called us."

Baptiste had been one of the first to install a telephone when the service was extended from Paris to the outlying towns. It meant no longer having to go into the city every time he wanted to contact his office. Leah still approached the instrument with apprehension, not quite sure yet just how it was that her voice could carry across the miles. She was relieved when Baptiste said he'd make the call.

Just as he reached his office, the phone rang. It was Mother Bernadette. They had missed Nicole at breakfast, but had not wanted to call and worry the family until they'd first

77

searched the whole building. They knew of Nicole's penchant for hiding whenever she was disturbed about something, and since no one had seen her leave, they had been sure they would find her either in the convent or in the church. When it seemed clear their search would not produce Nicole, they felt they had to call.

"That's all right, Mother Bernadette. She's here with us. I don't know how she traveled the distance in one night, but when we find out we'll let you know. And also why she left, if we can. Thank you for calling, and for all you've done. I'm sorry she put you to this trouble."

"It was no trouble, Monsieur Fontaine, except for the worry. She's a charming, delightful child, and we would be most distressed if anything had happened to her."

Gradually, a little at a time, Nicole told her story. While she talked, Blanchette kept plying her with all her favorite delicacies, and Nicole had to pause while she stuffed them into her mouth. There'd been nothing like them at the convent, and she'd forgotten how much she missed Blanchette's crullers and pastries.

She never said why she had left the convent school; in fact she kept insisting she'd been happy there. She simply preferred to be at home. She'd slipped out after the lights were turned off. She was never very clear about how far she'd walked, but she'd ridden most of the way with a farmer returning from the city. Before that, she'd slept a while in a barn and got water from a stream. The farmer had had some vegetables he couldn't sell, and she'd tried to eat them, but they made her sick. He was a very kind man who stopped when she became ill, and he'd brought her as far as the village nearest the château. From there she'd walked home. When Leah asked her why she hadn't come right to the house, she turned her head away and did not answer.

"You want to stay home?" Baptiste asked her.

"Yes, Papa."

"All right. But you must understand that you've given the sisters and us a great deal of worry. Much more than either they or your mother deserve. I won't ask you why now, but I'll make an agreement with you. You can stay home and study with Monsieur Balaine again. And the art lessons will continue. But you must promise never to run away again."

"For now, Papa, but never ask me what I will do tomorrow. Even I won't know until tomorrow comes."

She's a strange child, Baptiste thought, *almost like a*

changeling, but she is ours and we love her. We can only try to do what is best for her.

"All right, I'll understand that," Baptiste said. "But tell us when you feel like leaving. Then at least we won't worry so much."

Nicole only nodded. Promises were not something one gave unless one was sure of keeping them. It was good to be home, and she was quite certain she would stay this time. But then, she never knew when the strange, dizzy feeling would come over her and she would find herself first fighting it, then fleeing from it. It was not the same despair she had felt when she was deserted by Denise. This was something different; it was like the ghosts in the tunnel, there and yet not there, and it frightened her.

For a while Nicole seemed content to be home, and she no longer avoided Denise and Robert. She spent as much time with them and Lisette as she did alone. She rediscovered the doll house and devoted hours to repainting and redecorating it with scraps of material from Leah's remnant boxes. Nicole was not a child who looked to the future, or who reminisced over the past. She lived only for today.

And it wasn't long before Leah could sense the restlessness stirring in Nicole again. This time there were problems in the schoolroom. Monsieur Balaine finally admitted that Nicole was doing none of her assignments and never responded in class. Nicole's only explanation, when questioned, was that she hated the classroom. No, not Monsieur Balaine, just the room.

Among Baptiste's friends in Paris was Jules Ferry, Premier of France and former Minister of Education, during whose administration public education had been removed from the control of the church. He was dining at the château one evening when the subject of Nicole came up.

"Have you thought of sending her to public school?" Ferry asked.

"Why, no," Baptiste said. "We'd assumed that all our children would be privately educated."

"You've told me how much she enjoys playing with the children in the village. Seems to me that public school would be the answer," Monsieur Ferry said. "Send her to school with them."

"Public school?" Leah suppressed a shudder. "I don't know. Both Baptiste and I were educated privately."

"Don't look down on our public schools;" Monsieur Ferry said seriously. "There are some damn fine ones."

"I'm afraid I've insulted you," Leah apologized. "I'd forgotten you'd headed up the education ministry."

"Think nothing of it. But it's not my prejudice that says they're good. You've a fine young schoolmaster, Monsieur LaBorde, in the village. I know his family well. Nicole would be in good hands. He's strict and she'll learn, but she'll be among friends, too."

"What do you think, Baptiste?" Leah asked.

"I think it's worth a try. Just as the convent was. And she won't have nearly as far to run if she gets tired of it."

So Nicole began attending the village school, riding her horse in every day and carrying a pail with her lunch; she ate lunch with Monsieur LaBorde while the others went home for theirs. When she agreed to go, her only request was that she be allowed to dress like the other children.

My little moppet, Leah thought each time Nicole rode off, dressed in a rough peasant skirt and blouse and sturdy black boots or wood sabots. *Are you a real child or a will-o'-the-wisp who will disappear each time I think you've come home to stay?*

Chapter Ten

ALMOST FROM THE TIME HE'D ARRIVED in France as a little boy, Jean delighted in going to the city with his father. He considered it a special privilege to ride alone in the carriage with Baptiste and then spend the day among all the marvelous wonders in the firm's warehouse. It was his dream to grow up and work beside his father, eventually managing the export firm when Baptiste was ready to retire.

He was fascinated by the great conglomeration of goods of various sizes, shapes, and colors that were boxed on shelves or spread on tables. He loved the strange, foreign labels, the aroma of spices that pervaded and mingled with the heavy smell of ink in the accounting room, and even the account ledgers themselves. He admired the neatness of the entries, and he strove to imitate the fine cursive lines forming the words and numerals.

Then there were the lunches with his father's business acquaintances. The men never assumed superior airs or spoke down to him. Nor did they pretend he wasn't there or hesitate to talk business in his presence. The food, like the conversation, was always hearty, heavy, and masculine. He felt like a man among them. When bored by the conversation at his father's table, he listened to reports of the stock market, the money market, and the diamond market at neighboring tables. He wondered how many millions of francs were being traded in those guttural accents or lilting foreign tongues.

By the time he was fourteen, Jean was wise enough in the ways of the export business to be asked for advice by his father. Together, they'd go over the books and the orders from the previous year.

"We did well with that last year," Baptiste would say, "but I wonder if we haven't glutted the market."

With intense concentration, Jean would scrutinize the orders from several earlier years and then offer his opinion.

"Yes, Papa, I think you're right. Last year was an unusual one. Maybe we ought to handle only half, maybe two-thirds that amount."

Baptiste would nod his head in agreement, and the letter would be written to an office in China or India or Italy or Scandinavia.

Jean was also interested in the increase of import business from the United States. The quantity of raw products, such as hides, cotton, tobacco, and various ores, had accelerated rapidly and consistently since the end of the Civil War, and there seemed to be no end to the amount the States could produce. It would be fun to visit the States sometime, but he had no thought of living there or of working in the New Orleans office. Paris was his home, and the import firm of Bonvivier and Fontaine was as close to heaven as Jean wanted to get at the moment.

Today, he gathered his school books from the desk, bid Monsieur Balaine a polite good day, and then ran to his father's study. He was nearly seventeen, and he would soon be able to leave the schoolroom for good. He knew his father had plans for him to go to the university, but Jean had no heart for continuing his education. He was not a particularly outstanding student, except in math. He did his best, but he'd grown accustomed to having Monsieur Balaine shake his head over the papers and examinations he turned in. Maybe, just maybe, he could persuade his father that the university was not for him. If Jean had his way, he would go immediately to work. But doing what?

Over the years, Jean had often walked the surrounding fields and made the acquaintance of the farmers who worked them. He began to feel an attachment to the land. In late afternoons he found release from the tension of poring over his books by strolling between the rows of sugar beets and feeling the soil between his fingers. He learned to talk with the men about crops and weather, when to sow and when to harvest, and often, he took spade or hoe in hand to help them.

Then he'd go into the city with his father, and he realized he wouldn't really know what he wanted to do with his life until he spent some time with the firm. One thing was certain: He did not want to continue his formal education.

"Am I disturbing you, Papa?"

"Indeed not, Jean. Come on in. Wine? Dr. Boucher insists I have a glass a little while before each meal. Says it's good for the digestion, and who am I to argue with the good doctor?"

"Thank you, Papa, I think I will." His stomach had been churning all morning from anxiety over this talk he was determined to have with his father.

"I see you still have your books. Planning to do a little extra studying?"

Jean looked down at the books he was holding. He hadn't been aware he was still carrying them. Somewhat embarrassed, he placed them on the table and took the glass Baptiste offered him. "No, I—I was in a hurry to come in here."

"I have a letter from the university." Baptiste held it up in his hand.

"I know. I saw it come in the post." Maybe they would turn him down because of a poor recommendation from Monsieur Balaine. No, Monsieur would never do that. Although not superior, his work was more than passable.

"About what we expected," Baptiste said. "You're weak in some areas of the examination, but very strong in math. They will accept you for the next class, but they recommend additional tutorial work this summer."

Now was the time. Jean emptied his glass at one swallow, oblivious to his father's raised eyebrows.

"If you're that thirsty, Jean, I suggest you find something

other than wine to quench it with—and in not quite such an uncouth manner."

"I'm sorry, sir. No, I merely wanted to finish it before—before I begin what I came in here to say."

"Something you don't think I'll approve of, I gather." Baptiste was surprised. Jean was one child who never did anything startling or out of line. Usually, he was so predictable that Baptiste could frame Jean's answers to any question he might ask.

"No, sir, I hope you will approve, but it's not exactly what we'd planned. The truth is, I don't want to go to the university. I want to go directly into the office; I'd like to work for you in the city."

Baptiste did not answer immediately. The request was not entirely unexpected. He knew the boy's love for the business, and he was aware how much Jean had learned over the years. He was almost as expert in some areas as Baptiste himself. If that was what Jean really wanted, he might be wasting his time continuing with his education. And, in truth, Baptiste looked forward to having his oldest son take over eventually. It might be important to see just how serious Jean was.

"I have no position open for you in the firm at this time. Would you want me to fire one of the other men just to make a place for you?"

"Oh, no, sir. I only thought—well, perhaps I could begin by apprenticing in each of the departments. That is, go from one office to another, maybe spend a month or several months in each, and in the warehouse. Then I'd learn the business the way I really should. No one need be let go. I can still live at home, and I won't need much of an allowance, less than if I went to the university."

"You really want to go to work that badly and not further your education?" Baptiste pondered the boy's enthusiastic rush of words for a few minutes while Jean sat and waited on the edge of his chair. He couldn't remember when he'd seen his easygoing, phlegmatic son so excited about anything. Baptiste was pretty certain what his decision would be, but it would do the boy good to patiently endure a few painful days of waiting. Pierre LeDeux, the head bookkeeper, would be retiring in ten months, and young Jules Hébert should be moved into his position. An opening for Jean would be created without having to let anyone go. By that time, Jean would know enough of the business to take over the high stool and ledger books of Hébert's post.

"I'll be honest, Jean. I'm disappointed at your not wanting to go to the university. A good education is a valuable asset regardless of whether you need it for a profession. Nor am I giving short shrift to men who labor and work with their hands—or for that matter to men who've trained themselves to work with their minds. I can't understand your wanting to deny yourself the experience as well as the learning you'd receive. I have no quarrel with your wanting to come into the firm; in fact, I'm proud. If you're really ready. I'll have to think about it, but I will have a definite answer for you in a week."

Jean had to be satisfied with that. "Thank you, Papa. I hope you will come to see the request from my point of view."

"I'll look at it from all points of view—yours and the needs of the firm. Now, if you'll see when lunch will be ready, I will be most appreciative."

Jean spent the intervening week vacillating between hope and despair. At no time was their conversation alluded to, so Jean had no hint which direction his father's thoughts were taking. On the appointed day, he walked into the study, accepted the wine his father offered him, sipping it slowly this time. If it were to be the university, he had determined not to show his disappointment.

"All right, Jean, I'll agree to your entering the firm," Baptiste said, then told his son his plans for the aftermath of Pierre LeDeux's retirement. "But there is one condition: If any of the department managers feel you lack competency in any part of the business at the end of ten months, we'll talk about the university again."

"Thank you, Papa. You won't be disappointed." Jean managed to keep his voice calm even though he wanted to jump up from his chair and shout with relief.

"You'll start as soon as you finish this term with Monsieur Balaine, and I will expect you not to be derelict in your studies during these next few weeks. One word from him that you're slacking off, and I will change my mind. Is that understood?"

"Yes, sir." Just knowing that he'd never have to enter the schoolroom again, never have to pick up a textbook or study for an exam, made him feel that he wouldn't mind how many pages he had to read or how many papers he'd have to write in the next two months. He left the room as sedately as he could, then went yelling across the garden and through the nearby fields. He was free! He would show his father he hadn't made the wrong decision; he'd prove himself to be a real asset to the firm.

Unlike Jean, Henri was a superior student, the best in the family. The papers he turned in were meticulously neat as well as carefully argued. Monsieur Balaine considered him a joy to teach and never tired of telling Baptiste and Leah that they had a brilliant son. He would do them proud when he entered the university.

In reality, Henri was not particularly brilliant. He had a good, retentive mind, but he had something else as well: a compulsively competitive need to excel in whatever he did. He had to be the best in the eyes of his tutor, and his work had to be flawless. If two pages were assigned, he read four, and he memorized everything he read.

Since none of the other children gave much thought to their books after classes were over, they could really care less how well Henri did, and they felt no threat from him. Sometimes they teased him about his scholarly habits, but if it bothered him, he never let it show.

"Hey, professor!" Jean came into the room where Henri was scrutinizing a paper he'd finished writing on the Hundred Years' War. Jean slapped his brother on the back. "You're not going to spend the afternoon studying! The fish are biting, and Blanchette says she'll cook them if we catch them."

"I'm finished." Henri closed the book and reached for an old sweater to change into. Aside from his intense concentration on his studies, Henri was a normal boy pursuing normal, healthy exploits. "How do you like working in the city? And," he poked his head through the neckband, "what are you doing home this early? Been relieved of your position as office boy?"

"I'm no office boy," Jean said with a touch of pique, even though he knew his brother was teasing. "I'm a serious, hard-working apprentice. Papa called and said he needed some papers right away and suggested I bring them. He says I'm doing very well."

"You're lucky. I hope I can do what I really want in a few years." He had a secret ambition, but no one was going to know what it was until he successfully fulfilled it.

"But the university first, right?"

"I guess so." It was what they all expected of him, so he didn't argue.

"We'll be proud of you, little brother. You'll be the first in the family to graduate from a university. Papa went a year or two in Virginia, but of course Mama never went to any college. She did finish the convent, though."

"And I guess that was really something for a—for a—"

"Go ahead and say it, Henri. A woman of color. It's nothing to be ashamed of. Not over here anyway. Or even in New Orleans. She was free. So was our grandmother."

"I guess that makes a difference." But Henri still winced at the idea that his mother had Negro blood in her. And that he did, too. But someday . . . and this was part of his secret ambition.

They came abreast of an old storage shed. "Wait a second, Jean, while I check on the motor. Sometimes the girls play in here and mess up my things. Nicole loves to play house under my workbench, and then everything gets scattered all to hell and gone."

Jean moved impatiently from one foot to the other until Henri came out of the shed. "What do you plan to do with that motor? Make another contraption that does nothing but go round and round?"

"Those contraptions, as you call them, are very important for testing the energy efficiency of the motors. But I'll tell you a secret about this one. I'm working on making a dumbwaiter that goes from the kitchen up to the dining room. Then Blanchette and Nicolas won't have to climb the stairs during every meal. One can load in the kitchen and the other can serve at the table."

"Hell, you don't need a motor for that, just pulleys," Jean scoffed.

"Maybe so, but this would be a real improvement over that."

"If you say so." In spite of his teasing, Jean had genuine admiration for his younger brother's talent with motors and woodworking. A pity he would probably go to the university and end up studying law or medicine. If he stuck with his tinkering, he might someday invent something truly important.

"If Papa will only let me cut holes in the walls," Henri said.

Jean just shook his head at that idea. By this time they'd reached the river and were quietly baiting their hooks and casting their lines.

"I've got another idea, too," Henri said. "I'd like to run a small railroad through the tunnel from the house to the river. It would come out right about here."

"And what good would that be?"

"I don't know, but it's a real challenge."

"Henri, sometimes I think you have a screw loose. You make about as much sense as some of your inventions."

Henri didn't deign to reply. He reeled in his line, grunted in disgust at losing the bait, and tried again.

"You know what Henri wants to do now?" Baptiste called from the bedroom into Leah's dressing room.

"Turn the center hall into a workshop?" She was concentrating on trying to fasten the clasp of her necklace.

"No, but just about as crazy. Wants to cut holes in the dining room and kitchen walls so he can install a motor-driven dumbwaiter."

Leah walked out into the bedroom. "I don't think that sounds so crazy. It would certainly save a lot of steps for Blanchette and Nicolas. Neither of them is very young anymore."

"And have the whole house come crashing down on us! Leah, you're as crazy as the boy."

"Not if we have the contractor who built the addition do the actual work." She saw the skepticism on Baptiste's face. "At least let Monsieur Montand come and see if it's feasible. It's the least you can do for Henri."

"You win. That is, if Henri can show me it will work."

"Thank you, darling. His mechanical talent is just as important to him as music is to Lisette and art is to Nicole. Why, we might even have a genius on our hands."

"I'm more interested in encouraging his scholarship. It's important that he go to the university." Pleased as he was with Jean's progress at the office, Baptiste had never quite reconciled himself to the disappointment that he had not continued his education. "Tell Henri he can give us a demonstration whenever he's ready."

"No, Baptiste, you tell him. You're the one he told about his idea. It will mean more to him to hear it from you."

"I'm only speaking of a demonstration at this point. Don't forget that."

The whole family gathered around the storage shed to witness the maiden run of Henri's latest invention. He and Jean had conducted as many tests as they could inside the shed, but the small space hadn't permitted a real showing of what the device could do. Now Henri had constructed a scaffolding on the side of the shed from odds and ends of scrap lumber. Within the framework were the usual ropes and pulleys of a hand-worked dumbwaiter. A small platform, some two feet square, lay at the bottom of this makeshift shaft. Near it was the small, gasoline-driven motor.

Even Robert, now nearly four years old, jumped up and down in the go-cart where Denise had put him to keep him from running all over the garden. He sensed that something exciting was going on, and he wanted to know all about it. His conversation seemed to consist of nothing but questions. Especially the word *why*.

"If he doesn't tear down the house with that thing, he'll burn it down with the gasoline," Baptiste whispered to Leah. "Or create an explosion."

Blanchette and Nicolas stood to one side shaking their heads. Henri had promised them this gadget would ease their workload, but Nicolas already had visions of the lift getting stuck half-way up and his having to climb inside the walls to fix it. No, the stairs had been good enough for all the generations of butlers in his family, and they were good enough for him. Then he felt a twinge of arthritis in his knees, and he hoped young Henri would be successful.

Henri started the motor and let it hum contentedly for a few minutes.

"Is that all it's going to do?" Lisette scoffed. "Just sit there and make noise?"

"I'm letting it warm up, you ninny. A cold engine will choke down if you put it to work too fast."

"And meanwhile our supper will be getting cold instead," Lisette said and laughed at her own joke.

"Girls!" Henri said under his breath. "They think they're so funny."

"I think this is a wonderful invention," Denise said, moving to his side to console him. Lisette could be so trying at times, the way she thought she was so much better than everyone else because of her music. Denise looked down at the go-cart to make certain Robert hadn't pulled his sweater off. Lately he'd developed a habit of taking off all his clothes. He frequently tried her patience, but she wouldn't have given up his care for all the talent in the world.

"How much longer, Henri?" Baptiste, too, was beginning to get a little impatient. He was surprised to find he really wanted the device to work, for Henri's sake, even if it did mean tearing up the walls of the château.

"Right now." Henri slowly pushed a lever forward.

Not an eye moved from the two-foot square lift lying on

the ground; then, as it slowly moved upward, their eyes followed it almost without blinking. Nor was there any sound except for the purring of the motor and the creaking of the pulley wheels as the ropes went through them. It reached the top and stopped.

Then all was pandemonium. "It works! It works!" Jean shouted. "I told you it would, Henri."

"I knew it would all the time," Henri said matter-of-factly, but he was beaming over his success.

"How about bringing it back down," Baptiste suggested.

Henri reversed a second lever, and slowly the platform descended through the shaft. "It will work more smoothly and even faster," he said, "when we have the real shaft built inside. This one is so rickety I don't dare speed it up."

"If it went any faster," Leah said practically, "it would spill the food. And I can see Blanchette's face if one of her famous soufflés fell."

They all wanted to see it work again, and Henri obliged by sending the platform up and down several times. It seemed to work without a hitch.

"Well, Nicholas," Baptiste called out, "you think you can learn to work this thing?"

"Yes, sir, if Henri will show me how."

"All right. I'll talk to Montand in a few days about coming over to check the walls and install the shaft."

"I'll have to advise him how it should be built," Henri said, walking over. "It has to be done just right."

Baptiste laughed. "I can just see that master carpenter taking advice from a thirteen-year-old boy, but I suppose you could make drawings and show him how it's to work."

Henri felt deflated. This was his invention and he wanted to build the whole thing. With the right tools he could construct a beautiful, sturdy shaft that would work perfectly. "Why can't I do the whole thing myself after the walls are opened?"

"Henri," Baptiste told him, "you are about to learn an important fact of life. Architects design, but contractors do the building. You have one kind of talent; they have another. Architects may even do mockups, or experimental constructions like the one you showed us today, but when something is perfected, they turn to the next idea and leave the final building to someone else. Monsieur Montand will listen to what you have to say, and he'll respect your drawings and ideas, but he's the one to build the actual product."

"Yes, sir, I think I understand." Henri felt a new kind of

pride. He would do the designing and then others would do the building. But whatever was constructed, it still would be his.

Before Montand had completed the work on the dumb-waiter, Leah came up with another idea. She walked into Baptiste's study as he was going over the firm's latest financial report.

"Mind if I sit here and sew while you work?"

"Not at all, chérie. I'm always happy to have your company."

"Well, I'll be very quiet so as not to disturb you."

"I'm almost through, and then you can tell me what you came in here to talk about."

"Why, Baptiste, I did no such thing," she protested lamely. They'd been married too long; that was the trouble. He could see through her every time. She bit the knotted thread so vigorously, her teeth hurt.

"All right, that takes care of my business for the day," Baptiste said after working for a few more minutes. He swiveled around in his chair. "So now we can take up yours."

"I thought that as long as Monsieur Montand is here—" she began with a laugh, "there is something else he could do for us."

"Ah ha, I thought so. What devious scheme have you hatched up now?"

"I wanted to talk to you in private, because I thought it could be something of a surprise."

"For whom?" Baptiste asked. "Besides me, that is."

"For Henri. He needs a better place than that old shed for tinkering with all his machines."

"With the mess he makes and as dirty as he gets, that old shed is the perfect place," Baptiste said.

"And so all the garden tools and things we want to store get tossed out into the kitchen garden. No, he needs a real workshop. You said yourself the house would look more balanced with a second wing, and I told you then I had a feeling we'd someday need to add it."

"Certainly you're not suggesting he needs that big a room to work in! My God, he could build a full-sized locomotive in the place."

"He won't use all of the space," she agreed, "but I have a feeling we'll need the rest of it later for something."

"Oh, chérie, you and your feelings. All right, a second wing it will be—for Henri and whatever else comes up."

"You mean you're going to agree that easily?" She sat up straight, stunned at her success. "You're not going to give me time to marshall all my arguments?"

"Leah, I learned long ago to give in to you when I know I'm going to be bested." He grinned and reached for a cigar. "I don't know where you studied logic and persuasion, but it's bound to be the best school in the world."

"Not logic, darling, just living with you and knowing how to reach you." She'd been the one to scheme and economize during the difficult times. Baptiste had never complained, and now she loved to watch him indulge his fondness for spending the money his sharp business acumen was earning for them.

Henri couldn't believe he was finally to have the real workshop he'd dreamed about. The surprise that Leah had planned was thwarted when one of the carpenters asked him what he planned to invent next in the big room.

"But only half of the space is yours," Baptiste said when Henri came running to ask him if the man were right. "With the six of you needing all the upstairs bedrooms, Mama wants a room that can double as a sewing room and guest room. Also more storage area."

"Even half, Papa, will be so much more room than the shed." With that, Henri ran back to see how the construction was progressing.

Eventually Monsieur Montand wished his carpenter had kept quiet about the new wing. Henri offered unasked-for advice about every stone that was added to the walls and every tile placed on the roof. Finally, with the last of the exterior plastering finished, Montand breathed a sigh of relief and vowed he'd never build another thing for the Fontaines. At least not as long as Henri was around to supervise.

Within a week, the workshop was as crowded as the shed had been, and Leah wondered where in the world it had all come from.

91

Chapter Eleven

"BAPTISTE WAS OVER THERE AGAIN THIS AFTERNOON." Leah bit the end of her pen as she stared at the sentence she'd written. She didn't have to specify where he'd gone or whom he'd seen. It was the same sentence she'd written in her diary every day for the past month and a half.

Maybe she should stop keeping a diary if it made her as depressed as she was now, but old habits were hard to break. From the time she first learned to write, her mother had insisted she keep a daily journal, and through the enusing years, she'd seldom missed a day.

If only she could think of something else to write about— what the children had done or said, how the garden was coming along, or even what the weather was like. The trouble was, she couldn't concentrate on any of those things. That one thought dominated her so completely, nothing else mattered.

Some two months earlier, Simone Dubard, the widow of Count Emile Dubard, had returned with her three small children to her family's domain less than a kilometer away. Leah and Baptiste had called on her; she'd dined with them and they with her. Simone frequently came over for coffee in the morning after Baptiste left for the city, or Leah went there with Robert while the older children studied with the tutor.

Although Simone had been married several years, and her children's ages were between those of Nicole and Robert, she was considerably younger than Leah. *Strange,* Leah once thought. *I never think of her by name but always as "the young widow."* And this appellation had an ominous quality about it. Simone was pert and vivacious with a sweet nature, and she had a disturbing way of appearing helpless and strong at the same time, as if she understood intuitively that men were equally attracted to both qualities. While she exuded competence and independence, there was an ambiguity about her, as if she wanted it to appear that she was trying—albeit unsuccessfully—to hide her weaknesses and her need for assistance.

"Amazing," Baptiste had said one day, "how well Simone copes alone with those three children and manages the domain with no man to help her." Yet it seemed as if she were always needing assistance of some kind, and Baptiste was always thinking of ways to make things easier for her. Often they would refer to things or people Leah knew nothing about or hadn't heard mentioned before.

Baptiste never tried to conceal his visits to Simone. If he were at home, he'd announce that he was on his way to see her. If he'd spent the day in the city and arrived home later than usual, he'd casually remark, "I stopped by to see Simone." Yet Leah began to feel like a secret intruder into his mind as she tried to fathom his thoughts when she watched him casually check the time, glance over toward Simone's place from his office or the terrace, and call Nicolas to bring around the carriage.

And then came the day when he no longer mentioned to to Leah where he was going, and sometimes he didn't even bother to tell her he was leaving the house. She'd look for him and couldn't find him when a call came from the office or she wanted to ask him something. She knew he'd taken the gig, which he could harness himself. There was no point in wondering where he was. She knew.

A few times, especially when he was on the terrace, she watched him covertly while he seemed to be struggling with indecision over whether to go or stay. She imagined that if he could, he would be pacing the tile floor. Instead he wheeled his chair back and forth. In the end, he always went.

Leah threw down her pen. The pain in her chest couldn't be any worse if she were suffering a heart attack. Was Baptiste having an affair with Simone or was he merely infatuated with her? Intuition told her it was merely infatuation, but it was not knowing for sure that tormented her. A deeper hurt came from Baptiste's seeming unawareness of how upset she was at his visiting Simone daily. How could he not realize what it was doing to her to have him attracted to another, younger woman?

Amazingly enough, their life together went on as usual. Superficially at least, there was no strain between them. They made love frequently, with all the familiar passion and endearments. If anything, the endearments were more effusive and the passion more intense. But this had Leah wondering if the passion were born from his frustration at not being able to have Simone and if the endearments were caused by guilt over his feelings for her. Worst of all, Leah wondered if she were watching her husband falling in love with another woman. *Am I merely a handy vessel,* she asked herself endlessly, *into which he can pour all his pent-up feelings of desire for someone else?*

Twice before, Leah had endured the agony of seeing Baptiste infatuated with another woman. The first time had been in New Orleans. A pretty young seamstress, an unbelievable combination of naïveté and sophistication, lived in an apartment behind the house next door. She worked for a dressmaker in a shop near Jackson Square, but she did most of her sewing at home. Baptiste was also at home all day while Leah worked in the Federal offices. That time, Leah was less concerned. Baptiste did little more than look with sheep's eyes at the young woman whenever she walked by or came to the house for a chat. Leah knew that Baptiste, still recovering from his surgery, was flattered by the attentions of a pretty little thing years younger than he. Leah had managed to be more amused than hurt by his almost puppyish enthusiasm for the girl.

The second time was more serious, and Leah was still not certain how far that situation had gone. Baptiste had had to stay in Paris every night, except for weekends, for more than three weeks because of problems at the office. Leah, in turn, had been forced to remain in the country because two of the children were ill. Celeste Tourneau lived in the apartment building next door to Baptiste. Like Simone, she was a widow, and she had a quiet, appealing personality that gradually endeared her to everyone who met her. Baptiste was quite open about seeing her frequently and enjoying her company and, in fact, introduced her to Leah when she was finally able to leave the children and come to the city.

"I want you to meet and get to know her," he said while they were waiting for Celeste to join them for afternoon coffee. "You'll like her. She's a fine woman."

When Celeste walked from the hall into the living room, it was immediately obvious that she was completely familiar with at least part of the apartment. *What other rooms has she been in?* Leah wondered, and was then furious with herself for being suspicious. As completely at ease as Baptiste was with the two of them, there could certainly be nothing between him and Celeste. Not yet. Yet there was no disguising the hungry look in Celeste's eyes as she directed all her attention to him and hung on his every word. She desired more than friendship with him, and Leah wondered how far she would go, what tactics she would use to bring him to her.

Because Baptiste rarely stayed alone in the city overnight after those hectic few weeks, Leah's concern that Celeste might lure him into an affair subsided. All too soon, however, her emotional calm was shattered. She'd spent the day shopping in Paris, and she was taking a nap in the apartment before dinner. She woke up when she heard Baptiste open the front door. Leah got up from bed and walked toward the living room. Her bare feet made no sound on the carpet, and it was soon evident that Baptiste did not know she was there. She stopped for a moment when she heard him talking on the newly installed telephone. Business, no doubt. She took another step before she realized he was whispering. His words were indistinct, but the tone was too intimate for the feelings behind them to be misunderstood. Finally she caught a few words: "Go back to sleep. I'll see you later."

Leah was too hurt and stunned to cry out or let him know she'd overheard. Instead she returned to her bedroom and pretended to wake up when Baptiste came in. Leah was about to come to the obvious conclusion—Baptiste was having a daytime affair with Celeste—when he announced matter-of-factly that he had to go over and see Celeste after supper.

"Celeste has come to me about investing in some import goods for resale in the States," he said to Leah, "and I promised to discuss it with her this evening. I'd suggest you come along, but I think you'd be bored. I probably won't be more than an hour or two."

Could a man who was having an affair, Leah wondered, speak with such *sang-froid* about going to see his mistress? It was absurd to think he could, and Leah tried to convince herself she had been conjuring up something that did not exist. But always there was a lingering doubt.

Leah could never have explained how it was she finally knew that whatever had been between Baptiste and Celeste was over. It had been like watching the curtain fall on the last act of a play. Perhaps it was a slight easing of tension on Baptiste's part, the kind of satisfied relaxation that comes after one has made a hard but correct decision. Leah could almost hear his sigh of relief when he—not she—suggested they needed a larger apartment now that the children were growing up and would be wanting to come to the city with them from time to time.

Had Celeste tried to lure him into an affair he didn't want, Leah wondered, or was he relieved not to be living a lie any longer? Whichever, Leah had forced herself to make no comment to Baptiste about the brief episode.

Then, from a casual remark Baptiste made more than a year later, Leah discovered that he had been seeing Celeste for several months prior to those three weeks he had stayed in the city. The shock had Leah reeling with disbelief and convinced she had been deluding herself by thinking there'd been nothing serious between them. She'd then entered a period of depression that found her exhausted after the slightest exertion, weeping for no apparent reason, and often physically ill.

After three or four weeks of fighting not to lose her mind, she'd gone for a long walk alone to resolve the situation. She assessed her feelings, Baptiste's moods and actions, and their loving, happy, and more than satisfying life together since he'd stopped seeing Celeste. She finally decided that the immediate onset of depression had been a natural reaction but the prolongation of it had been her own doing. If she were to regain peace of mind, she had to bring herself out of it; no one else could do it for her. She must put those months, and her imaginings of what might have occurred, entirely out of her mind. They were in the past, and must no longer insinuate themselves into the present or influence the future.

And she could have kept those months out of her mind forever if Simone hadn't returned to her family's manor house.

Leah picked up her pen and reached for the sheet of paper beside her diary. It was the guest list for Lisette's supper dance. Life went on at the château even if her world was falling apart.

Lisette finished dressing for the supper dance and looked at herself in the mirror. She was pleased with what she saw. In her floor-length, blue silk ball gown, she was no longer a girl but a young woman, a beautiful young woman. But in spite of the reassuring figure reflected in the mirror, she couldn't control the flutters of anticipation in her stomach or the trembling fear she'd be a wallflower at her own party. She knew most of the young people who were coming; she'd known them from the time of childish birthday parties when they'd played silly games and had races in the garden. But this was different. Now they were grown up and had to behave like adults.

She looked grown up, but she felt like a little girl about to be thrust among strangers who knew all the rules of a game she'd never played. How would she make certain her dance card was filled with more than the obligatory "hostess" dances? Should she flirt and try to act seductive with the very boys at whom she turned up her nose for being too boisterous? Or should she act calm and poised? She just knew the other girls would get all the desirable partners, leaving her with the gangling misfits who couldn't dance.

"Lisette." It was Leah calling from below. "Do you need any help?"

"No thank you, Mama." This was her first dance, and she wanted to get ready for it by herself. For the past few days she'd spent hours arranging her long, blond hair in different styles—coming close to burning herself with the curling irons she heated over the gas lamp for her experiments with long curls down her back, over her shoulders, or rolled up in poufs. She'd frizzed the front of her hair with irons that were too hot, and was dismayed to see several burned strands clinging to the irons when she unrolled them. Fortunately, she was able to hide the short, seared ends among longer strands. Finally, in despair, she brushed it all out and let it hang straight with only a blue ribbon to hold it back. Some of the shorter hair persisted in not staying hidden, but at least it wasn't nearly so frizzy as it had been, and it lay in curls around her temples.

Lisette heard the first carriages arriving. It was time to go down. She pinched her pale cheeks until she saw a little color and pressed her teeth across her lips. Now she was ready.

Lisette need not have worried. Her card was filled for every dance even before the musicians had finished playing the light background music and the first waltz was announced. Nor were they the duty-bound, required "hostess" dances she had feared. She knew the young men's training and natural politeness would not let her sit out a dance, but she'd dreaded that that would be the only reason they'd ask. She was immediately assured by the men swarming around her and pleading for dances that they wanted to dance with her for her own sake.

The evening was one gigantic whirl from one partner's arms to the next, with scarcely time out to breathe. Lisette loved every minute of it. She wanted the rest of her life to consist of nothing but handsome escorts and gala parties. She decided that Papa would have to present her in Paris in two years so she could know the excitement of the great city and all the experiences it had to offer.

When it was time for the pre-supper dance, just before midnight, Lisette looked at her card. The name was unfamiliar—Georges LeClerc. A few of the guests were the sons and daughters of Baptiste's Parisian business friends. Lisette had been hurriedly introduced to them earlier in the evening, and she'd already danced with three of them. Georges LeClerc must be another, she decided, but she couldn't place him.

She waited for him by a tall urn of flowers. Not remembering what he looked like, she didn't know if he were one of the young men already milling around. She waited for him to approach her throughout the entire dance. He never announced himself. Never had she been so humiliated in her life, having to stand aside and watch the others whirl by in the fast gavotte that she loved. The dance ended, and the guests began to assemble near the doors to the sunroom where the buffet was arranged. Lisette tapped her foot impatiently. She was supposed to lead them in with her partner. Whoever this Georges LeClerc was, he'd feel her ire when he appeared—if he did. She was on the verge of tears. Was she going to have to go into supper by herself? Or should she plead sudden illness and escape upstairs?

Finally she saw a tall young man emerge from her father's office. Baptiste followed him. She was furious. Papa had no right to wander off with one of her guests. Especially the partner she was waiting for. When Georges finally walked up to her and bowed, she smiled coldly and took his arm. She certainly wasn't going to converse pleasantly with someone who'd stood her up. She glanced at him out of the corner of her eye. Why, he wasn't even looking at her!

The furniture in the dining room and salon had been moved out to make way for small tables that each seated four people. Once they sat down, Lisette swallowed her fury and determined to be the charming hostess again. She would keep the conversation going the way Mama had trained her to do. She turned over in her mind all the subjects of general interest that Mama had suggested would help avoid embarrassing silences. She needn't have bothered. Georges LeClerc spent the entire time talking with Monsieur Jacquard's son about horses and the upcoming races at Neuilly

98

and Longchamps. Lisette, in turn, tried to listen to Marie Beaumont's inane chatter about her latest visit to her couturier in Paris. She was afraid Marie would ask who her couturier was, and she'd be forced to admit they simply called in a local dressmaker. But again, she needn't have worried. Marie never paused long enough in her discussion of dress lengths and prices and styles to give Lisette a chance to say a word.

At that point Lisette considered Georges nothing more than an egotistical boor. She'd never met such a rude young man, but it piqued her that he paid no attention to her, and she set about to remedy that. She knew something about horses, too, and she loved to ride. So she began making comments, loud enough so that the two young men had to listen. It worked. Georges finally nodded his head in agreement with something she said. It was too late, however, for anything more than that. It was time for the party's final set of dances.

Well, she'd never see Georges LeClerc again, but there were plenty of others who said they wanted to come by the house to call. When she went to bed that night, she lay awake a long time thinking about all the fun she was going to have in the next few years. When she finally fell asleep, she dreamed of Georges.

It is definitely the young who should have children, Leah thought, watching Denise chase after Robert, who was heading pell-mell for the lily pond. *No woman over forty should have a baby unless there is a sister like Denise to care for him.*

Patient Denise. With her own concern over the problems of Nicole and Lisette, her involvement with the interests of Jean and Henri, and now these past few weeks of worry about the relationship between Baptiste and Simone, Leah found herself tending to take Denise for granted. The child sailed through life on such a steady keel that it seemed nothing could upset her. Usually bright and cheerful, she seemed at the same time to recede into the background of family life.

Denise never complained about having to spend her mornings in the classroom, but it was evident that any hours away from little Robert were meaningless to Denise and merely tolerated by her. He was the center and the love of her life, and Denise considered him her own child. Leah might as well not have given birth to him: it was Denise he called for in the middle of the night, and only she was permitted to dress him for their afternoon outings or play with him if the weather were too inclement for them to leave the house. Barely four, Robert was becoming a little terror with his constant demands for attention and a boundless energy that kept him racing from one end of the house or the garden to another. Yet Denise never seemed to lose patience with him.

Not until later that evening, when she saw Denise's shoulders droop and her face become weary at Robert's insistence on a game of hide-and-seek, did Leah realize how much she had imposed on her daughter. Almost immediately, though, Denise's face brightened, and she jumped up to play the game, but for just that moment, when she'd thought no one was looking, she'd revealed how tired she was.

I haven't been fair to her, Leah thought. *I've taken and taken without giving any thought to what her special needs are.* Denise had always seemed so happy caring for Robert and helping Blanchette in the kitchen. And she loved arranging the flowers and supervising the decorations for special occasions like birthdays and holidays. But did she have a secret talent concealed behind that calm exterior that she longed to have recognized and encouraged? Leah could scarcely remember talking with Denise about herself; when they talked, it was always about Robert or something to do with the house.

Denise was never going to be as beautiful as Lisette nor as vivacious as Nicole could choose to be, but she was a pretty child. She had Baptiste's wavy black hair, and her features were fine. Above all, however, it was her calm expression and sparkling brown eyes that would always enchant.

"Denise, I'll put Robert to bed tonight. You look tired." The game of hide-and-seek had ended with Robert collapsing on the floor in giggles and Denise flopping down beside him.

"No, Mama, I'm fine. Anyway, he'll have a tantrum if I don't tuck him in and read to him. I always do before he goes to sleep."

"Then let him have his tantrum." *If I can't control that,* Leah thought, *I'm not much of a mother. Nor have I been up to now. I didn't even know she read to him every night.* "Ask Nicolas to carry up some hot water and you have a nice, soaking bath. Better yet, go into my bathroom and use the English lavender soap. You are tired, and you'll feel much better."

"But, Mama—"

"Go, and then you can come in and kiss Robert goodnight. If he wants another story from you, all right, but I'm taking over for now."

Robert was too startled at the change in routine to make any complaint when Leah sat down beside him on the floor and told him it was time for bed. Without saying a word, he took her hand and docilely accompanied her upstairs.

Leah was embarrassed when he had to show her where his nightshirts were kept and the bag on the back of his door where he put his soiled clothes. She tried to overcome her feelings of inadequacy by teaching him a little song about a frog and an alligator while she got him ready for bed.

"Listen very carefully, Robert, and say each line after me. 'Here is an alligator'—"

"What is a lalligator?"

"Oh my, yes, you wouldn't see one over here. Well, it's a very long, green animal with very short legs. It lives near rivers and it likes to sun itself on the bank."

Robert's face took on a worried look.

"Not our river, pet," Leah said, "but other rivers, a long, long way from here."

"Good." Robert nodded his head.

"Now we'll start over. 'Here is an alligator sitting on a log. He looks in the pool'—"

"Our lily pool?"

"No, dear, you'll never see him in the lily pond. 'He looks in the pool and sees a frog. Off goes the alligator. 'Round goes the log. Splash goes the water. And away swims the frog.' "

Line by line Robert repeated it after her in his own unique fashion. By the time he was in bed, they'd said it together at least seven times.

"I know it," Robert said proudly.

"Very good. How would you like to learn the hand motions that go with it?"

"Show me," and he jumped up and down on the bed.

"All right, watch. When you say 'Here is the alligator,' hold your hand out like this with your thumb tucked under. That's it. Alligators have very long heads and very, very big mouths." Leah went through the motion of peering into the pool as if looking through opera glasses; she rolled her hands around for the log; she spun them rapidly for the splashing and spread them wide for the frog getting away.

101

Robert giggled as he followed every movement and then imitated her.

"The frog gets away?" He looked worried again.

"Indeed he does. Every time."

Robert pointed out the book he wanted her to read from, La Fontaine's *Fables*. Leah's mind went back a long way to the days in Indiana when she was teaching French to a group of delightful teen-aged girls. She'd chosen the *Fables* as a first reading assignment both because the girls already knew most of the tales, and because of the author's name. For a while it seemed to bring Baptiste closer to her during those long months she was away from him and thinking she would never see him again.

"Which one do you want?" she asked Robert.

"Read this." He turned the pages until he came to the one about the fox and the crane.

"Good, that's one of my favorites, too," Leah said.

They had almost finished the third tale when Denise came in after having her bath.

"Deenie, Deenie!" Robert threw back the covers and jumped off the bed. "I know a song."

"A song? How exciting." Denise climbed onto the bed and pulled him up beside her. "How does it go?"

While Leah watched and smiled, Robert went through the whole routine, words and hand movements, perfectly.

Denise kissed him. "Just for that, I'll read you another story. Kiss Mama goodnight."

Leah felt as if she'd been dismissed, politely but firmly. This was their last hour together each night, and she was not needed. But she had had her few minutes with him, and she'd do more from now on.

Leah started down the stairs, stopped, turned back, and went into Denise's room. This was the room Denise had shared with Nicole until Nicole gathered up all her things and moved into the former sewing room. While waiting for Denise, Leah looked around the neat room. When they were old enough, all of the children had been trained to make their beds and keep their rooms picked up. But only Denise always had her bed made before breakfast and her room cleaned before Monsieur Balaine arrived at nine.

Leah walked over to the dressing table and fingered the vanity set spaced evenly in its center. To the right was an oval lacquered box containing a few precious trinkets, and to the left, a picture of Baptiste and herself taken a few years earlier. All of these items sat on a clean, freshly ironed linen scarf, which was edged with coarse string lace that Denise had crocheted.

What a neat little girl Denise was! Smiling to herself, Leah walked to the wardrobe. There hung Denise's dresses, carefully arranged on the rod so none would be crushed. Her shoes and boots were placed neatly on their own shelf. How different from the rooms of the other girls, where everything was thrown helter-skelter. And the boys! No one could walk into their rooms without having to step over indescribable clutter. But the rooms were their own private domains, and if that's the way they wanted to live, Leah was not going to get upset. She demanded only one thing: The rooms were to be thoroughly cleaned and the beds changed once a week.

Denise was gone a long time for one story. Robert had evidently inveigled her into reading two or three. Denise was so tenderhearted, she'd do anything for anyone. Leah suspected she either helped the others with their chores or let them bribe her into doing them all.

"Mama, what are you doing here?" Denise entered softly and reached for her hairbrush.

"Waiting for you. Robert all tucked in?"

"And sound asleep."

"How many stories did you read to him?" Leah asked.

"Only one. But he had to teach me that new song and explain what a 'lalligator' was and why there weren't any in our lily pond."

"Crawl in and I'll sit here beside you. We so seldom get to talk, I thought I'd like to chat a bit."

"That's nice, Mama. Want to curl up on the bed against the bolster?"

"No, I'll stay here in the rocker." Leah plumped the pillow behind her until it fit just right in the small of her back. "My, I'd forgotten about this pillow. You embroidered it when you were seven—eight?"

"Seven."

"You did a beautiful job."

"You forget how many stitches I had to rip out and the tears I cried over it. I wanted it to be perfect."

"You like everything to be perfect and neat, don't you?"

"I—I guess I do," Denise said. "But it's just as easy to put everything right as it is to keep it messy."

"I wish the others felt that way," Leah said, sighing audibly.

"They have so many things to occupy their time."

"And you don't?" This was the opening she'd been waiting for. "There's nothing special you'd like to study or work at?"

"You mean like music or art or—or motors?" Denise dissolved into giggles.

"Something like that, yes." Leah laughed too, then became more serious. "Something besides taking care of Robert and helping Blanchette."

"But I love doing those things, Mama."

"Are you sure? Or have they just become habit? What I'm trying to say, Denise, in a very awkward way, is that maybe we've all been imposing on you and you're too generous to complain."

"Mama, do I have to have a special talent? Is it wrong to want to be only a wife and mother someday? I love everything to do with keeping house."

"Oh no, my darling, it's not wrong at all." Leah moved over to the bed and gathered Denise into her arms. "And don't ever say 'only' a wife and mother. It's all I ever wanted, and you know how contented I am." She thought a minute. "No, more than contented. I've been ecstatically happy. And all I can wish for you is that same happiness."

"Thank you, Mama." Denise rearranged herself under the covers and carefully smoothed them over her again. There *was* something she wanted to do, but she was afraid her mother would scoff at her. No, Mama had asked, and she never laughed at what the others did. "If you don't think I'm being silly, Mama, I'd like to start my hope chest. Just a few things to begin with, but at least I'd know it was mine. Something I could be adding to and taking care of."

"That's not silly at all. I think it's a wonderful idea."

"There's an old chest in the storage area next to the kitchen," Denise said excitedly. "I've looked it over and all it needs is to be cleaned up."

"No indeed. We're going to start your hope chest right. We'll go into Paris together and get you the handsomest one we can find." If Lisette could get a grand piano and Henri half an entire new wing, surely Denise could have her own heart's desire.

Leah was besieged by conflicting emotions as she prepared for the week-long stay with Denise in Paris. She had looked forward to giving Denise all her attention while they spent the days shopping, walking through the parks,

104

and visiting museums and other places Denise had never seen. In the evenings, Baptiste would be there for dinner, and they might take her to the theatre or the opera. Then Baptiste mentioned, somewhat casually, that he was troubled by pains in his hips, and he thought he'd stay at the château while they were in town.

"And I can be of some help to Blanchette," he added. "She'll be busy enough with Robert, and I'll be here if the others need me."

Leah couldn't disagree with him, but she wondered if it were his physical condition or the children, or Simone that kept him at home. Was he looking forward to a week in which he could see her as often as he wanted without Leah's watchful presence?

It was now two and a half months since Leah first noted in her diary his daily afternoon visits to Simone. Except that now all she wrote down was: "Over there again."

She tried desperately to understand and accept. Baptiste was still handsome and personable. Women had always been attracted to him and he to them. She'd known he was a charmer when she met him, and he hadn't changed a bit through the years. With flattery and teasing and wit, he had every woman around him eating out of his hand. He was as captivating and debonair at fifty as he'd been at twenty-five. Except for the situation with Celeste, she'd never resented the attentions he paid to female friends or the complimentary comments he made about some woman's figure. After all, when a man stopped looking and admiring, he might as well be dead. And he was always just as complimentary to her. She thought again about his handicap. Perhaps he needed constant reassurance that it did not deter other women from being attracted to him. And then he was fifty, and it must be very soothing to his ego to have his attentions welcomed by a much younger woman. Reaching fifty could have alarmed him, giving rise to a need to recapture his youth one more time.

Two or three times she'd started to speak to Baptiste about her worries, to ask him point blank if he were having an affair with Simone or if he were simply infatuated with her. Then she thought better of it. If there were nothing serious between them, she didn't want to plant ideas in his mind. And if he'd been innocent but had contemplated an affair, he could think that as long as she suspected him of being unfaithful, he might as well be exactly that. It was not a feeling of martyrdom that kept her silent. It was a common-sense approach toward preservation of their marriage.

The easiest thing would have been to put an end to her own friendship with Simone, but Leah continued to see her, sometimes by herself, sometimes with Baptiste. She maintained the friendship for the same reason she didn't speak about it to Baptiste. It was also her way of letting both of them know she was still very much an important part of Baptiste's life. But as the weeks passed she found it harder and harder to appear unaware of the special rapport between Baptiste and Simone, harder to conceal that her nerves were taut as violin strings.

When Baptiste was at Simone's, Leah often stood on the terrace and looked toward the distant house. Were they just talking? Were they aching to touch each other? Or were they already in each other's arms? At those times she wondered which would be the worse torment: to keep on wondering or to know they were having an affair.

Leah knew she appeared strong, and that she *was* strong in many ways, but it was a strength that ebbed and flowed. Although she presented a bold, indomitable self-sufficient face to the world, she was often frightened and in need of comfort and reassurance. Baptiste had always understood that. Now she felt as bereft as when James died and she'd thought Baptiste was lost to her, too. Since her marriage to Baptiste, she'd always been able to talk over her problems with him. Now that he was the problem, there was no one to talk to.

"Do you want to check my suitcases, Mama?" Denise's question interrupted Leah's reverie.

"I'm sure you've remembered everything, but I will if you want me to. Don't pack it too full; we'll be buying some things in Paris."

"Mama, I'm so excited I'm not sure I can sleep tonight. A whole week alone with you!" She danced around the room.

Denise's exultation would make up for her own worries about Baptiste, Leah thought. Why hadn't she considered taking the children into Paris one at a time before this? She would make it a point to do so, maybe once a month. She could not let her fears subvert their needs.

106

Chapter Twelve

Leah returned from Paris to find an ecstatic Lisette. Georges LeClerc had been around to see her almost every afternoon.

"Isn't that a bit often to be seeing one young man?" Leah asked.

"But he lives in Paris, Mama, and is visiting his uncle for only two weeks."

Since the supper dance, the young men had come swarming around Lisette, who entertained them on the terrace or went riding with them.

"I thought Papa and I agreed you should have callers only on weekends so as not to interfere with your studies and your music."

"What a bore that is!" Lisette exclaimed. "Nothing to do but wait for Saturday and Sunday."

"Have you forgotten that Papa and I allow visits from these young men as a privilege? We would hate to revoke it."

Lisette pouted but didn't dare say what was in her mind. Just then Denise ran up. "You should see what Mama bought me in Paris, Lisette. A big hope chest for all my linens and two beautiful dresses. There are some surprises in that new trunk for you, too."

"Pooh," Lisette said. "Who wants a hope chest or to think about marriage? I just want to have lots and lots of fun with dozens of beaux. And I will, too." She glared at Leah and walked off.

"Don't worry about her, Mama," Denise said comfortingly. "She'll come around."

"Thank you, dear," Leah said with a smile. "I'm glad you think so."

"Oh, Mama, I had such a wonderful time in the city. Now I can't wait for the chest to be delivered so I can put all my things in it. Maybe I'd better bring them down and press them all again so they'll be ready."

My little homemaker, Leah thought. *I hope when the*

time comes she'll meet a man who really appreciates her.

Because Georges LeClerc was going back to the city in just a few days, Leah and Baptiste relented and allowed Lisette to see him for a little while each day. Lisette couldn't get over her good fortune. Georges was not only very good-looking, but he was at least two years older than most of the boys she was seeing. As much as she liked him for himself, it was even more exciting to be called on by a university student.

Usually they sat on the terrace or in the sunroom, chaperoned by everyone in the house, from Robert who couldn't understand why they didn't want to play with him, to Henri going in and out of his workshop, and, of course, by Mama and Papa, who were usually close at hand. A couple of times Lisette and Georges walked across the lawn to the river, but were still in full view of the house.

Caught in a sudden downpour one afternoon, they ran for the summer house, where they sat on a bench and waited for the rain to stop. Then Lisette felt Georges' arm go around her. She shivered a little, partly from excitement, partly from awe at his daring, but she didn't want him to move it away.

"Cold, Lisette?"

She turned her face toward him and shook her head. When he kissed her, it was merely a gentle brushing of her lips, until Lisette put her arms around him. *This is more like it,* she thought, when he kissed her longer and held her closer. *If this is what it means to be a woman, I like it.*

They returned to the house when the rain stopped, but Lisette's thoughts were already on the next afternoon. The circular summer house had been built in imitation of an ancient Roman temple, with a series of pillars supporting the roof. Shutters had been installed between the pillars to be opened on warm days and closed to protect the interior on rainy days and during the winter. Lisette now made certain the shutters remained closed.

"Will you miss me?" Georges asked. It was the day before he was to return to Paris.

They had managed to slip into their retreat for a few hasty kisses the day before, and now there was just today and tomorrow. Lisette was quite certain she didn't love Georges, but she liked being kissed by him.

"Yes, very much," she whispered.

"I don't think I can stand being away from you." He had

his arms around her and now he pulled her closer to him.

They were standing in the middle of the small room. Lisette wanted to suggest they sit on one of the padded benches, as they usually did. It was uncomfortable standing on tiptoe while Georges kissed her, but he was holding her so tightly she could scarcely breathe, and he wouldn't stop kissing her long enough for her to speak. Her head was spinning from his forceful kisses and the strange sensation of having his body full length against her. She thought she was going to faint.

"I love you and want to marry you, Lisette," Georges said huskily, after releasing his hold on her slightly.

"Don't be silly, Georges, I'm much too young." She was still a little shaky from being held so tightly in his arms and from the strange feeling of exultation that had surged through her a moment before. But now at least she could breathe normally, and she no longer had that frantic desire for Georges to keep holding her.

"I don't mean right now," he said. "I mean after I finish the university."

"But that's years away."

"Only three. We could be secretly engaged."

Good heaven, she thought, *does Georges think he'll be the only man in my life?* She intended to have lots of beaux before she married and settled down. Nor was she particularly looking forward to marriage. Parties and kissing were a lot more fun than being tied down at home with babies.

"Let me think about it," she whispered. She'd been proposed to! That was excitement enough for one day. If only she could tell someone. None of her friends would believe her, and Mama would be shocked and probably forbid Georges to set foot in the house again. She stepped back and began smoothing her skirt. She'd keep him guessing for a while so they could keep on meeting like this.

"I like you, Georges, I really do. So don't forget me when you're in Paris."

"I'll come stay with my uncle every weekend so I can see you."

She backed off a little when he started to put his arms around her again, but then she stood on tiptoe and kissed him gently on the mouth.

Baptiste didn't walk often in the garden, but, despite the aching in his hips, he was too restless to stay on the terrace this beautiful day. Before he started back to the terrace, he'd rest in the summer house. He was getting old too fast, and he didn't like the idea. He resented everything implied by growing older—the aches and pains, the waning of youthful vigor and the enthusiasm for new challenges. Thank God he still had one pleasure left to him. Leah sometimes teased him by saying he'd be a lover until he died, and by God, he intended to prove her correct.

He wondered why all the shutters were closed. Maybe Nicolas had shut them during the rain a few days earlier and then forgotten to open them. It wouldn't take much of an effort, though, to push one open, and he really couldn't stand up much longer. Noting that one shutter was slightly ajar, Baptiste looked inside while he began opening it a little wider. When he saw Georges bend down to kiss Lisette, he slammed the shutter open with his crutch.

"Oh, Papa, you startled me." Lisette instinctively backed away from Georges and put both hands to her mouth, as if she'd suddenly discovered his touch was contaminating.

"I'm rather surprised myself," Baptiste said. He was trying very hard to keep from losing his temper and raising his voice.

"Georges—Georges was just leaving," she managed to gasp.

"And about time, I would say." What sort of young man had Lisette been seeing? And how did she dare behave like this, meeting someone in secret and acting the wanton? Baptiste found himself feeling betrayed by this daughter he loved so much.

"I'm sorry, sir," Georges said. "What Lisette was trying to say is that I'm returning to the city tomorrow. I—I just couldn't help myself."

How long, Lisette wondered, had her father been standing outside the summer house? What had he seen or heard? No, he would have barged in sooner if he'd seen anything more than this last kiss.

"You should be sorry," Baptiste stormed, no longer able to keep his temper under control. "You're a young man, but Lisette is still a child. I'm going to assume this is the first time you've kissed her." He paused. "But believe me, it is going to be the last time."

"Yes, sir," Georges said.

Lisette was too frightened to say anything. She knew her father's temper. She could only hang her head and hope he thought her flushed cheeks and flustered attitude came from being caught during that last, simple kiss.

110

"And you, young lady," Baptiste ordered, "back to the house. Your mother will have a talk with you later."

Monsieur LeClerc agreed with Baptiste that Georges should make no more visits.

"I apologize for Georges' behavior," LeClerc said, "but then you have to admit, Fontaine, that your Lisette is a most attractive young lady."

"She's still a child, LeClerc, and I intend to keep her that way for at least two more years." Baptiste swirled his brandy so viciously it almost spilled over the rim of the snifter.

"I don't blame you. I've suggested to Georges that he would do just as well at the University of Strasbourg as in Paris."

"I appreciate your understanding in this matter," Baptiste said, offering LeClerc a refill of brandy. "What I saw was really a very innocent kiss, and I would not be quite so upset about that. But from their acute embarrassment, I can only gather it was not the first. I want to protect both of them—Georges as well as Lisette—from anything happening they'd be sorry for."

"I agree heartily. If George feels the urge to sow his wild oats, he can do it in Strasbourg, or in Paris when he's home. I'll not have an innocent girl harmed. He knows how I feel, and he should have remembered what I've told him."

"Georges is not entirely to blame," Baptiste said. "Lisette is a flirtatious little wench. I saw that at the supper dance. Leah plans to have a talk with her and settle her down a bit."

What he didn't say was that he feared Lisette developing into another Catherine, a woman who would use her charms and beauty to lure men into her web. It was natural, he supposed, for her to inherit Catherine's traits, but he and Leah must see that Lisette grew up to be a more modest, less willful woman than her mother. He did not want his daughter to suffer—and cause others to suffer—as her mother had.

Lisette was restricted to the house for a month with no callers, and during that time Leah had several long talks with her.

"If you wish to consider yourself a young lady, Lisette, then you are going to have to learn to behave like one," Leah said at one point. "An unmarried lady does not allow men to kiss her. Nor is she alone with them except when

111

walking or riding, and then preferably within sight of others."

"Yes, ma'am." Lisette knew better than to argue when her whole future as the belle of Paris was at stake.

"Georges LeClerc is a very nice young man," Leah continued, "and I know he meant no real harm. But—young men get carried away and then—well, then things happen that shouldn't."

Bother, Lisette thought. *Here's that business again of something happening, but no one ever tells me what it is.* Georges had said the same thing as he took his arms from around her, just before he'd asked her to marry him. Or maybe it already has happened. Remembering all that had taken place in the summer house, Lisette felt herself blushing, and she hoped Mama would think it was because of the talk they were having.

"What I'm trying to say, Lisette, is you mustn't lead them on—flirt with them. Oh, I don't mean smiling and being charming. That's part of the game. And it can be fun. But—but don't let them take advantage of you—get you alone and try to kiss you."

"Why not, if I enjoy it?" Why was it that so much she liked was forbidden?

Leah started to laugh but stopped at a smile. Yes, the first kisses were fun and exciting. "That, Lisette, may be the unanswerable question. It's because men want their future wives to be innocent and pure."

Again Lisette felt a surge of that old closeness to Leah. Still, she couldn't ask Leah if having Georges touch her breasts and—and put his hand up under her skirt meant she was no longer pure. She'd have to wait and learn that for herself.

"I'll try to remember, Mama, but it is such fun to know you've made a conquest, that a young man wants to kiss you." She hesitated a minute and then thought it would be exciting to share part of her secret. "And you know what else? He asked me to marry him."

"He did!" Now Leah was really surprised. She took a longer look at Lisette. The girl was growing up faster than she realized. "And what did you say?"

"I said I was too young."

"Um, you're better able to handle things than I thought."

"The truth is, Mama, I don't want to marry him. Or anyone for a long time. Mama, do you think I'm pretty enough to have lots of beaux?"

"You're a very beautiful young lady, and if you behave

112

like one, you'll have all the nicest young men swarming around you."

"I hope so."

"When the right time comes, you'll meet the one you love and want to marry."

After Lisette left, Leah thought about their conversation. She would be all right now. She was a bit precocious, but basically she was a sweet and good girl.

In her room, Lisette was also pondering the conversation. Thinking about how she'd let Georges hold her so close and touch her made her tingle all over. Georges would never be allowed to see her again, or at least be alone with her. But there were other young men, and there were ways to escape from watchful eyes long enough to experience the same thrill. If she behaved herself and acted contrite enough, Mama and Papa might let her have callers again in a few weeks. Making more conquests, being alone with them, was worth the wait.

With all her concern over Lisette, Leah scarcely had time to dwell on her own problems. Baptiste had seemed genuinely glad to see her when she returned from Paris with Denise; perhaps she'd been foolish to mistrust him. Certainly, when they were alone that first night back, he was as ardent a lover as she could wish for. Yet the afternoon visits continued, and the hurt had returned.

Then one day, some two weeks later, Baptiste did not go to Simone's and continued to stay at home for several days after that. Leah was puzzled at the abrupt change in his routine, and at Simone's failure to come around for a visit during that time. Was the affair over or had there ever been one? Leah had all but convinced herself the latter was true when Simone drove up one afternoon.

"I came over to tell you good-bye," Simone said when she had alighted from the carriage.

"Good-bye?" Leah couldn't keep the surprise out of her voice.

"Yes, didn't Baptiste tell you? I'm going to be married and move to Provence."

"No, he didn't, but I'm very happy for you." Leah wondered if that was why he'd stopped seeing her—because she was in love with someone else. Or perhaps he'd made the break, and Simone had then accepted a proposal.

"And I'll miss you so much," Simone said. "I don't know what I would have done without you and Baptiste these past

113

months. I was so terribly lonely after my beloved Émile died, and you both made it so much easier for me to get over my grief."

"I'm glad we could help," Leah said. Would she ever know just how much and what kind of consolation Baptiste had given her?

"Please tell Baptiste good-bye for me."

"He's on the terrace," Leah said. "Why don't you tell him yourself? He'd be terribly disappointed to miss you."

Leah didn't know why she'd suggested it, except maybe to atone for how grateful she felt that Simone would no longer be around for Baptiste to see if he wanted to resume his visits or to think about if he continued to stay away.

Chapter Thirteen

AFTER SIMONE LEFT, Baptiste never mentioned her name again. Nor did he ever refer to the months she'd lived near them. It had been the same after the episode with Celeste: no mention of what had brought and kept them together for all those months. It didn't help to assuage Leah's doubts about him, their marriage, and herself, to have him exhibit no remorse—either time—for having devoted his attentions to another woman. Instead, his "accept and forget" attitude —his assumption he could behave as he wished with impunity and without incurring disaffection and distrust—made the pain more vivid. If he were at any time cognizant of Leah's feelings, he gave no indication.

The unnerving situation and accompanying misery, accentuated by the awareness she'd probably never know the truth, was something she had to keep to herself as well as the fact she would never "accept and forget." With Simone's departure, the immediate crisis was over, but it would take far longer for the effect of what she'd been through to dissipate.

Leah still loved Baptiste. They had been together too many years, and there was too much they had shared for her to stop loving him.

In most respects their life went on as it had before

Simone began to figure so importantly in it. She and Baptiste continued to laugh and joke together, to plan for the future, to worry about the children, and to make love. She needed Baptiste's love more than ever, and her love for him was in no way diminished. Only altered slightly. Having lost some of its buoyancy and its glow, it no longer had the power to lift her above the mundane, everyday world or to light up her heart. It was pointless to hope that they would ever again be as close as before. Baptiste might never have been physically unfaithful to her, but it was just as painful to accept the idea that he'd been unfaithful in his thoughts. And he must have been to have visited Simone every day all those months.

Strangely enough, with the belief that physical infidelity and mental infidelity were merely two sides of the same coin, she no longer felt a desperate need to know which Baptiste had been guilty of. Equally strange, it was a revelation that brought with it a type of peace that allowed her to acknowledge the fact that what is done cannot be undone.

Whenever he could, on weekends or after returning home from the Paris office, Jean walked through the surrounding fields and visited with the farmers in the village. He felt as at home in their crowded kitchen-parlors as he did in the spacious rooms of the château. As much as he enjoyed working in the city, he'd never lost his love for the land.

While he smoked a pipe with the men and inhaled the pervasive cooking odors of cabbage soup and spiced beets, he listened intently to centuries-old wisdom of how to work the fields, when to plant, and when to harvest. The more he heard, the more he felt stirring within him a primeval desire to possess and work his own land. Unlike many of the domains in the area, that of his family did not include acres of farmland. It probably had when the château was originally built, but later it was converted into a plaything, a charming place where one could escape from the rigors of court life and entertain in the bucolic manner popularized by Marie Antoinette's Petite Trianon.

There was never much farmland for sale, even if Jean had had the means to buy it. Most of the fields surrounding France's towns and villages were owned and had been owned for generations by the families now cultivating them. Or by large landowners like his father's friends. In most cases elder sons would inherit; little would be for sale.

Yet Jean continued to dream. One day he would own land. It would mean saving money for many years, for

115

right now he was being given a mere pittance of an allowance while he trained under his father's division managers. But if he worked hard and was rewarded with a regular position, there would be more to save. As long as he continued to live at home—and he saw no reason why he could not—his needs were few. What he had to do was convince his father that it was time he was given a regular position with full pay. Then the real saving could begin.

In Jean's mind, his dream was close to becoming a reality; he thought nothing but time stood in his way.

During his rambles through the countryside, Jean often passed the gristmill that ground the meal and flour for several of the nearby villages. He sat on the bank of the millstream now, watching the slow, deliberate, rhythmical turning of the wheel while he dreamed his dreams of the future. Much like the slow, methodical wheel, Jean went over and over his carefully laid plans for someday owning land like the soil he now clutched between his fingers. The good, rich earth that had nurtured people for more centuries than he could count. It had sustained life. It was life itself.

He looked across the stream to the pasture, where a dozen or so black and white cows munched the grass. Even as the cows were eating, an almost miraculous, internal force transmuted the fodder into the rich milk that would later be made into the sweet butter and tangy cheeses for which the area was famous. All it would take to make Jean content would be several acres of land, a few cows and goats, and a small cream-colored plaster house. Ten years. He would give himself ten years of stringent saving, and then he would begin looking for the acreage to buy. Nothing, nothing could stop those plans.

Restless, Jean began following the flow of the stream toward the spot where it entered the Seine, about a kilometer below the château.

He had almost reached the girl before he saw her. And then he saw only her head and shoulders rising above the drop of the miniature falls where the land sloped gently into the valley. With a second look, he saw that her shoulders were bare. For a brief moment, when she bent down, she was lost to view; she came up laughing and splashed handfuls of water on her face. Then it dawned on him. She was bathing, completely unaware she was being observed.

Jean stifled the urge to continue along the stream and and see more of the laughing eyes and long, glossy black

116

hair that already had him enthralled. Innately modest himself, Jean knew he would embarrass her; worse, it might prevent him from ever getting to know her. She would flee and that would be the end of it. But he could not turn and walk back. He had to see more of her. He had to know if her body were as beautiful as her face. The compulsion to watch her, to be a secret voyeur while she innocently continued bathing, was like a forbidden hunger eating away at him. Half hidden among the trees along the edge of the stream, he looked for a way to move closer and remain invisible.

Slowly, so no sudden movement would startle her, Jean moved deeper into the trees as he walked parallel with the stream and down the sloping ground. Now he was directly opposite her. He lay flat on the ground, with only his head raised. He could not take his eyes off the scene before him. She stood, like some Renaissance painting of a Roman goddess of nature, in the small pool that swirled among the rocks at the base of the narrow falls. Completely naked, she continued to laugh as she splashed water over her head and face and body.

Overcome by a confusion of wonder and delight and shame at the desire surging through him, Jean had to hold his breath to keep from gasping in adoration. He looked quickly from her full, milk-white breasts to her small waist, wide hips, and generous thighs, which were spread apart to steady her among the swirling waters.

Jean's hands ached to touch her body, to hold those magnificent breasts, and to move along those inviting thighs. Over and over again, more slowly each time, he let his glance move from her shoulders to her knees and back up again. Now he was actually writhing with an almost unbearably acute longing to hold her and possess her completely. He wanted to run to her and force her to submit to him right then. But he couldn't do that. Not from a sense that it would be morally wrong, but because he knew that as surely as he was seeing her, he was in love with her. He wanted to cherish as well as possess her.

At nineteen, Jean was still a virgin and an idealist. Twice he had come close to losing his sexual innocence, but both times he had been prevented from completing the act. The first time, at age fourteen, he and several boys from the village had been in a barn with a more-than-willing young woman. He had listened eagerly to his friends' exaggerated accounts of their sexual exploits, and he could hardly wait to find out for himself what having a woman was like. But when the time came, his senses rebelled at having an audience, and he had to slink away, ashamed that what he thought would occur so easily had not happened at all. He could still hear his friends' laughter, as they teased him for being a little boy rather than a man. He thought he never wanted to try it again.

The second time had been in Paris. He and several friends had gone to the theatre. The comedy, filled with lewd jokes and suggestive actions, had stirred up their juices, and they all thought: Hell, why not? They pooled their cash and went to one of the more famous bordellos. Unfortunately, Jean had taken several drinks to work up his courage, and he finally passed out. That was his one experience as a man-about-town.

He knew he could do it now. But not here, not this way. Instead, he watched as the girl stepped out of the pool, dried herself off, and then slipped into a gathered skirt and full, loose blouse. She casually pulled the strings of the neckline and tied them into a bow. But as shirred as her blouse was, her breasts filled it and swelled above it. She wore nothing but these two garments, and Jean continued, in his imagination, to see the body beneath them. He was so aroused by her body that he could hardly breathe. He stuffed his fist into his mouth to keep from panting audibly. Finally he watched her walk away, toward the grist mill, and he had to be satisfied with knowing where she lived.

Day after day Jean went to the falls, not following the stream anymore but approaching his hiding place through the trees. Not every day did she come, but when she was there, the empty hours of waiting were well rewarded. Her routine was always the same. She slipped out of her two garments and then splashed and played in the water for at least twenty minutes. Jean was filled with a secret delight that only he had trespassed on her and was privileged to view her innocent pleasure in bathing. Soon, very soon, he planned to approach her at the mill and introduce himself. It had taken him some time to think up a logical excuse for being there, but he had one now.

On Jean's second visit to the falls where she was bathing, Céline Larroque became aware of someone watching her from the trees. A single glance showed her a man lying there and staring intently at her. At first she was disturbed, but when he did not move or make any attempt to approach her, she continued bathing. It was no concern of hers if someone took pleasure in watching her. When she noticed him again, she was more distressed, but she took the opportunity to look at him more closely. Then, after describing him to friends in the village, she finally knew who her observer was. Jean Fontaine, son of the wealthy Baptiste Fontaine who lived in the beautiful château. While Jean was making his plans to meet her, she was laying some plans of her own.

She knew that at the moment he was still only a secret, and evidently shy, admirer. She would have to change that. She would have to draw him out of his hiding place and bring him to her. For sixteen years she had lived a miserable, penurious life. Jean Fontaine could well be the means toward realizing the wealth and pretty things that she dreamed about at night in the loft. She was wise enough to know that the differences in social class would forbid anything more than a casual liaison between them, but that could be enough. She had a beautiful body, a tempting body, and she knew what that body did to men and what it could do for her. It had already lured Jean to return again and again to watch her bathing, and she was not above using it to snare him into a subtle but powerful trap.

Céline was six when she was adopted by the miller, Guillaume Larroque. Before then she lived crowded together with other unwanted children in a foundling home. The mill, where she had her own bed in the loft above the warm and cheery kitchen, was like a palace to her. Helping Madame Larroque with the cooking and cleaning was not nearly so arduous as the heavy chores she'd had to do at the home. Most of all, there was the freedom to go outside, to walk along the millstream or into the woods just about anytime she wanted to. Madame Larroque was strict but not harsh in her demands that the work be done first, and Céline was eager to please. One of her favorite places was the mill itself, where she watched, fascinated, as the great stone wheels, powered by the waterwheel, ground the grain.

And Monsieur Larroque. Until she was eleven, he was beloved Uncle Gilly who held her on his broad lap, let her play with his whiskers, and told her fascinating tales of elves and werewolves. In her childish imagination, the kindly king of the elves was a miniature Uncle Gilly, generous, fun-loving, understanding, with a jolly chuckle that started as a low rumble in his huge stomach and then came out and set the whole world laughing. And how Céline laughed with him while she pulled at his whiskers and jogged up and down on his knees. Until she was eleven. Then he became Monsieur Larroque, a man to be feared, a monster more grotesque than any of the hobgoblins and ogres he'd described.

Uncle Gilly had always liked to play games, like tickling her in the ribs until tears came to her eyes and she had to beg him to stop. Or letting her "ride the horsey" on his knees. Sometimes when she stood in front of him, he slid forward on his chair, pulled something funny-looking out of his trousers, and tickled her between her legs. The sensation was a strange one, half exciting, half disturbing, but since she loved Uncle Gilly and he seemed to enjoy this game, she never moved away. Until the day she was eleven, a day she'd never forget as long as she lived.

"Want to 'ride the horsey'?" She'd been standing there letting him tickle her with that strange object, and then he pulled her up suddenly onto his lap. The pain was searing, violent. She couldn't scream. One huge arm held her face against his whiskered chin; the other forced her body to slide back and forth against his stomach. After long, terrible moments of agony, he released his grip slightly. The once-loving smile was now a grotesque leer. Céline wanted to run, to leave pain and fear behind, but she had no strength to move. After he pushed her off his lap, she waited numbly for him to say something.

"That game is our little secret, eh, Céline?" But his tone when he said this was not playful. Young as she was, Céline recognized the threat in his voice. "No word to Aunt Sophie. Because if you do—" He reached toward the fireplace for his heavy, knobby walking stick. "You're a pretty little thing, but you'd never walk again if I had to use this on you. Or there might be an accident with the mill wheel. Bound to happen if one gets careless."

With tears streaming down her face, Céline could only nod. No, no one would ever know.

"You're the daughter of a whore, Céline, and will make a pretty one when you grow up." He licked his lips. "I can enjoy you and make money with you, too."

Céline didn't know what a whore was, but it must be something dreadful to have Uncle Gilly treat her like this. She only knew she felt a dreadful shame and a burning hatred for Uncle Gilly. And the hatred was more intense because she had loved him so much. She did not yet know exactly what he had done to her, nor was she aware how

120

seriously her body had been violated, but she did know that her senses and her trust had been. And that was what hurt the most.

"Now scat!" he ordered. "Go wash your face and change your clothes. You look like a real hussy." No chuckle or kindly warmth this time. "Take your clothes to the stream and wash them, too, right away. Then if you're a good girl, we'll play this game again."

Céline was puzzled by the command to wash her clothes until she saw the blood on them. While she bathed in the stream, she scrubbed all evidence of the attack from her clothes. The cool water at the base of the falls swirled around her sore body, soothing the pain and easing her spirits. She vowed she'd never again get near enough to her once-beloved Uncle Gilly to let him touch her. It was only after overhearing two boys trading lewd stories that she realized what he had done to her. The revulsion sent her running into the fields, where she lay among a mass of wild daisies until the body-wracking sickness passed.

If once she had loved going to the mill and had eagerly awaited the time she'd be old enough and strong enough to help there, she was now relieved when Aunt Sophie insisted she was still needed in the house.

"More than ever now," Madame Larroque told her husband. "I'm so arthritic I can scarcely move for the pain."

Céline wondered about that. When her husband was away, Aunt Sophie had no difficulty bustling around the kitchen and the two other downstairs rooms of the small cottage. But Madame Larroque had seen how her husband lusted after Céline, especially after the girl's loosely gathered blouses became inadequate to conceal her developing figure. A violently jealous woman, Madame Larroque saw to it that her husband was never left alone with Céline, and Céline was grateful without knowing the reason.

Soon after she turned fourteen, Céline was working in the mill, feeding grain into the large millstones, and putting the meal into sacks. Monsieur and Madame Larroque had driven to a nearby village with a wagonload of meal, so she felt safe there. Monsieur Larroque had begun to find ways to touch her breasts with his soft, fat hands or lift up her skirts when his wife was out of the room. Céline knew it was only a matter of time before he made stronger advances and found a way to be alone with her long enough to rape her again.

Another one she feared was Marcel, the miller's apprentice, a brash, red-faced young man of seventeen. More than once he'd tried to corner her in the mill or in the dairy when she went to milk the cows. So far she'd held him off, and she sighed as she wondered how long that would last. As long, she knew, as Madame Larroque kept him satisfied. Oh, her adopted mother might scream threats of hellfire and damnation for anyone who thought about physical pleasures, but more than once Céline had seen Marcel sneaking out of his mistress's bedroom. She'd also seen the way Madame Larroque touched her husband invitingly when they bid Céline goodnight. And wasn't there a tiny space between two boards above their bedroom through which Céline could watch and listen to their nightly activities? So Céline knew that Madame Larroque might look stern and forbidding, but she was actually a lusty old crone who enjoyed the very pleasures she ranted against.

Well, Céline smiled to herself, she was safe this afternoon from Marcel, too. He was repairing a break in the rock dam that controlled the flow of water to the millwheel.

Suddenly she felt two strong arms go around her from the back and two hands clutching her breasts tightly enough to make her gasp with pain. Then came a harsh voice: "Feels good, doesn't it?"

She lowered her head in an attempt to bite the hands, but was thwarted when her attacker turned her roughly around. She found herself face to face with a stranger instead of Marcel as she had thought. The man was leering greedily at her.

"Marcel said I'd find you here alone. I paid a good price for that information. I expect you to be worth it."

There was no point in screaming. The Larroques had been gone for nearly an hour, and Marcel was undoubtedly counting the coins that had purchased his absence. "Let go of me, you brute," she said through gritted teeth.

She tried to lunge forward to push him away, but his strong arms were too quick for her.

"Hold on, my pretty. I'm famous for what I can do. So the pleasure will be as much yours as mine. And Marcel's coming soon to share with me."

"Oh, no! Not you or him." In spite of the helplessness of her situation, she began to scream.

"Won't do any good," he said in a surprisingly mild voice. "There's no one around."

Céline was too short to see over his shoulder, but she was familiar with every inch of the mill. If she had the strength to keep maneuvering him backward, she might get him as far as the stairs to the ground level. Even if she tumbled down with him, there was a good chance the fall would change his mind about molesting her.

With one arm around Céline and the other working to lift her skirts, the man seemed unaware of her intentions as she gradually moved him a short step at a time toward the stairs. She was concentrating so hard, she didn't realize they had changed direction slightly. Then, in one quick second, it happened.

Just as she had the sickening realization that she had backed him toward the wide door overlooking the water wheel, one of his feet slipped on the edge of the flooring. In order to regain his footing, he loosened his arms enough for her to move away, and then he fell onto the turning wheel. There was a scream, a thud as his head hit the water-soaked flanges, and then a splash when his body fell into the water.

Céline gasped when she finally dared to look down. The man had landed face down on the wheel but in its turning it had deposited him face up in the water. He lay there completely inert. She had no idea whether he was dead or alive. Should she try to move him or should she leave him there? If he were dead, it wouldn't make any difference what she did; she couldn't help him. No, he had to be alive. She'd wait until her heart stopped pounding and she was able to breathe more naturally before going down to see. Then she'd decide what to do.

"My God, you've killed him!"

Céline whirled around to see Marcel standing not five feet away.

"I did? I didn't mean to," she sobbed hysterically. "I just wanted to frighten him away."

Marcel quickly took in her flushed face, her body shaking from fear and exertion. No point in wasting time on pity.

"Come here, Céline. No one need ever know. I'll take care of the body and won't tell if—"

She was in his arms, and he was pushing her against a pile of grain-filled sacks. This time she was too tired and too desperate to resist in spite of the painful arching of her back against the rough sacks. She gritted her teeth against the memory of what it had been like with Monsieur Larroque. Surprisingly, it was not as abhorrent this time. She found herself clinging to him feverishly and biting his shoulder until she drew blood.

"Good Lord," Marcel said, "I never knew killing someone would get a woman so worked up." He was still leaning against her, letting himself enjoy the pressure of her breasts against his chest. No point in telling her now that his friend was unconscious but very much alive. Her belief she'd killed him would be Marcel's free pass to pleasure whenever he desired it.

"I don't know why I acted this way," she said.

"And another time?" His hand moved under her blouse.

In answer, she pulled Marcel's mouth down on hers in invitation. It was the price she thought she had to pay for his silence.

And she had paid. How she had paid! More often it was in apathetic surrender rather than real desire, and it didn't matter to her whether the act took place among the sacks of grain, on the floor of the dairy barn, or in the nearby woods. It happened wherever Marcel's demands took them. Until Madame Larroque had him dismissed for insubordination —meaning that he was furious because Marcel never came to her room after he had Céline in his power.

Céline was grateful for one thing. Monsieur Larroque never approached her again. Whether it was because of Madame Larroque's tartly threatening tongue, or because she was now fulfilling all his needs, Céline did not know. The important thing was that she no longer feared him.

Though Céline had no particular physical desire for Jean, she craved what he represented and what he could give her. In her mind there was only one way to get him, and that was by the allure of her body. It never occurred to her to tease him, to bewitch him, refuse to succumb until she had some promise from him. That was not the way of her world. She would give herself to him and then make her demands. With a more sophisticated man that would have been a grave mistake. She was fortunate that Jean was as naive in his way as she was in hers.

Jean finally worked up enough courage to walk directly to the mill and watch for the young woman to come out. When she finally appeared, he approached her hesitantly. Céline pretended not to recognize him.

"Pardon," Jean said, "but I—I just came to ask something."

"Yes?" She allowed herself a demure smile and a quick, modest lowering of her eyelids.

Jean focused on the long lashes lying against her pink cheeks. If he looked down at her blouse, he'd never be able to speak. As it was, he was afraid he'd only stutter. He clenched his fists behind his back.

"Do you—that is—does the mill sell any of the flour, or is all the milling done only for those who bring in the grain?" He'd said it, and he was still able to breathe normally.

So that was his method of approach, she thought gleefully. How different from others who boldly suggested a walk in the woods, already assuming she knew full well what they meant.

"Did you wish to buy some?" Had he come to see her or did he really want the flour?

"Well, yes, of course." He hadn't expected that question. "I mean, I wanted to find out, and then come back with the money. From my mother. She wanted me to ask."

"I'm sorry. We only grind for the farmers who keep it themselves."

'I see. Well, thank you. I'd best be going." But he remained standing in front of her as if forbidden to move.

Céline smiled to herself. He had come to see her. Now she had to make the next move, or he would leave and she might not see him again.

"If you're not in any hurry to get home," she said, "I was just going for a walk along the stream. We could find a place to sit down and put our feet in the water. It's such a hot day."

"Yes, it is hot," and Jean was glad of the excuse to wipe the sweat off his face. "I—I'd like to go for a walk."

"Wait here a minute," she said. "I'll bring something cool for us to drink after we find the right place." She already had a spot in mind for the seduction, a soft bed of pine needles under a huge fir tree. It was well hidden from prying eyes. Even if he had no intention of seducing her this first time, she knew what wiles to use to change his mind.

Jean watched as she walked into the cottage beside the mill, and was already envisioning how she would look lying down and waiting for him to take her. He would have to be gentle so as not to frighten her. And for just a moment the old fear returned that he wouldn't be able to perform as a man. But the sensations flooding his body assured him otherwise. His only concern now was how long he could wait before beginning to make love to her. He hoped they wouldn't have to walk too far before they came to a quiet secluded place.

Céline returned with a pitcher of cold buttermilk and two

mugs. Together, but not touching, they walked the short distance to the place where the stream curved out of sight of the mill and ran between two stands of fir trees.

"Here we are," she said blithely. She set the mugs on the grass. "Hold the pitcher while I take off my shoes. Then you can take yours off."

Jean sat as close to her as he dared. After he removed his shoes and put his feet in the stream, he felt grateful for the way the water cooled not only his feet but also the overwhelming desire to take her in his arms right there.

When she leaned over to pour the milk into the mugs, Jean could see almost all of her full breasts, their creamy whiteness accentuated by the dark red of her blouse. Once more he began to shake all over. Casually, with no apparent attempt at flirtatiousness, Céline pulled her skirt above her knees, as if to keep it from getting wet as she laughingly splashed her feet in the water. Jean could not keep from gasping. He knew she wore nothing underneath, and he waited expectantly for her to pull her skirt up some more. In his imagination he saw her thighs, now spread apart so she could lean over to rinse her hands, and the forbidden place between them that he had already entered a thousand times in his daydreams.

When it was Céline who suggested they find a more secluded spot, just in case the miller should see her and demand she return to work, Jean could hardly believe his good fortune. She was, he thought, unwittingly inviting him to seduce her, but he had to be careful not to act too abruptly and frighten her away.

While they were making their way toward the tall fir trees, Céline pretended to trip over a root; in an instant she was in Jean's arms, and he was hungrily kissing her face, her neck, and her eyelids. In another moment her mouth was opening against his, and Jean was completely lost. He didn't know when the string of her blouse was loosened; he only knew that, finally, his hands and then his mouth were on her magnificent white breasts.

"Please, Jean, stop," but her whisper was more enticing than pleading. Even as she pretended to struggle to get away from him, she made certain her body was rubbing against his to keep him aroused. When she felt his hand moving up her legs, she sighed and collapsed against him as if it were impossible for her to resist him.

Delightedly, Jean found himself lying on the ground with

126

Céline, completely unaware that it was she who had pulled him down with her. Not until they were finished did he wonder at his good fortune at knowing what to do and how to do it so perfectly the first time, and with someone as sweet and innocent as Céline. Nor would he ever know it was her expertise that guided him every step of the way.

Céline had early suspected Jean of being too naive and innocent to detect whether or not she was a virgin. When it became evident to her that this was his first experience, she found it no problem to feign surprise and pain at losing her virginity to him. Nor was it hard to begin crying piteously so that he had no alternative but to gather her into his consoling arms.

"Oh God, Céline, I'm sorry." He was sobbing now, too. "I didn't mean to do that. I wouldn't have hurt you for the world. Or—or done this to you. I just couldn't help myself."

"Please, Jean, don't say anything right now." He was contrite. That was good. It would make it all the easier to get what she wanted from him. She continued to sob against his chest. "I just don't know what to do now. I never thought this would happen. What—what are we going to do now?" She looked at him as if pleading with him to make things right.

When Jean heard the *we*, his stomach turned over. He had been afraid she would scream and run for help. Instead she was turning to him for guidance. It was more than he'd dared hope for.

"I love you, Céline." He'd wanted to tell her that from the first time he saw her. Now she had made it possible and indeed easy for him to get the words out.

"You what?" She could scarcely believe what she was hearing. She'd hoped he would want to keep on meeting her here in the woods, at least long enough for her to make her demands on him, but she'd never thought of love.

"I love you, and I want to see you every day," he repeated.

"I want to see you, too, Jean." She wouldn't say she loved him. She didn't love him, and she didn't want to be captured in the trap she had set for him.

Jean was propped on his side now and leaning over her. She reached up and brushed his cheek with her fingers. It was enough. He was on top of her again, and the heady feeling that overpowered him came not so much from the physical pleasure and release as from the thought that he

127

had made her his: She never had and never would belong to anyone else.

From then on, they met several times a week. Sometimes Céline allowed him to watch her bathing before she grabbed up her skirt and blouse and ran to their own special place beneath the fir tree. Jean always followed and let her lie down first; he enjoyed the feeling of power it gave him to stand over her and know she was waiting for him to drop down beside her.

So far Céline had made no demands. She could bide her time patiently because she knew he was not going to run away. Yet she began to feel she might need more than these daily tumbles to keep a permanent hold over him, to ensure that she got from him the means to live comfortably—preferably away from the country—for the rest of her life. His family had money, and she meant to get her hands on some of it.

Having heard Madame Larroque plead with her husband not to touch her when there was the danger of pregnancy, Céline figured out just when those times were. Now she decided to use that knowledge to make certain Jean was with her when there was a chance of conceiving. She insisted she could not go a day without their making love, and Jean was too enraptured to disagree with her. Often, it was after dark before he got home from the city, but she insisted the darkness only made their meetings more dangerous and exciting. It was true that the darkness seemed to bring out a wilder and more eager streak in her. Sometimes he bore the marks of her teeth on his shoulder or chest for days. He did not know that what he took for her ardor was actually her desperation to become pregnant with his child.

Finally the symptoms she'd been waiting for appeared, and she was all smiles when she ran toward him.

"Oh, Jean I have wonderful news."

"Nothing could be more wonderful than seeing you here each day." He took her in his arms and began unfastening her blouse. Each time they came together his appetite for her increased.

This time, however, she moved out of his reach and sat down on the ground.

"Not yet. You must hear what I have to say."

Like a child who's been caught misbehaving, Jean sat down with his legs crossed and his hands locked together in his lap.

"Here, closer." She patted the ground beside her. "And I won't deny you this." She finished pulling the string loose on her blouse, letting it fall open to her waist, and leaned over so he could caress her while they talked.

"You drive a man crazy, you know that," he said hoarsely.

"In a minute," she said, and put one hand in his lap. "But," she said, then hesitated. Maybe she shouldn't tell him so soon. Maybe he would run away instead of feeling he owed her something. No, she couldn't be that wrong about him. Jean was a good man who assumed his rightful obligations. "Jean, I'm going to have your child."

"What did you say?" He pulled his hand away as if her breasts were hot coals rather than soft flesh.

"I said I'm pregnant. I'm going to have your baby." Had Jean been so naive that he didn't believe such a thing could happen?

"My child? You're going to have my child?"

"Yes, Jean." She began crying. Was there even the slightest danger he might think she'd been with someone else? "Who else's could it be?"

"No, no, please, Céline, I didn't mean that. I meant it's such a surprise, such a shock." He wanted to marry her. From the very first time, he knew that eventually he'd ask her. But he was still no more than an apprentice in his father's office. Already he'd begun saving his money for the land he wanted to buy someday. His father had said that in another month or two he could assume a regular position, and there would be more money to put in the bank. But if he married now, if he had to support a wife, there was no way he could continue saving. He looked at Céline, curled now in his arms, and he knew he'd have to do what he'd really wanted to do all along, which was to marry her.

"Will you marry me, Céline?"

"What!" It was her turn to be stunned. She had expected offers of money, a trust fund, perhaps, for the child, and hopefully a place in town. But never this. She had found pleasure in being with Jean, but she never thought to marry him, to belong to him for the rest of her life. To her, marriage meant the constant bickering between Monsieur and Madame Larroque, not the loving she had known with Jean. Married people ended up hating each other, but in her dream world, lovers remained idyllically happy.

Then she looked more closely at him. He was a good and gentle man, and he seemed to want only her happiness and for her to know pleasure when they made love. She wanted to get away from the mill, and if this were the only way she could do it, she would be a fool to turn him down. More than that, she would be the daughter-in-law of the very wealthy Fontaines, with a château in the country and an apartment in Paris. And the clothes and the jewels! She could already see herself dressed in satin and attending exciting events in Paris. She might be bored silly by them, but she was very good at pretending. And wouldn't she lord it over the Larroques!

"Do you really mean it, Jean? You want me to be your wife?"

"I've loved you from the moment I saw you, and—and the first time we were here I knew I wanted to marry you."

"Then I will, Jean, but it must be soon." Now that she had made up her mind, she wasn't going to let the opportunity slip away from her. "What will your family say?"

"They won't like it at first because I'm so young. But I can make them understand. We'll live in Paris. Will you like that?"

"I'll like anywhere as long as I'm with you." There, that wasn't so hard to say, and she found herself almost believing it.

"I'll tell them tonight, and then you'll have to meet them."

Céline hadn't planned on that. She had hoped they'd be married quietly before his family knew about her. For the first time she was frightened. What if they argued him out of it after they saw her? No, she must make certain everything was planned before she went to the château.

"I'll—I'll see them before the wedding, Jean, but give me a little time first. Have everything arranged, and then you can introduce me."

"Just as you wish, darling." He pulled her face up to his. They had talked enough. He'd have to be getting back home, and he couldn't wait any longer to feel her respond to him. When he heard her sigh of contentment as he pulled up her skirt, he thought it was because she, too, had been impatient for him to make love to her. He couldn't know it was because she had at last got even more than she'd hoped for when she'd first set out to seduce him—so much more.

Chapter Fourteen

LEAH WATCHED JEAN follow Baptiste into the study, and she wondered what problem her oldest had now. She could tell by the furrows between his eyes and the set of his mouth that he was anticipating more than a friendly chat with his father. Even after he closed the door behind him, his image remained with her. Jean had developed into a stocky young man—if he were older he would be called portly—with a square face. He was much like Leah's father in his build, though not in personality. Her father had been jolly and fun-loving, whereas Leah thought of Jean as somber, unimaginative, unromantic, and so very practical. She wondered what in the world could be disturbing him. Something at the office, no doubt. He'd seemed rather introspective lately. Well, whatever it was, Baptiste would take care of it.

In the study, Baptiste sat stunned, an unlit cigar in his hand. Nothing could have shocked him more than Jean's news that he was in love and wanted to get married. It was the last thing he'd expected of his pliant, phlegmatic son. Baptiste shook his head and reached for a match. Not until the cigar was finally lit to his satisfaction did he express the thoughts that had been going through his head.

"There can be no talk of marriage at your age," Baptiste said. "And the affair must go no further. You will simply stop seeing her. You had no business getting involved with a woman of her class anyway. When you do marry, it will be someone from a proper family."

Jean decided to let the last remark go for the moment. There were more important considerations. "It's gone far enough already. She's expecting my child."

"And that's why you've offered to marry her?"

Lies didn't come easily to Jean, but now it was necessary to make Papa believe what he would say. "No. We—we didn't make love until after I asked her. We—we planned to wait to be married."

Knowing the sexual habits of many farm girls, Baptiste was tempted to ask Jean if he were certain the child was his. Realizing, however, that such a question right now would only cause a needless, irreparable rift, he held his tongue.

"Then we'll make arrangements," Baptiste said. "Pay all expenses and see that the child is adopted by a good country family. But no word to your mother. This would break her heart." There, that should take care of the situation. And he would urge Jean to stay in the Paris apartment and attend social functions with the daughters of his friends. He should have suggested it sooner, but he hadn't expected Jean to become involved in a serious love affair at such a young age.

"You don't understand, Papa." Jean was amazed at himself for being able to keep his voice calm and steady. "I love Céline and I want to marry her."

"No!" Baptiste insisted adamantly.

"Yes," Jean said just as determinedly.

Baptiste was completely taken aback. He'd never seen this son so defiant. "You're too young. You need my permission."

"She agreed to run away with me if you don't give it to me."

So, it was a *fait accompli*. Baptiste knew his son well enough to realize that Jean did not give his word lightly. If he'd asked the young woman to marry him, he meant it. And if he said he would run away, he'd do that, too. Baptiste would have to try another approach.

"To run away as your wife or—"

"Certainly as my wife. What sort of man do you think I am, Papa?"

"I am thinking more of what sort of woman she is. I know you would do the honorable thing, but she might be willing to accept less."

"Why? Why would you say such a thing about Céline? My God, you don't even know her." Furious with his father, Jean was having difficulty controlling himself.

"But I know her kind, her class, Jean. She's poor. She's uneducated. She's no doubt been forced to do hard, menial labor at the mill. You say she's adopted. You know what that means. She's probably the illegitimate result of some other farm girl's tumble in the hay. And you—you're the

132

son of a very wealthy man. Can't you see, Jean? You're money, you're position to her. She'd probably do anything to get a hold over you." Baptiste had another thought in mind—she might not really be pregnant—but before he could utter it, Jean exploded.

"Class! Illegitimate! How dare you say those things knowing the situation in our own family? Wouldn't I be a bastard if Mama hadn't gone North and married James Andrews? And Mama? Did you love her any the less because she was of a lower class, of almost the lowest class in New Orleans? I've never seen your proud Creole blood boiling over the fact she was illegitimate. Did you marry her? No, by God, you lived with her for years before you thought about coming over here where you could be married."

"That's quite enough!" Baptiste pounded his crutches on the floor.

"No, it's not. I love Céline, and I've asked her to marry me. I'm being more honorable than you thought of being all those years. And you had a wife at the same time. At least Céline is the only one."

"So you did ask her only after you knew she was expecting," Baptiste said. "You lied before, didn't you?"

"Maybe I did, but I'd still planned to ask her very soon. Only I was going to talk to you first and have you meet her. Then she told me about the baby, and I couldn't wait."

Baptiste looked at his oldest son, still so young and so vulnerable. Yes, the time had come to shock some sense into him, even if it meant Jean would hate him for a while.

"And you're quite sure the child is yours?"

Jean blanched and clenched his fists. "If you weren't my father, I'd kill you for that. Céline was a virgin when she came to me."

"Calm down," Baptiste said sternly. "I'm only trying to make you face some truths that you'd better be willing to face before you marry her. What makes you so certain she was a virgin?"

"I'm no fool, Papa. Of course I'd know the difference." Yet a faint doubt began to cloud his thoughts. It had all been so easy that first time. And she hadn't really fought him off. But no, there were other indications it was the first time for her, too. She hadn't lied to him. She couldn't have.

"I hope so, for your sake. Because Monsieur Larroque, is not known to be a generous man, and I can't believe she'd be living in his house all these years without his having his way with her."

133

"Papa! He's her father."

"Her *adopted* father, Jean."

Jean knew she'd been mistreated by the miller; Céline had told him all about the whippings and the hard work, but never— No, she would have told him that, too. Even if it were true, it was all the more reason to get her away from there.

"Papa, I don't care what you say to me or how much you try to malign Céline. I love her and I'm going to marry her. With or without your permission."

"If you do, it will be without." Baptiste's voice became sterner. "And without any blessing at all from this family. You are my son, and I was preparing to have you take over as head of the business within a few years. But if you leave here and marry that—that girl, you renounce your inheritance as well. There is no place for you in the firm. Is that perfectly clear?

That, thought Baptiste, should put an immediate end to the marriage. Céline would never agree to elope with Jean if it meant she couldn't get her hands on the Fontaine money and the Fontaine name.

"However," Baptiste continued, "the offer still holds to settle a generous sum of money on her and see that her child is placed in a proper home. Or," he hesitated, "I will even go so far as to set up a trust fund for her that should keep her comfortably for the rest of her life." Such an offer really ought to satisfy the girl.

"You seem to forget, Papa, that it's my child, too, and I don't want it in a foster home, to be mistreated as Céline has been."

"I said a good home. Or she'll be able to keep it with the amount of money I'm willing to give her. The choice will be up to her."

"No. I want to marry her, and I know she wants to marry me. You also seem to forget that we love each other."

"Give her the choice, Jean, and you'll see just how much she loves you."

"Damn you, Papa!" Jean shouted. "Damn you to hell. You say I'll be disinherited? Fine. I don't ever want to see you again."

Before Baptiste could answer, Jean stormed out of the room and out of the house. Blinded by tears of fury, he didn't see Leah waiting in the hall or hear her call to him.

At once, Leah rushed into the study. "Baptiste, what in heaven's name was that all about? Jean ran out as if pur-

134

sued by the furies." Then she saw her husband slumped in the chair, his head in his hands. "What is it, love?" Racing over to him, she put her arms around his shoulders. "What's wrong with Jean—and with you?"

"He asked my permission to marry and I refused." It was all Baptiste could say at the moment.

"Marry! At his age?" Who in the world had Jean met that they didn't know about? He was in the city during the day, but he was home every night and weekend. And she'd heard nothing from friends about Jean courting anyone's daughter.

"It's not his age that concerns me, Leah. It's his choice. He thinks he's in love with Céline Larroque."

"Larroque? I don't believe I know that name. Who are they? Business friends of yours in Paris?"

"No, my dear, he's the miller who has an establishment just beyond the village of St. Grièce."

"A miller's daughter? A farm girl? Then of course he must listen to reason. If it's just a case of adolescent love, then we can suggest he stay in the city and meet other young women. He'll get over it."

"It's not that simple, Leah. She's expecting his child." No point in confusing the issue by suggesting it might not be his.

"Oh." Leah was too startled to say more. Jean was still a boy in her eyes.

"Yes, that was my reaction, too." He waited for her to say something more, but she'd been stunned into silence. "So I made what seemed like a sensible suggestion, which was to give the girl a generous sum of money and see that the child is placed in a proper home. But, no, he insists he loves her and wants to marry her."

"And she wants to marry him?"

"So he says. She may change her mind when he puts the choice to her."

"Choice? What choice?"

"If they marry, he will forfeit all rights to his inheritance, and there is no place for him in the firm."

Leah couldn't believe what she was hearing. She was more aghast at Baptiste's ultimatum than she'd been when he told her about Jean's wanting to marry. "You told him that, you said he was no longer your son, and he still wants to marry her?"

"That's what he said when he left here."

"Do you realize what you've done, Baptiste? You've sent

135

him away." She was wringing her hands so hard they hurt. "You've driven him out of his own home. How could you?" This was a side of Baptiste she'd never seen before, and she didn't like it.

"No, Leah, the decision was his. I merely offered the options. Forget the girl or no longer be my heir. He made the choice."

"But he's so young, Baptiste." She walked toward the window, then turned around. "He's scarcely a man. He's not capable of making rational decisions about something like that."

"Stop thinking of him as a baby, Leah. He *is* a man now. Man enough at any rate to father a child."

"All right, physically maybe, but not emotionally. And look what you demanded of him. You didn't really give him a choice; did you try to reason with him at all?"

"Of course I did," Baptiste said impatiently. "But how can you reason with a boy who's so head over heels infatuated with—with the first girl he's ever had that he's blind to who and what she really is?"

"You mean more than just being a farm girl by that, don't you?"

"I certainly do."

"Did—did you suggest that to Jean?"

"I did, and that was the end of our conversation."

"Oh no! Let me talk to him, Baptiste. Maybe he'll begin to see some reason in another day or two."

"And he'll twist you around his finger like he always has. Talk to him but don't baby him. By God, if you had your way, he'd still depend on you for everything."

"That's not fair, Baptiste. I simply try to be more understanding. You—you get your back up immediately and lose your temper."

"All right, if you think you're so much more the understanding parent, try being that way when he says he'd rather marry that slut than remain one of the family."

"What I'll try to do is change his mind."

"If you can, more power to you. But be stern. You start sympathizing and he'll get to you. Before you know it, you'll be siding with him against me."

"Not this time, Baptiste. I think you were right to refuse permission. The only thing I hope I can do is make him wait a while, not force an immediate decision on him. I'll talk to him tomorrow, and I promise I won't give in to him."

"If he is here tomorrow."

"What do you mean?" She was gripped by a new fear that she'd never see Jean again.

"I have no idea if he plans to return. Not from the way he dashed out of here."

"We'll just have to pray he does. Or that Céline insists on time to make a decision. She'll have something to say about the choice he offers her. She may find the money more attractive than Jean."

"That's what I'm banking on," Baptiste said quietly.

"Well, I'd better see about supper. We can't all starve because Jean has turned this house topsy-turvy. I told Blanchette I'd be in the kitchen long before this." It was as good an excuse as any. She didn't know how much longer she could have kept her emotions under control if she'd stayed in the study. Baptiste had no right to issue such an abrupt ultimatum. Any boy would have made the same choice under pressure of the moment and the need to assert himself as a man. And Jean was just a boy in spite of what Baptiste said. So he'd had a fling with a girl. Come to think of it, what boy his age hadn't? Baptiste came on too strong, that was the trouble. Jean would listen to her; he always had. She could sympathize and still be firmly practical. When she got to the kitchen, she offered to help Blanchette with the yeast bread rising for the next day, and she pounded and kneaded it as if it were the Devil himself she was fighting.

Baptiste stayed in the study alone, not even turning up the lamps when it began to grow dark. He knew as sure as he sat there that Jean would not return. Nor was he as unmoved as Leah thought. How thrilled he'd been when he learned that Jean, the son he thought was James Andrews', was really his. And now he might lose him. As he had lost René, their first, to yellow fever. How he'd wept then, put his head on the kitchen table and wept until he was exhausted. He wanted to cry now, but all he felt was a cold, hard lump swelling larger and larger in his stomach. Even the third glass of brandy hadn't dissolved it. God knew, he'd miss the boy, at home and at the office. And damn, he'd been so proud to think that in a few years, Jean would be taking over the management of one department, then eventually of the whole business. Another Fontaine name to add to the firm.

But he'd been right—he just knew it—to make the boy see how serious the situation was. How the hell was he to know Jean would make the choice he did? Maybe he should have suggested setting Céline up in an apartment as Jean's mistress. No, that would only have prolonged the relationship. He refused to admit that Jean really loved Céline. There was only one hope, which was that Céline would choose the money rather than marriage. Jean had no training for any kind of decent work, and she'd be poorer with him than she was now. No, she'd never accept poverty to marry Jean. With that thought, Baptiste became calmer. Jean would be back. Céline would send him back in a hurry, and the whole affair would be forgotten. It would never be mentioned in the house.

Weeping and sobbing uncontrollably, Jean stumbled out of the house and raced across the open fields. He scarcely knew where he was running, but knew he had to get away from the house. He was like a blind man seeking something, anything, to get his bearings. Hatred for his father welled up in him like bitter gall, and he wished he could be sick so he'd be rid of the feeling. But it continued to choke him. Tripping over some branches at the edge of the woods, he fell to the ground and lay there panting. He made no effort to lift his face out of the mud. How dare his father suggest Céline was less than worthy to be his wife? He loved her as he'd never loved anyone or anything in his whole life. She *was* his life, and he was going to marry her. He didn't care how poor they'd be or what kind of work he'd have to do. He'd find some way so they could have a small house and enough to eat. That's all they'd need, at least for now. The important thing was they'd be together. It would be enough for both of them.

If only Céline would be at their secret place. He could hold her, and she would assure him over and over of how much she loved him. How he needed her right now! The thought of her warm body drove him nearly crazy. He couldn't just lie here on the ground. He had to walk or run to get rid of the anger and desire that had him ready to burst. It was idiotic, but he wished he had an axe so he could start chopping the trees around him or that a bear would suddenly appear so he could wrestle it. Instead, he screamed as loud as he could, over and over, and began walking toward their meeting place. Céline would come at their usual time, and he'd be waiting for her. He wasn't working at the office anymore, so he didn't have to report there in the morning. And he wasn't going back home.

138

By disinheriting him, Papa had said he was no longer his son. And by God, if that's what he wanted, that's the way it would be. Jean never wanted to see his father again.

There was no hurry now. Screaming had calmed him down, and he sauntered leisurely through the woods toward the stream.

Céline heard the screams from a long way off and sat up on the bed of leaves.

"Hey, Céline, lie back down. We got the whole night ahead of us, and I'm going to make the most of it. You're the best lay I've had in a long time."

"Shut up, Pépé. Didn't you hear those screams? Someone's coming."

"You're crazy. No one's anywhere near here. Just somebody beating up somebody else." He looked at Céline sitting up in the twilight. God, those breasts of hers were enough to send any man out of his mind. And the rest of her, too. He reached up and pulled her back down beside him. In another minute she was clutching him as hungrily as she had less than an hour earlier when she first brought him to this place.

Céline knew she was being foolish, but she couldn't help it. There was really little danger that Jean would appear. He'd said he was going to talk to his father tonight. When she met Pépé in the village and he'd suggested they meet somewhere, she couldn't resist him. Hadn't she been faithful to Jean all these weeks? And after tomorrow she wouldn't be seeing Jean again anyway. She knew what would happen. Monsieur Fontaine would offer a settlement to take care of her and the baby; then, once she had it, she'd be free and on her own. And wealthy. She wouldn't accept anything less than enough to live comfortably for the rest of her life. So why not a fling? She had to find someone else to take Jean's place and keep her happy. Right now no one could do it better than Pépé, who'd just come from Marseilles with a pocket full of coins from his last berth on a ship. And he was more fun to be with. Jean was always so serious, talking about nothing but his work when they weren't making love. She'd have sent him away long ago if it hadn't been for his family's money. Just the thought of what she would demand made her tingle all over. Monsieur Fontaine might not agree to her first request, but she didn't expect him to. Whatever she got would be more than she'd ever dreamed of having.

139

Céline had just reached over toward Pépé again when she heard another noise that really frightened her.

"Get up Pépé, someone's coming."

"They won't see us unless they trip over us, and who cares anyway?"

"I do. Get up right now and leave. I'll follow in a few minutes. Better yet, I'll see you at the café tomorrow afternoon."

"You expecting someone else to meet you here? Because if you are—"

She saw the threat in his eyes and knew he carried a knife in his boots. "No, no, Pépé. It's just—I remembered Madame Larroque told me to get back before dark, and it's almost that now. I've no mind to feel her whip again. She beats harder than he does."

She started down the path toward the mill, watched to see that Pépé started off for the village, and then turned back toward the trees. The sound might not have been Jean's footsteps, but if it were Jean and he'd found them, she'd be saying good-bye to all her hopes.

She stood by the stream where Jean could see her. In another few minutes the footsteps came closer.

"Céline! What are you doing here so early?"

"I just thought I'd go for a short walk. I miss you when you're not here." She breathed deeply. That explanation had better satisfy him.

"And I miss you. Come here. You're the best thing I've seen all day."

"You spoke to your father?" She was all impatience now to learn what Monsieur Fontaine had said.

"I did, and we'd better sit down while I tell you."

Céline smiled to herself. She knew what he was going to say. Monsieur Fontaine had insisted she give Jean up but would pay her to do it.

"Was he cross with you, my darling?" She reached out and put her arms around him. "Was he a mean old father?"

"He will disown me if we marry."

"Oh, dear, I was afraid of that."

"But it doesn't matter, Céline. I told him I was going to marry you anyway. There's nothing he can do to stop us."

"What!" This was not what she wanted to hear.

"Yes, aren't you pleased? We'll run away from here and live wherever we want."

"But your work, your place in the firm. We can't run far if you have to be in Paris every day. Unless—unless we live in Paris." That might not be so bad, even as Jean's wife.

"No! You don't understand, Céline. I've given that up. I've given everything up—my position, my inheritance, my place in the family—all for you."

"You've done what!"

"Yes, just to be with you, darling. You mean more to me than the whole world."

"So your father said if you married me, you'd be disinherited?"

"I don't care as long as we're together."

"He said nothing else? Just not to marry me or else?"

"That's all," Jean said. "What else did you expect him to say?"

Damn! Céline thought. What a miserly old bastard! And she'd been so sure he'd offer some kind of settlement and see to placing the baby.

Jean looked at Céline, who was now on the verge of tears. He knew he should tell her about the alternative, his father's offer to set up a trust fund, but he couldn't. Céline said she loved him, but would all that money finally prove to be more important to her? He didn't dare take the chance of losing her.

"I thought," Céline said, "he might have suggested I should leave and give the baby up for adoption."

"No. No, he made no such suggestion." Jean was finding it easier to lie now than when he was talking to his father. He'd make it up to her. By all that was holy, he would.

"Oh, Jean, what am I going to do?" This time her despair was genuine. She had allowed herself to become pregnant, had actually made certain she would, and now all her plans were collapsing around her.

"There, there, Céline." He reached to take her into his arms, and she was too disheartened to refuse. "There's no need to cry. That's why I'm here. We'll leave just as I said. This very night."

"And where are we going to live? And how? You've no money, no job." The last thing, the very last thing, she wanted to do was go away with Jean and live in some godforsaken hovel in another village exactly like the one she'd be leaving.

"I have a little money, enough for a month or so. And I'm strong. I can find work. Don't worry, you'll always be taken care of. I'll see to that. We'll be together and that's what's really important."

"No, I think I'd better stay here and make the best of it.

You can't leave your family and your position." She had a new idea. She'd stay right there at the mill and make certain Monsieur Fontaine saw her from time to time. She'd shame him into having to give her something.

"Have you not thought of what it will be like when Madame Larroque finds out you're pregnant? What will life with them be like then?"

She hadn't thought of that. And what if Pépé didn't want to take her to Marseilles with him? Or what if he decided to stay in the village and found out about the baby? He'd have nothing to do with her then, of that she could be sure. Maybe Jean was the only way out. Oh God, if she'd only known all this when she'd first thought of trapping him.

"All right, Jean, I'll go with you."

"You'll never be sorry, my darling. I promise."

"How soon?"

"Right now. Tonight. Go to the mill for your things, and I'll meet you at the station in time to catch the ten o'clock train for Paris. We'll spend the night there and then make plans."

Céline walked slowly toward the mill. So this was how the affair was to end—marriage to Jean and a life of living from hand to mouth. No, marriage was not the end of everything. She was still young and attractive; and once the baby was born, she'd find a way to make a new life for herself.

Leah stayed awake all night listening for Jean to return. When morning came, she still had not given up hope. By late afternoon, she was not so sure.

"He's not coming back, is he, Baptiste?"

"I don't think so."

"Well, I hope you can live with your conscience after sending him away. And don't look at me with that righteous expression. I don't know whether I'll ever forgive you for this."

"He's a man now, Leah. He'll make his own way all right."

"I'm glad you think so, because I'm not that sure. I'm going for a walk. If I'm not back when supper's ready, go ahead and eat without me. I don't think I could swallow anything anyway."

Baptiste watched her rigid back as she walked out. It was the first real quarrel they'd ever had. He hadn't been able

142

to make Jean see reason; he hoped Leah would come around to understanding why he'd had to do what he did. If not, he might lose his wife as well as his son. For now, he could only wait until she returned.

Chapter Fifteen

FOR A LONG TIME, Leah thought she'd never forgive Baptiste for sending Jean away. Then she finally came to realize her husband was genuinely distraught over the ultimatum he'd had to issue and equally hurt over the boy's decision. Baptiste had been right: Jean was old enough to accept responsibility for his actions. Then, too, Céline must have loved him to choose marriage over a settlement. Jean was a strong and willing worker; he should have no trouble finding employment. And Leah refused to let die the hope of seeing him again.

More and more now, Baptiste was suffering from excruciating pain in his thighs. He tried to ignore it, until finally he couldn't help wincing as Leah was helping him with his nightly regimen, which consisted of washing with warm water, a massage with salves, and then warm compresses. He had to admit to her then that he was in agony most of the time.

The Paris doctors agreed it was an arthritic condition resulting from the injuries he'd sustained in the explosion during the war. Not only had his lower legs been crushed, but his hips had been dislocated. They'd been reset satisfactorily, but through the years they had been abused by Baptiste's abnormal dependence on them and the awkwardness of walking with crutches.

"So I'm to be confined to my chair, is that it?" Baptiste said to Dr. Huget-LeClare as the physician prodded his truncated limbs. He made no attempt to hide the bitterness in his voice. As long as he was ambulatory and could ride a horse, he'd been able—though with difficulty—to accept his condition and not let anyone know how despondent he was at his inability to do the things most men—and most

143

fathers—could do. Things like helping to search for Nicole when she ran away. Or going tramping through the woods with his sons and teaching them to hunt. Or carrying the babies in his arms. The children had never known him any other way, but he felt that sometimes he was a burden to them. And to Leah.

But always, Leah would walk into the room, her eyes glowing just being near him, and her lips in that secret smile that said "I love you," and he would feel better.

Baptiste rose awkwardly to a sitting position on the examining table, and repeated, "Will I have to be confined to a wheelchair from now on?"

"I hope not," Dr. Huget-LeClare said. But Baptsite detected very little hope in his voice.

"You have something in mind?" Baptiste was ready to clutch at even the flimsiest possibility that he could continue walking.

"Your hips need rest from the burden they've been carrying, that is obvious," Dr. Huget-LeClare said. "More than that, they need strengthening. Rest would offer merely a temporary relief. At least the nerves have not been damaged. The normal aging process in your joints has been exacerbated by the strain you've put on them all these years."

"Now that you've given me the explanation," Baptiste said, "is there a cure?"

"No." Dr. Huget-LeClare shook his head. "I'd be less than honest if I said there were. But I think I can prescribe a regimen to alleviate the pain, maybe even slow down the degenerative process, and keep you on your feet for a few more years."

My feet, Baptiste thought. *My God, I left those in a garbage pail years ago. Thrown out with the offal from the bedpans and the bloody, discarded bandages.* But he knew the doctor meant well. He'd listen and follow any instructions that would keep him from wasting away in a chair.

"Whatever you say," Baptsite agreed. "I promise I'll be a good and obedient patient."

"First, I'm going to suggest you go to Aix-les-Bains for at least two weeks. Its reputation rests on its being a popular gathering place for the titled and wealthy, but its warm sulfur springs are thought to have strong curative powers. I've seen some long-term remissions of conditions like yours in patients I've sent there."

"Do I drink the waters or soak in them?" It sounded

more like a palliative than a genuine cure, but he was not ready to argue.

"Both. You'll bathe twice a day, for about an hour at a time, under the supervision of an attendant. He will massage your muscles while you're in the water and afterward on a table."

Doesn't sound too bad, Baptiste thought. It wouldn't be quite the same as when Leah rubbed him down after they went to bed, but it would feel good all the same.

"Really, Baptiste, you're fortunate. With the riding you've done, your muscles are actually in better condition than those of many men your age. You've just put a tremendous strain on them, and they're letting you know it. The baths will also help to reduce the swelling in your joints.

"Which brings me to the next part of the prescription. When you return home, you should continue to bathe at least once a day in warm water. That will keep the muscles relaxed, keep them from tensing up after using them all day. You'll learn from the attendant how they should be massaged and Leah can do that for you. She won't mind, will she?"

"No," he said matter-of-factly, "she won't mind." No need to tell him how she'd been doing it every night for as long as he could remember.

"I'll give you some powders, too, for when the pain gets bad. Don't hesitate about taking them. They're nothing more than a simple analgesic."

"Thank you," Baptiste said. "When should I leave for Aix-les-Bains?"

"As soon as you can get ready. I'll write to a colleague of mine there, and he'll be expecting you. I want him to see you before you start the treatment, as well as check you from time to time during it. I'd let him be the judge of how long you should stay."

Baptiste left the office a little more jauntily than he'd entered it. A few more years of walking were better than none at all; any extra time at all was a bonus. *Be grateful for that*, he told himself, *and don't ask for miracles.*

"Aix-les-Bains!" Leah exclaimed. "But that's such a fashionable resort, and I—"

"I know, you haven't a thing to wear," Baptiste laughed.

"Well, I haven't. I've read about the people who go there, and what goes on. Garden parties and teas and dinners and card games in the evening."

"Leah, we are not a part of that social milieu. We are going there for the cure, and we'll be staying in a very simple *pension*."

"I know that. But I want to look right—to be fashionable —when I go walking. I've read descriptions of the gardens. And we might—just might—be invited to some of the events. After all, you're a wealthy man and the firm of Bonvivier and Fontaine Importers is not unknown outside Paris."

"Well, just to please your frivolous heart, what do you need?"

"A morning gown, an afternoon gown—maybe two— and one new dinner gown. The two I have are almost brand-new. And, of course, hats to wear during the day. My serge suit will do nicely for traveling, but I'll need a new hat for that, too."

"And will two weeks be enough time to accumulate this grand new wardrobe? There's a special shipment of goods coming in from the Far East in ten or twelve days, and I want to be here to check it out. Otherwise, I can leave the office in Caron's hands."

"More than enough. I think I'll go into Paris with you tomorrow. Christine Richard is all right for most of my things, but I think I'd like to go to Worth and Doucet for these clothes. They'll be expensive. Do you mind?"

"I don't mind a bit." Leah was probably the least extravagant person he'd ever known. "You find the most stunning ensembles you can and have them send the bills to me. No one, royalty included, is going to outshine you at Aixles-Bains."

Her face glowing, she leaned over him and kissed him. "Our first vacation alone in years. I can hardly wait." Then she skipped out of the room like a child.

He touched the place on his cheek that her lips had touched, and he realized it had been a long time since she'd kissed him impulsively like that. How long had it been? Since Jean left? No, longer than that. There had been no lessening of her ardor when they made love, but there'd been no spontaneity at other times—no tender, unexpected caresses, no outbursts of laughter for no apparent reason, no lighthearted teasing or bantering to release the tension after some serious situation with the children. There was nothing in her manner he could criticize. They just never seemed to have fun anymore. If only he knew what had caused the change in her. Maybe she was just tired, or maybe their life together had become too routine. If so, this visit to the spa would benefit both of them.

Leah still had the magnificent amethyst necklace and earrings he'd given her on their wedding day. They were an exact duplicate of the ones he'd given her before the war and which she'd had to sell to keep them alive during the occupation. She also had the triple strand of pearls he'd bought for her when René was born. And the diamond lily-of-the-valley spray that celebrated the news that she was pregnant with Robert. It was time now, Baptiste thought, to get her the splendid gift he'd planned to buy when she'd insisted the small spray was all she wanted.

While Leah was visiting the couturier houses the next day, Baptiste went on his own shopping spree at Cartier's. He spent all afternoon watching the showing in the manager's office and selecting exactly what he wanted.

"These are all magnificent pieces, Monsieur Fontaine," the manager assured him. "You have made excellent choices. Madame Fontaine will be delighted beyond words."

"Either that or she'll take my head off for spending so much." Baptiste sat back in the gold and cut-velvet chair and lit up his cigar.

"Then we must be very discreet and not let her know," the manager said, smiling.

"Ah, but you don't know Madame Fontaine. I'll warrant she can appraise them for their true value within a hundred francs. But what the hell! She'll fuss, but she won't return them. To her a gift is to be cherished for the sake of the giver—whether it's diamonds or a hand-scribbled drawing from one of the children. She'll wear these and she'll love them."

"We'll have a rosewood box made and lined with velvet for them. It should be ready in a few days." He made a note of the size. "And how about you, Monsieur Fontaine? A ring? A set of studs and cufflinks?"

"Well, now that you mention it, I could use a new set to go with my evening clothes."

"Then let me show you this one set with diamonds."

"No—no, much too gaudy. Reminds me of a pimp I knew in New Orleans. Leave the diamonds for the ladies. Those opals are more my style."

"Very well. Will you take them with you?"

"No, you can send them to the office when the others are

ready." Baptiste got up gingerly. His hips were giving him more trouble than he liked to admit. Hopefully, this trip to Aix-les-Bains would take care of that and some other things as well. He walked out to the carriage, feeling very good about his purchases.

Leah finished modeling the gowns she'd bought in Paris, and Baptiste said that now it was his turn.

"You've bought a new dinner suit," she sighed. "Thank goodness. The old one is disgracefully cut of date."

"No, as a matter of fact I forgot. But Joseph has my measurements, and he can still tailor one before we leave. My purchase is for your new red dinner gown. I'm glad you chose red. You haven't worn it in years."

"I know. I really felt I was too old for it, but Monsieur Worth said it was perfect with the gray in my hair."

"He was right. And this will add the consummate touch." He handed her the rosewood box.

"My word," she said, looking at the size and shape of the container. "What could possibly be in here to go with the dress?"

"You'll never know until you open it. See, it has its own little gold lock and key."

Leah gasped and sat down on the bed when she saw what was inside. Seldom in her life had she been rendered speechless, but this was one of those times.

"Aren't you going to put them on?" Baptiste asked casually, while inwardly chortling with glee at her amazement.

"I don't think I can. Look how my hands are shaking. Oh, Baptiste, they are too magnificent for words."

"Slide over on the edge of the bed, and I'll do it for you. I can't wait to see how they look on you."

Carefully, he placed the diamond tiara on her smooth hair, pulled back as always into a large bun high on the back of her head. Then he fastened the four-strand diamond choker around her slender neck.

"You'll have to do the earrings," he said. "I'm hopeless when it comes to those."

"I—I think I can manage them now." She walked to the mirror and looked at herself. She looked and felt like a queen. How her grandmothers—Leilei, the simple Polynesian beauty, and Rachael, the mulatto ex-slave—would stare if they could see her now. And her mother, Clotilde, who had made certain she received a proper convent education. She took the earrings, which were matched marquise diamonds, and put their thin gold wires through her ear lobes.

"They are exquisite, Baptiste. I feel—I feel like—"

"Conquering French society? Appropriately dressed for the exclusive world of Aix-les-Bains?"

"Now you're teasing. But yes I do." She twirled around three or four times to make certain she could handle the train of her gown and then sat down on the bed again.

"You didn't buy anything for yourself? You make me feel very selfish."

"You needn't. I bought these." He showed her the set of opal evening studs and cufflinks.

"Very elegant. So much handsomer than pearls, even black ones. You'll definitely have to have a new suit."

"I'll see about it first thing tomorrow. Now, let's go show the children how very stunning their mother looks."

Leah slipped the train loop over her wrist and glided through the sunroom and the hall and into the salon.

Except for the short ride from the riverboat landing to James's home in Indiana and the ride from the French coast to Paris, Leah had never traveled on a train. Those journeys had been made by coach during the daytime. For the overnight trip to Aix-les-Bains she and Baptiste had a sleeper compartment. As the train entered the beautiful Loire Valley, the moon shone full on the river, and they followed its course for several miles. They stayed in the dining car, drinking coffee and cognac, until their double berth was made up.

"Oh, I don't know about getting undressed," Leah said later, eyeing the berth apprehensively. "I think I'll just lie down and maybe nap a bit until we arrive."

"Nonsense, chérie, you'll be miserably uncomfortable the whole time. It's just like being on the ship where you got completely undressed every night."

"This seems different somehow. People getting on and off at each stop. Are you quite certain the compartment door is locked?"

"It is locked, and no one is going to disturb us." Then he saw the determined look in her eyes. "At least take off your dress and loosen your stays. You won't get a bit of rest if you don't." He proceeded to take off his suit, shirt, and tie. Then he slid across the berth, ready to go to sleep.

149

"Do you think you should?" Leah asked. "What if something happens and we have to get off in a hurry?"

"Nothing is going to happen except that I am going to get a good night's sleep in as much comfort as possible. I suggest you do the same."

"If you insist," she murmured, but only her dress and shoes came off. She lay down flat on her back, ready to leap off the berth at the slightest sign of trouble. In less than ten minutes the gentle swaying of the car rocked her to sleep, and she didn't awaken until Baptiste shook her and told her to dress because they would be arriving in about half an hour.

"I wasn't asleep," she insisted, "not really asleep, that is. Just dozing."

"Oh? I'm surprised, then, that you weren't frightened when we went through the violent storm. You usually panic at thunder and lightning."

"No, I don't, I never panic." Nevertheless, she looked chagrined. She had slept through the whole thing, but she'd never admit it to Baptiste.

Their *pension* was small but clean and well run. It was near enough to the baths for Baptiste to walk if he felt like it, although carriages could be hired at any hour of the day.

"You going to try it today?" Baptiste asked after they'd got settled in.

"I think so. It's what we're here for." Although, after inhaling the strong sulfur smell pervading the town, Leah was dubious about anything that noisome being beneficial.

Leah soon learned to relax in the bath, moving her arms and legs just enough to let the water swirl around her. What would it be like, she wondered, to lie back, close her eyes, and float away? To be like a fish and move with the current? No, that would be under water, and she'd always feared being pulled under, being unable to breathe. Sometimes Baptiste teased her by drawing a blanket up over her head. At such times she became frantic, terrified that she would suffocate. No, she'd rather be a flower, like a water lily or a leaf, and just drift in the water. She succumbed to the sensuous touch of the water, like fingers caressing her body.

The waters were soothing, and she usually took a long nap before lunch; but afterward, she was ready for more energetic activity. She had tried one sip of the mineral waters and then declined to drink any more. Baptiste, however, was taking the full treatment—bathing, drinking, and a massage from an attendant.

Dressing for dinner one evening after they'd been there about a week, Leah asked Baptiste if he were really feeling any better.

"Yes, I do. The waters must have some magical power. I didn't want to say it before, but I haven't had any pain for four days."

"But you don't want to leave any sooner than we planned, do you?"

"No, I want to stay at least the full two weeks. This remission could be only temporary, and Dr. Huget-LeClare said such might happen. Let's see how I feel a week from now."

"We'll stay as long as you think necessary," Leah said. "I'm enjoying myself, and word from home says everything is fine there."

"I think I'll add riding to the regimen and do more walking. I'll be able to tell better after some exercise."

So Leah joined him in a short ride late every afternoon. She'd already found much to occupy her time while he took his afternoon baths. Walking in the gardens, she met a number of congenial people from England and Germany, as well as from other regions of France. Some of her English acquaintances invited her to have afternoon tea with them, and both she and Baptiste were invited to play whist or piquet in the evenings.

One Englishwoman whom Leah became particularly fond of—and found herself having tea with almost every afternoon—was Lady Cuthbert Westborne.

"I'm actually an American," Jane Westborne said, as they walked in the garden one day, "or rather I was before I married."

"What a coincidence," Leah said. "I'm from New Orleans."

"Really! What a lovely surprise to find another expatriate over here. Your husband is French?"

"No, he's from New Orleans also, but we came over when he decided to open a Paris branch of his firm, and we simply prefer to live over here."

"I thought perhaps you're like so many American wives."

"I'm not sure I understand," Leah said.

"Placed on the marriage market, with family money used to purchase a title and coronet. I've been more fortunate

151

than many in that my husband loves me, or at least tolerates my idiosyncrasies and demands very little in return. He allows me to go where and with whom I please."

Leah looked more closely at Jane Westborne. She seemed to be some years younger than Leah, yet strain had already caused age lines to appear around her eyes and mouth.

"Lord Westborne is not with you?"

"Good heavens, no. He's probably either grouse shooting at our country place or fishing for salmon in Scotland. You'd never get him to leave the bitter cold of England for some place as charming and lively as this. Monsieur Fontaine is here?"

"Yes, he's really the reason we came. For the cure."

"Well, it's said the waters help. I wouldn't know. I've tried them, but I much prefer the company." Then she suddenly changed the subject. "I've never been to New Orleans, but I hear it's very beautiful."

"Our French Quarter, yes. It, too, has a charm all its own."

"Well, I'm delighted you're over here so I could meet you," Jane said. "Now, how about tea. I suppose that's a strange custom to you, but I quickly learned to enjoy it as one of the few pleasures to be found in England."

"Where in the States are you from?" Leah had taken an immediate liking to this fresh, outspoken woman.

Before Lady Westborne answered Leah's question, she found them a table and ordered tea. "With all the trimmings," she insisted. "That means," she added to Leah, "that I want more than the simple croissants. I like cakes with plenty of icing." She spread the dainty napkin in her lap. "I'm from New York. My Dutch forebears made their fortune in furs and trade, and my father inherited the accumulated millions. I was in love with a very nice young man who would inherit his father's seat on the stock exchange, but my mother did not consider him good enough for me. Nothing would do but that I should marry nobility. So over I came to England, was introduced to society at the Queen's garden party— which, of course, the Queen did not attend—and soon thereafter met Lord Westborne at a ball given for just that purpose. His was a fine but impecunious family, mine had money, so a bargain was struck."

"You make it sound so—so commercial," Leah said. Or was it so different from the quadroon balls where young women of color went to meet wealthy white men and become their mistresses? The marriage market, to exchange commercial fortunes for titles; the *plaçage* market for security.

No, there was no real difference. In both, women were simply considered chattel, not human beings with feelings and desires and needs of their own.

"But, my dear, that's just what it was, a commercial deal. As to which of us got the better of the bargain, who can say? I like Cuthbert, and we get along pretty well the few times we're together. I also have other friends, if you will, and so does he. It works out rather well, on the whole."

Leah did not ask what she meant by "other friends." The implication was obvious. That night, at a large dinner party, Leah watched Jane on the arm of a very handsome, but much younger man, who was the focus of all Jane's attention.

Such romantic entanglements, however, did not in the least prevent a real friendship from developing between Leah and Lady Westborne during the time Baptiste said he would like to remain at the spa.

"Stay longer?" Leah was surprised—and concerned—when Baptiste returned from the doctor with that information. She was happy to stay, but she worried that while she'd been enjoying herself she had been unaware of whether Baptiste's condition was really improving. "You're feeling no better?"

"A good bit better, yes, but Dr. Joffre thinks another two weeks will assure there's no lapse—or at least postpone it longer. It would be like stopping the medicine when the symptoms disappear but the disease is still in your body."

"Then by all means we'll stay," Leah said. "I think I've had enough of the baths, but there's plenty to keep me occupied."

"You're quite sure you don't mind?" Baptiste asked. "We'll go back if you feel the need to return. Or you can go and I'll stay here."

Leah was tempted to agree that maybe she should return to the children, but something urged her to stay. Later she wondered what feminine instinct had decreed that decision. "No. We're here on doctor's orders, and it would be foolish not to follow his advice. Two more weeks away from home won't make that much difference."

Now that she'd given up going to the baths, Baptiste urged her to sleep late in the morning. "No need for you to get up," he said. "I leave as soon as I breakfast, so you might as well sleep and then order breakfast here in the room."

"It sounds luxurious and lazy enough for me to like it. I'll be completely spoiled when we do go back."

"You deserve to be, chérie."

Unfortunately, she found herself staying in bed more of

necessity than by choice. She caught a cold, which developed into a severe case of bronchitis.

"No, you continue with your treatments," she insisted when Baptiste said he'd stay with her. "All I need is bed rest and the medicines Dr. Joffre prescribed."

Jane Westborne came around each afternoon to detail the events Leah was missing, but Leah was too weak to care.

"But don't worry," Jane comforted her, "you'll be up in plenty of time for the ball on Saturday night. It will be the most splendid affair of the season."

Leah closed her eyes. She was getting tired, and Jane's chatter was giving her a headache. She vaguely heard Jane say something about wearing the red velvet to the ball so as to outshine a new arrival who was captivating all the men.

On her first day up, Leah tried a short walk in the morning and met Jane for tea in the afternoon.

"You and Baptiste will be at the ball tomorrow night, won't you?"

"For a little while, perhaps. Poor lamb, he's been so confined while I was sick. Treatments all day and with me every night after eating supper alone."

Jane raised one eyebrow. "Oh, I don't think he's minded so much. After all, he has charming company while he drinks the mineral waters as well as during supper. I'd hardly say he's been confined."

"Oh yes," Leah recalled, "he mentioned there were several interesting people taking the treatments, among them a German professor and an American businessman who's interested in what Baptiste exports."

Even if Jane loved a bit of titillating gossip, she was not malicious. She bit back what she had intended to say next, and said instead, "Yes, they are interesting, and there is—there are some others who've arrived while you were ill."

"Well, I look forward to meeting them." Leah was tiring and looking forward to a rest before dinner. "Best be going. Baptiste will be back from the baths. Enjoyed the tea, Jane. I'll see you tomorrow."

Baptiste was stretched out on the bed when she returned. "You're late, chérie. I expected to find you napping."

"I was having tea with Jane instead."

"Not trying to do too much your first day up, are you? I was hoping you wouldn't be too tired to have dinner in the dining room. I have a surprise for you."

"Oh!" Her face brightened. He'd planned something special to celebrate her recovery.

"Yes, you'd never believe who's here with her husband. He's very ill, and she's extremely worried about him, just as I've been about you these past days. We've been keeping each other company and trying to cheer each other up."

"So, who is it?" She remembered Jane's remark about his being with charming company during the day and at supper. Then it had seemed as if Jane wanted to say something more but had stopped.

"Didn't I say? Simone."

Damn! Damn! Damn! Leah swore to herself. How wonderful these weeks with Baptiste had been. His physical condition was improving; she'd experienced a joyful renewal of the special love she'd had for him before the episode with Simone. Now it seemed all for naught. Worse, she felt that love betrayed again, and this time the hurt was almost more than she could bear. She wondered if her face revealed the dreadful shock that was making her hands shake and her heart pound. So Simone was the charmer who had all the men captivated and was keeping Baptiste from being lonely.

"Simone is here," she said. If Baptiste noted it was a flat, despair-tinged statement rather than a question he gave no sign. It seemed to Leah that Simone must have arrived at about the time Baptiste suggested staying two more weeks. On doctor's orders. Or so he said. And he'd suggested she go back home.

"Yes, and she can hardly wait to see you. She didn't dare come up here while you were ill for fear of carrying the infection to her husband."

"How very considerate." Leah turned her back and walked toward the bathroom. She couldn't let Baptiste see her face, or the tears that were threatening to flow.

"Come here now, though." He raised up on one elbow. "There's still time before dinner for what I've been looking forward to all day." With exaggerated gestures, he smoothed his mustache, then widened his grin into a leer.

Leah was usually amused at his attempt to portray a lecherous villain, but now she didn't see the humor in it. "Not—not now, Baptiste." She couldn't bear the thought of his touching her. "I'm a little tired. Maybe I tried to do too much today."

"I'm sorry, darling." He sat up. "Here, lie down and rest instead."

He seemed genuinely sorry and concerned for her, but then he'd been solicitous all during the earlier episode with Simone.

"Maybe I will—in a minute or two." She wasn't even sure she could tolerate lying beside him. "I'll sit here and see how I feel."

"I've had my nap," Baptiste said. "If you don't mind, I think I'll dress and go into the bar for a drink before dinner. Why don't you rest a bit and then join me. We'll meet Simone later in the dining room. She always helps Jacques with his tray before she comes in."

Leah lay down after he got up from the bed. The last thing she wanted was to share with Simone her first night out after her illness, but it was preferable to thinking of Baptiste and Simone sharing a candlelit table without her.

"I won't rest long," she said, while Baptiste dressed. "I'm already feeling better."

"Good." He leaned over the bed to kiss her, and she stifled the desire to turn her face away from him. Her fighting spirit had been aroused. Simone was not going to win even a minor skirmish this time. Wherever Baptiste went—to the baths, to the mineral springs—she'd be right beside him. He was her man, hers and hers alone. And she'd be damned if she'd let anyone think otherwise.

After Baptiste left, Leah looked in the wardrobe and tried to decide what to wear. Not the red; she'd save that and the diamonds for the ball. Not the gray; she was still too sallow after her illness. The peach-colored silk and pearls. The soft tones would add color to her skin, and the pearls would remind Baptiste of the night he draped them over her breasts and they'd made love before going to the theatre. Leah dressed hurriedly but carefully. She wanted to meet Baptiste in the bar before anyone else—meaning Simone—arrived.

She was still too late.

Leah paused at the door to the bar and watched them, their heads huddled close across the table, as if drawn together by invisible strings. Baptiste's face was lit up like the face of a child who's been allowed to believe in St. Nicolas for one more Christmas. Seeing them together was like watching lightning dart back and forth between two clouds. The whole atmosphere was electric. Leah wanted to turn and run. Instead, she began walking slowly toward the table, back straight and head erect.

As soon as Simone saw her, she jumped up.

"Oh, Leah, how wonderful to see you again. You don't know what it's meant to me to find such good friends here. I thought I was going to be dreadfully lonely and depressed."

156

Instead you've been enjoying my husband's company, Leah thought, *when you weren't reveling in being the cynosure of all the other men's eyes.* Had Baptiste been going to the baths each day, or had he been with Simone while her husband was bathing?

"I'm glad we—or rather Baptiste—could be of such help." The sentence had a too-familiar ring. She remembered saying it once before, when Simone was leaving to be married. And wondering then what sort of comfort Baptiste had given her.

"I'm afraid I've imposed on him far too much," Simone said. "He's been very generous with his time. But now you and I can indulge in more feminine pursuits, and he won't be bothered with me anymore."

"It was no bother, I assure you," Baptiste said. "It meant as much to me to have company while Leah was ill as it did to you."

"You're being too kind, Baptiste," Simone answered, but the look she gave him was so filled with love and adoration that Leah wanted to claw her eyes out. "Of course, I have to spend most of each day at the baths, but late afternoons and evenings are free."

"Well, then, I'll see you at the mineral springs," Leah said. "I think I'll start taking the waters again."

"You will?" Baptiste didn't hide his surprise.

Was he merely surprised at her change of plan, Leah wondered, or was she putting the quietus on some of his own?

"Yes, I think they'll help rid me of this cough and congestion I still have. You don't disapprove, do you?"

"No, no," he said. "I just thought you hated the mineral water."

"I do, but one must often do things one dislikes if it is for one's own best interests. Right now, I think it is." She didn't particularly look forward either to sipping the vile mineral water or to spending endless hours with Simone, and she abhorred the idea of being entrapped in a subtle game of espionage. But she had come late into whatever intrigue was being played out, and so she had to use every device at her disposal to see that she won.

Chapter Sixteen

SIMONE AND LEAH SAT DRINKING LEMONADE while their husbands were in the baths. Leah had given up on the mineral water, still finding it impossible to swallow.

"I wouldn't touch it," Simone said. "Try the fruit drinks instead."

Leah went to the baths with Baptiste each morning and afternoon now. Rather than suggesting she might prefer doing something else, he was obviously pleased at her attention. When Dr. Joffre remarked that Baptiste was the best patient he had—"never misses a treatment"—Leah was forced to admit she'd erred in imagining illicit rendezvous between him and Simone during the time she was ill. But still— there was no denying the glances that passed between them.

"For fear of sounding repetitious," Simone said after signaling the waiter for another glass of lemonade, "I have to tell you how much it means to me to have you both here. Baptiste has been the strong support I've needed when I've found the going difficult."

"Oh?" If Simone caught the irony in Leah's voice, she didn't show it in any change of expression.

"Let me tell you why. I think you should know. If you will bear with a brief story." Leah merely nodded. Was Simone about to reveal what she'd suspected all along?

"Years ago, before I married Count Émile Dubard, Jacques and I fell in love. Unfortunately he was engaged to another, and it was a marriage he could not get out of for reasons not important now. Not long before Émile died, Jacques and his wife were in a serious accident. Their horses were startled into running wild and their carriage overturned. She was killed instantly, and he was seriously injured. Sometime later, Jacques learned that Émile had died, and he wrote to me several times. Eventually he asked if I'd consider marrying him. I would have said yes immediately, except for one thing: he'd been paralyzed from the waist down."

Simone paused for a moment and slowly sipped her lemon-

158

ade, as if wondering how to go on. "That's when Baptiste did so much to lift my spirits and help me make my decision. I loved Jacques, but I wasn't sure I could be happy married to him in his condition. I'm a coward about illness and infirmity. Then Baptiste showed me he could do everything any other man could do except walk normally."

Everything? Leah thought. The word covered a great deal of ground.

"And," Simone continued, "it was a joy seeing the two of you together, seeing what a beautiful life you have, how much you love each other. I knew that if marriage to Jacques would give me only a small share of such happiness, it was what I wanted. And I haven't been sorry."

All of this sounded very fine, but there was still something Leah had to know. "Simone, are you in love with Baptiste?"

"A little bit." The answer came so quickly and so naturally, Leah couldn't decide whether Simone was being open and ingenuous or very clever, in an effort to mask deeper feelings. "Most women who meet him are, Leah. He has a quality of caring, of being genuinely interested in a person. And he's very entertaining. But you're the only one he truly loves, There were certain times when I hoped—I hoped he didn't, but I was wrong."

Certain times. Two more words that, like *everything,* specified nothing but were ambiguous enough to include whatever imagination could conjure. She wanted to ask Simone point blank if she and Baptiste had been lovers, but no answer would satisfy her now. If Simone had said no, she wouldn't have believed her. If she'd admitted they had been, Leah didn't think she could stand knowing it.

"Your being here has given me the strength I needed again," Simone was saying. "Unfortunately, my husband's paralysis is degenerative. We had a very happy year together, but now we can no longer live as husband and wife. I was close to losing my mind until I met Baptiste here. I can't tell you how much being with him has given me new life."

And you have done the same for him, no doubt, Leah thought. More equivocal words to keep her wondering. Perhaps Simone was like Jane Westborne, who thought wives should expect and take in stride their husbands' extramarital affairs.

She wished Simone would stop talking long enough for her to collect her thoughts and put them into some perspective. Right now her mind was in a turmoil, swirling around a vortex of suspicion that Baptiste was guilty of infidelity. If she could force her mind to stay on the outside edge of the waters, she would not be sucked down and destroyed by that suspicion.

Simone continued to talk and Leah was forced to listen. "Jacques takes something to help him sleep right after supper, but he's insisted I go out and enjoy myself. I didn't really, at first, but I knew he'd be disappointed if I stayed in the room. Being with Baptiste occasionally made it easier for me. And then, when you were well enough to be with me—well, it's made all the difference in the world."

Simone was seemingly so open and honest, it would have been easy for her words to allay Leah's suspicions, if only she could erase from her mind the glances she'd seen pass between them.

After coming back to the *pension* from an afternoon walk, Leah paused outside her room. The door was slightly ajar, and for a moment she thought she was going to faint. Instead, she groped her way along the hall and into the dining room. She ordered a cup of tea and sat there a long time. Almost blinded by tears, she'd seen Baptiste and Simone standing and clinging so tightly together it was a wonder they could breathe. She could see only the top of his head and his arms around Simone, but it was enough for her to tell that he was kissing her. And all the while, Simone had her hand behind his head, forcing his mouth harder against hers.

The tea was too hot, and the first swallow scalded Leah's throat, but she didn't stop drinking. Maybe the pain would obscure the pain in her heart. Finally, she knew she had to go back and dress for dinner as if nothing had happened and she were not surrounded by a swirling miasma of despair.

Baptiste was sitting near the window when she arrived. She looked at him, and unable to rid her memory of what she'd witnessed earlier, she felt sick to her stomach. She walked to the dressing table and began removing her hat.

"Simone just left here," Baptiste said casually. "She came to say good-bye. She and Jacques are leaving earlier than planned. She said to tell you she's sorry she missed you."

Leah couldn't believe what she was hearing. Baptiste's easy dissembling hurt worse than if he'd told her what had actually taken place between Simone and him.

She averted her head just enough to say, "That was thoughtful of her," and turned back to the dressing table. "I stopped in the dining room for a cup of tea."

Something about Baptiste's appearance disturbed her.

With a jolt she knew what it was. When she saw him with Simone, he'd had on his black suit. Even through the blur of tears, she'd distinctly seen two dark coat sleeves against Simone's pale blue gown. Now he was wearing his light tan suit. There was only one conclusion to be drawn. They'd made love while she was drinking her hot, scalding tea, and he'd put on a different suit afterward. She swallowed hard. She was going to be sick if she didn't bring herself under control.

"There's—there's something I think you have a right to know," Baptiste said. "I don't want to tell you, but I think you should hear it from me. I only hope it won't change your opinion of Simone."

And of you? Here it comes, she thought, and she gripped the edge of the dressing table to keep from falling. "Nothing," she said more bitterly than she'd intended, "could change my opinion of her."

"She's having an affair with Charles Surrat. You might have seen him. About my size. Dark hair, mustache."

"What!" Leah swung around.

"Yes," Baptiste said, and Leah noted the tinge of sadness, of disappointment, in his voice. "They were waiting here for me—for us—when I returned from the baths. To say goodbye."

So Simone and Charles had been waiting in the room, Leah mused. That might explain something. "Was he wearing a black suit, I wonder," she said more to herself than to Baptiste.

"Why the interest in what he was wearing?" Baptiste asked.

"I don't know, except I might have seen them together earlier."

Baptiste looked down at his trousers. Charles had been wearing tan pants similar to his own, maybe a little darker, but certainly not what one would call black. But he himself had worn his black suit to the baths. And he'd changed just before Leah came in. Had she a reason for wondering what Charles was wearing? Had she come to the room, earlier, before going to the dining room for tea?

"You might as well know everything," he said. "They weren't really waiting for us. When I came up here a little while ago, I encountered them in a rather embarrassing situation, to put it mildly. I waited down the hall until Charles Surrat came out. Simone was all apologies and explanations. It seems he's been urging her to have an affair since Jacques became an invalid, but she held out until today when the

161

doctor told her Jacques didn't have long to live. In her desperation she succumbed to Charles's pleas. She insisted it was the first time. Maybe, maybe not."

"In our room? Why our room?" She really didn't care whether Simone had affairs with every other man in Aix-les-Bains. The thought it might have been Charles she'd seen with Simone was making her hope that all her anxiety had been for naught. Yet for the moment she had to find something unimportant to talk about. She couldn't bring herself to tell Baptiste how she feared their marriage had been disintegrating under the winsome smile and captivating eyes of Simone.

"She didn't say. They couldn't go to her suite with Jacques there and—well, maybe ours was convenient."

"And you don't remember what he was wearing?" She had to know. She had to be convinced it was Charles and not Baptiste she'd seen in Simone's arms.

Still that obsession about the suit, Baptiste thought. It could only mean that she had been outside the room earlier. "I think maybe it was a black one. I didn't look closely when he came out, and he had no suit on at all when I saw him with Simone." His laughter was strained. It had never been easy to lie to Leah. But the truth would hurt her worse.

Simone and Charles had been in the room when he returned from the baths, but fully dressed and preparing to leave. Simone had stayed behind to explain why they were there. She'd been so filled with shame and remorse, he'd taken her in his arms to comfort her. When she started crying, Baptiste found himself kissing her, and they'd been unable to stop with a few innocent caresses.

"Oh, Baptiste," Simone had whispered, "if only it had been you instead of Charles who brought me up here. Hold me very close."

"Isn't one lover enough for you?" Even as he'd said it, trying to sound censorious, his body had felt the demands of hers and was making demands of its own. It had all happened so quickly, and she'd made it easy for him. Her redingote-styled dress buttoned all the way down the front, and while he had his face buried in the warmth between her breasts, she'd unbuttoned the skirt. In a moment it was over. After she'd gone, he'd been so disgusted with his lack of self-control that he had an irrational urge to rip his clothes off, as if in getting rid of them, he was stripping away the weak part of himself that had succumbed to her.

Baptiste had become so quiet that Leah thought it must

have cost him a great deal to tell her about Charles and Simone. Leah was not a fiercely jealous woman, and they both had plenty of friends of the opposite sex. It was only her fear that Baptiste and Simone had been lovers, and that he had been and was still in love with her, that made Leah feel frantic and insecure. Looking at Baptiste's face, saddened now by what she assumed was hurt or shame at having found Charles and Simone together like that, she was ready to believe it was Charles whom she, too, had seen and not Baptiste.

Walking over to the chair, Leah knelt with her head on Baptiste's knee. "I love you so very much."

"No more than I love you, chérie. There's never been a moment since I met you I haven't loved you." That much was true. He didn't love Simone. She was more like an insidious disease that recurred from time to time, a succubus that entered him and cast a spell he could exorcise only by yielding to its demands, by allowing it to draw from him the life-giving fluid that was as important to a man as his own blood. He'd felt the same way that afternoon before she married Jacques. Simone had used him then as she'd used him today. He'd vowed that day never to see her again. This time he meant to keep that vow.

He sounded so sincere, Leah was filled with remorse for having doubted him.

"We've nearly an hour before we need to dress for dinner," she said. "Shall we rest or do something else?"

"I like all that 'something else' suggests." Baptiste pulled her up to stand in front of him.

Leah started to undress, while Baptiste made his way toward the bed. "Help me with these hooks, Baptiste. I don't know why I let Christine talk me into a dress with hooks in the back."

"To make certain you couldn't get along without me." He hoped he never saw another dress that buttoned down the front.

"Oh, I need you for much more than that." She slipped out of her dress, petticoat, and bloomers.

"Wait," Baptiste said. He looked at her standing there in her brief, wasp-waisted corset, long garters, and black silk stockings. "Don't take anything more off." He ran his hands along her thighs. "With just these on, you are maddeningly seductive."

"And I feel like a hussy!"

"Just the way I want you to feel." He fell back on the

163

bed and pulled her down on top of him. "You're my hussy, and you're never to forget that."

"How can I when you——" Baptiste's mouth on hers put an end to anything more she might have said. Leah couldn't remember when they'd last made love with such exuberance and such joy. It was as if they couldn't get enough of each other, as if they were discovering all over again how wonderful it was to be in love.

No, Baptiste thought, it was not the momentary release of passion with Simone that had broken the spell. It was Leah's love and her faith in him. He'd betrayed that faith, a fact he'd have to live with like a hidden, festering sore, but he swore by his love for Leah he'd never see Simone again.

When it came time for them to leave Aix-les-Bains, Leah urged Jane Westborne to visit them at St. Denis on her way back to England or whenever she was in Paris.

"Indeed I shall," Jane said. "I want to meet all those delightful children you talk about. I'll probably be in Paris within the month, and I promise to spend at least a few days with you."

True to her word, Jane called after she arrived in Paris to say she was hiring a carriage for a drive to the château.

Of all the family, Lisette was the most excited about having Lady Westborne for a visit.

"A real lady, Mama? Royalty?"

"A peeress, yes. She's married to Lord Cuthbert Westborne, Earl of Wayland. He's the twelfth earl, so I assume the title goes back at least two hundred years. I'm not certain just what constitutes royalty, especially since she's American by birth, but she's a fine woman."

"Tell me more of what she said about her country house and the parties and being presented to the Prince and Princess of Wales."

"All in one breath?" Leah asked. "Maybe you'd better wait and let her tell you. She does it with such flair, such *élan*."

"Is she beautiful?" With her hushed, awed tones, Lisette could have been asking if their visitor were Cinderella or Sleeping Beauty.

"Yes—yes she is. More than that, she's fun to be with. You're going to like her. Now, how about helping me get Jean's old room ready for her."

"Please, Mama, let me," Denise chimed in. "She can use the pillow slips I just finished embroidering."

"But they're for your hope chest. You really want to use them now?"

"For someone special like her, yes. And I'll arrange little bouquets for the room. It will be lovely having a guest like her."

"What do you say, Lisette?" Leah had already begun to feel that Lisette thought Lady Westborne was coming for her particular pleasure.

"Fine with me. I'll have more time to practice that new piece by Mozart that Madame Thiery gave me. If Lady Westborne likes music, I can play for her one evening."

From all Leah had said, Lisette was prepared to like Lady Westborne. She had not expected to fall in love with her. From the moment Jane stepped from the landau, Lisette saw her as the epitome of a regal lady. Of medium height, she walked with an erect carriage that made her seem taller, and she had a magnificent mass of reddish blond hair fashioned artistically into a high pompadour and full bun. Her elegantly simple morning costume was a shade of pale bronze almost identical to that of her hair; a single feather of deeper rust curled around her hat brim.

So entranced was Lisette, she barely remembered to curtsey when her mother introduced them, and from then on she was their guest's constant, silent, most obedient servant. Anything Lady Westborne desired, Lisette obtained for her immediately, whether it was a shawl when the sunporch grew chilly or a cup of tea when she came in from walking. Lisette listened to every word the beautiful woman said, and she wondered if she could ever learn to imitate her sparkling tones. Lisette had never delighted in learning English, although Leah insisted that all her children speak it as well as they spoke French. Now she was determined to practice it as much as possible, and she replied in English to everything Lady Westborne said.

"Aren't you sweet," Jane said, after listening to a rather long, halting sentence. "But I do speak French, so there's no need to use English."

"Please, Lady Westborne, I want to perfect it. That is, if you don't find I speak it too atrociously."

"Not at all. A few rough places here and there, but if you wish me to, I'll correct you as you go along."

"Will you really? That's most kind of you." From the moment Lisette saw Lady Westborne, she'd had the oddest feeling that someday she would go to England. Now she was more certain than ever that the intuition was valid. She was destined to visit their guest and maybe even live in England. Why she had this feeling, she didn't know; but it persisted so strongly, she felt she must do all she could to please this gracious woman in order to be invited.

Leah had raised her brows at Lisette's polite little speech. She knew her daughter's intense antipathy to studying anything except her music. Also, Leah disliked the implication that she had been lax in teaching her children English.

"We speak English every night at dinner, Jane, and the tutor devotes at least an hour to it each day, but I'm afraid Lisette has been less interested in the language than in her music. She is quite an accomplished pianist and is hoping to play for you," she added, to soften the criticism.

"I should be delighted to hear her." Lady Westborne spoke to Leah, but she smiled at Lisette. She had been as charmed by the girl as Lisette had been by her. Jane had no children, and she was already formulating a plan to take Lisette under her wing and introduce her to England. All of society would fall at the feet of this beautiful girl, and she herself could relive her younger years when she had been the object of all eyes at every ball and dinner. Yes, Lisette must come and live with her for a while, and maybe—just maybe—she would fall in love with a titled Englishman and remain over there. That men would fall in love with her was inevitable, but she sensed that Lisette was too independent a spirit to marry for anything less than love.

"Leah, you must let Lisette return to Paris with me and stay for a few days." Jane had already broached this subject a number of times, but always Leah had put her off.

"I'm afraid you'd show her a taste of life she cannot indulge regularly for some years yet. She's still a girl, not a young woman. She wouldn't be satisfied with life here at the château after being introduced to your life in the city."

"Is it fair to deny her even that taste?" Jane persisted. "Or me the pleasure of giving it to her?"

"I guess I'm being very narrow," Leah sighed. "All right, three days. It will certainly be the highlight of her young life."

It was indeed the most glorious three days Lisette had ever experienced: morning and afternoon rides through the Bois de Boulogne, races at Longchamps, the opera, a performance by Sarah Bernhardt at the theatre, and late supper afterward at Maxim's. Lisette could scarcely absorb the dozens of impressions bombarding her every day. Staying at a hotel was itself a Cinderella experience: a suite more elaborately furnished then anything she had seen before, her own room with canopied bed, and—most luxurious of all—a private bathroom. No more having to share with her brothers and sisters the one tiny room that Mama had finally had built at the end of the hall on the second floor. She could stay in the tub and luxuriate in the soapy water, fragrant with lavender or attar-of-roses bath oils, for as long as she liked without anyone banging on the door and insisting she hurry up. And the mirrors! There were long mirrors on the walls of both the bathroom and the bedroom, in which she could admire herself while she primped and dressed.

This is life, she thought, as she sat before the ivory and gilt dressing table and put her hair up in the same style affected by Lady Westborne. *This is the way I'm going to live once I'm old enough to leave home.*

Lady Westborne had already hinted that Lisette should visit her in England and had described the events that constituted the social season there. Mama and Papa just had to let her go if she received such a longed-for invitation.

Nor was Lisette unaware of the glances following Lady Westborne everywhere she went, whether walking through the lobby of the hotel or riding through the Bois. Lisette couldn't help but wonder if some of the glances were for her, and she determined she'd learn to carry herself with the same poise and wear the same slightly condescending smile as her hostess. Lady Westborne had a charm, as well as a beauty, that attracted every man to her, and she accepted their fawning like a queen receiving the obeisance of her particularly favored subjects. The men must love her manner, Lisette thought, since they surrounded her constantly. Nor was she unaware that one of them stayed each night in the suite.

The one discomfiting note in these three days was that Lisette had to wear the simple, almost childish gowns Christine Richard had made for her. True, they were now ankle length, but how she longed for the low necklines and sweeping trains that all the women wore to the theatre and the opera. Alone in her bedroom, Lisette tied a light spread around her waist as a train and practiced walking with it behind her and then looping it over her wrist as she pretended to dance with a partner. She knew that Mama would say, "When you are a little older . . . ," but she wondered if that time would ever come.

At lunch on the third day, Lady Westborne looked at her

across the table and said, "I have to go to Worth's this afternoon for some fittings. I hope you won't be bored."

Bored! How could anyone be bored when surrounded by all the excitement of a couturier house like Worth's? To see all the materials, to see someone as beautiful as Lady Westborne being fitted in the gowns that would be worn to the races and the dinner parties she'd described.

Lisette thought the highlight of the day would be watching Jane parading in her new gowns. It wasn't. It was her hostess insisting that Lisette accept two of the gowns, saying she would have them duplicated for her in the time before she had to leave for England.

Lisette needed no persuading. She and Jane wore almost exactly the same size, and the dresses needed only to be taken in a bit at the bustline. *That,* Lisette thought, *is my one figure fault. Oh, if only my breasts were larger. I could pad the dresses but Mama would never allow that.* So she stood there patiently while the darts and tucks were pinned to decrease the fullness in the bust.

Neither of the dresses had the train she longed for. One was a simple morning dress and the other a tea gown, but they did reach to the floor, not just to her ankles, and they were much more stylish than anything she owned. And best of all, Lady Westborne would be wearing ones exactly like them after she returned to England. Lisette could imagine her walking through a garden or pouring tea for titled guests.

Nor were the gowns the only gifts showered on Lisette. When Jane shopped for gloves, she insisted on buying her young charge several pairs. And when Lisette admired a music box with Limoges figurines of a girl at a piano and a man playing the violin, nothing would do but that Lady Westborne buy it for her.

"Please," she always said, "it is my pleasure. If I had a daughter your age, I would be buying all these things for her."

If I had a daughter, Jane would think. *If only my one little girl hadn't been stillborn. And never any more after her. Leah doesn't realize how lucky she is. Lovers are for the moment, but they can never take the place of a child, who is for always.*

How she longed to kidnap Lisette and keep the girl with her forever! Nothing would be good enough for her. Dukes and marquises would bow down before her. And if she should marry one of them, Jane herself would be mother-in-law to genuine royalty, not just wife to an earl whose ancestor had received the title for winning some battle or rescuing the exchequer from bankruptcy. She'd have to approach Leah and Baptiste diplomatically, but surely they wouldn't deny their daughter the opportunities Lisette would be offered in England.

"Welcome home, Lisette." Both Leah and Baptiste were on the front verandah when the carriage drove up.

"I can tell by your face," Leah said, "you had a good time."

"Oh, Mama, it was—it was like being in another world."

"I hope you won't have too much trouble coming back down to this one."

Lisette ran off to show her gifts to Denise and Nicole. Leah and Baptiste sat with Jane in the sunroom.

"Lisette is a charming and beautiful person, Leah," Jane said.

"Thank you. And thank you for giving her three such wonderful days."

"There could be more." She looked at Leah's face and knew only a forthright request would be respected. "I'd like to take her to England with me for a few weeks. The social season starts soon with the annual regatta at Cowes, and she'd have the experience of living on our yacht. Then there are the balls in London, and I always have a houseparty in the country over one long weekend. She'd have a glorious time, one she'd never forget."

Leah was both stunned and upset at the invitation. Lisette had already done more during the past three days than most girls her age, and Leah was disturbed at the gifts Jane had given her. She looked to Baptiste for confirmation of her feelings, knew she had it by the frown on his face.

"I don't doubt she'd have a wonderful time," Leah said, "and you're very generous to extend such an invitation. But I'm afraid we have to decline for her. Not only is she still young, but in France young ladies do not enter society until after they are married."

"I see." Jane could not conceal either her disappointment or her feeling that Leah and Baptiste were being unnecessarily provincial in their attitude. "It *is* a pity," she exclaimed. "Her beauty would grace any affair and have the men swarming around her."

"And that is just what we want to prevent—or at least postpone for a year or two," Leah said quietly.

"Lisette is very beautiful," Baptiste added, "but we're

trying to teach her that beauty alone is not enough, nor should she ever take advantage of the way it can sway people—especially men—into spoiling her and doing whatever she wants." He thought about Catherine and the way she had used her beauty to destroy. Lisette must not be allowed to develop her mother's penchant for using people.

"I understand, but my invitation remains open. As soon as you permit it, she must come to England. Do let her come at least once before she marries, just so she can have had the pleasure of an English season before settling down. She will be very well chaperoned, I assure you."

"I know that, Jane, and we don't mean to criticize your ways. We'll see. Maybe in a year or two."

When Lisette learned about her parents' refusal of Jane's invitation, she was furious. For the first time since she was a child, she threw an unholy tantrum.

"That, young lady, will do you no good at all," Baptiste said sternly. "Until you are married, you will live in this house and obey us."

"What a bore!" She remembered whispered conversations she'd overheard about marriages for convenience, lovers, and mistresses. She knew now what she wanted. If she had to marry before she could enter the social whirl, she'd certainly never let herself be tied down by her husband. Instead, she'd make certain that marriage meant freedom, freedom to go where she wanted and do the things that pleased her. She'd be like Lady Westborne, who spent as little time as possible with her husband and obviously had lovers everywhere she went. That would be living, not like being stuck out in the country with nothing to occupy her time but a garden and children.

"All right," she said, pouting to show her displeasure. "If I must marry first, then choose a husband for me."

"When the time comes," Baptiste said, "we will do just that, or at least approve your selection."

"You needn't bother worrying whether I like him or not," Lisette retorted, "because I don't intend to stay with him anyway. I shall travel and have men fawning over me wherever I go. Lady Westborne said I'm beautiful enough to have any man I want."

Leah was finding it very difficult to control her temper. She was furious with Jane for putting such ideas into Lisette's head. They should never have let her go to Paris.

"Marriage is a commitment, Lisette, not an open door to a free life."

170

"You're a fine one to talk," Lisette screamed. "You were my father's mistress while he was married to Marie-Louise before the war and then while he was married to my mother."

"Enough!" Baptiste shouted. "You're not going to slander Leah, who's been a mother to you since yours deserted you. Ours has never been a casual affair, but a life-long love."

"You never loved my mother," Lisette sobbed hysterically. "You hated her. I know she had a lover, so why shouldn't I be like her? Marry for convenience and then have some fun."

"There is always the choice of marrying for love," Leah suggested, knowing all the time she might as well be speaking to the wind.

"And then be tied down with one baby after another? No thank you. Either find me a husband soon, or I'll run away to England."

"In another year, we'll think about it seriously," Baptiste said.

"Meanwhile," Leah added, seeing the determined look on Lisette's face, "if you continue your musical studies, we'll make two promises. We will see about an audition at the conservatory; then, next summer, I will go with you to England for two weeks if Jane extends the invitation."

With that Lisette had to be satisfied. But she could still daydream about a future more in keeping with Lady Westborne's descriptions.

Chapter Seventeen

"WAKE UP, BAPTISTE." Leah touched him gently on the shoulder. When he only grunted and turned over, she shoved him harder. "Wake up!"

"Wha—what is it? Was I snoring again?" He snuggled deeper under the quilt and immediately went right back to sleep.

"Oh, for heaven's sake," Leah murmured. She shook him longer and harder. "Do wake up and open your eyes."

"I am awake," he growled. "How can I sleep with you pummeling me like that?"

"Then listen. I think there's someone on the back terrace."

"This time of night? Don't be foolish. You just had a nightmare."

"It's no dream," she insisted. "I've been sitting up and listening for at least five minutes." Shivering, she reached for the shawl at the foot of the bed and wrapped it around her shoulders. "There. Hear that? That is *not* my imagination."

Baptiste raised himself up on one elbow. "It does sound like something walking. Maybe it's just a stray dog." The village dogs were always wandering across their land on their nightly excursions, and one had no doubt found his way onto the terrace.

"I thought so, too, at first, but then it sounded like someone had tripped or hit something and fallen down. You know, a kind of shuffling, like someone trying to keep his balance."

"And Nicolas isn't here to check for us?"

"A lot of good he'd do at his age," Leah scoffed, "if it's someone trying to break in. Do you realize, Baptiste, we're completely at his mercy if it is?"

"Not while I still have my pistol and my deadly aim."

"No, you can't! You'd be no match for some thief determined to get in."

But Baptiste was already sitting on the edge of the bed and grasping the arms of his wheelchair. "I'm not completely helpless, Leah. If I can take him by surprise, the odds will be more even."

"Do be careful then." She knew better than to argue when he was determined to prove he was capable of doing what any other man could do. She wanted to follow him, but she knew that might put both of them in jeopardy. She could only wait until he returned—or until she heard something that demanded her attention. She prayed that if it were a shot, it would be from Baptiste's gun.

Baptiste wheeled out of their room and into the sunroom overlooking the terrace. There was no longer any doubt that someone was out there. At first he saw only a faint shadow from the moonlight, then the figure of a man leaning against a large stone urn. He checked the pistol lying in his lap. The rubber wheels of his chair made little noise on the wooden floor, but he knew that the man would be alerted to his presence the minute he turned the latch on the double glass doors. If only he could discover whether the intruder were armed. He rolled up closer to the door and squinted into the darkness.

The man didn't look very large or menacing. In fact, as

best Baptiste could tell, he was so thin as to be emaciated. Not that that made him any less dangerous. Even as Baptiste watched, the man clutched his stomach, staggered a few steps, and slid to the terrace floor.

Why, the man's sick, or half starved, Baptiste thought. He couldn't be pretending since he couldn't know anyone was watching.

Cautiously he turned the latch and waited, but the man didn't move. Baptiste opened the door a few inches and then recoiled against the surge of cold air he'd let in. He wished he'd taken time to put on his heavy smoking jacket. He'd have to rouse the man enough to get him inside or he'd freeze to death.

Baptiste opened the door wide enough to propel the chair through. He moved over to the man, who was now lying almost prone on the floor, his head resting awkwardly against the urn. Baptiste nudged him gently with one wheel.

"Ooooh." The shallow moan was so weak, Baptiste almost expected it to be followed by a death rattle.

"Can you—can you move at all?" Hoping the man would hear him, Baptiste leaned over as far as he dared, but the only response was another pitiful moan.

Baptiste looked at the filthy clothes, several sizes too large for the gaunt frame, and the equally filthy and unkempt long hair and beard. How in the world had this stranger made his way here? And why? Leah would be furious for his bringing this derelict into the house, but he couldn't just let him die out here.

"Can you move?" Baptiste repeated. The man raised his head slowly, as if even the slightest movement required his last bit of strength. Baptiste looked into the fever-blurred eyes, and the shock of recognition almost catapulted him out of the chair.

"Jean!"

"Yes, Papa." His voice was a little stronger now that he knew for certain he'd actually made it all the way home. For a long time, fever and exhaustion had confused him as to just where he was.

"For God's sake, Jean, we've got to get you into the house."

Jean merely lay where he was, waiting like a child to be told what to do.

"Can you reach the chair?" Baptiste asked.

Jean nodded.

"I'll lock the brake and you can use the chair to support yourself until you can stand. Then if you lean on the back, I think I can get us both into the house."

Slowly Jean pulled himself upright and then collapsed against the back of the chair. Baptiste leaned forward so Jean could let his head and arms fall over the back and be supported by it.

Not for the first time, Baptiste was grateful for the strength in his arm and shoulder muscles that had been developed over the years. Now he used those muscles to turn the wheels of the chair and drag Jean's dead weight as far as the sunroom. Somehow, he also managed to turn the chair and shut the door against the frigid air.

Jean finally let go of the chair and fell onto a couch.

"Leah!" Baptiste wheeled as far as the hall that led into their bedroom.

"Are you all right?" Her voice betrayed the fear that had been growing during the time he was gone.

"I'm fine, but I need your help. Put on a robe—it's cold out here—and come out to the sunroom."

Leah came running, and then retreated a step into the hall when she saw the man lying on the couch.

"Who is it, Baptiste?" She shuddered. "And what is he doing in here?"

"It's me, Mama." The warmth of the room, compared to the winter night outside, had already made Jean feel somewhat better.

"My God, Jean! What's happened to you? Where've you been?"

"The questions can come later, Leah," Baptiste said. "Right now he needs something hot to eat and blankets to get him warmed up."

"Can you make it to the salon, Jean? The coals are still hot, and I can get the fire going again in no time."

"I think so."

"Wait while I get a quilt to wrap around you," Leah said, "and then I'll help you."

Between the support of Leah's arm and the back of Baptiste's chair, Jean made it to the salon, where he collapsed once more on a couch. Leah poked up the embers, added more wood and coal, and in no time had a blazing fire.

"Mama, this feels good." Jean's face was still flushed, but his eyes were no longer so glazed.

"Well, lie there quietly while I get you some food. Hot tea

and the good vegetable soup we had for dinner. It won't take five minutes."

While she was gone, and after swallowing the brandy Baptiste had given him, Jean closed his eyes and fell into a restless sleep. Baptiste sat quietly beside him, never taking his eyes off the son he thought he'd lost. He didn't know what Jean had been through during the past months, but this time he'd listen to him. He didn't want to lose him again.

Both Leah and Baptiste sat and watched while Jean greedily spooned up the thick soup she placed before him on a small table.

"Drink the tea, too," she urged. "It's hot and full of brandy."

"I know. I can feel it already." Jean stopped eating only long enough to wipe some of the broth from his beard.

"Now," Baptiste said, after Jean had finished the soup and lain back against the pillows, "do you think you can tell us where you've been and what you've been doing to end up looking like a starving mongrel?" Baptiste kept his tone gently humorous.

"I need your help, Papa. Desperately."

"I can believe that. You're nothing but skin and bones."

"It's not just for me. It's for Céline, too."

Baptiste frowned and then nodded his head. "How about starting from the beginning, from the time you left here."

Leah and Baptiste listened attentively to his recital.

"Céline and I went to Paris and then south to Toulouse. We were married there." He waited for a comment, but there was none. "Work was harder to find than I thought it would be. Finally I got a job driving a fertilizer wagon. Shoveling it in from the slop dumps behind the houses in the villages, driving the wagon to the farms, and spreading it where the farmers told me to put it."

"Yes," Baptiste said, smiling to himself, "you do smell like a chamber pot. The next thing will be to burn those clothes."

"No, that's from the sewer. We stayed in the country till Céline took ill. I had to get her to Paris, to a good doctor there. No one in the villages could do anything for her, and I thought if we had to get to a city, it might as well be Paris. I thought there'd be a better chance of finding work. But it was just as bad as in the South. Now and then, when some part of the sewer got clogged, I'd get a job going down to loosen the debris and get it flowing again."

Baptiste thought about the sewers that spread like a

175

gigantic spider web under the streets of Paris, collecting all the refuse and offal and waste from the huge city. Millions of rats were said to inhabit the system, and more than one body had been dumped down the manholes to prevent a murder from being discovered.

"It made me so sick," Jean said, "I couldn't eat even if I had the money for food. Everything I made was just enough to pay for a room and food for Céline. And laudanum to ease her pain, but never enough for the doctor I wanted her to see. I'd thought our one-room hovel near Toulouse was horrible, but it was heaven compared to what we've been living in in Paris. So I came to you. I didn't want to do it, but I had to."

"You were right, whether you wanted to or not," Baptiste said. "Of course we'll help you. Good Lord, son, how long has it been since you've eaten?"

"I don't know. But Céline needs your help more than I do. She's dying, and I can't bear to watch her suffering. Or the thought of losing her and the baby."

"Then we can't waste any more time," Leah said in a matter-of-fact tone. "Go into my dressing room and take a bath, while I go upstairs and get some of your clothes. They won't fit but they'll be an improvement over what you have now."

"I'm surprised, Mama," Jean finally smiled, "that you didn't faint when you came near me."

"I've smelled worse." She wrinkled her nose and laughed. "But not much worse. I'll go right upstairs. You strip here while I'm gone. I don't want those smelly things in my room. Can you make it to the bath all right? There's a small charcoal fire going under the tub to keep the water warm for my morning bath, but Nicholas or Blanchette will bring me more when they get up."

"I can make it fine, Mama, thank you."

"Then strip and get into the tub while I'm gone. I'll lay out the clean things on my bed."

She hurried upstairs quietly, so as not to wake the others. She opened the wardrobe and chose trousers and jacket. Not until she was at Jean's dresser and reaching for underclothes and shirt did she break down. She could no longer control her tears. Jean had returned. She leaned her head on her elbows atop the dresser and cried for a long time. She'd been so sure they'd lost him for good. She didn't care that he was married to Céline. He had chosen to come to them for help, and that was what mattered. They were still important to him;

he knew he could still count on them. She dried her eyes on a pair of socks and hurried back downstairs.

"Well, what do you think?" Baptiste asked as Leah re-entered the salon and they waited for Jean to finish bathing and join them.

"I think we should do everything we can for him and—and for Céline. It's obvious he loves her, and since she did run off and marry him, we can only assume she loves him as well. And she is going to have our grandchild—our first."

Baptiste still had doubts about that, but he didn't voice them. Perhaps, since she had chosen Jean rather than the money, it *was* his child. He would prefer to think so, anyway.

"My first concern is for Jean," Baptiste said. "For his welfare and his happiness. If that includes Céline, so be it."

"Have you already given some thought to what you're going to suggest?"

"I'll offer him his job back as apprentice, and then if he proves himself—as he was doing before he left—there will be a regular position for him."

"An apprentice's wage will scarcely take care of all the expenses they have ahead of them."

"I thought I'd suggest they live in the apartment until they are better able to afford a place of their own."

"Baptiste, you are a good man." Leah rushed over and hugged him. "It will be just the place for them."

Jean was more than willing to return to the office, even as an apprentice, and ecstatic about living in the Paris apartment. "It's so much more than anything Céline's used to. She really will think it's heaven."

"And see that she gets the proper care," Leah said. "We'll take care of the doctor's fees."

It was a long time before Leah got over her mistrust of Céline, nor did she find it easy to like the girl. But like any grandmother, she doted over her grandson, Armand, and found all sorts of excuses for going into the city to see him. There was no question that he was Jean's child. He was the image of Jean as a baby, and even Baptiste was not averse to taking him to the office and showing him off.

As scheduled, Jean became a full-time bookkeeper, and then, some months later, when the section manager in charge of Far Eastern imports resigned to open his own office, Baptiste moved Jean into that position.

"There won't be any dissension in the office for promoting him over one of the assistants?" Leah asked.

"No, the boy deserves it. He's proved his mettle by hard work. Anyway, the assistant is thinking of going with the former manager, and I don't want someone in there who is not wholly dedicated to me. This may make up his mind for him. If he goes, fine; if he stays, I'll know it's because he wants to continue working in the firm. Then I'll think of him when another opening comes up."

About the same time, the elderly housekeeper at the apartment announced she would like to retire to the country to live with her daughter and grandchildren. Céline immediately suggested that instead of hiring a new housekeeper, she take care of the apartment so she and Jean could continue living there. It would still always be ready for the family whenever they came into town.

"It won't be too much work for you?" Leah asked.

"Work! Madame Fontaine, it will be a pleasure to take care of this beautiful place. And it's easy for me to take Armand to the park."

Leah was dubious at first, but finally agreed. And then, after she saw how well Céline took care of the place, she began to like the girl a little better. She was a good mother, and it was obvious that Jean was happy. Maybe the marriage would turn out better than they'd hoped, after all.

After Leah saw Jean and Céline comfortably provided for, and Armand growing into a healthy, laughing child, she was able to turn her attention to the other children over the next two years. Henri and Denise continued to divide their time between the schoolroom and their own pursuits; he worked hard in the workshop and she kept busy filling her hope chest and taking care of Robert. Lisette was still devoted to the piano, and Leah began wondering just how soon she would be expert enough to audition for the conservatory in Paris. With Jean and Céline living in the city, some of Leah's fears about letting Lisette go to Paris would be allayed. But no need to concern herself with that yet. Madame Thiery had said she would let them know when she felt Lisette was sufficiently accomplished.

It was Nicole whom Leah dwelled on more than the others. As Jules Ferry had suggested, she was attending the one-room public school in the village. She was not an exceptional student, but Monsieur LaBorde, the schoolmaster, assured them she was diligent and obedient. For a girl who would eventually marry rather than go on with her education, that was sufficient.

Leah had early recognized it was not books that commanded Nicole's attention, but her art. She continued to evince a genuine artistic talent, and Leah viewed with pride her watercolor scenes; Nicole seemed quite an accomplished artist for one her age. There was scarcely a level space in her room not cluttered with paper, paints, chalk, and other artistic paraphernalia. Three easels completely filled the area between bed, dresser, and door. Every other room in the château had at least one of her pictures, and Leah's bedroom and dressing room walls were covered with them.

"I think I know what we should give Nicole for her thirteenth birthday," Leah remarked to Baptiste while they were sitting in the summer house and enjoying the cool twilight.

"Well, she's long since outgrown dolls, and I can't think of anything she wants except more paper and paints, though God knows how she finds her way to bed at night for all the clutter—"

"That's why I came up with this idea. You know that feeling I had—"

"Which one? Your feelings have already cost me the price of two additions to the house."

Leah hesitated. She had to anticipate every argument Baptiste might come up with and then dismiss them before he even had a chance to mention them.

"I really had thought of letting her use Jean's old room, in addition to her own, but we really do need it when Jean, Céline, and the baby visit. Agreed?"

"Yes, but I have the feeling I'm doing so only to have to agree next with another of your hare-brained schemes. Like those two additions."

"But that's just it. You said the second one was much too big for Henri, even after I took part of it for a sewing room."

"And I was wrong. I never saw such a clutter of tools and engines and queer machines that move without doing anything."

"But he doesn't need all that space, and so I thought we could remodel half of it into a studio for Nicole."

"But she's only thirteen!" He lurched forward in his chair. "In another year, she'll find something else to amuse her."

"I don't think so. And remember, she's kept her promise

179

all these years not to run away again. I think we should reward her."

Baptiste could see that Leah was really serious about this. A studio for Nicole was not just an idle whim on her part. But then, he'd never known her to indulge in idle whims.

"How much remodeling?" He'd been outmaneuvered again, but somehow he didn't mind. Nor was it so much Leah's persuasive arguments as the thought of doing something that would please Nicole. Since fleeing from the convent and being allowed to attend school in the village, she had gradually returned to the sunny, vivacious child she'd been before Robert was born. That evidently had been more of a traumatic experience for her than any of them had realized at the time. She was moody occasionally, and still spent a great deal of time alone, but when she was with the family, she laughed and played games or entered into their discussions as if she'd never thought of alienating herself from them. Nor did she complain that Lisette had a room of her own where she could practice her music whenever she desired. Yes, Leah was right. Nicole needed a studio of her own.

"Very little needs to be done," Leah said in answer to his question. "The light is good from the long side, so I thought we would put in larger windows and a skylight in the sloping roof. Then, of course, she'll need shelves for her supplies, tables to work on, and so forth."

"Just another minor little project," Baptiste said, and grinned.

"Now you're teasing. Really, it won't cost that much. What I thought was that we'd make the major construction changes and then let Nicole tell us what she needs inside. After it's done, of course. I want it to be a surprise."

"And just how do you plan to make it a surprise when she's living right here in the house? I seem to recall we tried to do that with Henri."

"Oh, that's no problem."

Baptiste shook his head in wonderment. Whether it was finding a way to pay the enormous back taxes on the plantation when he finally recovered it after the Civil War, or planning how to surprise Nicole when major remodeling was going on, Leah remained undaunted. The amazing thing was, she always found a way; then when she explained it, it all seemed simple enough for any fool to have thought of it.

"What has that devious mind of yours come up with now?" Baptiste asked.

"Nicole has been longing to go to Paris and spend all the time she wants in the Louvre. Also, I happen to know there are several very fine art exhibits in smaller galleries in the city."

"Aha," Baptiste nodded, "I see where your mind is going."

"Yes, Nicole is very fond of Céline and she adores Armand." Leah remembered how Nicole had turned away from Robert and refused to hold him soon after he was born. She had declared then she hated babies and would never have anything to do with them. Yet from the time Céline had brought Armand to the château for his first visit, Nicole had been overjoyed to be allowed to help with him. And when he began to toddle and then run around, it was she who played patiently with him for hours, even foregoing her art while he was there. Perhaps, Leah mused, it was because he was no threat to her; he had not separated her from someone she loved. And at the same time, he was hers alone when he visited.

"How long do you think she'll need to be away?" Baptiste asked.

"I thought the exterior work could be finished in three weeks. There's not that much remodeling to be done. And Nicole will be able to explore the city and look at paintings to her heart's content."

"You don't think Céline and Jean will mind having her for that long?"

"I've already talked to Céline," Leah said, "and she's delighted at the idea. Don't forget, Nicole can also help her with Armand, and he's at a busy age now."

"You've talked to Céline? When?"

"Don't laugh," Leah said, "I finally screwed up my courage to call her in Paris. I found that the telephone wouldn't bite me after all, and the operators were very helpful."

"You never cease to amaze me, chérie. Undaunted by an office full of Federal officers during the war and then scared to death of a harmless telephone."

"Well, I can handle something I understand. But no one will be able to explain to me how my voice can go on that little wire all the way from here to Paris. Or to St. Denis, for that matter." Baptiste started to interrupt. "No, don't try to explain. It will only make me more confused. I'll use it when I have to, but I'll never feel really comfortable with it."

181

Baptiste continued to smile as she walked out of the room to go in search of Nicole.

Leah found her daughter just where she thought she'd be—in her room, surrounded by the most disorderly accumulation of things Leah had ever seen. As had been her practice since the children were old enough, Leah had left the care of their rooms entirely in their own hands. Denise's continued to be so meticulously neat it looked as if no one lived in it. Lisette's was usually strewn with petticoats and dresses, whereas her dressing table, with its pictures of Catherine, was kept as neat as a shrine. Nor was any dust allowed to accumulate in her music room. Her priorities were evident to anyone who took even a cursory glance at either room.

Henri's room always smelled like a zoo from the variety of live—and sometimes dead—creatures he was forever collecting and bringing home. Only in his case did Leah insist the room be aired and cleaned every week, and by him, too, since none of the maids would go near the place for fear of something crawling or jumping out at them. Robert, of course, was still too young to take care of his room, but already Leah wondered just what his particular penchant would be when he grew older.

"I don't see how you find your way around in here, Nicole, or know where anything is."

"It is kind of crowded, isn't it?" And Nicole looked around as if seeing it for the first time. But she made no move to pick anything up.

"If you could find a place for me to sit down, I'd like to talk to you for a few minutes," Leah said gently.

"Here, I'll just move these drawings," Nicole said and transferred them from the chair to the bed.

And back to the chair tonight, Leah thought, *when she's ready to go to bed.* "Thank you. I didn't really feel like perching on the corner of the table."

"Oh, Mama, it's not that bad."

"It is, but we won't worry about that for now. What I wanted to ask you was this: How would you like to go into Paris and visit Jean and Céline for a short time?"

"You mean really stay with them? Not just for one day?" Nicole nearly knocked over an easel in her excitement.

"For about three weeks, if you think you can find enough to keep you occupied for that long."

"Really, Mama? Three whole weeks? I can spend all the time I want at the Louvre?" She began dancing around,

182

somehow managing to avoid the sketches that covered the floor like a carpet.

"Yes, and I understand there are some very fine exhibitions at several of the other galleries."

"And Montmartre. I can go to Montmartre and see the artists at work. I can watch them while they're actually painting." She was completely lost now in her own dream. "And meet some of them. Do you think they will talk to me? Take me seriously, I mean?"

"If you talk intelligently to them about their work, I don't see why not."

"And walk along the Seine. Someday, Mama, I'm going to sell my paintings there. And then I'm going to have my own exhibit. Don't laugh. I know I will."

"I'm not laughing, Nicole. That's the very reason I want you to have this time in Paris. You need to become completely immersed in all the wonderful art that is there. And you need to see some that isn't so good in order to learn to distinguish what is good and what is bad."

"Maybe I can get permission to sketch in the Louvre. They do give permission, you know."

"You can try, but don't be disappointed if they consider you too young right now. You've plenty of time for that."

"But I can take my sketch book and—oh, think of all the things there are in the city to sketch. Enough to keep me busy for a lifetime."

"I really didn't think you'd go without it." Nicole would go without her clothes before she'd leave her art materials behind. "There's something else, though, I want you to think about. You'll be staying with Céline, and I don't want you to become a burden to her. Help her in the apartment and with Armand."

"You know I'll do that, Mama. We can walk to the gardens, and I can sketch while I watch him playing. And I can take complete care of him in the evening. I won't be any burden, I promise."

"I know you won't. But about the gardens. Don't be so busy with your sketching that you take your eyes off him. He could wander off or fall into the pond. He'll be your sole responsibility when you take him out of the apartment."

"I know, and you don't need to worry. I won't let him out of my sight."

Even as she packed her trunk with all the clothes Mama insisted she take, Nicole found it hard to believe she would be spending almost a month in Paris. Nor could she decide which she wanted to do first—go to the Louvre to feast her eyes on all the famous old masters and the art of antiquity, or go to Montmartre and watch real, live painters at work. Thinking of all she was going to learn in these weeks made her head spin. She could study the various techniques and then go back to the apartment to practice them herself.

Mama had said she would give her enough spending money to buy canvas and oils as well as paper and water colors. To be able to try her hand at oils! And there would also be a special fund, put away in a small, separate purse, for her to buy any one really good painting she wanted after she'd visited all the galleries. She would have to study them very carefully and make an intelligent choice so Mama wouldn't be disappointed. She was not unaware that for a girl of thirteen, she'd been given a tremendous responsibility. She wished she could let Mama and Papa know just how much she appreciated their understanding of her love for art, and how grateful she was that they took her work seriously and didn't think she was simply a little girl with a hobby she'd tire of. She knew she had real talent, and that someday she'd be able to pay back that understanding by making them proud of her.

The last item Nicole put into the trunk was Nissi, her beloved rag doll. She never went to sleep at night without it.

While the remodeling went on at the château, Nicole lived out her dream in Paris. Day after day she went to the Louvre, spending hours at a time in the Seven Metre Room with its seventeenth-century Dutch paintings by Frans Hals and Rembrandt and in the Salle des États, with such famous works as Leonardo DaVinci's *Mona Lisa*, Raphael's *St. George and the Archangel Michael*, Correggio's *Sleeping Antiope*, and Tintoretto's *Suzanna Bathing*. Then there was the Grande Galerie filled with Italian paintings from the thirteenth to the fifteenth centuries, the Van Dyck Room with its Flemish masterworks, the Medici Gallery, and so many more.

Nicole had passed through and then dismissed the rooms of Oriental antiquities. They held no interest for her. Nor did any of the sculpture aside from the magnificent, headless *Victory of Samothrace*, and two statues by Michelangelo, the two *Prisoners*. She spent hours looking at them from all angles, while trying to capture on paper the nearly perfect male figures wrought in marble by the sculptor.

Then there was Montmartre. Nicole was completely captivated by its Bohemian atmosphere and the fervid activity

184

of its artists. In the Place du Tertre, there were always a dozen to twenty artists standing in front of their easels, while patrons of the nearby outdoor cafés watched and sipped coffee, wine, or liqueurs. Sitting with Jean and Céline, Nicole was too enthralled to speak. She could only stare at everything around her and at the façade of the small church of St. Pierre-de-Montmartre a block away.

"How would you like to have your portrait done?" Jean asked.

"A portrait of me?" Nicole was breathless.

"Yes, many of them earn money by doing portraits and poor imitations of the old masters to sell to tourists. Then they have the financial freedom to paint what they really want to paint."

"But are they good? The portraits, I mean?"

"Some are," Jean said. "We'll study them this afternoon and then come back another time if you like."

"I want to come here as often as I can. There's such excitement in the air. Just think; some of the paintings being done by these very artists may someday be as famous as the old masters in the Louvre. They may even hang in the Louvre."

Jean looked closely at his youngest sister. Still such a little girl and yet when she talked about art, she spoke like an adult. Then he smiled. He'd gone into her room the evening before to kiss her goodnight, and he saw how she clutched her rag doll as she slept. With her long black hair still in braids, she looked no older than her thirteen years; but her eyes, almond-shaped like their mother's, were filled with a wisdom and a curiosity far beyond her years. A strange anomaly, this little sister of his.

On another afternoon, the afternoon she finally had her portrait done by a young artist who listened intently to all her serious questions and then answered them in the same spirit as they'd been asked, Nicole walked to the top of the hill that is Montmartre and gazed down on the city below. The roofs of Paris spread in every direction. Directly below was the Place Blanche. In the distance she could see the Seine and the Cathedral of Notre Dame situated on the Cité, the larger of the two islands in the river. This was a magic city. Someday she would live here and set up her easel in the Place du Tertre or the Place Emil-Goudeau. But she would never misuse her talent by painting cheap, tawdry scenes of Paris or hasty portraits for the tourist trade. She would concentrate on creating beauty.

One day, Céline asked a neighbor to care for Armand, and they went to Montmartre in the evening. Jean wanted Nicole to see it when the cafés really came alive. They ate a rich soup, hot, succulent meat pastries, and hard bread. Then they sat back with their coffee to watch the people sitting at the nearby tables or wandering through the square.

Nicole found herself fascinated by a man sitting several tables away. As a student of art she was intrigued by his scraggly red beard, the prominent bones of his face and his masterful hands that he kept clenched on top of the table. More than that, however, she was moved by the haunting, suffering expression on his face and the passion in his eyes. He had to be an artist. She had to meet him.

"Who is that man over there, Jean?"

"Please, Nicole, I don't know everyone in Paris."

"Then ask the waiter. Maybe the man comes here often."

Jean had come to know Nicole too well to try to dissuade her when she became inquisitive. Her curiosity was enough to drive to distraction anyone who spent more than ten minutes with her.

"Monsieur," he called to the waiter. "Do you happen to know the name of that red-bearded man sitting over there?" Jean nodded in the direction of the far table.

"That is Vincent Van Gogh." The waiter spat the name out.

"Is he an artist?" Nicole asked.

"He calls himself one, but hmmph," he made a gesture of disgust and disparagement, "no one will buy anything he paints. His paintings are nothing but junk, not worth the canvas and paints they're made of. More coffee?" His tone indicated he considered it a waste of time to talk about the man.

"Please," Jean said, "and another lemonade."

"Can we meet him, Jean?" Nicole asked.

"Who? That man Van Gogh? Certainly not. You can't just walk up and start talking to a stranger."

"I can." She stood up and began wending her way through the tables. Jean immediately jumped up to follow, saying, "Stay here, Céline. I can't let her approach him alone. God only knows what an unkempt character like that will say to her."

By the time Jean reached Nicole, the artist had already invited her to sit down. He nodded to Jean to do the same. His voice was amazingly soft, and Jean sat back and listened to the polite answers he gave to Nicole's questions. She was listening intently, but she was also hearing the sorrow beneath the words.

"I want to buy one of your paintings, Monsieur Van Gogh," Nicole said.

"Do you really? Then you are the only one. But maybe you'd better see them first."

"No, I don't have to. I know I'll like whatever you have done."

With that he threw back his head and roared with laughter. Then he saw the hurt in her eyes, but more than that, he saw himself reflected there. They were two of a kind, this little girl and himself. And in that moment a bond of understanding was forged between them. That it would last for only a moment did not matter. It had happened and that was enough.

"Come to the quay tomorrow, and I will paint a picture just for you. Oh, I have many for sale." He laughed again. "Many that will never sell in spite of my brother Theo's attempts to hang them in the Goupil Gallery where he works. Or those which my friends—to whom I am constantly in debt —hang in their cafés. But for you, a special one. You love Paris, don't you?"

"Yes, monsieur. Very much."

"Then you shall have Paris on canvas. Tomorrow. You'll find me easily enough, or just ask. Everyone knows where the crazy Vincent Van Gogh sets up his easel."

"I will. I'll be there. I promise." She started to walk away and then looked back. He was again as she'd first seen him, hands clenched on the table and eyes staring intently in front of him, as if seeing a world far different from the one surrounding him.

"You're not really intending to go to the quay tomorrow, I hope," Jean said after they'd returned to their table. "He won't be there."

"Yes, I am. I promised. And he will be. He's going to paint something just for me."

"If I say you can't?" Jean was finding that acting *in loco parentis* to his little sister could be wearing at times.

"I'll go anyway."

"Let her go, Jean," Céline said. "If Monsieur Van Gogh does not show up—well, she is not too young to learn the world is filled with disappointments."

"Thank you, Céline," Nicole said. "But I will not be disappointed."

"All right," Jean said. "But it was wrong to say you'd buy

something you haven't seen. It may be pure trash. Worse than anything you've been scoffing at."

"No, Jean, it will be beautiful. He couldn't paint any other way." Not with those warm, dark yet piercing eyes. For a moment, when looking into those eyes, she'd experienced an eerie feeling that she could see herself as he saw her, a kindred spirit with love for all that is beautiful. "He said he would give me the city of Paris on canvas."

"It's your money," Jean said. "I hope Mama doesn't blame me for letting you spend it foolishly."

Nicole played for an hour with Armand before he went to bed, but all the while her mind was on Van Gogh. She would see him again tomorrow, and maybe she would get to the quay in time to watch him work.

Directly after breakfast, Nicole packed a picnic lunch—enough for two—and rode in a cab from the apartment to the river, across a bridge to the Cité, and then across another bridge to the Left Bank. Céline had tried to dissuade her from going too early. She knew the tendency of artists to stay up drinking and then remain late in bed to sleep off the effects. But Nicole could not be budged from her determination to spend the entire day with the artist.

Since it was early when she arrived, only a few artists had begun putting up their easels, and Van Gogh was not among them. Nicole spent some time watching the *bouquinistes* setting up their stalls of used books and prints. She was neither worried nor impatient. Van Gogh had said he would be here, and he would not break his promise.

Nicole was not disappointed in him when he finally arrived. For most of the day she sat entranced while he painted with swift, sure strokes, not just the scene he viewed from his vantage point, but the very spirit of Paris. The spirit that Nicole had caught when she looked down from Montmartre. There was no traditional Notre Dame or Arc de Triomphe in this painting but there were the roofs, the cafés, and the flowers. There was the river winding a brilliant cerulean blue from one side of the canvas to the other, the very bloodstream of the city. All of the colors—the pure reds and blues and yellows—were brilliant, almost garish; yet the entire picture had about it the softness of a warm summer haze. Not a single object was delineated in its true form, yet the flowers bloomed on their stalks and people sat at the tables of the cafés.

Van Gogh worked quickly, almost feverishly, in short strokes of color. At times he seemed to be dueling with the canvas as he jabbed at it with the tip of his paintbrush to form the blossoms on a vine running up the façade of a house.

By midafternoon, the sun was hot and glaring over the quay, and Nicole watched Van Gogh anxiously as he wiped the sweat from his forehead or passed his hands over his eyes as if in pain. The finishing touch to the painting was that same glaring sun placed in the upper-left-hand corner of the canvas.

"There," he said quietly. "It is finished." He did not ask her if she liked it. He merely said, "It is yours. All of Paris."

"Thank you. It is as beautiful as I knew it would be." Nicole didn't feel it was necessary to ask how much she owed him. She simply gave him all the money allotted to her for buying a painting.

"Thank you, Nicole. This will keep me in canvas and paints for quite a while, even as fast as I use them up."

"And in food, too, I hope."

"No," he laughed. "I never buy food. I let my friends do that for me."

"I think you owe them a bottle of wine," Nicole said sternly. Then she shook his hand and bid him goodbye. Her stay in Paris was over, and she never saw him again.

Stunned silence was Nicole's initial reaction to the studio created for her in her absence. Then she ran around and around to check on all the things that had already been moved into it. After a few minutes she stared out the new and wider, floor-to-ceiling windows and up through the skylight. Only then did she speak, but more to herself than to Leah and Baptiste, who stood waiting to hear her reaction.

"It's mine, all mine. And it's almost as good as being in Paris." She seemed completely unaware of anyone else's presence.

"We thought we'd wait for you to suggest what you need for furnishings," Leah said finally. "Shelves and things like that."

Nicole looked at her as if she were coming out of a trance. "Yes, I suppose I will need things like that," she echoed Leah. "And I haven't said thank you, have I? But I do thank you."

"You're welcome, sweetheart," Baptiste said warmly.

Then just as suddenly she was herself again. "You did all this while I was in Paris, didn't you?"

"We did," Leah said.

"Is that why you sent me there? So this could be a surprise?"

"Partly," Leah said. "But we also felt it was time you had a chance to spend time in the city. I want to know everything you did and saw. You can tell us after dinner."

When Nicole showed them the painting she'd bought and described Van Gogh to them, Leah was more than a little taken aback. It was not at all the traditional sort of painting she'd had in mind, and she wondered if she should reprimand Jean for allowing Nicole to talk to the painter at the café and then spend an entire day with him. Of course they'd been on the quay with people all around them. But still, Nicole was only thirteen and very impressionable.

She looked at the painting again. Though too *moderne* for her tastes, it was really not so bad, and it might grow on her. The colors were certainly brilliant enough to enliven any room, and it did seem to capture the mood of Paris, as Nicole said it was meant to do. Well, she'd find some place to hang it so as not to hurt Nicole's feelings.

As for Nicole, there was no question where the painting was going. On the largest easel in her studio where she could study it and be inspired—as well as enraptured—by it while she worked. Leah was quick to agree, so that problem was solved. Somehow she couldn't imagine it in the salon or the dining room.

Nicole continued to attend the village school, and with somewhat more enthusiasm now that she could spend every afternoon in her studio.

Chapter Eighteen

AFTER HER BRIEF HOLIDAY IN PARIS with Lady Westborne, Lisette found her life again confined to the château. The hoped-for invitation from Lady Westborne never materialized; instead, there was a letter saying she was unwell, but that she would love to see Lisette whenever she might happen to be in England.

"What do you think she means, Mama?" Lisette was disappointed by the obviously chilly tone of the letter.

"I have no idea, unless she really is ill. But I rather suspect there's more to it than that. Marital problems, perhaps. Or a lover has deserted her for someone younger and more attractive. The life she described to you is not always as idyllic as she made it sound. I'm sure that such a social whirl would be fun for a few weeks, but having to keep up appearances every day? I like Jane. I like her very much, but I think she's afraid of growing old. She can't accept that age erodes the one thing she's depended on for security— her youthful beauty and charm—and she hasn't developed anything else to take its place."

"But you're older than she is, Mama, and you're still beautiful."

"Thank you, Lisette. But that's just what I'm talking about. She's afraid to acknowledge that one can still be beautiful when one is older if in a different way. She's clung to her youth, and to younger men, and now they're deserting her. I saw what was happening when she was here. She was very fond of you, I don't deny that, but what she loved most was your youth. With you by her side, she'd continue to attract young people. I think she was sincere in wanting to give you a good time, and I'm sure you would have thoroughly enjoyed a visit to England, but you would also have been the nectar to keep the bees swarming."

Lisette had seen enough while in Paris to accept Leah's explanation. She still wanted to go to England someday and she would certainly make it a point to see Lady Westborne while she was there, but now she'd be more aware of her mentor's situation.

Despite her reluctance, she returned to the daily routine of the château, in the hope that pleasing her parents would make them amenable to her wish to marry soon. Mornings were devoted to lessons in English and French literature with Monsieur Balaine, while the younger children struggled over grammar, history, geography, Latin, and science. At least those childish studies were behind her. Not that she didn't find most of her own assignments boring. But then she read Dumas' *Dame aux Camellias* and learned that many operatic librettos were based on great works of literature. Music was still her great love; the piano was her release from an otherwise humdrum existence.

Two afternoons a week were spent with Monsieur Poirier, her new music teacher, an eminent professor from the conservatory. At one time it had been her dream to become a concert pianist in spite of the strictures against women performers. The happiest hours of the day were those she spent in the music room, whether actually taking instruction, or playing for her younger brothers' and sisters' Tuesday afternoon lessons with the dancing master, or merely practicing.

Since her stay in Paris, her dream of being a great musician gave way to the dream of being an eager participant in a giddy, whirlwind social life. Her appetite had been whetted; now she watched, ferret-eyed, for any opportunity to go into the city. Several times she reminded Leah of her promise about auditioning for the conservatory. She would enjoy the lessons, but more important, it would be an excuse to be in Paris, maybe even live there. Now, she could go only occasionally when Leah suggested she accompany her to the dressmaker or to some of the shops. And she began to find it intolerable having to play for the Tuesday dancing lessons.

"I don't know why I should always be required to play for Monsieur Garnier, that simpering fool," she complained. "Just because he is too stingy to hire an accompanist."

"Monsieur Garnier is no simpering fool, and you will kindly not use such language again," Leah scolded. "He is an excellent dancing master who is very selective about whom he teaches. He comes here because he admires your father tremendously. His older brother, who emigrated to New Orleans, fought in the Civil War when he might rightfully have returned to France, and he was killed at roughly the same time your father was wounded trying to prevent the Federal boats from entering the Mississippi."

"I'm sorry, Mama," Lisette said, backing down at once. "I'll be happy to play for him. But what about your promise that I could audition for the conservatory? Monsieur Poirier says I'm ready, and he is a professor there. Think how it would benefit me. I'd be able to play with the concert orchestra, listen to others, learn new techniques."

Leah smiled at her daughter. She knew how Lisette longed to break free, for at least part of the time, from the confines of the house. "I haven't forgotten. I'll talk to Papa this very week."

In spite of her occasional outbursts, Lisette had a sweet and gentle side to her. She never hurt anyone intentionally; also, in spite of her growing sophistication, she was a person who could be easily hurt herself. If Monsieur Poirier agreed she was ready for the conservatory, then Leah thought she should be allowed to attend.

Before any decision was made about an audition, however, Lisette began suffering from violent toothaches, and Baptiste took her to the dentist in the city. In spite of the pain, Lisette was delighted to learn the work would take several days and that Papa would stay in Paris with her.

Baptiste knew Lisette was trying very hard to hide the discomfort she suffered after each visit to the dentist. "Do you think it would ease the pain," he asked, "if we dined tonight at Chez Madeleine?"

"Oh yes, Papa." This would mean she could avoid both Céline's fussing over Armand's refusal to eat every last morsel and the business discussions between Jean and her father. She loved Jean, but she would never understand how he had settled so placidly into a family routine.

In the richly appointed restaurant, Lisette gazed around at the bejeweled women escorted by men in well-cut evening clothes. Papa always looked so fine in his, too, and she wished again for a train she could loop casually over her wrist when she walked outside and then sweep along the floor once she was inside. The restaurant, she thought, was her true element.

Seeing how happy it made Lisette to enjoy some of the pleasures of Paris, Baptiste left the office every day in time for them to go driving in the Bois in the late afternoon. During one such drive, their carriage passed another from which the occupants, a young and a middle-aged man, tipped their hats to Baptiste. Lisette was immediately captivated by the handsome young man smiling at her.

"Who are they, Papa?" She tried to keep her voice casual, but all the while her heart was pounding. Maybe this visit to the city would provide more than a cure for her aching teeth. Certainly she'd have to find an excuse to prolong the stay. Then she remembered she had an interview with the director of the conservatory the next morning. *Dear God, please let me be accepted. Then I'll be coming here at least two days a week.*

"Monsieur Duchalais, the banker, and his son Philippe. Our firm does business with them, and he has become a close friend."

"He is very handsome, Papa. How old is he?"

"Who? Monsieur Duchalais?" Baptiste smiled to himself. He knew whom she meant, but he wanted to tease her.

"Oh, Papa, you know perfectly well I mean his son."

"Twenty-four or five. And to answer the next question coming to your lips: No, he is not married."

Lisette was embarrassed to find herself blushing. "Does he drive here every day?"

"And rides in the morning."

"You'd approve of my seeing him? If, that is, he wanted to see me." At twenty-four, Philippe Duchalais would certainly be a very experienced man about town. He might not be interested in a girl from the country who hadn't yet turned twenty. Suddenly her face and figure, of which she'd been so proud, seemed like those of a child. Her bust never had developed as much as she'd hoped it would, and she had to keep secret from Mama the fact she stuffed some of her gowns with gauze.

She did, however, have a smartly styled riding suit, and she knew she rode well and looked good on a horse. Of course it wouldn't be proper for her to ride alone. Maybe she could persuade Papa to ride with her.

"I would indeed approve," Baptiste said. "The Duchalais are a fine and well-respected family. And from the expression on Philippe's face, I'd say he would very much like to see you again."

"Then if I'm accepted at the conservatory, will you ride with me some mornings?"

"I'll do more than that. I'll persuade Mama to come to Paris with us, and we'll have a small dinner party that will include Philippe and his parents. We'll invite a few others as well, so as not to make the intention too obvious."

"Papa, you are a darling. In spite of those sessions with the dentist, this has been a wonderful few days." Lisette lay back against the carriage cushions. To think she was going to meet a man as handsome as Philippe Duchalais! And perhaps he would be only the first of many.

Lisette was certain she'd fail miserably at the audition. She dressed with special care that morning, not so much to make a good appearance as to try to calm her shaking hands. She hoped she'd be told to sit down immediately at the piano and play. If she had to talk or answer questions, her tremulous voice would reveal her anxiety, and the director would then feel she lacked the poise and assurance needed to become a student, and ultimately, a graduate of the conservatory. She must not give way. She must show him she was capable of playing before the audiences that regularly attended concerts at the school.

Even though she'd eaten no breakfast, she was nauseous while she brushed her hair and felt certain she'd be sick before the end of the morning. Again and again she tried to arrange her hair in a large bun on top of her head, but it kept falling apart under her trembling fingers. She finally gave up and pulled it back with a ribbon.

Brother! I did so want to look mature and self-assured.

By the time she had on everything except her dress, her hands were shaking somewhat less, and she began to think maybe she was going to be all right in spite of the awful churning in her stomach. Then she tried to close the front of the silk jacket. It had a dozen small buttons that fastened with cord loops. Not one button would slide into its loop. In abject misery, she began to weep.

"What's wrong, Lisette?" Céline stood tentatively in the bedroom doorway. She knew Lisette didn't like her very much. These visits always made her very nervous for fear she'd do or say the wrong thing and find Lisette's eyes fixed on her. But she didn't hate Lisette. In fact, she had a secret admiration for the beautiful young woman who was everything Céline herself wanted to be.

"I—I can't get this dress buttoned," Lisette sobbed. "And I don't feel well at all."

"I know. You're nervous. Here, stand up and I'll fasten them for you. Buttons like these are always pesky. But the dress is perfect, and you look beautiful in it."

"Thank—thank you, Céline." Lisette reached for a handkerchief to blow her nose and wipe her eyes. "I'm not at all sure I can get through it."

"Of course you will. You play too well not to be accepted."

"You really think so?" It was nice of Céline to say it, but she could hardly rely on her judgment. After all, Céline had never been to an opera or a concert in her life.

"I never heard real music until I heard you play," Céline said. "I thought it was only something to dance to when there was a fête in the village. Then I listened to you. I didn't know there could be such music or such beauty. You'll do all right." She smoothed the jacket peplum over Lisette's hips. "Now, about that sick feeling. The trouble is you didn't eat any breakfast. I have some hot tea and croissants in the kitchen."

"I couldn't, Céline. I just couldn't. They'll come right back up."

"Nonsense. They'll settle your stomach. And you don't want it to growl while you're playing."

"No, I don't," and Lisette began to laugh at the thought of the director's face if the delicate music were accompanied by a series of gastric rumblings.

By the time she arrived at the conservatory, Lisette was feeling somewhat better. The food had settled her stomach, and her hands were shaking less.

"Now don't think about the music," Baptiste advised as they walked in. "You know this piece, you've played it enough to have it thoroughly ingrained in you. Let your hands do the playing, and one note will follow the other with no problem."

"I know, that's what Madame Thiery and Professor Poirier say. Never think about the next note or you'll get completely confused."

"Right. So let your mind dwell on something pleasant, and before you know it, you will have finished the piece and done splendidly."

"I hope so, Papa. I'll do as you say and think about something else."

Lisette was immediately relieved of one fear. She did not have to talk to the director. He merely nodded to the piano and asked her to play.

Something pleasant, she thought as she took time to settle herself comfortably on the stool. *Don't hurry. This is your moment. Pretend you are already a concert pianist and you're playing before an audience.* It was all very well to pretend that, but she was grateful her back was to the director. He told her that he'd listen to her first, then study her fingering and her style later.

Something pleasant. Her fingers went into the opening measure of the pavane. She'd chosen it for her first selection because it was light and not too difficult. If he asked for more, she'd play a more intricate piece. The pavane reminded her of the drive through the Bois, and then she thought of Philippe. He had looked so handsome sitting in the carriage beside his father. And his smile! She knew it was for her, not just a polite acknowledgment of Papa's nod. Tomorrow she and Papa would go riding in the Bois, and if they should be so fortunate as to meet Philippe, Papa would introduce them. In her imagination she was already riding beside Philippe and then dancing with him. What would it be like to feel his arms around her while they glided with other dancers to the strains of a waltz or pavane?

"Very good."

Only the voice of the director brought her back to the present and the realization she had finished the piece.

"You play with great spirit, Mademoiselle Fontaine. During this next selection, I would like to watch you more closely."

He was asking her to continue playing! That in itself usually meant a student was accepted. She was no longer nervous. It wouldn't even disturb her to have his eyes on her hands while she played. She began a Brahms concerto. Papa was right; her fingers played as if they and not her brain had memorized the notes. Certain passages had sometimes given her trouble before, but today, it was as if she had written the music herself. When she finished, she rested her hands in her lap. She'd never known such calm.

"Well done," the director said. "There is much work for you to do with your fingers and wrists. You sit a bit too stiffly. If you played an entire concert that way you would soon have a backache. But we will teach you the proper techniques."

"I'm accepted?" Lisette could scarcely get the words out, but she had to know.

"Yes. Professor Poirier is right. You will be a good student. I want you to return next week for a series of auditions with various professors to determine which one you will study with. Bring all your music with you. They will decide what they want to hear you play."

"Yes, sir." She'd been accepted! That was all that mattered.

"There is one stipulation you must agree to if you are to be a student here. Nothing—nothing, I say—must come between you and your studies. Your music must be all and everything. You will be on time for every lesson, and you will practice the number of hours a day required by your teacher. The first time you fail to appear for a lesson without extenuating circumstances, you will be dismissed. Do you understand what I am saying?"

"Yes, sir, and I won't fail. I promise."

"Very good. I will set up the appointments for next week, and will inform you of the times when you return on Monday."

Lisette would have liked to hug the elderly man, whom she knew to be a real martinet when displeased, but she remembered to dip into a respectful curtsy instead. He had neither screamed at her nor slapped her fingers with his walking stick as she knew he was wont to do. Still in a daze, she followed Baptiste down the long hall and through the front door.

"I'm proud of you, Lisette," he said while they waited for their carriage. "You played better than I've ever heard. You must have really been inspired by the director's presence."

Lisette said she was pleased he thought she'd played well, but she decided it would be better not to tell him that Philippe had been her real inspiration.

"Now, how about an ice or some pastries to celebrate?" he asked. "I'm sure you must be hungry, and I could eat something myself."

"Are you saying you were nervous, Papa?"

"Very. I haven't been so nervous since I asked Leah to marry me. It's hard enough to force yourself to do something. It's even worse when you're praying that someone you love will do well."

"You didn't think I could?"

"I know how good you are, but I didn't know how the presence of the director would affect you."

"It wasn't hard when I did what you told me to," Lisette said. " 'Think of something pleasant and forget about the notes.' " They turned into the pastry shop. "We *are* going riding tomorrow morning, aren't we? You do remember your promise?"

"I do and we will. Now, which of these confections shall we order?"

Lisette concentrated on the selection in the glass-fronted counter and said she would like coffee with hers.

Riding through the Bois the next morning, Lisette scarcely noticed that the trees were leafing out or that the waters of Lac Supérior were sparkling in the bright sunlight. She only knew it was a beautiful morning to be alive. Would Philippe be riding? Would he stop to talk after Papa introduced them? *What will I say if he does? Please don't let me be tongue-tied.*

They hadn't ridden far when she saw him approaching. And, yes, he smiled when he saw them.

"*Bonjour*, Monsieur Fontaine." Philippe Duchalais reined in his horse.

"*Bonjour*, Philippe. A perfect day for riding, isn't it?"

Baptiste indicated Lisette. "I would like to introduce my daughter Lisette."

"*Bonjour,* mademoiselle."

Philippe turned his horse around and moved alongside Lisette. Since the path was too narrow for three, Baptiste dropped back and watched with interest as the conversation continued between the two young people.

"Only two days a week?" Philippe said at length. "Too bad, I'd hoped we could meet and ride every morning."

"Next week I'll be here every day while I audition for different professors." Then Lisette took all her courage in her hands and stated as a fact what she was hoping Mama and Papa would agree to. "When my lessons begin, I'll probably spend some of the intervening days here, too." She was finding it easier and easier to talk to him—as long as she didn't look at him. Never in her life had she seen anyone as handsome. Why in the world had she ever been attracted to Georges LeClerc?

"Do you like the theatre?" Philippe asked.

"I love it. And the opera. I haven't gone often—living in the country—but I go whenever I'm in the city. And you?"

"Two or three times a week or more, if something especially fine is being presented."

Lisette was astounded. "There are that many different productions?"

"No, but when I see something I like," he paused and looked directly at her, "I never tire of watching it."

Lisette felt herself blushing under his intense gaze.

Realizing he must return to the office, Baptiste rode up beside them. "Afraid we have to go back, Lisette."

"Monsieur Fontaine," Philippe asked, leaning across Lisette's horse, "may I have your permission to call on Lisette next week?"

"We will be honored. I'll probably be at the office, but my daughter-in-law will be at the apartment to receive you."

"Thank you, sir." Philippe looked straight into Lisette's eyes, and she thought she was going to melt right then and there. "If I'm not being too premature, may I also ask permission to escort Lisette to the opera next Wednesday? It will be *Rigoletto.* We will go with my parents, of course, so Lisette will be well chaperoned. If you are going to be in town, naturally we would be delighted to have you join us."

"Thank you, Philippe, but I think I will have returned to the country. If Lisette wishes to go, she may."

"Lisette?" Philippe turned to her.

"I'd be delighted. I haven't seen that opera, but I'm familiar with some of the arias and have been wishing I could hear them performed."

"Excellent. And may I call on Monday afternoon?"

"I'll be looking forward to it." Almost too late, she remembered to act calm and poised. She'd nearly given herself away over the invitation to the opera.

"You feeling better, Lisette?" Baptiste asked after Philippe rode away. "You looked a little green around the gills there for a minute or two."

"What do you mean, Papa?"

"I mean, you didn't eat any breakfast this morning, and I was afraid you were going to pass out when Philippe spoke to you."

"I was not going to do any such thing. You're a terrible tease, you know that. I don't see how Mama puts up with you."

"Because I'm so handsome and she loves me."

Lisette started laughing. "I do feel better, but I didn't know my earlier anxiety showed quite so plainly." For the next few minutes they rode along, chatting about nothing in particular. Then Lisette said, "I hope my husband and I are still in love after twenty years of marriage."

"And you hope that husband will be Philippe?"

"Maybe, maybe not. I like what I've seen so far, but I want someone I can feel comfortable with, the way you and Mama do."

"I thought you didn't want to marry for love, just be married so you could be free to do as you pleased."

"No, I can see that Lady Westborne is not as happy as I thought she was when I first met her. I want to live in Paris and enjoy all it offers, but I'd rather do it with my husband than have to worry about keeping a lover or finding new ones all the time."

"My, my, Lisette, you sound like quite a woman of the world. When did you acquire so much wisdom?"

"You're teasing again. But you do admit I'm right."

"I do, and I hope you find just the right man for you. If you feel he is, we will no doubt approve." At nineteen, Baptiste thought, Lisette was far wiser than her mother had been. Catherine had thought only of snatching from life everything that took her fancy, with no thought of how her actions affected other people. He hoped nothing would happen to Lisette to turn her into a greedy, self-serving person like Catherine.

When Philippe came to the apartment on Monday afternoon, he stayed only the brief time that etiquette demanded of a first call. He was polite and gracious to Céline, who was nominally his hostess, and he complimented her on the cakes and coffee she served. It was Lisette, however, who held his gaze and to whom he directed as much of the conversation as courtesy allowed. He had decided the first time he saw her that he was going to marry her. She was beautiful, which his own love for perfection demanded. She was young enough that her mind and her opinions could still be molded to please him. When they'd met again in the Bois, he was reassured that his first impression had been correct. For all her seeming poise and sophistication, she was still extremely naive and would willingly come under his tutelage. She no doubt had had a strict upbringing and was used to obeying her father. She would very naturally transfer that obedience to her husband. Yes, she would be the perfect wife, adoring and unquestioning. With her by his side, he would be the envy of every man in Paris.

Lisette tried very hard to keep from staring at Phillipe while he was talking to Céline, and she was not unaware of the way his eyes kept returning to her the whole time. It made her a little uncomfortable, and she wondered if something were wrong with her hair or her dress. Yet, even as he spoke to her, he was smiling, so she could only assume he enjoyed looking at her. He was bound to be a bit uncomfortable talking to two almost total strangers, although Céline was doing very well in keeping up her part of the conversation. Things would be better when they spent the entire evening together at the opera, even if his parents were with them.

When Philippe left, he held Lisette's hand just a little longer than necessary, and she could swear he squeezed it just before he finally released it.

"Until Wednesday night," he said, loudly enough for Céline, who was still in the salon, to hear. Then in almost a whisper he added, "You cannot know how much I'm looking forward to it."

"I am, too," Lisette whispered back.

Yes, Philippe thought, *I'll court her for a reasonable length of time and then ask for her hand. She's going to be the wife I've been looking for.*

During the next few weeks, Lisette felt as if she'd been whisked bodily from the mundane world of the château to a magic kingdom, where every wish was granted and every pleasure was within reach. The auditions went smoothly, and she was assigned to Professor Clare for two hours of lessons a week. She was at first disappointed that it was not Professor Poirier with whom she'd been studying for nearly two years, but he comforted her by saying it was time she worked with someone who could teach her new techniques. She'd learned all he could give her.

The night at the opera with Philippe and his family had Lisette feeling as if she were moving through a dream. Monsieur and Madame Duchalais were as easy to be with as her own parents, and there was never an awkward lull in the conversation. She was embarrassed by Philippe's extreme attentiveness: He helped her with her wrap, assisted her into the carriage, pulled out her chair in the box, and hovered close at all times. She found herself saying "thank you" until she began to feel like a mechanical toy. Yet, with all this, one thought kept running through her mind: *I'm with Philippe. I'm actually spending an evening with him,* and all that could make her happier than she was now was to see him again.

"Philippe tells us you are quite a musician," Madame Duchalais said during supper, at the fashionable restaurant they'd gone to after the performance of *Rigoletto*.

"I'm a student at the conservatory, yes, but I've only begun my studies there."

"Perhaps you would have dinner with us one evening and let us hear you play."

"I'd be delighted to." At least there was one more evening to look forward to.

"Would you be able to dine with us on Thursday next, Lisette?" Madame Duchalais then asked.

Thursday she would be returning to the château after her second lesson of the week. She could delay her return, but the better part of wisdom told her to pretend she had other plans.

"I'm afraid Thursday is not possible. Wednesday perhaps?"

"Wednesday is fine," Madame Duchalais said. "A week from tonight then. We shall be looking forward to hearing you."

Another advantage of Wednesday, Lisette thought, was that it was twenty-four hours sooner than Thursday.

Life now seemed like a carousel ride, complete with color, excitement, thrills, and music. Sometimes Lisette thought she'd never catch her breath, and yet she didn't want it to stop. Although she spent only three full days each week in the city, between Philippe and the conservatory lessons she had little time to rest. And, unfortunately, little time to practice, so he had to devote most of her hours in the country at the piano. As much as she thought she loved Philippe and as certain as she was that he would eventually ask her to marry him, she wasn't yet ready to give up her music.

Almost every morning when she was in the city, she and Philippe rode in the Bois, and then she returned to the apartment to practice or, if she'd been up late the night before, to rest. Tuesday and Thursday afternoons were her music lessons. As time went on, she began to approach them with greater trepidation. She knew she was playing well, but she feared she wasn't making any strides forward. She would simply have to work harder while in the country to overcome the weaknesses of which Professor Clare could so caustically remind her.

The evenings at the theatre, the opera, or at home with the Duchalaises were enchanted. Although she'd fallen in love with Philippe at first sight of him, her feelings grew deeper and stronger each time she was with him. She'd been immediately attracted to him because he was handsome. His medium height and slender build were less imposing when he walked beside her than when he rode a horse or sat erect in a carriage, but his face, especially his very large eyes, were spellbinding. Brown hair framed his finely drawn features, which in a certain light were so delicate as to be ascetic, and his large brown eyes had a mystical quality. Nor did his personality belie this impression. He was quiet and reserved, even moody at times, as if lost in his own thoughts.

Because they were almost always chaperoned by his parents, Lisette was not aware of just how quiet Philippe was until she noticed that while he would answer a direct question, he seldom expressed an opinion or initiated a conversation. Gradually she began to wonder what it would be like, should they marry, when they were alone.

Perhaps he was intimidated by his parents, who were

naturally convivial and outspoken. Monsieur Duchalais reveled in seeing the funny side of any situation, and his wife laughed loudly and exuberantly at everything he said, even when some of his jibes were aimed at her and her love for gossip. It occurred to Lisette that perhaps Philippe, more taciturn and introspective by nature, became even more subdued in their presence.

Yet even when they were with people other than his parents, Lisette began to feel as if Philippe were holding himself in, afraid to speak for fear of revealing something about himself he did not want her—or anyone else—to know.

But I love him. If it is his nature to lapse into long periods of silence, I can live with that. At least he is very gentle and considerate.

The few times they were alone, usually when riding, Lisette would steer the conversation toward his work at the bank, and he would become quite voluble about his ambition to follow his father as its president and his desire to have a home of his own. That was probably the clue, she thought. He did feel intimidated by his family, and things would be different if they married.

Leah and Baptiste saw Philippe several times when they were in the city, and their approval of him was obvious.

It was during a Thursday morning ride that Philippe made the request Lisette had been waiting for.

"Do you think it would be convenient for me to drive out and see your parents on Sunday?" They had been riding side by side; he reached over and took her hand, something he never did except after the lights dimmed at the theatre.

"I think they would be very pleased to see you. I'll tell Mama as soon as I get home this afternoon."

"Your father will be there?"

Lisette's heart was beating rapidly, and her mouth had become dry. "I'm sure he will be. He seldom goes anyplace without Mama. But I'll make certain he will be."

This is it, Lisette thought. *He is going to ask for my hand. No one could possibly be happier than I am right now.* She'd scoffed when Leah suggested she marry for love. How foolish she'd been! All thoughts of freedom or going to England or having lovers vanished when she looked at Philippe and knew he loved her. She was a little disappointed that he didn't propose to her before speaking to her father, but then he'd been properly brought up. It didn't really matter. His request to visit was the same as a proposal, and she continued to let him hold her hand until the ride ended.

Chapter Nineteen

LISETTE LOOKED AT HER WEDDING GOWN lying across a chair in Leah's sewing room, the room she'd used to lay out her wedding finery and pack her trousseau. Her own room, as usual, was strewn with discarded dresses, torn petticoats, and worn-out shoes. Denise was going through them now to see what she could salvage for herself. Practical Denise. What a waste of time it was when Papa would buy her anything she wanted.

Of candlelight silk, the wedding gown had been designed by Worth along the simplest lines. The tightly fitted bodice and waist flowed into a graceful skirt. Chiffon filled in the low-cut bateau neckline and rose to a high, stiffly boned collar fitting snugly around her throat. The bodice and skirt had a delicate overlay of ferns and ivy embroidered in pearls and brilliants. In a few minutes Mama would be in to help her put it on. On a table lay Mama's diamond tiara that would hold her five-yard-long veil in place. She hadn't believed it when Mama said she should wear it.

"But, Mama, don't you want to wear it at the reception?" she'd asked.

"No, darling. It's your day, and I want you to be the happiest, most beautiful bride there ever was. Then Denise and Nicole will wear it, too, on their wedding days."

She would be beautiful today. Lisette could hardly wait to see Philippe's face when she walked down the aisle on Jean's arm. Papa would be up front waiting for her, but the long walk was too much for him. Or so he'd said. But Lisette knew it was because he feared his awkward gait and crutches would mar the perfection of her appearance. Bless Papa's heart. She'd insisted at first that having him beside her was more important than appearances, but Mama had shaken her head. Finally Lisette had deferred to his wishes.

Lisette touched the silk of the dress, then felt unexpectedly frightened. In a few hours she would be Madame Philippe Duchalais. It was what she'd dreamed about for weeks, but now, suddenly, she was beset by doubts. Did she really want to be married? Or did she even love Philippe enough to spend the rest of her life with him? In many ways he was still a stranger. They'd ridden together; they'd gone to the theatre; they'd dined with each other's families. But they'd never been alone, not really alone. She had no idea of his everyday likes and dislikes, and she feared she'd displease him by expressing her own. Thank goodness she didn't have to worry about keeping house or cooking, since they'd have both a maid and a cook. But, oh, she wasn't ready to be a wife, to assume the responsibilities of running an apartment and pleasing Philippe.

Coming from Denise's room where she'd been helping the younger girls into their bridesmaids' gowns, Leah was distressed to find Lisette crying. Nicole had been so excited she was nearly hysterical, and Leah had had to calm her down and then find a vial of smelling salts for Nicole to clutch in her handkerchief. Now here was Lisette in tears.

"What is it? Are you ill?"

"No, Mama, just—oh, Mama, I'm so scared. I don't know whether I want to be married."

"Now, now, you love Philippe and he loves you. You're suffering from the flutters every bride experiences."

"No, I'm really frightened. I keep trying to imagine what marriage will be like, and I can't."

"Just like living with the family, the usual day-to-day routine. You're not sailing to some strange country."

"It seems strange to me. I don't know Philippe like I do the family. And when we'll be alone—"

"Is that what's frightening you? Don't worry, it will all come very naturally. At least you won't be ignorant like most young brides. I wouldn't let you go into marriage not knowing what to expect. Your wedding night may be—well, a little awkward, but soon everything will be easy and wonderful."

"I don't mean that, Mama. I know you've told me what I need to know. It's the thought of spending the rest of my life with Philippe and having enough interests in common and things to talk about."

"My darling, don't worry about the years ahead. Take it day by day. You'll have enough things to keep you occupied and to talk about. His work, your music. The things you enjoy doing together. Philippe is a fine young man, and it's evident he wants only to make you happy."

206

Lisette stood on tiptoe and kissed Leah on the cheek. "Thank you, Mama. I'll remember that."

"Now—do you think you're ready to get dressed? The carriage will be around in less than an hour." She knew what had Lisette worried. Maybe it was a mistake for young people to remain so closely chaperoned after they were engaged. They didn't really get to know each other until after they were married. At least this marriage hadn't been arranged as so many of them were. Lisette and Philippe loved each other, and that made all the difference.

After the wedding in the village church, the two families returned to the château for the wedding breakfast. Leah looked at Philippe and Lisette sitting at the head of the table, and thought about what Lisette had said earlier. Philippe was a fine young man, but he was extremely reserved. Nor did he ever reveal anything about himself. She didn't know him any better now than when she'd first met him.

Suddenly Leah wondered if the marriage had been his idea or his parents'. The Duchalaises were an old, established family in Paris, and she had been somewhat startled when they accepted the engagement so quickly. In spite of Baptiste's wealth, the Fontaine name was decidedly inferior to that of the banker, who was related to some lesser nobility. True, France was a republic now, but that didn't mean that former nobles had relinquished their titles or begun to consider themselves commoners. Leah was suddenly smote with the thought that perhaps all was not well at the bank and Baptiste would be called upon for more than the already generous dowry he'd bestowed on Lisette. No, that was foolish thinking. She was suffering from an overdose of the same flutters she'd soothed away in Lisette.

Late in the afternoon, the house and the gardens were filled with friends from Paris, the surrounding towns, and the nearby countryside. Tables of food were placed on the terrace and under marquees erected on the lawn. For an hour Lisette and Philippe stood in the hall to receive the best wishes of their guests; then they mingled among them in the garden.

As soon as Lisette had seen Philippe smile at her when she walked up the aisle, she'd felt her fears subsiding. From the moment they left the church, Philippe never let go of her hand, and she wondered if he, too, had been unsure of his feelings before the wedding. They were married now, and whatever problems they'd face would be worked out. She smiled up at him, and her heart turned over when he squeezed her hand.

"Would you like to dance?" he asked her.

They had danced together only once before, at a ball given for them by the Duchalaises after their engagement was announced. Lisette remembered how she'd felt being held in his arms as they waltzed around the room. It was the closest they'd ever come to an embrace. How much more reserved Philippe was than Georges LeClerc! Georges would have found any excuse to get her alone and kiss her.

The village band had been playing lively folk tunes, and now the orchestra from Paris began to play a waltz. The wooden platform between two marquees was then cleared of dancers to allow Lisette and Philippe to dance the first waltz alone. Lisette, who had never minded being the center of all eyes, knew they made a handsome couple. With her train looped over her wrist and her veil gathered over her arm, she felt she could dance until morning. Other dancers joined them, but then, all too soon, Philippe suggested they slip away to change and leave for Paris.

"This is it, Mama," Lisette said as Leah helped her into her going-away suit. "I'm actually leaving here and going to my new home."

"Be happy, darling. I think Philippe was very wise to suggest you postpone your wedding tour until he could get enough time for a long cruise to Greece."

"I think so, too, Mama."

"No more flutters?"

"No. Well, not too many, anyway."

"Good." Leah gathered Lisette into her arms. "You're a married woman now, and I promise I won't deluge you with lots of unwanted advice. But—Papa and I will always be right here."

"I know, Mama. Thank you." If there had been a time when Lisette thought she hated Leah, those feelings had long since vanished. She loved Leah and would always cherish the closeness that had developed between them.

Much to her later chagrin, Lisette fell asleep in the carriage during the ride to Paris, not waking up until Philippe shook her gently and said they'd arrived at the apartment.

"I'm so sorry, Philippe. I don't know what happened to me."

"That's all right," he said quickly. "I understand."

She'd expected him to be cross, but instead he was as gentle as always.

Philippe unlocked the door to the main entry, and they went up one flight to the door of their own apartment. The building contained four apartments, and theirs occupied two floors to one side of the wide, communal stairway. Inside, there was a narrower staircase connecting the living area with the bedrooms; Philippe led the way up.

Thank heavens they had separate dressing rooms, Lisette thought, after Philippe checked to make certain all her bags had arrived and that her clothes had been put away by the maid.

"I'll see you in a few minutes," he said, and Lisette sat down on a small boudoir chair before undressing. She was shaking, and she wondered if she'd be able to unfasten the buttons and hooks on her suit and all the ribbons on her undergarments. Nonsense, there was nothing to be flustered about. Mama had said everything would happen naturally once she and Philippe were in bed.

Lisette opened the door of her dressing room a crack and peered out cautiously. Good, Philippe had not come in yet. After tying her peignoir loosely around her waist, she stepped into the room and tried to decide where she should be standing when he came in. No place seemed right. Finally she sat at the round table near the window, where she pictured them having breakfast every morning, but that wasn't right either. When she heard him coming down the short hall from his dressing room, she pulled off her peignoir, threw it across the foot of the bed, and slipped between the sheets. That was the way she should be: sitting in bed waiting for him.

Lisette was surprised to see Philippe in a casual suit rather than nightshirt and robe.

"Aren't—aren't you coming to bed?" She tried to keep her voice from quavering.

"No, you're tired. I thought you'd rather sleep alone tonight."

"I'm not, Philippe, really I'm not. I don't know why I fell asleep in the carriage, but I feel completely rested now."

"Yes, Lisette, you are tired, more tired than you realize." His voice was still soft, but there was an almost hypnotic quality about it, as if he were commanding her to fall asleep.

"I'm not feeling very well," he continued, "so I'm going out for a short walk. Don't worry, I won't disturb you when

I come in." He bent over and kissed her lightly on the forehead. "I'll sleep on the day bed in my dressing room."

When Philippe had stood at the foot of the bed and looked at Lisette lying back against the pillows, he'd thought her very beautiful. With her blonde hair and delicate features, she was like a piece of rare porcelain or a painting by Watteau. She was his now. He had acquired her in the same way he'd acquired the rare antiques and tapestries that filled the apartment. No one else would ever possess her, and all men would envy him.

He wished he could love Lisette as he knew she wanted him to, but he couldn't. He loved someone else much too passionately to be unfaithful. Perhaps he'd been unfair to Lisette, but she was the perfect foil to keep his affair secret. He hoped she was too naive and innocent to know what usually took place on the wedding night. She'd probably been told no more than to submit to her husband. Well, she would, but in a far different way than most brides did.

Long after Philippe had gone out, Lisette lay in bed, angry and frustrated. Then her anger turned to despair, and she began to weep into the pillow. She remembered what Mama had told her after Papa had discovered her with Georges in the summer house. And what she'd told her just before the wedding. With Georges, Lisette had sensed that something more should follow all the caresses, and now that she knew what that something more was, she couldn't understand Philippe's reluctance to make love. What was it Mama had said? "There are times when men cannot, but you must make no comment. It would hurt their pride."

This must be one of those times, she thought, forcing herself to believe it. She'd heard him shut the downstairs door into the common hallway and then listened for the sounds of the outside door. She'd heard nothing. Maybe he had changed his mind about the walk. He must have come right back up and gone quietly to his dressing room. But tomorrow would be different.

After all the guests had gone home and she'd retired to bed, Leah could not get to sleep. It was not Baptiste's gentle snoring that kept her awake. Since he always fell asleep before she did, it had become like the rhythm of his breathing and the beating of his heart; it was a most natural accompaniment to the few solitary, reflective moments she had before she, too, dozed off. This was her time for sorting out the day's events—like tucking them away in their own pigeonholes—and doing a bit of thoughtful organizing for the next day.

But tonight there was something that would not stay tucked away.

The wedding had gone beautifully. Even Philippe's parents had been impressed with the simple ceremony in the village church—in spite of their wish to have it in their own, larger church in Paris—and with the reception at the château. The weather had been fair, the garden in full bloom. Lisette had made an enchanting bride, modest yet glowing. Her happiness was obvious enough to be almost tangible. Philippe had beamed with pride and the desire to protect and cherish her.

Leah looked at the bedside clock. Lisette was probably a real wife by now. Was that what was keeping her awake? No, she had prepared Lisette well—as well, that is, as one can prepare a virgin. But Lisette loved Philippe and seemed ready to consummate that love. And surely he would be as gentle with her in bed as he was in every other way. They were two young lovers who, after all their shared excitement, needed only to be alone together. To explore, to learn, to share, and to exult in their love for each other. They would think it unique, unlike any that others had known.

Leah touched Baptiste, and her love for him surged through her anew. *Yes, such love is unique,* she thought, *because each couple's love is unlike anyone else's. It is what they begin with and what they create through the years.* She prayed that Lisette and Philippe's love would become mutually reassuring and supportive, while always remaining exciting and stimulating. Like an embryo, it should grow and stretch with each day's needs.

Baptiste turned and threw one arm over Leah. Everything would be all right, she thought, and laughed to herself. It was she—not Lisette—who was suffering from wedding night jitters.

Philippe had already left for the bank when Lisette awoke and rang for breakfast in her room. No, said the maid Yvonne, there was no message from Monsieur Duchalais except that he would be busy all day but home in time to dress for dinner and the theatre. So that was how it was to be. By herself all day until dinner, when Yvonne would be standing by to serve them, out in public with him in the evening. Lisette donned a simple day gown and went down to practice her music. She'd taken a leave of absence from the conservatory during the weeks of preparation for the wedding, but now that she'd have her days to herself, she hoped to return to her studies there.

Before she began to practice, she went into the kitchen to check with the cook about dinner.

"Yes, madame," Eloise said, "everything is ready. I've already finished the shopping. Monsieur Duchalais planned the menu, and he informed me he will be giving me menus for a full week each Monday from now on."

"Monsieur said that?" Lisette was too taken aback to say any more.

"Yes, madame, he said he wanted to relieve you of the more tedious duties."

"I see. Thank you." So she wasn't even to supervise running the apartment. She certainly wasn't left with much to do.

She walked into the salon. Two days before the wedding, Philippe had brought her to this apartment he'd chosen for them. She'd walked with him through the rooms. From entry hall to her dressing room, everything was perfection. Not a detail had been overlooked—carpets, furniture, draperies, lamps, paintings, and accessories. She was delighted with his selections, and yet she'd felt she was walking through someone else's home. Like any young bride, she'd looked forward to furnishing her first home, and she couldn't help feeling a deep disappointment at not having selected a single piece. The only things that belonged to her were the toilet articles on the dressing table and the pictures of her mother. Two things consoled her: first, the magnificent grand piano that was Philippe's wedding gift to her and, next, the obvious pleasure he took in showing her the apartment. Perhaps she was being petty to fret over having no say in the furnishing of their home. He wanted it perfect for her, and it was. Yet one thought kept nagging at her. If the piano was a gift to her, then everything else in their home belonged to him. They were his, not hers.

"Are you pleased, Lisette?" he'd asked.

"It's beautiful," she'd said, convincing herself she was selfish to begrudge Philippe his pleasure in planning the rooms.

Now she went over to the piano and ran her fingers over the keys. She took out some of her music, and, except for lunch, practiced for the rest of the day. When Philippe came home, they went upstairs to dress for dinner, then went together to the dining room.

"How was your day at the bank?" Lisette asked when they were seated at the table. There had to be some way of starting a conversation.

"As usual. Nothing out of the ordinary. And what did you do today, my pet?"

Unconsciously Lisette shivered at his term of endearment. He sounded like a master speaking to a lap dog. She was not a pet to be fed and pampered and then ignored when he had other things to do. Or was she being overly sensitive after last night?

"I stayed at the piano most of the day. There were a number of pieces I hadn't worked with in a long time, and I found I'd gotten sluggish."

"Very good," he said. "I've decided you may continue with your studies at the conservatory. It's a proper accomplishment and will keep you from being bored. You can practice during the day, and I'll enjoy listening to you play in the evenings when we're at home."

"Yes, I'd planned to return to studying with Professor Clare." She decided it was time to assert more of her independent spirit.

"But only with my approval, I trust."

Under his sardonic gaze, Lisette cringed inwardly. For the first time she actually felt afraid of Philippe. "Of course, I wouldn't want to do anything you didn't approve of . . ."

"I don't think you quite understand, Lisette. You are to have my approval before undertaking any new project."

With a shock, Lisette now realized she was expected to submit to his complete domination, to acquiesce to his every wish. She knew that was the way with many marriages, but things had always been so different between Papa and Mama that she wasn't prepared for this. She didn't take easily to being dominated, but she would have to stifle her anger until she could find a way to ease out gradually from beneath his authority.

During the next few days, Lisette began to see Philippe as a frightening enigma. When they were with others, he was as gentle and considerate as always. He was so much the doting bridegroom that Lisette wanted to scream when she saw other people smiling at them. She knew people were thinking that she and Philippe were an ideal couple. He led her to their seat in the theatre box; he made certain she was warm enough or cool enough; he brought her refreshments at intermission. He hovered over her constantly, as if protecting her from a harsh wind or the unwanted attentions of others. She saw the glaring ferocity in his eyes when male friends of his spoke to her. They frequently rode together in the morning as they had before they were married. They didn't talk then, but if someone he knew were near them, he looked at her as if there were no other person he wanted to be with.

How different it was when they were home. Seldom a word between them except when Yvonne was serving a meal. Lisette was alone all day, yet she had no privacy. She soon learned that all invitations and letters—even those from home—were opened and read by Philippe before he gave them to her. He decided which dinners and other events they would attend. They seldom spent an evening at home together. When they were not going somewhere together, he usually excused himself and said he would be out with friends. Most baffling and frustrating of all was that he had not yet come to her bed. And he no longer offered any excuse.

One night Lisette lay awake longer than usual, wondering if Philippe were impotent. That would account for his irritability and quick flashes of temper, as well as his need to possess and dominate every aspect of her life other than the physical. Mama had tried to explain impotence to her, but she was still not exactly sure what it meant, only a man could not be a real husband. If that were true of Philippe, did it mean she'd never know what it was like to be loved? Then why had he married her?

She pounded her pillow, buried her face in it, and wept. The thought of Georges holding her close stirred up memories of the exquisite yearnings that had set her body tingling. The thought of how eagerly she'd responded to him made her ache all over now that she knew what might have followed, which was what she should be enjoying in this bed with her husband.

She wouldn't have any children, either. Not that she really looked forward to being pregnant. Mama had had such a dreadful time with Robert. But once you were married, you were supposed to have children, and people would think it strange if she didn't. They might ask questions, and how was she supposed to respond?

Sometimes it's temporary, she recalled Mama saying about impotence, and a wife should be patient. For how long? They'd been married more than a month. Would it be weeks or months more? Or forever?

214

Then she was stricken with a new thought. Perhaps impotence wasn't the problem; perhaps Philippe didn't love her. As impatient as he'd been to marry her, he'd never actually said "I love you." That was it. She had merely inferred from his smiles and the way he touched her—seeming so proud and possessive—whenever he could. True, he had kissed her, but only to brush her cheek or forehead with his lips. Never like Georges had, but she'd thought it was out of respect and propriety.

Why did he marry me if he doesn't love me? Lisette started crying again. *Or why not sleep with me?* Many marriages were not based on love. Like Lady Westborne's. And there were many others she'd heard about.

Did he perhaps have a mistress whom he really loved but could not marry? If that were the answer, if Philippe had married her for appearances, perhaps urged to do so by his parents, then she, Lisette, would have to win him over. She recalled some of the alluring and seductive wiles Mama had told her about. She'd tried none of them, thinking that being Philippe's wife was enough. Evidently it wasn't. She had an idea, and tomorrow night she would put that idea into action. Tomorrow night she'd make herself irresistible. She was sure now she knew what—if not who—her competition was, and that was challenge enough to stir her blood. She might be young and the other woman more experienced, but she would show Philippe what he was missing by not making love to her.

Philippe had to love her. She loved him so much it ached to think her love wasn't returned.

The next day, they spent one of their rare evenings at home. After dinner, Lisette played the piano while Philippe read the papers. At least he enjoyed listening to her and was usually complimentary about her playing. He was also in a more pleasant mood than usual.

"If you'll excuse me, Philippe, I think I'll go up to bed."

"Fine. I'll be going out in a bit anyway." So far Lisette had uttered no complaint about being left alone every night. He wondered how much longer that would last. She was not stupid. She might be ignorant of some things, but she must at least know that most husbands and wives slept in the same bed. And soon there would be questions from her mother about whether or not she were pregnant. As much as he dreaded it, he would have to make up his mind to tell her the truth, or to sleep with her if she insisted. Which was

215

worse, he wondered, to be unfaithful to the one he really loved or to risk losing his wife and have his secret known?

After going upstairs, Lisette left the door open between her dressing room and bedroom. She filled her bath water with fragrant oils, and she lathered herself with lavender soap. She waited anxiously, hoping the water would not get cold before he came up to give her his customary chaste goodnight kiss. Soon she heard his steps on the stairs, then heard him enter her room. He stopped when he saw her in the tub, but before he could turn and leave, she stepped out covered only by aromatic soapsuds. As seductively as she knew how, she reached for a towel. Philippe took in the picture at one glance. Lisette's pale, wet skin gleamed iridescently in the candlelight. Her blonde hair was piled high in captivating disarray with damp tendrils clinging around her face and neck. Her small but perfectly formed breasts invited him to come and touch. Any other man would have picked her up and carried her to the bed. Philippe looked and felt nothing.

"Sorry, Lisette," was all he said, "but you have neither the talent nor the—endowments for seducing me." He turned abruptly and left.

Lisette threw the towel across the room and then flung herself on the bed. How could he be so indifferent and so cruel? What did he want in a wife? What did his mistress have that she didn't? Or what could his mistress do that Lisette could not? If it were not a mistress, if he were impotent, he wouldn't leave every night. No, someone—or something—was taking him away from her, and she had to find out what it was. There must be some way she could learn who her rival was and be better able to compete. If she followed him some night? It would be difficult. She'd have to keep herself invisible, but it could be done. Between her desperation over his abandonment of her and her determination to find a way to follow him, she got little sleep that night.

As was her habit, Lisette sat down to the breakfast Yvonne set at the small round table in front of the bay window in her bedroom. Before now, she'd never felt particularly lonely eating by herself, but this morning she was bereft of everything that made life important. She was buttering her second roll when she heard someone opening the door.

"May I join you, Lisette?" Philippe asked as he walked in.

"Yes—yes, please do. I'll ring for Yvonne to bring more rolls and a fresh pot of coffee."

"No need. I've already eaten. I wanted to talk to you. About last night."

Lisette had been startled enough at his sudden appearance. Now she found it impossible to say more than, "Yes?"

"I'm sorry. I don't know what else to say except—I'm sorry."

Lisette saw what seemed to be a plea for understanding in his eyes, and she waited until she could speak calmly before asking, "For marrying me or for humiliating me last night?"

"Both. The marriage was a mistake. I knew that as soon as I asked your father. But it was too late then. Everyone was so pleased, and there were certain pressures—"

"From your familiy?"

"Yes."

Lisette took a deep breath and swallowed several times to keep from crying. She must not cry. "You love someone else, don't you? Someone you can't marry."

"I wish to God I didn't, Lisette. I wish I loved you. But I don't."

"Not even a little—just enough to make me your wife?" Love wasn't all-important in marriage. Maybe it would be enough that she loved him; perhaps she'd be able to know a certain satisfaction from sleeping with him and eventually having children who would love her.

"No—not even that."

"Then why did you marry me? Why did you choose me?" She could no longer control the tears. "Why put me through these weeks of torture?"

"I don't know, except that you're very beautiful, and I wanted you to belong to me. I had some foolish notion it wouldn't matter to you if we didn't consummate the marriage."

"You thought I would be ignorant of what it meant to be married?" What a wasted conversation this was—talking about something they should be enjoying.

"Or grateful I didn't force myself upon you."

"And you love your mistress so much you can't be unfaithful to her by being a husband to me."

"Until now, Lisette. We'll dine at home tonight, and I promise I'll do all I can to make up for the hurt I've caused you. You are my wife, and I don't want to lose you." He reached across the table for her hand, the first loving gesture he'd made in private since they were married. "You have a lesson today?"

"Yes."

"Then I'll leave you to your practicing, and I'll see you tonight."

After he was gone, Lisette couldn't stop the tears, but now they were tears of relief. Everything was going to be all right at last. She still had a rival, whom Philippe loved more than he did her, but with time she might be able to win him away. Especially if there were children. Once, she'd dreaded pregnancy; now she longed for it.

Philippe hadn't been lying when he said he didn't want to lose her. She was too important to him, not only for her beauty and her talent, but as the mask to hide the real passion that had him in its grip, the real reason he had to leave the apartment every night. For Philippe was compelled to go to someone who could give him what his body had first craved and now demanded. He knew he was in thrall to a vice that might someday destroy him, would surely make him an outcast if the truth were known, but he didn't care. The pleasure of the present moment far outweighed his fears for the future.

Until his marriage to Lisette he had lived at home. When his parents began to question his being away until late every night, he knew he had to get his own apartment. They, however, would not hear of his leaving. After all, their house was big and he was the last unmarried child. He knew then the only solution was to get married and have his own place. He'd met no one among his family's friends who seemed suitable as a wife; then, most fortuitously, he met Lisette and her father. He knew she'd be the perfect wife and the ideal hostess for the entertaining he planned to do to advance his political and business ambitions. Too late, he realized he would have to leave her every night. But Lisette would be less demanding than his parents. He would not have to account for his actions to a wife the way he did to them.

Now he also realized he would have to be a husband to her, if he were to continue with his charade and hide the truth from her. It would take all his determination to make love to her. By evening his craving had become almost unbearable, and he wondered if he would be able physically to carry out the act with Lisette. But if he kept in mind the

218

fact that he could leave immediately afterward, another half-hour would make no difference.

Dinner went off well. Lisette described her lesson at the conservatory.

"And I'm to play in a recital in little more than a month. My first public appearance, Philippe, and I'm quite frightened. The others are more advanced than I am."

"You'll do it well. I'm proud of you."

"Shall I play for you tonight before—before we go upstairs?"

She knew why she had played so well that day. A whole new life was opening up before her. She was going to be Philippe's wife in more than name only. And once she learned what pleased him, he would come to love her.

"I'm sorry, Lisette. I meant to tell you earlier, but just as soon as we've eaten I have to leave for Marseilles on business. I've ordered the carriage for eight-thirty so I can catch the night train."

"How—how long will you be gone?" No, she would not cry. He was not intentionally discarding her this time. If it were business, he had to leave. And he would be back. There would be other nights.

"At least three days. So you'll have all the time in the world to practice without having to worry about pleasing me."

"But I like doing things to please you."

"Then study hard, and you can begin making plans for having your family in for dinner soon after I return."

"Thank you, Philippe." Until now, he'd turned aside any mention of having her parents dine with them. And he had indicated quite clearly he wanted her to issue no other invitations to their apartment without his prior approval.

When he was ready to leave, Lisette moved to kiss him good-bye. She moved in close enough that he had either to put his arms around her or leave them hanging at his sides. She clung to him as long as he let her, but she was not unaware there was no physical response of any kind from him.

All during the day, Philippe had tried to put himself into the mood for making love to Lisette. Finally, in desperation, he told his father he would make the trip to Marseilles to handle some bank business that was to have been taken care of by one of the other officers.

"I'd rather have you go than anyone else, Philippe, but are

you sure you want to leave that beautiful bride for so long?"

"She'll understand, Papa, and I think it's important that I go. It will be hard to leave her, but three days is not forever."

"Fine. And when you return, the four of us will have dinner together."

"We'll look forward to it." Philippe breathed a sigh of relief. It had not been as hard as he'd feared. There were plans other than business ones to make for the stay in Marseilles, and he put his mind to those immediately.

Chapter Twenty

UNLESS INVITED, Leah seldom went into either Henri's workshop or Nicole's studio. To her, the rooms seemed the ultimate in disorder and confusion, but the children insisted everything was just where they wanted, and nothing—*nothing*—was to be disturbed.

"But they have to be cleaned sometime," she argued one day. She looked at Henri, who was covered with oil and heaven-knew-what-kind-of-grime from head to toe, and then at Nicole, who was so paint-splattered she looked like a clown.

"Why?" they chorused.

"Because—well, just because I'm sure they need it."

Nicole threw up her hands in despair at the ignorance of some people. "That's no reason," she said, and stalked off.

"Mama," Henri said more calmly, "those rooms are not like the rest of the house. If I cleaned the workshop today, it would just be messed up again tomorrow."

"And I could say the same about the rest of the house. How would you like to eat at a table that's never been dusted or cleared of dirty dishes?"

Henri grinned. "As long as I didn't have to eat off those dirty dishes, it wouldn't bother me."

"Oh, go along with you," Leah laughed. "I know when I'm licked. All right, I won't insist on getting in there with a pail and scrub brush, but you must promise one thing. There

220

must be nothing left around to cause a fire. I won't have you endangering the rest of the family."

"Mama, I'm not that foolish. When are you coming in to see the latest thing I'm working on? Come on now and bring the tad with you." He pointed to Robert, who was clutching Leah's skirts.

"All right. I'm curious to see what all that banging has been about."

When she walked into the workshop, Leah did her best to overcome her dismay at all the batteries, wires, motors, and other paraphernalia. "So what is the latest great invention?"

"It's not that great, Mama, but it is a challenge. I'm working on a miniature railway to run from the river to the house through the secret tunnel."

"Why?" Leah was amused. "What possible use could there be for that?"

"None, really. But, as I said, it's a challenge. I thought about it years ago when we went in there to rescue Nicole. It's easy enough for companies to make huge steam locomotives, but to miniaturize them is something else. I'm experimenting with both batteries and gasoline motors. So far I can't decide which is the most practical or which would run the longest, since they do have to be small. I have some of the track laid. Want to see it?"

"No, thank you, Henri. I don't think I care to go into that tunnel." She saw her youngest out of the corner of her eye. "Robert! No, don't touch anything."

"He's all right, Mama. He comes in lots of times to watch me. He knows what he can touch and what he can't. But you will ride on my train when it's finished, won't you?"

"Well, I'll see. But I make no promises. Now I'd better go talk to Nicole. She left in a huff, and I need to smooth things over. I wish she were as easy to talk to as you are. Come, Robert."

"Let him stay, Mama," Henri said. "He won't be in the way."

"You're sure?"

"Positive. He's a great little helper and good company. Aren't you, tad? How about getting me that small spool of wire we were using yesterday?" Robert ran across the room and brought back exactly what Henri wanted. "See, Mama, I can't do without him."

"All right. Just don't let him get hurt." Leah picked up her skirts so they wouldn't drag on the floor, then saw it was unnecessary since Henri kept the floor scrubbed clean. *He's a better workman than I gave him credit for,* she thought as she left the room.

Leah knocked tentatively on Nicole's door. Sometimes her daughter answered; other times she was so deeply engrossed in her work that she seemed unaware of anything beyond her own little world.

"Come in." The voice was neither welcoming nor forbidding. "Mama! What a pleasant surprise. You haven't been in here in ages." How like Nicole. Furious one minute at the suggestion her studio needed cleaning up and in the next minute, as pleasant as one could wish for.

"I know. I thought I'd like to see what you've been working on. It's been quite a while since you brought us a finished picture to hang."

"Well, as you can see," Nicole waved her arm around the room, "I've been trying out several techniques."

Leah saw half-finished watercolors, pastels, and oils. Even her ignorant eyes could see that Nicole had been experimenting with different styles—realism, impressionism, and some strange-looking ones she couldn't name.

"Trying to find your own?" Leah asked.

"Something like that."

Leah saw her looking over at the painting by the man named Van Gogh. "You admire him very much, don't you?"

"Yes. There's something about his work—I don't know what—that—is really magnificent. I start on a painting or drawing and then look at his and I'm disgusted with myself. I can never hope to be the artist he is."

"Give yourself time, Nicole. You're still so very young. And I think you do really fine work. You should finish these family portraits you started. I know Lisette would love to have hers in her apartment."

Nicole's face clouded over, and Leah knew at once she'd said something wrong. But whether about the portraits or Lisette, she didn't know.

"If you'll excuse me, Mama, I'd like to get back to work. I have an idea about how to get the feeling of more light into this one."

"Of course, dear. Lunch will be ready in about an hour."

"I'll see. I may be too busy," Nicole said and turned her back, as if dismissing her mother and all thoughts of food.

Nicole did not show up for lunch, and Leah brooded all afternoon about her youngest daughter. Each day Nicole seemed to grow taller and become more and more a physical

222

duplicate of Leah herself; in other ways, though, she was completely different. In spite of Nicole's usually placid exterior, Leah sensed an inner turmoil. And it was more than frustration over her inability to find an appropriate style for herself as a painter. Nicole had real talent, and she knew it. It was something much more serious than that. There was something about Nicole that could not compromise with reality. Leah feared there would be much trouble and heartbreak for Nicole unless she and Baptiste could get to the source of her problem and help her in some way. She would have to talk to him about it.

For the next few days, Leah watched Nicole closely whenever she could and often reviewed the conversation they'd had in the studio, trying to discern what had made Nicole's face cloud over so suddenly. Leah had said Lisette would love to have the portrait of herself for her apartment. When Robert was born and Denise began caring for him, Nicole had felt deserted and run away. Eventually, she'd turned to Lisette for comfort. The bond between the two had grown amazingly strong. Leah wondered if Nicole were suffering the same pangs of desertion since Lisette's marriage. It had never occurred to her, now that Nicole was older, to worry about her daughter's running away again. Yet that's just what she was doing—running to her studio and to her painting, burrowing deeper and deeper into a tunnel of her own making. But would she also seek a new way to express her insecurity this time?

The answer came the next afternoon. Leah was in her sewing room and Baptiste in his office when they both heard the unmistakable sound of shattering glass. Leah's first thought was that something had blown up in Henri's workshop, which was followed immediately by the fear he might be dead or seriously injured.

For a brief instant, Baptiste sat immobile in his chair. "What the hell was that!" he shouted.

Leah and Baptiste met in the sunroom, and Leah pushed his chair out the door toward the one leading into Henri's workshop. There was no smoke and his windows were intact. At the same time, Henri came running out.

"What in blazes does Nicole think she's doing?" Then he pointed at his sister, who was standing nearby holding a rock in her hand.

As they all watched in horror, she threw it toward the last of the unbroken windows, and they ducked instinctively as glass flew in all directions.

223

"Nicole, what's wrong with you?" Baptiste started propelling his chair toward her.

Instead of answering, she glared at him and walked into the house and up to her room.

"You'd better go upstairs with her," Baptiste told Leah.

"Not yet. I want to look in the studio." She opened the door and walked in, followed by Baptiste and Henri. Her heart sank.

Every painting, every drawing, had been carefully and methodically slashed from corner to corner. Leah looked at the paintings and wanted to cry. Here was the work of weeks destroyed in one afternoon. At first, she was especially upset that the family portraits, which Nicole had been so proud of earlier, were now ruined. Then she was more disturbed that Nicole had destroyed the pictures she was working with to find her own natural style.

Strewn over the floor were tubes of paint, brushes, trays of watercolors, and other paraphernalia. All had been squeezed, broken, or stomped on. Leah looked toward the corner where Nicole had placed the painting by Van Gogh so it would catch the right light. It remained intact, a solitary sentinel over the destruction in the rest of the room.

"What in God's name got into her?" Baptiste demanded.

"I don't know, and I doubt we ever will," Leah said. "I'll go upstairs now, but I don't think she'll see me. All I can do is let her know I'm there if she needs me."

As she'd expected, Leah found Nicole's door locked. Nor was there any answer when she tapped gently on it. She could hear Nicole crying hysterically, and she felt as if her own heart were being torn apart. She placed a comfortable chair next to Nicole's door and asked that her dinner be brought up to her.

It was Denise who carried the tray. "I've brought dinner up, Mama, but I think you ought to come down and eat with us."

"No, dear, I want to be here if she comes out."

"I don't think she will. Not until morning. She's done this before."

"You mean had hysterics like this?"

"Often, though not so bad as this. Sometimes she lets me in, and I'm able to quiet her."

"She's turned back to you then," Leah said quietly.

"A little. Enough to let me sleep with her when she's upset. But it's Lisette she misses now."

"I thought so. But she more than misses her."

"I know," Denise said. "Nicole has a desperate fear of being deserted. And I feel so guilty because it's all my fault. When Robert was born, I mean."

"But she got over that," Leah said. "Or seemed to."

"Because she had Lisette. Now she's not sure of anyone."

"That's not normal, Denise. In families people come and go all the time."

"But that's Nicole, and all we can do is try to understand her."

Leah looked at her middle daughter in amazement, the dependable daughter who never caused any trouble, who smilingly went her own way. How had she become so wise for her years?

"You're right, Denise. I guess we have to try a little harder."

"You go downstairs now, Mama. I'll eat the dinner I brought up and stay here until Nicole lets me in. She will after a little bit, and then everything will be all right."

Leah let Denise stay, but she knew everything was not going to be all right. They could learn to cope with Nicole's problem, but only the girl herself could find the means to accept life as it was. And Leah could only hope it would not be a means that destroyed her.

The next morning Nicole came downstairs to breakfast and greeted everybody cheerfully. She chatted throughout the meal and then excused herself to go to the studio. In another minute she returned.

"Well," she asked impatiently, "isn't anyone going to help me clean up that mess?"

"No, Nicole," Baptiste said calmly. "You did it, you clean it up." He was just as upset over Nicole's actions as Leah, but he was determined not to let his daughter know. She would have to learn he was not going to allow her fits of temper to upset the entire family.

Leah agreed with Baptiste, all the while deeply concerned that the mess in the studio was but a foreshadowing of future messes that only Nicole would be able to clean up.

"Go to hell, damn you!" Nicole screamed at them, and ran out of the room.

"I'll go help her," Denise said, rising from her chair.

"No, you won't," Baptiste ordered. "She has to learn she can't depend on anyone else to lean on or sweep away her problems. First it was you and then Lisette. She has to learn she was born into this world alone, and she has to go it alone if she's to find any happiness. And," he turned to Leah, "as much as she loves her art, you've got to stop her from running off to that studio and staying there all day whenever something upsets her. She's just running into another tunnel and hiding. She's got to come out and face the world."

"I'll do what I can," Leah sighed.

"And I'll help," Denise said. "I want to go into St. Denis for some things. I'll ask her to go with me."

Later in the morning, Denise walked into the studio. Nicole had been working hard. The broken windows were stuffed with old rags, and the floor had been swept. What had been paintings and sketches was now a pile of rubbish in one corner.

"Want to ride into St. Denis with me?" Denise asked. "I'm going to look at material for new curtains for my room."

"You're always redoing that room. Let me have the old ones for in here, will you? I don't know when Papa will replace the broken windows, and there's a draft."

"You can have them. But—you want to go with me?"

"Yes. Maybe I can find some of the things I need to start painting again. I really should go into Paris, but I don't know how soon I'll be able to."

"You want money for more paints and canvases?" Baptiste sat back in his chair and pulled on his cigar.

"Yes, Papa. I have to start all over."

"And why do you have to start all over?"

"You know why." She clenched her fists. This was ridiculous; he knew what had happened. "The ones I had are ruined."

"And who ruined them?" he asked, calmly and slowly.

"I did." Instead of hanging her head as he'd expected, she glared at him.

"And so I should provide more money to replace what you destroyed. Do you think that's fair?"

"Oh, Papa, you've plenty of money." She was getting impatient.

"That's not the point, Nicole, and you know it. I have enough to provide for all our needs and for many pleasures. But for *new* things. Not to replace willful destruction."

226

"I'm sorry, Papa, I don't know why I did it." That was what was causing this violent headache. She didn't know why she'd done it.

"Artistic talent is one thing, and I'm proud you have it. But artistic temperament—if in fact that was what caused you to destroy the studio—is something else, and you'll have to learn to control it. And you will learn that I will not tolerate waste. Is that understood?"

"Yes, Papa." Nicole turned to leave.

"Wait, Nicole. I'm going to give you the money, but you'll have to earn it. Agreed?"

"Yes, if it's something I can do."

"You can do what I have in mind. I want you to spend more time with other members of the family, like Denise and your mother. Learn a little something about household affairs from Denise and help your mother with Robert. You might also help her in the garden. You love beautiful things; you should enjoy working with the flowers. I'm not going to forbid you to go into the studio, but I am going to limit your time there to a few hours a day. And bring some of your friends home. You used to, and I miss seeing them around here. Do you think all this is asking too much of you?"

"No, Papa, as long as I can still keep on painting."

Nicole rubbed her hands across her eyes. She knew she'd been wrong to ransack the studio, and she wondered what had come over her to make her do it. Sometimes she was unaware of doing things until after they were done. Like that wild picture of the garden. She'd gone into the studio to work on one of the portraits, and the next thing she knew she found herself in front of another canvas filled with garish splashes of color. And yesterday. Not until Mama and Papa and Henri called to her did she realize she'd broken all the windows in the studio, and she'd been shocked this morning when she went back and found the ruined pictures. She shouldn't have yelled at everyone when they wouldn't help her, but she was frightened. These periods of acting without knowing what she was doing were occurring more frequently all the time, and she never knew what would bring them on.

She supposed this last one had started coming on when Mama mentioned Lisette's name. Maybe Papa was right. If she spent more time with the rest of the family, she might not have these strange periods when she was completely lost to the real world.

227

"No one wants to inhibit your creativity, Nicole," Baptiste said. "You have genuine talent, and we want you to pursue it. But you need to realize it is not the only thing in life. All right now, no more lecturing. Go shopping with Denise and have a good time."

The change that came over Nicole was like a miracle. She and Denise were as close as they'd been before Robert was born, and, wonder of wonders, she began to play with Robert every day and seemed genuinely to enjoy herself. She would never be as domestically inclined as Denise, but she puttered about in the kitchen with her whenever Blanchette allowed it, and she agreed to let Denise help her redecorate her bedroom.

At times, Leah actually thought she heard Nicole singing while she painted, but the change did not completely dissolve her fears that her daughter might retreat again into her moods if something really upset her. Maybe another trip to the city would help. Nicole had enjoyed her one stay with Jean and Céline. Or she might like to stay with Lisette and Philippe. Not right away, of course. They were still in the honeymoon stage and wouldn't welcome an overnight guest. But in a few weeks. She'd talk to Lisette before she suggested it to Nicole. At least one daughter was happily settled with the man she loved, and Jean seemed equally content with Céline and his work. Leah breathed a sigh of relief. It was good to know there were two she didn't have to worry about.

Chapter Twenty-one

AFTER PHILIPPE LEFT FOR MARSEILLES, Lisette wandered around the apartment. She picked up the new novel she'd bought some days ago, but it was so boring she couldn't concentrate on it. She went upstairs to the bedroom and spent some time experimenting with various hairstyles. That soon palled. One thing she could do would be to go through Philippe's wardrobe and make certain all of his soiled linens were ready for Yvonne to give to the laundress in the morning. When Lisette had complained that Philippe gave her nothing to do for him, he'd laughingly said she could make certain he always had enough clean linen and socks. He'd meant it as a joke, but she'd taken him seriously. It made her feel she was being at least a little bit useful.

It was his habit to fold his soiled linen and place it on a chair in his dressing room so that Yvonne would take care of it when she cleaned every morning. He didn't know that Lisette had taken over this duty, carefully checking his shirts to make certain he hadn't left his cufflinks in and looking for any stains requiring special care.

Lisette picked up the shirt he'd worn the day before, removed the cufflinks, and opened the cuffs. A small scrap of paper fell out. It contained only four words: "Marseilles, yes. Same location." They were like a knife in her heart.

So it was not business that took him to the south of France. He'd made that up in order to be with his mistress. Even if there were business to be taken care of in Marseilles, he was also planning to meet her there.

Worse than the knowledge he was with another woman was the thought that the trip might have been planned even before he'd promised to spend the night with her. How easy it had been to promise when he knew he wouldn't be at home. He was despicable!

Well, two can play at this game, Lisette thought. She threw his shirt on the floor, knowing how he cringed at rough treatment of his precious wardrobe, and ran to the writing desk in her room. A short note would do it. She wrote it quickly, sealed the envelope, and rang for Yvonne before she could change her mind.

"Yvonne, please take this and mail it right now. I want it received early tomorrow."

"Yes, madame. It should arrive in the morning mail."

Only after Yvonne left did Lisette begin to have qualms. Maybe she was being foolish. Maybe the note wouldn't have the desired result. Or if it did, would she know how to handle the situation? She picked up the discarded novel. Boring or not, it would take her mind off both her present misery and the worry over what tomorrow night might bring.

The next evening, Lisette went carefully through her wardrobe selecting and discarding. She finally chose a provocatively demure dress. The answer to her note had come in the afternoon mail.

While she bathed, dressed, and put up her hair, she thought about Georges LeClerc. He would be with her in less than two hours. They'd met a few times, at social events, after the disastrous episode in the summer house, and although she'd refused his proposals, they'd remained friends. Lisette wasn't sure just how he could help her, but at this point she needed some assurance she was an attractive and desirable woman.

Having told Yvonne she could leave for the night, Lisette went downstairs to answer Georges' ring herself.

"Good evening, Lisette." He looked a bit mystified, but his smile gave no hint of the real wonder he felt at being invited to call. "Is Philippe here?"

"No, he's out of town. Come in. If you want to fix yourself a drink, there's everything you need on the table over there."

"Thank you. I think I will. And you?"

"A little wine, please. In that crystal decanter."

Under Georges' quizzical gaze, Lisette found she couldn't come right out and tell him why she'd asked him to come over. She sipped her wine and asked how things were going now that he was in business with his father. Finally, she grew anxious to come to her point.

"Georges, am I beautiful? Am I attractive at all?"

Georges put his glass down and slid forward in his chair. "That's a strange question coming from you, Lisette. You need only look in the mirror to answer that."

"Please don't tease. I've always thought I was beautiful, been very vain about it, in fact. But am I—am I attractive to men, I mean?"

Georges was no fool. He'd certainly made his own feelings clear to her and there'd been all the other young men who'd swarmed around her even before she put on long skirts. She must know she was attractive. There was more to the question than appeared on the surface.

"What are you trying to say, Lisette?" But he already suspected what it was.

In spite of herself, she burst into tears. "I've never been so miserable in my life. I've been humiliated and debased. Vanity? I wish I could be vain; instead, all I can do is despise myself for being something less than a woman."

She looked at Georges, who was staring at her, bewildered and unsure of how to calm her. "I guess all I can do," she said, "is blurt it out. There's no easy way to say it, but

230

I've—I've never slept with Philippe. I'm married, but I'm not a wife."

"My poor Lisette. That bastard! I thought maybe he—" He didn't finish the sentence. "There's nothing wrong with you. You are a very beautiful, very desirable young woman."

"Then why does he leave me every night to go to that mistress of his? The woman he says he loves so much he can't love me. I think she lives right here in this apartment house because I never hear the outer door close. I've tried everything—I'm not ignorant anymore. I've humbled myself until I've destroyed every bit of pride I once had. He's with her now. Gone to Marseilles for three days. On business, he said. But I know she's with him."

"Please, Lisette, stop weeping. And listen to me." He tried to sit beside her and take her in his arms, but she got up and walked toward the window. All he could do was follow and stand directly behind her. "It's not a mistress that takes him away. It's a lover."

"A lover?" Lisette turned around in confusion. "I—I'm not sure I understand." Then just looking at him, she was struck by the truth. "A lover! Another *man* is my rival?" Then she was nothing more than an actress in a farce of Philippe's making! Suddenly it all struck her as so ludicrous, she began screaming hysterically, "A man! My God, I've been trying to compete with a man!"

"Calm down, Lisette. Here, drink this brandy. I know it's a shock, but nothing that can't be remedied."

Lisette suddenly became very cold and matter-of-fact. "How do you know?"

"He's managed to keep it a fairly well-concealed secret, but I have reasons for knowing. A friend of mine was Philippe's first paramour, and he committed suicide when Philippe told him the affair was over. He left me a note telling me all about it while asking me to say nothing for the sake of his family. When Philippe and you became engaged, I assumed he'd changed and wanted to resume a normal life. I'm sorry I had to be the one to tell you, Lisette, if you love him."

"Love him! Do you think I'm mad?" There was no way she'd let Georges know just how much she did love Philippe or just how deeply she'd been hurt. She could only hope the lie would allow her to keep some of her pride.

"Then why did you marry him?" he asked.

"An entrée into society. He is charming and witty and

intelligent, as well as handsome. But why—why would he marry me?"

"I told you: to hide the truth. He's an ambitious man; he wants to remain socially acceptable, to put a lie to the rumors. How better than to marry a beautiful young heiress whom any man would be proud to have as a wife." Georges looked around the room. "He loves beautiful things and he's very proud of his possessions. So—in marrying you, he acquired another desirable *objet d'art*. Be careful. He's a very jealous man where his acquisitions are concerned. I'm sure he appears to others as an ardent and loving husband. But I've seen him display the same love and affection for a fine painting or a piece of rare porcelain."

Oh, how right Georges is, Lisette thought. His words restored some of her lost vanity, but did nothing to ease the pain of loving Philippe. She'd been used, and that was humiliating as well as painful.

"Thank you, Georges. I don't know what I'm going to do now that I know the truth, but I'll find some way to straighten out my life."

"Then let me help you." He put his hands lightly on her shoulders.

In another minute she was in Georges' arms and letting him kiss her as he had that afternoon in the summer house. The pressure of his arms felt wonderful, and to respond would be to release all the anxiety she'd been keeping inside all these weeks.

But this should be Philippe holding her, not Georges. She wanted Philippe. She began crying again.

"There, there, Lisette. It's going to be all right." Now he was smoothing her hair with one hand and unfastening her dress with the other. Just as she realized he was leading her toward the couch, another thought occurred to her at the same time. She pushed him away.

"You lied to me, Georges. Everything you've said tonight has been a lie. It's not true what you've said about Philippe. Maybe he does have a mistress, but not a lover. You said all those horrible things to make me hate him enough to get me for yourself. You want me as much as you did that day in the summer house. How could you? How could you be so despicable?" *I'll get Philippe to love me yet,* she vowed.

"Believe me," he insisted, "I haven't lied to you. Every word I said is true."

"No, you're just angry because I wouldn't marry you. And when I told you about Philippe and me, you thought I would rush into your arms and take you for a lover. Maybe I've been fooled by one man, but I'm not going to be fooled by another."

"I'm sorry, Lisette, if you can't face the truth. But if you ever need me again, I'll come to you. Not as a lover but as a friend."

"Get out! And don't worry, you won't hear from me again. You're no friend of mine."

Lisette slammed the door behind Georges as he left. Men! They were no more than lascivious beasts just waiting for a girl to fall into their arms. And Philippe with his crazy ideas about honor for a mistress but none for his wife. Well, she hadn't lost yet. She'd fight her rival with every bit of cunning, every nuance of seduction Leah had taught her.

Philippe returned from Marseilles late in the evening and went straight to his dressing room. Tonight was his to do with as he pleased. Tomorrow he must again play the doting husband while he and Lisette were with his parents. He knew Lisette had heard him come in, but he was hoping any contact with her would be brief. Instead, just as he finished shaving, she came into his dressing room without knocking, something she'd never done before. She was dressed in a sheer gown that revealed every curve, every aspect of her body.

"Welcome back, Philippe. Weren't you coming in to let me know you were home?"

"I'm sorry. I have an engagement, and I'm late as it is."

"I thought you already had a prior engagement. With me." The sight of his slim muscularity as he hastily wrapped a towel around himself made her whole body ache. She loved him and she wanted him. She wouldn't care how many mistresses he had if only he would love her, too.

"Not tonight, Lisette."

"Not tonight? Will it be any night?" Amazed at her own daring, she snatched the towel away from him and wrapped her arms around him. "Please, please make love to me. Just this once, at least. I don't think I can bear it if you don't."

"For God's sake, Lisette, where is your pride?"

"Pride? Is that what a wife is supposed to have? I thought it was love. And I do love you. I don't care if you have a mistress or if you took her to Marseilles with you. I don't ask you to give her up. Just love me a little and be a husband to me. You must have felt something for me to marry me."

"Felt something for you? What I felt was a need to be married—to someone. And you happened along at the right time. Now get out! What I feel now is revulsion. You have no idea how your actions disgust me."

"Disgust you? Because I want to be your wife? Is there —is there something wrong with me?" Lisette hesitated. Maybe Georges had been right. "Or with you?"

"There's nothing wrong with me that a night away from you won't cure. As for Marseilles, we'll never mention that again. Now leave so I can finish dressing."

Angry and distressed, Lisette returned to her own room. She still didn't believe Georges; he was either mistaken or he'd been deliberately untruthful. The thought, however, didn't make her feel any better; in fact, she was more distressed than ever. The simple truth was that Philippe did not love her and never would. She was doomed to be a married virgin for the rest of her life. Unless. Unless she followed Lady Westborne's example and took lovers. Once she'd thought that was exactly what she wanted. But not yet. She wasn't ready yet to follow that path.

Incensed at how Philippe was forcing her to think like this, she determined to avenge herself in some way. When she heard him leave his dressing room and go downstairs and out the door, she had an idea. It was such perfect revenge for his behavior, she couldn't keep from laughing out loud. She would have to dine alone, with only the dull novel for company, but as soon as Eloise and Yvonne left for the night, she'd carry out her plan. Oh, how Philippe would hate her. He'd rant and rave, and she'd just laugh at him. How she'd laugh. He'd say mean things, but he'd never hurt her, not physically. He was cruel and arrogant, but he'd never strike her.

As soon as she knew she was alone, Lisette went down to the kitchen. There she searched the cupboards for what she wanted. It took two trips, but anticipation of the shock and consternation on Philippe's face made all the effort worthwhile.

She pulled all his suits out of his dressing room wardrobe, spilled open the drawers where his shirts and other linen lay so carefully folded, and arranged his shoes and boots in a neat row in the middle of the room. Then, quite methodically, laughing all the while, she poured meat sauce, vanilla, milk, vinegar, and melted butter all over everything. The *pièce de résistance* was the partially congealed roast beef gravy that she spread carefully over his new formal evening suit. In an additional fit of pique, she twisted all his ties into knots. Then she sat back and grinned at her handiwork. As proud as he was of his finery, this would show him exactly what she thought of him.

Carefully, she replaced every empty bottle, jar, and dish in the kitchen and returned to the novel that wasn't as dull as she'd first thought. At least the characters entertained her more than her husband did.

Lisette was sitting calmly at breakfast when Philippe stormed in.

"What in God's name possessed you to do that?"

"I'm sure I haven't the faintest idea what you're talking about."

"You know damn well what I'm talking about. They're ruined. Every single piece of clothing I own is ruined. I should kill you."

"But you won't. And you know why? Because I'm much too valuable to you. How would you keep your little secret if I weren't here to hide behind?"

"You mean my mistress? It's no crime for a man to have a mistress."

"A mistress?" she asked quite calmly. "Or is it a lover?" Maybe Georges had been right, after all. She felt calm and prepared to accept any of the possibilities.

Now it was Philippe's turn to be shaken. How in hell had she found out? "You want the truth? All right, I'll tell you. But—you won't ever reveal it, and you'll remain as my wife."

"Are you quite certain of that?" She didn't feel nearly as confident as she sounded. An annulment would not be impossible, but it would be quite difficult since the Church required proof and legal documents to substantiate that the marriage had not been consummated. And if he should make love to her, even once, which he might do to thwart such plans, all hopes of an annulment were destroyed.

"I am," he said, "because if you don't, your father will be ruined. Our bank holds notes for a business venture not going too well, and if I call them in, he'll be bankrupt."

Lisette didn't know whether or not he was lying, but she dared not take the chance. "All right, I'll say nothing and I'll remain here, but I can't live any longer without knowing why I can't be your wife in every way."

"Because you're a woman, and I despise women. I have a lover, not a mistress. Do you hate me?"

"No more than for the way you've treated me these past weeks."

"Do you want to take a lover?" He lounged against a chair.

How easily he says it, she thought. *Sloughing me off onto someone else as if I were a worn-out toy. Except I'm not a toy, and I'm still brand-new.* "I don't know. You've scarcely given me time to think.

"Well, don't. I forbid it. You're mine and I never share what belongs to me." He turned to leave. "By the way, we're going to the opera tonight with my parents. And have you asked your family to dinner?"

"Yes. Wednesday night."

"Good. Then we'll behave as if nothing were wrong between us." With his commanding tone he might have been speaking to one of his underlings at the bank.

Actually, the evening at the opera went better than Lisette expected. As usual, Monsieur Duchalais dominated the conversation, and all Lisette was expected to do was laugh or nod or put in an occasional word. The opera was *La Bohème,* one of her favorites, and when she wept at the end, no one knew it was for her own tragic life, not Mimi's.

Philippe had given her a small nosegay of miniature gardenias to wear on her cape and to hold during the performance. How touched she once would have been at his thoughtfulness. Now it was only a pose. Their cloying, sweet perfume was overpowering in the warm theatre, and she feared she'd be sick. Never again would she be able to enjoy what had once been a favorite flower. Philippe was, if anything, overly attentive, and she wanted to scream at him to stop play-acting and leave her alone.

"The evening went well, I think," Lisette said, only to relieve the gloom of silence that surrounded them when they got home.

"You didn't smile enough," Philippe scolded. "You should smile more. It's expected of a new bride."

"And is there any reason for me to smile?"

"You have this beautiful home, furnished just for your pleasure, a carriage with a fine pair of matched horses, and a wardrobe any woman in Paris would envy."

"And would they envy me my husband, too?"

"Some would, yes." He started down the hall, then

turned around. "By the way, I would prefer it if you ceased taking lessons at the conservatory. I've decided I would rather you didn't appear in a public recital, and I don't approve of the people you associate with at the conservatory."

"No! It's not fair to ask me to give up the one thing that makes me happy. You promised I could continue, and you said you were proud of me."

"I've changed my mind. There's no more to be said about it. Good night."

Lisette was now more distraught than ever. She'd counted on her music to keep her from losing her mind completely and to give some meaning to her life. If that were taken away from her, she didn't know how she'd get through the long days and nights. She enjoyed playing for her own pleasure, but it had been the lessons and the recital that made the hours of practice meaningful. Now she risked being completely overwhelmed by the tedium of living in a house where she was not allowed to take care of even the smallest detail. She would simply have to find a new interest to occupy her time, something that was a challenge and demanded use of her mind as well as filling up the hours.

Luckily, for two days she was busy preparing herself for her parents' visit. Philippe's parents might not see anything amiss between them, but Mama was much more observant. There would have to be more than smiles and tender gestures. There would have to be genuine rapport, and that would not be so easy to simulate. Her eyes would give her away if nothing else did, and how could she look at Philippe with wifely affection when in her heart frustrated longing and bitter hatred were battling for control?

Philippe, of course, had chosen the entire menu without bothering to ask if her parents had any particular likes or dislikes. But since his taste in both food and wine was impeccable, it was likely to be a fine dinner.

Wednesday morning, Lisette went for a short walk to the pastry shop to indulge her love for hot chocolate and éclairs. She had both in her own kitchen, but she had to get out of the apartment if only to prove she was free to leave whenever she wished. Philippe had already sent word to the conservatory that she would no longer be a student there, and she couldn't bear to look in the direction of the building where she'd spent so many pleasant hours.

When she returned, the salon and dining room were

237

filled with bouquets of flowers. Philippe had taken care of that. They had already been arranged in his crystal and silver vases, so she'd been denied that pleasure, too.

At least she could dress herself. So far that had not been taken away from her. She spent the afternoon selecting her gown and arranging and rearranging her hair. While bathing, she heard Philippe come in and go to his dressing room, so she knew it would be little more than an hour before her parents arrived.

How she yearned and yet feared to see them. She would have to act as if nothing were wrong and quell her longing to pour out to them how miserable she was.

"Mama! Papa! How wonderful to see you."

"Hadn't you better let them in, darling, before you smother them?" Philippe's voice was so gentle and soothing, she could scarcely believe it belonged to the same man who had ordered her to stop her music lessons.

"Yes, yes, of course, but I can't believe I'm finally welcoming you to my own home."

Leah looked around the salon. "How lovely it is. This is truly one of the most beautiful rooms I've ever seen."

"Philippe deserves all the credit," Lisette said, managing to smile at him. "He has such perfect taste."

"But you were the inspiration, my love," Philippe said. "It reflects your beauty." He turned to Baptiste. "Would you care for a cigar, sir? I believe these are your favorite brand."

"So they are. How observant of you. Thank you."

Yvonne came in with aperitifs, and Lisette felt the situation easing while they drank and chatted casually. Philippe could be a most amiable person when he felt like it, as he evidently did tonight. Thank heavens.

The dinner went off smoothly. At least superficially. When they rose to return to the salon for after-dinner coffee and brandy, Philippe went to Lisette's chair and put his hands on her shoulders. But he squeezed so tightly, she wanted to cry out from the pain of his fingernails.

"We apologize," he said, "for waiting this long to have you here. But Lisette is so beautiful and popular, we have yet to spend an evening alone."

How ironic, she thought. *He lies and tells the truth at the same time.*

"I hope you're not getting too tired, Lisette," Leah said. "Every night out can become very wearing."

"No, Mama, I get plenty of rest during the day. Philippe is so considerate, he breakfasts alone and lets me sleep late every morning."

Leah, however, had noticed the hint of tears in Lisette's eyes. Nor was she blind to the tension around her daughter's mouth. Maybe there was a good reason. She remembered how she frequently had felt close to tears during her first weeks of pregnancy, and she wondered how soon Lisette would know for certain and tell them. Then she looked again. Lisette was a good little actress, but she couldn't mask the sorrow in her eyes. Something was wrong—very wrong—in this exquisite apartment.

In truth, Lisette had all she could do to keep from crying while Philippe did everything possible to impress her parents with what a loving husband he was. It would have been better if he'd been snide and sarcastic.

While Philippe and Baptiste were deep in conversation about banking and the stock market, Leah asked Lisette about her music. When she saw her daughter involuntarily clench her fists as she explained that she was too busy to go to the conservatory anymore, Leah decided it was time to speak.

"Now that we've spent such an enjoyable evening here with you, it's time for you to return the visit. How about this weekend? You know the others are longing to see you."

Wondering if Philippe had heard her mother's invitation, Lisette held her breath. Thoughts raced through her mind: Would he agree to spending a night or two in the same bed with her? Or be away from his lover for those two nights?

Philippe had heard Leah. "Thank you, Madame Fontaine, but I'm afraid that would be impossible. Our evening calendar is filled." He turned to Lisette and saw immediately how dangerous a refusal was for their little farce. "We could come out for the day on Saturday. I know Lisette misses all of you, and perhaps a whole day with the family will ease her homesickness a bit. Will that suit you, darling?"

"That would be wonderful." Lisette released her breath. It was not what she'd hoped for, but it would assuage her pain somewhat. Maybe being with the family for a short time would make it less difficult to return to the city.

"Good," Baptiste said. "We'll expect you early in the morning. If the weather's fine, we'll plan a picnic on the lawn. We can talk about a longer stay later."

With their arms around each other's waists, Lisette and

Philippe saw her parents to the door. Immediately after the door closed, he let go and walked into the salon.

"Thank heavens they're gone," he said. "I've never been with such boring people in my life. Since I agreed, we'll go out there on Saturday, but from now on I prefer you see them during the day so I don't have to suffer."

For the first time since her marriage, Lisette dared to show how really angry she was. "They are my parents, and this is my home as well as yours. I shall see them as often as I please from now on. And when I please."

"As you wish, but don't expect me to play the charming host every time. If I'm not here, it will be up to you to make the proper—and most plausible—excuses."

For the second time in three days, there was no answer when Philippe knocked at the door of the first-floor apartment. When he waited and knocked again and there was still no answer, he vented his anger the only way he could: he broke his cane over his knee. He knew someone was inside. He could hear muffled sounds, as if someone were purposely trying to keep quiet. It was unconscionable that he, who was providing and paying for the apartment, didn't have a key. But that had been part of the agreement. At first it had been a game. He would come like any lover to his mistress, knock, and know the thrill of expectation as he waited for Adrian to answer. The titillation of that game had long since palled, but Adrian still would not agree to let him have a key. Now he knew why. Adrian had fallen in love with someone else, had perhaps been entertaining him during the day, and now was daring to have him spend the night.

Philippe turned away from the door and went slowly up to his own apartment. For a brief moment he was tempted to go to Lisette's room. He had no physical desire for her, but maybe, now that she knew the truth, he could talk to her, let her know how much misery he'd endured for so much of his life. It might be possible to work out a compromise that would make their marriage bearable.

He'd been wrong to marry her under false pretenses, and his cruelty to her since then could never be forgiven. He should have been gentler. It was not necessary to hurt her as he had done. Was he cruel to her because she was normal, or because he feared to let down his guard? But why lie to himself. He knew the reason. He'd suspected for weeks that he was losing Adrian, and he couldn't bear to lose anything that belonged to him. If he were jealous of every man Lisette met, it was because he feared the inevitable: that she would turn to someone else for the love he could not give her. Then he would lose her, too. And be lost himself.

Whatever, she would never listen to him sympathetically now. She'd only laugh, and he deserved whatever scorn she heaped on him.

Philippe lay on his back, his hands behind his head, and looked into the bleak darkness surrounding him. He was lonely and he was afraid, but loneliness and fear had been his companions for as long as he could remember. He thought about his boyhood days and the tutor he'd adored. No man ever had or would mean so much to him. François, with his love for learning and his passion for beautiful things, had awakened Philippe to the joys of acquiring fine and precious *objets d'art*. And he'd also awakened him to the joys of love, not the physical love that would come later, but the sharing and the feeling of oneness with someone so like himself that it was as if they had a single heart and a single brain between them.

François was sent away when the time came for Philippe to attend a private academy. Night after night he'd wept at the thought of being separated from François, but his tutor assured him he would find others to love, and that he himself would never forget his favorite pupil. But the letters had stopped soon after Philippe went to the academy and then the loneliness had overwhelmed him.

There were no others like François at the academy, nor any who welcomed Philippe's overtures of intimate friendship. At first he was unable to recognize just why and how he was different from the others. When other boys turned away from him, revelation came, bringing with it both fear and an unwillingness to accept what he was. Shame followed, as the desire to find a companion like François became stronger and stronger. At first he became withdrawn. Then, in order to overcome and mask his fears, he played the part of the cynical extrovert. He did it so well he became a leader at the school. While he inwardly became more sensitive to every slight, he overlaid himself with a veneer of cruel sophistication that was the admiration of all the other boys. It was an honor to be allowed to walk with Philippe Duchalais, or to sit next to him at the table. A reprimand from him was far more humiliating than one from the headmaster.

241

From time to time he found partners to satisfy him physically. But not until he met Adrian did he fall in love again as he had with François. Adrian became his life, his whole reason for existence. And now he was losing Adrian.

He could never be anything but what he was. Marrying Lisette had shown him that. No woman could be more beautiful or more desirable to a man than she, and yet he was not only unmoved by her feminine charms, he was actually repulsed by them. Yet he had to keep her from leaving him, from allowing even the whisper of a rumor that their marriage was not an ideal one. There would be other lovers after Adrian who would have to be kept secret, but even more important was his ambition to rise to prominence in the banking world and in politics. It must not be jeopardized in any way.

Lisette sat in her room a long time before preparing for bed. She had an important decision to make. She knew she could no longer go on living with Philippe as she had been. It was an impossible situation, made worse because she still loved him. If she could hate him, or if she could be indifferent to him, she might be able to bear this mockery of a marriage, but she couldn't when his nearness stirred her to depths of longing and despair.

It was nearly four in the morning before Lisette made up her mind as to which direction to go. She had three choices: to stay with Philippe as things were and simply learn to endure them; to return home and ask for a separation, promising not to tell the real reason she'd left him if he vowed not to carry out his threat against her father; or to remain in Paris and take a lover to assuage her aching need for physical affection. When she'd finally decided which would be the easiest and best for both of them, she went to bed and cried until she finally fell asleep from exhaustion.

Chapter Twenty-two

LEAH HADN'T REALIZED how much she was looking forward to Lisette and Philippe's Saturday visit until she found herself repeatedly changing the lunch menu. Baptiste had suggested a picnic on the lawn, but she needed to think about an indoor meal, too, in case the weather were bad. She wanted to see her daughter here at home. Perhaps Lisette had just been nervous the other evening, which was probably natural for a bride entertaining her parents for the first time.

Blanchette and the other children were excited, too. Denise wanted to show off her newly redecorated room, and Nicole was working on a special watercolor for Lisette to replace the portrait she'd destroyed.

"I thought I'd paint the summer house and the garden," Nicole explained to Robert, who sat on a stool and watched. "That way, if she gets homesick, she can look at it and feel better."

"What's homesick?" Robert asked.

"It means when you've been away for a long time and wish you were back home. I expect you'll feel that way someday when you're older."

"No, 'cause I'm not going to leave."

"Oh, but you will," Nicole said, "when you grow up and go to work."

"No, I think I'll work right here and live right here."

"If you like. I'm sure Mama and Papa would love to have their baby stay."

"I'm not a baby! Mama says I'm her big boy now."

"I'm sorry. I didn't know. Now hush and let me keep on working."

"I think I'll go see what Henri is doing. He always lets me help."

Lisette sent another note to Georges. To stay with Philippe under the present conditions would be impossible.

To leave him would endanger her father, since she knew her husband would carry out his threat to call in the notes. Philippe had forbidden her to take a lover, but if she were discreet, she could manage it. She was determined not to be a married virgin any longer. Of all the men she'd met, there were several she would prefer over Georges LeClerc; he was her friend, though, and he understood the situation. He would introduce her to the mysteries of love and then she could find someone else. How like Lady Westborne she sounded already. She would probably end up seeking out younger men. No, there must be some way to have a steadfast, loving relationship outside of marriage. And maybe, eventually, another marriage that would be a happy one.

Georges' answer came in the afternoon mail. He'd be there that night at ten.

Lisette dressed quite differently from the first time. This was to be an assignation, and she wanted Georges to know it from the moment he entered the apartment. It would make it easier, especially since she'd sent him away once before.

As soon as he came through the door, she put her arms around him.

"That's quite a welcome, Lisette." He smiled at her. "Why the change?"

"To show you how sorry I am for having doubted you last time. Philippe finally told me he has a lover, and I thought—well, if he has one, why don't I? If you wish to stay the night, we won't be disturbed."

"Do you really mean that, Lisette, or are you simply reaching out for someone—anyone—to ease the hurt?"

"I mean it, and I want you. If you want to, that is."

"You know how long I've wanted you. But don't rush into something you might be sorry for."

"Are you putting me off?" Lisette wanted to cry. It had never occurred to her that Georges wouldn't fall right in with her plans.

"No, Lisette, but let's have some wine and talk a bit first."

"Yes, I'd like that, too." She was shivering inside from both fear and expectation. She needed to be relaxed and completely at ease when the time finally came.

She poured the wine and sat down on the couch next to Georges, but making sure there was some distance between them.

"I know it was hard for you to believe me," Georges said, "when I told you about Philippe."

"But I shouldn't have accused you of lying. I wasn't at all sure you'd come tonight."

"I told you I would whenever you needed me. I love you, and for now it's enough you chose me when you needed help."

"Would you like more wine?" In some ways she wanted it over with; in other ways she wished she could postpone it as long as possible.

"We'll take the bottle and glasses upstairs, shall we?" he suggested.

Lisette turned off all but one light and led the way up to her room. She went into her dressing room, and when she came out, Georges was already in bed. She looked at his naked chest and shoulders above the quilt. This was the way she should have seen Philippe on their wedding night. Self-consciously, she turned her back while she took off her robe.

The lovemaking was not the rapture Lisette had thought it would be, but at least she was no longer a virgin. And perhaps it would get better in time. With Georges' arm still around her, she sat up in bed and took the glass of wine he handed her.

"As much as I love you, Lisette, why didn't you wait to marry me?"

"My parents chose for me." She wouldn't let him know she'd fallen in love with Philippe, that she still loved him in spite of everything.

"Now that you know the truth, you can get an annulment. I'm in business with my father, and I'll eventually inherit his estate. We can be married in less than a year if you apply to the Church for a divorce."

"Annulment? Divorce!" Of course, after tonight, it would have to be a divorce; there would no longer be proof the marriage had not been consummated. Surely Georges must know Philippe would never testify to the truth. "That idea is scandalous. How far do you think I could get in society if I were divorced? Now that I know about Philippe, I'm free. I'll still be his wife, but I can live and do as I please as long as I'm discreet. I can really start enjoying myself."

"Then tonight? Why did you ask me to come over? Why allow me to make love to you, if you didn't intend to—to marry me eventually."

"I needed you. Please believe me, Georges. I need *you,*

not just any man. But you wouldn't want to marry me. I'm sorry. I thought you'd enjoy being my first lover—as you almost were a few years ago. But my first, not my last or only. If you can't forgive me, I hope at least you'll remember me with pleasure and—and kindness."

"You know I will, Lisette. And I'll always be available when you want me. I don't relish the thought of being one among many, but if you tire of the others, I'll be ready to take their place."

Lisette eased out of his arms by reaching for more wine and a biscuit. Rather than answer him, she pondered the great awakening she'd just experienced—or was endured a better word? Being a virgin no longer was certainly a plus. Having no basis for comparison, she didn't know whether Georges was a poor or—heaven forbid—an excellent lover. She didn't find it so sublime. She wondered why people talked so joyously about having lovers. She began to have second thoughts about gathering a whole phalanx of them around her. It would be better to find someone she could really love, because she was suddenly aware of the difference between making love and being in love. The first was not very satisfying without the second.

Feeling Georges moving toward her, she slid to the edge of the bed and got up. "I'm going downstairs to—to get us more wine and biscuits. Suddenly I'm very hungry." Before Georges could argue with her, she snatched up her robe and ran from the room. As she reached the kitchen, she burst into tears. The full import of all that had happened to her—learning about Philippe, taking Georges as a lover —dawned on her, and she felt miserable. She'd married Philippe because she loved him, and she still did. Even now, she would still accept him if he would be a real husband to her. For even though Lisette's mind could accept the reason Philippe gave for finding her undesirable, her emotions could not.

She went back upstairs to tell Georges he had to leave. No sooner was she inside the bedroom than she heard the door to the apartment open. Philippe! But he always stayed out all night. Lisette wasn't aware he'd been returning home early the past few nights. She hadn't heard him sneaking quietly to his dressing room so as not to disturb her and have her ask embarrassing questions.

As quietly as possible, she closed the door behind her and signaled for Georges to put out the lamp by the bed. "It's Philippe, but he never comes in here. As soon as he's been

246

in his dressing room for a while, you can leave. I'll walk down with you in case he hears the footsteps and becomes suspicious. I can always say I was going to the kitchen."

Georges needed no further invitation to get out of bed and put on his clothes.

Lisette waited for the steps to pass her door. She knew Philippe's temper, and there was no telling what he'd do if he found her in this compromising situation. Even if she were decently dressed, the simple fact that Georges was in her bedroom was enough to disgrace her. To her intense relief, the steps continued down the hall, and she heard the door of the farther room open and then shut.

"It's all right, Georges. He's gone right to his room as I thought he would. We'll wait a few more minutes and then go down."

During those few minutes, Philippe went to his room and began getting ready for bed. He'd been through a devastating experience of his own that night. For the first time in several days, Adrian had greeted him with open arms, and it was as if there'd been no estrangement between them. Then came the blow. Adrian, a writer, announced he had an article to finish in order to meet a deadline the next day. Philippe would have to leave or he couldn't get anything done.

"I need the money," he'd said.

"I'll give you the money, Adrian, if you let me stay," Philippe had begged.

"It's not just the money. It's my reputation as well. This is the most important article I've written so far; after this, I'll be in demand by all the newspapers and magazines."

Philippe had accepted the inevitable and come back upstairs to his apartment. All the while he was undressing, he was thinking about Lisette. In his fear of losing her, he'd been too harsh with her. If he gave her more freedom, allowed her to return to her music, tolerated visits with her family . . . No, that was not enough. She was a normal young woman with normal desires. It was unfortunate she thought she loved him, since it would be easier if she didn't. But if he could find some way for her to meet someone else, someone he selected himself, he could keep an eye on their affair and thus make certain it never progressed beyond the physical level. He'd talk to her tonight before he lost his courage. He would have to approach her more humbly than he'd ever done before, and hope she would be understanding enough not to scoff at him. He would deserve it if she did, but he'd have to take the chance.

"I think it's safe to leave now," Lisette said. "I don't hear any sound from his room."

In another minute, however, she heard what she feared much more: footsteps on the hall carpet and a gentle tapping on her door.

"Lisette? Are you asleep? I'd like to come in and talk if you'll let me."

"There's no help for it now," Lisette sighed. "He'll have to know you've been here." She opened the door.

All Philippe's will to stay calm disappeared the moment he saw Georges standing beside Lisette, who wore her sheer gown and robe.

"What the—what the hell's going on here!" he shouted.

"I was lonely and Georges came over to keep me company." Her voice quavered, and she clenched her hands at her sides to keep them from shaking.

"And I see how appropriately you're gowned for entertaining him." He glanced around the room at the unmade bed, the decanter of wine, and the two glasses. "Wine, too. How nice." He turned to Georges. "You get the hell out of here before I really lose my temper and kill you. As for you, Lisette—"

This is the end of everything, Lisette thought. *My reputation, Papa's business, his whole future.* She was terrified at the thought of what Philippe was going to do to her and Georges.

"It's all right, Lisette," Georges whispered. "There's nothing he can do to hurt you."

"As for you, Lisette," Philippe sneered, "don't hope I'm going to order you out, too. No, you're going to stay here as my loving and obedient wife. You thought I was cruel to make you stop your music. You don't know how cruel I can really be. But be assured, you'll know soon enough. There is always your father and the notes the bank holds."

"I don't think so," Georges said in a surprisingly cool voice. "I don't think Lisette has to fear for either herself or her father anymore."

"I'm not bluffing, Georges," Philippe answered. "I mean every word I say."

"And I think you'll change your mind after you hear what I have to say. If you're thinking of threatening Monsieur Fontaine, remember that Lisette also holds a threat over you.

248

One word from either of us and you can say good-bye to your ambitions in the banking world and in government."

"She wouldn't dare." Philippe was growling like an animal faced with an adversary larger and stronger than himself.

"You underestimate Lisette's strength." Georges spoke as if in complete command of the situation. "And my astuteness. I've done some investigating since I was last here. Yes, you may well look surprised, but Lisette spoke to me earlier about your rather unusual marriage. Not that I didn't know the truth about you before this. Do you remember Anatole?"

"Anatole?" Philippe asked casually. "I've known several by that name."

"But only one who committed suicide when you discarded him. He was a friend of mine, and he left me a note." He paused. "Which, by the way, I still have. I've also had Adrian watched for the past few days. He's been playing you for a fool. All the while you're paying for his apartment—and how convenient for it to be right downstairs—he's taken at least one other lover. And during the day he pimps for some of the most expensive prostitutes in the Place Pigalle. Does all this surprise you?"

"You're lying!" Philippe glared at him, but he knew Georges was telling the truth. He'd long known that Adrian had more money than he could possibly earn from his writing. He'd been a fool to believe that Adrian's declarations of love were sincere.

"If you don't believe me, ask Adrian. He's already tired of you. He won't care if you leave him. He has a baron for a patron now, and will be moving to his country estate."

Philippe was so deflated and so miserable he could hardly stand. Only his pride kept him from reaching for something to support him. His life, as he'd known it up until now, had come to an end. Maybe it would be better if he ended his life altogether.

"I suppose you intend to reveal all this," he said.

"Not at all, Philippe. I think we can reach a compromise. Lisette will not request a divorce or annulment, since that would necessitate your agreeing to reveal the truth about the marriage. But she will no longer live here as your wife. She will be free to pursue her own life, with a generous allowance from you so she need not be dependent on her family. I'm sure she can make some acceptable explanation as to why you are no longer living together. In return, she will agree to say nothing about what she's been through these past several weeks. Nor," Georges pressed his finger against Philippe's chest, "will there be any action taken against her father. Is that understood?"

During the time Georges was talking, Lisette was struck dumb with amazement. How coolly he was handling the whole situation, and how perfectly he understood what would be the ideal solution for her. She was sorry she couldn't love Georges enough to have an exclusive relationship with him; she didn't, though, and to pretend she did would be unfair to him.

Philippe had no strength left to argue. The issue had been resolved, and he would have to be satisfied with the results. He would lose Lisette, but his ambitions would not be in jeopardy. With the acknowledgment that Lisette had won for now—but only for now—his fierce pride reasserted itself. He would begin making plans to avenge himself against her and Georges. Someday he'd delight in bringing them both down. He would destroy them as they were now destroying him.

"I'll agree. I'll expect, Lisette, to find you gone from here by the time I wake up in the morning."

"Not so fast," Georges said. "She's not leaving here until I ascertain you've taken care of the financial arrangements for her. You and I will go to the bank tomorrow, where you will set up a substantial trust fund for her, one she can draw on at her convenience."

"My father will question such a large amount," Philippe said stubbornly.

"That is your problem. Call it an investment, if you like, an investment in the security of your own future."

"Just as you say. I'll meet you there at eleven tomorrow."

Georges looked at Lisette, who had retreated to a chair at the far side of the room while the men were talking. "I'll come by for you Saturday morning. Can you be packed and ready to go by then?"

Lisette was too weak to do more than nod. She could scarcely believe all that had happened in the past half-hour. At first it seemed she would be ruined, but instead, Georges had freed her from an unendurable situation.

Philippe was the first to leave, and Georges followed as soon as he'd assured Lisette everything would be all right.

But will it be? she thought as she lay on the bed. It was the end of her life with Philippe, but what was her new life going to be like? She couldn't see herself staying with the family, and yet there seemed no place else for her to go. At least Mama and Papa were there, and they'd tell her what to do.

She couldn't tell them the truth, but she could make them believe she and Philippe had separated merely because they were incompatible. She could hint at a mistress and hope that would be a sufficient reason. Maybe she could say the separation was temporary; then, in time, it would come to be accepted that she wouldn't return to him at all. Well, she'd wait until she got home and hope that something would guide her to a right decision. A feeling of relief such as she'd not known in weeks, swept over her, and she fell asleep almost immediately.

Completely shaken from his confrontation with Georges and Lisette, Philippe sat on the bed in his dressing room. He could live without Lisette. The marriage had been one of convenience from the beginning, and had soon turned into a farce. But could he live with the fear that the truth about himself might be revealed? Lisette and Georges had sworn they'd keep his secret as long as Lisette was free to live her own life and received a regular, generous allowance.

Philippe had agreed willingly. He had to trust them. His threats to call in Baptiste's notes meant nothing in the face of having his true nature disclosed. Money. It would silence Lisette, yet he'd always live with the fear of being revealed. He'd lived with that threat for so long now, it had become as familiar as his own shadow. He'd simply go on living from day to day as he'd always done, concentrating on his ambition to become one of the most influential bankers in France, and to work his way into government so he could manipulate and control people as well as money.

"Georges! How thoughtful of you to bring Lisette out." Leah turned to her daughter. "Philippe is not coming?"

"No, Mama. I'll explain later." Surrounded by the other children, all wanting to hug and kiss her at the same time, she didn't think this was the appropriate time to say she'd left Philippe. "Oh, it is good to be home. You don't know how much I've missed all of you."

"Come to the studio and see what I've just finished," Nicole said.

"And then to the workshop," Henri pleaded. "You won't believe what I've invented."

"Did you bring me a surprise?" Robert asked, tugging at her hand.

"Indeed I did, tad, and I'll get it for you in a minute. How

251

about you, Denise? Haven't you something you want me to see, too?"

"Nothing as exciting as what Nicole and Henri have to show. Just a few new things in my room."

"And I'm sure they're very pretty things."

Leah watched Lisette closely as Georges said good-bye before departing for his uncle's. A look seemed to pass between them. Something was wrong. Her enthusiasm in greeting the family had been genuine, but forced at the same time. And no smiles could hide the strain on her face or the tension in her body.

After lunch Leah found herself alone with Lisette and Baptiste. Not one to equivocate, she came straight to the point. "I noted you brought a handbag alone. Are you planning to stay the night? If so, we're delighted, but also a bit confused."

"Not just for the night, Mama. Philippe and I have separated. My other things will be coming later."

"You've left him?" Baptiste was shocked. Not just at the thought of a separation, but at Lisette's daring to leave. French wives were expected to remain at home no matter what the problem. His face darkened, and he wondered if Philippe had cause to send her away.

"Yes. By mutual agreement, Papa. We simply did not get along, and we both thought it would be better if I did not stay."

"Is anyone else involved?" Seeing Georges again revived old memories of finding him with Lisette in the summer house, and he worried that she had taken him for a lover.

"On my part, no," she said in a positive tone. There was no need to involve Georges. Philippe had agreed to say nothing about that confrontation, which had been as unfortunate for him as for them. "If you're asking if Philippe has a—a mistress, yes. But that's not the real reason. I knew beforehand I might have to accept that, even if I didn't expect it quite so soon. We simply found our life together less than satisfying."

Or impossible? Leah thought. There was more to it than Lisette was expressing so calmly to her father. The child had already torn one handkerchief apart and was trying to hide the remains under her skirt. And again there were tears in Lisette's eyes, just the way they'd been the night at the dinner at the apartment. Now, if they questioned her further, the tears would spill over.

"Lisette," Leah said quickly, "I don't believe you've seen

the quilt I'm making from all our discarded dress scraps. It's going to be very beautiful. Now, don't tease, Baptiste. I know you insist I'll never finish it, but I will. You'll see."

Lisette followed Leah to her room and sat while her mother pulled out her scrap bag and the partially finished quilt top.

"Mama, it is going to be beautiful. All those silks and satins."

"Yes, but that's not the reason I wanted you to come in here. Don't tell me anything you don't want to—but I know you're not going to last much longer if you can't tell someone what's really wrong."

"You're right, Mama. It's much worse than I told Papa."

"Here." Leah handed her a handkerchief to catch the tears that had started to fall. Then she sat quietly and waited until Lisette could bring herself to speak.

"It's very hard to talk about," Lisette said. "It's not something one discusses easily. I really loved Philippe, and in some ways I still do. That's what makes it so difficult. But our marriage was wrong from the beginning." Lisette hesitated, remembering the promise she'd made to Philippe. "What I'm going to tell you must never, *never* be known by anyone else. Not even Papa. You have to promise that."

Seldom did Leah keep anything from Baptiste, but for Lisette's sake she would this one time.

"I promise. Not even to Papa."

"Philippe married me under false pretenses. He was never a husband to me. Our marriage was never consummated."

"What are you saying?" Leah was stunned. This was the last thing she'd expected to hear. "He's unable to? If so, there might be a way to correct that." There had to be. Lisette's happiness, her whole future depended on it. If only she hadn't promised not to tell Baptiste. He'd know what to do.

"Not unable, Mama, unwilling. Although I don't think he would be able to, either. In a word, he prefers men to women. He has a lover, not a mistress."

The thought that Philippe could be impotent had stunned Leah. But this news was so much more shocking, she felt drained of the ability to say anything to console Lisette. "My poor darling. He seemed so adoring, so obviously in love with you."

"In public, yes. That was part of the charade. To help keep his secret."

"I was going to ask why he married you, but the answer is obvious. Yet he agreed to let you leave?"

"Yes, under certain conditions. I'm never to reveal his secret, of course. If I do, he will have the bank call in the notes he holds on Papa. He never told me how much they amount to, but I assumed it was enought to cause trouble or even ruin him."

Leah thought about the investment Baptiste had made in the Panama Canal Company. He hadn't mentioned it in a long time, so she had no idea whether there'd been any returns or if he were pouring more money into the company. At any rate, she knew him well enough to feel sure he wouldn't endanger their future with foolish speculations. "Not enough to bankrupt us, you may be sure of that. But it would ruin his reputation to have them called in."

"That's why no one must know," Lisette said. "There will be no annulment or appeal to the Church for a divorce. Neither of us wants the scandal that would cause."

"What are you planning to do now?" Leah was amazed at how maturely Lisette was approaching her situation, but the kind of suffering she'd endured made one grow up in a hurry.

"I don't know. Stay here for a while. I'm hoping you can give me some guidance."

"Anything. You know that."

"I'll have no financial worries. Philippe has set up a very generous trust fund for me. I will say that for him. He didn't quibble over the amount. I can live very luxuriously for the rest of my life. So—I can travel or settle wherever I please. Right now, I don't know where that will be."

"And for right now, you're not going to have to decide. You're going to stay right here until you recuperate. You've suffered as much as someone who's been seriously ill, and I want you to rest and relax for as long as you like. Everyone is delighted you're here, and they'll find all sorts of ways to keep you amused."

"Thank you, Mama, for understanding. I am tired. The rest will do me good, and I'll enjoy working with my music again." It would be nice to be treated like a child for a time. Sitting in Mama's room, she could almost believe she'd never been away, never suffered through an untenable marriage.

Within a month, Lisette found she could go almost a whole day without thinking about her miserable time with Philippe. Although the rest had done Lisette a great deal of good, Leah had begun to notice the girl was increasingly restless.

"I have an idea, Lisette. How would you like to go to England for a while?"

"I don't know. I hadn't thought about it."

"Lady Westborne has written again, urging me to come for a visit. I can't go myself at this time, but I'm sure she would love to have you for a guest, and I know you'd enjoy being with her."

"Yes, I remember how much I liked her. How impressed I was with her and all her worldly ways."

"Well then, why not a taste of that life? It would do you good to be back among people again. Let me write to her, and I'll bet you receive an invitation before the week is up."

The invitation came, filled with Jane's exclamation-marked delight that Lisette was really coming to see her at last. There were several parties already planned, and there would be many more once people met Lisette.

"You see," Leah said, "you'll be so busy you won't have time to think of anything but the fun you're having."

Leah found it hard to say good-bye to Lisette when she boarded the boat train in Paris. She knew that Lisette would be very different after her first experience with the kind of social life Jane Westborne would introduce her to. Leah waited until the train pulled out before returning to her carriage. For some reason she felt very old, and she wished Baptiste had come along to give her some of his strength.

Chapter Twenty-three

As 1888 TURNED INTO 1889, Leah became less concerned about Nicole, who agreed to continue in the village school for one more year if after that she could concentrate on her art studies. If at one time it had disturbed Leah and Baptiste to have Nicole making friends among the village children, they now were pleased when she resumed visiting their homes and bringing them to the château after school. Her art continued to dominate her life, but at least she was no longer using the studio as a refuge from the real world.

In London, Lisette sat at the writing table in her room at Lady Westborne's. She was trying to compose her weekly letter home. She'd had an idea when she accepted Jane's invitation what a whirl of activity was in store for her, and for a while it had been fun to write pages of description of the events she attended both in London and at country homes, the men who escorted her, and the new gowns she was constantly having to buy. More recently, the letters had become her only outlet for easing the painful homesickness that smote her whenever she was alone. She had no desire to return to Paris, with its memories of Philippe and the suffering she'd endured at his hands, but she longed to sit down at the dinner table with the family, to talk freely with Mama about new worries besetting her, and to be assured that time would ease the pain.

When she tried to envision her future, Lisette could see only an empty, blank space; she feared she'd spend the rest of her life feeling alone while she was surrounded by people. Yet she needed the parties, the superficial people with their inane conversation, to keep from giving way to complete despair. Since Philippe's rejection of her, she had to be continually reassured of her beauty and desirability. She was miserable unless surrounded by admiring men. Let a man fail to smile at her when she was driving or riding through Hyde Park and she dissolved into tears. At the balls her card must be filled by a different partner for every dance, and she thought her evening a failure unless at least one man suggested it end in an affair.

So far, however, Lisette had not agreed to any of these suggestions. Held close in some partner's arms, she'd been tempted—until she remembered that a brief physical fling was not what she really wanted. It would satisfy only one part of her longing while intensifying the deeper need for someone who would really love her.

More than once, after retiring to her room at Jane's or whatever country home she was visiting, Lisette wondered why she had refused the latest invitation to share someone's bed. The society to which she now belonged condoned whatever went on in the bedroom as long as it was not made publicly evident. The Victorian moral code demanded modesty and reserve in the drawing room; the word *adultery* was never uttered above a whisper, although she knew the seventh commandment was being broken in most of the homes in which she had stayed. Maybe she was a fool.

At the beginning she'd found it fun and exceedingly flattering to catch an inviting glance across a dinner table. Sometimes it would be followed by an intimate *tête-à-tête*

256

behind the tall palms in a darkened conservatory or a stroll through the garden. There would be a few passionate kisses, some hurried caresses, and then she would insist it was time to join the other guests. Her refusals to indulge in more than these innocent pastimes were usually accepted manfully, but occasionally her partners were deeply hurt or insulted. She knew that most of the time they were only pretending to be wounded, even when they declared they couldn't live another day if their passion were not returned. It was merely their pride she had pricked. Only once, when a young baronet threatened to kill himself if she didn't submit to him right then and there in the garden, was she really afraid. She put him off with promises, and later that evening saw him leading another young woman through the French doors into the garden. Lisette shrugged her shoulders and hoped he would have better luck this time. She'd have hated to see him kill himself. Her flirtations might be the talk of all London, but her bedroom door remained locked at night.

Rereading her letter, Lisette was thoroughly disgusted with the inanities she'd written to her family. She tore up the letter and started another one, saying that she'd had a wonderful time in England, and the change had done her good, but she wanted to come home. Denise had written that all Paris was getting ready to celebrate the centennial of the fall of the Bastille and wouldn't it be fun if all the family could be together. Lisette looked at her calendar. There were two more dinners she was obliged to attend, but after that she'd be free to leave. With that she ended the note to her family, too excited to write the long letter she'd intended. She danced around the room as she licked the envelope, then rang for someone to take it to the post.

While Leah made preparations to welcome Lisette home and planned centennial celebrations for the whole family, Baptiste sat at the desk in his office and looked over a report on the Panama Company. Over the past two years he'd added regularly to his orginial investment. Not only had he used most of the import firm's surplus, but without Leah's knowledge he had borrowed considerable amounts from the bank. It was the first time in their marriage that he'd made such important decisions without her advice. But she'd been so wrapped up in Nicole and then Lisette, he'd hadn't the heart to burden her with more to think about.

He looked again at the report. For the past few months he'd been hearing rumors that all was not well in Panama, but a recent newsletter seemed to indicate that, although the construction was moving more slowly than originally projected, it had not stopped. Baptiste shook his head. Being an astute businessman, he realized he should have known something was wrong when he never received any financial statements. This latest news was bad and seemed to confirm the rumors that the entire canal project had been poorly conceived and organized.

It was hard to believe that DeLesseps, who had been so successful in building the Suez Canal, could fail in Panama. But Baptiste could not deny the words he was reading now. Enormous sums of money had been consumed in trying to conquer the mud and the jungle, and very little construction had taken place. To make matters worse, the labor force was constantly being decimated by yellow fever. So far there was no indication the project would be abandoned, but it was doubtful for the time being if the investors would recoup their original outlays, let alone receive any dividends.

Baptiste lit one of his long black cigars and sat back in his chair. He was not too concerned with having decreased the firm's surplus, although they could be in serious trouble without that basis for security if business declined even so much as a small percentage. No, what had him really worried were the notes held by the Duchalais bank. With an excellent credit rating, he'd been allowed to borrow on his signature alone. At the time, he was certain he could redeem the notes within a few years. When he'd mentioned to Monsieur Duchalais that specific dates be put on the notes, the banker had waved his hand nonchalantly and said that between friends such a suggestion was ridiculous. They were still friends, in spite of the estrangement between Philippe and Lisette, but he wondered how long that friendship—or their business relationship—would last if it became known that the Fontaine affairs were in jeopardy.

The decision facing Baptiste now was whether to tell Duchalais about the problems in the Panama Company and ask him to continue holding the notes until he could stabilize the import firm and then begin paying them off gradually, or say nothing and hope the banker hadn't heard the rumors about the Panama Company. Baptiste shook his head again. Duchalais was too good a businessman not to know what was going on across the Atlantic. Baptiste would simply have to tell the banker how he'd invested the money he'd borrowed and hope he'd be given enough time to pay it back.

He'd go into the city tomorrow. Since Jean had been promoted to assistant manager, Baptiste found it unnecessary to go to the office every day. Now he'd have to think of a reason for going in twice in one week. Above all, Leah must not know about the visit to the bank or the gravity of their situation.

"Baptiste, I need your advice."

He was so startled by Leah's sudden appearance just when he's been thinking about her that he jumped involuntarily.

"My goodness," Leah said, "you'd think you'd seen a ghost."

"No, I was thinking about asking you if you wanted to go into the city tomorrow and see Roland." Jean and Celine's second son was now six weeks old. "He's changing every day."

"I'd love to. While I'm there, I'd like to see about redoing Lisette's room. But should I get new draperies and everything —or should I just get new hangings for the bed?"

"You're sure she's coming home to stay?" he asked. "If not, there seems no point in spending all that money."

"I'd just like to welcome her back after being away all these months. You've never quibbled over money before."

"I'm sorry, chérie, if it means that much, but don't get too extravagant."

"Is there something wrong in the firm?" She'd noticed new lines in Baptiste's face and the way he'd been retreating into silence more often than usual. For a brief time she'd fear another episode like the ones with Celeste and Simone. But he seldom stayed in the city overnight, and when he did it was with Jean, so she'd immediately convinced herself she was being foolish. Now, she realized she should have considered the possibility of business reverses.

"Not too serious. Just a minor decrease in orders. I'm sure it will improve before long. But if we watch the budget, I won't have to go into the surplus for our personal needs." It was hard to keep things like this from Leah, but it was true they had to keep expenses down.

"I wish you'd told me sooner; I'd have been more economical about everything."

"It won't be for long. A few months of tightening the purse strings and we'll be all right."

"Good." Leah thought about Philippe's threat if Lisette revealed the truth about him. Baptiste had never told her about the bank held notes against him, but she hadn't worried. She was certain he wouldn't endanger the family. Now she wondered how long there had been problems in the firm. He'd borrowed to keep it going and hadn't wanted to worry her. She'd do all she could to keep expenses down, but it wouldn't be easy with Henri at St. Cyr and Nicole wanting two art lessons a week. They could all make do with the clothes they had—that would save some money. There were other areas where she could economize, too.

"Anyway," Baptiste said, "I hope you'll still come with me to the city tomorrow."

"You know I don't need a second invitation for that. I'll spend the whole day with the grandchildren. Do you suppose all grandmothers are as dotty about their grandchildren as I am?"

"They might be, but you're the most beautiful grandmother I've ever seen."

"Thank you, darling." Earlier that morning Leah had noticed an alarming amount of new gray hair. But as long as Baptiste still thought her beautiful, she was satisfied. She had indeed been foolish to worry about another woman in his life.

As soon as Leah was settled in a chair with Roland in her lap and Armand beside her, Baptiste left for the bank.

"Come in, come in, Baptiste," Victor Duchalais greeted him. "It's good to see you. You're in town so seldom now. We can have lunch together, can't we?"

"I think so. Leah's happily ensconced with the grandchildren and won't miss me all day."

"Yes, I heard Jean had a second son. I also hear he's doing very well as assistant manager. It won't be long before you'll be putting him in complete charge."

"Caron has at least three years before he'll want to retire. But Jean is doing well, and I expect to keep giving him more responsibility." Baptiste fidgeted in his chair. There was no point in postponing the inevitable. "However, I expect to be spending more time in the office from now on."

"You sound as if you think there are problems only you can take care of. Business not going well?"

Baptiste wondered if Duchalais were thinking of calling the notes in. "No, doing fine," he said. "I want to look into the possibility of expanding."

"That's good news, Baptiste."

"Not quite as good as it sounds, Victor."

"Want a brandy?" Duchalais walked to the liquor cabinet.

"Thank you, I would."

"As soon as you came in, I sensed you had something on your mind."

Baptiste turned the snifter in his hand. "Is it that obvious? I hope I did a better job of keeping my worries from Leah."

"Want to tell me? I'm not only your good friend, Baptiste, but your banker. You know I'll do all I can to help you if you have financial problems."

"That's a very broad, inclusive statement, Victor. And a generous one. You might want to take it back when I tell you why I came in here today."

"Let me be the judge of that."

Baptiste finished off the brandy and placed the glass carefully on the table beside his chair. "It's the notes you hold."

"I haven't called them in. Don't intend to." Duchalais smoothed his mustache and frowned. "Philippe hasn't said anything to you, has he? I'm sorry he and Lisette have separated—I'm genuinely fond of her—but personal affairs have nothing to do with business."

"No, he hasn't said anything. Nor did I think you were planning to call them in. But I did think you should know now why I borrowed the money and why I might have difficulty repaying it anytime soon. You're familiar with the Panama Company?"

"I am," Duchalais said. "Invested several thousand francs in it when it was first organized."

"Then you've heard the latest news." Baptiste relaxed. It would be easier to talk to Victor knowing he'd put money into the company, too.

"I have, but I suspected the problems soon after they were organized." He looked quizzically at Baptiste. "Is that where you put the money you borrowed?"

" 'Fraid I did, Victor. With DeLesseps behind it, I didn't see how it could be anything but a success. The worst of it is that, after an initial investment, I continued to buy shares."

"I doubt you'll ever see your money again."

"I know. That's why I have to find some way to expand the business. I no longer have a large enough reserve fund to draw on, and I don't like running a business that way."

"I'm surprised at you, Baptiste. You're too good a businessman to keep investing in something that doesn't send regular financial reports. I wish you'd consulted me."

"I should have, Victor, but it's too late now. I won't default on the notes, but I'll need time."

"There's no time limit on the notes. I know you'll pay them off," Duchalais said. "Now—how about lunch?"

"Great idea. I'm ready to relax with a good meal."

"I hope so, because you're still as tense as a young man on his first visit to a bordello. You're not too old, I trust, to appreciate the analogy."

Baptiste threw back his head and roared with laughter. "No, no indeed. I remember that night very well. Between the champagne and the women, I was almost completely undone. I barely made it out of the place on my own two feet. I hope I'll do a little better this time. The truth is, I'm worried about Leah and the children. I don't know how much longer I'll be able to take care of them."

"What is it, Baptiste?" Duchalais leaned forward attentively in his chair. He was no longer joking.

"You remember I went to Aix-les-Bains a few years ago for the waters?"

"I do, and I thought you came back a new man."

"Only temporarily, Victor. The arthritic condition returned within a few months. I've learned to tolerate the pain in my legs, but now it's attacked my hips so viciously I can hardly walk. Leah's going to have to know soon. That's why I don't want her worrying about the money. And I have to make plans for the future, for when I'm confined to a wheelchair or bed—or worse."

"I see now why you want to give Jean more and more responsibility," Duchalais said. "Have him come to lunch with us one day soon, and we'll sit down and make some plans. He should know the situation and be included in the decision-making."

"Fine. I'll talk to him in a few days. Right now we're all involved with the centennial and waiting for Lisette to come home."

"Home to you or to Philippe?" Duchalais missed her beautiful face and her vivacious personality.

"To us, at least for the time being. But maybe while she's in Paris—"

"I hope so. I'd really like to see the two of them back together."

While Duchalais gave orders for a carriage, Baptiste reached for his crutches. It was good to have someone he could confide in. He'd never be as close to Victor as he'd been to Pierre in New Orleans, but then he and Victor hadn't been boyhood friends.

The frivolous atmosphere of the centennial celebration in Paris was intoxicating. For Leah, with all her family around her, each day was like a holiday. Together they stared in awe at Monsieur Eiffel's tremendous steel tower erected at the opposite end of the Champ-de-Mars from the École Militaire, but it was Henry who became completely involved in the details of its construction. To design and build something so magnificent was his lifetime dream. He'd do something just as great someday.

Leaving Robert with Armand and Roland's nurse, the rest of the family spent an evening at the Moulin Rouge. Lisette could not decide what entranced her more, the sight of the demimonde mingling with the aristocrats, or the wildly enthusiastic dancers shocking many of the patrons with the daring new can-can.

"Look, Mama," Henri whispered, "you can see their petticoats and their pantaloons."

"I know. I suppose it's very naughty, but aren't they good?" She gasped in amazement as one of the dancers lifted her leg up until it was level with her forehead, while another dancer leapt up and came down into a split on the floor.

"Wicked," Baptiste mumbled under his breath.

"You want to leave?" Leah asked. She waited for him to take his eyes off the dancers and look at her.

"What? What did you say?" he asked.

"I said, do you want to leave?"

"No, no, you and the children are enjoying it."

Leah and Lisette burst into giggles.

"And you're not, Papa?" Lisette asked. "You haven't taken your eyes off that redhead since we came in. And I think it's dyed, too."

"That's what I've been looking at," Baptiste insisted. "Her hair."

"Don't believe a word of it," Leah laughed.

"She'd make a fantastic subject for a painting," Nicole said. "With that hair she could be in the center with the other dancers a swirl of color around her." Nicole immediately pulled out the small sketch pad that always accompanied her and made a few hasty lines with her pencil. "See what I mean? Of course, color will really bring it alive."

"Looks like you have something there, baby," Baptiste

263

nodded. "You should study some of the paintings of Monsieur Toulouse-Lautrec. His posters are spectacular."

"I already have, Papa. I like his use of strong colors. That's what I want to try with this one."

Nicole had already spent much of her time at the galleries showing the works of Rosa Bonheur and Mary Cassatt. She'd been impressed with Bonheur's powerful paintings of horses and with Cassatt's magically delicate impressionism. If she could just move to Paris where she could meet and discuss painting with other artists. But since Roland's birth, there wasn't enough room for her to stay with Jean and Céline for any length of time, and Papa had put his foot down about her living alone in a rooming house. But someday she'd live here, perhaps in Montmartre with other artists. And she'd be one of the great ones. It was her only dream, and one she was determined to see come true.

Denise's favorite pastimes in the city were walking in the Tuileries with Robert or attending the small open-air theatres along the Champs-Élysées. She enjoyed Paris for brief spells, but it didn't hold the special excitement for her that its society did for Lisette or its art for Nicole. Denise was always ready to return to the quiet life of the château.

As they were returning home one night after attending the circus and watching a fireworks display, Leah said, "Well, I must say we've had quite a time during this centennial, but I'm glad it doesn't happen every year."

"Can we go back again tomorrow night?" Robert asked. He was still breathless from watching the acrobats and clowns and from all the colors exploding in the sky.

"No, pet, you've stayed up after your bedtime too many nights already. It's time we settled back into a more normal routine."

"Next week?" he pleaded.

"We'll see, but I make no promises."

"I've never had so much fun in all my life," he said, snuggling against her and falling immediately to sleep.

In all your very long life, Leah smiled to herself. *But it has been fun, having all the family together again.*

Chapter Twenty-four

THERE WERE ALMOST AS MANY foreign visitors as Parisians celebrating the centennial of the fall of the Bastille, which had marked the beginning of the French Revolution. Among them was Lady Westborne. Leah and the girls had met her for tea a few times, and she'd shared their box at the theatre on two occasions. Both times she'd asked Lisette when she was planning to return to England.

"And you, too, Leah?" Jane asked. "When are you going to accept my invitation? All of you, in fact. I've plenty of room and would love to have you. Lisette can tell you what a whirl of activity there is."

"She's told us all about that," Leah said. "And I know she had a wonderful time. Maybe soon." As carefully as Baptiste tried to hide his pain, she knew he was suffering more than he had been before they went to the mineral spa. His place was at the château where he could remain fairly quiet and there were few demands on him. And her place was with him.

"Lisette?" Jane asked again.

"I'll be back, never fear, if only for a short visit. But I want to be with the family for a while. I hope you'll understand."

"Indeed I do," Jane said, "and I envy you such a family. But the invitation is there whenever you want to come. I'm having a costume ball in a few weeks. Maybe that will tempt you. Meanwhile I'm giving a dinner party here next week. Do say you'll come to that."

"I wouldn't miss it," Lisette said.

"And you, Leah? You and Baptiste?"

"I'd better decline. All this excitement lately has put something of a strain on both of us. We're neither of us as young as we used to be. But Lisette can stay at the apartment with Jean and Céline that night."

"Very good. I'll send a carriage for you, Lisette. And I have a very special partner in mind for you. I think you'll be pleased." Jane Westborne smiled secretly to herself. If she knew Lisette—and the special partner—Lisette would be taking the first boat train to England after the dinner party.

"Are you always this quiet, mademoiselle?"

Lisette was amazed at her dinner partner's fluent French, but she answered him in the precise English Leah had insisted she learn and which she'd perfected while visiting Jane. "I'm sorry. Sitting next to Your Royal Highness renders one as young and naive as I quite speechless."

"Young, maybe," the Prince of Wales said, "but not too naive, I trust. And very beautiful."

"Thank you, sir."

When Lisette learned that the special partner to whom Jane Westborne had referred was His Royal Highness, Edward, Prince of Wales, she nearly fainted. Laying her hand on his arm as they prepared to enter the dining room, she prayed he wouldn't notice how it was shaking. *What in the world does one say to a prince?* she wondered. Somewhere she'd heard one should always wait for royalty to speak first. During the first course he'd been occupied with the woman on his left, who kept asking all sorts of stupid questions to which he'd responded politely. Obviously he'd become bored, and now he'd turned to Lisette. Well, she certainly had no intention of boring him. She only hoped she wouldn't say anything improper or gauche, although from what she'd heard about the Prince, he was not a man concerned with propriety.

"Now tell me," Edward said, "what was going through your head as you sat there so pensively."

"If I may be so bold, Your Highness, I was thinking how much you remind me of a former monarch—Henry the Eighth."

Edward's response was a hearty laugh which put her immediately at ease. "Because of my penchant for beautiful women?"

"Partly, perhaps, but more because of your grand style, your aura of undeniable greatness. You could almost be his descendant, though we know, of course, he had none. A pity. Such a great brain. A man of violent passions, true, but a magnificent mind."

"And I remind you of him?" Edward asked. "You're just flattering me, I trust."

"No, Your Highness," Lisette said, with her most beguiling smile. This was fun. This was the kind of challenge she'd enjoyed before meeting Philippe and making the mistake of falling in love. If she could captivate the Prince of Wales, she could conquer the world. The other men she'd met in England were just playthings compared to a real prince. Not that she had any intention of going beyond a mild flirtation, but through him she might meet someone she could love. It would make up for all the agony she'd suffered with Philippe.

"I seldom flatter," she continued. "I was brought up to speak the truth and to abhor dissembling."

"Then I thank you," he said. "I, too, admire the man who, as you say, could not possibly be my ancestor."

"A very fine king. You will make as great a one, I think."

"And you say you're not flattering me?" He frowned, but Lisette could see the smile behind the ferocity. "My dear mademoiselle, don't underestimate my faculty for recognizing unctuousness."

"I am neither a toady, nor a sycophant, Your Highness. You wound me deeply." With a twinkle in her eye, she grinned mischievously at him. "But do you think flattery so harmful? Far better surely than cruel honesty. Better to praise than to demean. If I had a wart on my nose, I shouldn't like to be reminded of it. I'd rather be told how becoming my new gown was."

"And if you had a wart on your nose, mademoiselle, you would not be sitting at this table. Jane knows me too well not to pair me with the most beautiful woman of the evening. Ah, you *are* naive, I fear. I am so surrounded by flatterers, I'd love a good dose of that cruel honesty you speak of. Tell me now, what is the 'wart on my nose' you refuse to mention?"

"I haven't found one yet." She paused just long enough. "But then, I've known you such a very short time, scarcely an hour."

"Should I let you think I have no faults, or should I allow you the opportunity to discover them?"

The conversation was progressing as she'd hoped. A little faster, perhaps, than she'd planned, and it frightened her a bit; still, Lisette was never cautious when daring were required to get what she wanted.

"If you offered me such an opportunity," she said, "I should be the flattered one."

"Please, Lisette, don't play the coquette with me." He shook his regal head. "I liked you better when you were honest. You're a beautiful young woman who's attracted my attention, and you know it."

His use of her first name did not go unnoticed. "Then will

you allow me to be honest and say I'm both pleased and touched that you take pleasure in my company?"

"You may." He waited for his wineglass to be refilled. "Your reference to Henry the Eighth gives me an idea. Lady Westborne is giving a costume ball to raise funds for one of her charities—Lord only knows which one. Are you invited?"

"I am." Lisette remembered Jane mentioning a costume ball she was giving, and she only hoped it was the same one.

"Good. No matter, though, I would have asked her to invite you. I understand from her you're free to travel as you please. That you're separated from your husband."

"Yes, unfortunate but true." From all she'd heard, Lisette knew it didn't really matter to Edward whether a woman be married, separated, or single, just so long as she was not divorced.

"As guest of honor," he continued, "I planned to attend as King of Thieves. During medieval times, a cutthroat was usually given the honor of wearing the king's crown for a day."

"I know. I've read all of François Villon's poems. He loved the women, too. Remember 'Where are the snows of yester-year?' "

"I'm not a reader of French poetry, but if he admired beautiful women, then I agree with him wholeheartedly."

Lisette heard the note of warning in his voice. Light chatter, yes; literary discussions, no. She would not forget.

"Then," she said, "going to the ball as the poet-thief would be most appropriate."

"But I've changed my mind. I think I'll go as my esteemed predecessor, Henry the Eighth."

"You'll be perfect," and Lisette had to prevent herself from impulsively clapping her hands.

"More perfect still if you go as Anne Boleyn." He smiled as he spoke. "You'll have to get a wig, of course. She was known as the dark-haired beauty. Sometimes as a witch." He watched to see if this shocked her.

"I know. Shameful, wasn't it? I can't think of anything more delightful than to go as that fascinating woman. Oh, but—" She was struck by the full import of what he might be suggesting. "The implications! Won't there be gossip and innuendoes if you go as Henry and I go as Anne?"

"There's always gossip when I devote an entire evening to one partner, as I intend to do with the Lady Anne. Does gossip disturb you?"

"When applied to me? I don't know." *Perhaps it's time I found out*, she thought.

"As Jane is holding the ball at her country estate and I'll be among the guests staying for the weekend, can I look forward to spending a number of interesting hours with you?"

Here it is. The decision left entirely up to me. There would be no second offer, but was she ready for it? She'd often wondered if someday she might find herself having an affair with an earl or a duke, but she had actually captured a prince —*the* Prince of the land. His reputation for very brief affairs banished any illusions about his being in love with her. But through an involvement with him, she would gain a social eminence from which to view all likely prospects for a permanent liaison that might provide her with love and help her forget Philippe. Being mistress to the Prince of Wales for even a brief time was the equivalent of an accolade. It bestowed immediate entrée—as well as lifelong membership—into an élite circle of society.

"I, too, look forward to seeing you there," she said. "As Lady Anne."

"Until then, Lisette. I see that Her Royal Highness is indicating she wishes to leave. She tires very easily, and I'm most solicitous of her health. She'll be leaving soon for the south of France to take the waters and then to Denmark to visit her family. She will be gone for at least two months."

With that, Edward, the Prince of Wales, departed. The words about Princess Alexandra were said with complete sincerity, for Lisette knew that there was love as well as genuine respect and admiration between the two. Nor did she miss the implication of his last words. He looked forward to more than a weekend, or he would not have mentioned how long the Princess would be away.

How often would she see him, Lisette wondered, and how would she manage it? Perhaps much of that depended on her. Not just pleasing him; she felt certain of her ability to do that. But it must be made convenient for him. Until after the ball, she'd be staying with Jane Westborne. Then, perhaps, it would be time to get her own place. A small house in Mayfair would be ideal. She'd go over to London as soon as she could pack and arrange for some of her things to be sent over.

"I'm going back to England, Mama." Lisette was having morning coffee with Leah.

"I rather thought you might accept Jane's invitation. Especially when she mentioned the costume ball."

"Yes—yes, I'm looking forward to that." Mama would never know how much or with what trepidation.

"Did you enjoy the dinner party last night?" Leah had wondered why Lisette returned so early this morning instead of spending part of the day in Paris. Now she thought she knew. Lisette wanted to prepare for her return to England.

"Very much. It was quite splendid. The Prince and Princess of Wales were there."

"I hope you remembered to curtsy when you met them."

"Mama, I'm not so gauche as to forget that."

"Not gauche, perhaps, but thrilled. I would be." Leah had never outgrown her childlike awe of royalty, even if she did not necessarily admire them. "Did you speak to them?"

"Yes. In fact, I sat next to the Prince at dinner." She thought it better not to say he was her partner.

"I hope you were polite and remembered all your manners."

"I assure you, Mama, I behaved quite properly. You will be pleased to know the Prince hopes to see me again when I'm in England."

"Oh?" Now they were getting nearer to the truth of why Lisette was in such a hurry to return to England. "I hope you will limit your acquaintance with him to well-attended functions."

"I'm an adult, married woman. I think I'm old enough to make my own decisions about my friends."

"Friends, yes." Leah looked at Lisette and thought about what the girl had been through with Philippe. She wanted only happiness for her, no more pain. But she couldn't plan Lisette's life for her. The young woman would have to make her own decisions from now on. The best Baptiste and she could do for this daughter was to let her know they loved her and to always be there when she needed them. Perhaps that was what parents were for: to let go of when the time came, but to keep their hands available to be grasped when wanted.

Lisette was to spend a week with Jane Westborne in London before the ball in the country. As yet, Lisette had not met Lord Westborne. With a casual wave of her hands, Jane would say he was up in Scotland or someplace.

"Another shopping spree?" Jane asked when Lisette hurried in breathlessly, just in time for tea.

"A few things for the ball. I had to see a dressmaker."

"Are you going to tell me what you're wearing, or must I wait for that night?" Jane asked coquettishly. Lisette noted the new lines in Jane's face. She was getting too old to play the coquette, even with her.

"If you don't mind, I want it to be a surprise. I'm not being evasive. It's just there's a special reason for not letting you know."

"I see," Jane said, pretending to be hurt. "Piquing my curiosity like that will make me all the more eager to see you."

In opening her doors to Lisette and acting as a surrogate mother to her, Jane also had hoped to be the recipient of all Lisette's confidences. It hadn't worked out quite that way. She learned that Lisette was a very private person and not at all ready to reveal the details of either her failed marriage to Philippe or of her present affairs. And Jane was quite sure there had been several of them during Lisette's earlier visit to England.

"I don't think you'll be disappointed when you do see me," Lisette said, "or at the stir I'll make among your guests."

"Nothing grotesque, I hope." Jane shuddered. "It should be something to enhance your beauty." In inviting Lisette to England, Jane had sincerely hoped to launch her into society. But she had also expected to realize social benefits for herself. With Lisette in her home, they were constantly being visited by the same men who once had swarmed around Jane herself. She thought that once the men were there, they'd surely be attracted to her again. But instead, Lisette was the center of all eyes, while Jane fumed inwardly at the polite acknowledgments of her presence.

"Not grotesque, I assure you," Lisette said. "And I hope I'll appear beautiful. It's necessary for the full effect."

"Then you'll continue to enjoy your immense popularity. My, what an impact you've made. But no more that I prophesied the first time I saw you."

"And I appreciate what you've done for me." This was the opening Lisette had been hoping for. "I also think I should begin reciprocating all the dinners I've attended. You've been a more than generous hostess, and I hate to seem ungrateful, but I really feel I should find a place of my own."

"I understand completely, my dear." Jane came close to breathing a sigh of relief. Lisette would remain in London but not close enough to become irritating. "You'll be want-

271

ing to entertain, but smallish things at first. No one will expect anything lavish from you. And I'll be nearby to give you any assistance you need."

And be ready to receive invitations, Jane thought, for she knew that even though Lisette provided no amusing gossip, she must continue to bask in the light of the girl's popularity. Jane had finally come to admit that no amount of creams or hair dye could disguise the fact she was past forty and could no longer hope to attract the young men she needed so desperately to maintain her pride.

"Then will you help me look for such a place?" Lisette asked.

"I'd be delighted to. I think I know of just the place, too. By the way, speaking of entertaining, I've received word that His Royal Highness has accepted my invitation to stay the weekend. I had so hoped he would. At first he said he thought he'd have to return to Windsor right after the ball. On orders of Her Majesty, I suppose. A shame the way he's under her thumb, as if he were still in short pants. But anyway, he will stay, and it is a real feather in my cap. I'll have to figure out new sleeping arrangements, but that's a minor matter if it means having him there. The Duke of Cadbury will simply have to be satisfied with the smaller suite in the east wing.

So he hadn't originally planned to stay, Lisette thought. That's not what he said the night of the dinner in Paris. Had he changed his mind after meeting her? Lisette knew all too well what that could mean, and she wondered what the new sleeping arrangements would be.

"But back to you, my dear." Jane turned in her chair and picked up a small book from the table. "I'm engaged for tomorrow morning, but in the afternoon we can begin house hunting. I'm as eager as you to find just the right place." Then Jane hoped she hadn't sounded too pleased to be getting Lisette out of her house. "It must be close by so we can see each other often." There, that should cover up any such implication while also hinting that she wanted to be included in all the young woman's plans.

"Yes," Lisette said, "I do want it near you. I don't think I could manage alone if I couldn't count on running to you for advice."

"And I'll be right here to help you. Now, if you'll excuse me, I must relocate each of my guests for the weekend. So many with such idiosyncrasies—no sun in the afternoon, no sun in the morning, not too far away from the stairs. I hope

272

you won't mind, dear, since you're young and spritely, if I leave your situation until last and put you in whatever room is left over."

"Not a bit, Jane. I'm just thrilled to be included."

Lisette didn't see Jane until the following afternoon when they set out to look at houses.

"I finally have all the rooms designated for the weekend," Jane said. "You'll be in the west wing. I'm afraid the room is rather small, but I think you'll find it quite pleasant and attractive."

The west wing, Lisette thought, and the Duke of Cadbury had been moved to the suite in the east wing. Did that mean that the Prince's accommodation would be near her room? Had he asked Jane to make certain it was? Jane gave no hint. Or had she been arranging rooms for lovers and would-be lovers so often it was no longer important enough to mention? No, this was foolish thinking. Jane had said she would put her in whatever room was left over, and it was merely coincidence that it was in the west wing. That was the way she must continue thinking. The Prince had said he enjoyed her company and looked forward to seeing her again. She was the one who had read more into his words than he probably meant. His idea of having her appear as Anne Boleyn was a gesture designed to titillate the other guests and set tongues wagging. Or to make his present mistress, a very beautiful and titled woman, jealous for the evening. The ball would be exciting, but she must concentrate on meeting and making new friends; that was why she'd come to England, not to become the Prince's mistress. She was furious with herself for hoping he might want to have an affair with her.

"Any room will be fine, Jane. Remember, I've seen them all, and there's not a single one less beautiful than the others."

"Well, with all I've planned, you won't be spending much time in it anyway," and her enigmatic smile set Lisette wondering again what the Prince had written in his letter of acceptance.

"Now," Jane said, "there are several houses we can look at, but I've learned this morning that the Sheldon house, a half-block off Berkeley Square, is available for a year's lease. I think it will fit your needs precisely. Shall we go there first?"

The house was exactly what Lisette had pictured. It was on a short street ending at the square, three blocks from Jane's home in one direction and no farther from the Shepherd's Market in another. She could easily walk to Piccadilly as well as to both Green and St. James's parks if she didn't feel like ordering her brougham. The monthly deposits into her bank from the trust fund Philippe had set up for her were more than adequate for her to maintain a London address. He'd been right when he suggested that money would keep her quiet. Not for the world would she jeopardize the life she was rapidly becoming accustomed to.

From the entry foyer of the four-story house, Lisette saw a formal living room on the left and a smaller sitting room on the right. With some rearrangement of the furniture it would make a perfect music room. She must have her piano sent over immediately. Behind the living room was the dining room; and behind the music room, a library. The second floor was devoted entirely to the master suite of bedroom, dressing room, morning room, and bath. More bedrooms and baths were on the third floor, and servants' rooms were above that. Stairs from the back hall led to the kitchen area below street level. She would have to see about hiring a housekeeper, a cook, and one parlor maid. Her coachman could double as butler, and she would simply have to hire more by the evening when she entertained. There was a coach house with rooms above for him, so there would be plenty of room for the three female servants on the fourth floor of the main house.

"Do you like it?" Jane asked. Lisette hadn't said a word since they'd walked through the front door, and Jane wondered if the young woman were going to be difficult to please.

"It's perfect, Jane. Just what I wanted."

"Good. Then we won't have to take time to look at the others. We can drive to the house agents right from here."

"I'm going to need your help, too," Lisette said, "in hiring servants. It's not something I've ever done. Mama and then Philippe took care of that."

"No problem," Jane said, readjusting the bow of her toque. "I'm glad you asked. Believe me," she sighed in mock exasperation, "I've had plenty of experience in hiring servants, and I know what questions to ask and what to look for. So leave it to me."

"I'll be glad to," Lisette said.

With the lease signed and the servants hired, Lisette returned to Jane's house exhausted. She and Jane had gone to an employment agency specializing in domestics, and if it hadn't been for her experienced friend, she would have hired the first women interviewed. And made a serious mistake. As it was, she now had an elderly cook with the very best references, and an efficient but not officious housekeeper who seemed pleased with the thought of running a household with no children. "Not that I mind children," she said, "but most of my experience has been in homes that cater to entertaining at dinner parties and teas rather than birthday parties and nursery suppers." Lisette assured her that was exactly what she would be doing. The new parlor maid seemed very young, but Mrs. Mabering, the housekeeper, assured Lisette, "I know exactly how to train her, Madame Duchalais, so you will be completely satisfied."

"I think Mrs. Mabering is impressed with your French accent," Jane said later. "She thinks all wealthy French who come to England are titled, or would be if the revolution hadn't put an end to all that."

"That's silly."

"No, it's not, and you must use it to your advantage. Otherwise she'll get the upper hand. Keep in mind it's your home to be run the way you want it. Oh, she'll be a very good housekeeper, or I wouldn't have chosen her, but don't let her run you as she does the house."

Lisette laughed. "That sounds just like what Papa told me about the cook on his plantation in Louisiana. He said she and the butler might have been slaves before the war and servants afterward, but woe to anyone who tried to cross them or interfere with how their domains were run."

Lisette moved to the house immediately, and once everything was arranged to her satisfaction, it felt more like her own home than the apartment in Paris ever had. Then she and Jane left London early Thursday morning, though the ball wasn't to take place until Friday night.

"I need a whole day to get myself ready as well as the house," Jane said. "When there's so much to see to, I'm never sure everything is in readiness unless I supervise it myself."

"I don't see how you do it all," Lisette said sympathetically.

"The right servants and—above all—the right guests. It's a matter of having certain parts of each day planned for them, while leaving them to their own devices the rest of the time. That means people who are congenial and can find their own amusements. I hate to harry them around all the time like a shepherd with his flock. As long as card tables are set up, the tennis court is ready, and the croquet field arranged, I can relax. The main thing is checking all the menus with the cook and making certain the provisions have arrived."

"I think a single dinner at a time in London will be all I can manage. And a few people in for afternoon tea from time to time."

"And no more will be expected of you," Jane said. "One thing, do be ready for unexpected guests at tea. Never for dinner, but teatime is more informal; when women have been out shopping or at some charity event, they're very apt to think of dropping in for a bit of tea and a visit. But Mrs. Mabering will handle that for you. She'll always be prepared as far as the food is concerned. Just be sure you're ready to receive them."

"But what if I'm out myself? Do I always have to be at home at that time?"

"Oh, they'll understand, leave their calling cards, and go somewhere else. You'll be doing the same thing the afternoons we go out."

My, Lisette wondered, would she ever become familiar with all the demands of English etiquette?

The weekend guests began arriving early Friday afternoon, and Lisette met most of them at tea. The Prince and his party would arrive in time to dress for the ball, and he would not appear before he made his formal entrance. Some twenty guests were spending the entire weekend, many of whom Lisette already knew and with whom she felt comfortable. Among them was a man to whom she found herself disturbingly attracted: Lord Gerald Boswick, heir to the Duke of Highcastle. Some years older than she, he had a quiet assurance so vastly different from the superficial patina of most of Jane's guests. With no Lady Boswick in attendance, Lisette wondered if he were widowed, separated, or single. She'd done no more than speak to him for a few minutes after they were first introduced, but she already felt he was a man she would enjoy having as a friend. Maybe something more than that. Because she was not free to marry, it didn't really matter what his situation as long as her feelings were reciprocated by him. She looked at him across the room, where he sat in deep discussion with the Prime Minister. It should be an interesting weekend in many ways, much more so than she'd anticipated.

Lisette watched Lord Boswick closely at tea, and she was more impressed with him than ever. Somehow all she wanted to do was please him, to appear desirable yet innocent of any intrigue. She might never see him again, but making the right impression seemed terribly important to her.

Later that evening, Lisette stood a long time before her mirror. She had some serious second thoughts about the costume she'd just donned, which was an exact duplicate of one in a portrait by Holbein. The idea of appearing as Anne Boleyn to Prince Edward's Henry the Eighth had seemed exciting at first. All she'd considered was the effect she'd have on the other guests. Now she wondered if it were a mistake. The Prince might regret her choice, even if the suggestion had been his. Two weeks had passed since that dinner party, and maybe a passing thought had been replaced by a wish not to be so closely associated with her. No, what she was really worried about was the impression she'd make on Gerald Boswick. What would he think when he saw her, especially if she danced with the Prince? The implications would be obvious.

She looked at the formal dinner gown she'd bought for Saturday night. She could wear that with her mask, with perhaps the addition of a lace scarf draped over her head as a mantilla. Or maybe if she didn't wear the black wig, she'd look like any Elizabethan lady, not one in particular.

Then she glanced at the door leading to an adjoining room, a room in the Prince's suite. Jane had not given her this room as the last one available. It had been purposely chosen for her. If the Prince were disappointed in her, there was no telling how he might react, what he might do or say to make her *persona non grata* in society. She knew he could be a very good friend to those he liked, but a deadly enemy to those who incurred his wrath.

Turning her back on the dinner gown lying on the bed, she placed the brunette wig carefully over her pinned-up hair; then she adjusted it and the headdress until they sat comfortably on her head. She might in no way resemble the Lady Anne in her features, but there was no doubt who she was supposed to represent. Taking as deep a breath as she could manage in the heavily boned bodice, she made ready to go down to the ballroom, which was the entire first floor of the west wing.

Amidst all the gaiety, no one seemed to give her more than a passing glance when she walked in. The Juliets, the Cleopatras, the Indian maidens were so much more obvious. Not seeing Jane Westborne, Lisette walked over to a group of people she knew and was standing with them when the entry of His Royal Highness, Edward, Prince of Wales, was announced. Everyone, including Lisette, gasped at the imposing figure he made in his Henry the Eighth costume, and like the others, she dropped into a deep curtsy when he passed her.

As Master of Revelry for the evening, Edward made an appropriately jocular speech and urged all to join in the fun and dancing. Then he announced: "I shall begin the proceedings by dancing with the lady of my choice."

It was expected the Prince would ask his hostess, Lady Westborne, who wore the garb of an early Dutch ancestor. To everyone's surprise, and Jane's chagrin, he chose Lisette. A one-time favorite of his, Jane had hoped this weekend would bring the return of a close, if not intimate, relationship. She not only had a number of favors to ask, but wanted an invitation to his box at Ascot as well. Now all she could hope for was the obligatory hostess dance.

Edward had been discreet this time about his intentions. He hadn't requested that his room be near that of anyone else, as he sometimes had in the past, so ostensibly, Jane could have had no idea he had his eyes on Lisette. But now, all that Jane needed was one look at the two of them dancing, and she had no doubt of their intrigue. Lisette had said Jane would be surprised at her costume; that, Jane thought, was decidedly the understatement of the year.

Nor was anyone else ignoring "Henry" and "Anne" as they swept around the dance floor. Before they made the full circle one time, the whispers began.

Lisette heard the whispers and saw the glances, but she steeled herself to ignore them. This was her final revenge against Philippe, a moment to savor for the rest of her life. He would learn whose mistress she'd become—gossip traveled rapidly to the Continent—and he'd never dare to bring harm to her or her family. *Lose yourself in the moment,* she told herself, *and forget about the future.* Following her own advice, she had a wonderful time throughout the evening. When she wasn't dancing with the Prince, who was a superb dancer, she had no lack of other partners. Including Gerald Boswick.

"You and Edward make quite an outstanding couple," he told her while they danced.

"It—it was his idea," she said quietly.

"I rather thought it might be, although he's usually a little more temperate in letting the world know who his latest affair is with."

"We're not having an affair, and I'd appreciate your thinking otherwise. Our dressing like this was just for fun."

"Oh!" The single word was as perfect an expression of

278

disbelief as Lisette had ever heard. "How long have you known him?"

"I met him at a dinner party in Paris two weeks ago. It was then he suggested our costumes. I'd mentioned how much he reminded me of Henry, and that gave him the idea. I think he merely wanted to amuse the guests."

"He's done that all right," he said, but there was no hint of a smile in his voice. "You may be sure. And I understand he's staying the weekend."

"Yes, I believe he is." Oh, if only Gerald were not spending the weekend, or she were not, or if Gerald would ask to see her when they were back in London. Even if she did please the Prince and he paid a great deal of attention to her, she still wanted to look forward to seeing Gerald again.

"I understand you've leased the Sheldon house in London," he said.

Good, Lisette thought, *he's gotten off the subject of the Prince.* "Yes, for a year. I do hope you'll come around some afternoon for tea. Jane Westborne tells me people simply come by informally without an invitation, so I would be pleased if you'd feel free to do so."

"I'll look forward to doing just that." And now Lisette was relieved to see a smile on his face.

It was the last Lisette saw of Gerald for the evening, but she was now able to give herself over to complete enjoyment of the ball.

The dances with Edward included the supper dance, and while she sat with him, she found herself liking him more and more. He was as excellent a conversationalist as he was a dancer, and it delighted him to tell others at the table how he'd met her and how she claimed never to flatter or tell a lie.

"Then you're a rare one in this world," one of the men said. "But I see I'll have to watch what I say and do if I'm not to become a victim of your Cassandra-like tongue."

"Oh, please," Lisette laughed, "I don't pretend to foretell the future or do anything so dire as forecasting the downfall of a city. I guess I was just brought up to speak my mind."

"It's still a good thing London is not Troy," the man said. "But beware, Edward, she doesn't have you picked to play the role of Agamemnon. I'd hate to see you stabbed in your bath."

"Have no fear," Edward assured them. "As long as Her Majesty is alive, there's little danger I'll be guilty of too much pride. She can prick it with a single word or glance."

He said it jokingly, but Lisette knew all too well that it rankled Edward to have Queen Victoria treat him, her eldest son, as if he were still a child.

Since royal etiquette forbade anyone to leave before the Prince, he excused himself while the orchestra was still playing. His last words to Lisette were simply that he looked forward to seeing more of her during the weekend.

Good, Lisette thought. *He's created the stir and excitement he wanted, but it will go no further than that. Let people think what they will, I'll know the truth, and I'll be able to convince Gerald Boswick of it.*

Lisette had barely finished undressing and turning down the bed, when she heard a light tap on the door to the adjoining room. For the moment, her heart sank. Nonsense, this was what she had been hoping for since she met Edward in Paris. If people were going to think they were having an affair, it really made no difference if they actually did. And secretly she was rather looking forward to finding out what kind of a lover he was. Tying her robe around her waist, she went to the door with a very special smile on her face.

Although they appeared to be no more than casual friends when around others, the affair between Edward and Lisette was intense and all-consuming from the beginning. The morning after the ball, Lisette was convinced everyone would know simply by looking at her that they had spent the night together, even though Edward sought her out no more frequently than he did anyone else. There was no surreptitious holding of hands, or any loving glances passed between them, and Lisette was free to join Gerald in a game of croquet and to converse with other partners at luncheon and dinner. When Edward asked her if she played cards and she said not very well, he didn't press her to sit at his table, but seemed delighted to find others who played as demonically as he and for stakes as high.

For nearly two months after she returned to London, Lisette saw Edward every night when he had no obligatory social affairs. Sometimes they dined at her house, and often they spent a quiet evening during which she played his favorite pieces on the piano, which had arrived from France. All he asked of her was that she be at home when he was able to come around, or to let him know if she had made other plans. He in no way discouraged her from attending dinners and the theatre with other escorts. As she had hoped, her association with him had put her name on the most exclusive guest lists and afforded her entrée into London's innermost circle.

During those two months, Lisette came to love Edward in a very special way, quite different from the love she'd felt for Philippe. Edward was a good friend as well as an exciting lover, and she enjoyed every moment she was with him. She was happier as Edward's mistress than she'd thought possible when the affair began. She could always be herself, laughing when she felt like it, or quiet if that were her need. Edward was not a man of difficult moods, and she soon learned the few things that did displease him. She could tease him about his gargantuan appetite, but she could never scold or contradict him. He was a fascinating companion, who taught her much about breeding horses and ruling an empire. Considering that Queen Victoria allowed him absolutely no say-so in British affairs, he was amazingly astute in his perception of various domestic and foreign political situations. Often, after one of their more serious conversations, Lisette thought it a great pity his abilities should be held in abeyance until after his mother's death.

One evening, Lisette sat playing a Brahms concerto while Edward reclined, as though asleep, on the large couch in the music room. Running her fingers lightly over the keys, she moved into a Beethoven sonata and continued playing as softly as possible. She knew Edward was not asleep, only resting, but she didn't want to disturb his mood.

Without changing position, Edward opened his eyes. "You are very good for me, Lisette."

"Thank you, Edward. Why am I?"

"When I'm with you, I don't have to pretend to be someone I'm not."

"I don't know why you should ever have to pretend," she said. "Why can't you just be what you are?"

"Ah, that shows how little you know about being a prince of the realm. There are times when I have to be regal whether I feel like it or not." He sat up and stretched. "I must never appear bored or uncomfortable or irritable. Above all, I must not yawn or stretch as I did just now. Both would be unforgivable in public."

"I was under the impression you acted very much as you pleased most of the time," Lisette said, smiling impertinently.

"More of your ignorance, my love. You sound like Her Majesty when she upbraids me for enjoying myself on the Continent. But I walk a very straight line here in England."

"Indeed you do." She knew very well why Edward could

invite her, along with others, to share his box at Ascot, but could not invite her to parties at Sandringham in Scotland or to his magnificent pavilion at Brighton. His actions, and the rumors of his various mistresses, had brought him under maternal fire, and this was a period when he was trying to show Her Majesty that he could be a good boy.

"That's why I appreciate your letting me visit here in the evening and waiting for me whether or not I'm able to come. I couldn't get through this period without you."

Lisette merely nodded her head. Princess Alexandra was still in Denmark; despite his proclivity for seeking out beautiful women, she knew that Edward's wife remained the one stable aspect of his life. He might cavort at wild parties with some of the most notorious women in London, or spend his evenings with a current mistress, but he wanted Alexandra there when he needed her.

Not all of their evenings ended in lovemaking and Lisette was pleased she could comfort and satisfy him in ways other than the physical. She sensed his need for a few genuine friendships, people with whom he could, as he'd said, be himself. Why he felt that way with her, she didn't know, but it was deeply gratifying.

Almost every time he came to the house, Edward brought her a gift, nothing very elaborate or expensive, but something he'd obviously chosen because he thought it would please her. It might be a small bouquet of flowers, a tiny enameled pin surrounded by pearls, a book, or a piece of music he wanted her to play for him. Then one night he brought her a magnificent sapphire-studded silver box with a miniature portrait of himself on the cover. She'd said sapphires were her favorite stone. The gift indicated that their love affair, if not their friendship, was coming to an end.

Knowing from the beginning that the intensity and the constancy of their affair could not last, Lisette was less upset than she might have been when Edward mentioned he would not be visiting as often. She would miss him, because she had grown genuinely fond of him, but he promised he'd return from time to time, if only to hear her play. The one consolation were the doors, heretofore closed to her, that he'd opened. And she would always be one of the guests invited to special functions. She was to stay on his yacht during Cowes and join him in his box at Ascot. She now had her ticket to society, and she only hoped the price she'd paid was not too dear.

Gerald came by for tea one afternoon while she was still seeing Edward. Fortunately no one else dropped in, and they had a pleasant hour together. He made no mention of the rumors she knew were going around Mayfair about her and the Prince, and she hoped he thought them merely that—rumors. Anticipation of future visits, however, came to an abrupt end almost immediately.

"I was wondering," he said, "if you would go to the theatre with me on Tuesday next. It's a lively farce I think you'd enjoy."

"I'm sorry, Gerald, I'd love to, but I already have an engagement." Tuesday was the one night Edward always knew he'd be free to visit.

"I'm sorry, too. I think then I'll leave sooner than planned for High Tor in Cornwall. I've neglected the place badly, and since my uncle, the Duke, is not well, he has pretty much entrusted the running of the estate to me. He's right, of course, in thinking it would be foolish of me to neglect my future inheritance."

"Will you be gone long?" Had her refusal put the truth to the rumors, or had Gerald been planning all along to leave London? She'd probably never know.

"Several months at least," he said. "I have a number of obligations to fulfill."

Lisette had learned by now that there was a Lady Boswick, from whom Gerald was recently separated. Additional rumors suggested it was because his wife had taken a lover. Were the obligations he referred to an attempt at reconciliation?

"Well, at least," Lisette said, "I can hope you'll come by when you do return."

"I'll look forward to it." It was not a promise, but at least it was not an outright refusal. With that she would have to be satisfied while she continued hoping. "I'd best be going," he said. "I have some appointments, and I'm meeting my brother at the club for dinner."

"I'm happy you came by, and I do hope you will again." She did her best not to sound flirtatious so that Gerald would know she was sincere about wanting to see him again.

Chapter Twenty-five

UNTIL 1889, the precarious financial situation of the Panama Company had been hidden from the public and small investors like Baptiste, who were courted because they would not inquire too deeply into the legal and financial aspects of the company. When, early in the year, Baptiste had heard first the rumors of trouble and then read newspaper accounts about the company's serious financial straits, he'd still hoped to recoup his original investment if not any dividends. Victor Duchalais had been pessimistic about recovering any of the money, but he hadn't thought it impossible. The company might yet make a turn-around once the jungle was conquered and actual construction of the canal begun. It was on that chance Baptiste placed all his hopes.

But now a new report had come in, a report sent not only to the investors but headlined in all the newspapers as well. The Panama Company had filed for bankruptcy. Names other than DeLesseps appeared, such as Jacques de Reinach and Dr. Cornelius Herz, who had been responsible for raising the original money and for the public relations work that had everyone thinking all was well when the Company was actually being decimated by bribes and payoffs as well as yellow fever.

To Baptiste the news was a staggering blow. The worst, of course, was the loss of all the money he'd sunk into it over the years. The import company would be in serious danger if business should slow down and there were a need to dip into the surplus. A surplus that no longer existed and which would take years to replace. In addition, there were the notes for the money he'd borrowed to invest in the Panama Company. Victor Duchalais had said not to worry about them, but Baptiste *was* worried. He was not a man who liked to be in debt, and he'd allowed himself to borrow the money only because he'd been so certain the returns would not only pay off the notes but give him financial security as well. He'd also had a dream, and now he had to see that dream vanish completely. With the Suez Canal opening up new routes between Europe and the East, he'd hoped, once the Panama waterway was completed between the Atlantic and the Pacific, to expand his import business to the west coast of the United States with an office in San Francisco. It hadn't been feasible as long as ships had to go around the Horn.

Baptiste slumped behind his desk. No, he would not consider the dream destroyed, only postponed. There had to be a way; he would find it and have that office in San Francisco. Right now, though, he had to figure out how to increase the business they had from their present sources in Europe and Asia and get his company back on safe ground. He'd go back into the office, and with Jean as assistant manager, he'd figure out some way to double their business.

Jean knew he'd done well as assistant manager, particularly in handling the European division, and he wondered at his father's sudden daily appearance at the office.

"Something's worrying Papa," he told Céline one night. "I wish I knew what it was."

"Maybe you should ask him, if it's disturbing you that much." Céline looked across the table at her husband. He was not the romantic hero she'd once visualized as having for a lover, and she'd become pregnant only in the hopes of getting her hands on some of the Fontaine money. That desire had been dashed, and she'd lived through months of hell before Jean went to his father for help just before Armand was born. She still had nightmares about the damp basements they'd lived in, the nights Jean came in stinking of the sewers of Paris or of the manure he'd gathered and spread on farmlands. She also couldn't forget how a lack of food finally brought on the illness that sent Jean back to the château.

If life since then had not been as luxurious as had been her dream, they did at least have this beautiful apartment. They still had to economize to live on Jean's salary, and she had to welcome the rest of the family whenever they came to Paris, but if she really thought about her life, she had to admit she was happy. She no longer tried to decide whether she loved Jean or just found living with him comfortable. And she had her two sons. She'd never thought of herself as possessing intense maternal feelings, but when she held Roland or played with Armand, she knew she felt a deep need fulfilled.

285

It was important to Céline that Jean be appreciated for what he did at the office. When he was hurt, she too felt the hurt, and she wanted her husband to be happy. Now she waited for his response.

"I can't ask him," Jean said. "If he's chosen not to confide in me, then I have to respect that decision."

"And our plans?" Céline asked. "Are you going to talk to him about them?"

"This week. I had to find out if the property I saw is for sale."

"And?"

"It is." A wide grin spread across Jean's broad face.

"Wonderful!" Impulsively, Céline got up from the table and ran around it to hug him.

"Well," Jean said, "I should come home with surprising news more often."

"I know what this means to you. I've watched how restless you've become over the past few months."

"What does it mean to you, Céline?"

"I've enjoyed it here in Paris. I really have. And I know I'll be giving up this apartment for a very small house. But it will be my house. And look at me. I'm a country girl at heart."

He pulled her down on his lap and buried his face in the warm spot between her throat and shoulder. "You're my girl, Céline, and you always will be. I fell in love with you the first time I saw you. I thought then I could never love you more than that. I was wrong."

"The boys are both in bed," she said, unfastening the front of her dress and putting Jean's hand inside.

"God, Céline, how is it you can always sense when I need you?"

"Because I need you, too." And she did. Marriage had not dulled her appetite for physical intimacy, and Jean's ability to keep her satisfied was another positive aspect of her life with him; it made up for her feelings of inadequacy with the rest of the family, for her occasional feeling of being trapped in a situation she had not wanted.

Later, after they'd made love, Céline said, "Your father has to agree to your plans. If he's come back to the office, it must mean he's missed it. Think how much easier it will be to ask him. He probably feels he's in the way now."

"That's what I'm hoping." Jean thought of the notations

286

he'd made. To others they might look like a number of simple sentences. To him they were the fulfillment of a dream.

It was no use. No matter how Baptiste arranged and rearranged the figures the only way the company could get on solid ground was to expand, and that meant finding more money for capital investment. He doubted that Duchalais would lend him what he needed unless he had specific, well-founded plans. That was what he had to come up with.

Baptiste looked up to see Jean standing at the door of the small office off the shipping room he'd taken as his own.

"Come in, Jean. Something up front you need me for?"

"No, but I'd like to talk to you, Papa. If you have a minute."

"Always. Come on in." Glad for the interruption, Baptiste reached for a cigar and sat back. "What's on your mind?"

"I was wondering if you were planning to return to the office on a permanent basis."

"Why? Does it bother you that I'm here? Am I looking over your shoulder too much?"

"No—no, sir, nothing like that. It's just that if you were, I have a proposition I'd like to present."

"Tell me your proposition," Baptiste said, "and then I'll answer your question." Baptiste wondered what the boy had in mind. Jean was a good worker but was somewhat lacking in imagination and inventiveness.

"You know it was always my ambition to work in the import firm."

"How well I know. From the time you were barely tall enough to reach the counters, you begged to come in with me every day."

"And I've enjoyed the work here. I really have. I think I've done well."

"You have, Jean. I'm proud of you. All your promotions and raises have been because you deserved them, not because you are my son. I hope to see you manager before long."

"Thank you, sir. But the truth is, I'd like to make a change."

Baptiste's eyebrows rose with displeasure. "You're thinking of going with another firm after I've trained you so carefully?"

"Oh, no, sir, nothing like that. I would never do that to you."

"Thank goodness," Baptiste said. "Though I didn't really think you would. What do you have in mind?"

"Sometime before I left home—I can't really say when— I began to think I'd like to work on the land."

"Yes, I remember what one of the farmers said one of the times we were looking for Nicole. He said the two of you often visited him and talked about how to work the land. I'd forgotten that until now." But what could the boy possibly have in mind now that there was no farm land connected with the château?

"Well," Jean said, no longer fearful about broaching the subject, "I've become interested in the cultivation of grapes and the production of wine. I've read everything I could get my hands on. With the right vineyards, there's good money in it. Especially if one can find mature vineyards that are already producing successfully."

"Grapes, hum? Never thought of you as a vintner, Jean. Since you're bringing the subject up now, I presume you have found the right vineyards."

"I have, Papa. Several acres are for sale near Villedommange, not far from Rheims. It's champagne country, and the harvests are said to be unequalled.'"

"So you've been doing a lot of reading. How about experience? You haven't a damn bit of experience in working any kind of crop, let alone grapes. I don't know much, but I do know they and the soil require constant attention while they're growing and a very special knowledge of when to pick them."

"Surely I can learn all that as I go along," Jean insisted. "More, I mean, than what I've already read."

"Grapes are scarcely a crop to experiment with. How many years do you think you can afford to lose money if the first and then the second crop fail?"

"None, sir, but I don't intend to fail. I intend to be a success."

"That's easy to say." Damn! Baptiste thought. He hadn't seen the boy this adamant about anything since his insistence he was going to marry Céline.

"And just as easy to do if I put my mind and back to it, as I intend. I want to get back to the country and so does Céline. I always appreciated your taking me in when I needed this work so desperately, but I don't want to be held to it forever."

"Nor do I want you to stay if you feel so strongly about leaving," Baptiste said. "I can appreciate your longing to do what you really want, and I'm not going to hold you back. How soon do you have to make a decision about buying the vineyards?"

"By the end of this week. I only learned recently they were for sale, and the present owner said he would hold off selling to anyone else until then. But that's as long as he can wait."

"I see," Baptiste said. "And who do you propose to take your place here?"

"Henri should be thinking about coming in here."

"No, Henri is at St. Cyr, and he wants to graduate from there. I don't know what other plans he might have, but I gave you the chance to do what you wanted. He should have no less."

"Maybe I can handle both jobs," Jean suggested. "I can take the train in from Rheims every morning. Most of the other vintners have full-time jobs in addition to the fields, and the grapes won't require my attention all the time."

"No, you can't divide yourself that way. At least not until you have more experience with the vineyards." Baptiste realized that in a way he owed this opportunity to Jean. He'd lived uncomplainingly on a small salary, and Céline had taken care of the apartment in place of a paid housekeeper. "If you will plan to come into the city when I need you, I'll come back on a full-time basis. I've begun to vegetate in the country, and I think it will do me good to be here more often."

"You're quite certain, Papa? It won't be a hardship?"

"Oh, your mother will fuss for a while, but then she's always fussing at me—in her gentle way—for not having anything to do around the château." No point in worrying Jean with the fact he was confined more and more to his wheel-chair.

"The next point, Papa, is about the money. I—I was hoping you would be willing to invest in the vineyards. I'd pay you back, of course, once I begin seeing a profit. And Céline and I will live frugally, so that should be within a few years."

Baptiste had wondered how long it would be before the question of money would be raised. He'd had a wild hope that Jean would change his mind during their conversation, but inevitably, the time had come to tell his son there were no surplus funds in the company from which to draw.

289

"I'd like to think about it, Jean." Baptiste played for more time. "Till the end of the week, you say?"

"Yes, I put all my savings down as earnest money."

"And the amount?" Baptiste looked at the slip Jean handed him. "Hmm, seems like a fair price for good champagne fields. Let me think about it overnight. I'll tell you tomorrow morning."

"Thank you, Papa. I promise you this, you'll never be sorry if you do decide to invest." Not until he left his father's office did Jean allow his shoulders to slump. If Papa didn't agree, there was no place else for Jean to turn. Papa had to agree, he had to. There was more than enough money in the import firm's surplus fund which his father kept in a secret account. He hadn't seen those books lately, but if the money were increasing at the rate it had a few years ago—and it should be, the way the business was going —there could be no question of using part of it for the vineyards. Yet Jean knew his father was a shrewd businessman, and he could only hope he'd convinced him he'd succeed as a vintner. In one more day, he'd know if he'd be returning to the country or staying in Paris instead, until he was able to save the money for some other good opportunity.

Immediately after Jean left his office, Baptiste phoned Victor Duchalais and asked him to have lunch with him.

"You must be a mind reader, Baptiste. I was just thinking about you."

"Good thoughts, I hope."

"Always," Duchalais said. "About lunch. Let me come by and pick you up at one."

"I'll be ready."

For the time being, Baptiste put the idea of a San Francisco office out of his mind. If Jean were right about the vineyards, that might be a better place to put new capital investment. Duchalais had offered to be his business advisor, and now was the time to take him up on the offer. For the next two hours, Baptiste was busy with a new set of figures, starting with the purchase price of the vineyards. To that, at least a year's living expenses for Jean had to be added, plus a substantial amount for costs connected with the vineyards until they produced. The question of having their own winery hadn't come up yet, but he'd have to look into that possibility. They were more likely to sell the grapes to an established winery in the district until they could see their way to building their own. Probably, that meant they would see a return as soon as the grapes were harvested, rather than having to wait until the wine aged and was sold.

When Duchalais came by in the carriage, Baptiste was waiting at the front door of the company's building.

"Did your family enjoy the centennial celebration?" Duchalais asked.

"Almost too much. Little Robert thinks he should be coming to the city every night to watch the fireworks. After seeing some of the art exhibits, Nicole is hounding me to let her move here and live in Montmartre. We finally came to a compromise when I agreed she didn't have to go to school anymore and could have an art instructor three days a week and spend as much time as she wanted in her studio."

"And Lisette? Philippe mentioned he once saw her driving through the Bois."

"She's returned to England. She doesn't write often, but she's leased a house in London and seems to be enjoying herself."

"I'm sorry," Duchalais said. "I was still hoping she and Philippe would get back together. He's never said what the trouble was, and I don't ask."

"The same with us and Lisette, although I have the feeling she's told her mother more than she told me. But as you said, maybe it's better not to ask."

Baptiste postponed any talk of business until after they'd ordered their meal and were sharing a bottle of wine.

"Tell me, Victor, what do you think of the champagne industry?"

"Just curious or asking my advice?"

"It's the advice I'm after. I've been trying to think of a way to expand the import business to increase the profits. I had hoped, of course, to open a San Francisco office when the Panama Canal was finished. Since that's now out of the question, I've been thinking about something else. Actually, it was Jean who gave me the idea. The boy is tired of the city, and it seems he's always wanted to be a farmer of sorts. It was news to me; I thought he liked the office. Anyway, he has a chance to buy several acres of vineyard not far from Rheims."

"That's good champagne country," Duchalais said.

"But would it be a good investment? Jean claims he's read everything he can find, but, of course, he's had no experience whatsoever."

"I know some of the vinters in that section. One, who has

291

borrowed from the bank several times, lives in Mont-Chenot. He'd be happy to give Jean all the advice he needs."

"How far is that from Villedommange?" Baptiste asked.

"Twelve, maybe fifteen, kilometers."

"But how about the champagne business itself? Is it doing well? I'm not thinking about an investment that may take years to bring returns."

"Doing better all the time," Duchalais said. "Especially now that champagne has become so popular in England and the States. The vintner I mentioned has paid back every loan right on time. And each loan was to expand his acreage."

"Popular in England and the States, you say?" Baptiste asked.

"Very. It's considered the queen of wines."

Baptiste's mind was busy with new calculations. "If I invested in the vineyards, what do you think the possibilities would be for our firm to export wine from the vintners in that area?"

"I'd say very good. We'd have to look into it, but if you're one of the growers and offered them good terms, I should think they'd be agreeable."

"Now comes the hardest question of all," Baptiste said. And he smiled to himself to think that the trepidation shuddering through him was a duplicate of what Jean must have suffered earlier. "Is my credit good enough to borrow the money for such a large investment—considering the purchase of the vineyards and the capital needed to run them for at least a year?"

"For at least two years, Baptiste, and more likely three. Isn't that what you planned on when you re-established your plantation after the war?"

"You're right. And we were able to count on a good harvest the first year."

"Speaking of harvest," Duchalais said, "what is the condition of the vineyards right now?"

"Jean says they plan to harvest within the next two weeks. The original owner would, of course, reap the profits from that. Then Jean would take over."

"Then I suggest we all go to Villedommange and see for ourselves." Duchalais raised his wineglass. "Here's to you and the future of the vineyards. May you both prosper."

Within two months, Jean and Céline were settled in a small, half-timbered house on a street of winegrowers in Villedommange. When Jean wasn't in the fields preparing the vines for winter and checking the soil, he was visiting all the wineries in the area to learn more about wine production. Evenings, he visited with other growers, absorbing their advice and information as avidly as one who has just regained his sight delights in the beauty of the world around him. He had no intention of simply being a grower and harvester of grapes. Someday, and not too far into the future, he would have more acres of vineyard, and he would see his own grapes go from the first stage through the bottling of the wine.

The work was hard and the hours were long, but Jean discovered a new kind of contentment from working with the soil. This was the life he'd dreamed about for years, and now he was a part of it.

He thought his happiness was complete when Céline announced she was pregnant again. Then, when she gave birth to a daughter, Fleur, Jean could scarcely contain himself.

Nor could Leah. As soon as Jean wired her that Céline had gone into labor, Leah picked up her already packed bag and took the train from St. Denis to Rheims, where Jean had a carriage and a driver waiting for her. She arrived just minutes after Fleur was born.

"Oh, Céline, she's beautiful," Leah said as she helped the midwife bathe the baby and wrap her in warm blankets.

"But she's so tiny, Mama Fontaine."

"With your rich milk, she'll soon put on weight."

At the end of her short visit, Leah returned to the château with an easy heart. Jean was doing well with the vineyards and looking forward to his first harvest. He and Céline seemed truly happy, devoted to each other and their children. Best of all, Fleur had put on weight and, although more delicate, would soon be as plump as her brothers had been at that age.

Chapter Twenty-six

NEVER A GIRL to do just one thing at a time, Denise was relaxing on the terrace overlooking the back garden and embroidering a linen pillow sham for her hope chest. At the same time she was watching ten-year-old Robert fighting imaginary enemies with his wooden sword and cautioning him against getting dirty. She was also listening for the sound of carriage wheels on the front drive. Her beloved oldest brother, Jean, was coming for a three-day visit to report on the success of the first harvest from his own vineyards.

Villedommange was not that far from the château, but from the time the vines flowered, over three months earlier, he had stayed close to the vineyards to watch every step of their progress. This was, after all, his first full season as a winegrower. It would be so good to have him at home for three full days. A pity Céline would not be with him. Denise had been her ardent admirer and staunch advocate since she'd married Jean. Now she was openly envious of Céline for having three children. But Jean's note had said that Fleur was still sickly and frail, and Céline would neither leave her nor come and bring her.

Denise knotted the embroidery thread and bit it off close to the material. Then she carefully folded the linen inside a towel to keep it clean until she could put it in the hand-carved chest. Although the chest was nearly filled with linens, enough for every room in the home she hoped to have one day, she was no closer to marrying than she'd been when Mama had bought it for her in Paris.

It wasn't that she was eager to leave home, and she knew from her few visits to Paris that she didn't want to live in the city. Her greatest wish was still to marry and have a houseful of children. She could imagine nothing more ideal than having a baby every year until the house was overflowing. Which meant, she thought, she should not wait too much longer to get started. So far, however, Mama and Papa hadn't been in any hurry to introduce her to eligible young men. Perhaps, she thought, it was because of Lisette's tragic marriage. But it was not right to let one person's mistake affect another's future.

Although she was uncomfortable among large groups of people, and became almost physically ill at the idea of meeting strangers, Denise thought that perhaps she should let Mama and Papa know she would like to have a party at the château. She would try her best not to be shy and tongue-tied when introduced to the young men from the families of friends in the city. She knew that was why she'd never appealed to the few Papa had brought to the country or she'd met in Paris. Nor was she as beautiful as Lisette, who could immediately charm every man who came near her. *Oh dear,* Denise thought, *there isn't a thing about me to appeal to a man, so why should it be that all I want is to marry and have a home?*

"Come, Robbie," she called, "time to go in and get ready for dinner. Surely Jean will be here in a few minutes," she added impatiently.

"Will he bring us some of his wine?"

How much like Papa he looks, Denise thought. *Nicole looks like Mama and Lisette looks like her mother. And I don't seem to look like anybody but myself.*

"Goodness no, not yet. The grapes have to be pressed at the winery and then—oh, it's a long process. Maybe he'll explain it to us tonight."

"I don't want him just to tell. I want to see it. When can we visit him again?"

"Why don't you ask him? I'm sure Céline would love to have you spend a few days and play with Armand and Roland."

Denise heard the sound of wheels on the drive just as she entered the rear door, and she ran down the long hall to the front. Leah was already there with her arms outstretched, so Denise stepped back to wait until she could greet Jean in her own way.

"It's so good to see you," Leah exclaimed as she hugged him. Then he stood back to look at him. She could never get over how mature and settled this oldest son of hers had become.

"And happy to be here, Mama. I've brought you something, too." He handed her a package.

"Oh, Jean, you know how I love surprises. What is it?"

"Open it up and see," he said, and a brief smile flitted across his usually serious face.

She opened the round, flat package. "How did you know I've been longing for some of this wonderful Brie cheese?"

"And rousselet pears to go with it?" He handed her a string bag.

"We'll have them tonight." She looked at Denise who had moved up quietly and put her arm around Jean's waist. "Denise, please take these to the kitchen."

"I'll put them on a platter and set them on the table." She smiled up at Jean, waiting for a word from him; when he winked at her, she started to leave.

"Wait," Jean said, "there's someone I want both of you to meet. A friend I brought with me. He's outside talking to Nicole now. By the way, how's Nicole doing?"

"We see her at meals," Leah said, "but she spends the rest of the time in her studio or walking the countryside with her paints and easel. Other than that, she seems content, but I worry that she keeps so much to herself."

"Content or too passive?" Jean remembered how vivacious and excited Nicole had been when she'd visited them some years earlier in Paris.

"I know," Leah said. "I wish something would bring her out of her shell."

"I'll see if she'll go back to Villedommange with me. It would at least be a change of scenery and new material for her to paint. Now, let me call Edouard in." He stepped outside the door. "Edouard, come in and meet the rest of the family."

Hearing all the voices, Baptiste had wheeled himself from his office. Except for moving from the house to the carriage, Baptiste used the wheelchair all the time while at home. By marshalling his strength there, he was able to continue walking with crutches when in the city and to give the appearance of still being hale and hearty. It would not be good for business if people thought he was becoming feeble and unable to run the firm.

After the introductions, Blanchette appeared to announce that the roast was done to a perfect turn. Everyone immediately went into the dining room to avoid insulting Blanchette's creation. Denise kept her head lowered while she ate. The one time she'd looked across the table at Edouard Valcou, she found his eyes staring straight into hers. Now she was afraid she would blush. As shy as she was, she'd never felt quite this way around any of the young men she'd met. She could usually manage to say something, but now she found herself grateful the others were carrying on an animated conversation that allowed her to remain quiet. Not until halfway through dinner did she realize that Edouard had spoken very little himself.

"Papa," Jean was saying, "Edouard has vineyards between Versenay and Verzy. We met at a convention of winegrowers in the section, and he's been of inestimable help to me. He inherited the vineyards, and he's been supervising them and his own winery for more than twelve years. You can't imagine the number of problems he's been able to solve for me."

"I appreciate that, Edouard," Baptiste said, "considering I have something of a stake in Jean's success."

Before Edouard could answer, Jean was talking again. Leah thought she'd never known him to be quite so voluble. "Oh yes, we can credit much of our success to his advice. But then, Edouard is one of the most prosperous vintners in all the champagne country."

"Jean," Robert piped up, "when are you going to tell us how wine is made? Denise said you'd explain it all while we ate."

"In a few minutes, Robert," Leah said. "I want to hear about Fleur. How is she? Your note worried me."

"There seems to be nothing medically wrong with her," Jean said. "She just doesn't eat much, and often she can't keep down what she does eat. But she is gaining weight, and the doctor in Rheims says it's something she'll grow out of. Just to be patient."

"That's good. I miss her and the boys."

"Then come back to Villedommange with me," Jean said. "We can put you up at the inn. I wish all of you would come for a visit. It's been a long time; Papa, you haven't even seen the vines this year."

"Later, perhaps, Jean. Right now things are pretty busy at the office." He didn't want to admit he was not up to such a trip. "But some of the others can go if they wish."

"Now, Robbie," Jean asked, "what is it you want to know about making wine?"

"Let's move to the library for coffee," Leah suggested, "and then you can tell all of us."

Once they were seated around the fire that had been lit to relieve the evening chill, Jean said, "I think Edouard should take the floor now. After all, he's the prosperous winemaker here, and I'm only a tyro. I haven't done more than watch, while he's spent years supervising the process from beginning to end."

As quiet as Edouard had been during dinner, he came into his own as he explained the detailed and delicate procedure of turning grapes into the finest champagne in the world. Denise hung on every word, and not because she was that fascinated with winemaking. As she watched and listened, she wondered if this were what people meant by falling in love at first sight. It made no difference to her even when she heard Jean mention that Edouard was a widower. He was a good many years older than she was, too, which she realized when Jean referred to him as "old sobersides." But she was so much happier being in the same room with him than she was with younger men who tried to impress everyone with their dashing ways and good looks. Others might not call Edouard handsome, but if he were not a smooth, sophisticated dandy, there was something very appealing to Denise in his honest face and workman's hands. He obviously did more than merely supervise the work in the fields, and Denise liked him for that.

She hadn't spoken more than a few words the entire evening, but when Jean suggested both he and Edouard had had a long day and he'd show their guest to Henri's room, Edouard told her he looked forward to seeing her in the morning. Was there a special look in his eyes for her, or was she just imagining it?

For the first time in years, Denise found it hard to fall asleep. She tried to visualize Edouard in various ways around a house: sitting across from her at breakfast, coming in after a long day in the field or the winery, and lying beside her at night. He and Jean would be here for three days. Was there a chance he would fall in love with her during that time? She couldn't play the flirt like Lisette. Or make light, meaningless conversation. If he did fall in love with her, it would have to be because he liked her the way she was.

By the time Denise came down to breakfast the following morning, Jean and Edouard had already been up for an hour.

"Good morning, sleepyhead," Jean greeted her. "You'd never make a good farmer's wife."

Oh, dear, Denise thought, *why did he have to say something like that?*

"I don't know," Edouard said, "as pretty as she is, she'd be worth waiting breakfast for."

He thinks I'm pretty! Unconsciously Denise smiled. She didn't know it then, but at that moment Edouard completely lost his heart to her.

298

"I've been trying to show Edouard the garden," Jean said, "but as much as I've learned about grapes, I can't tell a rose from a weed. You work out there with Mama all the time. How about taking him around?"

"I'd be pleased to." This was like an answer to a prayer. The garden was something she could talk about quite easily.

"For shame, Jean," Edouard said, "she hasn't had her breakfast yet."

"Well, I could use a second cup of coffee," Jean said. "We can sit with her, and then she can show you around."

Denise was scarcely able to do more than nibble at her croissant and take a few sips of coffee. The way the butterflies were flitting in her stomach, she knew she'd be sick if she ate or drank more. "I've had enough," she said. "I seldom eat much in the morning."

For the first few minutes in the garden, conversation was limited to Denise's identification of the various plants and Edouard's appropriate comments. When they reached the bank of the river, Denise started to explain about the secret tunnel, but Edouard was scarcely listening.

"Jean said you'd never make a good farmer's wife. Have you ever thought about being one? A farmer's wife, I mean."

"I've never thought about being a wife to any special person." *Only to someone I could really love,* she thought. *To someone like you.*

"You don't wish to marry?" Edouard's heart sank.

"I didn't mean that," Denise said. "I just meant no particular type of man. Of course I want to marry someday." This was discouraging. He sounded exactly like Jean, like an older brother getting ready to counsel a little sister.

Of course, Edouard thought, *someday, but not while still so young or to someone as old as I am.* "And I'm sure you will when the right man comes along." He turned as if to suggest he was ready to return to the house.

The right man has come along, Denise wanted to cry, but she turned and followed him across the lawn without saying a word.

Baptiste stayed at the château throughout Jean's visit, and most of the time they and Edouard were closeted in his office discussing the details of the vineyards. Victor Duchalais, after his visit to Villedommange, had invested some of his own money in the property. He joined them at the château for an entire day.

Denise returned to her usual regimen of helping with the

299

house and supervising Robert's studies after the tutor left each noon. Unknown to her, Edouard was aware of her every move, and the more he saw of her quiet, gentle ways, the more he was in love with her and knew she would be the perfect wife for him. But it was no use, he thought, she'd never be interested in a man as old as he and a widower as well.

On the morning of the third day, when Jean and Edouard had only a few hours left at the château, Denise was in the garden picking fall flowers for the luncheon table. Edouard saw her there. Without saying a word to either Baptiste or Jean, he left the office and strode out as if he'd decided that it was now or never.

He reached Denise's side and took the flower basket out of her hands. "Denise, I hope you'll forgive me for being rash, but I can't hold it in any longer. I love you and I want to marry you. If that disturbs you, I'm sorry, but I couldn't return home without telling you."

"Disturb me!" If he hadn't taken the basket, she would have dropped it from her shaking hands. "Oh, Edouard, you'll never know how happy you've made me. I love you, too, but I was so sure you thought me still a girl."

"No, you're a beautiful young lady, and I promise I'll always do all I can to make you happy if you'll say yes."

Denise found it impossible to say a word, but she moved into Edouard's arms as if those arms were the ones she'd been waiting for all her life.

With her face still half buried against his chest, Denise said shyly, "I think I knew I loved you as soon as I saw you. But why did you fall in love with me?"

"Because you have the most beautiful eyes and sweetest smile I've ever seen." He lifted her face, and Denise stood on tiptoe so he could kiss her.

"My God, Papa, look out there!" Jean shouted.

"Out where?" Baptiste looked through the office window. "What in the world has gotten into you?"

"In the garden. It's Denise and Edouard."

"Why I do believe he's proposed to her and she's accepted." Baptiste grinned. "You mean you didn't see it coming?"

"Good heavens, no. Why, he's years older than she, and he's been married before."

"All the better for Denise," Baptiste said. "He's just the

man for her. I knew that as soon as I met him. She needs someone settled, who has a good home for her already."

"But wait until Mama hears," was all Jean said.

When Edouard and Denise announced they wanted to be married as soon as possible, Leah was outwardly calm, but the minute she could, she got Denise off in private.

"You hardly know him, Denise. How can you be so sure you love him?"

"I just know, Mama. I love him very, very much, and I want to marry him. I can't think of any greater happiness than being his wife."

"Then wait a bit to make sure. Don't be too precipitous in something as serious as this. Maybe it's because you want to be married, and he's the first man you've cared for."

"I don't need to wait. I am sure." Oh bother! Why did they have to go through all this? "I suppose to you he doesn't look like the handsome, dashing lover you'd choose for me, but I see him as a good husband and father. And that's what's important to me."

"Tell me, Denise, are you really in love with him, or do you just feel comfortable with him?"

"Is there a difference, Mama?" Determinedly single-minded, Denise was ready to fight for what she wanted. Easygoing, placid, and content with her life, she had never had to assert herself before, and she was shaking inside with the thought she might have to defy her mother. But defy her she would in order to marry Edouard.

"Maybe you're right," Leah said. "Lord knows, Lisette learned that looks and style don't insure a happy marriage. That's the one thing I've wanted most for all of you girls. Now Lisette is miserable in England while she tries to prove to everyone she's having a good time, and Nicole is so absorbed in her art, I don't think she'll ever be interested in a husband. If marrying Edouard is what you want, then you shall marry him with our blessing. Papa seems delighted, and he's an unusually good judge of men."

"Thank you, Mama." Denise bent over to kiss her. "And you know what? Edouard thinks I'm pretty." With that she ran off to tell him that nothing stood in their way now and that they could be married as soon as the banns were read.

So someone else considered her Denise pretty, Leah thought. *I've always known she was, but it took Edouard to bring out the radiance in her eyes and the color in her cheeks. Dear God, do let this marriage be right.*

Lisette came over to France for the wedding, and once more the whole family was together. During all the pre-nuptial festivities, Lisette managed to mask her tremulous feelings of depression and loss with a façade of gaiety, but Leah sensed the tension Lisette was under, with memories of her own wedding surely being stirred.

Her sisters and Céline helped Denise dress in the gown and veil that Lisette had worn, but Leah came in and shooed them all away so she could have a minute alone with the bride. "Be happy, darling. I think Edouard is going to make you a splendid husband."

During the three weeks of preparation for the wedding, Leah had come to realize that no one could have chosen a better husband for Denise than she had found for herself. Edouard Valcou was gentleness itself, and it was obvious he was deeply in love with her. At first Leah had feared he was merely looking for a wife to replace the one who'd died in childbirth six years earlier. And since the baby had died, too, she worried that he might simply want someone to bear him more children. But her fears were put to rest when she saw him with Denise.

Both the wedding and the reception were smaller than Lisette's, but it was exactly what Denise wanted. When Edouard suggested she might like to go to Paris or the south of France for a honeymoon, she said she'd really like to go right back to his house if he didn't mind.

"Anything you want, darling. We can take a trip later, if you like."

"I want only one thing, to begin being your wife in every way as soon as possible. And I *can* get up early, in time to fix your breakfast."

Jean had continued to tease her that she had a lot to learn about being a farmer's wife, but she would merely laugh and continue with whatever she was doing.

"Only if you want to," Edouard said. "I'm quite used to taking care of myself."

Leah happened to overhear the last of that conversation as she passed the sunroom, and she was reminded of James Andrews saying the same thing soon after they were married. How very much like James, Edouard was. Well, if Edouard brought the happiness to Denise that James had given her during their brief marriage, then she had nothing to worry about.

If it had been hard for Lisette to hide the pain she felt during the days before the wedding, she found it almost impossible to hold back the tears as she heard Denise and Edouard exchange their vows. How blithely she had spoken hers in her own wedding to Philippe, and how full of hope and expectation she'd been. How could something that had seemed so right come to naught? The affair with the Prince, the gay life she led in England—none of it could take the place of what she had wanted, and still wanted, with Philippe. If only she could stop loving him. It wasn't enough to hate him. She had to learn to feel indifferent to him, to stop being haunted by the memories of the days before they were married. Only one man might help her do that: Gerald Boswick. But he'd never returned to her house again after that one afternoon, and she saw him only occasionally in the company of other people. And then he was merely polite.

"Are you going to stay a little while this time, Lisette?" Leah asked, after they'd seen Denise and Edouard off in the carriage to the railway station and the guests had all left.

"I don't know, Mama. It doesn't seem to matter whether I stay or return."

"Is life really as empty as all that for you?"

"That's as good a way as I know to express it. But at least over there there's always something going on. There's a lull now until the pre-Christmas parties begin and the winter season opens. There are a few country weekends I've been invited to, where the men go hunting in the morning and the women sit and gossip until it's time to go into the fields and eat the lunch that the servants bring them. I've learned to play cards, and I'm really very good at it. It's something to do during the long evenings."

"Do you gamble?" Leah looked worried.

"Don't frown, Mama, it's never for high stakes. And I can afford it. Lord knows, Philippe has been generous with money. I can't fault him for that."

"Yes, you look very well dressed." *But so very tired and worn.*

"Going to the dressmaker is the favorite female occupation in London. And then to someone's house for tea. I've heard all the gossip so many times, I'm almost convinced most of it is true."

"Any about you?" Had Lisette had an affair—or affairs

—to ease the frustration of Philippe's failure to consummate their marriage?

"No, Mama, I'm being a very good girl." *Or almost,* Lisette thought. "If you hear I'm flirting with Lord So-and-so, that's as far as it goes." There was no point in worrying her mother and father over the fact that some of the flirtations had, indeed, gone quite a bit further.

"It wasn't Lord So-and-so I was thinking of," Leah said. "I heard something about the Prince of Wales."

"I'm fortunate to have him for a friend—and that is all. He's introduced me to some people I really enjoy knowing." It was true. As of now, he was a good friend and nothing more, so it wasn't an actual lie.

"I'm relieved. And, I might add, very pleased to have you here."

"I'll stay a few more days. I've missed you and Papa and the others. Hasn't Henri grown into a handsome young man? He'll be fluttering hearts before long."

The conversation continued on that light note, and if Leah were still concerned about Lisette's style of life, she was at least relieved she'd found a place for herself that she'd never had in France.

Denise had not been to Edouard's home before the wedding, and she was amazed when she saw it that night. It was nothing like the small house Jean and Céline had in Villedommange; instead it was a country house almost as large as the château. Several centuries old and constructed of the traditional plastered stone, it nestled among beech trees at the foot of a sloping plateau. Surrounding it on all sides were Edouard's vineyards.

Long after they went to bed, Denise and Edouard lay and watched as the blaze in the fireplace burned down to red and then dusty pink coals. Wrapped in his arms, Denise suddenly and inexplicably began to cry.

At first Edouard was too upset to find words to say. Finally, when the tears stopped and she had buried her face against his chest, he was able to ask, "What's wrong, love? Have I—have I made you unhappy? Have I hurt you in some way?"

"No, no, just the opposite. It's because I am happy and I love you very much. Is it wrong of me to hope to get pregnant tonight? I can't think of anything more wonderful than to have a baby conceived at the same moment I know what it means to be really in love."

"And then hope he doesn't come early," Edouard smiled at her, "and have everyone counting on their fingers."

"I wouldn't care, would you?"

"Not if it made you happy. I was afraid I'd hurt you, or —or it had been unpleasant for you."

"Not loving you as much as I do. When Mama and I had a long talk, she told me to be happy. I wish I could tell her right now that I am."

"You really look forward to having children, don't you?" He drew her closer and began kissing her forehead and cheeks.

"I used to say I wanted hundreds, but I'll settle now for a few less."

Edouard thought about his first wife, who'd died in childbirth. *Dear God, don't let me be cursed that way twice. I loved Aileen but not the way I love Denise. She is the most precious thing in my life.*

Denise raised her face so Edouard could reach her lips and waited for him to begin caressing her again. She hadn't been wrong when she'd seen him walk through the door and knew he was the man she wanted to marry.

Chapter Twenty-seven

ALTHOUGH NICOLE WAS NEVER AGAIN as close to Denise as she'd been before the birth of Robert, she'd been able finally to establish an easy relationship with her sister. Often she found that Denise was the one person in the house who could understand and comfort her when things seemed to be going all wrong. Maybe because Denise was such a shy person, she could sympathize with Nicole's need to be alone much of the time, a need apparently not shared by others in the family.

Nicole still suffered occasionally from trancelike states from which she emerged disoriented and terrified, unable to recall what she'd been doing for the preceding hours, but never again had she been as destructive as after Lisette's marriage. Now, she would often waken to find she'd painted

305

something she'd been thinking about consciously; other times she'd find she'd painted something from a nightmare.

It had been several months since she'd had a really bad attack, and Nicole was beginning to think she'd overcome whatever had been disturbing her. Then, some weeks after Denise's wedding, she had another. It did not manifest itself in any violence, but during it she painted a grotesque, almost obscene, picture. She immediately splashed paint across it, so no one else would see it. Then she stood in the studio, shaking as if from chills and fever.

This time there was no Lisette to cheer her up as there had been after Robert's birth, and no Denise to comfort her as after Lisette's wedding. She was alone.

Inspired by Mary Cassatt, she'd been working on an impressionistic Madonna and Child. Now she turned to finishing the Madonna—a young peasant woman nursing her baby in the fields—and planning for more in her series of young mothers with children. Madame Schumann, the baker's wife with whom she'd stayed the time she ran away from home for several days, had recently had a new grandchild, and Nicole hurried into St. Denis to sketch the young mother still in bed with the infant at her breast. Nicole was delighted with the way she caught the tender, laughing smile of the mother when the baby pulled a little too hard. If only she could capture it in oils. With all this work, the feeling of having been once again deserted dissipated little by little, and she was able to sing while she painted and to converse easily with the family at dinner.

"I was worried about Nicole for a while," Leah mentioned to Baptiste one evening. "She seemed to be heading for that same depression she suffered after Lisette's wedding. She and Denise had grown pretty close."

"And you think she's fine now? I'd hate to have to replace all those studio windows again." Baptiste spoke in a light, bantering tone, but he was as worried about his youngest daughter as Leah was. Strange how she was the image of Leah and yet was so different.

"At the rate she's going with her new series of paintings," Leah said, "I think so. And you see how amiable she is at dinner. Have you been in the studio lately?"

"No, it's been several weeks. Not since the wedding."

"You should," Leah said. "You will really be impressed. I think we should plan for a private showing of her work. Do you think one of the galleries would agree?"

"I think so. But why private, if you think she's that good?"

"I really meant by invitation, rather than open to the public. I'd like her to have some critical response to her work, and I'd be proud for our friends to see what she's doing."

"I'll talk to Monsieur Berthoud tomorrow," Baptiste said. "He has one of the best galleries, and he'll know exactly whom to invite."

"Then I'll wait to mention it to Nicole until after you've talked to him. I do hope she'll be pleased if he agrees—or suggests a more suitable gallery for a showing like this."

"I don't know why she wouldn't be," Baptiste said. "If she really wants to pursue art seriously, it's time to find out how good she is—or can be."

After Baptiste came home the next evening with the news that Monsieur Berthoud had agreed enthusiastically, Leah mentioned to Nicole at dinner that she and her father would like to talk to her.

"More private stuff?" Robert asked. "Why do I always get left out?"

"More private stuff, tad," Nicole said. "When you're a little older, you'll be involved in private conversations, too."

"Yes, but then you'll be gone and there won't be anybody left to have them private from."

"And what makes you think I'll be leaving?" Nicole asked.

"You'll get married and go away like Lisette and Denise." He pouted as he swirled cake crumbs in the soupy remains of ice cream.

"And you'll be off to school like Henri."

"Or in the office with Papa," Robert said. "I think I'd like that better. I'm tired of studying."

"Well, you've still years of it ahead of you," Leah said, patting him on the head.

"Mama, don't do that." He tried to squirm away. "I'm not a baby anymore."

"You're my baby, and don't ever forget it. Nor are you a young man yet. So up to your room and those hated books. If you want to work with Papa, you'd better improve your arithmetic."

After he left, Leah, Baptiste, and Nicole went into the library.

"A showing!" Nicole exclaimed when told of the plan. She'd been so certain she'd done something wrong, she had prepared herself to run if need be. Now she jumped up and ran over to her parents. "A real show of my very own?"

"All your own," Baptiste assured her, "with no one else. Monsieur Berthoud said one of his rooms would be available in about two months. Will that be time enough to finish up what you're doing and get them all ready?"

"Plenty of time, Papa. And the critics will be there?"

"Several will be invited along with Monsieur Berthoud's list of clients who are interested in new, young artists."

"Look at me," Nicole said, "I'm shaking all over. I don't know whether it's from excitement or fright."

"Berthoud says you're the youngest artist he's ever exhibited in a one-man show."

"Please, Papa, that doesn't help these jitters."

"But you do feel you're ready, don't you, Nicole?" Leah asked.

"Yes, I feel very good about the last few things I've done. And I can retouch some of the others."

"Will your Madonna series be finished?" These were the paintings that had so impressed Leah. Nicole had captured a universal yet unique quality in each one. In some it was pure happiness; in others, love; still others, anxiety about being a mother for the first time.

"I have only one left to execute. The sketch is complete, but I haven't started the painting. The others just need some finishing touches. Yes, I can have them all ready."

"Then Papa can tell Monsieur Berthoud to go ahead with the plans. You'll want some of your friends from around here to be invited, won't you? You can give me your list."

"Can I really ask them? Madame Schumann and her daughter? And the others I used as models?"

"Of course, Nicole, this is to be your show. You can ask anyone you wish. The exhibit will run for two weeks, and we'll have a gala party the night of the opening."

For the next several days, Nicole felt as if she were walking on air. There weren't enough hours in the day for all she wanted to do, especially for paintings she would like to start and finish before the show. Instead she concentrated on the ones already at hand, knowing she'd be foolish to hang anything done in a hurry. She even agreed to go into Paris with Leah and have a new gown made especially for the opening. It was probably the first time in her life that Nicole really cared about how she was going to look.

Nicole was in the studio, when Leah walked in with the

telegram in her hand. How was she going to tell Nicole that the showing wouldn't take place after all? The news could disturb her far worse than either of the weddings had. This, Leah feared, was a reality that Nicole could not face.

"Mama! Come in. See how I've changed the color in this dress, made it a little softer." She pointed to one of the Madonnas.

"Yes, yes, it looks better."

"Then that one's finished and ready to be framed. Goodness, do you think we'll get it all done in time?"

"There's no hurry now, Nicole. The show has to be postponed."

"Why?" Nicole collapsed against one of the benches. She should have known it was too good to be true.

"This wire. It's from Jean. Fleur is very ill. She's always been frail and unable to eat enough to get strong. Now it's more serious. She can't retain a thing, and she's running a high fever. Céline plans to take her to the doctors in Paris to see if they can diagnose the problem."

"Poor Fleur. And poor Jean." As disappointed as she was, Nicole tried to accept that everything had to be put aside until they knew about Fleur.

"It's only a postponement, Nicole. And maybe you can get a few more of those things done you had in mind."

"I suppose so." Then she saw the strain on Leah's face. "That's exactly what I'll do, Mama. You have enough to worry about with Fleur. Don't think about me."

"I will be thinking of you because I know how disappointed you are. It isn't fair, but then life seldom is. I'm going into Paris to keep Céline company. Jean can't leave the vineyards right now, and Céline shouldn't have to go through this alone. Papa is going to stay out here most of the time, so I count on you to keep him company. All right?"

"All right, Mama. I won't let him get too lonesome for you." Only postponed. That's what she had to keep in mind. There would still be a show. She'd be all right as long as she didn't have another of her attacks. If she did— She wouldn't think about it, because she had the feeling that if she did have one, she would do something much more violent than wrecking the studio.

Leah had not been entirely honest when she told Nicole she was going into Paris only because she thought Céline should not have to go through the ordeal of Fleur's illness alone. After the wire came, she'd paced the floor in her room. She was extremely worried about her granddaughter, but she was also trying to make a decision: Should she go to Villedommange and stay with Jean and the boys, or should she go into the city to be with Céline?

As upset as she'd been by Jean's marriage, she'd grown genuinely fond of Céline over the ensuing years. Céline had proven to be a good wife and mother, and there was no doubt about Jean's love for her. Leah, however, had not been as naive about Céline as Jean was. There were things one woman recognized about another woman that a man could not or—blinded by love or infatuation—would not see. Fortunately there was no question about Armand being Jean's son; at the time they ran off to be married, though, Leah had wondered whether Jean had been tricked into the marriage to cover up another man's pleasure.

Céline claimed to be all in favor of Jean's wish to return to the country, but Leah wondered if her enthusiasm had been sincere. Leah found it hard to believe that the country, which was sure to remind her of her unfortunate life with the miller, wouldn't set Céline to longing for the more exciting life of the city. There might, just incidentally, be a man she'd met while living there. Leah was cross with herself for having these thoughts, but she could not make them disappear. So she would go to Paris. Jean had said there was a woman who would come in every day to keep house and take care of the boys, and he would be with them at night. Paris was definitely the place for Leah to be.

"Oh, Mama Fontaine, I'm so glad you're here." Céline fell into her arms the minute Leah opened the door to the apartment. "You won't know Fleur when you see her. You won't believe she could lose so much weight and still be alive."

"She's in the hospital?"

"While they run some tests, yes. Then the doctors say I can bring her back here. I can give her as good care as the nurses, and I'll only have to take her back for certain treatments. I don't even understand what's wrong with her."

"Can we go there this afternoon?" Leah was furious with herself for thinking what she had about Céline. Her daughter-in-law was absolutely distraught and on the verge of collapse. "It's a good thing I came when I did. You don't look as if you've eaten anything yourself for days."

"I haven't. I couldn't swallow. Everything just stayed in my throat and choked me. Yes, I was going to leave in about an hour. The doctor will meet me at the hospital then. Maybe he can tell us something more definite."

"We'll go to the hospital, and then we'll come back and I'll cook you a good dinner," Leah said. "And stand over you until you do eat it. It won't do Fleur any good for you to get sick."

"Again, thank heavens you're here. When Jean said he didn't dare leave the fields now, I didn't see how I could go through this alone."

"Well, you're not alone now. Perk up so Fleur won't see you've been crying. Even a child can tell when something's wrong." *And I'll do the same,* Leah thought. *This little girl whom Jean loves so much simply has to get well.*

Leah could scarcely keep from crying out when she saw Fleur. Céline had been right. She wouldn't have recognized her. Fleur could hardly lift her hands to take the soft doll Leah brought her. Leah turned toward the window so neither Fleur nor Céline would see her tears. She turned back again when the doctor came in.

His explanation was anything but simple or satisfactory. "There are two possibe reasons why she can't retain her food. The first is that there is a blockage at either the entrance to or exit from the stomach. I'm inclined to think it's the latter, since she does swallow the food and retains it for a time. If that is the case, it means surgery, very delicate surgery, and right now she's too frail to undergo it. The other reason is that her system is simply refusing the food, cannot tolerate whatever she's eating. It's a rare illness, but I've seen other cases."

"And?" Leah had to know the prognosis.

"Madame Fontaine—young Madame Fontaine—tells me Fleur has never been strong, but she was gaining weight when fed soft foods as an infant. We can put her on such a diet. Again, whether her system is able to tolerate that diet, or if there is enough of an opening to let liquids through, we still won't know. But we would be able to keep her alive, and maybe strengthen her enough for exploratory surgery."

"You mean go in there and look around?" Céline wailed.

"There, there, Madame Fontaine, it can be done, and it might be the only way to find the answer. I want to keep Fleur here one more night, but you can take her home tomorrow. She'll be more comfortable and responsive with you. I'll suggest a diet for her, as well as some medicine to counteract any spasms that might occur when she eats, and

311

then I'll want to see her at the office every other day. More often if you think you need me."

And so began the round-the-clock regimen of feeding Fleur a few spoonfuls of milk alternated with a watery gruel and soft custard. At first, Fleur could still not keep anything down. Then came the joyous hour, at two o'clock in the morning, when Leah aroused Céline to tell her that it was time for the custard, and that the milk was still in Fleur.

"What do you think, Mama?" Through all their travail together, Céline had gradually dropped the "Fontaine," and Leah felt a new bond of closeness and fondness growing between them.

"I think we have a long way to go, and we won't know for days, maybe weeks, what the future holds, but at least it's a start."

"Now for the custard," Céline said, "and let's pray it stays down, too."

The next few days were anxious ones, waiting after each feeding to see if Fleur were tolerating her food. And she did. Leah knew Fleur would never be strong on a diet like this, but at least she was still alive.

Jean thought that if he had not had his work in the vineyards to keep him busy during the day and exhausted at night that he would have lost his mind. Thank heavens for the boys. Sometimes they followed him around the fields, and then at night fell asleep over their supper plates.

Poor little tykes, he thought, *they can't understand what's wrong with Fleur and why their mama isn't here.* He himself couldn't understand why a child was unable to eat perfectly natural, wholesome food. Heaven knows, the boys were growing like weeds. Every day he waited for some word from Céline. He'd be forever grateful to his mother for going to Paris to be with her; but if only he'd hear from one of them, he could at least be relieved of some of his anxiety.

On one of the days when he took the boys with him to the vineyards, a sudden storm came up, drenching them to the skin before he could get them back to the house.

"Get out of those clothes, right now," he ordered. "Armand, help Roland. I don't need you two getting sick." The housekeeper had left a pot of stew warming on the stove, and he forced them to eat it and to drink tea as hot as they could stand. What would Céline do if they became ill? Oh God, if only she were with them. She always knew exactly what to do in an emergency, and was always so calm about it at the same time.

He looked in the storage chest and saw the strips of flannel. That was it, hot flannels on their chests. And rub them with some of the salve he found in the medicine box. He heated bricks over the stove, wrapped the flannel around them, and prepared to lay the bricks on the boys' chests.

"No, Papa," Armand wailed, "not the bricks! Just the flannel when it gets hot. I wish Mama were home."

"I wish she were, too, but you'll have to make do with me. She does something with the hot bricks," Jean muttered.

"Puts them at our feet," Armand said, "in more flannel."

"Oh, yes, of course." He'd gotten the boys in bed, and now he tucked the bricks in near their feet. "Too hot?"

"No, just right," Armand said. "You're doing fine, Papa." Roland merely nodded and continued sucking his thumb. Someday, Jean thought, he'd have to put an end to that habit, but not tonight.

"The flannels are getting cool, Papa," Armand called out. Jean had just sat down in front of the parlor fire with his first pipe of the evening. Usually he was into his third by this time. And there was a new article on testing grapes for sweetness he wanted to read.

"Take them off then," he said, "and hand them to me." *How often do they have to be reheated?* he wondered.

As if Armand had read his father's thoughts, he said, "Mama usually comes in several times during the night to check on us. Will you do the same?"

"If Mama does it, then I guess I will."

"And she tells us a story, too, so we can go to sleep."

"How about my reading an article on grapes, instead? Wouldn't you like to learn more about them?"

"Sure. All right with you, Roland?"

Roland said something, but his thumb impeded the full import of it, and Jean could only assume he'd agreed. The boys were asleep before he'd barely started the article, and Jean was able to go back to the fire and finish it.

In spite of Jean's hourly ministrations during the night, by morning the boys were flushed and both had a hacking cough. Worse still, the housekeeper sent word by her daughter that she couldn't come over that day. Jean was frantic; he had to see to the vineyards after the heavy rain of the day before.

313

"I can stay, Monsieur Fontaine, if you like. I'm a good cook, and I'd be happy to take care of the boys."

"Would you really? I may have to be gone all day." He looked at the young woman in her wide skirt and full, freshly ironed apron. Thank heavens for at least one bit of good luck.

"Don't worry about a thing," she said. "I'll give them lunch and have a good supper waiting for you."

"Thank you, Mademoiselle—?"

"Josette."

Jean went to the fields with a much lighter heart than he'd had a few minutes earlier. If only there would be some good news from Paris.

For the next four days, Josette appeared every morning with the word that her mother was not feeling well and that she would continue to take her place. There was no need to tell Monsieur Fontaine that she had encouraged her mother to stay home after she came to the house the first time.

At first the boys seemed to be getting better, and then suddenly their temperatures shot up again. Jean began to wonder if he would ever know another good night's sleep. Between caring for the boys and working in the vineyards, he was close to collapse.

In Paris, Céline and Leah were enduring the same turmoil. Fleur would seem to be improving slowly, even gaining a little weight, and then she would be unable to retain food and rapidly begin losing everything she'd gained.

"There can be no thought of an operation now," the doctor told them, "and I'm convinced a blockage is the problem."

"But why?" Leah asked. "Why was she able to eat for a while?"

"The blockage is getting worse. Something is closing up. If it had been a matter of her body not tolerating the food, she wouldn't have begun to improve for that time."

"So what do we do? Just sit and watch her die?" Leah was beyond tears.

"No, we continue with the milk and with foods mashed and strained to a liquid state. If we can bring her weight up a few pounds, I might venture to operate."

So a new regimen began. Milk, meat broth, vegetables mashed, strained, re-strained, and diluted with the broth. Once again, Fleur began to improve.

"If she continues doing this well," the doctor said after several days, "I think we can operate next week."

Do we really want them to operate? Leah thought. *Cut open that little body and try to find among all her tiny organs that one place threatening to kill her?* Of course there could be only one answer. They had to do whatever was necessary, to take the one chance that would mean keeping Fleur alive.

Leah and Céline had finally worked out a schedule that allowed both of them to get some much-needed sleep. Four hours on, feeding Fleur every hour, and four hours off. They managed to alternate the visits to the doctor between morning and afternoon, so neither had the burden of always being the one to take her. Whichever one went, she usually came back exhausted and ready to collapse. The other immediately took over, no matter whose turn it was.

"I'm going to put a pallet in the kitchen and spend the night," Josette said after Jean received word that things were not going at all well in Paris.

"No need for you to do that," he said.

"I insist. The boys are getting better, but you'll soon be the one lying sick all day in the bed."

I wish I could do that right now, Jean thought. *I could collapse on that bed and sleep for three days without turning over.*

"I won't argue with you, Josette. But the couch in the parlor would be more comfortable. The back folds down to make a daybed."

"Thank you, sir. I'll be close to the boys there, too, so I can hear them in the night." *And closer to you,* she thought. So far things were going exactly as she'd planned. How fortunate her mother hadn't been able to work here that one day, and that she'd agreed to let Josette take her place from then on.

While the boys recovered from the inflammation in their chests, word from Paris kept getting worse. The latest was that the doctor might have to operate.

No! Jean swore to himself. *No one is going to cut open my baby. She has to get well without that.* Leah had promised she'd send word to him daily, and just as soon as the vines were in good shape, he'd go to Paris to be with Céline and Fleur. He didn't see how he could stand waiting to see Fleur again. She was his baby, his precious little girl. For the first time in years, he broke down and wept.

315

Life had been so good to him and Céline the past few years, and now this. He guessed it was just retribution for thinking his happiness with Céline would never end.

Before going to bed, Jean went in and kissed the boys for the second time that evening. They were already asleep, but he had to reassure himself that they were still with him and getting well.

In later years, Jean would try to make himself understand why he went from the boys' room to the parlor that night, instead of to his own room. He did not try to rationalize his actions; he simply tried to understand what had driven him to it. Was it despair over Fleur's condition? Was he so lonely for Céline that he was past the point of enduring her long absence? Or was it simply a craving that came over him when he thought about Josette lying asleep in there? Whatever, when he walked into the room and found Josette still awake, he broke down in tears again, and she began to comfort him. After that, it was easy to lie down next to her on the couch and feel the joy of her warm body beside his. Like an animal finding release with another of its kind, he gave no thought to what he was doing. All he knew was that all his frustrations were vented, and for the first time in nearly a month, he fell into a restful sleep and didn't wake until morning.

The next day, there were no words spoken about their union, but it was tacitly accepted by both that he would return to the parlor that night and she would be waiting for him. If Jean were suffering any pangs of guilt, he did not let them interfere with the pleasure he found with Josette. She welcomed him eagerly, and her passion was such that no matter how tired he was, she could always arouse him.

"Don't go, Jean," Josette begged one night when he'd started to get off the couch. "Stay and I will please you as you've never been pleased before."

"More than what we've already had together? You wear a man out, Josette."

"Ah, but what I will do now will not tire you, but make you so relaxed and satisfied, you will think you are floating on a cloud. Josette knows what a man needs when he's tired."

"No, I'd better be in my own bed if one of the boys should wake up and come in there. It wouldn't do for them to find me in here."

"Until tomorrow night then. Think of me all day, and think about the very special treat you have waiting for you."

316

Josette smiled to herself after Jean left the room. How jealous Auguste would be if he knew about this affair she was having with Jean Fontaine. But he didn't need to know. It was upsetting him enough that she was staying in this house. Enough, she hoped, for him finally to admit he couldn't live without her. The affair and the pleasure it gave her would be her own secret.

There was no tomorrow for Josette and Jean. The next day brought the wire that said Fleur was to be operated on, and Jean made preparations to leave for Paris. Edouard and Denise, now pregnant with her first child, came to stay with Armand and Roland for as long as Jean had to be gone.

"This is good of you, Edouard," Jean said, "to leave your fields and come over at this time."

"No problem, Jean. I have good workers and an excellent manager."

"What is family for," Denise said, "if not to help out in times of need? You go to Paris and don't worry about a thing here. The boys will be fine."

"And I'll look at that winery you mentioned was for sale," Edouard said, "and see if it's worth buying."

"Thank you, Edouard." Jean was fighting back the tears. "Thank you, Denise."

Denise came up and put her arms around him. Jean had always been special to her, the more so since he'd introduced her to Edouard. "Give our love to Céline, and—and we'll pray for Fleur."

Jean looked at Fleur as she was being wheeled to the operating room. Céline had begun crying and Leah had gone back to Fleur's room with her to offer some comfort. Alone with Fleur for a brief moment, Jean kissed her pale cheeks. He brushed her soft brown hair away from her forehead. So tiny. And such a sweet child.

"Don't worry, Monsieur Fontaine." The doctor had walked up unnoticed by Jean. "She's strong enough now. She looks weak, perhaps, but she's much better than she was when she first came here."

Somewhat heartened by the doctor's words, Jean walked back down the hall to join Céline and Leah. He was not entirely unprepared, however, when the doctor, accompanied by a priest, joined them two and a half hours later to say he was sorely grieved to tell them Fleur had died on the operating table.

"It was her heart," he said. "It simply gave out under the stress of the operation. There was nothing we could do."

Not until Jean returned home after the funeral did he realize just how abominable, how utterly despicable, his affair with Josette had been when his child was dying and his wife needed him with her. He had needed Céline, too, but he hadn't been strong enough to endure the separation alone. He'd turned to another woman. He'd been unfaithful at the very time he should have been completely loyal. If the worry and loneliness had been hard on him, the guilt he felt now was almost unbearable. Worst of all, he knew it would remain with him for the rest of his life. He could feel remorse, he could be a better husband to Céline, but the abomination of that dark, bleak, shameful period in his life, that time of succumbing to temptation, could never be obliterated.

Chapter Twenty-eight

"I DON'T SEE HOW you were able to keep going during all those days of helping Céline," Baptiste said. Leah was spending her fourth consecutive day in bed, so tired she found it impossible to move. "And then to bear up as well as you did throughout the funeral."

"I had to, Baptiste, for Céline's sake. But now look at me. Absolutely immobile. Grief is a strange thing. You can keep going during the worst of it, and then collapse when you should be getting over it."

"It's not something to recover from so quickly."

"I think it was not having you there," Leah said. "I really needed your strength, especially when the doctor came in and said Fleur had not survived the operation. I reached out for you, but all I found was emptiness. That's what took the last of it out of me."

"It wasn't easy staying here." Throughout the worst of the ordeal in Paris, Baptiste had been suffering from one of the most painful attacks in his legs and hips. As much as he'd wanted to be with them, he knew he'd be more of a burden than a help.

"I know, and I'm sorry if it sounded as if I were accusing you. I wasn't. I just wanted you to know how much I need you all the time."

"Well, rest is what you need now, and I'll be right here."

"No," she insisted, "rest is not the answer. I need to be doing something."

Nicole came in carrying Leah's luncheon tray. "How are you feeling, Mama?"

"Much better and ready to get out of this bed." Seeing Nicole made her realize she'd get over the grief of Fleur's death faster if she put her mind to something else.

"I think we should start planning for your art exhibit again."

"So soon, Mama?" As if she'd had a premonition of Fleur's death, Nicole had begun some sketches of her from memory as soon as her niece became ill, and now she'd nearly completed the painting she planned to give Jean and Céline. In concentrating on it, she'd almost forgotten about the show.

"Right now." Leah reached for her robe.

"Don't get too impatient," Baptiste said, "or you'll be right back in that bed."

"Nonsense, you know how I perk up when I've got something to keep me busy." She turned to Nicole. "We'll go into Paris tomorrow and talk to Monsieur Berthoud."

"Should I take one of my paintings?" Nicole feared he might change his mind when he saw her work, but she wanted to know before the show whether she was a good artist rather than wait for the critics' opinions.

"I don't think that's necessary," Baptiste said. "He's already agreed to sponsor the show, and he'll want to have all of them ahead of time to plan for the arranging."

Several days after she and Leah returned from the meeting with Monsieur Berthoud, Nicole stood in the middle of her studio trying to decide which paintings, in addition to the Madonna series, should be in the exhibit. When she felt herself suddenly engulfed by an overpowering sensation to destroy them, she knew that she was experiencing the onset of one of her attacks. But never before had she known anything at all until it was over. Did this mean they were getting worse, or would she now be able to control them? Or at least control her actions during them? It was as if some elemental force deep inside her were fighting the urge to destroy what she had so lovingly created. The agony was like a physical pain, and her body doubled over with the pressure of the forces that seemed intent on destroying her as well as her paintings.

She had to flee. She had to get away from the contradictory desires that seemed impossible to reconcile. Perhaps that's what she'd wanted all along, a reason to flee from home and find a place for herself in Paris. Not when she was a little girl and hid in the tunnel; yet in some ways there was a similarity between then and now. Always she had been fleeing from some intolerable situation. Only later did Paris become the focal point, the destination toward which her subconscious took her when she was not allowed to go there in reality. But now she could. Before anyone knew it, she was gone from the studio.

Nicole stood in front of the Church of the Sacre-Coeur, still under construction, and looked out over the roofs of Paris. She had no idea how she'd gotten there. Her last memory was of looking at her Madonnas and knowing she had to leave them. Somehow she'd gotten to her room without anyone seeing her and found the birthday money and the additional sum Papa had given her for buying whatever she would need to finish the paintings for her show. She still had on the peasant skirt and blouse she always wore when she painted, but she must have removed her smock at some point. Whether she'd taken the train from St. Denis or begged a ride with some farmer as she had when she left the convent, she didn't know. But she was here now, and here she was determined to stay.

The rays of the setting sun, mingling with the smoke from thousands of chimney pots, enveloped all the roofs in a rosy glow. Nicole remembered herself at thirteen and the awe with which she had viewed the city from this same spot, during her first real stay in Paris. She had fallen in love with Paris then, and she was still in love with it. This was her city. This was where she belonged. Her heart and her soul were here. No, this *was* her heart and soul.

"She's not in the studio?" Baptiste asked.

"No," Leah said, "and her painting smock is on the floor in her bedroom."

"She's just gone into the village, or maybe to St. Denis to get some supplies, and simply forgot to tell you."

"I hadn't thought of that," Leah said. Nicole had missed lunch, which was unlike her now that they had so much to talk about concerning the upcoming show. Leah hadn't begun to worry until she looked for her in the studio and then her bedroom without result. "She should be getting home soon, though."

"If she did go into St. Denis, she would have needed some money," Baptiste suggested. "Did you check on that?"

"No, I'm not sure where she keeps it, but I'll look." Leah remembered that one drawer of Nicole's dresser had been partway open. When she looked inside, she found all her underclothes pushed to one side and a small metal box with the lid open.

"I think that must be it," Leah said when she came back downstairs. "Her canvas bag is gone, too, so she must be doing some shopping."

When Nicole had not yet returned by dusk, Baptiste said he'd take the carriage into the village and see if she had decided to spend the night with one of her friends. He didn't tell Leah what he feared: that Nicole had run away again. "If she's not there, I may go on into St. Denis. You know how fond she still is of Madame Schumann and her family."

"Yes, and she'd planned to invite them to the show."

"So she's just forgotten how late it is," Baptiste said. "Don't worry if I don't get back right away."

But Leah did worry. It was not like Nicole to leave without telling them where she was going or to stay away this long except—except when she ran away. With her excitement over the exhibition, what in the world could have possessed her to leave now? Anxiety over having her paintings displayed in public, or a belated reaction to Denise's marriage? When they found her—and Leah never doubted they would—she wouldn't be able to ask her. Nicole would never tell her.

Well, the first thing I have to do is find a place to stay, Nicole thought, *and then get something to eat.* She walked back toward the Place du Tertre, where the artists were beginning to fold up their easels and pack their paintings. She saw the café where she'd sat with Jean and Céline the night she met Monsieur Van Gogh, and she thought maybe she'd better get something to eat before looking for a room.

"What will it be, mademoiselle?" the waiter asked.

321

"Some good, thick vegetable soup and a glass of wine? The soup will fill you up and ward off the chill. It's going to be cold tonight."

"Sounds fine. Just what I need." The tantalizing aromas from the kitchen had started her stomach growling.

"Ah, *oui,* I thought so. You look hungry, and," he bent down to whisper to her, "it is not expensive. I will bring you some good wine. It is not the best, but it is good."

Well, Nicole thought, *I must already look like a starving artist.*

The soup and the wine were good, and like other diners around her, Nicole ignored the knife beside her plate and broke off chunks of the hot, fresh bread to dip in the soup and soak up all the broth.

"And how do you feel now?" The waiter stood smiling beside her. "Better?"

"Much, thank you." Looking around, Nicole realized she had absolutely no idea how to go about finding a room. "Tell me, monsieur, are there rooms for rent near here? I've just come to Paris—to paint—and I have no notion of where to start looking for a place to stay."

"No problem, no problem at all. Do you have money?"

"Yes." She started to say enough for several weeks, but something warned her to be cautious about mentioning that. She must learn to be wary, even of someone so kind as the waiter, or she'd have her money stolen from her. Worse, she might be physically attacked for it. "Enough at least for a room for the night."

"You see the house down there?" He pointed toward the corner, down the row of attached buildings. "That yellow one?"

"Yes, I see it."

"It is Madame Franconne's. I live there myself, on the second floor, but I think she has a room available on the top floor. It is not large, but it will be sunny."

"Thank you. I'll go right now." Nicole sighed with relief. She hadn't realized how anxious she'd been about finding a place to stay.

"She'll want the money in advance, but just tell her Claud sent you."

"Thank you, Claud. I'll probably see you here tomorrow."

Nicole's knock on the door of the yellow house was answered immediately by a tall, imposing woman enveloped in a huge white apron. Her black hair was pulled straight back from a face whose high, austere forehead, beaklike nose, and wide, generous mouth fought for domination.

"Yes, I have a room. It's five flights up and under the eaves. But if you want it, it's cheap." When Madame Franconne named a price, Nicole did some quick figuring and knew she could stay here at least a month, maybe two, before she'd have to find a job or see about selling a painting.

The room was small, smaller even than she'd imagined it from Claud's description, but it did have a large skylight and a tiny window with an even tinier iron balcony. At least she could open the window and look out over Paris while she ate breakfast. The bed, table, and single chair were plenty of furniture for her needs. As long as she had room to set up her easel, she was satisfied.

"Very good," Nicole said. "I'll take it. And I'll pay you for a month in advance." A week was all she needed to pay, but this way she'd know exactly how much she could spend every day for food and supplies.

"There will be no cooking in here," the concierge said sternly. "You may bring food up, but no cooking. And try to keep the scraps to a minumum or you'll have the rats for company."

"I'll remember. I'm really a very tidy person." With only the clothes she wore, she thought, she didn't have much to keep tidy.

Nicole lay down on the bed. This was to be her home for at least a month, time enough to find out if she wanted to stay or return home. But she knew the answer. She would never return. She had reached her Mecca.

When Nicole was not to be found in either the village or St. Denis, an intensive search began.

"I think she's gone to Paris," Jean said. He'd hurried to the château at the first word that Nicole was missing. "She was fascinated with the city when she visited Céline and me."

"But she was to have her showing there," Leah said. "Why would she leave us now?"

"I don't know," Jean said, "but I've seen it coming for a long time. Maybe she felt she had to do everything on her own, not be dependent on you for anything."

Throughout the next few weeks, both Jean and Edouard scoured Paris looking for Nicole. Henri joined them when he could get leave from St. Cyr. They intensified their search around the Place du Tertre, but there was no sign of her. Either she had disappeared completely or she had sworn to silence those who had seen her.

"It's uncanny, Edouard," Jean said one evening as they sat over dinner. "I can feel her presence there in Montmartre as surely as if I were looking at her. She's there, but she doesn't want us to find her."

"I've felt the same way," Edouard agreed. "And I don't think there's any point in continuing the search. At least not for a while."

As the months passed, only the impending birth of Denise's first child kept Leah from breaking down completely over the loss of Nicole, the child who needed her the most and whom she loved the most for that reason. Her real sorrow came from the realization she hadn't been able to meet that need. Leah forced herself to accept the fact that the situation was the same as when Nicole was in the convent. They could help her only when she herself recognized and would admit her need for them.

Well aware that her family would eventually come to Paris looking for her, Nicole had indeed sworn everyone she met to silence, as her family had suspected. Since such need for secrecy was not unusual among the inhabitants of Montmartre, they agreed with no questions asked. She looked out her tiny window one day to see Edouard and Jean walking along the street and stopping people, obviously asking them if they'd seen her. For a brief moment she felt a tug at her heart. Not for having left home, but for worrying the family. If there were some way she could let them know she was all right without seeing them, she would. Instead, she shrugged her shoulders and turned away from the window. No, this was the better way. Let them think she was lost to them for good. They would get over it sooner. It would be easier for her, too, to make the break final.

The days became weeks with Nicole scarcely realizing how time was passing. When the weather was fine, she worked outside. When it wasn't, she stayed in her room and worked from the sketches she made every day. There was so much around her to paint—enough subjects to last a lifetime. She strove to capture the colors of the buildings, the plants, and the people she saw. She talked to other artists and compared their techniques to her own. She knew she was still learning, and at night, under the glow of a single gaslight, she labored to find new ways to express the feelings she had from being a part of the life around her.

She'd been in Paris nearly a month when she decided to venture away from Montmartre, which was as familiar to her now as the grounds of her home in the country. She walked the crowded streets that seemed trapped between huge buildings; she ambled more leisurely along the Champs-Elysées and the Place de la Concorde. She'd save the Louvre for another day. She moved ahead toward the banks of the Seine, where artists were exhibiting their paintings for sale to tourists. This was where she would have to bring her paintings when she felt they were ready to sell. If people were buying some of the things she saw here, she knew hers would sell. These were nothing more than enlarged picture postcards, and hastily done at that.

For a long time she stared at one painting of the Pont Neuf and part of the Cité. She looked from the painting to the artist, who was standing nearby, with a hopeful look on his face. Taking some coins from her bag, she counted out the price. Even while the young man was thanking her vociferously—never before had anyone paid the first price he quoted—Nicole reached into her bag again, took out a palette knife, and began slashing the picture.

"What the hell are you doing!" In his fury, the artist tried to grab the knife from her and attack her at the same time. With an amazing presence of mind, she simply backed away.

"Destroying something obscene," she said with complete aplomb.

"Obscene! My masterpiece? *Que Diable!*"

"Masterpiece? You smeared so much paint on it, it looks like a whore wearing too much rouge."

"And I suppose you consider yourself a bona fide critic." He was panting so hard he could barely talk, and he clenched his fists to keep from striking out at her again.

"No, a painter." She slipped the palette knife back into her bag and began walking away.

"Wait a minute, you bitch!" he yelled. "A painter, eh? And I suppose you think you can do better."

"Yes, all but this part." She picked up the picture again and cut out one section. "This is magnificent, this use of light and shadow. But the rest? Faugh! Ugly. Just ugliness." She threw the pieces on the ground.

"You really think you can do better?" Now he was intrigued by her attitude and her perception of what he, too, knew was the best part of the painting.

"I know I can." If this young man hoped to challenge her to some kind of contest, she was ready for him.

"Where are your paints?" he asked.

"I don't have them with me. I didn't come down here to paint but to look. I can bring them with me tomorrow, and I'll show you how something as beautiful as the Pont Neuf should be done."

"No, I want you to come with me now. You're going to prove what you've said."

Nicole shrugged her shoulders. Why not? She watched as he picked up his canvases and placed them carelessly under one arm. Then she followed him wordlessly through the streets to a building not far from her own.

"You think you can manage four flights up?" he asked.

"I climb five to get to my room," she replied succinctly.

He didn't answer her but turned to lead the way. His room was somewhat larger than hers, but with fewer furnishings. There was a mattress on the floor instead of a bed, and hooks instead of shelves for his few clothes.

"Here," he said, pointing to the table. "Here are the paints, and there's a canvas over there. First, tell me your name, then show me how you paint. I am Jules, by the way."

Nicole muttered her name, took off her sabots, and stood barefoot by the window. Quickly she sketched in the scene of the opposite window, with its dingy, grayish white curtain and the pots of brilliant red flowers on the sill. Then she carefully selected the colors she wanted and began to paint.

At the same time, the young man found a second canvas and started painting her. The light was good for another two hours, and during that time they worked steadily and wordlessly.

Finally, Nicole put down her brush, flexed her fingers, and looked around the room at some of the man's work. Not too bad, except for the nudes leaning against the wall. She walked over to see what he was doing, and saw he'd been painting her.

"Your nudes are disgusting," she said. "Stiff and unnatural."

"They're as I see them." He didn't look at her but kept on painting.

"Is that supposed to be me? You've made me all bones. My arms aren't that skinny."

"That's how I see you. Now go away and don't bother me."

When angered, Nicole was not to be ignored, and she was irate now. She ripped off her peasant blouse and skirt and then her underdrawers, all that she was wearing, and posed naked before him. Then she stamped her foot, and he looked up.

"What are you doing?" He was stunned but not displeased. Her body was all shimmering gold, and her long black hair, covering but not concealing her breasts and small, pink nipples, flowed into and mingled with her equally thick black pubic hair.

"Showing you what a woman really looks like. Not like one of your hideous Norman cows."

"No, no. You're beautiful." He put down his paints. Without another word, she was in his arms and they were lying on the shabby mattress. She made no protest when she realized he was making love to her. It had all happened too fast for Nicole to be frightened; she had tensed at his first touch, then relaxed and allowed herself to enjoy the new and stimulating sensations. When it was over, she lay quietly and looked at the ceiling.

"You didn't tell me you were a virgin," Jules said.

"You didn't take time to ask. Anyway, virginity is more of a fetish with men than with women. Even then, it's only a state of mind." She shivered involuntarily.

"Are you cold?" He rolled over on his side to put his hand on one breast. He was enjoying this little interlude.

"A little." Jules pulled up a ragged, dirty quilt. She pushed it away. "This thing is filthy!"

He ignored her complaint and wrapped the quilt around himself. "Will you stay with me? Pose for me?"

"And sleep with you?" She'd liked it, and she liked the way his hand had caressed her breast and was now moving down her belly toward her legs, but she didn't want him to take for granted that it would be part of the arrangement.

"Unless you can afford a second mattress." He rolled easily back over on top of her. Her mouth had opened under the pressure of his, and Nicole could feel his sharp teeth nipping at her tongue. When his hands went under her back to lift her slightly, she raised her knees to make it easier for him. In a moment her hips were undulating, and with her hands on his buttocks she was urging him to in-

327

crease the rhythm and the force of his motions. She had not climaxed the first time, and when she experienced orgasm now, she shouted for joy. With a low moan, she reached for the quilt, pulled it over her, and turned on her side.

"You're staying, aren't you?" was all he said.

For a long time she said nothing. She needed the time, not to think or to decide, but to savor the feelings still swirling through her. Finally, she sat up, wrapped the quilt around her, and looked down at Jules, who lay grinning up at her.

"If you'll let me paint, too. And clean this place up!" She stood up and put her clothes on. She was under no illusions that Jules would be able to pay her for posing, but even if she had to share the rent of the room, she would still be saving money. Even at a moment when she was feeling sensual and satisfied, she could be practical.

"I don't even know your last name," he said.

"It's just Nicole." There was no need for Jules to know her last name, and this way she could feel completely divorced from her past.

"No last name?" Jules was mystified.

"It doesn't matter. I have no family."

"Congratulations. Neither do I." He looked toward the table. "Want to go out and get something to cook for dinner?"

"I need to go to my room and get my things. And bring my paintings over here." With luck she might be able to get back part of the advance payment on her room.

"We'll go together," he said. "You have any money?"

"Some. Why?" What had she got herself into? Maybe she'd better leave by herself and not come back. Jules was an artist, but he might be a thief and cutthroat, too.

"I'm broke. Haven't sold a painting in days."

"No, you're not," Nicole said crossly. "You have the money I gave you."

"I forgot." He saw the frown on her face. "No, honestly, I forgot. What with everything else we've done today," he added with a grin.

"All right, but it's fifty-fifty from now on. Either that or I don't stay."

"Won't work, Nicole. There'll be times when you have money and times when I do. Traditionally around here, whoever has it does the paying."

"Tradition, huh? All right, but you start trying to live off me and I'm leaving. Is that understood?" Nicole stood with her hands on her hips, glaring at him.

"I'll be damned," he said, "if I'm going to let you think you'll sell more paintings than I do. I'm better than you are, and I'll prove it."

"You do that, and I'll help you celebrate," she said. He was challenging her again.

"Agreed. The first one to sell five paintings gets to buy the bottle of champagne."

"You'd better let me know your favorite brand," Nicole said smugly, "because that's one bottle I'm looking forward to buying."

"Come here, Nicole." She walked to him and let him take her in his arms again. "I don't know how long we're going to stay together, but damn, I think we're going to have a good time."

"How hungry are you?" she asked, nibbling at his ear. His nearness excited her, and already had her gasping with desire to be taken again as quickly as possible.

"Very, but not for food," he said, pulling her toward the mattress.

Never before had Nicole known the delight of such ecstatic abandonment to pleasure. His hands and his mouth were all over her; in her frenzy, she bit him on the shoulder until she drew blood.

"God damn, but you're a tiger cat," he said, and began nipping her on the stomach until she screamed. In another moment they reached the peak together and then lay limp, Jules still on top of her, both of them completely exhausted.

"Remind me to buy a new quilt," she said, after they'd stood up and straightened their clothes.

With her usual lack of concern for anything material, other than food and painting supplies, Nicole settled easily into life with Jules. He demanded complete silence when she was posing for him, but quiet had never bothered her, so days went by when they hardly spoke to each other. The only times she threatened to leave—and did walk out on him one time—were when he lost his temper and went into violent rages. But she soon learned to handle his rage by luring him to the mattress and letting him subdue his

wildness by making frenzied love to her. She had plenty
of time to paint during the day, and in the evenings they
frequently joined other artists in their rooms or in the outdoor cafés. Everything she'd envisioned about living in Paris
was proving to be true.

Chapter Twenty-nine

LEAH SHIVERED and pulled the shawl tighter around her
shoulders. There was a feeling of fall in the wind that was
blowing across the fields. She should walk back to the
house before she took a chill, but the château seemed so big
and empty now. She'd been thinking back twelve years, to
her fortieth birthday, and how upset she'd been then to
learn she was pregnant. Yet what wouldn't she give to return to that year when all the children were still at home,
gathering each night around the dinner table to compete
with each other in telling the events of the day. Now she
and Baptiste usually had a simple supper in front of the
library fire.

True, a new, very special intimacy had developed between them now that, as Baptiste said, there were no
longer any little "chaperones" in the house. They could
do whatever they pleased whenever they pleased. Yet
there were moments like this when she wished she could
hear their voices, even if those voices were raised in argument. She supposed it was because Robert had only recently
left for the private boarding school recommended by his tutor.

"I'm not suggesting I'm displeased in any way with his
work," Monsieur Balaine had said, "or that I don't enjoy
teaching him. It's more because I think he needs the com-
panionship of other boys. Nor is he like Nicole, who could
get by with going to the local school. Robert has a fine mind
and needs to be preparing for the university."

Nearly as tall as Leah, Robert was still her baby. She
smiled and thought how furious he became when she said
that. More than either of the other boys, he could hardly wait

to become a man. She supposed it was natural for the youngest to feel that way.

Leah knew her loneliness was accentuated by the loss of Nicole. After all these months, she was trying to accept the idea they might never see her again. Leah refused to believe she was dead. No, Nicole had at last found the refuge from the world she'd been seeking for so long, and, Leah could only hope, some happiness with it.

Some had scoffed when Jean and Edouard said they felt Nicole's presence in Montmartre, but Leah, clinging to the hope that her youngest daughter was still alive and she would see her again, believed them. In the past, she herself had experienced the same sensation of knowing someone was nearby when there was no one in sight.

At least the pain of Fleur's death was easing, and Jean was doing very well with the vineyards. Aided by Edouard, he was looking for a winery to buy so he could be involved in the entire process from tending the vines to bottling the wine. Céline said they were hoping to have another baby, but there as yet was no sign that she was pregnant.

Letters from Lisette came every week, and if they were a bit repetitious in the names and places she mentioned, it appeared she was still enjoying herself. Too bad she couldn't be divorced from Philippe and find someone else to give her the happy marriage she deserved. Philippe's threat to have the bank call in all Baptiste's notes must no longer be a real danger. It had been nearly five years, and surely Baptiste had them paid off by now. Well, she wasn't going to think about it now. She was only wishing there were some way she could help Lisette.

If two of her children had her worried, the other four were flourishing. Denise was excitedly awaiting the birth of her first child; Henri would soon be finishing at St. Cyr and going into business with Baptiste; Jean was doing well; and Robert's letters from school were filled with as many enthusiasms as misspelled words.

"Madame! Madame Fontaine!"

Leah turned to see Blanchette waving to her from the door of the sunroom. Leah was tempted to pick up her skirts and run, until she remembered that running left her gasping, with her heart beating wildly. So, instead, she walked as fast as she could.

"What is it, Blanchette?"

"Monsieur Edouard just called. The doctor says Mademoiselle Denise will have her baby within three days."

"How wonderful! Thank you." In spite of the twinge in her knee—when would she remember she was fifty-two?—she grabbed Blanchette and twirled her around the terrace. "Another new little person coming into the family. It's something to celebrate. We'll put a bottle of champagne on ice. I wish it were from Jean's vineyards, but we'll have to wait a few years for that."

"Should we, madam?" Blanchette looked distressed. "I mean, should we celebrate before the baby gets here? It could be bad luck."

"Don't be so superstitious, Blanchette. If you had your way, Denise wouldn't have a layette ready. The idea of waiting until the baby gets here to start sewing—it's absurd."

"Yes, madame," Blanchette said, but Leah saw her cross herself several times as she walked back down to the kitchen.

"And don't forget the champagne," Leah called. *I'm going to celebrate even if no one else will, she told herself . . .*

"So Denise is about ready to whelp," Baptiste said as he refilled his glass with champagne.

"Baptiste! Such language. And about your own daughter, too."

"It's a perfectly good expression. She isn't doing anything every other animal doesn't do." The angrier he saw Leah becoming, the more he grinned to himself. He was just as thrilled as she was at the thought of another grandchild. Especially Denise's child, since all she'd ever wanted was to be a wife and mother.

"This will be a child of love," Leah bristled, "not of—

"Lust? Is that the word you're looking for?"

"Well, whatever it is they call it with the 'other' animals you so obscenely referred to."

" 'The natural continuation of the species' is probably a more reasonable term," he said.

"No," Leah insisted, "with Denise I call it love, and I'd always assumed it was the same with us."

"It was, my darling, and it always will be. I was only teasing. You get so—so otherworldly where the grandchildren are concerned. As if you thought they floated to earth on little pink clouds."

"I don't, either. I know perfectly well how they get here —just like mine did. Sometimes, Baptiste, you can be so—so aggravating."

"But you'll never give me up," and this time he grinned broadly at her.

"Never, darling." She smiled back. "Now, to be more practical. Are you going to go to Denise's with me?"

"I don't see why not. Things are going well at the office, and I want to spend time with Jean, too, and check the vineyards. How long did you plan to stay?"

"At least two weeks, or until she's on her feet. She has a good housekeeper, but I want to wait until she's able to care for the baby."

"I can't plan to be away more than a week. I don't think I can leave the office for any longer than that." Leah looked fretful. "Don't worry. You stay," Baptiste added. "Blanchette and I will get along fine right here."

"Only if you promise not to overdo." If she knew Baptiste, he'd be scurrying back and forth between here and the office every day.

"I promise." Baptiste held up his hand and crossed his heart.

"Just to make sure you keep it, I'm going to suggest you and Blanchette move into the apartment. I wish we'd gotten a housekeeper after Jean and Céline left. Blanchette may be glad of the change and a chance to see the city."

"Don't trust me, huh? Think I'll spend all my nights in Pigalle?"

"It's not the women I'm worried about, it's the work. But if Blanchette tells you to be home for dinner by seven, I know you'll be there."

"And I'll be glad to see her—and her dinner," Baptiste assured her. "Then I'll put my feet up before the fire and fall asleep until it's time to go to bed."

Leah sat back and enjoyed the train ride to Rheims. She loved riding through the countryside and seeing all the small villages, sometimes no more than a dozen houses clustered under the protection of an imposing, gray stone church. Around them, in all directions, lay the fields that had been worked by the same families for many generations. The scene evoked the serene continuity Leah felt when she thought about her grandchildren. They were man's visible immortality. She reached for Baptiste's hand.

Denise had a long and difficult labor before Edouard, junior, was born. He was a strong, healthy baby, but Denise was so weakened by her travail, Leah was glad she'd come prepared to stay as long as she was needed.

"And you *will* go into Paris with Blanchette," she said for

333

the fourth time, while helping Baptiste to the carriage that would take him to Jean's for a few days.

"I will. I will. I will," Baptiste said. "There, does that satisfy you?"

"I think you omitted one 'I will,' but I'm satisfied. And don't forget to lock the château good and tight and make sure Nicolas knows to come and check on things every day. I gave him a key before we left."

"Bon Dieu! I'm not one of the grandchildren, Leah." Baptiste handed his crutches to the coachman and let the man help him up the step and into his seat.

"I'm sorry, but I just want to make sure you'll be all right. If you need me, now, be sure to phone and I'll leave here."

"I am not going to need you, and you stay as long as you think Denise does." He leaned forward to kiss Leah goodbye. "But I will miss you. Now, Joseph, let's go before Madame Fontaine changes her mind and makes me stay."

Of course Baptiste would be all right, Leah thought, as long as he stayed at the apartment in Paris. Maybe they should think about moving there, now that all the children were gone and they didn't need a large house. The almost daily drives into town were beginning to wear on Baptiste. He never said anything, but she knew he was in constant pain, and she could tell by the way he walked that his hips were badly affected. She'd talk to him about it when they were together again.

Baptiste opened the door to the Paris apartment and made his way slowly through the entrance hall to the living room.

"A fire would feel good, Blanchette, if you wouldn't mind," he said.

"I'd be happy to, sir. Would you like me to get your wheelchair from the bedroom?"

"No, I think I'll sit right here by the fire." He suited his action to the words. The wheelchair was necessary for mobility, but the large, soft club chair would be comfortable to sit in for the entire evening, which was exactly what he intended to do. "Don't worry about dinner anytime soon. You might check and see what shopping you need to do."

"I'll get the fire going first," Blanchette said, "and then look into the kitchen. You're sure you'll be all right if I leave you for a while?"

"Dammit, Blanchette, you're worse than Madame Fontaine when it comes to worrying about me. I'm perfectly capable of taking care of myself, as I have been doing for more years than I like to remember."

"Then I'll see about the fire," Blanchette said, and shambled off in a huff.

Baptiste lit a cigar and opened the paper he'd brought with him. There was nothing in it of great import, and he thought he'd take a short nap while Blanchette shopped. He'd just dozed off when he heard her shouting from another room.

"Monsieur Fontaine!"

"What is it? Rats again?" The damn things were always coming up from the sewer to the first floor.

"If it was, they stood on two legs. Every cupboard's been opened, and blankets are missing from the bedrooms."

"Any clothes?" Baptiste had an idea who the intruder might have been. There'd been no signs of a break-in, and all the children had their own keys to the apartment.

"Not that I can see." Blanchette walked into the living room. "Do you want me to bring your wheelchair so you can come back here and look?"

"No, just check the room where Mademoiselle Nicole usually sleeps."

"Yes, sir." She was gone for less than five minutes. "I don't know what all she had there, but the wardrobe and dresser don't look like they've been touched. Everything is hanging or neatly folded in place."

That put the quietus to that theory, Baptiste thought. Then again, it might not. She hadn't taken anything with her when she left the château, and she would certainly have packed up clothes if she'd wanted them. She always preferred dressing like the people she associated with. He remembered how she'd insisted on wearing homespun skirts and cotton blouses when she was going to the village school. If she'd created a new life for herself here in Paris, she would be dressing appropriately. Blankets were blankets, the same everywhere. At least now he felt certain she was in the city. But she had chosen to conceal herself from them rather than ask to live in the apartment, as if rejecting her former life.

Maybe now that he was going to be in the city every day and night until Leah finished at Denise's, he could do some looking on his own. Nicole probably felt safe to come out late in the evening, and he might see her then. He wouldn't

335

say anything to Leah, as it would merely get her hopes up again.

Baptiste made his way into the restaurant and crossed the room to the table in the rear, where Simone was waiting for him. He paused to look at her before she saw him. She was younger-looking and more beautiful than ever.

Simone glanced up when he approached the table, and her smile lit up the whole room. "Baptiste, you look perfectly splendid."

"Thank you, and you're—you're too beautiful to describe." He let his eyes rest on her, as if he could think of nothing more to say or he'd already said too much. He signaled to the waiter.

"The usual, sir?" the man asked.

"Please. Another for you, Simone?" He noted her glass was almost empty, and he was sorry he'd made her wait alone.

"Yes, to keep you company." Her words came through her brilliant smile.

"I apologize for being late."

"No need. Anticipation brought me here a bit early. Now, tell me what makes you look as if you'd just won a million francs at Monte Carlo."

"Sitting here across the table from you, being able to enjoy looking at you."

"Thank you, monsieur, but there's a new look I haven't seen before. Come, fess up, what is it?"

"Must be pride over our third grandson," he said. "Nothing like grandchildren to make one swell like a pouter pigeon."

"A third! How wonderful. Jean's?"

"No, Denise and Edouard's. Their first. I've just spent a few days there, and Leah is still with them." He waited until the waiter set down their drinks before he went on. "Enough about me. What have you been doing?"

"Looking forward to seeing you again."

"No, seriously. How's everything at home? With Charles? The children?"

"All fine. Charles is very busy with his various pursuits, which take him all over the Continent, and the children are in private schools. So, *seriously,* waiting out the months until I have a reason to come to Paris is my most strenuous occupation."

Baptiste reached across the table and took her hand.

336

"Don't—don't make these meetings take on too much importance. I look forward impatiently to them, too, waiting for your letters, being with you. I wouldn't have written to you this time if not, but—"

"I know. You have Leah. You love her, and she is completely devoted to you."

"Yes, but you give me something she cannot. Something precious, but momentary. It's as fleeting as the brief time we spend together. If it's not the same for you, I don't think we should see each other again."

"Please, Baptiste, I couldn't stand that. You give me something important, too. Momentary, also, but with a long-lasting effect. I have a good life, but—less than stimulating. Seeing you is—is a *soupçon* of excitement, of something slightly forbidden."

Baptiste felt the waiter hovering near. "Ready to order yet?"

"Not quite," Simone said, "but I'd love another aperitif."

"Two more, please," Baptiste said. "We'll order a little later."

Simone had placed her hands in her lap, but now she lifted one and reached for Baptiste's.

"These are special moments for us, Simone. This table is our world, 'For love all love of other sights controls/And makes one little room an everywhere.' "

Simone immediately recognized the lines from John Donne. "I didn't know you read poetry."

"I don't often, but I heard that poem once and never forgot those lines." He didn't say it was Leah who'd read Donne to him soon after she became his *placée*.

"Our little world," she said. "I like that."

After they finished their drinks and were halfway through dinner, she suggested they drive into the country and have a picnic the next day.

"A picnic! You *will* make me feel like a young man again."

"Isn't that why you see me?" Baptiste detected a faintly plaintive tone in her voice.

"Partly, only partly," he said.

"I'll have the hotel pack a picnic lunch, and we can spend the whole day together. That's more than we've done in a long time."

"I like the sound of it," Baptiste said, smiling back at her.

As they rode toward Simone's hotel in a handsom cab,

her head on his shoulder and his arm around her, Baptiste reflected on his long association with his companion.

When, years earlier, Simone returned to her childhood home, Baptiste had been attracted to her for one very simple reason: she was someone new. Suddenly she'd appeared—refreshing and novel—in what had become an ordinary, mundane, routine life. Her face, her clothes, her voice, her point of view: all were different from what he'd been seeing and hearing every day for as long as he could remember. He enjoyed talking to her. She always listened intently, as if genuinely interested in what he was saying. Perhaps, he admitted to himself, because everything he said was fresh and new to her. She hadn't heard it a dozen times before. She valued his opinions and asked questions that showed him she really wanted to know how he felt; she wasn't just humoring his ego. They could take opposing sides without having their debate degenerate into an argument. Instead, their discussions often ended with Simone laughing, an easy, lilting, infectious laugh. In turn, Simone had a sparkling but subtle wit that captivated him and had him laughing with her.

When they were together, there were no household problems, no Panama Canal, no fretting over nagging, day-to-day decisions. Instead, they moved from one challenging or humorous or lighthearted topic to another.

At first, Baptiste would have been surprised to discover that anyone might consider the relationship between them anything more than platonic. Later he wondered if it were possible for any relationship between a man and a woman to be—or to remain—platonic.

At first he'd been less attracted to Simone physically—sexually—than for the mental stimulation she offered. Then she began entering his thoughts while he was at home. He'd wake up in the middle of the night thinking about her, and after a time, fantasies began to emerge. He'd hear Leah breathing deeply beside him, and he'd reach for her, as if by making love with her he could quench the unwanted desires teasing him. Gradually his subdued longings became more lustful. It was almost as if, through his fantasies, a new Baptiste were emerging from the old shell. Had Leah wondered sometimes at his increased passion, his more frequent need for her?

Then ordinary happenings with Simone began to take on new significance. Their hands met as they reached for the same thing. Their knees touched accidentally under the table. They discovered they both liked things that no one

338

else they knew liked. Glances passed between them after innocent-seeming words had been spoken, and the words began to take on a deeper meaning.

Yet he had been able to sublimate his physical desire for Simone until he'd arrived for one of his late-afternoon visits, and she appeared wearing a dressing gown. "I'm sorry," he said, "if I've come at a bad time."

"No, it's I who should apologize. I was resting longer than usual. I didn't sleep well last night. A disturbing letter yesterday, but that needn't concern you."

It wouldn't have, except that she dissolved into tears, and Baptiste's only intent, when he moved over to sit next to her on the couch, had been to comfort her. Instead, he found himself making love to Simone, who, rather than denying him, responded with ardor.

When she told him she was going to marry Jacques, a childhood sweetheart, he was not only deeply hurt but felt used as well. She hadn't mentioned her hesitation about marrying a man who was partially paralyzed; but when she told him she'd accepted Jacques' proposal, the truth became evident. Baptiste had been nearly torn apart by the feeling that she'd allowed him to make love to her only to be certain that a man who was handicapped could perform in bed. He hadn't seen her again until Leah sent her out to the terrace to say goodbye the day she left for Toulouse.

It had been hard seeing her. His hurt had been compounded by the guilt he felt over being unfaithful to Leah. Having Simone sitting beside him had intensified both feelings.

"Wish me happiness, Baptiste," she'd asked.

"I do. You know that."

"I can't go without telling you I love you. If your wife were anyone but Leah, I would have done everything a woman could to make you my lover. I would have stayed in my home here and become your mistress. But Leah is a very special person—as are you. Don't ever forget that."

With that she'd left, and he'd been certain he'd never see her again. Then had come Aix-les-Bains and the few hours they had alone together. He had been delighted to see her and as pleased as an adolescent boy, when Dr. Joffre suggested he stay two more weeks. Again, he had sincerely intended for them to be friends, nothing more. But she had come to his room, had waited for him after Charles left, and the hasty coupling—it could scarcely be called love

339

making—had been a frantic, cataclysmic climax to their reunion.

After Aix-les-Bains, Jacques had died and Simone had married Charles. "I almost didn't marry him," she told Baptiste at their first, accidental meeting. "I hated him for seducing me the day I learned Jacques would soon die. I was desperately unhappy—grief-stricken—and he took advantage of that. But I need to be married; I need a man close by."

Baptiste had thought about how she'd gone right from Charles' arms into his that afternoon, as if a second seduction could obliterate the shame of the first. Except that he, Baptiste, had been the one seduced. *No, don't try to exonerate yourself,* he thought. *You were quite ready and much more than willing.*

Anyone who saw them in the hansom would assume they were lovers. If asked, Baptiste would admit he loved Simone in a unique way. Yet, since Aix-les-Bains, they'd merely held hands or shared an innocent embrace. It hadn't been easy. Only by exerting all the willpower he could muster had Baptiste kept their *tête-à-têtes* from exploding into a fiery, passionate love affair. He knew Simone was finding it just as difficult to keep her desires under control. When he felt himself weakening, when a touch of Simone's hand on his arm or the increased pressure of her lips on his cheek threatened to send him into her arms, he recalled her words, "Leah is a very special person," and he remembered how very much he loved his wife. Even though temptation was kept to a minimum by never going to Simone's hotel room, he wondered how much longer he could resist giving into the need he felt for her. He vowed after each encounter that he'd never see her again—it would be better that way—and then would come her note saying she would be in Paris. And this time he had allowed himself to write to her, to let her know that Leah would be with Denise for at least another week. He knew he was opening a door that should remain forever locked.

There'd been no change in his love for Leah. She was his life. His meetings with Simone were something completely separate from his marriage; they belonged to a different world. They were something fragile and delicate—ephemeral, like a flower that blooms once a decade and only for an hour. She gave him a precious gift—the gift of his youth for a sweet, brief time.

"Do you love me a little bit?" Simone had asked him once.

"I love these hours with you and what your presence does for me."

If she wanted more, she hid the desire behind a smile; and since she continued to see him whenever she could, he thought she was satisfied to keep their relationship on the precipitous but tantalizing edge between an affair and a deep-seated friendship.

They drove into the country the next morning and found a grassy spot near the river, partly sheltered and partly open to the warm sun. While Baptiste sat and watched her, Simone picked wildflowers and then set out the lunch. Afterward, he reclined against a tree. She was lying on her stomach, resting on her elbows, her chin cupped in her hands.

"I'm feeling sleepy," he said. "Want to take a nap?"

"No, I don't want to miss a minute of this perfect day."

"It is perfect," he agreed. *So perfect, I wish Leah were here to share it with me.* In the next second he wished he hadn't thought of Leah. It was wrong to be enjoying this beautiful day with someone else. He missed her terribly and felt an urgent longing to see her.

Simone sat up and leaned over him, her face very close to his. "You're looking too serious. What are you thinking about?"

"Nothing worth mentioning."

"Then think about this." She leaned closer and kissed him.

In another minute, his arms were around her, and he was kissing her as he'd wanted to since he'd first seen her in the restaurant the night before. As he'd dreamed of kissing her all the months, the years, since Aix-les-Bains. She slid down to lie beside him. His arms tightened around her waist, and he could feel her straining against him. When she opened the front of her dress, he put his hand inside and felt the warm, enticing cleft between her breasts. Her lips and tongue were inviting him to take her right then, to enter her as quickly as possible. His hand touched her, and she moaned in expectation. His desire for her was now all-consuming, and they frantically shifted into a more comfortable position.

As swollen and erect as he'd been from the moment she kissed him, he suddenly and inexplicably went limp. For a minute he lay there, his head on her breasts. Then he moved away and sat up.

"It's all wrong, our being here," he said. "I can't explain what happened, but—" He looked across the river to the meadow beyond. He didn't dare look at Simone's face or the way she lay, bewildered and yet still tempting, beside him. The momentary failure, the body's refusal to act, could be overcome, he knew, by a few caresses, by another kiss. "We can't see each other again," he said before desire could dominate his reason.

"Why not, Baptiste?" She was sitting up, too. "Are you embarrassed because of—because of what just happened? There's no need to feel humiliated, to think you're less than a man. I understand."

"It's not that."

"Then what? Please, I need you to make love to me. If it's Leah, it's just as unfaithful to be here with me like this, wanting me, as it is actually to make love."

"I know." He felt wretched. "You don't need to remind me."

"Will not making love to me this time negate the other times? If then, why not now? I need you, Baptiste."

No more than I need you and want you at this moment, he thought. "Those times were different. Another would only compound the wrong. We came too close. I can't see you again."

"After this week, you mean," she said hopefully. There would be another day, another evening to be alone, when his conscience might not take command.

"After today," he said. "I couldn't be with you and not make love to you. But it would be hurting you as much as it would hurt Leah. There'd be no meaning to it beyond satisfying a moment's desire."

"I see." Simone stood up, walked to the picnic things spread on the cloth, and began gathering them up. "I think I understand now."

They were silent for most of the drive back to the city. Just before they arrived at her hotel, Simone said, "Don't feel guilty, Baptiste. Not for Leah. You haven't done anything to hurt her. Nor for me. I love Charles. I'll return tonight, and he'll be surprised and delighted. So delighted, he'll— Well, I look forward to that."

After telling Simone good-bye, for the last time he was sure, Baptiste returned to the office.

"I won't be in the rest of the week," he told his manager.

"I'm going back to my daughter's to spend some more time with my new grandson." *And my wife,* he added to himself. Leah would be surprised and delighted, too.

In the spring of 1894, Henri graduated with honors from St. Cyr. He had hated every minute of his years there; but, still determined no one would best him at anything, he had stayed at the top of his class. He'd taken awards in fencing, riding, and marksmanship; and it was assumed he would accept a commission in one of the élite cavalry units.

For his part, Baptiste was hoping Henri would prefer to resign his commission and come into the business with him. He was looking forward to giving him a few months of training and then turning the import business over to him. Henri had never shown as much interest in it as Jean and now Robert, but still it was the family business and it would establish Henri for the rest of his life.

"We're mighty proud of you, son," Baptiste said when they'd returned home after the graduation ceremonies.

"And it's good to have you home for a while," Leah added. She looked at her tall, handsome son. With his military bearing and newly acquired mustache, he would be setting plenty of hearts on fire. There might be another wedding in the family before long.

"I hope it will be for longer than a while," Baptiste said. "Unless you have plans to continue with a military career, I'm counting on you to start coming to the office after you've had a short vacation."

"I'm afraid not, Papa. I do have other plans."

"The army?" Leah asked. She wasn't afraid of his being killed. There were no threats of war—except for the Boer War and that was all England's problem—but she'd hoped he would be home from now on.

"No, Mama, I've had enough of uniforms and strict regimens for now. The military is not for me, and I learned plenty of other things at St. Cyr."

"Then what are your plans, son?" Baptiste asked. "You're not thinking of being a farmer like Jean?"

"Heaven forbid!" Henri exclaimed. "No, I want to do something with my mechanical talent. I want to invent things, and I've plenty of ideas in mind."

"Then you're going to stay right here in your workshop?" Leah asked. "That's it, isn't it?"

"No, Mama, I'm not. I'm going to New York."

"New York!" Baptiste and Leah were completely stunned.

343

"Why New York?" Baptiste asked.

"Because France is decadent. It's a dying country. America is alive and vital." Henri began pacing up and down the room to emphasize his words. "America is just coming into its own. There's a real future there for a man with my talents."

"There's a future here too, son," Baptiste said. "Maybe you can be the one to help lift France out of this sorry situation you think she's in."

"No, industry is really booming in the States. There are factories for everything imaginable, just crying out for someone to come along and invent better and faster ways to do things. Here, some old president of a company would look at my ideas and shelve them for ten years. In America, they ask how soon you can have it finished."

"But America," Leah said. "That's so far away. Why not England? There are new things coming from there all the time. And Lisette is there."

"I'm sorry, Mama, but I've made up my mind. This is something I really want to do. I've always done everything you asked me to; now I need to be my own man."

"But you'll come back? From time to time, I mean." Leah was deeply upset. She would never understand how two of her children, conceived with such love, could turn their backs so completely on their family.

"In the future, perhaps," he said, "but don't expect me very soon. You came over here from America to seek what you wanted, to find something you couldn't have in the States. I want to do the same thing, if for different reasons."

Leah knew perfectly well what he referred to. She'd never hidden from the children her Negro heritage and the fact she and Baptiste could not be married in Louisiana. It was their heritage, too, and one she hoped they would be proud of as long as they did not suffer as she had.

"Then I hope you'll be as successful as I was," Baptiste said. "And as happy as we've been here."

What Henri didn't want to tell them, because he didn't want to hurt his mother, was that rather than being proud of his African heritage, he was ashamed of it. He wanted to go someplace where no one would know about it.

"Have you made any contacts over there?" Baptiste asked.

"Not yet, but I have letters to some industrialists in New York and New Jersey. And I have sketches of the first inventions I hope to patent. I don't think I'll have any problem finding a job."

344

"Then all we can say is good luck," Baptiste said. "How soon do you plan to leave?"

"In about two weeks. I want to see Jean and Denise and their families before I go, but I'll spend the rest of the time with you, Mama. You can clean out the workship if you want to use it for something else."

"With all the empty rooms there are now?" She stifled a sigh. "No, I'll leave it in case you do decide to return and work here."

"I might work in there before I leave," Henri said, "and put that railroad in the tunnel."

"Whatever for?" Baptiste asked. He hoped his son's other inventions made more sense than that crazy idea.

"For the fun of it. And to correct some problems that bothered me when I had to stop work on it. I hate to leave anything half finished."

Leah hid her sorrow as best she could by fussing over Henri during those two weeks, making certain his linens were all in order and he had enough warm clothes. She'd heard that New York could get terribly cold.

On his arrival in America, Henri set out with his letters of introduction, and immediately found a place with a carriage-maker in New Jersey. The man was experimenting with internal combustion engines, and he was particularly interested in one of Henri's inventions.

"I'm all set over here," Henri wrote home, "and I've already sent three designs to the patent office. By a year from now, I should be running the manufacturing side of this business."

"Nothing modest about that boy," Baptiste said.

"No, he'll do fine." With that, and the regularity of his letters, Leah had to be satisfied. But suddenly the house seemed very empty again.

Chapter Thirty

NICOLE WAS SURPRISED at how content she'd remained during the months of being Jules' model, mistress, and housekeeper. So far, those three jobs had kept her too busy to do much painting, but she didn't feel as pressured about working at her art as she had at home.

She had been serious about replacing the filthy quilt Jules used as a bed cover. At first she tried washing it, but when not even the strongest soap would dislodge the bugs that had taken up residence in it, she bought one at the Saturday market. It was secondhand, but it was clean. When the weather got colder, it was time to get a second one. She looked into her purse. In spite of living frugally and sharing expenses—which she continued to insist on—the coins were going faster than she liked. She needed to paint something that would sell quickly. Meanwhile, she had to find them more bed covers.

"I'm going out, Jules. I'll be back after a bit."

"Why now?" Jules grumbled from behind a curtain Nicole had insisted on putting up to make a separate dressing-room area. There were times when she required privacy. "I wanted you to start posing."

"Not on an empty stomach. I won't be too long, and I'll bring you something back for a surprise." In looking through her large, canvas, carry-all bag, she'd seen something she didn't know she still had. It had got stuck to the bottom of the bag by the minute remains of a piece of toffee and then covered with a scrap of paper.

It was the key to the family's Paris apartment. Instead of heading for the market, she'd go there. There would be plenty of bedclothes. They'd never miss what she'd take.

Before she reached the apartment building, she looked to see if the concierge were around. Usually he was at the corner café for coffee this time of morning, but she wanted to make certain. If he saw her, he'd be sure to tell her parents. When there was no sign of him, her next move was to

346

ascertain if any of the family were staying there. She tip-toed to the door and listened. There was no sound from within. She tried the key in the lock, listened again, and opened the door partway. The place was empty. All the dust covers were still on the furniture.

She headed directly for the linen chest. As long as she was getting quilts, she might as well get sheets, pillows, and pillow cases as well. Living in Montmartre didn't mean she had to give up all of life's comforts. Passing her room, she looked in. No, she didn't want any of her clothes. They were a symbol of the life she'd left behind. She'd feel out of place now in dressmaker designs. She did take an old shawl that would come in handy when it got colder.

She'd have to hurry and get to the market. Having had no breakfast, she was getting hungrier and hungrier. Maybe she'd find something in the kitchen to eat before she left.

Nicole opened the cabinets and felt like Aladdin entering the cave. Flour, meal, sugar, and rice could be taken with her, if she'd only brought a basket to carry them in. She looked in another cabinet and stepped back. It was filled with canned fruits and vegetables that Blanchette had put up the year before. This was like finding the Horn of Plenty. There had to be a basket or large satchel someplace. She went to the storage room off the kitchen. Just as she hoped, Mama had used one of her big gardening baskets to bring some things in from the country. It wouldn't hold everything she wanted to take, but she could come back the next day for more. She arranged several jars of fruits and vegetables among the bags of flour, meal, rice, and sugar, and covered them with a set of sheets, pillow cases, and a blanket.

The basket was heavier than she'd anticipated, but she was determined not to leave much behind. Not even for one day. Tomorrow she'd insist to Jules that he come with her to help carry more things. She lifted the basket to her head to see if she could carry it the way she'd seen farm women bring their produce to market. It was still heavy, and unless she kept it balanced, it would fall; but she managed to make it out of the apartment and to the street.

She adjusted the basket until it was comfortable enough for her to walk all the way back to the room. Jules would be pleased with what she'd found. Having saved all the money she'd been going to use for food, she stopped at the market long enough to buy a few pieces of meat. She'd make a good stew with the canned vegetables. She also bought two pieces of the chocolate torte she loved so well.

"Jules, come see what I've got for us."

He helped her get the basket to the floor, and then she pulled off the blanket and linens.

"What did you do," he asked, "rob a store?"

"No." She started to tell him about the apartment, then remembered she didn't want him to know about her past or her family. "No, I found some money I didn't know I had." This put an end to her plans for having Jules return to the apartment with her. She'd have to find another excuse for getting more things out of there.

"We sure could have used it these past weeks when you kept us on such skimpy rations."

"I'm sorry, Jules, but at least we can eat well for a while. And if I sell something—"

"You won't, if you don't start painting."

"Well, who is it keeps me so busy posing I don't have time?" she shouted.

"It's not the posing," he shouted back. "It's all the time you spend fooling with this place. It suited me fine the way it was."

"It didn't suit me. I'm not going to live in filth when I don't have to." She picked up the blanket and linens.

"Where did you get these?" he asked suspiciously when he saw the lace on the sheets and pillow cases.

"In—in the flea market. I didn't ask if they were stolen. They were cheap." She hoped he didn't ask more questions when he took a closer look at the jars of food. Fresh vegetables came to market every day, but not many canned goods.

"How about putting them away and fixing breakfast," Jules growled. "I want to get back to the painting."

"I'll pose for a while, but I'm going to get out my things. From now on, I'll pose for half a day and paint the other half."

"Don't start making rules now the place is looking fancy. I don't like living by a schedule."

"No," Nicole said, "you'd rather sleep all morning and make love all night. Enough of that goes a long way."

"It's your fault. Your body drives me crazy."

"Then start painting me with my clothes on." Nicole put a pan on the one-burner kerosene stove. She'd make coffee first and then cook up some batter cakes. She felt Jules grab her from behind. "Stop that! How can I get breakfast?"

"That can wait. I want something else first."

"Damn you, Jules! Why do you do this to me?" There were times when she hated him, hated being used by him and having to clean up after him, but she couldn't leave him. He had aroused something in her that only he could satisfy.

Jules ran his fingers lightly over her body, until she was quivering and aching with anticipation.

"You want it, don't you?" he said. "Then beg me for it. I like to hear you beg."

"Please, Jules, I can't stand it any longer." She pounded him on his back with her fists, and then in a brief frenzied moment it was over. It never took long, and she despised herself every time; but she couldn't live without it.

During the next few weeks, Nicole insisted they hold to her schedule of posing in the morning and painting in the afternoon. Finally she finished a number of what she called "enlarged picture postcards"—almost photographic reproductions of Paris scenes in garish, unreal colors, the kind that were bought eagerly by the tourists. She signed them with the name "Michele." If she ever did succeed as a real artist, she wanted no one to associate these works with her. Then, too, should one of her family see them, they wouldn't know she was in Paris.

"Take them with you this morning," she told Jules. "I'm not going to the quay. I don't want to see who buys them."

"What difference does it make as long as we get the money?" Nicole certainly had some weird notions, he thought.

"It makes a hell of a lot of difference to me."

He shrugged his shoulders in agreement. It was easier than arguing with her.

As soon as Jules was gone, she got out another canvas and began organizing her paints. With both their paintings to sell, he wouldn't be back until dark. She had plenty of time to do what she wanted. She was going to start a real painting, one she'd had in her mind for a long time. It would cleanse her artistic soul of the filth she had been doing. For the first time in months she sang as she worked. She was happy. The picture was emerging as she hoped it would. She was doing the scene she saw from the window, the one she'd started the day she came to live with Jules. But this time she was making it more impressionistic, with that rosy haze over the roofs she'd seen the day she arrived in Paris.

It was detailed and yet there was nothing clearly defined. By the end of the day, she was satisfied with what she'd accomplished. She hadn't lost her touch.

Jules returned with one of her paintings and two of his. "Here you are," he said, handing her a fistful of francs. "Down to the very last coin. I spent only enough of mine for some tobacco and this." He showed her the bottle of wine. "Better than we've had in a long time, isn't it?"

She grabbed him around the waist and let him twirl her around the room. "I did it, Jules! I sold one of my paintings. My very first."

"You don't sound now as if you hated them."

"That doesn't matter. I've finally sold something. Oh, what that does for me. I'm an artist now. Open the wine and I'll get the cups."

Nicole didn't know she could feel such exhilaration, such elation, from finally knowing that someone wanted and was willing to pay for something she'd created. Now she could really put her heart into her work as she never had before.

"Want to go to the café for dinner?" Jules asked.

"Yes, let's. I want to celebrate as if this were Christmas, Bastille Day, and my birthday all at the same time."

They ate at one café and then spent the rest of the night visiting the others. The whole of Montmartre seemed to have converged around Place du Tertre that night. There was talk of the Galerie Durand planning an exhibit of Monet's work in the near future. Nicole met Paul Cézanne and Camille Pissarro, two artists she'd heard much about; and Edouard Vuillard came by and sat at their table.

"I hear Gauguin will be coming to Paris soon," Vuillard said. "You ever see his work, Nicole?"

"No. I've never heard of him."

"Good but weird. You might like him, though."

"Why?" she asked. "Am I supposed to like weird things?"

"Well," Vuillard said, "you're always talking about Van Gogh's work. And he never sold anything."

"Yes, he did. I bought a painting of his when I was only thirteen years old."

"Really?" Vuillard look dubious. "He never mentioned it. He was crazy, you know. Cut off his ear, and then died a raving maniac. Killed himself."

"I don't believe it," Nicole said. "About being a maniac. He was unhappy, but he wasn't insane."

"Don't get upset," Vuillard said. "I liked him, too. I'm only telling you what I heard."

Nicole became reflective. She knew Van Gogh was dead, and she'd already heard the stories of his madness. She thought about the haunted expression on his face and the passion in his eyes the night she'd first seen him. During that brief conversation and while watching him paint the next day, she'd been acutely aware that they were two of a kind. A bond of understanding had been forged between them. A bond so strong that, although she had never seen him again, he had remained her mentor, become a part of her. Was his madness also a part of her?

She hadn't had any of her attacks since coming to Paris, but that didn't mean they were gone for good. She knew how violent she could become, and she often wondered if someday she might turn that violence upon herself. She had no wish to destroy herself, but then she hadn't consciously wanted to slash those pictures to pieces years before. At least this last time, when she'd fled to Paris, she'd felt the attack coming on and been able to do something about it. For now, anyway. But what had she done during those lost hours between leaving home and arriving in the city? Someday she might enter that dark world and never emerge from it.

With more money in her pockets, Nicole could go to the apartment to get more things and then plausibly tell Jules she'd bought them. They could use additional bed covers now that winter was really here, and all those jars of food she'd left behind continued to exert a strong temptation to return. This time she took two baskets, one to hold on her head and another to carry with her free hand. She was going to bring back all she could manage.

As before, Nicole checked to make certain the concierge wasn't there. She opened the door to the apartment cautiously. She was still safe. First she found the bed linens she wanted, and she left the wardrobe door open in case she found, before she left, that she had room for more. Then she went into the kitchen to pile jars of food into the baskets. When she saw new bags of flour and other staples, she knew that someone had been to the apartment since her last visit.

She was putting the last of the jars in the basket when she heard someone at the front door to the apartment. All she could do was hold her breath and wait to see who it was. There was a rear entry, but she'd never get to it before whoever it was came in and heard her. She listened without

351

moving. Someone was turning the door handle. Then nothing.

"Fools," she heard someone mutter. "Always think they see someone snooping around."

It was only the concierge, and he'd come to check the door. She could breathe again, but she dared not leave by the front door, and she thought she'd better go quickly. There was no time to put things in order. She'd have to leave the kitchen and wardrobe just as they were.

Nicole piled the linens and quilts around and over the food and headed for the rear entrance. Not until she was several blocks away did she feel safe from discovery. Nor did she dare return. It was a good thing she'd thought to bring the second basket and been able to get as much as she had. They'd be warm now, and the food would last a good while.

This time Jules didn't ask where everything came from. If she were buying things, fine; if she were stealing them, that was all right, too.

In early spring, Nicole and Jules were again celebrating the sale of several paintings. They were sitting at a table under the café's awning when she saw a heavyset man walking toward them.

"I've got to leave!" She nearly knocked the table over in her desperation to get away.

"Why? We've already ordered!" Jules glared at her, and she knew he'd like to strangle her. Right now, though, she was more frightened by the threat of the man approaching than by Jules' violent temper.

"Then stay here and eat it yourself," she said. "I have to get back to the room." Her eyes involuntarily moved toward the man now coming nearer. She turned away immediately, but not before Jules saw whom she was staring at.

Nicole ran until she reached their rooming house. Furious at her for running off, Jules followed right behind as she stumbled up the stairs.

"Who is he?" Jules demanded as soon as he'd slammed the door behind them.

"No one of any importance," Nicole said, but she was still shaking from the near encounter. "I just didn't want him to see me."

"Who is it, I said." Jules grabbed her around the neck. "Who have you been seeing behind my back while I'm on the quay? That's why you won't go with me, isn't it?" He squeezed his hands tighter around her throat.

Nicole felt her eyes bulging and her chest filling with pain. Finally, she managed to get her hands on his and force them apart so she could breathe. "My brother, dammit! Let go of me."

"You're lying. You said you had no family." Livid with fury, Jules tightened his grasp again. "He looks too prosperous to be any relative of yours. You're his whore, aren't you?" He released his grip slightly.

"No! For me there is no family any more, but he is my brother Jean."

"I don't believe you. He's been paying you and giving you linens and food." He kept tightening and releasing his hands. She was like a butterfly, beautiful to look at but more satisfying to torment.

"No! No! Believe me," she cried. "There hasn't been anyone else." Nicole was terrified at the deranged look in Jules' eyes.

"And there won't be, either." He reached behind him for a palette knife.

Nicole could see he was aiming the knife toward her face and eyes. He was going to kill her, but not before he tortured her. Could she plead with him or was he past reason?

"Afraid, aren't you?" he leered. "That's good. I want you to be." He ran the knife along her cheek just deep enough to draw blood. "Should I slash your throat or just cut you up a little bit?"

"Please, Jules." She freed herself just enough to open her blouse. "Isn't there something else you'd rather do with me?"

"You bitch! You always know how to reach me."

She had stopped him for the moment, but how long would it be before something else enraged him? Jules had been fun, but she didn't need him anymore. She didn't need anyone.

When Jules next went to the quay—as calmly as if he hadn't tried to kill her—she tied together her canvases, put her paints and brushes into the bottom of her carryall, and stuffed her extra skirt and blouse on top of them. She'd lose whatever money Jules got for the paintings he sold, but it was a small sacrifice compared to being killed, or being severely beaten with his leather belt while they made love. Her body was still covered with red welts from Jules' outburst. Pulling clean sheets from a shelf and two quilts off the bed, she rolled them into a bundle. Then she stood back and surveyed her worldly goods. It wasn't much, and she had almost no money, but she would manage.

Four blocks away was the rooming house where she'd stayed when she first arrived in Paris. With luck there'd be a room. If not, she'd have to start looking, but at least she knew where to look now and how much to pay.

Madame Franconne was standing in the street and arguing with the baker over the price of two loaves of day-old bread.

"Good morning, Nicole." Madame Franconne tucked the loaves under her arm after paying the price she's insisted on. The baker went off grumbling, and she laughed at his discomfiture. "He should know by now I always win. Things going well for you?"

"No, madame, they're not. Do you have a room?"

"Your old room is vacant, if you don't mind living where a young man committed suicide night before last. Jacques and I were just shaking our heads over the tragedy of it."

Nicole shuddered. What had brought him to such despair? Did he know what he was doing? She was haunted constantly by the fear she'd kill herself during one of her attacks if there were nothing else around for her to destroy.

"I'll—I'll take it. How much do you want in advance?" She was too tired to look any further. Not having known the young man, there'd be no ghosts to haunt the place.

"One week," Madame Franconne said. "And remember—"

"I know, no cooking in the room and watch out for the rats."

After counting out the money, Nicole checked her purse. If she were careful, she could eat for two weeks at the most. Her room was paid for one week. The conclusion was obvious. She had to start earning money right away. Damn! She should have had the courage to wait for Jules and get either the money from the paintings he'd taken to the quay or the paintings themselves. But she hadn't, so she'd better get to work. She'd follow the same schedule, turning out rubbish in the morning and painting for herself in the afternoon. Some other artist would be glad to earn a percentage by selling them for her.

The "postcard" paintings progressed rapidly, and in a week she had two ready to sell. That would take care of her physical needs. More important, her emotional and spiritual needs were being met by the work she was starting to do in the afternoons. For years she had been searching for her own style, and now she felt she was finding it.

She wouldn't sell her afternoon paintings on the quay; she'd wait until she had enough to take to a gallery in hope of having them shown. She worked with such fury, she barely took time to eat or sleep. She was driving herself too hard, but she had two demons goading her on: the need for money to stay alive and the more urgent need to create something that would satisfy her soul.

In one way, turning out the salable paintings was easy because they required no thought. Like a machine, constructed to move automatically from one step to the next, she drew the lines and painted in the colors. However, the very drudgery and boredom of the task exhausted her. She'd get more satisfaction—and more money—from scrubbing floors. But she refused to let the work defeat her. From Leah she'd inherited a tenacity that gave her the energy and determination that drove her even after she'd reached the point of collapse. She had a goal: to achieve recognition as a great—not just good but a great—artist. She would do whatever had to be done to devote her afternoons to expanding her talent, and she had a talisman—the painting by Van Gogh.

Whenever she got depressed or felt she couldn't paint another garish scene with the Eiffel Tower in the background, she thought about the beautiful oil that so perfectly captured the soul of Paris—and the soul of the artist. Van Gogh had captured a single, perfect moment. He'd revealed something else, too. She'd been allowed a brief glimpse through his confused, tormented mind into his beautiful heart.

How could she still envision that painting and not work to unleash the talent she knew lay dormant within her? Each afternoon she labored to recapture on canvas one of the Madonnas she'd left at home. At times the exhilaration was like making love, with all its heart-pounding, breathtaking tension, the mounting crescendo toward a consummate instant suspended in time, the release and relief that followed. At other times, she felt like a woman in travail, straining to bring forth a child. Always, however, at the end of the afternoon, she viewed her accomplishment as a work of love and was relaxed and at peace.

Chapter Thirty-one

LISETTE GATHERED UP THE CROQUET MALLETS and stacked them in the rack. The sun was hot, and perspiration was oozing from all her pores beneath her immaculately white, high-necked, long-sleeved blouse, and stiffly starched petticoats, and white linen skirt. Someone else could hunt for the balls. She was ready to return to her room, bathe, and change for lunch on the terrace. Starting toward the massive country house, she suddenly couldn't remember which door to go in. For just a moment she forgot whose house she was visiting. Over the years, she'd been to so many that now they had all blurred into one gigantic labyrinth of stately halls, overfurnished drawing rooms, and long galleries. And then there were the bedrooms, which were all referred to by the predominating color or the famous personage who had slept in them centuries earlier.

"You will have the blue room, Lisette" or "I think you'll enjoy sleeping in Sir Walter Raleigh's room." Then there was, "You don't mind staying on the third floor, will you? You are so much more agile than the others who are coming." What that meant was, she was always willing to take what was left over, and the same held for the assignment of dinner partners.

Here she was cleaning up after the croquet game, and sometimes she felt that was the only reason she was invited for weekends. She could clean up the messes someone else had created, like entertaining a man no one else could tolerate but for political reasons had to be invited.

"Just ask Lisette," she could hear them saying. "She'll keep Harold or John or Albert occupied and out of our hair." Or, "Cecil's had a fight with his mistress and needs a little diversion." Or, "Reginald has some peculiar tastes in his pleasures, and the women I've invited are tired of locking their doors against him and fending off his advances. But we need the loan from his bank. Lisette can handle him and will

adore to do it for me. Oh no, she won't know, of course; I'll
just seat her beside him the first night."

Yes, she would handle him. She'd mastered the technique
of making any man think she had eyes for him alone and
then turning off the charm just at the right time without hurting his pride. It had taken years of practice. So many of the
men she'd met wanted only a night of submission, and more
than once she'd had to remind them that she, too, was a guest,
not a paid *soubrette* to be pawed over. Her bedroom door
continued to remain locked.

Lisette was really nonplused only once. Having been escorted into dinner by an elderly peer of the realm who could
barely totter to his place and who was almost totally deaf,
she was anticipating a dreadful weekend. Instead, she was
rescued by the charming and entertaining young earl who
sat on her other side. Nor did she try to dissuade him when
he made plain his intentions of occupying all her time. He
was a superb tennis player, and for once she didn't have to
pretend to let a man win. Later, they went boating on the
river, and she was genuinely enjoying herself. She began
thinking seriously that Lloyd might fill the place in her life
that Gerald Boswick obviously did not want to occupy. She
still saw Gerald from time to time—it was impossible to avoid
him when the same people were invited to all the important
functions. She'd waited for him to suggest coming by for tea
again, but beneath his rigidly polite manner was a coolness
that bordered on disdain or disapproval.

Instead, she found herself listening to Lloyd enumerate
the virtues of his mistress.

"You'd really like her, Lisette," he said. "I can't wait for
the two of you to meet."

Well, there goes any chance of developing a relationship
with him, she'd thought.

"Not only will you like her, Lisette," Lloyd was saying,
"you will love her. And she will love you. She hasn't liked
the other women I've brought home."

The other women! Why in the world would he take other
women to meet his mistress?

He was rowing toward shore when he made his shocking
proposal. "Yes, with the three of us everything will be perfect." In explicit detail, Lloyd went on to describe the delights
of being aroused by two women. Presumably, Lisette would
experience the quintessential pleasure of watching him with his
mistress, who in turn would delight in watching him with

Lisette. "But only the right one, you understand. And you are that woman, Lisette."

"Oh no, I'm not!" Never in her life had she been so insulted; she was sick with disgust at his obscene suggestions. Without waiting for him to beach the boat, she leapt out and ran trembling toward the house. She didn't care that her skirts were muddied and her kid boots ruined. Once in her room, she wept until she could cry no longer. What had she been reduced to?

At that point, Lisette wanted nothing more than to return home and let Mama and Papa comfort her. She'd never reveal all the details of the life she'd been leading, but they would understand if she said she was exhausted and needed a rest.

Leah read the letter a second time. Lisette seldom came home unless something were troubling her. Rumors of her numerous affairs had spread across the channel, and Leah wondered how much truth there was in them. No matter, she'd greet Lisette as warmly and naturally as always. And she would invite Denise to visit with little Edouard; the two sisters had always gotten along so well together.

"Mama, you always stay looking so young," Lisette greeted her. "How do you do it? I'll probably be old and wrinkled before you are."

"Nonsense, Lisette, you're more beautiful than ever." Nor did Leah have to lie. If Lisette were troubled in any way, she didn't show it. She was as vivacious and lively as ever.

"Then we'll just have to get together and trade our feminine secrets, so I can stay beautiful and you can stay young."

Baptiste looked at Lisette, more and more the image of Catherine. If only she didn't become hard and cynical like her mother. Unlike Leah, he could see the beginning of a coldness in her eyes and a tension in the way she held herself that hinted at some of Catherine's less desirable traits.

"How long are you going to grace us with your presence this time?" he asked.

"A month or two, anyway, if you'll have me." She followed Leah and Baptiste into the library, where Blanchette had set out the tea service.

"Have you!" Leah exclaimed. "We're absolutely delighted. This place is as quiet as a mausoleum with all of you gone."

"What do you hear from Henri?" Lisette had automatically

resumed her habit of adding cream and sugar to her father's cup and handing it to him. "I was stunned when you wrote that he'd gone to the States."

"He's doing very well, according to his letters. He's already received one promotion, and the owner of the carriage firm has set him to experimenting with various gasoline engines."

"Nothing he'd like better, if I know Henri," Lisette said. "Remember the motor-driven dumbwaiter he invented?"

"Don't laugh," Baptiste said. "Nicolas is still using it."

"Even after the 'infernal machine,' as he called it, blew up?"

"Henri made some minor adjustments," Leah said, defending it, "and it works fine now. You don't know what else we have. A small steam engine with two cars that runs through the secret tunnel from the house to the river."

"What in the world is that for?" Lisette reached for a second slice of cake.

Nothing is wrong with her appetite, Leah thought.

"Nothing," Baptiste said. "About as useless a contraption as I've ever seen, but Henri insisted he needed to finish it to prove some theory he had. It's all fueled and ready to go anytime you want to drive it."

"No, thank you." Lisette shook her head. "That tunnel gave me the creeps when I crawled through it. I wouldn't enjoy being stuck in it behind a broken-down steam engine. The last time I was in there was when we were looking for Nicole." She paused. "I don't suppose you've heard anything from her."

"Not a thing," Leah sighed. "All of us keep our eyes open when we're in the city, but she might as well be invisible."

"You do think she's still in Paris?" Lisette asked.

"Your mother does," Baptiste said, "because she has an intuitive feeling about it, and I do, because I think Nicole has been to the apartment."

"Baptiste!" Leah almost dropped her cup. "You never told me that."

"I didn't want to get your hopes up. But from time to time some things have been missing. When Blanchette and I stayed there while you were with Denise, some linens and most of the food were missing. Wardrobe doors and kitchen cabinets were still open."

"Why Nicole?" Leah asked. "Why not a thief?"

"Because there was no sign of forced entry. True, a professional thief might have found a way, but the concierge

359

said a neighbor had seen a young woman who looked like Nicole entering the apartment house."

"If she wants to stay in Paris," Leah moaned, "why doesn't she live at the apartment? We'd know she was safe, but she'd still be independent."

"I don't think being independent is all she craves," Lisette said. "I think she wanted to enter a whole different world from what she was used to."

"Was her life with us that miserable?" Leah asked.

"Mama, don't feel guilty. You must not take that burden on your shoulders. Nicole is her own person, just as I am. What she does with her life is her problem, not yours. She had a lovely home here and an adoring family. If it's not what she wants, you should not assume you were wrong in any way."

"That's so easy for you to say, Lisette, but she's my daughter just as you've been since you were a baby. Your father and I do worry about you girls."

"Be concerned for us, yes, but don't worry. If we decide we don't like the lives we're leading, we can always change. You trained us to make our own decisions. Now let us abide by them."

"I'll try, but it's not easy." Having Lisette home assuaged some of the ache Leah felt whenever she thought about her life in London.

Soon after Denise arrived for the promised visit, Jean and Céline surprised them by coming for a day with the boys. Once again the house was alive with the laughter of children; the halls resounded to the footsteps of the older boys, while little Edouard toddled behind and tried his best to keep up with them.

"It is good to have you all here." Leah looked at her three daughters sitting around the library fire. Jean was playing with the children in the garden while Baptiste watched from the terrace. "I'm just sorry Edouard couldn't come, too."

"It's harvest and pressing time," Denise said, "so he doesn't dare leave. He said he'd come and get us, so maybe he'll be able to stay a few days then." She reached over and poked a log. "You're looking especially lovely, Lisette."

"Yes, that's a beautiful gown," Céline added with some envy. Living in a small village and being so involved with the children, she seldom gave much thought to how she looked. Remembering how Lisette had snubbed her when she first married Jean, she still felt a little uncomfortable in this family setting.

"Thank you, both of you. It's one of my new ones." She wanted to tell them that visits to the dressmakers were as common in her life as trips to the baker were for them. They'd think her life was very exciting, even though she'd long since realized how shallow it really was.

"I saw what came out of all those trunks you brought," Denise said. "Where in the world do you wear them all?"

"Dinners, luncheons, shopping—so many places."

"A different gown for lunch and shopping?" Céline's eyes were popping.

"Lisette," Denise said hesitantly, "do tell us about your life in England. The little bits we read in your letters sound fascinating, but I'd love to hear the details—who, what, where."

"Oh, goodness," Lisette said, "I'm not sure where to start."

"London," Céline said, eager to indulge vicariously in Lisette's extravagant life. Her sister-in-law was being so much kinder to her on this visit, she was no longer afraid to talk in front of her for fear Lisette would think her crude and gauche.

"London. Let's see. I usually breakfast in bed and read the morning mail. That's when I decide which invitations I'm going to accept."

Leah sat back and smiled. For all her busy days and new-found friends, it was evident Lisette had been lonely. There was neither vanity nor braggadocio in the descriptions of her life in England. Obviously, she'd sorely missed having someone with whom she could talk naturally and honestly.

"Then," Lisette continued, "if the weather is nice, I go riding along Rotten Row or driving through the park. Sometimes it's luncheon at home, but more often it's with friends. The same with afternoon shopping."

"You shop every afternoon?" Denise asked, appalled at the amount of money Lisette must be spending on clothes alone.

"Almost. It doesn't do to wear the same gown more than two or three times, and never more than once if you know the same people are going to be there."

"What do you do with them when you're through wearing them?" Leah asked.

"Oh, give them to charity or to my maid. She has several sisters, so they get well worn in the long run."

"You never make them over?" Leah asked again. She

361

thought about the four years of Federal occupation in New Orleans, when she'd turned and remade the few dresses she owned until there was scarcely a whole thread in any of them. She'd even supported Baptiste and herself by remaking gowns and hats for other women for the few dollars they could afford to pay her. She still could not bear to discard a dress until there was absolutely no way it could be worn again. How fortunate Lisette was not to suffer such stringencies. And how unaware of hardship it made her, too.

"Occasionally, if it's a special favorite, but then only to wear at home."

"And do you have tea every afternoon?" Céline asked.

"Either at home, when someone usually drops by, or at a friend's house," Lisette said. "It's a rather informal time, with a great deal of chatter, mostly gossip. Then I dress for dinner and perhaps an evening at the theatre or cards in a private home."

"And those weekends you wrote about," Denise sighed. "All those fascinating people you meet."

Fascinating, Lisette thought. *If only Denise could meet them and see how really dull most are.* "That's when I really need the clothes. A morning gown for breakfast. Usually the men go hunting, and the women sit around and try to keep from boring one another. Then change for lunch, which might be out in the fields with the men. Another change for afternoon tea and then again for dinner. You spend a long weekend in the country, and you need twelve or sixteen gowns. Not to mention having something special made if the hostess has planned a costume ball. Sometimes the balls are historical, sometimes fanciful, and it takes all one's imagination to come up with something every other woman won't be wearing. And of course, you can never wear the same one twice."

Throughout all these descriptions, Leah noted how exuberant Lisette seemed to be. Almost too vivacious. Watching her daughter closely, Leah realized she was on the verge of frenzy, of an almost manic state. *She is about to break,* Leah thought.

"My," Denise said, "with all that gadding about, you must have a thousand friends."

"Not quite," Lisette said. "It's really the same ones wherever I go."

"Mama said you'd met the Prince of Wales," Céline said. "Do you really know him very well?"

"Yes—yes, we're friends. That is, I know both him and the Princess."

"And does he have all those mistresses we hear about?" Denise asked in almost a whisper.

"I—I don't know." Lisette was more disturbed by the question than she wanted them to know. "There are so many rumors about the royal family."

Denise caught the hesitation in Lisette's voice. She'd sensed from the beginning there was something more to the estrangement between Lisette and Philippe than she'd been told, nor was she so naive as to think that Lisette was living a totally abstemious life within a society notorious for its affairs. If the Prince had indeed been—or was once—one of her lovers, Lisette was really mingling with the highest social stratum. But was she happy? Denise, too, noted how Lisette would nervously twist her wedding ring and pull on one of her curls. Lisette had always been too poised and too fussy about her appearance to do that before. Maybe Mama would know what had Lisette so unnerved.

Only Céline, listening avidly to all of Lisette's descriptions, was unaware that her sister-in-law was not herself. She was dreaming that maybe someday Lisette would bring to the château some of those nobles she talked about so casually and Céline could meet them for herself.

"Do you want to talk about it, Lisette?" Leah had come upstairs with fresh linens. When she entered the bedroom she found the floor strewn with clothes and Lisette sobbing on the bed.

"I'm sorry you found me in such a state, Mama. I don't know what got into me. I haven't cried like this for years."

"Then it must be something serious," Leah said quietly.

"I don't know whether it is or not. Maybe I'm just being silly and infantile."

"I'm here if you want to talk, or I'll leave if you prefer." At this point Lisette might need privacy more than conversation.

"No, please stay."

"It's not all fun and games, is it? You had Denise and Céline thinking your life was continuous pleasure."

"That's not what's bothering me. I do enjoy the social life. Well, most of the time, that is." She sat up and took the handkerchief Leah handed her. "And you know how I love to spend money. Philippe knew what he was doing when

363

he offered money instead of a divorce for the price of my silence."

"Then what is it? A man? A man you can't marry?"

"You're closer than you realize," Lisette said, "except that he wouldn't marry me even if both of us were free."

"I can't imagine anyone not wanting to marry you. I assume from what you've said that he's married, too. And, I take it, he doesn't want any other kind of alliance."

"He might, and I would probably agree. He's the only man I've met I think I could be really happy with—married or not. Unfortunately, I'm not the woman he wants. The truth is, I'm not the woman he thinks I am."

"Now I'm confused, Lisette."

"It's those rumors Denise referred to. I'm unattached—no husband, no permanent escort. As the extra woman, I'm paired with whatever man is also at loose ends at the time. I'm not really a flirt, but I'm entertaining and obliging to a degree. I like to make the man I'm with feel appreciated and liked, if you will. So—rumor has it I have affairs with each of them. None of the men denies it. They like having people think they've made another conquest. I can't very well go around shouting to the world that it's all a lie, that I don't sleep with every man I meet. But Gerald has stayed away from me ever since I spent most of one evening dancing with the Prince of Wales. In his opinion, I'm a loose woman, and I have no chance with him at all."

"Are they all rumors, Lisette?"

"Mama, I'm twenty-six and a married woman, whose marriage was never consummated. If you're asking if I'm still a virgin, the answer is no. I haven't been promiscuous, but there were times—long weekends, close proximity, a few caresses—when I couldn't stand it any longer. None of them wanted a long-term relationship, so there were no emotional entanglements."

"I won't say I approve," Leah said gently, "but I don't condemn you."

"I guess maybe I am what Gerald thinks of me—a loose woman. When I do see him, he's so cold and formal, it tears me apart."

"Are you in love with him?" Leah asked.

"I don't know. I admire and respect him. Strange, at this point it's his good opinion I want. If nothing more than friendship developed now, I think I would be satisfied."

"Yet, you really feel it could go further?" Leah could sense the tension easing in Lisette. This was what she needed. Some one to talk to, someone who would not chatter inanely, and carry her confessions out of the house as gossip, or condemn her. "Stay with us a while. Maybe, if he were attracted to you once, he's forcing himself to maintain that cold and formal attitude to hide his real feelings."

"He was. I know he was."

"If you are away for a month or so, he might realize you're a finer woman than rumor has led him to believe."

"I'll stay for a few weeks," Lisette agreed. "If Gerald's attitude has changed when I go back, I'll know you were right. If not, I'll simply try to forget about him, and—and maybe I'll meet someone else. I can't go on alone much longer. I need someone to love me."

Leah recognized this as a genuine cry from the heart. "We all do, Lisette. I wish you could marry again. I'm not sure you'll find what you're looking for with a married man like Gerald. There are always the shifting hands of uncertainty underlying the relationship."

"But you and Papa were happy for many years."

"Yes, but if being his mistress had been enough I never would have left him and married James Andrews. I needed to be married. I needed that sense of belonging totally and completely to someone. That's why we came to France after Catherine—after your mother died. Twice I was willing to leave the security of my past and give up all that was familiar to find a new kind of security. I know you aren't free to marry—at least for the time being—but don't start seeking love in the wrong places."

"Please don't moralize, Mama."

"I'm not, but I watched your face when you spoke about the Prince's affairs. And you say there've been others. A brief affair with Gerald or anyone else is no substitute for love."

"Gerald's not like that," Lisette insisted.

"You don't know for sure."

"No." She began brushing her hair. "I think I'd like to go into the city for a few days. Will it be all right if I stay at the apartment?"

"You know it will. You can drive in with Papa tomorrow, if you like."

Lisette looked into the mirror over the dressing table. She'd dressed carefully for her two o'clock appointment, and now she was checking for the fifth time to make sure her hair curled properly under the brim of her hat.

What's the use? she cried to herself. *He doesn't care how*

I look. But it mattered to her. She had to appear completely self-assured and totally in control of the situation. Nothing haggard or self-pitying about her appearance, not if she hoped to get what she'd come to Paris for. This time Philippe was going to listen to her and meet some of her demands. She wasn't going to take just whatever he chose to hand out. She picked up her handbag and walked down to the waiting hansom. During the short ride to the bank, she tried to concentrate on the people hurrying along the streets instead of the approaching confrontation.

Philippe greeted her at the door of his office. "You're looking lovely, Lisette."

"Thank you, Philippe." One look at his smile and all the love for him she thought had been destroyed came surging back. Her heart pounded, and any determination she'd had to remain cold, strong, and unmoved evaporated like snow under the bright glare of the sun.

"I was surprised to receive your note," he said. "I thought you were in England. At least that's where the accountant says he sends your quarterly checks."

At the mention of England, Lisette thought of Gerald, and some of her determination returned. The reference to the money was all it took to harden her heart against Philippe once again. She was nothing more than a kept woman. The only difference between her and a mistress was that the money was to insure she stayed away from Philippe rather than be available to him.

"I came home for a short visit," she said, "and it seemed an opportune time to see you and renegotiate our arrangement."

"Oh!" Philippe's brows shot up. "You are displeased with it in some way?" God knew he'd made the settlement as generous as he could afford. The trust fund was set up in such a way that it could be dissolved only upon her death. And his present lover was making more and more extravagant demands.

"Yes. I want a divorce." There, she'd said it, and she hoped Philippe could not see how much she was shaking.

"Impossible! I'm slowly gaining a reputation in city politics, and I intend to be an important figure in the national government within a few years. A divorce would ruin me."

"Then a quiet annulment. And—you could find someone else to marry you who would be happy with the arrangement you had hoped to have with me. There must be someone whose silence you can buy."

"No. An annulment would require my testimony, and I'll never do that." As he looked at her, his eyes darkened. "And remember, no hint of the truth, or I'll ruin your father."

Lisette knew that the financial situation in the import office had improved, especially now that Victor Duchalais had personally invested along with her father in Jean's winery and the firm was exporting champagne to England and the United States. She was still not certain, however, whether Philippe could call in notes or whether he were bluffing.

"Also," Philippe added, "I'd like you to stay in Paris for a while and live at our apartment. People are beginning to speculate over our long separation."

"Never! That I will never do, and you cannot force me. I know the terms of the agreement and the trust fund. You can refuse a divorce, but I can also refuse to stay with you."

"If we live as husband and wife?" Philippe suggested.

Lisette's heart turned over. Could he be feeling something for her at last? Was it possible for someone like him to change?

"Are you serious, Philippe? As your wife, your real wife?"

"I need you, Lisette." It was true. He would never love her as a man loves a woman, but as one loves some beautiful precious possession. He knew her too well to think she'd gone this long without lovers, and his heart darkened at the thought of some other man touching her and making love to her. She had been defiled by groping hands and panting bodies, but he would be like a priest granting her absolution if she returned to him. If he were a husband to her, and he treated her more gently and considerately than he had before, she might not object if he also had a lover.

Philippe walked toward her and held out his hands in supplication. "I know I was insufferably inconsiderate and sometimes cruel, but I was jealous of every man who looked at you."

"Jealous? How could you be jealous when you wouldn't have anything to do with me?" She was the one who'd been consumed with jealous fury at his leaving her every night.

"You were mine. You are mine. I should never have let you go to England, but seeing you with Georges—well, I lost my mind. Will you stay?"

Philippe had once before offered to spend the night with her, but he'd gone off to Marseilles instead. The disappointment and frustration had been almost more than she could bear. She was more wary now of any promises he made. She knew why he said he needed her; it was for his own protection and for his ambition. He needed a wife by his side, a wife who could charm the people he courted and be a gracious hostess for the entertaining his position required.

"I make no promises of staying permanently, Philippe, but I will remain in Paris for a week and see how we get along. Then I'll let you know."

"If that's all you can say for now, I'll have to be satisfied with it. I'll send word to the cook to have a fine dinner prepared for two, and you can play for me afterward the way you did before."

"No, not at our place," Lisette said. "There are too many bitter memories—at least for the present. I'm staying at the family apartment. We can dine out and then return there. I think it will make it easier for both of us."

"As you wish." He could afford to defer to her wishes as long as it kept her here in Paris. And it would be good for them to be seen dining together tonight. "I'll pick you up at seven-thirty."

After Lisette agreed to spend the night with him, Philippe began preparing himself for this most important encounter. During the preliminaries, he could close his mind to the fact it was Lisette he was lying with and not Steven, the young English artist he'd met in Montmartre. Steven was small and slim like Lisette, who had narrow hips and tiny breasts. Those were probably among the reasons he'd been attracted to her. But then, would he be able to continue—and finish? Would his body respond to her as it did to Steven? Steven had slept with women and said that it could be very enjoyable. If only he could talk to Steven before he met Lisette for dinner. But now they had become lovers, the younger man would never understand Philippe's turning from him to his wife. Philippe remembered with a shudder his one visit to a bordello. His acute embarrassment. His humiliating departure. No, he mustn't think about that now. He must concentrate on consummating his marriage to Lisette, so she could never claim it had not happened. That would put an end to any attempt on her part to gain an annulment or divorce through the Church.

At the restaurant, it was as if they were courting all over again. Philippe could not have been more attentive or solicitous. *But then,* Lisette thought, he *was always a superb actor when we were in public. What will it be like when we're alone?*

From the first time she saw Philippe, Lisette had wondered what kind of lover he would be. As she undressed, she realized she would at long last find out.

Lisette slipped into bed beside Philippe. She wore only a peignoir that could be easily removed. He turned off the gas lamp. It would be easier in the dark. His first overtures were hesitant and awkward, as he was still trying to blind himself to her sex and pretend it was Steven lying beside him.

As subtly as possible, Lisette used first one technique and then another to arouse her husband. She was rewarded with a few tentative caresses. With her newly awakened love for him, she could hardly wait for him to take her.

But it never happened. His body remained unresponsive to her.

Philippe rolled over and began tearing his pillow apart as if it were something he had to annihilate before it destroyed him. He flung himself off the bed and reached for his robe.

"Philippe!" Lisette cried. "You can't do this to me. You can't leave me like this."

"Do you think it's any easier for me? Do you think I like doing this to you or to myself? Don't you realize that from the time I knew what I was, I wanted to be a man, a real man?"

"I don't know." Lisette wanted to believe him. She could almost reconcile herself to living with him and perhaps taking lovers, if she thought there was any chance for happiness between them. "You always seemed very satisfied to take your pleasure elsewhere."

"On the sly." He seemed to be talking more to himself than to her. "Afraid every moment I'd be found out, and knowing I could never have a real relationship with anyone."

"I'm sorry, Philippe. I mean it. I'm truly sorry for you. I wish there were some way I could stay with you and we could work things out. But I love you too much to live with you, to see you every day, and never have us make love. To know you're leaving each night to be with someone else. Whether lover or mistress, it would be intolerable."

"How can you love me knowing what you do?"

"That's something I can't answer. I'd managed to put you out of my mind after I went to England. Seeing you again was a mistake. The only salvation for me is to return to London."

"And your affairs?" Philippe was engulfed by another wave of jealousy. He waited for her to deny them.

"They are some compensation for not being loved by you."

She watched him run his fingers through his hair as he stared out at the stormy sky. "I think you'd better go now," she said. "I'll leave for London in a few days."

"Do you need more money?" He pulled on his trousers and carefully tucked his shirt inside.

"No, the trust is ample. And you can be sure tonight will remain a secret—as secret as the past has been." For the first time she realized how genuinely tormented Philippe was and why he'd behaved so cruelly to her after they were married. But she could never see him again.

"Then I think we have nothing more to say to each other." Philippe picked up his coat and hurried out the door. Steven would be waiting. Steven would be able to calm the upheaval that had him shaking like an alcoholic in desperate need of a drink.

Lisette turned over in the bed. She had failed. She'd been so certain that if she could obtain an annulment, Gerald would understand that her erratic behavior was caused by not just an unhappy marriage, but by an impossible one.

She was obsessed by the thought that her failure in the confrontation with Philippe was a dark omen that she'd also fail with Gerald. She felt like a child who had wandered too far and become lost. There was no going back, and she had no idea of which direction to take to move ahead. Papa and Mama were generous with their love, but they didn't understand her. It had been pleasant to visit them, but the château was no longer her home. Nor was France. She had to get out of the country where she was suffocated by unhappy memories.

She supposed she could travel. She'd often thought about touring Italy, maybe even going as far as Egypt or Greece. At the moment, however, such trips held no appeal. She'd just be running away instead of facing up to her problems. *Admit it, Lisette*, she told herself, *what you really want is to go home.* And home now meant England and her house near Berkeley Square.

Having decided to remain on their country estate, the Sheldons had given her a ten-year lease with an option to renew. Lisette had delighted in furnishing the place to her own tastes. She was seldom happier than when sitting in her small parlor. Decorated in white and shades of blue, it was a haven of tranquility to which she could retire when the hectic social whirl became too much for her. She loved her music room, too. She could sit at the piano and play alone for hours without ever feeling lonely. Just thinking about her house decided her. She would go back but move at a slower pace. If a future with Gerald was not to be, she could learn to make a life for herself.

Chapter Thirty-two

THE YEAR 1895 produced shock after shock in England. The first was the bitterly cold winter, with the lowest temperatures and deepest snows anyone in London could remember. Others would be the trial of Oscar Wilde, charged with indecent and immoral acts of sodomy, and the often obscene, titillating drawings—published and unpublished—of Aubrey Beardsley.

In January, Lisette returned late from a dinner party. It had been snowing all evening, and when she alighted from the fiacre, she stepped into a snow bank. By the time she got into the house and up to her room, her satin slippers were soaked through and her feet nearly frozen. Marney, her personal maid, answered her ring with a pot of hot chocolate and a few biscuits.

"Please, Marney, get a towel. My feet are so wet and cold I can't feel a thing when I try to move them."

"You need more than a towel, ma'am, you need a hot tub. I'll fix it for you right now."

"Thank you, Marney. I'm sorry I'm keeping you up this late, but I feel chilled all over."

Lisette let Marney help her into the tub. The water was as hot as she could stand it, yet she continued to shake with chills.

"A good rubdown will restore the circulation, ma'am, and I've put the bedwarmer between the sheets."

"I've never been so cold as I was coming home in the carriage." She'd wrapped her furs around her, but even those had failed to keep the chill out.

"You should have worn your fur-lined boots, ma'am."

"I know. Next time I'll listen to you." She slid between

the warm sheets and stretched straight out, her feet touching the spot where the warming pan had lain. When her eyelids became too heavy to keep open, she knew Marney had put laudanum in her second cup of cocoa. Good, she'd go right to sleep and not worry about the fiasco at dinner, where her partner, like so many others before him, had assumed she was available for the entire night. This time a simple no had not been enough, and she hated to be rude. It had ended whatever pleasure she was having.

Instead of sleeping peacefully until morning, Lisette suffered through one nightmare after another as her fever rose. First she was in Gerald's arms, and he was urging her to have an affair with him. Just as she was about to succumb, he turned into Philippe. He was caressing her and she was responding eagerly; but all his attempts to make love to her ended in failure. He was physically unable to complete the act. Worse, they were no longer alone in bed, but in the middle of a ballroom, and all the men she'd ever known were standing around, laughing. They were pointing their fingers at her and jeering as if it were her fault that Philippe was impotent.

"It's not my fault!" she screamed, and the sound of her own voice woke her up. She turned over and buried her head in the pillow so Marney, who was sleeping in the next room in case Lisette needed her, wouldn't hear her. She was shaking with chills now and she knew she had a fever, but there was no point in calling Marney. She couldn't do anything for her this time of night. In a few minutes, Lisette went back to sleep.

She continued to dream. First of Gerald and then of Philippe, and always there were the faces taunting her. When she awoke again in the morning, she found the blankets wrapped all around her like a cocoon; but she was still cold and her teeth were chattering.

"Marney." She tried to call loud enough for her maid to hear, but she could scarcely get the single word out because of her sore throat.

"Oh, ma'am, you're burning up with fever. Let me straighten your bed and get you some hot tea. Then I'll send for the doctor."

By the end of the day and after two visits from the doctor, Lisette was still feverish and shivering with chills. Most of the time she was too delirious to know what was going on.

"Where is her family?" the doctor asked Marney while writing out some orders.

"Her only family is in Paris."

"Then I think you'd better send a wire to them. She's a very sick woman and needs all the care she can get."

"I won't leave her side," Marney assured him.

"I know, but you'll need to rest. I advise you to send the wire."

Leah looked at the telegram that had arrived as she was packing her trunk to stay with Denise, who was expecting her second child any day. MADAME DUCHALAIS ILL WITH PNEUMONIA was all the wire said. After Denise's difficult time at little Edouard's birth, Leah wanted to be with her. She felt like a puppet being pulled by two sets of strings. Denise was counting on her to help with little Edouard, yet she had a competent nursemaid who could do that. It was Denise herself who had Leah worried. Was it intuition or superstition that told her Denise would survive only if she were with her? Leah paced the floor. It was just as well she had to make a choice in a hurry. If she had days, or even hours, to make up her mind, she would merely torture herself with indecision. But she had a train to catch whichever direction she went.

"Baptiste, what shall I do? Which one should I be with?"

"Pneumonia is serious, but the wire didn't indicate she was in any danger. Or even that she needed you."

"I think that's implied. The wire wasn't merely to let us know."

"Lisette has friends and many good doctors. We both know that even though Denise wants this baby, she's afraid. I think your place is with her. I'll wire Lisette's house for someone there to keep in touch with us."

"Then why do I feel guilty about not going over? Is it because Denise is my own child and Lisette is not?"

"Don't be foolish," Baptiste said. "No one would ever think that."

"I hope not, but Lisette seemed so different, acted so strangely, when she returned from Paris, I began to feel we'd lost contact again."

"Nonsense. She was just anxious to get back to London. You go to Denise. I'll wire you if there's further word from Lisette, and you keep in touch about Denise."

"And you'll be all right here?" Leah asked.

"Blanchette and I will go into Paris as we did before.

Don't worry. She keeps me on a tight leash and sees to it I behave myself."

"All right. The carriage is here, so I'll take the train for Rheims. And I'll give Denise your love." She bent over his chair to kiss him good-bye. "Do keep in touch."

It was with a heavy heart that Leah boarded the train. She had the uncanny feeling that Lisette not only would never understand but also would never forgive her for the choice she'd made.

When Marney received the wire saying that Madame Fontaine had to stay with another daughter, she merely shrugged her shoulders. It was no more than she'd expected. But she would not desert her lady. Madame Duchalais was the finest, most generous employer one could ever work for. Didn't she give Marney all her gowns after two or three wearings, even though she might have had them made over or sold them in the secondhand shops, as even some duchesses did? After Marney made her selection, she sent the others to her family and therefore was adored by her sisters. And wasn't she the envy of the other maids she saw on her days off? No, she'd take care of her employer herself, and then she'd be assured of a position in the household for the rest of her life, not a minor consideration in these days when every country girl preferred to work in a home rather than in a factory—or worse, take to the streets for a living.

With regular visits from the doctor and Marney's constant ministrations, Lisette began to improve. Nothing was said to her about the wire to Paris or the reply. There was no point in worrying her, Marney thought, and it was enough that Madame Duchalais gave her all the credit for her recovery.

"I don't know what I would have done without you, Marney."

"It was my only wish that you get well, ma'am. Your friends have also brought you good things to eat. I'm sure they helped, too."

"You're far too modest." Lisette smiled at her. "I know who took care of me night and day. There will be a generous raise for you as soon as I can get to the bank."

"Thank you, ma'am. That's not necessary, but it will be most appreciated." Marney was happy. She'd firmly established her place in the house.

Within a few days, Lisette was able to sit up in bed or on

the chaise longue. Jane Westborne came by frequently to say how dreadful it was that Lisette should have to miss out on so much of the winter season. "And the gossip, my dear. It will take several visits for me to catch you up on all of it."

"Anything really scandalous? I'm still too weak to go anyplace, but not too tired to hear all about everything."

"The worst is about Oscar Wilde." Jane settled herself in the chair for a good hour of gossip. "All those horrible rumors of his love affair with Lord Alfred Douglas. You know, the Marquess of Queensberry's son."

Shades of Philippe and his friends, Lisette thought. "I always thought him a strange man," she said aloud.

"But, oh, so talented and so very witty. They're talking of closing down *The Importance of Being Earnest,* and it's such a brilliant play. Do get well in time to see it."

"I'll do my best," Lisette said. "What else is new?"

"The things we're learning because of the gossip about Wilde. Everyone is shuddering to learn about the number of male prostitutes there are on the streets of London and the number of cheap hotels that pander to them and their companions. As often as I've visited Paris and seen what goes or in the Place Pigalle, I never thought it would happen in England."

"I guess human nature is the same everywhere," Lisette said. "Whose dinner parties have you been to?"

Jane began to enumerate them in detail.

"I hadn't realized how much I was missing," Lisette said.

"Speaking of which, I must go." Jane made a point of consulting the ostentatious watch pinned to her jacket. It was encrusted with pearls and rubies. "You're beginning to look tired, and I have to dress for another dinner party."

"That's a beautiful watch," Lisette said. "New?"

"I hoped you'd notice. Yes, from a simply charming young Italian. New to London and speaks scarcely a word of English. My Italian is not very good, but it's enough for us to get along marvelously. I'm not sure I want you to meet him. With your pale, wan appearance, he'd succumb to you immediately. But I will have you over soon, and I'll find just the right partner for you to keep Sergio at bay."

"Thank you, Jane. I can always count on you to find the right one for me." Lisette hoped she hadn't sounded too sarcastic.

"I'll be back in a few days, and if there's anything—*anything*—you need, send Marney around."

So Jane had a new, young lover. Lisette could only wish

her a few weeks or months of pleasure with him. After that, his eyes would begin to wander to younger women, and Jane would be forced to return to the Continent in search of another impoverished title. At least she hadn't been reduced to struggling artists or writers.

Lisette picked up a novel and then laid it down again. She didn't feel like reading.

"Madame?" Marney opened the door a crack. "Are you awake?"

"Yes, and bored to tears. Come in and give me a back rub while you tell me more about your family."

"I came to tell you, you have a caller. Lord Gerald Boswick."

"Gerald! Lord Boswick is here?" She couldn't believe she was hearing correctly.

"Yes. Do you wish to receive him?"

"Yes, but first get me— No, wait, go down and tell him it will be but a few minutes. Then come back and help me into something pretty and fix my hair a bit."

Marney helped her change into a pink ruffled robe to bring out some color in her cheeks and tucked across her lap the new embroidered afghan Jane had brought. Lisette looked at herself in the hand mirror. She was still very pale, but there was something attractive about that. Gerald couldn't help but be moved by her weak and innocent appearance.

There was an assured knock on the door. "May I come in, Lisette?"

"Yes, and how very nice of you to come." She smiled at him, and hoped her pleasure was not too obvious. Although a good-looking man, there was nothing of the dandy or the poseur about Gerald. He seemed as solid, as steady, and as genuine as the cliffs of Cornwall near his home.

"I heard you were ill," he said, "and I came to offer my services if there's anything you need." He sat down in the chair Marney had placed near the chaise longue.

"Thank you, Gerald, that's kind of you." His services! He hadn't come because he really wanted to see her. He'd do the same for anyone or anything he thought needed help, even a cat caught up in a tree. She wanted to cry.

"If you wish, I can have my driver take your maid shopping," he suggested.

"No, there's nothing I need. Jane and others are keeping me well supplied." She pulled at a loose thread on the afghan.

"Too bad," he said. "I thought it would be a good excuse to stay here and talk to you while she was gone."

Lisette caught the twinkle in his eyes and would have kicked herself under the afghan if she could have managed it.

"You don't need an excuse for a visit. I love seeing you again, and I'd like you to have tea with me if you will." Maybe she was being too bold, but he had indicated he wanted to stay.

"I'd like that, too. I thought maybe I'd become *persona non grata* with you since I never accepted your earlier invitation to return."

"But you're here now." She rang for Marney and asked to have tea served immediately.

"You're being very gracious, Lisette, when I know you must have thought I was deliberately ignoring you."

She still could not believe he was sitting beside her. "Yes, after—after we seemed to get along so well at first, I was certain I'd done something to offend you." Better to find out now than to get her hopes up.

"Not offend, Lisette, but discourage me. I'm not a prude, but when I kept hearing about all the affairs you were having—"

"Not so, Gerald! Rumors, nothing more." He had to believe her.

"I know that now, Lisette. As I said, it wasn't because I'm that circumspect that I didn't seek you out. I simply thought I could never compete with the others."

"You're worth twice all of them put together, Gerald." There, she'd said how she felt; if it were the wrong thing, then let the Devil take the hindmost.

"That's the most encouraging thing I've heard in a long time." He reached over as if to take her hand, but then Marney walked in with the tea tray . He waited until Lisette poured and they both settled back with their cups. "There were other reasons, too, why I stayed away. Problems with the estate in Cornwall demanded much of my time. The few times you've seen me were about the only times I've gotten away. Then there is Lady Boswick. She and I have lived separate lives for many years, but there are certain responsibilities I have to take care of and often they are not pleasant."

"You don't need to say anything more. I understand." Lisette began to hope that all those problems he mentioned were in the past, and he would ask to see her again.

Gerald put down his cup. "I'm going now. You look tired. But I'll be back soon, and this time I mean it."

"Don't wait too long. Your visit has really cheered me up." He would never know just how much.

From then on every day brought delivery boys with gifts of flowers, candy, and all types of delicacies, or Gerald himself with his arms laden with special treats. Her room began to look like a hot house, and she laughed with him at the thought she was going to get fat when he insisted she eat everything he brought.

"Gerald, this is all too much," she insisted one day when he walked in with a huge, tissue-wrapped bouquet in one arm and freshly baked tarts in the other.

"If I had four arms, I'd bring twice as much if it meant seeing you smile like that." He bent over and kissed her lightly on the forehead.

"And this plump figure that will hardly fit into this dress." But she was secretly pleased at the way she filled out the bodice.

"Better than that skinny look you had for so long."

"Skinny! What an insult after working so hard to keep a fashionably tiny waist."

"Anyway, it's good to see you up and dressed." He took her hand in his. "The weather has cleared. Would you like to bundle up in your furs and go for a drive?"

"I'd love it. I didn't know I could get so tired of this perfect little house."

"The carriage is waiting out front. I thought you might be ready to get out. Shall I ask Marney to get your things?"

"No, I have a fur cape right here." She walked to the wardrobe.

"And something for your head," he cautioned.

"I have that, too." She wrapped a long silk scarf around her head and shoulders and handed the cape to Gerald. He started to put it over her shoulders and then impulsively turned her around and took her into his arms. It was the first time he'd held her that close, and Lisette began trembling.

"What's wrong, Lisette? Feeling a sudden chill or—or have I done something wrong?"

"No, please, don't let go." She buried her face in his shirtfront. "Please, don't ever let me go, Gerald."

"You mean that, sweetheart?"

"I've never meant anything more in my life."

He kissed her gently on the mouth and then stepped back.

378

"Let's go for the ride." He held the door open for her and waited for her to walk ahead of him down the stairs.

Oh, dear, Lisette thought, *I've done it now. I've shown him how I feel and it's frightened him away.* But she wasn't going to let worry over that spoil their ride. She kept the conversation light, and had him laughing over some of the foolish antics of her family.

"You're lucky," he said, "to have such a big family. And to be so close. Mine was one of nursemaids and tutors; then I was sent away to school."

When they returned to the house, they sat by the fire in the small parlor.

"Everything about you is always so cheerful, Lisette. These rooms, the whole atmosphere. It brightens up my whole day to walk in here."

"Thank you. I despise drabness. Life so often seems to be full of unhappiness, but there's no point in not doing all you can to make it pleasant."

"You sounded rather bitter then." He leaned forward. "That's unlike you."

"Did I? I don't suppose with all I have I should be. Or maybe what I see is merely superficial, and somehow the really important things have eluded me."

"Lisette, I wanted to come back here and talk. I'm not usually an impulsive man. I need my feet firmly on the ground, and I need to know where I'm going."

"Yes." She nodded her head. "You've always impressed me that way." And it was why she was drawn to him; his steadfastness appealed to a deep need in her.

"That's why it's so important you understand how I feel. You've come to mean a great deal to me. If—if things were different, I'd be down on my knees right now proposing to you. But I can't."

Lisette was both pleased and disturbed. He wanted her, but he was holding himself back. She could only sit there and wait for him to go on.

"The natural assumption, I suppose," he said, "is that I'd ask you to become my mistress—or companion, as it's put so euphemistically nowadays."

"Are you asking me, or is this merely an exercise in rhetoric?"

"I'm sorry. I did sound very cold and pedantic, didn't I? Believe me, I didn't mean to be. I guess I forgot something. I forgot to say I love you, and I want you with me more than anything else in the world."

379

"Say it again, Gerald, and then you can go on in your logical manner." She reached for his hands. "Does this make it easier?"

"In a way, yes, and in a way, no." He slid forward in his chair to grasp her hands more tightly. "I love you, and I know you're trying to understand what I want to say."

"Not really." She shook her head and then let her smile become an impish grin. "It would be much more fun to see you down on your knees."

"Dammit, Lisette, you're going to make me start laughing, and then I won't be able to get it out at all."

"I'm sorry, but I was trying to imagine your trousers with a wrinkle in them. They're always so impeccably pressed."

"I know now why I love you. I am too serious, and you won't let me be. If I had my way, I'd pick you up right now and whisk you off to Cornwall. We'd walk along the cliffs and then come in to sit by the fire. Just the two of us all day long."

"Is there a thick rug in front of the fireplace?" she asked.

"The thickest. Why?"

"I've always wanted to lie in front of a fire and make love."

"You're not making this any easier for me, you know." He frowned.

"No, I don't know, Gerald. What is it you're trying to say?"

"I want us to think about it for a while, not rush into something we'd be sorry for. If—if we should decide we want to be together, it must be a total commitment. I had two brief affairs after my wife and I separated. They were most unsatisfactory. I am a man who must give himself totally and completely, without reservations. I need the same in return. Another brief affair, no matter how much fun it might be for the moment, is not what I want for us."

"Nor I, Gerald, nor do I. I've been hurt too many times to want to suffer like that again."

"I know," he said. "That's why I want both of us to do some serious thinking. We need more time together, a real courtship, if you will."

"I'd enjoy that." It would be fun to learn what his idea of a courtship was.

"But it won't be a long one. I love you and need you too much."

"Then it's me you're uncertain about, isn't it?" Lisette asked. Like so many others, he thought her flighty and unable to remain faithful or settle down. She had to prove him wrong.

"Only for your real feelings for me."

"And the thought I might tire of you and want to move on to someone else?" She supposed she had to accept that he'd think that after the reputation she'd earned.

"A little, yes."

"Then I'll honor your wish to take time, because when I do say yes, I want there to be no doubt in your mind that I mean it."

The next few weeks were a time of revelation for Lisette. Knowing that Gerald loved her, she could enjoy being with him without feeling that her every word and action were being judged. After long deliberation, she decided to break part of her word to Philippe and confided to Gerald that her marriage had never been consummated, but did not tell him why. As she hoped, Gerald was all sympathy. He seemed to understand what she'd been through and why she'd behaved as she had when she first came to England.

During those weeks, Lisette was engaged in intense self-evaluation. All her life she'd been the maker of her own rules, often seeming to flout society's accepted mores, yet she was acutely moral. In that way she differed from so many women of her age and station. Whether she wore the contrived mask of a cool, self-controlled woman of the world or that of a whimsical, childlike tease, there lay beneath it an intense passion and desperate need to be loved for herself. One disappointed would-be lover had told her she was like dry ice. The closer he got, the colder she became, but to touch her was to be burned.

She wanted to be loved for herself, but she did not know what her real self was. The charmer who sought admirers everywhere she went? The girl still bitterly hurt by her experience of marriage? A woman who wanted to be faithful to one man but who would soon be attracted to another? Or were these all merely façades that could be stripped away to reveal a woman ready to devote herself to someone who loved her as much as Gerald did?

She knew these were the questions Gerald wanted her to ask herself; she also knew that unless she came up with the right answers, there was no point in going on with him. A total commitment, he'd said. There'd be no trying it for a few weeks and then changing her mind. In the first place, she wouldn't hurt him that way; and in the second, he'd know the truth the minute she spoke. When—if—she agreed to

381

become his mistress, her sincerity must be absolute. Gerald was everything she could want in a man. She was truly fond of him and respected him tremendously. Yet she couldn't honestly say she loved him.

After probing her own feelings and bringing up every possible argument against living with him, she knew she would say yes and hoped everything turned out all right. She couldn't go on the way she had and there was no hope of a divorce from Philippe. She wanted to be with Gerald, and she'd do her best to make him glad he asked her. She could never be the Duchess of Highcastle; but being with him, whether in London or Cornwall, was worth all the coronets in the kingdom.

They were sitting quietly in her music room.

"Do you think the time has come, Lisette?" he asked.

"For what?" She knew what he meant, but she had to hear him ask her.

"To make a decision about our future."

"There you go being pedantic, as you call it," she said. "As serious as the step may be, I would like a touch of romance."

"I'm sorry. That's one of my failings you'll have to help me correct if— Hell! It's easier to propose than it is to ask someone to live with you. No one's invented the right words yet."

He stood up and, stuffing his hands in his pockets, walked across the room.

"Yes, they have. Tell me you love me and then see what I say. And it would be easier if you put your arms around me."

She walked over to where he stood leaning against the mantel.

"You're right," he said, holding her close. "It's much easier this way. I love you, and I want you with me for always. I've just been afraid you'd refuse."

"Stay the night, Gerald."

"And let propriety be damned?"

"Propriety? That's an old-fashioned word, dreadfully out of date," Lisette said teasingly. "I'm not quite sure what it means."

"Propriety means I don't leave my fiacre in front of your house all night, and that I walk home in the wee hours of the morning instead of having the driver return for me." He looked lovingly at Lisette. "I'll tell him to go home, but I'll have him come back some time before noon. That should titillate the neighbors."

"Then you will spend the night?" Somehow she'd sensed that as much as Gerald desired her, he was waiting—and would wait—for her to say she was ready.

"I can't refuse you anything right now, darling. Especially something I want, too."

To Lisette's surprise, they walked upstairs and undressed as if they had been married for years rather than just beginning their life together. She found being in Gerald's arms as natural as—but far more exciting than—sitting across the table from him at dinner. She knew immediately she belonged to him, and she'd be making no mistake in living with him.

They decided Lisette should keep her house in London, although they would be spending the greater part of each year in either Cornwall or Scotland. As Lisette prepared herself for living a secluded country life, she was surprised to feel relieved at not having to contemplate a succession of dinner invitations, theatre parties, or evenings at the opera. She looked forward to solitary walks with Gerald along the cliffs or through the heather, and learning to hunt the fields and fish for salmon and trout in Scotland. Marney, her personal maid, would accompany them, while the rest of the staff remained behind to care for the house and have it ready for their brief visits to the city.

"I want you with me all the time," Gerald said, "and that wouldn't be possible if we tried to follow the seasonal circuit of social events." Lisette knew why; he didn't have to tell her. Lady Boswick was still very much in evidence at most of the functions. "Will you mind very much missing such things as Cowes, the Derby, and country weekends?" he asked.

"Not at all. They were beginning to bore me anyway. And I'll never be bored with you." Surprisingly, she knew she meant it. Leah had spoken of a very special kind of security, and even though she and Gerald could not be married, she felt as if she would find that security with him.

Before they left for Cornwall and his home at High Tor, Lisette received a letter from Leah. In it, Leah apologized for not having come over when Lisette was ill, and said she was relieved to know Lisette was completely well again. Denise had had a difficult time, but she was now completely recovered from the birth of Gilles, a strong, healthy baby. Lisette was puzzled at the reference to Leah's not coming over, until Marney told her about the wire she'd sent. Then Lisette was momentarily hurt that Leah had chosen to be with Denise instead of her, until she realized that the choice had really been in her favor. If Leah had been there to nurse her, Gerald might not have come to see if she needed help. She really ought to thank Mama for having stayed away.

Chapter Thirty-three

LEAH WALKED INTO NICOLE'S STUDIO, left just as it was the day Nicole fled. Half-finished paintings on their easels lay under layers of dust. Others rested against the furniture, and a few hung on the walls. Leah didn't often go into the studio. The place was filled with ghosts, and at times she seemed to hear Nicole's voice—raised in anger or trilling with laughter —and see the tall figure carefully arranging her easel before a window.

Baptiste had suggested that some of the finished paintings, such as the Madonna series, ought to be framed and hung in the house. But Leah could not bring herself to do this; nor could she explain the feeling that as long as she left everything just as it was, Nicole would someday return. If one thing were moved, one picture dusted, the spell would be broken and Nicole lost to them forever. She thought of Orpheus, who had been warned not to look back while he led Eurydice out of Hades. But he had been unable to resist turning to see if she were still with him as they approached the end of the long, dark tunnel. And then she disappeared immediately into the black night of the underworld. Leah must do nothing to lose Nicole.

It had been three years, three long and painful years, since Nicole ran away; and there was no assurance she was still alive. True, Jean thought he'd seen her one time, and Baptiste had finally told her about the food and linens missing from the Paris apartment; even then, though, Leah could not be certain it had been Nicole. Many were the hours she'd walked the quay where the artists sold their paintings, and once, a particular painting had caught her eye.

384

From the style and the subject matter—a mother and child—she was certain it was Nicole's. But it was signed *Michele,* and she had to turn away to hide her tears of disappointment. She'd mingled with the artists at the Place du Tertre, knowing instinctively this would be Nicole's natural milieu, but there was no sign of her, and seemingly no one knew anything about her. Yet Leah could feel her presence as surely as she did in the studio. Sometimes she turned her head suddenly, as if by doing so she would see Nicole looking out a window above her or disappearing around a street corner.

After each such visit to Paris, Leah came home more subdued and sorrowful than ever, until Baptiste said he would forbid her to go into the city if she continued suffering so deeply. Nicole was gone, and she must accept her loss just as she would a child who'd died.

"I can't, Baptiste."

"You didn't give up on life when René died."

"This is different. I *know* she's still alive, and I think she needs us but can't admit it even to herself. If I knew for certain she was alive and happy, I think I could accept not seeing her."

Baptiste said no more. Most of the time Leah was occupied enough with the other children and grandchildren to keep her concern for Nicole from tearing her apart.

"Want to visit Jean or Denise for a few days?" Baptiste asked.

"Maybe in a week or two. I know what you're doing, so don't think you can fool me. You're trying to tell me in your own subtle way I should be grateful I have a big, happy family and that none of the others are giving me cause for worry. And I am. I love the grandchildren to distraction. But right now, I think I'd rather stay here with you."

"Another letter came from Henri," Baptiste said.

"He doesn't write as often as he did, but I guess he's very busy."

"Indeed he is. Another promotion, two more inventions patented, and what sounds like a hectic social life in New York. I think he's getting to be quite a man about town, one of the city's most eligible bachelors."

Leah absorbed that bit of information with interest. It meant just one thing if he'd been accepted into New York society: he was passing as white, the same as she'd done in Indiana. She knew Henri had been ambitious as far as his career went, but she had no idea he was also socially ambitious. He'd never hinted at being ashamed of his Negro

385

heritage, but his letter seemed to say it for him. That was why he'd wanted to leave France and had chosen to try his luck in a Northern state. Well, good luck to him if it was what he wanted. He might find it difficult to continue with the deception if he fell in love and wanted to marry. Further letters should prove interesting.

"And Robert is doing satisfactorily in school," Leah said, "so I should think about all of them and forget about Nicole."

"Not forget, Leah. Just not dwell on her so much. It's not loneliness tormenting you, it's guilt. And you haven't a damn thing to be guilty about. None of us does. She was as much loved as any of them. Whatever the problems, they are hers, not yours."

Denise had told her the same thing. "I'll try to remember that. And I'll consider visiting the children and spoiling the boys."

Leah thought about her four grandsons, all handsome boys, every one, from one-year-old Gilles to ten-year-old Armand. It would be nice to have a granddaughter, too, but little boys were just as much fun to spoil.

Although she was finally earning substantial amounts of money from the pictures she sold to tourists, Nicole was frustrated at not being able to spend all her time developing her style with more serious painting. Just when she felt pleased with something she was attempting, she had to stop and dash off several more of the garish Parisian scenes. She'd learned how to paint one scene, of a garden or a street or a building, from life, and then make a dozen or so copies.

Since Jules, she'd both modeled for and been mistress to a few other artists, but she never again left her own place to move into theirs. It was easier that way to keep her independence and make the break when she got tired of them or they began bringing new models and bedmates home. There was an intensity about her that demaded an all-or-nothing relationship with someone, even if that relationship lasted only a few weeks or months. On one point she was adamant: when she was an artist's model and mistress, she would not accept payment. She did it because she wanted to, and for that time, she'd think herself in love with him. The morality —or immorality—of it never disturbed her; as long as she took no money, and, in fact, paid her own way, she was not prostituting herself. She was an artist living by her own code of right and wrong.

Finally one night, after her friend who took her paintings

to the quay for her returned with no money and word that tourists were simply not buying anymore, she sat down to have a long conversation with herself.

For as long as she could remember she'd wanted to be an artist, to be recognized by the greats as one of them. When only thirteen, she'd been inspired by Van Gogh and the scene of Paris he'd painted for her. If he could capture the true feeling, the intensity and beauty of the city, she could strive to do no less with her own subjects. She wished she had the painting with her now. Always, whenever she'd been tempted to compromise her talent, she'd thought about it and forced herself to do her best, even with the junk that brought in the money. That was what had been wrong all along. She'd left her talisman at home. She'd refused to prostitute her body, but she had prostituted her natural gift. No more. If she couldn't have the painting hanging on her wall, she could compel it to be with her in her imagination. She would stop wasting her time on the postcard paintings and concentrate on something she wouldn't be ashamed of.

There was only one problem: how was she going to live? And buy the paints and canvases she needed?

The answer came sooner than she expected, and from a source she'd never thought to explore: the numerous art schools in Paris. Some were academies which accepted only students with some talent and whose training was as thorough as that required by Lisette's music conservatory. Others pandered to anyone with money who wanted to dabble in watercolors. The important thing was that they all needed models and they paid well.

Nicole had no difficulty working as many hours as she wanted. She had sat for enough artists to fall naturally into the standard poses and to remain motionless for nearly an hour at a time. However, the real reason she was hired immediately wherever she applied was that, with her long black hair, dusky skin, and almond-shaped eyes, she had a unique beauty that captivated everyone who saw her. In spite of her years in the art world of Paris, she had remained untouched by its more sordid aspects, and there was still a naive, ingenuous quality about her, far different from the prostitutes who were the usual models.

For Nicole, it was no different posing for a class than for a single artist, whether nude, dressed in her usual peasant skirt and blouse, or a costume provided by an instructor. But when, at one so-called school, it was suggested she would be posing with a nude male in lewd and explicitly sexual positions she stormed out in a fury. There would be no more assignments there, and they had paid better than any of the others, but she'd be damned if she'd be exploited to amuse the students, who obviously were more interested in watching the antics of the models than in getting anything sketched on paper.

Even with that job lost, she still had enough assignments to support herself. The rest of the time she gave herself over entirely to expanding her skills and working on new techniques. She often thought about the show she would have had if she'd stayed home. She'd still have a show someday, but merit, not friendship with the gallery owner, would bring it about.

At one of the better schools, Nicole was attracted to the work of a young student. In some ways he reminded her of herself years ago. He was unsure of his talent but determined to be an artist. Without telling the instructor, she often gave Étienne a few pointers. She would have been dismissed immediately if it became known she was talking to the students, let alone giving suggestions about how to paint.

"I don't think I'd better say any more," Nicole told Étienne one time, after the instructor had returned to the studio sooner than expected.

"But you've helped me so much," Étienne whispered. "Will you meet me after class?"

"At the café on the corner, if you'll buy me hot chocolate and rolls."

Étienne nodded, and Nicole returned to the bench where she'd been posing *á la* David's portrait of Madame Recamier.

"I don't feel I'm really learning anything," Étienne said later, after he'd ordered the chocolate and rolls. "Monsieur is a good teacher, I'm sure, but I feel he wants us all to paint alike, and exactly like he does."

"That's his one weakness. Leave the school, Étienne. You don't need a teacher; you need to paint. Hours and hours every day until you get the feel of what's right for you."

"But I can't. My parents will insist I go to the university unless I continue with these lessons, and Monsieur assures them I have a future as a painter."

"How old are you, Étienne?"

He blushed and then stammered, "Six—sixteen."

"Too young to leave home, so you'll have to do what your parents want for a few more years. Stay at the school. It can't hurt you. But you can paint what you want when you're not there."

"I—I could if you'd help me," he pleaded.

"Not during class. I can't afford to lose the assignments there."

"I meant in your studio. I know you're a painter, too, and maybe we could work together. I could afford to pay you for the time and the lessons."

Nicole thought a moment. The time she had to herself was very precious to her and not nearly as much as she wanted. But by his clothes and the carriage he arrived in, she knew Étienne was wealthy. Maybe she could give up some of her modeling and work with him.

"Can you pay me by the hour the same as I'm getting at the schools?"

"That and more," he said firmly. "After all, you'll be my teacher, not just a model."

"You want me to model, too?"

"Please. You're—you're very beautiful, and I think my best work is my sketches of you."

"We'll see." She took out a scrap of paper. "Here's my address. Come by tomorrow afternoon after your last class."

Nicole returned to her room and, while concentrating on her latest work, immediately forgot all about Étienne. She was quite surprised when he arrived promptly at four the next afternoon.

"Come in, Étienne. I'll put water on for tea. I'm not supposed to cook up here, but Madame Franconne doesn't say anything as long as she doesn't smell food. Fortunately, water had no odor. While we're waiting, you can set your sketch pad up on that easel over there."

Étienne had remained standing in the doorway, reluctant to enter the room. With her invitation, he finally came in and put his things on a table.

"This is very generous of you, Nicole."

"I'm not doing it out of the goodness of my heart. I'm doing it as much for the money as to help you."

"I've brought some oils, too," he said. "I thought I'd like to try painting one of the sketches I did of you."

"That will come later. You're going to find me as strict a teacher as Monsieur. You can start sketching that scene out the window."

For nearly an hour, Nicole worked on her painting while Étienne sketched. Occasionally, she looked at his work and made suggestions.

The routine continued for several days. Étienne came

389

directly from the school, and the two of them worked quietly side by side.

"You're making some real improvement," she said as she looked at his latest sketch.

"Thank you. Do you think I could try something in oils now?"

"I think so," she agreed. "The change from sketching would do you good."

"I'd like to do that one of you I started at the school day before yesterday."

For a brief moment Nicole wondered if it had been a mistake to continue posing for the class while she was also acting as Étienne's teacher.

"All right. Let's see what you can do with the human figure in oils."

"I'll need you to pose again."

Nicole hadn't counted on that. It had been all right posing for the class or for other artists, but this request made her feel uneasy. Nonsense, Étienne was an artist like the others and would look upon her as a study, nothing more. She slipped out of her clothes and settled on the bed in the same position she'd assumed on the bench at the school.

Étienne placed the sketch on the table beside him, brought out his oils and brushes, and arranged the canvas on the easel. He tried a few strokes and then threw his brush down.

"I can't do it." He buried his face in his hands and began to tremble all over.

"What in the world is wrong with you?" Nicole grabbed up her robe and jumped off the bed.

"I lied to you. I didn't come up here to learn to paint better. I thought you were like the others—and if I came up here and you modeled for me, you'd go to bed with me. I—I love you, and I can't stand looking at you unless—"

"Unless I get into bed with you?"

"Yes—yes." He was almost crying.

"I'm not like the others, Étienne."

"I know that now, and that's why I hate myself."

"Come here." Nicole walked toward him and held out her hands. "You're only sixteen, Étienne. Have you ever slept with a woman?"

"No. I thought it would be best to start with someone like —like—"

"A prostitute? And do you know what could happen if you did?"

"Yes, I know." He hung his head and scraped his foot

390

back and forth like a little boy. "I could become infected. But I didn't care; I wanted to know what it would be like with you."

"I'm flattered." She loosened her robe enough to reveal the length of her body and then put her arms around his neck. "Kiss me, Étienne." His was the kiss of a little boy, until she opened her mouth slightly and moved one of his hands under her robe.

"Oh, God," he whispered, "I can't tell you how much I love you."

"No, you don't. You only want to make love to me."

"Yes, yes, I do." He began clutching at her frantically and trying to remove his clothes at the same time.

"Take it more slowly, Étienne. Don't be in such a hurry to have it over with. Here, let me." She stepped back out of his arms and started unbuttoning his shirt. She knew now why she had sensed danger in having him come to her room. She was as attracted to him as he was to her, and she'd been aware all along it would lead to this. After all the men she'd known, it was his innocence that appealed to her. She was only twenty-one herself, but she was a woman and he was still a boy. It would be exciting to teach him how to make love as well as how to paint. She would be creating a lover in the same way she created a scene or a portrait on canvas. Each movement, each nuance would be sketched first in her mind and then transformed into reality through her touch.

An eager pupil, Étienne was more than willing to give himself into her hands. He'd waited a long time for this moment, and he could wait a little longer now that his dream of being with her was coming true.

"You have a very beautiful body," she said, moving her fingers across his flat stomach and down his thighs. "I couldn't have stood it if you were ugly."

"Please, Nicole, don't put me off any longer."

"No, it's time." She lay back on the pillow and closed her eyes. She could always lose herself completely in the feelings and sensations of making love, but she could never bear the sight of it. She thought her abhorrence of the sight of two bodies clinging and moving together went back to the time she'd been walking through the fields and passed a barn, where a couple was lying in a pile of hay near the door. She didn't know then what they were doing; she'd only known it was grotesque and obscene. She'd begun running as fast as she could, afraid she was going to be sick before she got home.

Not until Étienne was again lying beside her did she open her eyes. And then he looked as beautiful as he had before.

"Will you go out for dinner with me?" He turned on his side so he could look at Nicole. "I told my parents I might be late tonight."

"Why tonight? Did you think this would finally happen?"

"No." He grinned sheepishly. "I've told them that every day since I began coming here. They were always pleased when I was able to get home on time."

"And you want to come back here after dinner?" she asked.

"Please. I don't think I could stand it if I didn't."

"All right, but just for tonight."

"You mean we won't see each other again?"

"I don't know. I'm not sure this is good for either of us. You've accomplished what you wanted with me—you are a man now."

"Not just that, Nicole. I was sincere when I said I loved you."

"You're too young for me. I'm sorry if that hurts, but it's true. We could have a brief affair, but it wouldn't be any easier for you to say good-bye a month or three months from now than tonight. We'll eat and come back here and then—well, we'll see."

Nicole had meant it when she said it would be better for Étienne not to return to her room again, but she had forgotten one thing. Unwittingly, like Pygmalion with Galatea, she *had* created a lover, an almost perfect lover, and she found she wanted him as much as he wanted her.

The end of their affair came not when they tired of each other but when a certain army officer was accused, tried, found guilty of treason, and sent to Devil's Island. Like so many other artists and writers, Nicole became caught up in the Dreyfus affair. With them, she firmly believed that Captain Alfred Dreyfus had been condemned and found guilty not because of anything he had done but because of what he was: a Jew. In December of 1894 he was convicted of betraying French military secrets to Germany. Almost from that moment on, there were those who, convinced of his innocence and seeing a gross miscarriage of justice, demanded he be given a new trial. These Revisionists, as they were called, never let up in their attempts to bring one about. Although it could be proved that Dreyfus had been convicted on false testimony, each time new testimony was revealed by pro-Dreyfus groups to try to force a retrial, it was suppressed or thrown out by the army, which in turn was supported by the government, the Church, and most of the press.

Nicole joined enthusiastically with those who were marching and shouting against the injustice of this affair. Étienne, on the other hand, was the son of a government official, who had gained position through his wealth and who was a strong supporter of the status quo in the army. He had indoctrinated his son thoroughly in his beliefs. Nicole urged Étienne to march with her and to get his father to use his influence to bring about a new trial. When Étienne refused, Nicole told him in no uncertain terms to get out. She never wanted to see such a lily-livered pinhead again.

"Please, Nicole," he begged. "Politics has nothing to do with us. Don't send me away. You're the most beautiful, the most wonderful thing that's ever happened to me."

"Then you must go before we get tired of each other. You'll remember me with pleasure, and I'll like that."

"You're saying it's really over, aren't you? And not just because of the Dreyfus business."

"Yes," Nicole said. "I was going to tell you soon. I did what you wanted; I took you for a lover."

"And you made me a man, Nicole. I guess that's the greatest thing a woman can do for a boy like I was."

"A very handsome man, Étienne. Now you can go out into the world and capture the hearts of all the young women. But, you are still an innocent in the ways of the world—and a coward."

"Is that how you're going to remember me?" he asked.

"No, much more pleasurably." *As the lover I created, my first perfect work of art.* But to say this aloud would destroy his self-confidence, so all she said was, "Now kiss me good-bye."

"Just one more time?" He looked toward the bed.

"No, that would demean everything we had together."

It wasn't easy watching him walk down the stairs without looking back. Now she'd be alone again. He filled an enormous void in her life, but she could ease the longing by working twice as hard at her painting.

Leah bent down and picked up the basket. She had more than enough flowers to put in every room. She was particu-

larly pleased with her roses this year. They had never flowered so abundantly or with such magnificent blossoms.

Passing the studio on her way to the terrace, she thought
again she heard something inside. She wondered if the time
would ever come when her imagination stopped playing such
heart-rending tricks on her. Strange how a large, empty room
could have life and sounds of its own. She hurried toward the
terrace. A strong cup of coffee would clear away the ghosts.
And some brandy. Baptiste usually had a glass just before
lunch, and today she'd join him.

But there was another sound, and it wasn't her imagination.
Someone was definitely in the studio. She'd forbidden the
servants to go in there, but maybe one of them had gone
into Henri's workshop to sneak a smoke or a short nap,
causing sounds to echo through the studio. She opened the
door. The workshop was empty. She walked through it to the
studio.

"Good morning, Mama." Nicole turned from the easel.
She'd picked up a brush to work on an unfinished painting.
She spoke so casually, it might have been any morning in the
past. There might have been no three years in between.

"Nicole!" Leah wanted to weep and throw her arms around
her daughter, but she sensed that was the last thing Nicole
wanted and the one thing that would send her flying again.
"It's good to see you. Have you come home to stay for a
while?" Leah almost choked on her words and had to grasp
the doorjamb to stop her hands from shaking. "How is the
art going?"

"Just for a little while. Just to see Papa." She saw the pain
on Leah's face. "And you, of course. But to ask Papa's help
with something. The art is going well. I sell a lot of junk—
you've probably seen it on the quay. But I'm doing some
serious work as well."

"Will you—will you come and have lunch with us? Papa
is home from the office today."

"As soon as I do a little bit here. I was always sorry I
hadn't finished this painting. It was one of my favorites."

Now Leah did walk over and gather Nicole into her arms.
"Oh, Nicole, it is good to have you here."

Moved by her mother's welcome, Nicole put her arms
around Leah and rested her head on her mother's shoulder.
"It's good to be here, Mama."

"There's so much to talk about. We want to know everything you've been doing."

"Not much to tell, Mama. It can wait until lunch with

394

Papa. But you can tell me now about the rest of the family." After carefully removing brushes and tubes of paint from a bench, she pulled Leah down beside her.

In a few minutes, Leah covered the years, from the time Jean and others began searching for her, to the present, with the news of Denise, pregnant with her third child.

"I miss you all, Mama, but—"

"Then don't lose touch so completely again, because we miss you, too."

"I'll see, Mama." Even as she said it, Leah could see her withdrawing inside herself. Then Nicole stood and walked over to the easel.

Forewarned by Leah, Baptiste stifled his desire to give Nicole a good tongue-lashing for all the worry she'd caused them.

"Well, it's good to see you, Nicole," he said as he took his place at the table.

"Thank you, Papa. It's good to be sitting here again."

"And to know you're alive." He felt he had to say something. She couldn't just walk back into the house as if nothing had happened and not be made aware of how much they, and particularly Leah, had suffered. "We were worried about you, you know."

"There was no reason to. I'm perfectly capable of taking care of myself."

"I'm relieved to know you think so," Baptiste said. "It would have been more considerate of you to share that belief with us."

Leah saw she must change the subject before the conversation became unpleasant. "You say you sold paintings on the quay. I often looked for some of yours but never saw any."

"I signed them *Michele*. I didn't want anyone to see my own name on those horrid things. They're just junk, but they earned me enough to give me time to paint what I want."

"I saw one with the signature," Leah said, "and I thought I recognized your hand. It was really a very good study of a mother and a little girl. Not junk as you say."

"That must have been the one of my neighbor and her daughter. It was pretty good. I finally sold it."

"I started to buy it," Leah sighed. "I wish now I had."

"When I finish enough paintings that I think are really good, I'll have my own show. You can buy something then." She wished they'd let her concentrate on eating instead of making her talk. She'd forgotten how good Blanchette's vegetable soup tasted. "You really feel you're doing that well?" Baptiste asked.

"Someday I'll be great, Papa."

"You could still have the show we planned before you left," Leah suggested. "There are enough paintings in the studio, and if you have others—"

"No! I'll know when the right time comes, and I'll do it on my own." Then her voice softened. "But thank you, anyway."

"Mama said you wanted to talk to me about something," Baptiste said.

"Yes, about Captain Dreyfus. It's criminal the way he was tried illegally—on false evidence—and sent to that awful Devil's Island. Our voices—those who believe him innocent —are so weak compared to the army and the government and most of the press. You have influence in Paris. Can't you use it to see he gets a new trial?"

"I don't have that kind of influence, Nicole." He was startled by her request. "I'm part owner of a successful business, but that's all. I'm not in politics, and I have no connection with the army."

"But you know important people, Papa. You could contact them, or at least write to them. Your word would mean something."

"I'll see." Baptiste had read all about the trial and its aftermath, but he had no wish to become involved.

"Better yet, come to Paris with me and meet with the people who are working to free Dreyfus. Let it be known which side you're on. You know what it is to suffer for a cause, and you're a hero to more people than you realize. You could rally so many to our side. If just one substantial businessman like you, and maybe Monsieur Duchalais at the bank, would speak out, others might follow."

While the two were talking, all Leah could do was look at Nicole and mourn over how thin and pale she was, how faded and torn her clothes were. What kind of life had this child been living to put those dark circles under her eyes, that cynical tone in her voice beneath her apparent enthusiasm? If only they could persuade her to stay home for a few weeks so that Blanchette's cooking could fatten her up.

"I'm not that sure Dreyfus is innocent," Baptiste said. "He was given a trial; evidence was introduced."

"False evidence, Papa," Nicole insisted. "He is innocent."

"I don't believe the army would do that."

396

"Then you're blind to what's going on." Nicole could barely control herself.

"Please, Nicole," Leah said quietly. "Don't lose your temper. Maybe if we knew more about it."

"That's why I want Papa to come back to Paris with me, right now."

"Stay here a few days," he said, "and let me think about it. Even a few more weeks isn't going to make that much difference."

"No, not to you sitting here in this clean house and eating this kind of food every day. But every day that passes on that island for Captain Dreyfus could mean his death." She jumped up and threw her napkin down. "Forget about coming back with me then. But I'm going, and you don't need to think about seeing me again."

"Sit down, Nicole," Leah said in the voice she had used when the children were small. "Papa has said he would think about it. Go back to Paris today if you wish, but why not stay at the apartment? Then we'd know you were safe, and we could see you occasionally."

"Never!" Nicole exclaimed. "I prefer to lay my head wherever I can find a place among people who really understand me. You never have and you never will."

"We love you," Leah said. "Isn't that enough?"

"I love you both, too. I honestly do, but—no, it's not enough. I can't find here what I need. It's in my one room overlooking the roofs of the city. And it's among my friends who think and believe as I do. I don't hate you now, but I would if I stayed."

She reached toward the plate of rolls and put one in each pocket. Leah watched her walk out of the room but had no voice to call after her.

Wordlessly Leah got up and walked into the library. Baptiste followed soon after.

"We should have promised to do something—anything—to keep her with us," she said. "She came to us because she needed us. As independent as she is, do you know what it must have cost her to admit she needed us? And we sent her away again."

"I don't think so, and you mustn't either. Maybe we could have helped her in some way this time. But what about the next time? She's not going to change her way of life or be close to us again. That is something we are going to have to accept."

"I'll try, but I think she was reaching out her hand, and

397

we slapped it instead of grasping it. I think I'll go for a walk, but I won't be gone long."

After Leah left, Baptiste cursed the fact that he, too, couldn't get up and walk. His sorrow over the loss of Nicole was as great as Leah's. He wheeled himself miserably out onto the terrace and then back to his office.

Leah walked along the river a short distance and then returned to the studio. It hardly seemed possible that Nicole had really been there a few hours ago. As she looked around, she realized something was missing. One of the easels was empty. Then she remembered. It was the painting by that crazy man, Van Gogh. If Nicole had taken that instead of one of her own, it must have a very special meaning for her.

Baptiste sat at his desk for a long time, all the while thinking about writing to Simone. He desperately needed to see her. He needed her youth, to hear her laughter and to have her make him laugh. He picked up his pen and then put it back down. If he saw her now, it wouldn't stop with laughter. He wouldn't be able to leave her as he had during the picnic outside Paris.

Hearing Leah come in and go to her sewing room, he thought how much he loved her. How could he love her as deeply and devotedly as he did and still want Simone? He'd heard it said that men were naturally polygamous, but he wondered if that were a simplistic rationale for a deeper, much more complex aspect of the male psyche. Perhaps the male character was naturally ambivalent: demanding and craving a stable, constant, immutable relationship with one woman, while at the same time having an urgent need for variety and the thrill of forbidden pleasures, which carried with them the danger of being found out. Perhaps, subconsciously, he wanted to write the note to Simone so that Leah would find it. Or maybe he was simply bored, and the unfortunate visit from Nicole had filled the house with gloom as well.

He wheeled into Leah's sewing room. What he needed was a large dose of her tender, loving care. "Would you like to go for a drive?" he asked her. "Have dinner by candlelight at some country inn and then come back here and go to bed early?"

"I don't think so. I don't feel in the mood for any of those things."

"Just thought you might like to get away from the house." She didn't answer, and he went back to his office.

Nicole's visit seemed to create an impenetrable wall between them that Baptiste could neither breach with loving overtures nor knock down with attempts at firm logic.

Baptiste folded the note he'd finally written and put it into an envelope. He didn't read it over. If he did, he might lose the courage to mail it. He wanted to mail it. After all, it was Leah who had turned away from him. As was his style, the note was short and to the point: "Please come to Paris on Thursday. I need to see you."

Damn! he thought. *I should have said "I need you."* It sounded too impersonal, and he did need her. Without Leah's love, he was lonely and desperate. Nicole was *his* daughter, too, and if at times he failed to understand her, he loved her as much as he did the other children, as much as Leah did. It was Leah's love and understanding he needed right now, but there seemed no way to reach her.

He held the envelope in his hand, the flap still unsealed, and removed the note. He'd write it over. If he expected Simone to meet him in Paris after all the time that had passed since the picnic fiasco, he had to write a more personal, more loving note.

In a state of euphoric anticipation, Baptiste walked down the carpeted hall to the hotel suite. His knock was answered by a stunned Simone. Baptiste could tell she had hastily tied the sash of her silk robe at the waist. Her brown hair fell long and full over her shoulders.

"You're early, Baptiste. I haven't finished dressing yet."

"I know. That's why I came when I did." Her robe had parted slightly; through the thinner silk of an undergarment, he watched the rise and fall of her soft, full breasts. *"May I come in?"*

"Yes, of course." She let him pass and then shut the door. *"Some wine?"* She pointed to a table where an unopened bottle and two glasses had been set on a silver tray.

"Not yet. I want to look at you. I could hardly believe it when you said you'd come here." He remained standing, braced by a huge sideboard.

Simone walked over and caressed the sides of his face with her palms. "I told you once, Baptiste, I love you and I would do everything a woman knows to do to become your mistress. After the picnic, I thought I'd never see you again. Your note said you needed me, so I'm here. But never again, unless—"

In answer, Baptiste took her in his arms. He ran his hand

through her hair, all the while kissing her lips, her throat, and then her lips again. "I do need you. I need you more than I can say."

Simone pressed herself hungrily against him. She put her arms around his waist to support him and free his hand to caress her.

"Oh God, Baptiste, do you know what it's like to want you every day we're apart, to dream about a moment like this? And to know now that you want more of me than an amusing companion for a few brief hours."

"I wouldn't be here now if I didn't," he whispered. With both hands on the small of her back, he pressed her more tightly against him, and he heard her catch her breath.

"I want all of you, right now," she said hoarsely. "I can't wait any longer."

"I wish I could carry you into the bedroom, but—"

"It's all right."

They walked together into the darkened room. The moment Baptiste lay down, Simone was in his arms, and, as he'd known he would since the day they'd said good-bye in Aix-les-Bains, he was feeling her warm, soft flesh open up to let him enter.

Baptiste wiped the sweat from his forehead. It would be so easy, but it must not happen that way. In a fury made more potent by frustration, he tore up the note and then the envelope. Placing the scraps in a large ashtray, he reached for a match. He didn't love Simone. He needed her, yes, but he didn't love her. Reverie and erotic fantasies were one thing; turning that dream into reality was something else. He couldn't use her that way to alleviate his despair over Leah's coldness. Mere physical release with Simone was not the answer. Finding a way to reach Leah was.

It did not ease Baptiste's misery to realize that by indulging in lustful longings he was no less guilty of adultery than if he lay every night with Simone. His conscience, however, would not let him convince himself that he might as well carry out in deed what he had so often enjoyed in memory and wishful thinking.

In all honesty, he had to admit it was not Simone who haunted his sleepless nights and restless days. Rather, it was the spectre of a young man, strong of limb and whole of body, who sat a horse with ease, danced with all the belles of New Orleans, and got under the skirts of more than a few on carriage seats, garden benches, and in his apartment. It was also the ghost of the man who had three times rescued a beautiful octoroon and made her his mistress.

He slammed his fist on the arm of the chair. Damn! He needed Leah.

Chapter Thirty-four

THE EMOTIONAL ESTRANGEMENT between Leah and Baptiste, and the gloomy atmosphere pervading the house, might have continued for months instead of a few weeks, if word hadn't come that Denise had finally had the daughter she longed for. This time all went easily, but she would love to have Mama and Papa come for a visit to see their beautiful new granddaughter.

"Life does go on, doesn't it, Baptiste?" Leah was half crying, half laughing as she read the wire from Denise and Edouard.

"Yes, it does, Grandmama, so let's be off."

"Not until I tell you how sorry I am for being so moody these past weeks."

"No sorrier than I am for not being able to dispel that mood." *And for indulging in daydreams about Simone,* he thought. He wheeled over to where she stood. "I've missed you. I haven't had my back scratched in a long time."

"And you haven't brushed my hair." She walked over to her dressing table. Slowly, she took the pins from her hair and let it fall around her shoulders. Then she picked up the brush and handed it to him.

"Why, Madame Fontaine, you shock me. In the middle of the afternoon?"

"Why not? There's no one around, and it's a beautiful afternoon, with the warm breezes coming through the window. Can't you smell the roses?"

"I'd rather smell that scent you put behind your ears and in other tantalizing places."

In Baptiste's arms, Leah quickly dismissed all the worries that plagued her and thought only of how much she loved

401

him. He was husband and lover and friend, and she was never quite certain which was the most important to her.

During the week they stayed with Denise, Leah spent hours doing what she enjoyed most—taking care of the baby Éliane, who was indeed a beautiful little girl, with Denise's curly dark hair and tremendous brown eyes—while Baptiste went with Edouard to the winery and the fields, all the while discusssing new ways to improve the crops and the wines they produced. When Leah and Baptiste returned home, they brought the two boys, young Edouard and Gilles, with them for a two-week visit at the château. Leah delighted in having them all to herself, but she'd forgotten what it was like to care for a three-year-old, who demanded constant attention, and a one-year-old, who in the joy of learning to walk was toddling all over the house and pulling onto the floor everything he could reach. After Edouard came to take them home, she collapsed onto the chaise longue in the sunroom.

"What's the matter, Grandmama?" Baptiste asked. "Tired?"

"I am worn to a frazzle. I think I could sleep for a week, but don't you dare laugh at me. I loved every minute of it."

"Read that first part again," Baptiste said.

Leah re-read the first sentence of Henri's letter. During the seven years since he'd left home, he'd written quite regularly at first; then the correspondence had dwindled to cards at Christmas and an occasional note for a birthday. To get a real letter from him was almost as much of a shock as the news it contained.

" 'Dear Mother and Father.' How very formal." Leah frowned.

"How very American," Baptiste said. "Go on."

" 'I am moving to Detroit, Michigan, to take a position with a small firm that manufactures precision component parts for several larger industrial companies. Several of my patents have been bought by them, and I am to be a vice-president. Also, I am being married.' "

"How like Henri." Baptiste shrugged. "Business before pleasure."

"Well, he always was the practical one. All that about his work and nothing about her. Except that she comes from Boston. Do get that map you keep in your office, Baptiste. I thought Detroit was a small town in the wilderness."

"Not for a long time, chérie. Not with the industrial expansion and the new interest in the manufacturing of motor cars."

"Abominable things! I'll take a nice, pretty, clean carriage any time over all that smoke and dust."

"You're old-fashioned, Leah. It's the twentieth century now and a whole new way of life."

Baptiste spoke casually, not knowing the drastic changes that would be taking place before the year was out, changes that would affect every member of his family.

"Strange," Leah said, "that he didn't even comment on the fact that Robert went to St. Cyr because he wanted to follow after his favorite brother."

"Henri is many things," Baptiste said, "but sentimental is not one of them."

"No, I'm surprised he was able to work up enough emotion to fall in love. I thought he was married to his machines and inventions."

"Never underestimate the reserved, studious type, chérie. He might be a terror in bed."

"Baptiste! You can talk like that about your own son?"

"Well, being the son of my loins, I should hope he'd be as good as I am."

"You have no modesty and no shame."

"And aren't you glad of it. Are you blushing, Leah?"

"No, it's hot in here by the fire." Here she was a grandmother five times over, and Baptiste's grin could still set her heart pounding and her thoughts dwelling on the night before. If Henri were as good a lover as his father still was, he'd make his wife very happy.

Although Henri waited until he was thirty to marry, his courtship of Louise Carlyle was somewhat more romantic than his letter implied. He'd been attracted to many women since coming to the States, but he'd never felt he was in the position to marry and have the kind of home he'd been determined to have from the beginning. There would be no small cottage for two and only enough money to pay for necessities. Life in the château had convinced him he wanted to be well established and have a generous bank account before he settled down. He had finally reached that point.

When he met the tall, stately, serene Louise Carlye at a Thanksgiving debutante ball in New York—to which she had been invited as the older, still unmarried sister of an honoree—he knew immediately she was the woman he wanted as his wife. Not only was she wealthy and possessed

403

of a classic beauty but she was also extremely poised and self-assured. Within five minutes of opening his mouth to talk to her, Henri found out that she was intelligent and was not afraid to let a man know it. She was exactly the kind of woman he needed beside him as he rose to the top. Henri had never doubted for a minute that he'd eventually take his place among the industrial giants of the nation. What surprised him the most was that after dancing with Louise, he realized he was in love with her.

Two years older than Henri, Louise Carlyle had shocked everyone by choosing to remain unmarried until she met an ambitious man she could wholeheartedly admire. It mattered little to her whether she loved him as long as she could guide him along and stand beside him throughout his career. She recognized immediately that Henri was such a man. In the past, many would-be suitors had been frightened off by her obvious intelligence and her refusal to defer to a man when she knew he was wrong about something. She could not play the flirtatious coquette. She asked Henri knowledgeable questions about his business and his inventions. Unlike most other young ladies of her generation, her intent was to learn what he was doing, not to bolster his ego by urging him to talk about himself.

"How do you know so much about industry, particularly automobile manufacturing?" he asked, after leading her back to a chair and bringing her a glass of punch. He supposed he should go and ask his hostess for a dance, but Louise Carlyle fascinated him, and he wanted to get to know her better.

"I listen and I read. And," she allowed the hint of a smile to cross her face, "I have an avid curiosity."

Henri had a daring thought. If he asked the question he had in mind, she might be infuriated and never speak to him again. On the other hand, it might be just the one nobody else had ever asked her, and she would be intrigued by it. Her response might answer another question as well.

"Miss Carlyle, do you ever wish you were a man so you could take part in the industrial explosion we're experiencing now?"

"No." Just the one word. Henri looked at her closely to see if the question had insulted her, but her expression remained as inscrutable as ever. She might not have been pleased with the question, but she hadn't been insulted enough to turn away or get up and leave him.

"No?" he asked. "I'd have thought being denied a part in

the business world would make you eager to take it on as a challenge."

"There are other challenges just as exciting but more appropriate for me as a woman. And I happen to like being a woman."

"May I be so bold as to ask what those challenges are?" The more she talked, the more Henri was determined to marry her no matter what obstacles of money, status, or her lack of affection for him had to be overcome.

"To be the wife of a man who sees the opportunities in that explosion you mentioned and has the strength and the ambition to grasp them." She looked directly into Henri's eyes, and he wondered if she were offering him another kind of opportunity, one implied but not uttered.

"I admire you very much, Miss Carlyle. I have to fulfill the obligations on my dance card, but may I call on you tomorrow?"

"I should be disappointed if you did not." Henri was somewhat taken aback at the same time that he was pleased. Most young women would have simpered and said they would be honored to receive him. "My home is in Boston," she said, "but don't be alarmed. I don't expect you to go all the way up there. I'm staying with friends." She took a small gold pencil from her beaded purse and wrote an address on the back of his dance card. "Shall I expect you at three?"

"I look forward to it." Henri bowed and went to seek out his next partner, all the time wishing he'd kept his dance card blank so he could spend the rest of the evening with Louise.

Henri called promptly at three and handed Louise a small bouquet.

"Flowers, how nice. I haven't received any in a long time." There was nothing demure or dishonest about Louise, and he liked that. "You're right on time, too, and I admire promptness in a man. There's absolutely no excuse for people being late for appointments. I never am, and I expect others to be just as considerate."

"Would you like to go for a drive?" Not yet in a position to own a carriage—every cent he earned over and above his modest living expenses went into a bank account—he'd hired one for the occasion.

"Yes, I'd like that. I need some fresh air. My friends keep this house so dreadfully hot. Such a waste when all one needs to do is put on a flannel petticoat or a shawl."

Henri's brows shot up. No woman of his acquaitance would utter the word petticoat in mixed company, and few would even consider enduring a little discomfort in order to be economical with fuel. Everything Louise said merely strengthened his resolve to marry her.

During the drive, Louise asked more about his work and expressed an obvious admiration for the number of inventions he'd patented. Henri started to mention the possibility of going to Detroit and then thought better of it. He would wait until the move was definite.

"It's gotten colder," Louise said as they approached the house. "Won't you come in for tea, or a drink if you'd prefer."

"Tea would be fine. I drink wine but seldom anything stronger."

After the maid had set the tea things on the small table between them, Louise asked, "Where are you from, Henri? I detect the trace of an accent." She had pronounced his name as he'd been pronouncing it since coming to the States —as if it were spelled "Henry."

"Paris. That is, a country place outside Paris."

"How long have you been over here? You really have very little accent, and it doesn't seem all that French. I had a French governess, and she had much more of one."

"Only a few years, but I've worked very hard to eliminate the accent. Actually, there may be a trace of English in it. We had an English tutor, and we spoke the language during the dinner hour. My parents insisted we should know it well."

"They, too, are French, I assume. Is your father in business?"

This was the moment Henri had been dreading. Until now no one had probed any further into his origins than to find that he had come from France. He saw no need to mention New Orleans, but could he lie about his mother and carry out that lie for the rest of his life? He knew she had passed as white when she went to Indiana as the wife of James Andrews. The only danger he could see, if he did marry Louise Carlyle, would be if she insisted on going to France and meeting his family. Somehow, in some way, the truth would be bound to come out. He would simply have to make certain that they never went abroad.

"Yes," he said, "they are both French. My father owns an import-export firm. Unfortunately, I'm estranged from my family and don't ever plan to see them again. My father was extremely disappointed when I chose to come over here rather than go into the business with him. It was a 'you do it or else' confrontation, and when I left there were very harsh feelings on both sides."

"I'm sorry, but I agree it's important for one to follow one's own inclinations. Perhaps someday the situation will ease between you."

"I doubt it. I've written a number of times but have never received an answer." It was amazing how easily the lies came after the first one was spoken.

"I can sympathize with you. I've lived under a somewhat similar cloud of disapproval since I refused to marry immediately after making my debut. Fortunately—or unfortunately—I continue to live at home. To have my own place is, of course, untenable, although I can't think of anything that would give me more pleasure."

Henri knew there were some women who considered the idea of being married, of having a physical relationship with a man, totally abhorrent, and for a moment he feared Louise was one of them. Then he remembered her remark about wanting to marry a man with ambition. He would see her again, even if it meant trips to Boston; then, if he continued to feel as he did now, he would ask her to marry him.

Louise returned to Boston quite certain she'd met the only man she could ever consider marrying. It did not occur to her to wonder whether she were in love with him. That was an unimportant consideration. As long as she admired and respected him, she could live with him and be a dutiful wife. So many of her friends had been foolish enough to fall in love with men they did not respect, who were profligate wastrels living off the money their fathers had earned. Now those women were miserably unhappy. Henri was not wealthy yet, but with his drive and ambition, he would be someday. In the meantime, a small inheritance from her grandmother would allow them to live in moderate luxury. Henri had said he would get up to Boston as soon as he could, and she took this as a good omen.

When Henri received an invitation to another debutante cotillion in New York during the Christmas holidays, he was certain Louise had suggested he be invited in the hopes that he would ask to escort her. He smiled to himself. She was still enough inhibited by the proprieties not to invite him herself. He immediately answered the invitation and sent a note to her in the same mail.

It would not do, before they were engaged, for him to fill her dance card with his name; but he did make certain they had the first, the supper, and the last dance. When the evening was over, he knew it would be only a matter of time before he asked her to marry him. When he brought her back after the ball, he wanted to linger in the hall of her friends' home, but she gave no indication that she wanted him to stay. All he could do was hold her hand a little longer than necessary when he bid her goodnight and thanked her for a most enjoyable evening.

"Will you be in New York over New Year's?" he asked. "I was hoping we could welcome in the new year and the new century together."

"No, but it's really not that difficult to get to Boston."

She was right. He should visit her home and meet her family. It would mean the extra expense of the train and renting a hotel room, probably very expensive during the holidays. He would have to ask her to reserve a room at one of the better ones, too, in order to make the right impression.

Henri waited so long to reply, Louise was afraid she'd been too forward. This was only their second date, one she'd arranged.

"I'd be delighted to come up there," Henri said at last.

Before he could ask where she would like to go for dinner and dancing, she suggested, "Our boating club is having a New Years's Eve party. Would you like to attend that?"

Henri hoped she hadn't heard his sigh of relief. He'd been mentally adding up the cost of dinner and an evening at an expensive restaurant.

"That sounds very agreeable. I hope it won't be too much trouble if I ask you to reserve a room for me at whichever hotel you recommend."

"Oh, no," Louise said, "you'll be staying with us. We have plenty of room, and Mother would be offended if you didn't. We'll all be going together to the party, so it would be foolish of you to stay somewhere else."

Henri hadn't quite visualized an evening with the senior Carlyles, but there was no way he could suggest something else now.

"It sounds like a very pleasant evening. I'm looking forward to it."

"There's a train that arrives at five. You'll be in plenty of time to dress before we leave for dinner at the club. I—I think I'd better say goodnight now. Someone may talk if you remain in the hall much longer."

Henri reached for her hand again and raised her fingers to his lips. "Until I see you in Boston."

Every time Henri tried to visualize what New Year's Eve was going to be like, he saw the same thing: he and Louise sitting with her parents, and maybe others, around a big table at the club. The conversation would all be of sailing or business among the men. The women would either be listening quietly or suggesting that the men sit together on one side so the ladies could sit on the other and talk about their own interests. He would be with Louise only when they were dancing, and that wouldn't be every dance. He'd have to ask Mrs. Carlyle, too, and any other women in their party.

Then came the letter from Detroit he'd been waiting for, and it gave him the courage to make some changes in the plans for the night in Boston. First he decided to splurge on new evening clothes. Baptiste had sent him black pearl studs and gold monogrammed cufflinks for Christmas. The first impression he made on the Carlyles would be important for his plans, and he must appear at his very best.

Henri looked at himself in the long mirror at the tailor's shop. He was not displeased with what he saw. Not quite as tall as his father, he still stood nearly six feet and had a slim but athletic physique, which he'd developed during his fencing days at St. Cyr and maintained since then by walking everywhere he went. His black hair was as wavy as his father's and his mustache was smooth and neatly trimmed. His eyes were as dark as his mother's, with just a hint of the almond shape inherited from his Polynesian great-grandmother. Then he looked at his skin. It was darker than Baptiste's but not quite as dark as Leah's; he was actually lighter than many Frenchmen he'd known in Paris. He could pass even among the most proper Bostonians. He'd never known which disturbed him the more: the fact that he carried Negro blood, or the knowledge, arrived at when he was still quite young, that he was a love child, conceived before his parents were married in Martinique. Both of the thoughts made him feel unclean, and only gradually, since he'd come to the States, had he begun to consider himself cleansed of the twin taints of miscegenation and adulterous lust.

Having been spared the costs of renting a hotel room and paying for both dinner and a New Year's morning breakfast at an expensive restaurant, Henri decided on another luxury that would allow him some time alone with Louise. He wired Boston to have a hired carriage waiting for him at the station. He was not going to share Louise with her family the entire evening.

Henri enjoyed the party at the boating club more than he thought possible, and his practical mind realized he was making contacts with men who could be important to him in the future. They all toasted the new century—the new mechanical and scientific age—with champagne.

"All you younger men will be millionaires before the end of the decade," one of the older Bostonians said, speaking in the deep all-knowing voice of a prophet. "Combine business acumen with mechanical inventiveness and you can't lose."

He's speaking right to me, Henri thought. He'd not only received the letter from Detroit, but had found in the same mail the patent on his latest device. He had hundreds more ideas incubating in his brain. He'd been shrewd enough to know which ones to patent before someone else came up with a similar idea.

In Detroit, he'd have more time to work and better tools than he'd had in the New Jersey shop. Better yet, he'd be able to build a workshop in the house he planned to buy, and he could devote all his spare time to his inventions. Up until now, he'd been satisfied with his single room in a boarding house and the use of the owner's shop facilities. He hadn't been wrong, though, in remaining in the room even after he could afford a better place. It meant he now had a sizable bank account, one even his father would admire.

At the table, with himself and Louise, sat her parents and two other, older couples. She was wearing a delicate fragrance that was very disturbing, and it was all Henri could do to keep from reaching over and taking her hand. Thank heavens he'd thought about hiring the carriage. At least there he could sit closer to her than here at the table. He had something very special he wanted to ask her.

Then something happened that very nearly spoiled the entire evening.

"Do I understand that you come from France?" asked one of the older men.

"Yes, sir, from Paris. My father is head of a large export-import firm there." Later he wished he'd had sense enough not to mention his father, but he'd been trying to impress them. It was very nearly his undoing.

"Export firm, hm." The man put two fingers under his chin and nodded. Henri had already learned the man was president of a large chain of mercantile establishments. "I started out in my father's small general store," the man continued, and Henri sat back, prepared to listen to the man's self-aggrandizing tale of how he worked hard and rose to be head of one of the country's largest business firms. Instead, he found himself startled into stiffening his back to keep from revealing his discomfiture.

"I thought the name Fontaine sounded familiar," the man said. "There was a Bonvivier import house in New Orleans we bought from and later the name Fontaine was added to it. Many of our better stores still purchase goods from them. I don't suppose they are any relation to you?"

"They could be distant relatives." Henri was amazed at how calmly he was able to speak. "So many people fled France and settled in New Orleans during the various revolutions. I believe I might have heard my father speak of them, but they are certainly not close relations. Fontaine is quite a common name."

"Yes, I suppose so. Seems like an interesting coincidence, though, both being in the import-export business, I mean. I suppose it's a natural choice in a port like New Orleans." Henri began to relax, then sat up quickly again. "Has your father's business been in existence long?"

"The firm was established by my great-grandfather." At least that much was not a lie. He just hadn't said it was founded by his Bonvivier great-grandfather, not the Fontaine who owned the plantation on the Mississippi.

"And you chose not to go into it?" Mr. Carlyle asked.

"No, sir, I've always had an aptitude for and an interest in things mechanical. That's why I came over here. So much more of an opportunity for advancement."

Mr. Carlyle nodded sagely.

"And Mr. Fontaine has had another of his inventions patented," Louise said. "We should all be hearing great things from him in the future."

And you'll be the first to hear and to share in my success if things go as I hope, Henri thought, patting the letter in his pocket.

"If you'll excuse us," Mrs. Carlyle was saying, "I think we'll go home. We old fogies need our sleep. But you stay for a while. It was very thoughtful of you, Henry, to bring

411

your own carriage. I know Louise is enjoying herself too much to want to leave now." Hearing Mrs. Carlyle speak his name, Henri had a new thought. It was time to begin spelling his name, as well as pronouncing it, the American way.

"It's been a very pleasant evening, Mrs. Carlyle. Thank you for including me in your plans."

"I'll see you in the morning, Henry," Mr. Carlyle said. "I want to talk to you some more about that stock issue."

Henri began to think it would be a wise idea to invest a portion of the money he had in the bank. Some of Mr. Carlyle's suggestions looked very tempting, and the man himself had made his millions in the stock market. It would do no harm to listen to him.

"It's been such a pleasant evening, I really hate to see it end," Louise said once they'd gotten into the carriage. They'd stayed until the final waltz.

"It's snowing a little, but if you're not too cold, we could go for a short drive."

"I'd like that." The falling snow blurred the lights of Boston, and there was an ethereal quality about the night. Henri tucked the fur rug across Louise's lap and then took his place beside her.

"There's something I want to show you," he said a little later as he pulled up under a street lamp.

"Another patent?" Louise tried to sound enthusiastic. The evening had gone well. She knew her family was impressed with Henri, and they'd danced almost every dance together. Nor was she unaware that Henri had held her closer than necessary during some of the waltzes. She knew he had respected her opinions on the various subjects they discussed, but she also knew he would have to feel some physical attraction for her if he were to think about marrying her. So far she'd felt none of the rapid beating of the pulse or the fluttering in the stomach she'd heard her sisters talk about. But to Louise that was unimportant. Henri was going to be a success, and his good looks were merely an added point in his favor.

"No," he answered, "a letter." He described the correspondence he'd been having with the manufacturing firm in Detroit. "They want me to come out there as vice-president in charge of the tooling division. Most important of all, they want me to keep on with my inventions. The offer is a generous one. The company will share fifty-fifty with me on anything I patent, whether for use by them or by other companies. In addition, I'll have my salary as vice-president."

Louise's heart sank. Detroit was nearly halfway across the continent. She'd probably never see him again. "How—how soon do they want you to be there?"

"Within the month. I've already given my notice here. I gave it before I came to Boston."

Louise wanted to cry. If only it were two or three months, there might be a chance Henri would come to love her, or at least come back for frequent visits after he went to Detroit.

"I'll miss you," she said. "Even in this short time I've come to admire you very much." Louise was grateful the inside of the carriage was dark. She was blushing at having dared to speak so boldly.

"Will you really?" Henri folded the letter and replaced it in his pocket. "Enough—enough to say you'll marry me and come out to Detroit after I've gotten established?"

"Oh, yes! I think I'd have died if you hadn't asked me."

"I love you, Louise. I may not be able to give you all you're used to right away, but I promise you won't be sorry you married me."

"I know I won't, and I'll be right beside you all the way up." She could see herself now, urging him on with his work and being hostess at the dinners and other functions required of a young executive.

"Would six months be time enough?" he asked. "I know from my sister's wedding all the planning and dressmaking that goes on."

"I don't want to wait six months, Henri. I want to go with you. I don't need a big wedding to be married, and I've been through all that with my sisters, too." Louise feared that, even though they'd be engaged, he'd find someone else out there and forget all about her.

Henri had not been surprised at her immediate acceptance of his proposal. She was too honest to pretend it was so sudden and she'd have to think about it. However, her suggestion that she go to Detroit right away was more than he'd dared hope for. He hadn't been looking forward to the separation. "We'll have to live in a rooming house until we can find our own place. Will you mind that?"

"Not if I'm with you. And I can do the looking while you're at work. And do the furnishing, too." Their home must be absolutely perfect from the beginning. She had the feeling Henri might object to her using some of her own money. He had a pride about him that came not from family background or wealth but seemed to be of his own

413

making, as if to hide a failing she had yet to discover. Whatever, it must be something that disturbed him more than it ever would her. She'd ask her father to say the money was his wedding present to them rather than telling Henri she'd inherited it from her grandmother's trust. In that way Henri could have no objection to her using it for their home.

Though small by some standards, the wedding, which took place in the family's drawing room, still included more than a hundred guests and had the Episcopal bishop of Boston officiating. Louise had never asked Henri about his religion, and he decided that, since he hadn't been a practicing Roman Catholic since coming to the States, he would join the Episcopal church with her in Detroit. They'd find out which was the most prominent, most prestigious congregation in the city and become members of it. The right associations on Sunday could be as important as any he made in the business world.

Louise had never looked forward with either dread or anticipation to her wedding night and the nights that would follow. Physical intimacy was merely a part of being married; and in that, as in all aspects of marriage, she would be a dutiful and loving wife. She was pleased to find Henri a gentle and not overly demanding lover. Although she did not find herself aroused by his lovemaking, she was able to feign an ardor that seemed to satisfy him. While she did not particularly look forward to the two-nights-a-week routine he established, she did not shrink from it. As with everything else in his life, Henri was methodical in his approach to lovemaking, and she knew exactly what to expect from the time he reached for her every Tuesday and every Saturday night, until he finally rolled over on his back and went to sleep. If Louise felt that something was missing, she did not waste time deploring it. There was too much else to occupy her time and mind. Tuesday was the one night Henri allowed himself to relax and spend the evening with her rather than in his workroom, and on Saturdays they dined at the most exclusive club in town—membership to which was tantamount to success. Henri's name had been submitted by the president of his company, and he'd been accepted immediately. He had crossed the invisible color barrier, and there would be no going back.

On arriving in Detroit, Louise immediately made it her business to find the most suitable part of town in which to live. It must be in one of the better neighborhoods, yet not one that would make them appear to be living above their means or make them seem too ambitious about rising in Detroit society. Later they could build a home in one of the suburban areas developing to the east and north of the city.

She finally found just the place she wanted, a small but elegant house near East Grand Boulevard, a good but not ostentatious neighborhood. It was also only a few blocks from Henri's office, which was in the plant between Jefferson Avenue and the river. Henri could walk when he chose, which meant they would need only one carriage for the time being.

Louise was content to stay in the boarding house until she had the new house furnished precisely to her liking. And she was not one to rush when it came to selecting furniture, carpeting, draperies, and accessories. She had to create the perfect setting for themselves and for the wedding crystal and silver she'd brought with them.

At first Henri blanched at the thought of using all the money Mr. Carlyle had given them for a wedding gift. It had been a most generous amount, and Henri planned to invest at least half of it and spend the rest sparingly. But when he saw the first frown cross Louise's face, he knew immediately there would be many times in the future when he'd have to defer to her wishes. She was not a martinet, but she was a woman determined to get her way in certain things; he saw it would be easier living with her if he did not argue.

Henri was not displeased with the final results. She had refused to let him go inside the house until it was ready for them to move in. He'd been so busy getting established in his new position, he'd been more than willing to let her handle all the details of setting up housekeeping.

"It's perfect, Louise. You've done a splendid job." He meant every word of it. This was the right home for an up-and-coming executive. Not too lavish but everything very correct.

"I'm glad you're pleased. Your approval was all I wanted."

Henri released a satisfied sigh. Life was moving along exactly as he'd planned. He was married to the right woman, and he was well established as vice-president in charge of redesigning the precision parts the company manufactured. He was on his way to becoming a very wealthy man.

Much to Louise's surprise, he took her in his arms and suggested they go upstairs. It was a Wednesday evening. So far, of course, he'd had to spend his working nights at the plant rather than in his own workshop, but the Tuesday-Saturday routine had already been established.

"I want to celebrate," he said, "and I can't think of a better way. Put on the gown you wore on our honeymoon. The pale blue one that matches your eyes." When—if—they had children, he hoped they would be blue-eyed like Louise. That would put an end to any questioning of his heritage.

For the first time—and for almost the only time in their marriage—Louise found in her husband a passionate, even animal-like, nature, which had her gasping for breath and then collapsing with exhaustion. Yet, somehow, she experienced a satisfaction like none she'd had before, though the feelings it aroused had her blushing with shame. That night, a proper three and a half months after their marriage, she became pregnant with their first child.

Chapter Thirty-five

LISETTE'S LIFE WITH GERALD did not always go smoothly. There were times when, in his official capacity as duke apparent, he had to attend functions to which he could not take her. One such had been Queen Victoria's Diamond Jubilee in 1897, with all its attendant events. Then there were others to which he had to escort his wife. The situation, Gerald insisted, was as unpleasant for him—and for Lady Boswick—as it was for Lisette.

"I don't give a damn," Lisette cried, "about her dissatisfaction at having to be with you, or yours at having to escort her, but I do get upset at being left out completely." Her usually well-modulated voice rose to a scream. "And viewing your apparent connubial bliss from a distance."

"There, there," he said, trying to soothe her as he always did when they had this argument. "I love you, but you knew what it would be like. Maybe you should visit your family." It was his perennial suggestion whenever she was upset.

"No," and her response was always the same. "I'll find something to do until we can return to Cornwall or Scotland." Nothing Gerald ever said could assure her that her hold on him was more than tenuous, liable to snap if she were away from him for any length of time. As long as she was in England, he would return to her.

Being forced to sit on the sidelines during the Queen's jubilee had really galled her and continued to infuriate her whenever she thought about it, which was often. She'd looked forward to it as a time when they would leave the picturesque but rather dour surroundings of Cornwall, and she would have an excuse to buy dozens of new gowns for the dinners and galas. She bought the gowns and she went to several dinners and other events, but always on the arm of some escort Gerald had chosen for her, some dull person to whom she was in no danger of being attracted. She might have considered indulging in some mild flirtations, nothing serious but enough to make Gerald a bit jealous, but not one of the men was worth the effort. It took all her strength just to be civil to them while she watched Gerald from a distance. They couldn't even sit near each other or dance together as long as he was with his wife. Lady Boswick was a vicious person who would use being insulted in public as an excuse to get more money out of Gerald, even though she flaunted her affairs wherever she went.

To view the jubilee procession, Gerald had arranged an excellent vantage point for her. She sat with a number of his commoner friends on a balcony overlooking the parade route to St. Paul's. Lisette was as open-mouthed and awed as the rest of the onlookers. All the dominions and colonies were represented by premiers in carriages of state, but they were not nearly so impressive as the cavalry troops that had come from every quarter of the globe. It was they who illustrated just how far-flung and universally important the British nation was. They exemplified in living flesh and brilliant colors the proud boast that the sun would never set on the British Empire. Troops of English, Scottish, Irish, and Welsh cavalry regiments were followed by others from Australia and Canada, and mounted infantry from the Cape. Each group received appropriate applause as it marched past, but the really overwhelming huzzahs and hurrahs were saved for the turbaned lancers from various states in India, the befezzed Zaptichs of Cyprus, and the fantastic, costume-ball uniforms from Jamaica, Nigeria, Hong Kong, Singapore, the West Indies, and Sierra Leone. The color and the pageantry

417

were overwhelming, and Lisette felt almost dizzy as her eyes took in one company after another.

Then a hush fell over the onlookers, followed almost immediately by an ear-splitting cheer. At the very end of the procession, in her landau emblazoned with the royal coat of arms and pulled by matching cream-colored horses, came the Queen. Very tiny and very frail, she smiled warmly on those who stood watching, as if all of them were truly her children. She was dressed in her customary black, but cream-colored feathers in her bonnet nodded as she bowed in response to the good wishes of her people. Although it was June, overcast skies had been forecast, and there was a chill in the air. As soon as the Queen emerged from the palace, however, the sun broke through and everyone agreed that the appearance of "Queen's weather" was a good omen for the future of Great Britain.

In the past, Lisette would have been delighted beyond telling to have attended all the functions in celebration of the jubilee, even in the company of an ape. Being in the same room with Gerald, however, and seeing him pay court to other attractive women, while she had to pretend to be enjoying herself put a distinct pall over the whole fortnight they stayed in London—she in her house and he in his.

"Only a few more days," he whispered. He had managed to get her aside during one ball after his wife disappeared on the arm of a Spanish grandee. "Then we can return to Cornwall."

"I don't know whether I'm going back with you."

"But you will, won't you? I couldn't stand being there without you."

"Since you put it like that," she said smiling up at him, "I guess I will." There was certainly no point in staying in London, and Gerald *did* love her.

The jubilee was neither the first nor the last time they had to be separated, and she knew it would be that way as long as she remained with him. It was amazing how their relationship was tacitly accepted in society, and yet there was real protocol about where they could be seen together and where it would be more discreet for her to be with someone else.

During one such interlude, in the spring of 1900, when Gerald had taken guests to his lodge in Scotland while she remained behind in London, she had a confrontation that sent her reeling into the depths of despair. Her dinner partner put his hand on her knee and then began moving it up her leg. Before she could stab him with her fork—since her glaring disapproval had made no impression—he leaned over and whispered in her ear. In her fury she could never remember his exact words, but he said something like "I understand you are always available."

Lisette immediately jumped up and excused herself from the table, leaving the impression she was either ill or extremely rude. She didn't care which they chose to think. She called for her cloak and carriage and hastened away before anyone could see her tears. How could those rumors still be cropping up after all these years? Was she never to live down the reputation she'd had, if not deserved?

At home she sat at her dressing table, but her hands were trembling so badly she couldn't unfasten the clasp of her necklace. In another minute her whole body was shaking violently, and she was afraid she was going to faint. She rang for Marney, but while waiting for her, she was overcome by a clammy, nauseating cold sweat. Shaking uncontrollably, she stumbled to the bathroom. In a few minutes she felt somewhat better and tried resting on the bed, half lying, half sitting up. *Thank heavens*, she thought, *I had sense enough to put in modern plumbing when I remodeled the dressing room.*

There was a timid knock on the door. "Marney? Come in."

"Are you all right, ma'am? You looked so pale."

"Just a touch of something. Maybe the lobster I had for dinner. I'd like tea—very hot and very sweet. And some toast, please."

No, it wasn't the lobster, though she might wish it were. Something more poisonous and tainted than any lobster had made her ill. She had once sworn she'd use men to gain what she wanted. Instead, she'd been allowing men—even Gerald—to use her from the time she met Philippe. As did all the hostesses and the people she thought were her friends.

She'd entered upper-class British society, all right, but by the back door. She could live with Gerald in Cornwall or Scotland, when no one else was invited, but she had to sit on the sidelines at the very times when she would be proud to be seen with him. No more of that!

Getting off the bed and walking over to the dressing table,

Lisette looked into the mirror. Barely past thirty but already she needed creams and lotions to keep her skin smooth and a bit of tinted rice powder to hide the circles under her eyes.

I've got to get away from here, she thought. There had been moments of depression before, but now she felt as if she were fighting to keep from going under, to keep from having a complete breakdown. It was like fighting to save her life while caught among churning waves threatening to pull her farther and farther out to sea. She was actually finding it hard to breathe, and her heart was pounding in an erratic rhythm. The room was spinning around her again. Where was Marney with the tea? Once more she dashed for the bathroom, where she suffered through stomach-tearing spasms of dry heaves. Weakly, she made her way back to the bed.

"Here, ma'am," Marney said, bringing in a tray. "The tea is good and hot."

"And sweet?" She couldn't stand tea to be the least bit bitter.

"I put in two teaspoons and brought more. I left the toast unbuttered. Better for an upset stomach."

"Thank you, Marney. Let's just hope it will stay down." If it didn't, at least it would be better than the bitter gall of this last attack.

"Do you want me to call the doctor, ma'am? Maybe he could give you something."

"No, but you can find the laudanum in the medicine cabinet for me. It might help me sleep." That was what she needed, hours and hours of peaceful, restorative sleep. Not until morning would she begin to think about what she ought to do.

Lisette slept until nearly noon, but sometime during the night she'd made up her mind. She had to get out of London. She didn't want to go alone, but she definitely did not want to visit any of her friends. There was only one person she really wanted to be with. As soon as she finished the light brunch Marney brought her, she reached for her writing case.

"Baptiste," Leah said, coming into his office, "I've received the most surprising letter from Lisette. She wants me to come to England and spend a few weeks with her."

Baptiste swiveled around in his chair. "Is she ill again?"

"I don't think so. At least she doesn't say she is. Only that she wants to get away from London and wouldn't I like to share her vacation with her."

"Sounds like a pleasant enough idea. Why so surprised?"

"After all these years? She hasn't even come home for a visit since she—she began seeing Gerald."

"Became his mistress, you mean." Baptiste had never gotten over the failure of her marriage to Philippe.

"What else could she do since Philippe refused to give her a divorce?"

"Live with him like a proper wife. Whatever the problem was, she didn't give herself—or him—time to work it out."

"I don't think it was that simple, Baptiste." If only she could tell him the truth, but Lisette had sworn her to secrecy. "I think it was something so irreconcilable no amount of time would bring a solution. But back to this letter. Something's wrong. Maybe she's left Gerald."

"And maybe she just wants to see you. Do you want to go over?"

"Yes. Yes, I do. I've always felt I let her down before. Anyway, I'd enjoy seeing England. We never did take up Jane Westborne's invitation to visit her. Do you want to come along?"

Baptiste read Lisette's letter. "I think it's you she wants to see. If all is well, and she wants me to, I might come over later for a few days."

"I hate going off and leaving you."

"I won't be alone. I'd already planned to spend some time with Jean. Since he's acquired those additional fields, this will give me an opportunity to see how they plant the new vines, as well as to observe all the processes in the winery. Jean has some new ideas for improving the color and the flavor of the champagne we're exporting. It seems there's a growing demand for a sparkling rosé."

"Then I'll write Lisette and tell her I can be there by the end of the week."

Leah had been touched by Lisette's wish to see her, and now she found she was excited at the prospect of seeing England for the first time. She tried to imagine what London looked like; also, she'd heard so much about the beautiful countryside, she hoped they'd do some touring. She sang while she packed her trunk, and then was ashamed of herself for being so happy at going on a trip that she and Baptiste had often talked of taking together. If he were disappointed that Lisette hadn't included him in the invitation, he wasn't showing it; still, she'd insist he join them before she returned to France.

The channel crossing was smooth; then, once on the train to London, Leah spent all her time looking out the window and gazing at the verdant country and quaint towns they passed through.

Lisette met her at the station, and for a long time they stood with their arms around each other, saying nothing.

"Mama, it is good to see you. I wasn't really sure you'd want to come when I wrote."

"Nothing could have kept me away."

"It's been too many years, hasn't it?" Lisette wiped a speck of soot from her eyes.

"Far too many." Leah was also finding that the smoky station made her eyes water.

"So," Lisette said as she led Leah to the waiting carriage, "you must tell me all about everyone—Jean, Denise, their children. And Papa. How is Papa?"

"Fine. Not as active as he once was, but he gets along quite well. He's spending this time with Jean and learning all the new tricks in the champagne business."

Leah looked long and hard at Lisette. If she were troubled about anything, it didn't show in her face. In fact, she seemed calmer and more at peace with herself than when she'd last been home.

"And while we talk," Leah said, "I want to see all of London, all the famous places I've heard about."

"For a few days, but I have other plans I hope you'll approve of."

"Nothing too exciting, I hope. I didn't come over here for a round of social activities."

"Not one tea or dinner," Lisette assured her. "In fact, just the opposite. But here we are. I'll tell you all about it later."

"Oh, Lisette," Leah said while she wandered from room to room, "this is a beautiful home. Are you still leasing it?"

"Yes, the Sheldons don't want to sell, but their agent has assured me I can stay here as long as I like."

"Is all this furniture theirs or yours?"

"Mine," Lisette said proudly. "When I signed the second lease, they moved all their things out, and I had the most glorious time furnishing it just the way I wanted."

"Then I have to compliment you on your exquisite taste."

"Come see the music room. I've saved it for last. I'll play for you tonight if you like."

"I'd enjoy that. I'm pleased you've kept up with your music—even if you didn't get to the concert stage."

"I guess the piano is the one genuine, consistent pleasure in my life. When I play, I forget about everything else. Amazing the restorative as well as relaxing powers music has. Life takes on a whole new perspective after hours of sitting here alone and letting the music take me where it will." Never before had Lisette revealed to anyone just how much music meant to her and how dependent she'd become on its healing force.

After a four-day, lightning-paced tour of London, Leah was ready to accept Lisette's suggestion they spend the rest of their time together in the country.

"We'll take the train to Truro in Cornwall," Lisette said. "That's about ten miles from the cottage I've rented. It may seem rather bleak and lonely at first, but I think you'll find after a few days how really lovely that section is."

"Will we be making any stops along the way?" Leah looked forward to the days with Lisette, but she hadn't come to England to spend the entire time in a cottage hidden in the rocky crags of Cornwall.

"I hadn't planned to. Any place you'd especially like to see?"

Leah listed a few sites, and the itinerary was altered immediately. With Leah playing tourist and wandering entranced through the grandeur of Salisbury and Wells cathedrals, the remains of legendary Glastonbury Abbey, and the beautiful city of Bath, it took them five days to reach Cornwall. Lisette had thought she'd be bored traipsing after Leah—cathedrals and historic remains always bored her—but she found herself equally awed by the sense of tradition and continuity pervading each place.

When they'd boarded the train for the final leg of their trip, Leah philosophized on her own experience of continuity. "From each generation," she told Lisette, "comes a new one that will carry on when we're gone. It's the same thing each woman must feel at times. Within her—within us—are the seeds of every generation that will follow. That, to me, imparts a greater sense of immortality than the thought I might have an immortal soul. I sensed it a bit when I had each of the children, but much more so when I look at my grandchildren.

If death should be an ending rather than a beginning, they will be my immortality."

"That's all very well for you to say, Mama, but what about someone like me? I have no hope of ever seeing a child of my own, let alone a grandchild."

"I'm sorry. It was thoughtless of me to speak as I did. And very selfish."

"That's all right," Lisette said with a smile. "I didn't bring you over here to burden you with my troubles. We're going to have a good, cheerful visit."

And that it was. The cottage Lisette had rented—a good distance from High Tor, Gerald's estate—was perched almost on the edge of the cliffs. In the night they could hear the surf pounding at the base of the cliffs, and the sound lulled them into deep, restful sleep.

The first day they walked along the cliffs, climbing down to the shore where the footing was less precarious, and brought back armloads of wildflowers from the meadows to the cottage. On other days, they rode in a dogcart to some of the nearby towns.

"A dogcart!" Leah exclaimed when Lisette told her she was renting one from the milkman after he made his morning rounds.

"That's only its name," Lisette laughed. "It's really pulled by a pony. But with it we can go across the fields or along the roads, whichever way our fancy takes us. Much more convenient than a larger conveyance."

Following Lisette's example, Leah hitched up her skirts, climbed in, and tied a scarf around her hat to keep it from blowing off. Lisette took the reins in her hands and said, "Well, where to?"

Off they drove, over the rolling hills and the windswept moors with their banks of yellow-flowered gorse and fronds of bracken. When the sun grew hot, they stopped for a picnic lunch in the cool shade afforded by a spiney of trees and later stopped to follow an estuary to a pleasant site by the water's edge. They stared in awe at the granite-topped tors, black against the sky, and rode along lanes little wider than the cart itself, between gray stone walls.

Hiring a carriage with a driver, they went to Penzance and looked across the water toward St. Michael's Mount; also, they rode to St. Ives, a town of medieval buildings and cobbled alleys, with a jumbled cluster of fishermen's dazzlingly white-walled cottages on the peninsula.

When inclement weather forced them to remain inside,

they sat before the small peat fire and sewed or read. Above all, they talked and got to know each other as they never had before.

"What are you working on?" Leah asked Lisette, who was sorting through some strands of embroidery floss. "I've never known you to enjoy handiwork."

"A dressing-table scarf. It started out as a gift for Denise, but with all the mistakes I've made, I think it will end up in my room. If I ever finish it, that is."

"She'll appreciate it, in spite of its mistakes. How long have you been sewing?"

"Not long," Lisette said. "Just for the fun of it I started a sampler. Then I found how relaxing it was, how it helped me wind down after a hectic day."

"So you do have some homely attributes in spite of your attempt to deny them. Your beautiful house and now this."

"You've found me out, Mama." Lisette laughed nervously.

"You miss having a real home, don't you?" Leah felt completely a loss as to how to comfort her. "If only Philippe—"

"But he won't, so there's no use talking about it. I tried that last time in Paris."

"Can you tell me about it?"

"I'll try. I thought I could keep it all inside but the memory is slowly tearing me apart."

Hesitantly Lisette described the meeting and then the night with Philippe.

What do I say to her? Leah thought. *How do I help her?* "Being with Gerald hasn't been enough to obliterate that experience?" she asked finally.

"No, at times it only makes it worse. That's why I had to get away—from London, from him. Being here with you, Mama, has helped. It really has. I've enjoyed every minute of it."

"But it will soon be over. What are you going to do then? Return to London?"

"Yes, I love my home there, and I do have some good friends. I don't think I'll see Gerald for a while, though. I need to re-evaluate our relationship."

"You wouldn't consider coming back with me? Papa would love to see you." Baptiste had written that it was impossible for him to get away.

"Not just yet. But," Lisette put her arms around Leah, "don't be surprised if you get a letter saying I'm on my way."

The weather cleared the next day, and they rode as far as

Tintagel, where they climbed the stone steps cut into the side of the cliff and viewed the remains of an abbey on the site where, according to legend, King Arthur was born. On their return, Lisette found a letter waiting for her. It was sealed with the royal crest.

"It's from Edward!" Lisette exclaimed. "How in the world did he know where I was?"

"Open it," Leah said. "Maybe the answer is inside." The familiar use of his first name strengthened Leah's belief there had been—and might still be—more than friendship between the Prince of Wales and Lisette.

"Yes," Lisette said, "he writes that he found out from Marney where I was." Reading quickly, she found that he, as well as all her friends, had been missing her, and wasn't she about ready to return to London? He especially wanted her to be his guest on his yacht during the regatta at Cowes.

There was no mention of Gerald in the letter, and Lisette wondered why it was Edward and not Gerald who'd written. True, she'd sent Gerald only a brief note saying she was vacationing with her mother; still, if he missed her and wanted her to return, he could have found out where she was the same way Edward had. This shored up her resolve not to see him again, at least not anytime soon.

Knowing Lisette was hesitating about cutting their vacation short for fear of hurting her feelings, Leah spoke up to make it easier for her.

"It's time for me to be returning home. Thank you for inviting me over; I loved every minute of our visit, but I miss your father."

"After all these years?" In spite of her light, bantering tone, Lisette was serious.

"After all these years. Being with him is a very strong habit, and not one I have any desire to break."

"Good for you, Mama. I'm ready to go back, too."

Leah noted how the sparkle had returned to Lisette's eyes and the color to her cheeks. Maybe that was all she'd needed, just to get away for a while.

Her first night back in London, Lisette was surprised by a visit from the Prince. She'd seen Leah off on the train, then gone to the house to unpack, eat a light supper, and get into bed early. Her plans for a quiet evening ended when Marney announced she had a caller.

"Have I come at the wrong time?" Edward asked when he saw she was in a dressing gown.

426

"Not at all. I was simply relaxing after the long journey up from Cornwall and seeing my mother off to Paris. The music room?"

"You haven't forgotten my favorite place, have you?"

"No, although it's been a long time since you've sat in that chair over there. Something to drink?"

"A little brandy," he said, "if you have any."

"Only the best, in anticipation of seeing you again." She rang for Marney, and aked her to bring brandy, wine, and glasses. "Now, what brings you here tonight?"

"Is it enough to say I've missed seeing you around town? We all have."

"I was feeling a bit under the weather," Lisette said. "I needed a change of scene."

"Nothing serious, I hope." He waited for Lisette to pour his brandy and then some wine for herself.

"No, the fresh sea air helped."

He looked over toward the piano. "Will you play something for me?"

"I'd be delighted to, though I'm a bit rusty. I haven't played in all the weeks I was gone."

She sat down, ran her fingers over the keys, and then played several of his favorites. Suddenly, without warning, she stopped and put her head down.

Edward put his glass down and came over to her. "What's wrong, Lisette?"

"I'm sorry. Just more tired than I realized, I guess." Yet it was more than exhaustion that had her feeling as if she were going to faint.

"It's my fault," he said. "I shouldn't have come here so late. I see now you're really very tired. Also," he stood back and looked at her more intently, "you're much too thin."

"I'm not really physically tired. It's—I don't know—I'm just all confused."

"Can you tell me?" He lifted her off the piano bench and took her in his arms. "I have very broad shoulders."

"And very comfortable ones." She'd forgotten how much, and how often, she'd depended on his strength in the past.

"Then let me play father confessor. It might help just to talk it out."

"You're a good and true friend, Eddy."

"Those are kind words for a past lover to hear. Now—what's wrong?" He sat her down in a chair and settled himself comfortably in a chair facing her.

"Everything—the whole life I've been leading. It was fun at first. Gay Lisette! But I don't like what I see in the mirror, and I'm terrified of the future. I don't mean I fear for my immortal soul. It's just that in spite of being surrounded by people, of finding dozens of invitations waiting for me, I'm dreadfully lonely. And I know it can only get worse."

He reached in his pocket for a cigar. "Mind?"

She shook her head.

"You need to marry, Lisette. You have so much to offer the right man. A pity Gerald's not free. You're right for each other."

"It wouldn't matter if he were. How could I? I'm married to Philippe, and the Church would never sanction a divorce."

"If the Papal Rota knew the truth?"

"The truth? What do you mean?" *How much does Edward know?* she wondered.

"Philippe's private life is not as private as he thinks," Edward said. "Don't look so surprised, Lisette. It's a matter of simple deduction. You left him after—what?— less than two months? A Frenchman is often known by his mistresses. Philippe has none. The conclusion is obvious."

Lisette was stunned—and bewildered. She had suffered all these years while maintaining her silence. And all the while there were others who knew. If Edward were to be believed she could have applied to the Church for an annulment—except there were still other considerations.

"We made an agreement," she said, "and Philippe has been fair with his end of the bargain. I can't fault him for that. I have everything I need." She laughed ironically. "Just look around. I lack nothing."

Edward nodded understandingly. "Except the security of a good marriage. Don't be disillusioned; there are good marriages. And you know what it takes to make one. Write to Philippe. He might agree. Who knows what Gerald might be able to do."

The last was a bold statement for Edward to make. He thoroughly disapproved of divorce; any divorced person, whether the guilty or innocent party, was automatically excluded from all royal functions. Was there something she did not know about the relationship between Gerald and his wife which would allow for an annulment? Right now, however, that was less her concern—after all, she hadn't seen or heard from Gerald in several weeks—than her own freedom.

"I have written Philippe," she said, "over and over. I've

428

pleaded with him, said I was willing to be named the guilty party, would agree to be cited for adultery."

"Which of course would not be necessary in an annulment suit," Edward said. "What has he said?"

"No personal word from him. Only a copy of the agreement we signed. I've torn up and burned a dozen of them."

"And you need his financial support?"

"Yes. Don't think I haven't lain awake nights thinking it all out. So I meet someone who wants to marry me. The minute—the very minute—I start proceedings through the Church, Philippe will withdraw my allowance. Then it could take one, two, or even three years for the annulment from Rome. Philippe will never admit to having gone into marriage fraudulently, deliberately unwilling to consummate it. I'd have to find witnesses. And I can't ask a future husband to support me and wait all that time. I'm trapped and Philippe knows it. That was one thing about my relationship with Gerald. I have remained financially independent, and that has been important to me." She did not say aloud that it kept her from feeling like a prostitute.

"Your family?" Edward suggested. "Surely they would give you the support you need."

"I could return home," Lisette agreed, "but I hate to ask them for help. Then there would be the shame for them. If a scandal ensued it could ruin my father's business. My mother knows the truth, but he doesn't. He—he just thinks I left Philippe because he had a mistress and never really loved me. He doesn't know the truth."

"Then you should tell him," Edward said. "He'll respect you more for trying to protect him."

"I don't know." Lisette poured herself a second glass of wine and offered the brandy decanter to Edward. If only they'd had this conversation years earlier, how different her life might have been. She knew Edward was trying to help her, but one thought dominated her mind: it was too late. "I'm so bewildered now, I can't think straight."

"Then let me think for you." He reached over and took her hand. "Go home for a while. You'll have a breakdown if you don't. I can see it in your eyes. When you're with your family, you'll know what to do."

Lisette stood up and bobbed a small, almost impertinent curtsy in his direction. "Thank you, Your Majesty."

"Your Majesty?" He stiffened and sat upright, but the twinkle in his eye told her how much pleasure the words gave him. "Aren't you a bit premature?"

429

"I was remembering a ball where I danced all night with a king." She was smiling again.

"And I with a queen. It was a brief affair, Lisette, but I loved every minute of it."

"And I loved you. I still do, you know, but not as a lover. Does that make sense?"

"More than you know," he said, "and it pleases me. Now, kiss me goodnight and go straight to bed. Think over what I've said."

"I will. I promise."

Lisette lay awake for several hours after she'd bade Edward good-bye. This time, however, the sleeplessness was not due to anxiety or a fear of nightmares, but to a new calm that allowed her to consider Edward's words and plan her future rationally rather than emotionally. She still had four years to go with the present lease on the house, but homes in that section of London were in such demand, she was certain the Sheldons would release her from the contract. She'd like to take a few pieces of furniture with her, though much of it she could sell at a good price, especially the fine antiques. The piano, of course, would go back with her. What would Mama and Papa say to having two pianos in the music room? Maybe she should sell it, after all. It had been a gift from Philippe and if she got rid of it, she would be cutting her last ties to him. She'd talk to an auctioneer about handling the sale for her. Then, at least, she wouldn't be completely dependent on the family for financial aid.

The hardest part would be telling Papa. Each time she began thinking about that, she forced her mind to turn to some other subject. If only she could keep from hurting him. But she'd need his help in getting the best lawyers. She wasn't afraid he'd be disillusioned about her, but knowing what Philippe had put her through would tear him apart. He was such a soft-hearted, sentimental man, and all he'd ever wanted for her was a happy life.

In the morning, Lisette sent off a short note saying simply she was coming home; then she set about the business of putting England and the disappointing years there behind her, just as she'd once done with France and its bitter memories.

Chapter Thirty-six

NICOLE STOOD BACK and scrutinized the paintings hanging on the walls of the small room. The lighting was poor, nearly nonexistent in fact, since the sun was blocked by the half-broken shutters. At night it was worse. The paintings reflected what dim light came from the bare, dirty bulbs, and most of their details were lost in the glaring pale yellow circles.

She sighed. She should be grateful to Monsieur Ébert for allowing her to display some of her work in his café. It wasn't the Louvre or one of the galleries where she'd dreamed of having her paintings shown, but at least here she had an audience that appreciated the real artistic talent she felt these oils revealed.

Montmartre was also a mecca for tourists, and occasionally one of them had an eye for genuine art. She might be fortunate enough to have such a one walk into Monsieur Ébert's café and like her work. Since returning from her last visit home, she no longer cared if one of the family saw her. She could ignore them or talk to them now without feeling pressured about returning home. She'd said her piece and now felt completely free of them. One by one they had rejected her, and if occasionally she found it hard to swallow the lump in her throat when she thought about her brothers and sisters, about Mama and Papa, it was only the last remains of her old love for them.

"Hey, Nicole! How about splitting a bottle of wine to celebrate your first showing?"

Her eyes had become accustomed to the dim interior, and she put up her hand to shield them against the bright sun that came in when the door was opened. "Who—?" Her voice was tremulously inquisitive. She believed and yet she could not believe who she was seeing.

"Étienne, is that you?" She looked at the handsome, self-assured young man who had been still a boy when she sent him away from her room. Had it been four years ago?

431

"In the flesh," he said, spreading his arms to show himself off and offer himself for an embrace. "Am I so changed?"

Nicole stood back to survey him for a moment, then accepted the offer of his arms. There was nothing hesitant or boyish about the way he held her close and kissed her firmly on the lips.

"Yes, in many ways," she said when she finally caught her breath. "What brings you to this dismal den of cheap coffee and even cheaper wine?"

"Your paintings. And you. Word came to me by way of, ah, one of the models and frequenters of a bar near the university that you had a showing."

"And when did she tell you? In the bar or in bed? I thought I'd cured you of soliciting favors of that kind."

" 'Fraid not," he laughed. "Just whetted my appetite for more."

"I'm ashamed of you, Étienne.

"I didn't come here for a lecture on morals, Nicole. Anyway, what do you expect a university student to do when he needs some relaxation from his books and classes?" He tried to appear worldly wise and succeeded only in looking chagrined.

"Be a little more particular about the company you keep," she said. "What did she or the others give you besides a half-hour tumble on the mattress?"

"Nothing. I'm not as stupid as you think," and he patted his pocket. "Now, teacher—now that I've had the lecture, how about that wine?"

"You paying?" She was particularly low on funds and couldn't even afford a bottle of Monsieur Ébert's cheapest.

"I invited you, didn't I?" He acted hurt. "Can we get anything decent in this place?"

"If you bribe Monsieur Ébert, he'll bring out something from his private cellar." She watched Étienne while he spoke to the proprietor, who'd been eyeing them from behind the bar. As long as he'd allowed her to hang her paintings in the café, it would hardly do for her and Étienne to leave and go someplace else. At least he would bring out his best when Étienne showed him the money.

"Now," she said, after Étienne returned with the bottle and two glasses. "Tell me what you've been doing."

"Going to the university, like a dutiful son."

"No more painting?" Nicole accepted the glass he'd poured.

"Not since the night you sent me out into the big, dark

432

world. Your rejection was like being thrown into an ice-cold pond. It was a terrific shock, but it was what I needed. Once I realized I wasn't going to die, I knew you'd done the right thing." He held up his glass. "Here's to you and your career."

"And to yours," she said, "when you tell me what it is."

"Law, I think, and then politics. With my father's position in government to sponsor me, I can get into just about any firm I want and start making a place for myself in politics. It didn't take me long to learn that it's not what you know that counts but who you know."

"That's my good old Étienne. You never were an idealist except when it came to women." She hoped she didn't sound too cynical.

"And what's wrong with being a realist if it gets you what you want?"

"Nothing, as long as it's what you want," she said. "And you can live with yourself."

"I haven't found that a problem yet, and I'm doing very well with my studies. If I know law and use my father's position to be hired by one of the best firms, why should I feel I'm compromising myself?"

"You shouldn't. As long as you don't mind having to pay the debts you accrue along the way."

"Oh, hell, Nicole, don't sound so pious. You know what politics is like: a little back-scratching among friends is the accepted thing."

"And when you see someone being persecuted and you can't do anything, because that would arouse the wrath of one of these so-called political allies? What then? I'm sorry, Étienne, but I value my independence and my private moral values too much to compromise them for any reason."

"Still full of righteous indignation, aren't you? And what good does it do? I suppose you're still weeping over the fate of Dreyfus. If it hadn't been for him, we might still be together."

"No, we wouldn't. He was only an easy excuse for me to end an affair that never should have started."

"Well, a hell of a lot of good it did for all of you to march and carry on about a new trial. He got it in Rennes last year and what happened?"

"I know what happened. He was found guilty again, a real travesty of justice. But at least he didn't have to return to Devil's Island. Someday—someday—his name will be completely cleared. I only hope he lives to see himself vindicated."

433

"Enough of him," Étienne said. "He spoiled things for me once. I'm not going to let him do it again. I came back to see you because I've never forgotten you. I told you once you were the most beautiful thing that ever happened to me, and you still are. I—I want to see you again." He twirled the wineglass in his hand, and for a moment Nicole thought he was going to snap the stem.

"It's true, Étienne; we did once have something very wonderful. I won't deny that. You did as much for me as I did for you. But that was four years ago. Don't try to resurrect something that's been long dead. Things that die become rotten and then they stink."

"I didn't say I wanted to sleep with you again. I said I wanted to see you. To be friends."

"Do you really? I'd like that." She couldn't remember any man wanting to be her friend without a lascivious motive hidden behind his engaging smile. "Then turn around and tell me what you think of my paintings. You said you came to see them."

"I can tell you without looking. They're damned good. Those I saw in your room were, and these are, too. Sold any?"

"No. But I never give up hope." Still, though, she was tired of the feeling in the pit of her stomach, sort of like holding her breath, while she waited for someone to appreciate her talent.

"Then I know someone who should see them. Jerome Trowbridge. He's an ex-lawyer, a remittance man from England."

"A what?"

"A remittance man. He got involved in some kind of legal scandal at home in Manchester, so his family shipped him off to Paris and sends him a remittance every month to keep him here. He's still considered one of the shrewdest legal minds on either side of the channel," Étienne said, "and so he was invited to lecture at the university. More to the point, he's a real art enthusiast with enough money to support his enthusiasm."

"How did you learn all that?" Nicole asked.

"We got to talking over a few drinks after one of his lectures. I wanted him to clarify some points he'd made, and we ended up talking about his past and his love for art. I'll bring him up here one evening."

"Bring him along, especially if he's in the mood to buy. If I'm not here, you know where to find me. I haven't moved."

434

"I'll do that, and—and, Nicole, it's been good—no, it's been wonderful seeing you again. Can I come back?"

"I'm always happy to see my friends, even unreconstructed, pragmatic ones like you. Aren't you afraid, if you hang around me, you'll turn into an idealist?"

"Never," Étienne laughed. "You keep living in your flea-infested rathole, and maybe I'll invite you to the grand apartment I plan to have someday when I'm established."

"I might bring some of the fleas along with me."

"They won't bother me any more than some of your crazy ideas. If they're yours, they'll be welcome." He looked at his watch hanging from its heavy chain. "Good God, I'll be late for my next lecture. See you in a few days."

Nicole smiled as she watched him stumble over a chair. In spite of looking like a man, he was as much the boy as ever. She felt a bittersweet longing for him after he'd gone. Had he really come wanting to be no more than a friend? Or had he said that to keep from showing his disappointment? It would have been so easy to invite him up to her room, but what she'd said to him applied to her as well. To resume as lovers might rekindle their former pleasure, but it might also prove disillusioning. And it would most certainly lead to another, more painful, separation.

Nicole soon forgot about Étienne's promise to bring his lawyer friend to see her paintings. But true to his word, Étienne knocked on her door late one afternoon. In tones usually reserved for more portentous events than the visit of an amateur art connoisseur, he announced that Mr. Jerome Trowbridge was at that moment viewing her canvases in Monsieur Ébert's café.

"And what am I supposed to do?" Nicole asked. "Rush right down and inform him he'd better buy one or else? Or fawn over him for deigning to look at my pitiful display?"

"Don't be asinine, Nicole. I simply thought you'd like to meet the man."

"Not really. But, then again, maybe he'll buy a bottle of wine while he's looking." She tried to sound flippant, but inside she was quivering. She wanted so desperately to have someone appreciate her work. She wiped the cerulean blue off her brush with her skirt.

"Don't you think that's being a—a bit messy?" Étienne asked.

"It's not me I want him to be impressed with; it's my work. At least," she said, eyeing the various spots of color on her skirt, "he'll know I'm a real painter, not just a dabbler."

Failing to find her hairbrush among the trinkets on the shelf—cheap jewelry was her one weakness—Nicole ran her hands through her hair and left three smears of blue from forehead to crown. Near her temples were yellow and red smudges she'd made while pushing her hair behind her ears as she worked. If Leah had been there, she might have been reminded of herself when she'd worn the make-up of a voodoo priestess back in New Orleans. As it was, Étienne gasped at the eerie, almost mesmerizing sight Nicole presented.

"What are you staring at?" Nicole asked.

"You have paint all over your face and in your hair."

"So? I'll wash it off when I get back. Let's go."

She hurried down the steps in front of him, as if she intended getting this meeting over as quickly as possible so that she could return to her work.

If Étienne were startled at the way Nicole looked, Jerome Trowbridge was positively stunned, but with admiration, not shock. Never in his life, he thought, had he seen anyone as beautiful as this young woman. She walked like a queen, head held high with a pride bordering on disdain for everyone around her. Her glossy black hair hung straight to below her waist and her skin was like dusky old ivory. He caught himself staring into her eyes and noting their haunting, vaguely Oriental shape. Although he'd never seen her before, Nicole was so tantalizingly familiar that he strained to think of whom she reminded him. Then the haphazard splashes of color on her skirt—as if she'd been casually wiping her brush on it—gave him the clue. He'd seen some of Paul Gauguin's Polynesian paintings. Now he knew. This young artist standing before him did not belong in Paris; she was a Tahitian queen.

All Nicole saw was a man who might or might not be interested in buying one of her paintings. She was oblivious to his short, slim physique, and to his awkward, English-accented French.

"How do you do," Jerome Trowbridge said when Étienne introduced them. "Your paintings are magnificent, Mademoiselle Nicole, or it is Michele? Étienne has mentioned both names."

"Nicole."

Although she'd spoken only the one word, Jerome Trowbridge was enchanted by the way her voice lingered on the vowels.

"I'm very much impressed with these," he said. "Do you have others?"

"In my studio." If he wanted one of these, Nicole thought, why did he need to see others? She had the feeling he was merely whiling away a dull afternoon, and she didn't have that kind of time to waste.

"Would it be possible for me to see them?" He had to find a way to see more of this young woman, and if her other paintings were as good as these in the café, he thought he knew how it could be done. He was not without influence in the Parisian art world.

"Follow me." She turned and strode toward the door. Better to get it over with as quickly as possible.

"I have to get back to the university," Étienne said, but it appeared as if neither of them heard him. He shrugged his shoulders, followed them out, and proceeded down into the city.

Jerome Trowbridge was not only captivated by Nicole as a woman but genuinely interested in her work. Inside her studio, his eyes went from her to the various canvases she showed him.

"These are even better than the others," he said after he'd studied them all. "You have a bold touch with color, and yet there is a finesse about it." He pointed to a large canvas. "You've really captured the spirit of Paris in this one." He indicated one of the smaller Madonnas. "And the quality of motherhood in this one is very poignant."

"Thank you. I think these are my best, too, but I didn't think they would appeal to the casual observer." Gratified as Nicole was, part of her remained wary of him. His words sounded sincere enough, but so had others she'd listened to before learning not to be disappointed when no sale was forthcoming.

It was the longest speech Nicole had made since they'd met, and Jerome listened intently to every word.

He said, "I think Étienne told you I'm a lawyer by profession, but art is my avocation. I've purchased a fair quantity of contemporary art. And I'd intended to buy one when I saw yours. Now I want to do something more."

"Buy more than one, you mean?" she asked. "I'm flattered."

"I may buy several, but that's not what I had in mind. I have connections with a number of galleries in Paris, and I want to sponsor a showing of all your work. Would you be agreeable to that?"

"Agreeable?" Now it was Nicole's turn to be stunned. "It's

437

what I've dreamed of since—since as long as I can remember." Then she began to have second thoughts. What was behind this man's wish to sponsor a show for her? She'd learned quickly that men are not altruistic by nature. There was nothing she wanted more than a gallery exhibition of her paintings, but what would be the eventual cost to her? "Why do you want to do this for me?"

It was all Jerome could do to keep from saying, *Because you are the most beautiful woman I've ever seen and I'm in love with you.* Instead he answered, "Because your paintings are worth a show of their own—a gallery show—and I think I can arrange one for you. We'll have to see about having some of these framed, but I can take care of that." He could feel a new power sweeping through him. Handling the framing would be only the beginning. She'd be so busy with her painting, she'd be glad to have him do it. Then, gradually, he'd assume other responsibilities, until she'd ceded every aspect of her life to his control. Her beauty had captivated him, but it was her talent he would shape and mold until he was indispensable to her. Without knowing it, people would be admiring him when they praised Nicole's paintings.

"How soon do you think it can take place?" Nicole asked. So far, he seemed perfectly businesslike, and it would be a dream come true to walk into a gallery and see her paintings hanging in the right light and being admired by people who were real art enthusiasts.

"Most galleries are booked from six months to a year in advance, but I might be able to get you into the right one in about four months. It must be one of the best." He knew of one with a room that would become available in less than two months, but he needed more time to insinuate himself into her life so that her dependence on him would be total.

"Good. That will give me time to finish a few things I have in mind." For a moment she thought about going back to the château and getting the paintings she'd left there. Then she put that idea out of her mind. It would upset her parents to learn she was allowing someone else to sponsor a show for her. Also, her recent work was much better than what she'd left at home.

"Now we have that settled," Jerome said, "how about going out to dinner with me?"

"I'd like that very much." *But dinner only,* Nicole thought. *I owe you that much, but no more.*

"I'm glad the show is already decided on. Otherwise, I'd

think you accepted the invitation because of what I might be able to do for you rather than because you want to."

"I accepted because I'm hungry for a good meal," she said matter-of-factly.

Jerome waited for her to smile at her little joke, and then realized she was deadly serious.

"Well," he said, "honesty like that deserves the finest dinner in Paris. Put on your best gown and we'll celebrate the forthcoming debut of France's newest artist. You'll have the whole city at your feet before long."

Without answering, Nicole slipped behind the screen and changed into another skirt. She left on her blouse and sabots.

"That—that's your best?" Jerome tried hard to keep from sounding shocked.

"Yes, it's the clean one." She reached for a shawl that was thrown over the back of a chair and proceeded him out the door.

"I promised you the best dinner in Paris, and the best it will be," he said, closing the door behind them. He no longer cared what people might think. Nicole looked more stunning in her full skirt and loosely tied blouse than any other woman could possibly look in silks and laces.

During dinner, Nicole paid little attention to what Jerome said. She was concentrating on the dishes the waiter placed before her. Not so much because she was hungry, but because she was filled with a strange uneasiness whenever she looked up and met Jerome's eyes. She'd heard about snakes immobilizing their prey by staring unblinkingly. Jerome didn't look like a snake, but his eyes had the same hypnotic quality. They were deep set, under heavy lids, in his long, saturnine face. His thin lips were a straight line under his proud, aquiline nose. *He wants something of me,* she thought, *and I don't think it's what most men want.* What she saw was something more dangerous, more insidious.

"And so you see," Jerome was saying, "that's why I left England. My parents will say it was because I had to, but actually the choice was mine. If they want to send me a remittance check, which is really more like conscience money, every month in addition to interest from the trust my grandfather set up for me, I'm not going to refuse it."

Nicole had absorbed so little of what he'd told her, she had no idea what he was talking about. Why he'd left England, by force or choice, was of little consequence to her. Jerome Trowbridge was important to her only as a means of

439

getting a gallery showing, no more. She'd see as little of him as possible between now and then. And once the showing was over, she'd rid herself of him as totally as she had her family.

While they rode back to her rooming house, Nicole waited with some trepidation for Jerome to suggest he'd like to share more than dinner with her. After his explanation about his self-exile in Paris, their conversation had rarely strayed from art for the rest of dinner. She would have enjoyed the evening had it not been for the way he stared at her, with his almost lidless reptilian eyes, as if willing her to relax her defenses and submit to him. Yet, in the cab he neither sat too close to her nor tried to hold her hand. Once again, it was not his sexual advances she feared, but something more malignant.

Jerome helped her down from the cab and said he'd be in touch as soon as he'd contacted some of the galleries.

"I'll be waiting to hear," Nicole said. With a sense of relief, she walked up the five flights of stairs and then wondered why she was as breathless as if she'd run the whole way.

Jerome got back into the cab and asked the driver to take him around for a while. One look, one word, and he would have followed Nicole up to her room; however there'd been no hint he'd be welcome. All evening he'd had to force himself to keep his eyes focused on her face. The ties of her blouse had loosened, and through the narrow opening he could see the soft curve of her breasts. It unnerved him to realize she wore nothing beneath the blouse, and in his imagination he saw the complete fullness of her breasts. He couldn't get the picture out of his mind, and in the cab with her it was all he could do to keep from putting his hand on her blouse and feeling her respond to his touch.

Jerome Trowbridge wanted Nicole more than he'd ever wanted a woman, but he wanted more than her body. He wanted to possess all of her, to have her completely under his power. But intuition told him it was not yet time. Right now she would not allow anyone to possess her. She might appear to give of herself, but she still retained the very thing he desired most—control over her own thoughts and emotions. The affair in England, the reason he'd had to leave—and he had been forced to in spite of what he'd told Nicole—had been but a hastily drawn sketch, a poorly per-

440

formed rehearsal, for what he intended to enjoy with Nicole.

After Nicole caught her breath, she put all thoughts of Jerome aside. In spite of her excitement about having her own show, she fell asleep as soon as she got into bed.

It was different in the morning. She began to make a careful study of the oils in her studio. Some needed a bit of retouching and these she'd tend to first. Several sketches would be the basis for additional oils. All in all, she should have about thirty paintings ready for the showing if, as Jerome had said, it would be a matter of some four months before they could expect to find an opening at one of the better galleries.

But once his name had entered her mind, she could not dismiss it: *Jerome Trowbridge.* Nicole was surprised to hear herself saying the name aloud. What sort of man was he really? His features were starkly clear in her mind, as if impressed by a heavily indented seal, but what dominated was the burning intensity of his eyes. She couldn't remember exactly what, but something he'd said suggested that when something stirred him, it took precedence over everything else. She'd sensed almost immediately his complex nature: he seemed to possess the sensitivities of an artist and the zeal of a fanatic. Nicole had met others like him, and she knew they could be as gentle as puppies when pleased and dangerous as poisonous snakes when aroused. She had no intention of compromising herself, her beliefs, her mode of living, or her art to please him; at the same time she'd do nothing to deliberately stir up his enmity, either. She would simply be wary in all her dealings with Jerome Trowbridge.

Four days passed without a word from him, and Nicole was finding it more and more difficult to concentrate on her work. Nothing was going right. The sketches looked all wrong when she transferred them to canvas. With the skies clouded over and rain threatening, she didn't have the light she needed to blend her tones. Finally, when she'd squeezed the last from several tubes of paint, she threw down her brush. It was just the excuse she needed to get out of the studio and walk off her frustrations. She reached for her shawl and ran down the stairs. Passing Monsieur Ébert's café, she decided impulsively to stop in for coffee before buying her paints.

Just inside the door she hesitated. She didn't know whether she wanted to go in or return straightaway to her room. Jerome was sitting at one of the tables near the back. If he were here, why hadn't he come to see her?

Before she could turn around and leave, he looked up. "Nicole! I've been sitting here hoping I'd see you." He stood up, pulled out a second chair, and came forward to lead her back to it.

"I've been busy." She couldn't trust herself to say anything more. His broad, generous smile showed he was truly glad to see her, and his eyes looked less forbidding than previously. Perhaps exhaustion and excitement at the thought of having a show had made her see things that didn't exist.

"I know," he said. "That's why I haven't bothered you." Let her think he was concerned only about her work. Let her wonder why he hadn't come to see her. It was all part of his plan. "Would you like coffee? Or maybe some wine?"

"Coffee, please. Then I have to get back to work."

Nicole was aching to ask if he'd contacted any of the galleries, but she dreaded what the answer might be. No one was interested in exhibiting an unknown artist, and a woman at that. If he had good news, surely he would tell her right away.

Instead he asked, "How is the painting coming?"

"Slowly. I'd used up some things I needed. That's why I came out. Except," she laughed, "I just realized I forgot to bring any money with me. I don't know where my mind could have been." *On you,* she thought, but didn't say it aloud. Sitting across from him, she realized how very much she'd wanted to see him again. Never before had she felt so ambivalent about anyone, dreading to become involved and yet longing to do just that. If she did, she'd be lost. She'd once vowed that no one would ever again be as important to her as Denise and Lisette had been. She would remain free of any emotional ties; yet, when Jerome looked at her, she could feel the threads of need and loneliness tightening around her. She must break them before they became chains, before she relinquished herself to him completely.

"Don't worry about the money," Jerome said. "I'll go with you and get what you need."

"Fine. I'll pay you back when we get to my room."

"No need for that." He frowned at the way she flaunted her independence. "I'm glad to do it."

"No! I prefer to pay for my supplies." She walked over to Monsieur Ébert. "I'll bring you the money for the coffee next time I'm in here."

Damn the woman, Jerome thought. *She's going to make certain she need be grateful to me for as little as possible. No,* and he smiled to himself, *she's afraid to owe me anything.*

"Nonsense," Jerome said. "I invited you to my table, and I'd be a sorry host if I didn't pay for your coffee." If her façade of independence was so fragile it could be pierced by the cost of a cup of coffee, she would soon be as supple as soft clay in his hands.

"Thank you," she said coolly. She'd insist on his taking the money for the supplies; she'd not be bound to him by gratitude.

"You might like to look at what I've done," she said when they reached her room, "while I look for the money."

Jerome tried to examine each of the paintings with an art expert's shrewd, analytical eye, but all he could see was Nicole clutching and releasing the folds of her skirt as she paced from the window to an easel and then to a table. Finally, he walked to where she stood and took her in his arms. When he kissed her, her response left him no doubt that she'd soon be completely in his power.

He felt the warmth of her body through her clothes, and he knew her desire for him was as strong as what he felt for her. She was offering herself to him; he hadn't had to find a way to seduce her. He would possess her body first; then, gradually, he'd claim complete mastery over her. He could now tell her he loved her without the danger she'd use that knowledge to bend him to her will instead of the other way around.

"No more than I love you," and Nicole was startled to realize he was the first man she'd ever said that to. She was also frightened, but there was no taking back the words or denying the feelings that gave rise to them.

Slowly, she withdrew from his arms and began undressing. Jerome stood moved but unmoving as he watched her shed skirt and blouse. Her body was perfection. There was nothing about it he would change, but now he must mold her mind and soul to be equally as perfect. And to be his to command.

He let her lie on the bed a long time before he approached her. Instead of becoming impatient or furious when he didn't at once lie down beside her, Nicole was supremely at ease. Under his intense gaze, she felt her whole body swept up and moved by an inexplicable ecstasy. In another moment it was suffused by the blissful warmth and lassitude she usually experienced after reaching a climax.

Without touching, with only their eyes, they had made love, and for the moment she was satisfied.

"I love you," she said, reaching her arms toward him.

"I know," he said, as he eased himself onto the bed. He was ready to enjoy her body now that he'd demonstrated his power over her mind. His will had guided her through an intangible erotic experience as easily as he would now take her physically. He would have no trouble commanding her to do as he wished from this time on.

Chapter Thirty-seven

"I THINK YOU SHOULD MOVE INTO MY APARTMENT," Jerome said while they dressed. "It's not large, but at least there's a kitchen so we won't have to go out to eat."

"I'd rather stay here, if you don't mind." Right now Nicole needed to hold on to something all her own. "Nor is there enough room here for you."

After her swift acquiescence and her obvious pleasure at making love with him, Jerome was startled by the resurgence of her independent spirit. Living apart would delay getting what he wanted from her, but he could afford to let her have her way for the time being.

"I hope that doesn't mean I won't be welcome here," he said with the subtlest hint of importunity.

"Of course not," she said casually. "You're always welcome. Come often, but leave me a little time to work."

"Speaking of which," Jerome said as he squinted at himself in the cracked mirror and struggled to get the knot in his tie just right, "I can't believe any woman would be so lacking in vanity as to have only a single, broken mirror."

"What does vanity have to do with my work?"

"It doesn't. It was just a gratuitous statement. What I started to say was that Monsieur Engle is delighted at the idea of showing your work."

"Jerome! How could you! How could you keep that from me all this time?"

"I didn't mean to," he said. "I intended telling you right

444

away." That was not true. He had deliberately put off telling her until the most propitious moment. "But I got sidetracked by other interests."

"Yes, I guess we both did. But tell me now. Everything. Don't leave anything out."

"Over a bottle of wine during dinner," he said.

"Fine, but let's hurry." She grabbed up her shawl and ran her fingers through her hair. "I can't wait."

Jerome slowly and deliberately undid and reknotted his tie several more times while she waited impatiently at the door. She must learn to wait for him. Finally he walked over and slid his fingers through the length of her hair. "Now I know why you never need a mirror—and don't ever become stupid enough to use one. You're naturally beautiful and must never change."

"Thank you, but don't worry. Mirrors frighten me. I don't like to see the changes that take place."

"You know what you looked like when I first saw you?" He held the door open for her. "A queen. You reminded me of something else, too, one of the Tahitian women Paul Gauguin painted."

"That's not so strange," Nicole said. "My great-grandmother was a Polynesian. Another was a mulatto. My mother is an octoroon."

"That accounts for your hair and those eyes. And your lustrous skin. I knew there was something different about you."

"You're not shocked?"

"Why should I be? You're the one who's important to me, not your ancestors."

"My great-grandfather was a ship's captain, and he was disowned when he brought his Leilei home from the islands to his very proper parents in France. Nor could my father and mother be married as long as they lived in the States."

"I'm not a very proper person, Nicole. I'd like to hear more about your family." The more he knew about her, the easier it would be to bring her completely under his influence.

"No, you never will. I have no family. Not anymore." He'd already drawn more from her than she'd intended.

For the moment Jerome was willing to abide by her wishes.

"To your show and the fame that will come after it," Jerome said after he poured the wine.

"Now," Nicole said, "the details."

"Not many, really. Engle has always been interested in young artists. He checked his calendar, and he'll be able to exhibit your paintings for three weeks."

"How soon?" *Three whole weeks!* She hadn't dared hope for more than a week.

"Early in September. He could have made it in August, but that's not a good time. Too many people still away. So I chose the second date."

"Three whole weeks!" Nicole repeated aloud. "How long does that give me?"

"Nearly four months. Enough?"

"Plenty. And enough time to spare for you."

Jerome had figured on that when he chose the second date. The more time there was before the show, the more certain he'd be to become indispensable to her. He'd never lose her then. "And after the showing," he said, "you'll move into my apartment."

"We'll see," she said. She couldn't let him know how torn she was between maintaining her independence and succumbing to the emotional comfort of his protection.

Jerome smiled to himself. When the time came, she'd move.

Nicole worked without interruption during the daylight hours. Evenings she was ready to put down her brushes and enjoy the rest of the night with Jerome. Rarely did he come in the afternoon; but if he did, he sat quietly watching her work. He might not have been there for all the attention she paid him, but he knew his presence was enough to remind her of his importance in her life.

Jerome was as stimulating a conversationalist as he was a lover; they often talked for hours on end, interrupting each other with opinions on art, politics, music, and the prevailing attitudes toward women. Nicole thought women should be equal to men in all ways; Jerome said that women were created to be submissive.

"Only to someone they love," Nicole said, and the conversation came to an abrupt but passionate conclusion.

Only one subject was taboo: Nicole's earlier life. Jerome was frustrated at not being able to probe into her past, to learn her weaknesses, but he convinced himself that time would reveal all.

When Jerome came to the studio one afternoon and Nicole was not there, he was livid with anger.

446

"Where have you been?" he demanded when Nicole returned half an hour later.

Then it was her turn to be furious. He had no right to question her in such an imperious tone. Her time was, and always would be, her own.

"I don't really think it's any of your business," she said quietly, "but as a matter of fact, I went out for some lemonade. It's very hot in here."

"Don't ever do it again without leaving me a note."

She turned away from his probing gaze. "This is my room, Jerome, and I come and go as I like. I don't intend to be questioned as if I were a child or an errant wife."

He put his hands on her shoulders. "Look at me, Nicole. I don't ever want you to do it again. Do you understand?"

She looked into his eyes and felt herself wilting, her strength eroding, under their powerful force. "I'm—I'm sorry, Jerome, I'll never do it again."

"That's more like it, darling. Believe me, I worry about you because I love you. Your happiness is my only concern. So let me be the judge of what is best for you at all times."

"I will. I promise." It was gradually becoming easier to relinquish her freedom in favor of his care. Independence had a sorry counterpart: loneliness.

As she knew it would, the afternoon ended in a wild abandonment to sensuality. She sometimes wished Jerome would realize there were more ways to resolve differences and to understand each other than making love. He gave the impression that, once it was over, everything was settled and there'd be no more problems. Always, she was made to feel like a child who'd been given a lollipop and told to be a good girl from now on. Jerome always seemed to think their differences had been resolved firmly and finally, while she would feel they'd reached only a momentary truce, which would have to be renegotiated time and time again. She had not yet begun to realize, however, that Jerome was getting his way more and more often.

Near the end of July, Nicole made a discovery that both disconcerted and pleased her. She was pregnant. According to her personal calendar, she must have conceived almost as soon as her affair with Jerome began. She alternated between despondency and elation. As much as she loved Jerome, and had come to depend on him, she'd never thought of their relationship in terms of lasting a lifetime. A child would force her to think along those lines.

447

Nor had she ever thought of herself as having a maternal drive, and she wondered how a child would affect her career. She looked into her cracked mirror and this time she liked what she saw. Already her face was fuller, and her arms had become plumper. Did such changes really take place so soon? She patted her belly. How odd to think about the little human being growing in there. Was it a boy or a girl? And could she possibly wait more than seven months to find out?

You precious little thing, she thought, patting herself again. *You're all mine.* It was exhilarating to see a painting come to life on canvas, but this creation was a wonder above all wonders. *I am happy, and Jerome will be, too. Won't he be surprised when I tell him!*

She dashed out, remembering this time to leave a note, and bought a new skirt and blouse and a bottle of very good wine. She never doubted he'd want to celebrate her announcement.

"Well," he said as soon as he came in, "look at the new clothes. Turn around and let me see."

"And this." She held up the wine.

He put his arms around her. "There must be a special reason." He kissed her. "Don't keep me in suspense."

"Tell me you love me first."

"I love you and you are the most important thing in my life."

"I'm pregnant."

First she felt his arms drop from around her, and then she saw his face go white.

"Don't be so shocked," she said. "It happens all the time."

"Are you sure?" He jammed his clenched fists into his pockets.

"Very sure. I have all the appropriate symptoms. Aren't you pleased?"

His eyes seemed to darken and recede into their sockets, and his mouth tightened into a narrow slit. "No. It will spoil everything. It will ruin you."

"Spoil? Ruin?" She couldn't stop the tremor in her voice or the shaking of her body. "Our child? The child of our love? What are you saying, Jerome?"

"You are an artist, Nicole. With my help you will become the greatest artist in France, maybe in the world. But a child will only get in the way. You think you have worked hard in the past, but from now on, you must devote every hour of the day to your art. A child will dissipate your energies."

"No, it won't. There'll be time for both. Anyway," she

turned aside and put the wine on the table, "it's too late to talk about it. I'm already pregnant."

England, he thought, and rubbed his hand frantically across his forehead. *It's England all over again.* Only it wouldn't be the same this time. He'd make certain of that. In Manchester, he'd defended a young woman accused of killing her infant by suffocation. In spite of all he did, she'd been found guilty and hanged. She'd been so beautiful, too, and such a talented writer. What no one knew was that the child had been his and he'd convinced her that her career as a writer, the career that he'd intended would afford him control over the minds of her readers, would be ruined by a child. The mistake had been to let the child be born and then killed. Only his parents had suspected the truth and insisted he leave England. The decision, of course, had been his own. This time would be different.

"It's not too late." He reached out and turned her around to face him. "Look at me, Nicole."

She did, and once again she felt her flesh and bones dissolving and her soul being drawn through his eyes into his mind. Her mind became one with his. "Yes, Jerome."

"You are not going to have the child. I know a doctor. We will go there tomorrow and it will be over in a few minutes."

"What are you suggesting?" She couldn't believe what she was hearing. "I'm not going to lose this child." It would take all her force of will to defy him. But what he wanted was both illegal and immoral. She was not concerned about flouting the law or religious enough to worry about committing a sin. Rather, she already loved the baby inside her and she wouldn't kill something she loved.

"Yes, you are." He clutched her shoulders. "You love me and you will do exactly as I tell you."

The worst of it was she loved him, too. She didn't see how she could live without him. But to deliberately destroy the seed of their love! "I can't do it, Jerome. Please don't ask it of me." She began sobbing uncontrollably.

"Yes, you can, my darling." He took her in his arms and rocked her gently back and forth. "Just love me and let me make all the decisions for you. Abide by them and everything will be all right. I promise you."

"I love you. I love you," she heard herself whispering over and over again.

"I know you do, and I'm going to take care of you and never let you be unhappy."

Jerome picked her up and carried her to the bed. Even as she clung to him, she hated herself for loving him as much as she did, and for giving herself so completely to him that she no longer had control over her own thoughts and actions.

When he left her later that night, Jerome kissed her gently. "Good night, my darling. I'll see you in the morning, and we'll make an appointment with the doctor. You know, of course, I can't let you make any other choice. Because if you should . . ."

He left the sentence unfinished, but Nicole knew what he meant. Any other choice would mean losing him, too. She didn't answer him, but shut the door quietly behind him.

There was no sleep for her that night. She was faced with a decision no woman should have to make—whether to keep her lover, the only man she'd ever loved, or her child, the child she already loved as deeply, as passionately, as she did Jerome.

Chapter Thirty-eight

"OH LORD, LISETTE," Baptiste said, "why didn't you come to me right away? We could have started annulment proceedings as soon as you left Philippe." He pulled at his mustache. He still found what his daughter had told him hard to believe. How she must have suffered those two months in Paris! And what sort of life had she been enduring since then? He loved all his children equally, but there'd always been a special tie with Lisette, perhaps because her mother hadn't wanted her and he felt he must somehow make up for that.

"I told you," Lisette said. "Philippe threatened to call in the notes. I had no idea how many or how much or the financial condition of the business. I didn't dare take the chance. Then there would have been the notoriety, the shame for you of having my marriage a failure. Philippe would refuse to admit he was at fault, and I'd have to try to find witnesses." She threw up her hands. "I came to you now because I could no longer stand the way things are. I need your advice."

"Victor—Monsieur Duchalais—would never have called in the notes on me. He would have been shocked to learn about his son, but he's a businessman, too, and he knew I'd be able to pay them back."

"I—I didn't know. How could I?" Lisette wrung her hands.

"My advice," Baptiste said, "is to proceed with the annulment. Lawyers can find witnesses, especially for a price. A little discreet investigating, and we can locate the right ones. It's unfortunate that you—that you've been living with Gerald. A doctor's examination would be the best evidence we could present that the marriage was not consummated."

Lisette knew there was no point in telling him she'd lost her virginity to Georges before she left Philippe, or about the few affairs she'd had between then and Gerald. Fathers rather liked to believe their daughters were angels, free of all human passions.

"How about the notes?" she asked. "Does the bank still hold some?"

"Not the same ones Philippe was talking about, but a few later ones since Jean bought the vineyard and we opened the winery. But they don't add up to enough to worry about. It's unfortunate, perhaps, that Monsieur Duchalais is dead and Philippe is now president of the bank, but I could always appeal to the board if he tried anything so foolish as to demand immediate payment. The business and the vineyards are doing too well."

"There, you see," Leah said. "I told you Papa would agree you should go ahead." She didn't know which had been more difficult: listening to Lisette tell Baptiste about her marriage or watching his face while she listened. She knew why he was more upset and disturbed than when Lisette ran off to England. He'd been blaming his daughter all this time for the failed marriage, no doubt comparing her to Catherine, her mother, and his tormented union with her. Baptiste had never spoken of that union, and she'd never asked about it. She long suspected, however, that Catherine had found the marriage intolerable. When Leah knew her just before her death in New Orleans, Catherine had taken a lover. From a few things Baptiste said, but more from his attitude toward Lisette, Leah sensed that Catherine had never wanted the child. Had, in fact, hated her.

"So," Lisette asked, "what do I do first?"

"Let me think about it a bit," Baptiste answered. "We should probably talk to lawyers whose primary cases are with the Church. There are several in the city. Some deal mostly with land or business suits, but I'm sure there are some who specialize in annulments. They're not as uncommon as you might think."

"We don't go to the bishop first?" Leah asked.

"No, I think we should have a lawyer make all the contacts, do all the talking for us. I don't think we should do a thing without his advice. Otherwise there's no point in having a lawyer."

"Well," Lisette said, "I asked for your advice, and I'm ready to take it, so I'll do the same with a lawyer."

"Give me a little time to ask around and find the best," Baptiste said. "Meanwhile, it will give your mother and me a great deal of pleasure having you here."

"Thank you, Papa. I'm glad I came. This is where I belong right now." For the first time in years she felt at home with them. Maybe it was because she was neither apprehensive nor anxious about returning to England. There was no reason to return now. She'd written to Gerald, telling him only that she was going home for a visit; there had been no answer from him asking her to stay. For better or for worse, that chapter in her life was over.

Baptiste talked to a number of Paris lawyers, but at the end of a week wasn't satisfied he'd found the right one. Each seemed to raise the same points of difficulty—mainly getting proof that the marriage had not been consummated—and he was disgusted at their refusal to take Lisette's word for it.

One lawyer said, "In the final analysis, your argument is not with me, it's with the Church. I'm not ready to appear before the Rota, or even submit a request to appear, with the scant evidence we have."

"Damn!" Baptiste said. "Then I'll find someone who is." If only he could have stalked summarily out rather than limping away on his crutches, he might have felt a little better. He was determined, though, not to give up. If his little girl wanted an annulment, he was going to get it for her.

Meanwhile, Lisette helped Leah in the garden, did a few unnecessary chores around the house, and wished she had something to keep her totally occupied.

"How's Robert doing at St. Cyr?" Lisette asked while she and Leah were sorting through some old linens. "I can't believe he's a man and old enough for military college."

"Not nearly so well as Henri did," Leah sighed, "and he's always involved in one scrape or another."

"Gambling? Drinking?" She was shocked.

"A little, but mostly just pranks. Henri was—is—always so serious about everything, whereas Robert thinks all of life is a joke."

"Sounds like he enjoys it more, though."

"Papa and I aren't exactly complaining. Robert has indicated a definite interest in the import business, and after Papa's disappointment in having neither Jean nor Henri join him, he'd approve of almost anything Robert did, short of murder or rape."

"Then he's not going to take a commission?" Lisette asked. "Why did he choose St. Cyr?"

"Probably because Henri went there. In spite of the differences between them, Robert adores Henri. But I can't decide if he reminds me more of Don Quixote or one of the Three Musketeers, ready to take on anyone or anything if he thinks the cause is noble—or there's a good fight involved. When you see him, note the scar over his left eyebrow and the one near his chin."

"Dueling?" Lisette was amused.

"Right."

"To protect the honor of a fair lady?" Lisette was almost laughing at the image of her brother flinging back his cape and brandishing his sword. Except men no longer wore capes except in the evening and the sword would now have to be a slender fencing épée.

"One I think was over a woman," Leah said. "The other had something to do with a horse. Don't ask me what. And I don't know how many other duels he's fought and come out of unscathed. He inherits the proclivity for a good fight from his father. Sometime I'll tell you about the duel he fought in New Orleans. Or at least the most serious of many."

"What do you mean, sometime? Now you have my curiosity aroused, I want to hear about it." Lisette set aside the pile of handtowels she'd intended to mend, and Leah tucked up her skirts and sat on the floor beside her.

"I don't know all the details, but I think he defamed a young woman's reputation—called her 'Mademoiselle Round-heels'—in the presence of her brother and several other young men. As I understand it, they had all enjoyed her favors, but it was not something to be mentioned aloud. So, naturally, the insult had to be avenged. Fortunately, neither of them was seriously injured, although, as your father so charmingly puts it, if the bullet had gone in two inches higher, he wouldn't be the father of six children."

"Oh, no!" Lisette laughed and rocked back on her heels. "I don't believe it. My own father!"

"So you see, we never know quite what to expect from any of the boys."

Or the girls, Lisette thought. How often, she wondered, did they think about Nicole and wish they knew how and where she was? Only Denise seemed to be enjoying a calm, placid, uneventful life that caused them no worry.

"You know what I think?" Leah said one day. "I think you should have your own apartment."

"Mama, I like staying here. Unless I'm in the way."

"Never that, Lisette. I didn't mean that. It would be right here. I just think you'd be happier in a place you could call your own."

"I'm confused." Lisette shook her head. "There are no apartments around here."

"I was thinking of turning Henri's workshop and Nicole's studio into an apartment for you. They—they're never used, and I don't think they will be again." She had to turn away to hide the tears that came whenever she thought about Henri in the States and Nicole, lost somewhere in Paris.

"Don't say that, Mama. They'll both be back sometime."

"I don't think so, Lisette. From his letters, I can see that Henri has a good marriage and a successful career. He doesn't need us anymore."

"There may come a time when he does. Look at me, independent Lisette who thought she knew exactly what she wanted."

"It's different with him. He's now a white man succeeding in a white man's world. His family no longer exists except to write to occasionally."

"Oh." As Catherine's daughter, Lisette had seldom given much thought to her stepmother's Negro heritage. Leah was Leah—and her mother, really—but the other children must have wondered sometimes if there would be any stigma attached to their ancestry. Henri obviously did and had chosen to exile himself in America.

"Still," Lisette tried to comfort her, "I'm sure he'll be back sometime. And you said Nicole came back once. She probably will again, and this time you'll be better able to understand her."

"Perhaps, but I no longer let myself dwell on that hope. Now, about the apartment. I'd really like to do it for you and for another reason, too. I've long wanted to close off the second floor, except when the family comes to visit. It will save a great deal of trouble for Blanchette, as she now finds it difficult to climb the stairs."

"Would it be much trouble to remodel those rooms?" Lisette was suddenly intrigued with the idea. She'd be able to bring over from London the few pieces she hadn't sold and furnish a charming parlor and bedroom.

"I don't think so. The rooms are large, but we could divide them up so you'd have a dressing room and bath and still have a good-sized sitting room and bedroom, or whatever you wanted. I think you'd probably like a fireplace in at least one of them."

"You make it sound quite ideal, Mama. If Papa agrees, we can get started right away." It would not only give her privacy, but something to do while awaiting the outcome of the annulment proceedings. If ever the proceedings got underway!

"Oh, Papa will agree," Leah said. "He never argues about something that is already a *fait accompli*. He'll fuss a little and then grin because he knows when he's licked."

Baptiste realized he should have known something was up when Leah wheeled him into the library and Lisette poured his brandy and handed him a cigar. *Someday*, he thought, *if I live long enough, I'll learn about the women in this family. And the tactics they use.*

But as Leah had predicted, he grinned and agreed to their plans. "Why do you always bring them to me worked out to the smallest detail?" he asked.

"It makes it so much easier to get you to agree."

"And now you're training Lisette to be as clever as you." Baptiste shook his head over the devious nature of his two females, all the while admitting to himself how much he loved them.

While the contractor went forward with the remodeling, Baptiste was making equally rapid progress with the lawyer he'd finally selected to handle the annulment case.

"I've talked extensively with Madame Duchalais," the attorney told Baptiste, "and I've gone over and over the deposition I prepared for her to sign and submit to the Rota. I don't know that they'll doubt her word, but it would be much simpler if we could get a statement from Monsieur Philippe

Duchalais. Even one saying he entered fraudulently into the marriage, unwilling to consummate it, without going into further detail."

"That's impossible," Baptiste said. "Lisette—Madame Duchalais—met with him only a few days ago. He stubbornly insists he will make no such statement, but in turn will file a countersuit claiming she is lying. You know his reputation in this city. It's impeccable."

"On the surface, yes. That simply means we must find witnesses. It will take time, but it can be done. Meanwhile, I suggest Madame Duchalais do nothing and say nothing that could be detrimental to her case. No word of why she is here, not the slightest hint to friends."

"She won't say a word, I can promise you that," Baptiste assured him. "This annulment means too much to her."

Baptiste was certain she hadn't said anything since coming to France, but he wasn't so sure about what she might have told friends before leaving England.

"No, Papa," Lisette said when he questioned her. "I didn't tell anyone, not even Gerald, why I was coming home. I simply said I wanted to get back here."

"And selling your things—that wouldn't make them suspicious?"

"No. If anyone asked, I said I was tired of them and would buy new things when and if I returned. They think me flighty enough to believe I'd do just that." Lisette changed the subject. "Does the attorney really believe he can find witnesses, people who will swear to the truth about Philippe? It could put them in jeopardy, too."

"Not the ones he's going to find. They won't be men who fear losing their reputations."

Lisette remembered what she'd heard about male prostitutes in England during the trial of Oscar Wilde. Philippe was such a fastidious person, she doubted he'd ever allowed himself to stoop so low. She would not bank her hopes in that direction. It would be her word, and her word alone, that would have to carry the case. She had to be believed. She could look forward to two, three, maybe even four years of waiting. Years during which papers were filed away for future examination, the numerous examinations themselves, and then maybe—just maybe—the case would be deemed worthy of presentation to the high tribunal. At any time, at any step along the way, it could be thrown out and it would be all over. Now she returned to selecting materials for the curtains in her new bedroom, but how would she occupy her time after the decorating was completed?

"Jean! What a pleasant surprise." Leah greeted her oldest with a kiss, and he responded with his usual bear hug. "But where are Céline and the children?"

"Home, and you might not think it's such a pleasant surprise when I tell Papa why I'm here."

"Is somebody ill?" Leah's hand went to her heart.

"They're fine."

"I'll call your father then." Céline and the children were Leah's concern. Business was Baptiste's affair. "Go on into the library. Papa is finishing breakfast, and I'll have Blanchette bring you coffee and hot rolls." She hurried down to the kitchen.

As he awaited his father in the library, Jean paced back and forth. He thanked Blanchette for the tray, but continued pacing while he drank the coffee and munched on a roll.

"For heaven's sake, Jean, sit down while you eat," Baptiste said as he rolled his chair in. "You'll get indigestion."

"Pacing helps me think," Jean said, but he automatically obeyed his father and sank down into the nearest chair.

"Will we be shipping a good quantity of wine this year?" Baptiste lit one of his long black cigars and poured himself a cup of coffee.

"Almost twice what we did last year, and of much superior quality," Jean said. "We'll soon have the reputation of sending the best champagne to the States."

"How about the harvest?"

Jean's face darkened and his eyes narrowed. "That's why I'm here. In one section, more than one-third of our acreage, the vines have split at the base, just above the ground. It's uncanny. Not one undamaged."

Baptiste thought for a minute. "A disease?"

"Could be, but I don't know which. It's nothing I've seen before."

"What does a one-third loss mean to us?"

"Well, we usually use two-thirds of the harvest in our own winery. The rest we sell to others. If we don't sell any, there'll be no revenue from the vines this year, but we'll earn it when we sell the champagne. If we do sell any of the grapes we harvest, there will be less champagne to sell in the future."

"Which decision do you advise?" Baptiste asked. He'd been leaving the management of the vineyards and the winery in Jean's capable hands, and he didn't want to take it away from him now.

"That's why I came to you. I don't know which would be best."

"I'd like to look at the vines. It's been a while since I've spent some time with you, and I think we have a problem here that needs my attention."

"Good. I was hoping you'd go back with me. I'm worried about the rest of the vineyards as well as puzzled about the damaged ones."

"Then," Baptiste said, "I'll ask Leah to get my things packed. Mama will ask lots of questions. Just tell her there's a small problem at the winery."

Baptiste and Jean left early the next morning on the train to Rheims. Jean's wagon would be waiting there for the drive to Villedommange. During the trip, they went over the figures of the past years' harvests and charted the increasing profit from champagne sales. "I think we'll keep all we harvest for our own winery," Baptiste said. "I see no need to sell any of the grapes." He paused a moment. "Have you asked Edouard to come and see what's damaging the vines?"

"I have. I told him I was hoping you'd come back with me, and he's coming over later today."

"Good," Baptiste said. "If it is a blight that's struck, he might know what to do about it."

After leaving the train, Baptiste and Jean rode southwest toward Villedommange. "I'm afraid this wagon isn't as comfortable as your carriage," Jean said, "but it's more practical. We don't really have any need for anything fancier here."

"It's fine, Jean." Baptiste braced himself with both hands, refusing to admit that the jolting sent excruciating pains through his legs and hips. *I must remember,* he told himself, *to give Jean and Céline a buggy for Christmas.*

He tried to forget his agony by watching the countryside they were passing through. They'd crossed the flat-topped Montagne de Rheims with its magnificent beech forest interspersed with dry gulleys and springs. They had now descended onto the plain and were driving along the winding road linking the various wine villages. On either side of the road, lush vineyards spread in all directions to the horizon.

It was a magnificent sight, as full of richness as the grapes themselves were of juice.

Céline welcomed them with open arms. "There's wine in the parlor, and lunch will be ready as soon as you've rested."

Céline grew plumper with each year, but she still had a sparkle in her eyes and a captivating smile for the two men. Jean had done well for himself, Baptiste thought. Céline was the perfect wife for him. In love with her husband, her sons, and her home, she asked nothing more than to be allowed to care for all of them. Baptiste smelled some spectacularly delicious aromas coming from the kitchen, and he drank his wine in pleasurable anticipation.

"The boys are in the vineyards," Jean said, "but they'll join us for lunch. They're really looking forward to seeing you."

"And I to seeing them. It's been far too long."

Baptiste didn't realize just how long until the boys walked in. At fourteen, Armand was nearly as tall as his father, but built along slimmer lines, more similar to Baptiste himself. And he had Céline's twinkling eyes and vivacious smile. "Welcome, Grandpapa," he said rather formally, "it's good to see you again." He took his seat and placed his napkin neatly across his lap.

Short and stocky, twelve-year-old Roland was a miniature of his father but with Céline's rich, reddish brown hair. His greeting was an exuberant hug, and he unashamedly kissed Baptiste on the mouth as well as on both cheeks. "what fun to have you here, Grandpapa." He knocked over his water glass when he reached for his napkin, used the linen to wipe up the spill, and then forgot about getting a dry one.

Céline placed a huge tureen of *pot au feu* in the middle of the round table and told them all to help themselves, while she cut off great chunks of bread hot from the oven and passed the freshly churned butter. When they'd finished the soup, she brought in a grilled chicken stuffed with its own liver chopped and mixed with garlic, onions, and herbs. Another platter held several trout delicately braised in wine and covered with a sauce of shallots, butter, and champagne. All this, along with vegetables and a dandelion salad, made Baptiste think he was sitting down to a feast in the palais-royal instead of a stone cottage.

"If you eat like this every day," Baptiste said, "I don't see how you can get up from the table and go to work in the afternoon."

Céline beamed at the compliment, and Jean patted his stomach. "Céline may have done a little more in honor of your being here," he said, "but you can look at both of us and see what a superb cook she is."

Edouard Valcou arrived in mid-afternoon, and the men immediately made plans to visit the damaged vineyards.

"I can take you part of the way in the wagon, Papa," Jean said, "but the walk through the vineyards may be too much for you."

"Let me try it. I want to see as much as I can."

"How about one of the harvesting carts?" Edouard suggested. "He could sit in that, and we could push him."

"Would you mind that?" Jean asked. "It wouldn't be very comfortable, but—"

"Sounds like the perfect solution," Baptiste said.

They rode from the house to the first of the vineyards. Pushing a small wheelbarrow Armand and Roland ran along beside the wagon. There were a few uneasy moments while Baptiste was transferred from the wagon to the barrow, where he had to sit with his knees drawn up. "I'm fine. I'm fine," he laughed, "although I'd be a damn sight better off if I'd left half my legs back at the house."

"Oh, Grandpapa," Armand wailed, "how can you joke about something like that?" The boys were so used to Baptiste's infirmity, they seldom thought about it. Only now did it strike Armand that perhaps they should feel pity for him.

"Better to joke, Armand," Baptiste said, "than to bemoan something that can't be helped. Now, let's be off."

They moved slowly up the hillside and among the hillocks of vines entwined around supporting posts and wire.

"See there," Jean pointed out to Edouard, "damaged just above the ground."

"I don't see any signs of disease," Edouard said, examining the vine with eyes and hands.

"It almost looks as if something, some animal" Baptiste said, "has come along and methodically chewed every one of them."

"I don't think so," Edouard said. "Look here." He pointed to one vine. "These vines have been cut, probably with an ax."

"Cut!" Baptiste exclaimed, looking at his son-in-law. Edouard was too knowledgeable about the cultivation of grapes for him to doubt his word, but such a verdict seemed absurd. "Are you quite certain?"

"I can't think of anything else that would damage them like this," Edouard said. "Look, each one was chopped in the same way."

"But who? Who would do this to us?" Jean asked.

"Is there anyone around here who would like to see our business ruined?" Baptiste asked.

"Absolutely not," Jean said firmly. "The other vintners have gone out of their way to help us and cooperate in every way possible. They've given advice when I asked for it and come over to see that things were going right at the winery. We've all helped one another out that way."

"Anybody who's wanted you to export their champagne whom you've refused?" Edouard asked.

"None that we've refused," Baptiste said. "Not all have been interested in doing that. I'd welcome more. We can handle all we can get."

"We must post watchmen for the next several nights," Edouard said. "This could be the work of some crazed person or someone you don't realize has been hurt by your success."

"We'll stay out here, Papa," Roland spoke up. "Armand and I will be glad to watch all night."

"Thank you both," Jean said, "but we'll also need men with guns."

"I'm still a good shot," Baptiste said, "if you have an extra gun."

"I don't know, Papa," Jean said. "It gets mighty cold out here at night."

"Nonsense, I'll sit in this barrow and wrap myself up in a blanket. Don't think you can leave me back at the house." Baptiste was ready for an adventure. He was tired of being forced to lead a sedentary life. He remembered the night, so many years earlier when the plantation had been threatened. He'd got up on a horse for the first time since he'd lost his legs and ridden all night and the following day to track down and kill the man who'd set fire to the cabins and outbuildings. He'd said then that no one destroyed what belong to Baptiste Fontaine, and he felt that same passion to protect what was his surging through him now.

"If you insist, Papa." Jean knew better than to argue when his father's mind was made up.

After dinner, Céline fixed baskets of food and jugs of hot coffee for them to take to the vineyards. Four of Jean's workers joined the crew of sentries, and his sons took dogs

461

along with them. They set up look-outs at strategic points in the undamaged fields. The quarter moon was covered by clouds from time to time. It was a good night for someone to sneak among the vines. But no one came. They maintained the watch for two more nights, seeing no intruders, although they heard wagons on the nearby road.

"What do you think, Edouard?" Baptiste asked on the third morning.

"I think we had visitors, but something frightened them off. Either they saw us or they heard the dogs barking. I don't think we need to spend our nights out there any longer, but I would ask some of your workers to alternate watching, along with the dogs, until harvest."

"Good idea," Baptiste said. "I'm exhausted, and Leah is going to worry if I don't get back soon. We may never learn the answer, but I think we need to save ourselves for the harvest. I'll be back then with Leah and Lisette." He turned to Edouard. "Expect a visit from them, too. I think Leah has some things for the children."

"Doesn't she always," Edouard said. "We'll be glad to see Lisette, too. Denise will be delighted to learn she's coming for a visit." He said it was time for him to be returning to his own vineyards.

Baptiste clapped his grandsons on the shoulder and told them what a fine job they'd done during the three previous nights. He kissed Céline good-bye. "I've probably put on ten pounds, thanks to your cooking. Leah will be pleased, but I'll have to have all my trousers let out."

"Thank you, Papa," Céline said. "Come again soon, and maybe next time it will be more of a pleasure visit."

"Oh, I enjoyed every minute of it." He had, too.

The answer to the question of who wanted to destroy the vineyards came almost as soon as Baptiste returned home. More tired than he realized after spending his nights in the fields, he decided to stay home from the office for a few days and leave the running of the Paris firm to his able managers. He was at the château when the post brought a letter from the bank. Philippe, now president, was demanding payment, in full, of the outstanding notes.

"Damn!" Baptiste exclaimed after reading the letter twice.

"What is it, dear?" Leah asked. She'd been reading a note from Denise.

462

"He wants payment in full immediately. He can't do that."

"What are you ranting on about?" Leah was still smiling over Denise's descriptions of the children's latest accomplishments and how much they all looked forward to her promised visit.

"It's from Philippe. We took out notes at the bank to buy the winery and additional ones later when we needed new equipment. We've been making regular payments on the principal as well as interest. When Victor died, Philippe assured me he'd honor his father's agreement for us to take as long as we needed to repay them. Now he's demanding full payment."

"Can he do that?" Leah asked.

"Unfortunately he can. They were signature loans and as such are demand loans."

"I thought Victor had invested in the vineyards, too."

"He did," Baptiste said, "and as his heir, Philippe inherited his share of the vineyards and the winery. It's only a small percentage, but—"

"But what?" Leah asked impatiently.

"I guess it's right you know. Jean came here and took me back to Villedommange because at least one-third of the vineyards have been destroyed."

"Oh, no!" Leah moaned. "Disease? Can the rest be saved?"

"Not disease. Someone deliberately chopped them off near the ground. None of us could figure out who would do such a thing. Now I wonder. Could it be Philippe's doing?"

"But if he has a share, isn't he hurting himself as well?"

"No," Baptiste said. "His share comes off the top before any distribution of the revenues. That was our agreement with Victor when he invested with us."

"Why is he demanding payment of the notes now? Will you be able to cover them?"

"I don't know yet, but I think the export business has enough in the surplus fund. The sales of champagne will provide the income for Jean. If Philippe is behind the destruction, it's the damnable, insidious nature of the action that infuriates me. Ruining good crops! Making threats."

Damn the man! Leah thought. *First he ruins Lisette's life, now he threatens ours and Jean's.* "There must be a solution."

"There is," Baptiste said, "in the last paragraph. He won't call in the notes if Lisette agrees to withdraw her petition for an annulment."

"He's a beast," Leah fumed. "That's the whole reason for all of this—the damage, the notes, everything. Using the rest of the family to blackmail her into doing what he wants. What are you going to do?"

"Not say a word to Lisette. She's going to have her annulment."

"Good for you, darling." She went over and kissed him. "But I knew you'd say that."

"Not a word to Lisette."

"No, no," Leah promised. "She'd insist on agreeing to his demands."

They both turned, startled, as the library door opened.

"You don't need to worry about keeping it a secret," Lisette said. "I heard enough to know what I have to do."

"You are going ahead with the annulment," Baptiste insisted. "And you're not to argue about it."

"I think that's my decision, Papa. I'm not going to let anyone worry or suffer for my sake. You and Mama are doing enough for me already, taking me in and supporting me." She'd been notified earlier that her allowance had been stopped and the trust fund dissolved the minute she instituted annulment proceedings.

"You're very generous, Lisette," Baptiste said, "but I think this is a family decision, not yours alone. We're all involved—in the vineyards and in your happiness. I'll go into the city tomorrow. If my memory isn't faulty, I think there's enough in the firm's surplus accounts to take care of most of what we need."

"I'll go in with you. One way or another I need to talk to the lawyer. But, Papa, the final decision will be mine."

Leah looked at the two of them, father and daughter, facing each other with love and determination. *Baptiste always says I'm stubborn*, she thought, *but I can't hold a candle to either of them when their minds are made up*. If only there was a solution that was right for the whole family. Lisette had been a different person since freedom from Philippe had become more of a possibility than a dream. She must not be denied that freedom. At the same time, Leah well knew the dangers inherent in decreasing the firm's surplus to a point where they couldn't weather a loss either in trade or any of the company ships. Two had foundered and been sunk in the past six months.

Leah left Baptiste and Lisette talking and went to see Blanchette about lunch. A good meal could often help settle things.

Chapter Thirty-nine

NICOLE HAD NEVER CONSIDERED HERSELF a religious person. She'd attended church as a child with the same attitude she'd had when she sat down to the dinner table or gone to bed: It was a familiar routine. When she grew older, the mysticism implicit in parts of the Mass moved and fascinated her; however, she never felt strongly that God took a personal interest in her and so considered prayers of supplication a waste of time. If she wanted something, she either found a way to get it for herself or she accepted the fact it was not for her.

Since coming to Paris, she'd visited a number of churches, but merely to be inspired by the artistry of the stained-glass windows or the magnificence of the sculpture and the structures themselves. Often, she did sketches of the worshippers she saw, aged women in black shawls, fingering their beads with the sure knowledge that what they asked would be granted, or old men, painfully lowering themselves to their knees on the cold stone floors. Seldom did she see any young or middle-aged worshippers.

It came as a distinct shock then, when she realized that one reason she didn't want to get rid of the child within her was her horror at committing the sin of murder. Her immediate reaction to Jerome's suggestion of an abortion was an incredible sense of loss, not only the loss of something belonging to her, but of something she'd created. It would be like destroying a perfect work of art. She would have had the same feeling if she'd watched her mother or father tear up one of her first childish sketches. Being hers, the child was precious. Only later came the fear of committing an unforgivable sin; it was a fear that reawakened in her conscience the inexorable power of guilt.

Then she thought about losing Jerome, and she knew the pain of that loss would be no easier to bear. She remembered the look in his eyes when she told him she was pregnant, and she began to wonder if he were mad. Not angry, but insane. Only madness would demand the killing of an unborn child.

The words *killing* and *child* kept repeating themselves in her mind, and something began to emerge from the recesses of her memory. The night they met. Sitting at the table in the restaurant when she'd been so intent on eating and avoiding his eyes, she hadn't really listened to him. Now, though, what he'd told her came through as clearly as if she'd memorized it. He'd defended a woman accused of killing a child. He'd lost the case and had fled to France. Why had that case been so important to him? Why had he been so moved or upset by it that he couldn't stay in England? He'd said something about his parents' insisting he leave and that they sent him money every month to stay away. They had known something.

Oh, it was all clear now. The child must have been Jerome's. The woman, his lover. But why had she killed the child? Because he'd insisted on it. The woman? What was it he had told her about the woman? The answer remained tantalizingly out of reach. She wasn't married; but that hadn't been the problem. She was young, and Jerome had said something about her being beautiful. Yet there was something more. An artist like herself? No. Nicole found herself pacing the floor. She walked to the window and then back to the table. Casually, she picked up a book Jerome had left behind, and then she tossed it back down again. She was in no mood for reading. But she was in no mood for painting, either, and she had to do something besides walk back and forth. She looked at the title page on which the author had written a brief inscription to Jerome. That was it! The young woman had been a writer. Nicole felt better now that she'd thought of it, although what the woman had been didn't really matter; it was not being able to remember that bothered her.

A writer and an artist. What did they have in common that would attract a man like Jerome? Maybe the woman was a free spirit like herself, with an independence that challenged Jerome's desire to dominate.

"No!" Nicole screamed aloud. She would not be destroyed like that tragic young woman in England. She would not subjugate her will to Jerome's.

She looked at the clock. Jerome had said early in the morning. He would be there soon, and she dreaded seeing him. She was frightened. If he touched her, if he looked at her, she would again become as pliant in his hands, as easily tamed, as a puppy. Nor did she mean any more to him than that, something cute and lovable, something to be fondled and cherished—as long as she obeyed.

No, she wouldn't be waiting for him. He'd have to come and find her. He would find her, but the fact that she had disobeyed him by leaving the room would shake him up, weaken his power over her. Hurriedly, she put on a clean skirt and blouse and went to the café. She was staring at her coffee cup when he walked in.

"Good morning," he said, bending over to kiss her. "You're looking especially lovely this morning."

Nicole was the one taken aback. She'd expected him to be furious, not complimenting her on the way she looked. "Thank you," was all she could manage to say.

"I'm glad to see you're up and ready to make our little visit this morning." He smiled as benevolently as a priest; in the past, though, priests had officiated at sacrifices.

"I'm not going. I've decided against it."

"Yes, you are. Don't let's start that again. It makes everything so unpleasant." He signaled to Monsieur Ébert. "I'll have some coffee with you. There's no need to hurry. I've already made the arrangements."

"Just as you say, Jerome." She couldn't bear to quarrel with him here. She'd find an excuse to return to her room and then send him away. She didn't dare look at him, not because she was afraid of what his eyes might do, but because she was going to lose him, and she loved him so much it hurt.

She began to sip her coffee slowly as Jerome told her more about the plans for her showing. "Monsieur Engle has suggested I help with the hanging of the paintings. He values my opinion very highly. He has assured me there will be a number of critics there as well as buyers." He reached over and took her hand. "You will soon be a very famous artist, Nicole. We will then have to be thinking about a touring show. You will like that. We'll travel all over France and perhaps to England."

Yes, I would, Nicole thought. But if the show were successful, she could do that on her own, with Monsieur

467

Engle's help, of course. She wouldn't need Jerome. But she did need him; she needed his love and reassurance. If only she could convince him that a baby would not be in the way, would not keep her from working. No, that was not the reason he wanted it destroyed. He simply wanted her to do what he asked without questioning him.

"When can I meet Monsieur Engle?" she asked.

"He's a very busy man, Nicole. You'll meet him the day the show opens."

"And I'm to have no say as to how the paintings are hung?" After all, they were hers, and she knew which ones she wanted grouped together.

"No need for you to worry about that, my darling. That is one thing I can take off your hands."

There seemed to be no way to fight him, to regain control over herself.

"If you're finished," he said, "we can go."

She stood up and followed him meekly out the door. He merely shrugged off her suggestion of returning to her room. There was still time, though. She'd go to the doctor's; then, once there, she'd refuse the operation.

She thought, of course, they would drive down from Montmartre into the city. Instead, she found herself following Jerome through a number of narrow streets and back alleys. Finally he stopped at an old, decrepit house. There was no brass plaque on the door, no indication it was a doctor's office. They went into a dark, low-ceilinged hall and walked back to another door in the rear.

"I—I thought we were going to a doctor's office," she whispered.

"This man is a doctor. You'll see. Everything will be all right. You trust me, don't you?"

It was no longer a matter of trust, but of fear. In England he'd had a child killed, and the mother was hanged as a murderer. Was he about to solve this problem by having her killed in addition to the baby? No one would know, not here in Montmartre, where transients and violent death were as common as the rats.

She had to find a way to escape. There was a rear door, partly open, through which she saw courtyard, but Jerome was gripping her arm so tightly, there was no hope of freeing herself. It would have done little good anyway; the courtyard was walled in and she'd be trapped.

Jerome knocked on the door of the back room, and it was opened by a stooped, elderly man with thin, yellowish white hair, heavily wrinkled skin, and sagging jowls. Jerome pushed Nicole in ahead of himself.

"No, monsieur," the old man said, "you stay out here. It will take only a few minutes."

Jerome growled something under his breath, but did as he was told. Nicole was surprised; she expected him to insist he be allowed inside. "And the money, monsieur?" The man held out a skeletal hand. Nicole watched as Jerome peeled off a number of franc notes. She had no idea such an operation was so expensive. But then it was illegal, and crime was costly.

The old man, or doctor as Jerome had referred to him, led her inside and told her to lie on the bed. Everything about the room was filthy: the curtains, the bare floorboards, the one table. The quilt she was to lie on was no cleaner than the one she'd got rid of when she went to live with Jules. In stark horror, she watched as the doctor picked up a stiletto, tapered at the end like a knitting needle, and wiped it on his trousers. That was what he would use to destroy the child she carried inside. She cringed as if already feeling the pain of insertion. He laid the instrument on the table again and poured something from a brown pharmacist's bottle onto a soiled cloth.

"You won't feel anything, my dear," he said in a voice meant to be soothing but evil-sounding and malicious. "When you wake up, it will all be over."

He held the cloth near her face, and she smelled the sickly sweet aroma of chloroform.

"No! Please, I don't want it done. I don't want to lose the baby. Please, please, let me go!"

The odor grew stronger as he laid the cloth across her mouth and nostrils. She tried to struggle against it and against him, but the last thing she remembered was the bed spinning beneath her as she lost consciousness.

In spite of Baptiste's insistence that a way could be found to pay the bank notes, Lisette informed her lawyer she wanted the annulment proceedings dropped.

"It's not fair to you," Leah said. "Philippe is being beastly about the whole thing."

"It's not really that important to me, Mama. If I were in love with someone who wanted to marry me, it would be different. It was just the idea of being free of him that appealed, and in a way I've been free for a long time. Papa

469

won't have to worry anymore, and Philippe may re-establish the trust fund. I won't be dependent on you."

They were in the remodeled apartment, attending to some final touches. It had been wonderful, Leah thought, having Lisette with them. She hoped she wouldn't decide to return to England after they'd had all this done for her. Not that she regretted the work or the expense; it had been fun. The apartment would be useful when the others came to visit. But she'd miss Lisette terribly.

"This has really turned out to be a beautiful room," Leah said, looking around the parlor now furnished with Lisette's things.

"The whole apartment is perfect. I'm really going to enjoy it." She walked into the tiny kitchen they'd installed as an afterthought. "And you must come every afternoon and have tea with me."

"Then you're staying?" Leah asked. "You're not going back to England?"

"I see no reason to. There's nothing, no one, over there to take me back. I'd like to spend some time in Paris, renew old acquaintances, make new ones. If it doesn't sound foolish, I might even see if I can study at the conservatory again."

"Not foolish at all," Leah said. "I think it's a wonderful idea." She rearranged some figurines on the mantel of the fireplace they'd had built in the parlor. "One on each end, Lisette, or grouped together? I can't make either way look right."

Lisette stood back and surveyed the mantel. "Put them together on this end. I have an idea." She went into the bedroom and looked in her trunk. "Here, we'll put these on the other end." She handed Leah a pair of tall, carved ivory candlesticks. "And the Limoges clock in the center. It never did look right on the end table."

"Madame Fontaine?" Blanchette rapped gently and walked in. "There is a caller, a gentleman caller, for Mademoiselle Lisette. I've shown him into the library."

"A caller! Who in the world would be coming to see me here?" Her heart fell at the thought it might be Philippe. But, no, he'd never come to the château to see her. Anyway, Blanchette knew him and would have told her right away if it were he.

"Yes, ma'am. A Monsieur Boswick."

"Gerald! Here?" Lisette was as stunned as the day he'd shown up when she was recovering from pneumonia.

470

"Go see him," Leah said. "I'll come along in a bit. I'm looking forward to meeting him."

Lisette picked up her skirts and ran down the hall to the library. She didn't care if it were unladylike; she couldn't wait to see him, and she didn't stop running until she was in his arms.

"What are you doing over here?" she asked when he finally stopped kissing her.

"Seeing you. You can tell me you don't love me and don't want to come back to me, but I couldn't stay away any longer."

"I don't understand, Gerald." His arms around her were warm and comforting. She let her head rest against his chest. "Our separation was your doing, not mine. You were the one who went off to Scotland and stayed God knows how long."

"Only because I had to. I explained that. When I got back to London, you'd gone off with your mother. Before I could get in touch after you returned, you'd come over here. What was I to think except you didn't want to see me anymore?"

"But not a note, not a word all that time. I could only come to the conclusion that you didn't want to see me."

"I'm sorry, Lisette." He gathered her into his arms again. "I'm a stupid, thoughtless man."

"No." She touched his lips with her fingers. "Just a bit careless at times."

"And you'll forgive me?"

"I forgive you." Gerald was back and all the disappointment over the annulment was forgotten. That there could be no marriage no longer seemed to matter.

"How would you like to celebrate?" he asked. "By going on a long trip? We could tour Italy and Switzerland and Germany."

"I'd love it. And there are lots of places in France I haven't seen."

"We'll be gone as long as you like," he said. "And we'll not come back until we've seen everything we want to see."

There was a tentative knock at the library door.

"That's Mama," Lisette said. "We were in my new apartment when Blanchette said you were here."

"I like her sense of timing," Gerald said, kissing Lisette on the nose and letting her go.

"She is very understanding and tactful. You'll love her."

471

She walked over and opened the door. "Come in, Mama, and meet Gerald."

"Welcome to France," Leah said. "I hope you'll be able to stay a while."

"For a few days, yes. I have reservations at a hotel in Paris."

"No indeed," Leah said firmly, "you must stay here with us. We've plenty of room. If you and Lisette want to spend some time in the city, you can stay at our apartment there. No need at all for a hotel."

"Thank you, ma'am. I can't think of anything that would give me more pleasure."

"Lisette," Leah turned to her daughter, "wouldn't you like to show Gerald the new apartment? And he might like to take his luggage along with him." She'd seen the suit-cases in the hall. So he'd come here before going into the city. He must have been very anxious to see Lisette.

"To the apartment, Mama?" Lisette looked a bit stunned.

"Yes. As long as he's going to stay here, he might want to unpack and change after the long trip." She noted the smile on Gerald's face. Well, she was not going to play the hypocrite. She knew they wanted to be together, and she might as well let them know right away she didn't mind if they shared a bedroom. She'd prefer that to having them tiptoe around the house in the night. Her own mother had moved in with her and Baptiste while they were in New Orleans and had accepted their relationship. She could do no less now herself.

Baptiste was just as enthusiastic as Leah in his greeting to Gerald. "Consider this your home as long as you're over here," he said. Anyone who could bring that look of joy to Lisette's face was more than welcome. He'd been stunned when Leah had announced that Gerald had ar-rived and had already settled into the apartment.

"Not a word about it," Leah said sternly. "Don't play the enraged father. They want to be together and they can't be married, so that's that."

"Am I likely to forget those years we had together before we came to France?" he asked.

"I didn't think you would, but I also didn't think it would hurt to remind you."

In the afternoon, the subject of the vineyards came up.

"I'd like to take a look at them and the winery," Gerald

said. "I've always been fascinated by wine production, especially champagne. Do you suppose Jean would mind showing me around and explaining it all to me?"

"Not at all," Baptiste said. "I'd like to go back with you. We could go on over to Versenay where Denise, another daughter, and her husband live. Edouard's been a prosperous vintner for many years."

"Would you mind?" Gerald asked Lisette. He was actually asking if she objected to postponing their trip for a little while.

"Not if I can go with you. I'd planned to visit them later in the fall, but I'd rather go now."

"Then we'll make it a family outing," Leah said. She certainly wasn't going to be left at home.

"How soon can we leave?" Gerald asked. He had an idea in the back of his mind, and the sooner he discovered whether it were feasible, the sooner a lot of problems would be solved —for him and for Lisette's family.

"As soon as the women look over their wardrobes and see if they have the right clothes," Baptiste said with mock seriousness.

"Two hours, then, no longer," Leah said, half cross and half teasing. Baptiste could be so infuriating in his opinions of women.

"Then let me send wires to Jean and Edouard. We can take the morning train to Rheims day after tomorrow. You women might be able to get ready in two hours, but I think we should give Céline more time than that to prepare for our visit."

Gerald was no stranger to Rheims, with its magnificent cathedral of Notre Dame and its basilica of St. Remi, but like so many other tourists, he'd never traveled south into the magnificent countryside where the world-famous champagne was produced. As they drove in the hired carriage through the plain where the wine villages nestled, he looked up toward the vine-clad slopes and felt an eager stirring in his blood. Even the air was lush and fecund. His life in England had become sterile and useless. He was tired of London, and even Scotland and Cornwall could no longer rouse him from the apathy that seemed to have taken hold. Life was bursting out in the fields around him, and he wanted to be a part of that renewal. More and more his plan seemed a good one. He'd look at the vineyards and the winery and then talk to Monsieur Fontaine.

"This is a good time to come," Jean said to Gerald after

473

Baptiste explained why they were there. "We won't be harvesting for a few weeks, and the winery is fairly quiet, but that will give me more time with you. I can explain the processes and some you can see for yourself."

"I want to know all about it," Gerald said. "Why this land is so good for wine and how each successive step contributes to the final product."

The whole family had retired to Jean's parlor after one of Céline's breath-stopping meals. Armand and Roland had asked to be excused, and now the conversation turned serious. Céline brought in chilled bottles of champagne, and Jean was pouring. "Taste this," he said, handing a glass to Gerald. "It's a near-perfect example of what you're asking about."

Gerald sipped it slowly. "I'd say it was more than near perfect. It's excellent."

"Never perfect," Jean said. "There are always ways to improve. Now to answer your first question. The slopes of the higher ground cover vast deposits of chalk, I believe they were once cliffs, like your cliffs of Dover. The roots of the vines go several yards deep into those chalk deposits, which seem to offer just the type of soil our vines require. Those ancient cliffs offer another advantage. There are over a hundred miles of cellars under the roots in which the champagne is stored and matured. We'll go down there while you're here."

"Sounds fascinating," Gerald said.

"Here," Céline said, passing around a plate, "try another delicacy of our region." On the plate were arranged slices of Brie cheese alternating with quarters of rousselet pears and plump cherries.

"Thank you, Céline. Between you and Jean, you make a man want to settle down here."

"You could do worse," Jean said. "It's not London or Paris, but it offers a contentment not to be denied." He looked lovingly at Céline, who blushed under his gaze. "Stay with us awhile and you won't want to leave."

"Speaking of leaving," Baptiste said, "I wonder if we should make certain there's room at the village inn for us."

"There's room right here," Jean said. "The boys are sleeping in one of the *vendangeoirs*." He saw the confused expressions on the faces of Lisette and Gerald. "Those are buildings located throughout the vineyards where the grape pickers live during harvesting. The winepresses are there, too. Grapes must be pressed as soon after picking and sorting as possible. Tomorrow I'll show you how the presses work."

"We don't like putting the boys out," Leah said.

"Nonsense," Jean assured her. "They're thrilled at being allowed to sleep out alone all night. Céline and I will sleep in the small room under the eaves, so two of you can have our bed. No, no," he said, when he saw Leah about to fuss again, "we often do when Denise and Edouard come over."

"We'll take the boys' room," Lisette said quickly, as if sleeping in two single beds would mitigate the impropriety of sharing a room with Gerald.

"Where do you want to go first?" Jean asked Gerald the next morning.

"Somewhere to walk off that enormous breakfast Céline fed us. I thought the French ate only rolls and coffee for breakfast."

"Not the farmers. There's too much hard work to do between dawn and dinner. The vineyards, then. You said you wanted to follow the process from the beginning, and that's where it starts."

"I'll stay here with more coffee and a cigar," Baptiste said. "My memory of being hunched up in that barrow when we guarded the fields is still strong and painful."

Gerald followed Jean up the road from the village to the slopes. The blazing September sun was alleviated somewhat by a cool morning breeze, but Gerald began to sweat before they'd reached the first row of vines. *Just getting up here is hard work,* he thought.

"These are *Meunier Noir,*" Jean said, holding a heavy cluster of fruit in his palm. "Only three species of vine are grown here in Champagne. Called the *cépages nobles,* they are this *Meunier Noir,* and *Pinot Noir* and *Chardonnay.*"

"And the variety determines the taste or bouquet?" Gerald asked.

"Not entirely. Grapes from this area produce a robust and full-bodied wine. Those from the Marne Valley have a powerful, fruity bouquet, whereas the wines from the Côte des Blancs area are very delicate and fresh. We produce champagne from only our own grapes, but many of the champagne houses in Rheims and Épernay blend the wines from different harvests and different areas to produce their own particular brand. A real wine connoisseur can tell by taste exactly which grapes from which sections are blended in any one champagne."

"Very interesting," Gerald said. "So the grapes you sell to a champagne house rather than processing them yourself may end up in combination with any number of others."

"Exactly," Jean said.

"And your father tells me you won't have any to sell this year because of the damage to a third of the vines."

"We haven't decided about that yet. I'd like to keep them for ourselves, but that may not be possible."

I think it will, Gerald said to himself. He was becoming more and more convinced that his idea was a good one. After he'd seen a little more, he'd approach Monsieur Fontaine about it

"This is a *vendangeoir,* the building where we press the grapes and where the boys slept last night." He walked over to the press. "These wide, shallow presses are designed to ensure the juice will not be colored by the skins. Only the first pressing will be made into champagne."

"And it flows into these vats?" Gerald asked.

"Yes, the first fermentation—up to six weeks—takes place here. During the winter, the wine will be racked several times until it is clear. If we're going to do any blending, we do it in the spring. This results in what is called a *cuvée.*"

"At what point in this process is it bottled?" Gerald asked.

"First we must add the *dosage,* a carefully measured amount of cane-sugar and yeast enzymes. Bottles are then stacked on their sides in those deep cellars I told you about. We'll go down there a little later. They'll stay there for three to five years while the sugar is transformed into alcohol and gas to make the wine effervescent. During this second fermentation, sediment forms. We get rid of that by placing the bottles neck down in *pupitres,* or wooden stands, and every day a highly skilled *remur* rotates the bottles. This increases the angle so the sediment will come to rest on the corks."

"And you have such skilled men?" Gerald was especially interested to learn how large the family-owned operation was, compared to the large champagne houses in Rheims.

"Yes, me. We can't afford many full-time employees, and the most important of those work in the vineyards. Along with all the other help Edouard gave us, he spent hours training me."

"How do you get that sediment out if the bottles are corked?"

"That was only the first corking. During the *dégorgement,* during which we freeze the necks of the bottles, the sediment is frozen into a small block of ice, and when the bottle is uncorked, it will be shot out by the carbonic gas. Finally, we top them with cane-sugar dissolved in mature champagne and cognac. The amount of sugar we add will determine whether the wine will be dry, *demi-sec,* or sweet. Then we do the final sealing and the wine is left to settle. The sooner it is drunk after the *dégorgement,* the better it will be. If in doubt about how long since the *dégorgement,* buy a jeroboam, the equivalent of four bottles, rather than a magnum. The bigger the bottle, the longer the wine will remain in top condition. So, if you're serving a large party, one rehoboam, or six bottles, or a mathusalem, eight bottles, is better than three or four magnums."

"I'll remember that," Gerald said. "I appreciate the information."

During this conversation, the men had been walking from the vineyards to the small winery, where the bottles were labeled and the general running of the business was taken care of. From there they went into the deep caverns beneath the fields, the cellars where the champagne was stored while it matured, and Gerald watched as Jean examined previous years' harvests and gently turned the bottles.

"What do you think of it?" Jean asked as he and Gerald walked back to the house.

"I'm impressed. I'll enjoy drinking it even more now that I know all that's involved."

"Wait until you see Edouard's operation. It makes mine seem very small. Having those vines destroyed will be a serious drawback for several years. It's not only the time it takes to replace the topsoil in all the vineyards—that's something we have to do by hand—but when we do replant, it will be four years before the vines bear fruit. Four years before we can sell those grapes or at least seven years before we'll see champagne from them. I wish I could be optimistic about recovering."

Gerald listened quietly, his mind made up.

"Did you enjoy the tour?" Baptiste asked when Jean and Gerald returned.

"Very much. It's quite an operation."

"That's how I felt the first time I saw all that Jean had accomplished with Edouard's help. There are problems now, but we'll manage."

"Yes, I saw the damaged vineyards. A tragedy, a real

477

blow." Gerald looked toward Baptiste and wondered how to approach this proud man.

"We'll simply have to tighten our belts. We've done it before."

"If I may, sir," Gerald said, "I'd like to offer a suggestion. I was impressed enough by what you and Jean are doing here to want to be a part of it. If you would accept me as a partner, I'd like to buy those notes from the bank. You can either consider the money as my share of the partnership or you can pay me back over a number of years."

"Are you serious?" Baptiste asked. This offer would be a lifesaver for the business and for Lisette. It didn't seem that Gerald had made the offer lightly. He wasn't in either the mood or the position to turn it down, so he wasn't about to pass it off as a momentary gesture of good will.

"Very serious. I like what I've seen and I want to share in it."

"You're not doing it just for Lisette's sake?"

"Not at all. If you'll accept me as a partner, I mean to be an active one. To live near here and learn all I can from Jean and Edouard so that I can be of real help."

"Then welcome aboard." Baptiste held out his hand, and Gerald walked over to shake it. "Your being here will be as important as the money you put into it."

"I still want to visit with Edouard and Denise," Gerald said. "I want to see his operation, and I know Lisette wants to see her sister. Then, if you agree, we can see a lawyer to draw up the papers, and I'll see Philippe at the bank."

"Just what I was going to suggest," Baptiste said. "Jean is completely in charge of the business here, and I have only a one-fourth interest. His share is one-half. You might not know that Philippe also inherited one-fourth of the business from his father. He may try to cause trouble, but Jean and I can outvote him. Be prepared, however, for some arguments from him."

"Why don't I try to buy that share from him, too?"

"If you can," Jean said, "it would solve many problems. Then you and I can split the three-fourths share between us. How does that sound, Papa?"

"Very good, if Gerald agrees. He'll be putting a great deal of money into the business if he gets Philippe's share as well as buying the notes."

"That's all I want," Gerald said. "In fact, it seems like more than it should be as long as Jean is running the business."

"Not so," Jean said. "If you do come in as an active partner, you'll do your share of the work."

"Agreed," Gerald laughed. "You know, I actually look forward to getting out and working in the vineyards. It will be quite a change from getting my exercise stalking deer or riding to the hounds."

"More hard work than just exercise," Jean said. "You'll find muscles hurting you didn't even know you had."

"But exhilarating, because the work is productive." He leaned back and took one of the long black cigars Baptiste offered him. Now that all this was settled, he had one more hurdle to overcome. How would Lisette accept the news that he was planning to live here in a small village and become a farmer? He'd come to France to try to persuade her to return to England with him after their long Continental tour; now, here he was getting ready to settle down in the French countryside. He only hoped the shock wouldn't be too much for her.

"You're going to do what!" Lisette exclaimed when he told her the news.

"I'm going into partnership with Jean and your father." He waited anxiously for her next words.

"Then I did hear you right. Oh, Gerald, I think that's fine, just fine."

"You do approve? I wasn't at all sure how you'd feel about it."

"How could I be anything but pleased?" she asked.

"You can proceed with the annulment if it all works out."

"I don't care that much about the annulment. Philippe be damned! But I do care that Papa and Jean won't have to worry anymore."

"You ready to start looking for a house near here?" It was a less than subtle means of telling her his plans to be an active partner, but he could find no better way to broach the subject.

"How often do you plan to be here?" Lisette was puzzled. Gerald and she could always stay with Jean when he thought it necessary to visit.

"I plan to live here. I'm going to be working right alongside Jean. It's not just the money I'm putting into it, but myself as well. Will you be with me? It won't be Paris or London."

"I went to Cornwall, didn't I? I think I'd love having a house of our own." A house of their own. They'd never had one before. It had been hers and his in London and only his in Cornwall. It would be almost as good as being married.

"And we won't be far from Rheims or Paris. We can visit them when we find the bucolic life boring. Or to St. Denis when you want to see your family or I need to talk business with your father."

"The apartment. All that time and work Mama put into it, and I won't be living there." She hated the thought of disappointing Leah after assuring her she'd be staying at home from now on.

"Disappointed?" Leah said, when they told her the news. "I'm as pleased as I can be. After all, when Gerald came over here to see you, I assumed you'd be returning to England. Now, with Robert going into business with his father when he graduates, most of the family will be together again."

Most, but not all. Neither Nicole nor Henri were ever very far from her thoughts. Henri she missed but did not worry about. Success was evident in every letter he wrote. Baptiste kept hoping he and Louise would come to Paris soon, for a short visit at least, but Leah knew why they would not. Henri would never run the danger of exposing his mother's heritage to Louise. With Nicole, it was different. There was no point in worrying about what could not be helped, but she could mourn quietly for the loss of a daughter who'd always had a very special place in her heart.

Philippe refused unequivocally to allow Gerald to buy up the notes the bank held against Baptiste. "They're my one guarantee Lisette won't continue with the annulment proceedings."

"Aren't you being a bit shortsighted?" Gerald suggested. "If Monsieur Fontaine decides to pay off the notes, you will have lost that guarantee anyway."

"But he can't do it and pay me my share from the vineyards. I know his financial standing, and he hasn't the surplus to do that and carry both the champagne operation and the importing firm for the seven or eight years it will take him to recover from the damage to the vines. I made certain of that."

By destroying the vines yourself, Gerald thought. But there was no proof, and to suggest it would only challenge Philippe to bring a suit for defamation of character.

"Perhaps he can't," Gerald said aloud, "but I can buy

into the business as a partner with enough money to pay the notes. You can't stop that."

Philippe rose up from his chair behind the desk. "Not without my permission. I inherited a share from my father."

"Try it and you'll be outvoted." Philippe was beginning to infuriate him. "The Fontaines own three-fourths of the business or two votes to your one, whichever way it is set up."

"You're doing it just so Lisette can obtain an annulment, aren't you?" Philippe sneered. "Well, don't try to buy my share. I still want a voice in the wine business, and if you go ahead with this, it will be a voice you wish you could silence."

"I wouldn't dream of it," Gerald said. *So much for that idea,* he thought, *but at least Philippe will be outnumbered.* "As for the annulment, Lisette has no intention of going ahead with it. As your wife, of course, she'll eventually inherit that share you're so greedily hanging on to, as well as a good bit of this bank." He looked around the office as if already anticipating what changes could be made.

"Never! I'll outlive her just to make certain she doesn't." Philippe slumped back into his chair, but not before his face became so inflamed, Gerald feared he was having an attack of some kind.

"It doesn't really matter as far as she's concerned," Gerald said. "Now that annulment proceedings have been dropped, you have to restore her trust fund and allowance. I think she'll manage nicely."

"You can leave now," Philippe said, almost under his breath.

"Thank you, but not before I give you this." He handed over a check for the full amount of the notes. "You will see it is signed by Baptiste Fontaine. We anticipated you might object to my buying the notes, so I brought three checks. One of mine has already been deposited in Monsieur Fontaine's account, just so there'll be no question that it might be overdrawn for even a few minutes." He reached into his pocket. "Since I won't need my check made out to you, I'll destroy it." He slowly and meticulously tore it apart before Philippe's eyes and dropped the pieces onto the desk.

"You've thought of everything, haven't you?" Philippe knew he'd lost and he looked it.

"I always try to. Good day." Gerald left without a backward look. He'd just as soon Philippe didn't see him grinning from ear to ear.

Chapter Forty

"YOU LOOK HAPPIER than I can ever remember seeing you," Denise said to Lisette. The two young women were looking over materials Lisette wanted to use for draperies in the house Gerald had bought.

Lisette had spent Christmas with her parents and Jean and Denise's families at the château; but now that the New Year's holidays were behind her, she was eager to get her home furnished. With nothing available to rent or buy in Villedommange, she and Gerald had just about given up hope of settling near Jean when they found a delightful cottage half hidden in a small beech-tree forest. On the road between Villedommange and Mont-Chenot, it was only four kilometers from the vineyards, an easy distance for Gerald to travel every day. Not so easy was keeping farmer's hours: up at sunrise and not home until after dark. For the first two weeks, Gerald declared he'd die if he had to keep up the pace. Within two months, he insisted he'd never felt healthier or stronger in his life.

"Happy and fat," Lisette said in answer to Denise's comment. "Have you ever eaten as much in your life as we did over Christmas?"

"No, and I wish this bulge in front were something other than food. Five years since Éliane was born and no sign of another."

"You're lucky, Denise. You have three handsome, healthy children. I used to say I didn't want any; now I wish I could. But, living as I do with Gerald, it wouldn't be respectable."

"How do you—do you keep from becoming pregnant?" Denise asked hesitantly. She was mystified at the thought any woman would not want children and curious as to how they were avoided.

Since Gerald's entry into the wine business, the two sisters had seen each other frequently, and Lisette found it much easier to share confidences with Denise than she had with either Leah or Jane Westborne.

"Actually, it's not that hard," she said. "Ask any girl in an expensive bordello. There are several ways. But—and sit down because this will really amaze you—we use something made by the family doctor in Paris and distributed by our very proper father."

"Papa! Papa makes something for birth control? I don't believe it." Denise did sit down and dropped half-a-dozen swatches of material onto the floor.

"Ask him. Or Mama. Funny-looking little skins made from lamb intestines, but they work. Papa tried to export them to England and the States, but the fuddy-duddy customs officers wouldn't let them in. Not officially. They do get to England, though, in boxes of medical supplies. I don't know about the States."

"I'd love to see one." Denise giggled like a schoolgirl hearing her first dirty joke.

"I'll go get one. Gerald has boxes—fancies himself a great lover."

"And is he?" Denise asked with an impish grin.

"All the hard work in the vineyards has actually increased his ardor—I get exhausted just seeing him walk through the bedroom door."

"But you love it. I know I do. Edouard may be a lot older than I am, but he has a young man's stamina."

Lisette disappeared into the bedroom and returned a moment later. "Here, see for yourself what they're like." She handed Denise one of the skins.

"Ugh." Denise shuddered. "It's all wrinkled and gray."

"Not when it's all stretched out and in use."

Denise stretched it out between her fingers and then suddenly began to blush. To cover her embarrassment, she asked, "Do you ever wonder about Mama and Papa? Now, I mean, as old as they are."

"If I know Papa, he'll never be too old," Lisette said. "Nor Mama. She's just as lively as ever, and I'm sure Papa thinks she's as beautiful as the day he met her."

"She really is very beautiful. She still stands so straight and proud. And that clear skin and fantastic mane of white hair. I wish mine were that thick."

"At least, Denise, you inherited Papa's curls. And Papa is certainly as handsome as that picture of him in his cavalry uniform. Yes, I imagine they still make love frequently. I've seen Mama's nightgowns. No heavy granny gowns buttoned up to the neck for her. They're as sheer and revealing as anything you'll find."

483

"So I guess she doesn't wear them just because she likes to sleep in them."

"What a conversation we're having!" Lisette said. "My God, if they could hear us."

"Mama would blush and Papa would grin and say every word of it was true," Denise laughed. "And it all started because I said how happy you looked."

"I am, for now, but I won't take any bets on how long it will last."

"Why, Lisette? Gerald loves you, and you seem so perfect for each other."

"There's still his wife. Just when I feel things are going smoothly, she'll step in and foul up our life. So, I live for the moment and enjoy it. Yes, I am happy, and I mean to make the most of whatever time we have together."

"You really think something will go wrong?" Denise asked.

"Just a feeling, nothing more." As if to avoid further discussion of the subject, Lisette went back to looking at the materials. "I think I'll use this *toile de joie* for the draperies in the parlor and carry out the red in upholstery for two of the chairs. Maybe a stripe for the couch . . ."

After a few days, Denise returned to Versenay, and Lisette settled into a quiet, peaceful routine of being a housewife and spending long hours in Céline's kitchen learning how to cook. Her earlier dislike for Céline had turned gradually to admiration as she spent more time with her. Céline might be the daughter of a peasant, but, living in the country without any servants, Lisette needed her talents as a housewife more than the blasé airs of any aristocrat. Her kitchen soon became as aromatic as her sister-in-law's.

"Um, that smells good," Gerald greeted her one afternoon.

"You're home early. No more bottles to be turned or corks to be popped?"

"The word is not *popped* but *dégorged,* my dear."

"I'm sorry," Lisette said, kissing him. "I'll try to remember. You came home early just to see me."

"No, I wish it were something as pleasant as that. We have to go to St. Denis. I received a wire from your father asking us to come immediately."

"Why? What's wrong?" All sorts of tragic visions flashed through Lisette's mind.

"He didn't say. Just to come immediately."

"It's Mama. I know it is," and Lisette began crying. "She's ill or dying."

"There, there, love." Gerald took her into his arms. "I'm

484

sure if anything were wrong with her he would have said so. So it must be something about the business, and he simply made it sound more urgent than it really is. Wires tend to do that."

"How soon are we leaving?"

"On tonight's train from Rheims. Can you get packed?"

"With a summons like that?" Lisette said. "Immediately."

"We have time to eat whatever smells so good."

"I couldn't eat a thing." Lisette couldn't dismiss the feeling that something was seriously wrong with Leah. If it had been her father, Mama would have sent the wire. Maybe it was Robert. He was always getting into scrapes, and Mama had mentioned he'd fought duels. . . . All the time she packed, during the carriage drive to Rheims, and on the train to St. Denis, Lisette could not ignore the intuitive feeling that someone she loved was either seriously ill, hurt, or dead.

Paris was very cold this time of year, and Nicole shivered beneath her heavy shawl. It was night and she was walking along the river, scarcely knowing where she'd been or where she was going. This was the fourth time since she'd learned she was pregnant and Jerome had left her that she'd come out of one of her spells and not known where she'd gotten where she was or how long she'd been there.

She'd lost Jerome, but she still had her baby, thanks to a greedy but sympathetic old man. She had evidently not been the first young woman to balk when she was actually about to destroy her baby. The man already had the money, so it mattered little to him whether or not he performed the operation. He'd gone into the hall and told Jerome that there'd been complications and she would have to lie on the bed and rest for several hours before she could safely leave. Evidently the amount of bleeding he'd described had caused a frightened Jerome to flee the premises. Nicole herself had stayed no longer than to thank the man, who then showed her a gate through the courtyard wall and gave her directions back to her room.

Surprisingly, she didn't miss Jerome as she'd thought she would. The visit to the doctor had destroyed her love for Jerome as completely as the surgery would have destroyed their child. But her thoughts soon turned to the showing of her work that Jerome had promised. It took great courage to seek out Monsieur Engle at his gallery.

"Since Mr. Trowbridge no longer represents me," Nicole said immediately after introducing herself to the man, "I thought I'd come and talk to you myself about the show. How soon do you want to see the oils?"

"I won't be needing them now, mam'selle. There isn't going to be a show."

"What do you mean? I thought it was all arranged."

"Why, my dear young lady, you didn't think I was offering my gallery to you for nothing, did you?"

"You mean—?"

"I mean Monsieur Trowbridge would have been paying the rent on that room for those three weeks, and he'd be guaranteeing the purchase of at least a fourth of the paintings. You may be very good, mam'selle, but you are not yet known."

Damn him! Nicole thought. *Damn him for the miserable worm he is.*

"You have seen Monsieur Trowbridge then?" she asked.

"Yes, indeed. He came here nearly two weeks ago and said there would be no show. He implied you had left Paris. In fact, he mentioned something about going to Italy. I assumed you were going with him."

So he'd left Paris, had he? Well, at least she need no longer fear seeing him.

"Thank you for your time," she said.

"You're quite welcome. When you do begin to sell and get a name for yourself, I'll be delighted to arrange a showing."

She walked hurriedly away before the tears could come. Jerome had lied to her, had said her work was good enough for a show. Instead, he'd intended to buy her way into the art world and would have bought her as well. It would have been his way of getting her completely in his power. *Well, no more, Jerome Trowbridge. I'm well rid of you and the influence you had over me.*

From that moment on, Nicole resolved to devote all her days to painting and to selling enough to take care of her expenses and begin buying a few things for the baby. She had not expected the resumption of her attacks, but she'd been quite mistaken about that.

The first time she'd awakened curled up tight under her bed. It was dark and for a moment she imagined she was back in the dark tunnel leading from the château to the river. She could hear the sounds of water and of footsteps coming closer. Then she realized it was raining hard and that water in the downspout from the roof was splashing on her balcony. The footsteps were those of Monsieur Gaillard who lived in the room across the hall. It took her several minutes to uncurl her cramped body, so she must have lain there for a long time; and it was only with a real effort that she was able to crawl out from under the low bed. She looked around her studio. Everything was just as it had been before the attack; nothing had been destroyed.

Not so with the second attack. Just before its onset she was so weakened by nausea, she had to lie on the bed all morning. She was running low on money, and it was imperative she get some paintings finished to take to the quay to sell. She'd had attacks of morning sickness before, but never one so enervating. Hating the baby for keeping her from her work, the last thing she remembered was lying on the bed and wondering how she would manage. When she woke up, some hours later, she was horrified to see she had slashed all the hated postcard paintings, the very ones that would have brought her the money she so desperately needed. The only ones not touched were those she was proud of but which no one wanted to buy. In desperation, she cleaned the place up and then worked on a new series of tourist pictures day and night until her strength almost gave way. But during the following week she sold them all.

The third attack was the worst, at least in its consequences. She was six months along and long since over her brief wish to destroy the child. In fact, she was looking forward with hope and anticipation to having the baby. But one thing bothered her. She had put on so much weight that when she looked into the mirror all she could see was her swollen face and bloated body. She was ugly. No one would ever love her again. She wanted to hide from everyone, and she agonized over every trip outside to buy food or supplies. If only she could run away someplace where no one knew her, where no one would speak to her and force her to answer.

When she woke up that time, she was horrified to find herself in bed in a strange room. Next to her a man she'd never seen before lay snoring. She looked around the room, one much like her own, with almost no furniture but several easels with partly finished paintings. She was terrified. She reached for her skirt lying on the floor beside the bed. That was evidence enough of what had taken place during the blank hours. Before she could put it on, the man half awakened and reached for her again.

"Let go of me!" she screamed. She was struggling to get off the bed and get dressed at the same time.

"Come, come, sweetheart, you were a lot more friendly in the café when you let me buy you supper and wine. And very friendly when we got back here. We had us quite a time, didn't we?"

"I don't know who you are," Nicole said furiously, "but I'm getting out of here." Before he could stop her, she was out the door and down the steps into the street. She found she was in a strange part of Paris, miles from her room. She reached into her pocket. At least he hadn't taken her money. But what kind of a man was he to want to take a pregnant woman to bed? The whole episode was revolting, and only after days of hard work and nights filled with terrifying dreams, did she begin to get over the experience.

Yes, it had been the worst attack until this one. Nicole looked at the river. Coming to her senses, she'd found herself standing on the quay and looking into the water. For all these years, she'd had one fear: that she would take her own life during one of the spells. How close had she come to doing it this time? And what instinct for survival had saved her?

She continued walking and found herself on the steps of Notre Dame. She had no idea what time of night it was, but the doors were open and she walked into the darkened sanctuary. A few votive candles supplied the only light. Taking some coins from her pocket, she selected a candle from the rack and placed it before a small shrine of the Madonna. It had been years since she recited a "Hail Mary," but the words came easily to her lips.

"Hail Mary, full of Grace, the Lord is with thee. Blessed art Thou amongst women and blessed is the fruit of thy womb, Jesus. Holy Mary, Mother of God, Pray for us sinners now and at the hour of our death. Amen." *And pray for me during my travail,* Nicole added silently.

She stayed on her knees a long time, then got up awkwardly and made her way from the cathedral. For the first time in months, she felt at peace with herself. Mary would watch over her now and not let anything happen to her or the baby. She'd have her child and find some way to keep it with her. With someone of her very own to love and care for, there'd be no more attacks.

"And how are you feeling today, Nicole?" Madame Franconne greeted Nicole, who was on her way back from the market. Nicole no longer made any pretense of not cooking in her room, and the concierge made no complaints. She was either ignoring it or being more understanding because of Nicole's condition.

"Fine, but wishing my time would come. I get tired just walking a block or two, and these steps leave me exhausted."

"There's a room coming vacant on the second floor. Would you like to move down?"

"Thank you, but I'm used to my room. It won't be so bad after the baby comes." She didn't want to say she couldn't afford the more expensive room.

"I can let you have it for the same rent," Madame Franconne said, as if reading Nicole's mind.

"You mean it?" The concierge nodded. "But it's so much bigger."

"Bigger, but there aren't as many people looking for rooms. This cold winter has sent them running to the south."

It's true, Nicole thought. She hadn't seen several of her artist friends recently. The warmer climes had drawn them away.

"I'll take it then."

"The room will be ready day after tomorrow. The tenant left it a mess, including several obscene murals that will have to be painted over."

Nicole knew well the young man who'd lived there. He was a foul-mouthed artist who, since the popularity of Aubrey Beardsley in England, thought the world was waiting eagerly for his lurid drawings of grossly distorted human figures. Unfortunately, he had neither the talent nor the style of Beardsley, and his work was merely obscene.

The new room was not only larger than her old one, but it had much better light as well. Nicole set up her easel next to the wide, floor-to-ceiling window. In the flea market she bought two more chairs, one for the table and a comfortable armchair. She would need that for holding and nursing the baby. Against one wall stood the new possession of which she was most proud: a crib. There hadn't been room for one upstairs, and she'd thought she was going to have to put the baby on a pallet until it was old enough to sleep with her. Now her baby would have its very own bed, one large enough to use for a few years. Her paintings were now bringing in enough to enable her to buy the linens and small clothes she needed for the baby. They were piled neatly on a shelf near the crib.

A few days later, on a warm, sunny February afternoon with a hint of spring in the air, Nicole's daughter was born. It was Ash Wednesday, February 20, 1901.

"Her name is Mary," Nicole said before falling asleep after her long but not difficult labor. While the midwife bathed the baby, Madame Franconne deftly remade the bed with clean sheets and laid a light quilt over Nicole. Since Madame Franconne had five sons but no daughter, she'd begun to look on Nicole as the girl child she'd never had. Unlike most of her tenants, the young woman never caused any trouble, except for the cooking, and that was easily overlooked. But she always seemed so sad. Madame Franconne thought her a good, if not a great, artist, and she beamed with pride every time Nicole told her how many paintings she'd sold. If Nicole wanted to keep this baby, and it was obvious from all the preparations she'd made that she did, Eloise Franconne would do everything she could to help her.

Nicole woke up, felt her flattened stomach, and smiled. "May I see her now?"

"She's just been waiting for her mother to wake up. I think she's hungry." Madame Franconne took the baby from the midwife. "Now, Marie, your mama's ready for you."

"Not Marie," Nicole said, "Mary."

"But that's English." Madame frowned.

"Mary is her English grandmother's name. I want her to know she's half English." She'd never know her father. Jerome Trowbridge would never learn he had a daughter, the daughter he'd wanted to murder before, she had any chance at life. But still, Mary should know who she was.

"She's a fine, healthy baby," the midwife said. "And you came through it easily. You should have no problems. But if you do, you know where to find me. Rest in bed a few days, and you'll be fine."

"Thank you," Nicole said.

While she nursed Mary, she examined her from head to toe. Mary had Jerome's coloring, dark-brown hair and fair skin, but her features were very like Nicole's own. Her body, though plump and sturdy, was long. *She'll be tall, like me,* Nicole thought. *She's beautiful. The most beautiful thing I've ever seen.* She was going to love her and find a way to take care of her until Mary grew into a beautiful young woman.

Over the next few months, Nicole painted every morning while Mary lay in her crib and then gradually began playing with the soft, flannel toys Nicole made for her. Nicole made hundreds of sketches of Mary and based a number of paintings on them. At first she wanted to keep all of them, but with the added expenses of Mary's needs, she took a few of them to the quay. Surprisingly, they sold better than the city-scapes did, but she kept a few of her favorites. In the afternoons, they went for long walks, Nicole pushing Mary in the old pram Madame Franconne lent her. More and more frequently, Nicole brought Mary to dinner with Eloise Franconne and spent the evening with her.

When Mary was eight months old, Madame Franconne died of a heart attack. The new concierge announced that rents would be going up, and that she would require immediate payment.

"Pay now or get out," was all the response Nicole got when she said she'd have to sell a few paintings before she had enough money. She'd fallen behind on the rent after Mary was born, but Madame Franconne had been letting her make it up gradually each month.

Nicole had already had one argument with the stone-faced woman about the furniture she'd bought herself. "It's my crib," Nicole insisted, "and my chairs."

"If they're in this room, they belong to the house." Most of the furniture in the rooms did belong to the owner of the building, and he'd told the new concierge she was simply to take possession of everything.

"I'll be damned if that's so," Nicole had said. "They're mine and I mean to have them."

"If you touch one piece, I'll accuse you of stealing. How would you like to be sent to prison for several years and have your precious baby taken away from you?"

The woman was right, Nicole thought. Let her be accused of theft, and who would believe her? She felt completely defeated. The argument had left her so exhausted she could hardly get up the single flight of stairs to her room. She hadn't enough money to pay the rent, so she'd have to look for another place. One requiring only a small deposit so there would be enough money left for her and Mary to eat.

Because the old pram had also come into the possession of the new concierge, Nicole had to carry the baby while she looked for a room. Out of desperation, she took the first affordable place she found. Mary could sleep on a pallet as long as the weather stayed warm and then sleep with her when it turned cold.

For another few weeks, Nicole struggled as best she could, painting as long as she could stand and trying to keep up with Mary, who was now crawling all over the room. Morning after morning, Nicole walked the blocks from her room to the quay, the paintings under one arm, and Mary, securely fitted into a knapsack, strapped to her back. Days often went by with no sales. Paris was virtually deserted of tourists, and local people were not buying.

Finally, Nicole awoke one morning and knew she couldn't go on any longer. She no longer cared much about herself, but Mary deserved a better life than any she'd be able to give her. Nicole looked into her change purse. She had enough for either breakfast for herself or a short ride into the country. After feeding Mary the last bit of milk and a little gruel, Nicole wrapped a few of the baby's things in a clean crib sheet and set out for the train station.

When she returned a few hours later, she was alone. Before succumbing to the attack she felt coming on, she burned all the sketches of Mary. The paintings she left untouched. They were her bequest to the world that had forced her to give up her child and brought her to the final edge of despair.

Chapter Forty-one

BY THE FALL OF 1901, Lisette finally recovered from the shock of the scandal that followed the tragedy that had sent her and Gerald rushing to St. Denis. For a while she thought she could never again look any of her friends or acquaintances in the face, and for weeks she dreaded opening the front door for fear she'd find another reporter from one of the tabloids that fed on disaster, depravity, and juicy tidbits of scandal among the wealthy and prominent.

Baptiste had met Lisette and Gerald on the porch and led them immediately to the library, where Leah sat trying to work on a piece of embroidery.

"What is it, Papa?" Lisette had been relieved to find both parents well, but she knew by their faces that something was seriously wrong.

"Something with the business?" Gerald asked.

"No," Baptiste said. "I almost wish it were."

"Robert?" Lisette asked. "One of the others?"

"They're all fine. Sit down and let me tell you as best I can. Philippe is dead."

I should be elated, Lisette thought. *I'm free from him at last. So why do I feel like crying? Because I never really stopped loving him in spite of all he did—of what he was.* She pulled a handkerchief from her small bag.

Gerald couldn't help noticing, and was surprised at her reaction. He'd known she loved Philippe when she married him, but he had no idea she still had any feeling for him. Perhaps one never did quite get over a first love.

"Was he ill for long?" Gerald asked. *Better to talk about it,* he thought. *As soon as Lisette can bring herself to mention his name, she'll begin feeling better.*

"He wasn't sick at all," Baptiste said. "If it were as simple as that, I would merely have wired you the news and suggested that Lisette come here in time for the reading of the will. Unfortunately, he committed suicide."

"Suicide!" Lisette jumped up from her chair. "Why?"

"It's a situation that could be very embarrassing for you, I'm afraid. Philippe's body was found in his apartment next to the body of a young man he killed just before he shot himself. The authorities know it was not the other way around—the young man killing Philippe and then himself—because the gun was clenched in Philippe's hands."

"I don't believe it." Lisette put her face in her hands and began rubbing her forehead.

"There are going to be some difficult weeks ahead for all of us," Baptiste said matter-of-factly. "Gerald and I are going to be involved because of our business and banking connections. Though it seems to be a clear-cut case of murder and suicide of two lovers, the authorities will not be ready to accept that verdict until every aspect of Philippe's life is investigated. The relationship between the two of you will be under scrutiny. Husband deserted, wife living with another man. That sort of thing. If you're to keep from having the mantle of guilt placed on your shoulders, Lisette, that it happened because your husband could no longer live without you, you're going to have to reveal some aspects of your marriage."

"That seems so unreasonable," Leah said, speaking up for the first time. "That young man lying there like—like he was should tell the whole story."

"What do you mean 'like he was'?" Lisette asked.

"Your mother said that because they were both naked. She's right, of course, but only the truth will put the quietus to the notion that he took a lover because he could not get Lisette back."

493

The next few days were a nightmare. First there was the funeral, which Baptiste insisted she attend. Dressed entirely in black with a long, satin-bordered widow's veil over her face she sat in the church and stood beside the grave in a site fenced off from the large cemetery of the church. Murderers and suicides could not be buried in consecrated, hallowed ground. Madame Duchalais having recently died, Lisette was the only member of the family in attendance. Baptiste was at her side, while Leah remained at the château with Gerald.

From the time Lisette heard that Philippe was dead until after the funeral, she was in a constant state of depression, unable to carry on a conversation and bursting into tears if anyone so much as looked at her.

Gerald was deeply concerned for her, unable to determine whether she was mourning for Philippe or dreading the questions that would be the aftermath of his death.

"Would it help to talk about it?" he asked her finally. They were in her apartment at the château, and she was nervously arranging and rearranging books, figurines, and other bric-a-brac.

"I don't know. I feel so confused. I loved Philippe when I married him, and then I hated him for what he put me through. Should I continue to despise him for the way he treated me—and my father—or should I remember the man I once loved?"

"It's your ambivalent feelings that are bothering you, isn't it?"

"Yes." She laughed self-consciously. "Maybe because he was such an inconsistent person, such an enigma. He could be so sweet and attentive at times that it really hurt when I realized his behavior was a mask he wore while we were with other people. Yet, he shielded himself behind that mask for so many years, I wonder, now, if he realized he was wearing it. I think he was really bewildered that I didn't understand why he was loving at some times and so unconscionably cruel at others. Or so very jealous and possessive even though he never desired to possess me as a wife.

"I think," she continued, "I can understand him and forgive him now. He was a very lonely and frightened man and that influenced everything he did. I don't really know why he thought I'd understand him then and be willing to live with him, but I fulfilled a need. And I don't mean just a need to show the world that he was a normal man with a wife. I think it went deeper than that. His other relationships were ephemeral, insecure, never stable or permanent. Strange

494

as it may seem, I think that's what he wanted from ours. Not love in the physical sense, but security and perhaps friendship. And I let him down. I deserted him."

"You did the only thing you could, Lisette," Gerald insisted. "You couldn't continue living with him any longer than you did. You mustn't feel guilty about that."

"I don't any longer, not since he's dead."

"Strange," Gerald said, "that he should choose such a way to die. He must have realized the truth about him would come out, the very truth he labored so hard to conceal all those years."

"No, I don't find it strange," Lisette said. "I think at the last he realized he was finally going to be free of the secret he'd carried all those years. How many of us wish we could say, 'Look at me. This is the person I am, not someone you think I am or that you want me to be. I am me. Accept me for myself.'"

"And so you wonder how you should remember him? I think as the man you married, the man you loved and in many ways still do."

"That doesn't upset you? That I would still carry some feelings for him?"

"Lisette, I love you. If it were at all in my power for us to be married, I'd do anything to make that possible. Your happiness is the only thing that matters to me. I would be a sorry man if I could not accept your earlier love as part of you. And I think I like you more because you do still carry some feeling for him."

"Thank you, darling." Lisette walked over and sat on Gerald's lap. "I feel much better now. Hold me very close. I think the worst is over, but I couldn't have got through it without you."

As much as she'd dreaded being questioned by the police, Lisette found them understanding and supportive. They accepted her word that she'd left Philippe because he would not be a husband to her. Yes, she'd seen him a few times since then, but only to discuss financial affairs. Yes, she had sought an annulment on the grounds he'd entered into marriage fraudulently. No, she hadn't stopped the proceedings because she intended returning to him but because of family reasons. At that point, Baptiste interrupted to say it was part of the business affairs he would discuss with them after she was excused.

The reading of the will was handled circumspectly, in a lawyer's office. There were a few irregular bequests, such as the generous amount of money left to the young man Philippe had murdered; it would now go to whatever family of the victim could be found.

"That will be up to me as executor of the estate," the lawyer said. Certain properties went to cousins, but all of the furniture in the apartment went to Lisette.

"Please see that it's sold," she said. "I don't want to see any of it."

"As you wish. I can take care of that, too."

For Lisette, the most important clause in the will left Philippe's share of the vineyards and the winery to her. Now all of the business was in the family.

"There is a rather unusual request I need to discuss with you, Madame Duchalais," the lawyer said. "You may or may not know that he was not sole owner of the bank. His father had been, except for a small number of shares held by bank trustees. Upon the elder Duchalais's death, he bequeathed a portion of his ownership to a number of employees who'd worked for him for several years. It was necessary then, of course, to change the structure from single ownership to partnership. Philippe himself was but one of the partners—with, however, a fifty-one-percent share. His will asks that his share be divided among the other partners and three other long-time employees. As his widow, you have a right to challenge that part of the will."

"Is the trust fund he set up for me altered in any way by his death?" Lisette asked.

"No, and that is completely separate from the will. In a sense the money in there was no longer Philippe's to bestow. It was already yours."

"Then I have no wish to challenge the will."

"Thank you, madame. The beneficiaries will be most grateful to you."

Then came the reporters. The newspapers all had given lurid headlines to Philippe's suicide and the murder of his companion. Some had even managed to get pictures of them, but no one had approached Lisette until after the funeral. Many of their questions were the same ones the authorities had asked, but not so gently put. She couldn't believe she was being asked about such personal aspects of her life. When she refused to answer, thinking they'd soon forget all about her, she was doubly shocked to read lurid, intimate details that could only have come from the reporters' imaginations.

"I'm taking you back home," Gerald finally said one afternoon, after a reporter had Lisette weeping uncontrollably. He had asked her what it was like to share her bed and home with her husband's lover.

"Where do they come up with such questions?" she sobbed.

"In the sewer," Gerald said. "You've had enough. We're leaving tomorrow."

The strong support of Jean and Céline, and the frequent visits of Denise with the children, helped Lisette get through the next few months. She no longer grieved over Philippe, but was tormented at times by the same thought she'd had early in their marriage: Perhaps, if she'd been more attractive as a woman, he would have been able to love her. Gerald, sensing her feelings, could always bring her out of these moods by buying a little bauble "for the most beautiful woman in the world." At other times, she'd began to tremble if she saw a stranger, and then force herself to realize that no reporter was going to follow her this far from Paris.

"Where are the children?" Lisette asked Denise as she arrived for one of her visits.

"Edouard said he'd keep them while I came over here for a few days." Denise took off her bonnet and reached over to receive Lisette's kiss on the cheek.

"Does he know what he's let himself in for?" She took her sister's bonnet and wrap and led the way to the guest bedroom.

"No, and he'll probably never offer to keep them again. But I just had to come alone so we could talk without the interruptions of curious offspring. Guess what? I'm pregnant again."

"How wonderful," Lisette said. "I'm happy for you."

"If only you were, too. It's a pity now Philippe's gone that you and Gerald can't be married."

"Nothing we can do about that. As to a child—heaven forbid! I'm too old now."

"Now," Denise said once they'd settled in the parlor, "how is Gerald doing in the business?"

"You'd think he'd been born in a vineyard. Seriously though, he's made a number of valuable suggestions, especially concerning the selling and exporting end of it. That part is really his forte, though he loves working in the fields, too. He has a good many contacts here on the Continent, so he's been traveling some. He and Papa and Jean are thinking of buying another small winery and expanding."

"So there are no plans to return to England?"

"None, unless his uncle dies and he has to go back to see

497

about the estate. He'll be the Duke of Highcastle then, and I suppose there'll be more obligations for him to fulfill." Lisette sighed to herself. Gerald's uncle was past ninety and would not live much longer. She dreaded his death because it would take Gerald away from her for long periods of time, unless she swallowed her pride and returned to her former position on the periphery of his life, touching but never quite a part of it.

Lisette didn't tell Denise there was another occasion that would take Gerald away from her for at least two weeks, another of those splendid royal affairs in which she could not participate. Some months earlier, on January 22, 1901, Queen Victoria had died and Edward became king. But because feelings were running so high about the Boer War—both pro and con—he had not yet been crowned; however, when the date was set for the coronation, Lisette knew Gerald would have to return to England to fulfill his duties as a peer of the realm.

As Denise was about to leave a few days later, Lisette reminded her again, "You must let me come and help when the baby arrives. I may be all thumbs with infants, but I can certainly keep young Edouard, Gilles, and Éliane occupied."

"I'll remember; come over whenever you can. I think Mama is already planning to have us all for Christmas again. Papa keeps threatening to sell the château and move permanently into Paris, but she'll never let him as long as she can gather her chickadees around from time to time."

Even with Henri in America and Nicole somewhere in Paris, the family was amazingly close, Lisette thought. She had strayed from the fold for a while, but these past few months, with all her problems and all the comfort the family afforded her, had made her realize how grateful she was for them.

King Edward's coronation was finally set for June 26, 1902.

"How soon will you have to go over?" Lisette asked Gerald.

"Only a couple of weeks ahead of time. Once the coronation is over and I attend a few festivities connected with it, I can return."

"We'll be separated a good part of the spring then. You remember, I promised Denise to help her when the baby comes early in May." Lisette held up the tiny sacque she was embroidering.

"No reason I can't come popping over to see you while you're there. Edouard and I always have plenty to talk about. Amazing man. I can see why Jean is so indebted to him for getting the vineyards and winery going well."

"You're not sorry, then that you've stayed over here?" Gerald had never been enamored of the social life, but he did have a host of friends in England, and she could remember with what pleasure he looked forward to the hunting and fishing seasons in Scotland.

"I'm happy as long as you're with me," he said. "But to answer your question, I'm really enjoying this life. I think, though, that when I return I'll see about getting a small apartment in Paris. It would do us both good to have a bit of city life now and then."

During the first two weeks of May, Lisette stayed with Denise and her new daughter, Jeannine. She returned in time to help Gerald prepare for his trip to England early in June.

"I suppose," she sighed, "your wife will be with you during all the rituals and festivities." It wasn't fair. She was much more his wife now than Lady Boswick had ever been, and how she would love to be standing proudly beside Gerald throughout the majesty and grandeur of the coronation.

"For the sake of appearance, yes. She is, after all, wife to a duke apparent, and it would be most unseemly for her not to attend with me. I'll wish it were you, Lisette, the whole time. You'd look so splendid in the robes of a peeress."

"I think it's beastly that I have to stay here and she has all the fun." She walked to the window and looked at the wildflowers now in full bloom at the edge of the woods.

"You won't be out of my mind a single minute, and I'll bring back a very special bauble, just for you."

"Will you sleep with her?" Right now any bauble or trinket was far less important than the threat of Gerald and his wife being reunited and perhaps even reconciled.

"No. That I can promise you. She doesn't want me any more than I want her. She thinks I'm dull and stodgy."

"But if she does want you?" Gerald must have loved her at one time, and she must have loved him. If there were not a lover for Lady Boswick to return to after the coronation, what sort of power did she still hold over Gerald? After all, she would soon be a duchess—the old duke couldn't live much longer—and she might be more than willing to forego certain pleasures if she had a coronet within her grasp.

"We won't be seeing each other except at certain requisite

functions. When we're in London, I stay in the townhouse and she stays with her sister. Believe me, darling," he said, taking her in his arms, "no one can ever lure me away from you. Now, kiss me and tell me you'll miss me."

Lisette willingly let him hold her close for a long time. "I'll miss you every minute, too."

"If you're too lonely here, stay with Denise or your parents for a while. They'd love to have you. Three weeks, four weeks at the most, and I'll be back."

But it was to be much longer before Gerald returned.

In the middle of June, King Edward began suffering from intermittent chills and fever. The doctors immediately diagnosed appendicitis, and peritonitis developed almost at once. In spite of the danger to his health, the King continued with the plans for the coronation on June 26. On June 23, he was told that if he didn't have the appendectomy immediately, he would die. Insisting he didn't want to disappoint his subjects, he suggested the operation take place after the coronation. Finally, after much persuasion by the doctors, he agreed to postpone the coronation only so long as it took him to recover. He was operated on the next day, June 24.

Gerald's letters chronicled the deeply emotional reaction of the British people when they heard their king was ill. The area around Buckingham Palace, where the operation was taking place, swarmed with prayerful well-wishers awaiting word the operation was over and successful. In Westminster Abbey, where those involved with the coronation had gathered for a dress rehearsal, the Bishop of London officiated at a service of intercession while the operation was in progress.

"You've never seen anything like it," Gerald wrote. "If Edward knew he was loved by his people when he became king, he must surely be overwhelmed by their feelings for him now. We are not certain yet just when the coronation will be, so it seems best I stay here until it is over. Miss you terribly and will come home the very minute I'm able."

As Gerald suggested, Lisette divided her time among the members of her family. She missed him dreadfully; more than that, she was concerned that his extended stay in London would put him too often in close proximity with his wife. He said nothing in his letters about seeing her, but they couldn't help but meet at various social events and the homes of mutual friends. Lisette could only hope that Lady Boswick wasn't, as Jane Westborne so often found herself, between lovers and ready to settle down with her husband. One consolation was that Gerald spent some time with his uncle in Cornwall, and

Lisette knew Lady Boswick would die before she'd bury herself in what she'd once told Gerald was the most godforsaken place God ever created.

The coronation finally took place on August 9, and four days later, Gerald wired for Lisette to meet him at Calais. He was returning at last and had a very special gift for her.

Lisette was waiting on the dock as the boat from Dover came in. She saw Gerald immediately, but there were no packages under his arm. The gift was a new phaeton then; it had to be.

His boisterous greeting and bear hug put to rest her fears about his wanting to stay in England or return to his wife.

"Now, where is it?" she asked as soon as she could talk.

"You'll see soon enough, Miss Curious. We have to go to the shed where they're unloading cargo."

Whatever it was, it was too big to fit in his trunk or valises. Lisette held her breath again, waiting for someone to lead the pair of horses down the ramp. She was watching for them so eagerly, she didn't see what else emerged from the hold.

"There it is," he said. "How do you like it?"

Lisette almost fainted. A motor car! A shiny, dark green motor car, with narrow gold trim.

"Oh, Gerald, it's—it's fantastic." She clutched his arm. "I never dreamed. Never expected— And it's mine?"

"It's all yours. I wanted to bring you something very extra special for all the disappointments you've had."

"You did, that's for sure." Beside herself with excitement, she couldn't move from where she stood.

"Don't you want to go over and look at it?" Gerald was smiling at her reaction. He'd been looking forward to this moment through all the weeks since he'd ordered it.

"Yes, of course, I do. I just can't seem to move."

"Then let me help you." He took her arm and led her over. Lisette ran her hands over the tufted, tan leather cushions and the shiny wheel spokes.

"Will I ever learn to drive it? It's . . . awesome."

"You'll learn quickly. Let me go in here and get the papers from customs. Then we'll put our bags in the back and take off. I'm having my trunks shipped through."

"You mean we're going to drive it home? All that distance in a motor car!" She didn't know whether it was elation or fear sending shivers up her spine.

"Certainly. Think what fun it will be to drive through the country, stopping whenever we feel like it," Gerald said. "There's no hurry, is there?"

"None that I know of." There was a gleam in her eye. "Can we go to St. Denis first? I can't wait for Mama and Papa to see it."

"We'll go wherever you want, darling. The car and the itinerary are yours."

"My, if we sit in the open like that how will I ever keep my hat on when it gets windy?"

"I'll show you." Gerald went into the customs shed, returning with his suitcase and a large box under his arm. "This is for you, too. Open it."

Lisette pulled out a long, lightweight coat and a hat with a huge veil around it. Wrapped in a separate piece of tissue paper was a pair of goggles.

"The coat's called a duster," Gerald said, "for obvious reasons, which you'll see when we start motoring along the roads. The veil will keep your hat on and protect your face as well. If it gets very dusty, you can put the goggles on."

On the rear seat of the car was a second coat, a floppy hat similar to a large tam with a brim in front, and another pair of goggles. Lisette stood back and laughed as Gerald put them on. "Don't we look a pair," she said.

They had a glorious time driving through the countryside, laughing at the chickens that scurried, squawking, out of their way and the cows that looked at them curiously, as if wondering who these fools were in that noisy contraption. They stopped at one roadside inn for lunch and another to spend the night. Each time, they were surrounded by people who ran to look at the motor car and exclaim over it.

"I don't know when I've had such fun," Lisette said as they approached the château.

"Then you forgive me for running off and leaving you all this time?" Gerald asked, reaching over to hold her hand.

"After last night," she replied, squeezing his fingers, "do you doubt it?"

"No man could ask for a finer welcome home." He leaned over to kiss her and they swerved off the road. "Oh, no," he said, "I keep forgetting this isn't a carriage with a horse that knows enough to stay on the road."

Leah and Baptiste were duly impressed with the automobile, and Baptiste immediately climbed in for a ride with Gerald.

"Not today," Leah said when Gerald insisted there was room enough for her, too.

"What she means," Baptiste laughed, "is she's scared to death of it and doesn't trust it not to run away with her."

"I'll stay here with Mama," Lisette said.

The men were gone nearly an hour; when they returned, Baptiste was sitting behind the steering wheel.

"Baptiste!" Leah shouted. "Get down from there. You don't know a thing about motor cars. You might have been killed."

"I know all I need to now. Gerald showed me everything. I'm going to put my order in for one tomorrow."

"You'll do no such thing," Leah said. "How will you ever manage to get around once you get where you're going?"

"You'll be there to help me." Leah could see the grin spreading across Baptiste's face.

"Never! You'll never get me in one of those things."

"Really, Madame Fontaine," Gerald said. "They're perfectly safe and entirely hand driven, so Baptiste has no trouble at all driving it. Or he could train your coachman to be a chauffeur."

"No," Baptiste said, "if he goes at all, it will be for the ride. Driving that motor car was too much fun for me to let anyone else do it."

"Come on," Gerald coaxed Leah, "go for a spin with me. You'll enjoy it. Lisette, give her your coat and veil. I guarantee that when we get back, you'll be just as eager as Baptiste."

"No, don't try to persuade her," Baptiste said. "When Leah makes up her mind, she's as stubborn as a mule. There's no budging her. She used to be fearless, but she's getting jittery in her old age."

Leah glared at him. This was a challenge she couldn't resist. She'd always been proud that nothing could daunt her; fear was to be overcome, not succumbed to.

"Give me that coat," she said to Lisette. Without another word, she put it on, tied the veil under her chin, and stomped toward the motor car. She sat on the seat as straight and stiff as Marie Antoinette riding to the guillotine. She looked neither right nor left, but clutched her hands in her lap while Gerald cranked the motor and they started off.

When they returned, all she said was, "Gerald is going to show me how to drive it tomorrow." Then she walked into the house to check with Blanchette about supper.

Chapter Forty-two

WHEN ROBERT GRADUATED from St. Cyr in 1903, Leah and Baptiste heaved a simultaneous sigh of relief. Never the student Henri had been, Robert preferred getting away to Paris as frequently as possible and enjoying the wilder side of city life. He excelled in fencing and athletics and was popular with all his classmates, but he opened his books only when an imminent examination drove him to it. There was no opposition from the administrative officers when he announced he had no intention of taking a commission.

"How soon will you be ready to come into the business?" Baptiste asked. They were driving home in the motor car, which Robert had pronounced "absolutely ripping!" Leah shuddered at his slang, but was too glad to have him coming home to comment on it.

"Let him have a little vacation," she said. "He should get some reward for managing to graduate."

"I thought I'd combine business with a vacation," Robert answered. He'd finally persuaded Baptiste to allow him to drive, and they were careening along the road at top speed. He turned to look at his mother in the back seat.

"Good God, Robert!" she screamed. "Keep your eyes on the road. Baptiste, make him slow down."

"Loosen up a bit on the throttle," Baptiste suggested. "Your mama loves to drive, but she thinks ten miles an hour is flying. Now, what did you mean about combining business with a vacation?"

"Go over to the States and see Henri. Then maybe spend some time in the New Orleans office, learn the routine there. You said the manager would be retiring in a few years. You've got good men here, and I don't see any advancement in this office for years unless you let one of them go, and I know you don't plan to do that."

"Not you, too," Leah sighed. Why was it the children wanted to get away from home as soon as they were ready to spread their wings?

"Not like Henri, Mama," Robert reassured her. "I'll be back frequently. I just have a yen to see New Orleans and the places I hear you talking about."

"I think it's a good idea," Baptiste agreed. "We'll be needing a member of the family over there. Robert can see his cousins in Martinique on the way over, and Pierre will take him in hand when he gets to New Orleans."

"Pierre Delisle's your former brother-in-law, isn't he?" Robert asked.

"Yes. Catherine was his sister, but he was my good friend long before she and I were married. Marcel Bonvivier, the present manager of the office, is your mother's cousin, and it's true he's been saying he'd like to go back to Martinique when he finds someone to take his place."

"So, just like that it's all set," Leah said. "Well, I've helped the others pack, and I suppose I can help you, too."

"Mama, the firm's ships go back and forth every week. You'll see me often."

"I know. I think maybe it's because I envy you a bit. I'd love to see New Orleans again. I wonder if I ever will."

"Not until the laws are changed," Baptiste reminded her. "We'd be arrested the minute we set foot on land. Maybe you could go with Robert on a return trip after he's been back here."

"No, I wouldn't want to go without you." She thought about the little house Baptiste had bought her and where she lived so many years as his mistress. She kept it rented; she could never bring herself to sell it. She couldn't go back without Baptiste. It would remind her too much of the misery she'd suffered at not being able to be his wife while they lived in Louisiana. "But Robert can be our eyes and tell us what it's like now."

Just as Nicole was the image of Leah from the time she was a little girl, Robert was a duplicate of Baptiste. He sailed from France clean-shaven; on the voyage over, however, he let his mustache grow. By the time he arrived in New Orleans, he was able to trim it exactly like his father's.

Both Pierre Delisle and Marcel Bonvivier were at the levee to meet him when the ship docked. Pierre spotted him among the passengers coming down the gangplank and walked right over.

"*Bon Dieu*, Robert," Pierre greeted him and crossed himself dramatically. "I never thought to see Baptiste again; for a moment, I imagined I had."

"Look that much like the old man, do I?" Robert grinned with delight at the stunned look on Pierre's face.

"You smile like that, and you'll have all the belles of New Orleans on your trail, the same as your father did. But none of them could hold a candle to your mother. How is she?"

"Yes," Marcel said, "how is Leah? I haven't seen them since they were married in Martinique. I couldn't have been more than eight or nine. Good Lord, how long has that been?"

"I don't know," Robert said, "but long before I was born. I was the last of the litter, and an afterthought at that."

"I know," Pierre laughed. "I remember the letter I got from your father announcing your forthcoming birth. I couldn't tell whether he was more pleased or shocked. A little of both, I think."

Over drinks at Le Coq d'Or and dinner later, Robert was kept busy telling Pierre how Lisette, Pierre's niece, was getting along and detailing to Marcel the life that Leah and Baptiste led in the country. In turn, Pierre regaled him with some of the escapades he and Baptiste had got into during or after an evening at their favorite bar.

"I was surprised," Pierre said finally, "to learn you were arriving so soon. I thought you'd planned to come here after a visit with Henri in Detroit. We've all been disappointed he's never come South to see us. I thought being Baptiste's son and all—"

"I'd planned to spend a few days with him. Before I left France, he wrote saying he was very busy right now, bad time of year for me to see much of him. And his wife is expecting their second very soon. Somehow I gathered through it all that he wasn't overly eager to see me."

"Have you any idea why?" Marcel thought he knew, and if he were right, it was a decided insult to his cousin Leah.

"Mama has never said anything, but I think Henri is passing as white since coming to the States. My sudden appearance could definitely put a crimp in his grandiose style of life, because I never have sense enough to keep my mouth shut. Or to forget I have as much pride about my mother's side of the family as my father's." Robert's words confirmed Marcel's suspicions.

"I think most of us have the same feeling about Henri." Pierre nodded toward Marcel. "Especially since he married the heiress from Boston."

"Ah, yes, the elegant Louise," Robert said. What he kept to himself were the hurt and disappointment over Henri's not wanting to see him. Henri had been Robert's favorite brother since he'd toddled behind him and been allowed to play and then assist him in his workshop. He's gone to St. Cyr —even if he hadn't emulated his brother's study habits—only because Henri had. He would just as soon have gone right into the business the way Jean did.

"Well," Pierre said, "you won't feel any lack of welcome here. My son Ambrose had plans for this evening, but he's eagerly waiting to meet you and make some introductions."

"And," Marcel added, "he knows everyone in the *Vieux Carré* worth knowing."

"What he means," Pierre said, "is all the most beautiful young women. There won't be any dearth of companions during your leisure hours."

"That's great," Robert said, "but I'm also here to learn the rudiments of the business." He turned to Marcel. "How soon can I start in there?"

"Tomorrow morning if you like," Marcel said. "Your father may have told you I'm looking forward to returning to Martinique. I've enjoyed it here, but my wife is from Martinique also. She's homesick for her family and my family needs me to take over the reins at the main office. We're hoping you'll stay with us until you find an apartment of your own."

"I think there's a vacancy in the Pontalba Apartments," Pierre said. "You'd be right in the middle of things, overlooking Jackson Square. I think you'd like it. Ambrose can take you to see it tomorrow afternoon."

"Fine," Robert said. "I'm in your hands now." He'd been somewhat anxious about how well he'd get along with Pierre Delisle, whom his father spoke of with such admiration and genuine fondness. Often, long-time friends of the family were a disappointment; in this case, though, Robert felt close to Pierre already, in spite of the very great difference in their ages.

Most of Pierre's children were nearer in age to Jean and Lisette than to Robert, but Ambrose, the son of Pierre by his mistress, Cecile, was only a year older than Robert.

"It's good to have you here," Ambrose greeted him. "We're going to have some great times together if you're anything like your father."

"I see Papa's reputation hasn't lost any of its shine during all these years," Robert said, laughing.

"Not as long as my father is still alive to talk about him.

507

Come, I want you to meet my mother and then we'll go look at the apartment he mentioned. It's just a couple of blocks from mine."

Robert walked with Ambrose along the *banquette* and followed him into a large couturier establishment. Robert found himself being introduced to the owner, a petite, vivacious woman with sparkling black eyes and masses of strikingly beautiful gray hair styled in a high pompadour. She was dressed in a simple gray silk gown, but there were real diamonds glittering in her ears and several strands of pearls around her neck.

"Mama, I want you to meet Robert Fontaine. He's come from France to be associated with the Bonvivier-Fontaine import firm."

"Ah, yes," she exclaimed, talking as exuberantly with her hands as with her voice. "I remember Monsieur Fontaine. And the beautiful Leah is your mother?"

Robert nodded. "Yes, ma'am."

"How are they?" she asked.

"Very well, thank you." He was a little discomfited by the intense way she stared at him.

Cecile walked around him as if taking his measure, smiling all the while. "But you are so young!"

Robert laughed. "I was an afterthought—or an accident—born after my mother was forty."

"Ah, but such a handsome afterthought. You look, I think, just like your papa."

"Thank you. So it is said, yes." At times Robert wondered if he liked being such an exact duplicate of Baptiste, but it was so evident how much his father was admired here in New Orleans, he was rather glad for the resemblance.

"I remember your mama so well," Cecile continued. "I saw her before she married Mr. Andrews and again before she became Madame Fontaine. She was happy both times, but—I think—happier the second time. Your father has always been the man she really loved. I'm so pleased they have had a good marriage. I can tell by looking at you it has been a happy one."

"And how can you see that?" Robert was puzzled.

"Because," her eyes twinkled, "your mama was not so young when you were born. When there is a baby after forty—ah, they are still lovers.

Ambrose watched Robert blushing. "You weren't so young yourself, Mama, when I was born."

"So? Should I be ashamed that your father and I are still

508

lovers? I wish you both the same happiness. You will never know any greater. Now—go along and look at the apartment. Then supper at my house."

Robert's acceptance into the business community of the *Vieux Carré* was immediate. The import firm had been one of New Orleans' most prestigious establishments ever since Claud Bonvivier opened the office more than thirty years before the Civil War. Here, being Leah's son made no difference. *Gens du couleur,* free men of color, had owned property—including plantations—and stores and run their own businesses for a hundred years before Bonvivier's opened its doors.

Acceptance into the social life, however, was limited to Baptiste's few remaining close friends or those who remembered him with respect as one of New Orleans' beloved war heroes. Here, though, the color line was clearly and unmistakably and irrevocably drawn. He was invited to small family dinners or large, formal receptions, but never to an event that would occasion intimate, one-to-one, personal contact with daughters and granddaughters. There were invitations to attend the races, but none to dances. He could converse with the young women in the lobby of the theatre or opera, but he could not join them in their private boxes.

Robert waited with some trepidation for someone to make a derogatory remark about his mother or himself, and wondered how he would respond. He finally mentioned it to Ambrose.

"Don't think about it," Ambrose said. "If you hear something, ignore it the way I ignore remarks about being a bastard. I could let people hurt me—and I have been hurt, especially when I was a child—but then I decided I didn't want to know those people anyway. Most of our generation don't give it a thought. My God, Robert, you're what—onesixteenth Negro? I'll bet a third of the *Vieux Carré* that claims to be Creole is, too."

"Well, I can't be like Henri and try to change who I am, but I won't dwell on it, either."

Robert remained content to limit himself to the social life proscribed by his color. A few young white women, titillated by the forbidden, indicated they would be charmed to have him as an escort. However, in spite of that and what Ambrose had said about changing attitudes in his generation, Robert knew it was unwise for him to become involved with white daughters of New Orleans. He was enjoying himself, and becoming emotionally entangled or falling in love was not part of his plans.

Leah read and re-read the latest letter from Robert. He was good about writing lengthy weekly letters and describing in detail his work with the firm. Most of that was for Baptiste's benefit, and she usually skipped over it on the second and third reading. She was more interested in his personal and social life. Certainly his letters indicated he was enjoying himself and not missing the nightlife of Paris. It delighted her that Ambrose was the son of Cecile, her former friend and *modiste*.

It had been good of Baptiste's friends to make Robert welcome, but Leah worried whether it was right, whether it would lead ultimately to unhappiness for him. He was her son as well as Baptiste's. Robert was both proud of and unconcerned about his mixed heritage, and she knew he'd go merrily along, until someone or something brought him up short.

Leah was particularly concerned about the young women he was meeting through the Delisles and Bonviviers. If he fell in love with a Creole and wanted to marry her, tragedy would result. Leah was torn between wanting to warn him against such an outcome and thinking it would be better to let Robert's life run its own course. She finally decided on the latter.

With their passionate addiction to both racing and gambling, Robert and Ambrose spent every Saturday afternoon at the race track, followed by dinner and a night of drinking with their cronies. On one such Saturday, Ambrose began talking to a young woman Robert had not seen previously at the track. In a minute, Ambrose brought her over and introduced them.

"Isabella, I'd like you to meet Robert Fontaine. Robert, this is Isabella Quinsarro. She's just returned with her family from a lengthy visit to Spain. Isabella, the *Vieux Carré* has been abysmally dull without you."

Although of pure Spanish heritage on both sides, Isabella was blond with skin so fair it seemed translucent. In startling contrast, as if to make up for a lack of color elsewhere, her large, deep green eyes immediately commanded one's attention.

"If I believe that, Ambrose," she said. "I'd be as great a

fool as all those other girls you keep dangling with your cache of never-ending compliments."

"Isabella loves to tease," Ambrose said. "Be careful, Robert, she has her own cache of tricks."

"Hush up, Ambrose, and turn around," Robert said. "The race is starting, and I've bet heavily on Gallant Major."

Between that race and the next, the conversation between Robert and Isabella focused on their mutual love for horses. It continued in the intervals between the next three races, and Isabella asked him if he rode often.

"I hate to brag," he said, smiling into her eyes, which stared openly at him, "but I'm probably the best rider in the *Vieux Carré.*"

"Not bragging? Just stating an opinion, I presume," she said. "But that's a statement you'll have to prove. My family lives in the city, but we also have a plantation on the Mississippi where I keep several horses. I drive out to Casa Verde at least three days a week to see the horses and go for a long ride. Perhaps you can get free one afternoon and join me."

Having decided that Isabella Quinsarro was the most beautiful young woman in New Orleans, Robert thought no prayer of his had ever been answered so quickly. "Which day would be most convenient for you?" He was already thinking up excuses to get away from the office. Marcel had been turning more and more of the management details over to him in preparation for Robert's replacing him, and his days were long ones. Surely Marcel wouldn't mind if he took one afternoon off.

"Wednesday? I drive out in the morning to exercise all of the horses, and then go for a ride in the afternoon. About three o'clock?"

"I'll be there. Give me the directions, and you'll find me on your doorstep promptly at three."

"And then we'll see who is the better rider." Her deep green eyes sparkled with delight, and Robert was ready to offer his heart then and there. "Casa Verde is only a few miles out along the river. Follow the river road and you can't miss it."

Not until then did Robert realize what a quandary he'd got himself in to. He had no horse. He could borrow one from Pierre; however, after the ride to the plantation, the horse would be in no condition for a fast gallop. But he was not about to renege on the challenge.

"Of course," Isabella said, as if reading his thoughts, "you

511

might not want to ride your horse out to the plantation and then hope to put him through his paces. You can ride one of ours."

Robert hoped she hadn't heard his sigh of relief.

"Don't worry," she laughed, "I won't take advantage of you by giving you an old nag. Ours are all very spirited Andalusians. Papa had them sent over from Spain."

"Thank you. I appreciate the offer."

When the races were over, she returned to her carriage, and Robert reminded Ambrose they were to have dinner together. He wished he were looking forward to an intimate, candlelit tête-à-tête with Isabella, but there would be another time. He meant to make the most of his afternoon with her.

The Spanish Creoles of New Orleans, descendants of the earliest settlers of the Delta, considered themselves vastly superior to the French Creoles, who did not arrive until some years afterward. Their daughters were far more sheltered and protected, and the Quinsarros seldom let Isabella out of their sight. When she drove to the plantation in the landau—it would have been unthinkable for her to ride that distance—her duenna was by her side. Tia Martina, her father's older, unmarried sister, had early assumed total responsibility for Isabella, whose mother produced a child a year during the early years of her marriage.

The first person Robert saw when he drove up to Casa Verde was Isabella, looking provocatively beautiful in a riding habit of a slightly deeper shade of green than her eyes. He started to reach out for her hand, then suddenly pulled it back. The second person he saw was Tia Martina.

"This is my aunt," Isabella informed him. "She will be riding with us."

Robert could only stutter, "How d–d–do you do." He wanted to weep, but strong men didn't weep. Swearing would have helped, but gentlemen did not use coarse language in front of ladies. All he could do was smile pleasantly and follow them into the house. He had discerned a mischievous twinkle in Isabella's eyes, and he cursed himself for being made to play the fool.

"If you're ready to ride," Isabella said, "we can go right to the stable. Or would you like to see the grounds? We have very beautiful gardens here, though not much is blooming now."

Although not a garden enthusiast, Robert agreed. He'd noted the difficulty with which Tia Martina was keeping up with Isabella's surprisingly long strides. The elderly woman was obviously loathe to walk any farther than she had to. A stroll through the garden could be very pleasant.

Isabella suggested to her aunt that she might like to sit on the verandah while they were gone. "We'll walk only as far as the river, Tia, and be back in a few minutes."

Robert looked at the broad expanse of lawn sloping gently down to the river. On either side were plantings of towering azalea bushes, but nothing disturbed the vista between the house and the water except for a few intricately designed flower beds, empty now of spring and summer flowers, and a number of camellia bushes. He felt strangely moved. It was more than the natural beauty and the placid atmosphere; he was overcome by a sense of *déjà vu,* as if he'd been here before. As if he were being welcomed back to a place where he belonged. Then he shrugged the feeling off. He was being influenced by Isabella's obvious love for the place and his own desire to be wherever she was.

Beyond a bank of azaleas, he saw a small white garden house with peaked roof and latticed walls. On the edge of the water, it commanded a startling view of the river and the opposite bank. "That looks like a nice place to rest for a minute," he suggested.

"The gazebo? Tia would have a fit. She will anyway if we don't go back immediately."

"And she's going to ride with us, I suppose," Robert said, thoroughly discouraged at the turn the afternoon was taking.

"Naturally, but I don't think you'll mind." Her eyes as well as her lips smiled at Robert. "Come on, let's find you a horse."

Tia Martina heaved her bulk off the wicker settee and followed them to the stables.

"There you are," Isabella said, "you've seen them all." They had walked the length of the building between the rows of stalls. "Take your choice."

"That's hardly fair," Robert said. "One glance at each doesn't show me anything. I could pick out the slowest. I dare you to choose the one you know is best—next to yours, of course."

"And I'll challenge you," she retorted. "You say you're a good judge of horses. Look at them again—closely—and find your own mount."

"All right, I'll take that challenge." Robert strode up and down. Stopped. Returned to another. Moved on. "I'll ride this one."

"You devil, you," Isabella laughed. "How did you know Skylark is my favorite?"

"I'm not a devil, but I talk to horses. Didn't you see him tell me to choose him?" He didn't mention he'd seen her tense each time he paused at Skylark's stall. Then he saw real disappointment in her eyes, and suddenly he wanted only to please her so he could see her again. "You ride Skylark. I wouldn't feel right riding your favorite. I'll choose another."

"Will you really?" Her eyes lit up again. "You're a darling." She ignored Tia Martina's disapproving frown at her easy use of the endearment. "Just for that, I'll give you a hint. Ride Sorrento. He's the fastest we have."

"You're offering me the chance to outride you?"

"I am, but beware. I said he was the fastest. I didn't say you would win on him."

Now what the devil does she mean by that? Robert wondered, and he remembered what Ambrose had said about watching out for her cache of tricks.

Isabella called to the stable boy and told him to get the horses ready, including the slow, steady mare for Tia Martina.

With the chaperone following a few lengths behind, Isabella and Robert walked the horses almost a mile before urging them into an easy canter.

"Are you all right, Tia?" Isabella looked back.

"Fine," Tia puffed.

After another two or three miles, Isabella slowed down. "Wait here," she said to Robert. She turned her horse and rode back to Tia, now nearly a half-mile behind them.

Robert waited and watched. Soon a smile crossed his face. He saw what Isabella had meant when she said he wouldn't mind having her aunt with them. She was helping the elderly woman off her horse and urging her to sit in the shade of a huge water oak. Then Isabella mounted up and rode back to Robert.

"She always rests while I go for a good gallop. It was a little harder persuading her today, but I managed. I told her she'd see us the whole time. I didn't remind her that she always falls asleep while I'm gone."

Robert looked at Isabella's pixie grin and wanted nothing so much as to lean over and kiss her right then and there.

"And now to find out who's the better rider?" Robert asked. If Tia Martina were watching them, there was no point in walking the horses and trying to hold Isabella's hand. He'd save that for another day.

"Right. We'll start here. Just around that curve," Isabella pointed with her crop to a spot about a mile and a half away, "is a deserted wharf. The boats used to stop there to load, but the plantation house was burned during the war, and no one lives there now. The land is still worked, but the owner lives in the city. He's a Yankee." She shuddered involuntarily. "One of those who came and bought the land for taxes. Anyway, we'll race to that wharf, turn around, and come back here. Agreed?"

"Seems like a good distance," Robert said. If Sorrento really were the fastest horse in the Quinsarro stables, he'd have no trouble beating her back. This time he wasn't going to give in and let her win. He sensed she'd be more disappointed if he did.

"Are you ready?" He nodded, and they both snapped their reins at the same time. Sorrento took off immediately. If he'd been a motor car, like the one his father had, Robert would have said he started off in high gear. All the way along the river, around the curve, and to the deserted wharf, he was well ahead of Isabella. *This is too easy,* Robert thought.

At the wharf, Robert pulled the reins easily to the right to turn Sorrento around. It was not to be. Instead, Sorrento quickened his pace and raced across the open cane field. There was no stopping him. For the next twenty minutes Robert found himself tearing through underbrush and trees grown so close together he thought his legs would be scraped raw. He had to duck his head under low branches that threatened to knock him off the horse, and more than once, smaller branches flicked across his face and drew blood.

"Damn that girl!" he swore aloud. Never before had he been unable to control a horse. So this was what she meant when she said Sorrento was the fastest horse but not a guaranteed winner. They didn't stop until Sorrento, panting and blowing, slowed down on the other side of the woods. When Robert turned him, he was a docile as a kitten. "Well, damn you too!" Robert swore again. "Now we go back in humiliation and defeat, and I'll bet she'll never stop laughing at me."

For a moment Robert wondered if he were lost. Sorrento was ambling along as if out on a joy ride. Then Robert realized if he gave the horse his head, he'd get them back. Sure enough, in another few minutes, Sorrento brought him

515

to the tree under which Tia Martina was still sleeping. Isabella sat next to her aunt, waiting for Robert.

"I thought you were going to win our race," Isabella said with her impish grin.

"And you called *me* a devil." Robert urged his sore muscles to lift him out of the saddle and onto the ground. "I don't know whether I can walk."

"Look at your face! What happened?"

"Sorrento likes the woods. He especially like to race between trees and under low-hanging branches."

"Here, let me." She took a handkerchief from her pocket, walked over to the river's edge, and dipped it in the water. Coming back, she began wiping the blood from his face.

Robert smiled under her ministrations. He'd welcome being wounded every day if she'd care for him like this.

"I hope these scratches don't leave scars," she said. She was touching the one along his cheek "Where did you get this one?"

"A saber scar. Dueling."

"Dueling? How dreadful. Was it exciting?"

"Not particularly. Not when you're up against the best fencer at the academy. But he came away with more scars than I did."

"Good." Isabella sat back and watched while Robert brushed leaves and twigs from his suit and inspected a rip in his trousers. "Was it over a girl?" she asked. "The duel, I mean."

"What if it was?" He had no intention of giving her the details of having been challenged over the attentions of a cabaret dancer.

"I'd think it terribly thrilling to be fought over."

Before the conversation could go any further, there was a loud snore from Tia Martina, followed by a huffing noise, and she sat straight up. "Well," she said, "I'm glad to see you came right back as promised."

Robert and Isabella merely looked at each other. "Ready to go back, Tia?" Isabella asked.

Fortunately, Tia's myopic eyes didn't discern the scratches on Robert's face, or that might have been his last ride at Casa Verde.

From then on, Robert drove out to the plantation at least twice a week, and he and Isabella went riding. No more fast gallops, but easy walks or canters so they could hold hands once they were out of Tia's sight. They also spent

516

hours inside the house, where Robert admired rooms echoing with loneliness.

"I love this house," Isabella said one afternoon. "I don't know why the family prefers to remain in the city. If it were mine, I'd live here all the time. When I marry, I'm going to ask for it as a wedding present."

"What if your husband doesn't feel the same way?" Robert asked.

"I'd never marry anyone who doesn't love this place as much as I do."

Robert knew what she meant. He felt a special attachment to it already, and not simply because of his growing love for Isabella. It was a strange sensation, as if he were coming home, each time he rode up to the house or walked through the gardens. The feeling was most intense when he sat quietly like this with Isabella in one of the sparsely furnished rooms.

"Has the plantation been in your family for many years?" he asked.

"No, not the several generations as have so many of them along here. The Quinsarros have been in New Orleans since the first Spanish came over here, but during the war both my mother's and father's families, as Spanish nationals, fled to Spain. Mama and Papa were born over there, although they did not meet until they returned here. When they were married, my grandfather bought this place and gave it to them for a wedding present. They named it Casa Verde. I have no idea what it was called before then or who owned it."

"I suppose whoever did was forced to sell," Robert said, "or maybe none of the family was left." Robert was saddened by the thought, but he had no idea how close to the truth he'd come. He was walking on Fontaine land, his own father's land, the plantation Baptiste and Leah had fought so hard to regain after the war.

In the same way that Isabella did not know to whom the land had once belonged, the Fontaine name meant little to the Quinsarros. When their families returned from Spain, Leah and Baptiste had already left for France. Señor and Señora Quinsarro met and accepted Robert as cousin to Marcel Bonvivier and friend of Pierre Delisle. In the closely knit Spanish Creole world of the *Vieux Carré*, the few who had heard Robert's name thought of him only as one of the family who owned the Bonvivier and Fontaine import firm. Which of the family were his parents was of little concern.

The Quinsarros' only disappointment—and their only reason for encouraging Isabella to see other young men as well—was his descent from French rather than Spanish Creoles. However, he was welcomed in their home, and they made no objection to his calling on Isabella. Either Señora Quinsarro or Tia Martina was, of course, with the young couple at all times.

Not so when they went riding. Tia could always be persuaded to rest under the tree, and they'd have at least an hour to be alone together. The deserted wharf became their trysting place.

Sitting on the wharf one afternoon, Isabella hugged her knees and leaned back against one of the decayed pilings. Robert was lying on the sun-warmed boards with his head in her lap.

"How long have you loved me?" she asked.

"From the time you looked straight at me and challenged me to the race. You have the most beautiful eyes I've ever seen."

"I love you, too." She lowered her head and kissed him. "I didn't really like you at first, though. I thought you were conceited. And much too handsome."

"And now?" He took her hand and slipped it inside his shirt so that she could feel her fingers against his skin.

"You're still handsome and much too sure of yourself, but I love you anyway."

Robert sat up and leaned on one elbow. "Will you marry me, Isabella?"

"I—I can't answer that." She'd known Robert was leading up to a proposal, and she didn't know whether she was pleased or worried. "That will be up to Papa."

"And if he says yes?" Whether because or in spite of the fact Robert was wildly in love with Isabella, the color barrier between them had been completely erased from his mind as if it had never existed.

"I don't know," she said. "You might have to return to France to your father's business. You said neither Jean nor Henri was interested in the firm."

"You wouldn't be willing to go with me? If you love me?" He couldn't understand her hesitation.

"I told you once, Robert, I'd never marry anyone who didn't love Casa Verde the same way I do. I could never live anywhere else."

"There's a good chance I could stay here and head the New Orleans office."

"Your business would still be in the city—"

"I could go in every day. With a motor car it would be simple." He put his arm around her. "I love the land, too. I feel so—so complete when I'm here. It's a strange way to put it, but I feel as if I've gone full circle and come home again. I'd never leave it, if that's what you want. My father has managed without me all these years; the firm won't founder without me."

"Talk to Papa then. I'm not superstitious, but I'm afraid if I say yes first, he'll refuse."

But she had said it whether she meant to or not, and it was all Robert needed to hear. They were later than usual getting back to Tia Martina, and she scolded them severely.

"Tonight?" Robert asked as he prepared to return to the city.

"Tomorrow night," Isabella said. "Mama and Papa have a dinner party tonight. I won't tell him why you want to see him, but I imagine he'll suspect when he learns you want to talk to him."

"Until then, darling," Robert whispered. He wanted to kiss her one more time, but Tia Martina had not taken her eyes off them since their return from the ride.

Feeling somewhat like a bachelor on the night before his wedding, Robert suggested to Ambrose they make a night of it. After tomorrow, he hoped to be devoting all his evenings to Isabella. Ambrose was always ready to have a good time. They started out at Le Coq d'Or and made steady progress from bar to bar. Along the way they picked up several of their friends. Finally, deep in their cups, they headed for a late supper at a favorite restaurant.

While they were walking up the stairs to a private dining room, Robert hinted to Ambrose that he hoped to be asking for Isabella's hand the next day.

Ambrose let his glance linger for a moment on Robert, but he kept his thoughts to himself. Either Robert was going to get a severely disappointing shock when Señor Quinsarro told him none too politely never to see Isabella again, or the Quinsarros were going to surprise all of New Orleans. Whichever, it was not his place to bring up the subject. "Congratulations, old cock," he said instead. "Maybe we should go someplace other than home after we eat. You'll have your, ah, wings clipped once she says yes."

"No," Robert said, weaving slightly as he made his way to a place at the table. "I shall remain eternally true to my lady love. True and pure." He looked around. "Where the hell's the wine?"

"A toast! A toast!" Ambrose shouted. "To the first of us about to know the sweet delights of debudding a rose in a marriage bed."

"Who?" Émile LeRoque asked. He'd drink toasts all night as long as someone else furnished the wine.

"None other than Robert here," Ambrose said, slapping him on the back.

The announcement was acknowledged with appropriately vulgar remarks about Robert's virility and what the fair young virgin might expect on their wedding night.

"And who is the charmer who makes you so willing to give up this life of debauchery and endless nights at Madame Eugénie's?" asked one of them.

Robert hesitated. He'd told Ambrose in strictest secrecy, and he didn't want to mention Isabella's name until he'd spoken to her father.

"That, my fellow debauchees, is a secret for now. I do not wish the fair lady's name to be bandied about in this degenerate gathering."

"Are you insulting us, Robert?" Émile asked. Drunker than the others, he was in a surly mood.

"Never that, Émile, old friend." Robert was sober enough to realize he had to soothe Émile "It's just that I haven't spoken to her father yet. It's a bit early for congratulations. But," he said, noting the frown on Émile's face, "there are plenty of other things to drink to." He called to the waiter. "Champagne for all." That should quiet Émile.

"You'd better not insult me, Robert Fontaine, you black son of a bitch. I know what you are, even if these others don't care."

Robert moved forward in his chair, then sat back. It wouldn't do to start anything.

"You're a bastard," Émile mumbled. "A son-of-a-bitch mulatto bastard."

Ambrose and the others immediately leaped from their chairs and surrounded Émile, hoping to shut him up.

"Don't lay a hand on me," he growled.

"Who are you calling a bastard?" Robert shouted. He saw the fury on Ambrose's face, who was just as ready as he to strangle Émile.

"You, you bastard. Your parents aren't married. Not over here. And who's your mother? Bastard daughter of a slave

520

who should have been a slave herself. Consorting with Yankees. Even had one for a lover."

Robert was seething. How dare Émile? That was his mother, his beloved mother, whom this drunken, no-good degenerate was defaming. He sat for a fraction of a second, his hands clenched around the stem of his wineglass. It snapped. He felt the sweat beading on his forehead. His palms were clammy, his stomach churning; his temples throbbed and pounded. A strange numbness came over him, a sudden physical paralysis, while his mind boiled with energy. He felt his face going red from the blood rushing to it. It wouldn't be enough to hurl insults at Émile. He had to act; he had to do something violent.

"I'm going to kill you," Robert said. He slapped Émile across the face with his bare hand. "Choose your seconds because I'm calling you out. I'll see you in the morning."

"No, you can't," Ambrose said, trying to calm him down. "You'd only make more trouble for yourself. You know dueling's illegal."

"Goddammit, Ambrose, let go of me. I'm going to kill him. Are you going to second me or not?"

"Yes, but only if you come home with me now." Ambrose had an idea, and, God help them, it had to work.

Still unsteady on his feet, Robert followed Ambrose down the stairs and out into the street. After getting Robert home and onto a bed, Ambrose went to find his father.

Pierre was asleep, but as soon as Ambrose started talking, he was sitting up, wide awake.

"He can't do it," Pierre said. "He'll be arrested and banished from New Orleans." He shook his head. "He can't marry Isabella, either." He'd thought the young man had enough sense not to fall in love with a Creole.

To Pierre's surprise, Robert agreed at once to withdraw the challenge. He'd done some thinking while Ambrose was gone, and he'd come up with an alternate plan to avenge the insults to his mother and himself. The new plan was deadlier in its way and would give him a great deal more satisfaction.

As to Pierre's fears about Robert wanting to marry Isabella, they were soon set to rest. Before noon the next day, Robert received a formal statement from Señor Quinsarro forbidding him to see Isabella again.

Chapter Forty-three

LISETTE WAS IN THE KITCHEN when she heard Gerald come in, and her stomach tightened involuntarily. He'd been staying with Jean for four days—something to do with the latest shipment of wine—and she hoped he was in a pleasant mood.

"Hello, darling." Gerald strode into the kitchen and kissed her on the cheek. "What's for dinner? I'm starved."

"Grilled lamb chops and our first asparagus from the garden." Not a word to say he'd missed her or was glad to be home.

"Sounds wonderful. Have I time to change? We were in the fields all day, and I'm covered with mud."

"Plenty of time," Lisette said. "Everything's ready. Let me know when you are."

Lisette breathed deeply and tried to ease the knot in her stomach. Everything was going fairly well so far. Now if only she didn't say or do something to cross him.

"Lisette!" Gerald called from the bedroom.

"Yes, dear?"

"I don't suppose you remembered to change the buttons on my shirts." The tone of his voice had changed very little, but as attuned as she was to his moods, Lisette could detect the trace of sarcasm.

"I'm sorry. I've been so busy I forgot."

"Busy? Doing what?" His voice implied that taking care of a small house should not have kept her busy all the time he was gone.

The knot began to tighten again. "I've been going to the village every morning. Playing the piano for the schoolchildren. They're rehearsing for the festival."

"I don't know why you bother," he said from the bedroom. "They don't appreciate it, and the teacher can do it just as well."

Maybe because I enjoy it, Lisette thought, but she didn't say it aloud. "I'll change the buttons after supper."

522

"You should have taken them back to Madam Gerow. After all, she's the one who made the buttonholes too small. I don't know why you're so hesitant about doing it. It was her mistake, not yours."

"But she'd be terribly embarrassed, and I hate to hurt her feelings." Poor Madame Gerow. Her eyesight was failing, and she received very few sewing orders now.

"So you take on the job," he said, "and then don't get it done."

"I told you, Gerald, I'll do it tonight. If you're ready, I'll put dinner on the table."

At least Gerald was all compliments about the meal. "Delicious. You outdid yourself this time. I'm glad we thought of putting asparagus in the garden."

"Thank you, dear."

"By the way," he said, "I need to go into Paris for a few days. Care to go along?"

"Care to? I'd love to." It had been months since they'd been to the city, to the apartment Gerald had found for them after returning from England.

"I'll be busy most of the time, but you'll probably want to take a side trip to see your parents."

Not until they arrived in Paris did Lisette realize how very much she wanted to see Leah and talk to her. She'd reached the point where she had to talk to someone, and it couldn't be either Denise or Céline. They wouldn't understand.

"You go along and have a good time," Gerald said as she was leaving. "Stay two or three days. The change will do you good."

"I might. But I'll be back in time for Emily Berthold's dinner. I'm looking forward to that."

Still unsure about driving the car any real distance by herself, Lisette took the train to St. Denis and was met by Leah.

"Mama! You put me to shame. I'm afraid to drive from Paris by myself, and here you are meeting me with the car."

"It's all in your mind, Lisette," Leah said firmly. "Just tell yourself that nothing will go wrong and nothing will. I drive all over the countryside and never have a problem."

"Well, you've always had more courage than I have." She looked at Leah, still as erect as a sergeant major, her beautiful mass of white hair protected by a veil, and her long, supple hands encased in fine suede gloves.

"Now," Leah said after they were settled in the house, "we can talk." She never talked while driving. "How is everything with you?"

523

"Fine."

"Well, you don't look fine. You're too tense. Come, come, what's wrong?" If Lisette were still a child, Leah would have approached the subject indirectly, but now she saw no point in wasting words.

"I didn't know it was that obvious."

"Too lonely in the country?" Leah picked up her knitting, ready to settle down for a good heart-to-heart conversation. She recognized in Lisette the symptoms she'd suffered during problem periods early in her marriage.

"Not the living in the country. I love it there. I'm blissfully happy puttering around the house and my small garden." She laughed. "I have it filled with flowers that are guaranteed to grow no matter what I do or don't do to them. Then the minute Gerald walks in the door, I become tense or develop a headache. Or both. In spite of the fact I look forward all day to seeing him."

"Are the arguments that serious?" Leah had never been one to argue. She thought it very common and unladylike.

"Oh, we don't argue. Maybe it would be better if we did, but Gerald doesn't even like discussions if I take an opposing view. Instead, I store all my antagonism inside."

"If you enjoy being in the country and look forward to Gerald's coming home each day, I don't see what's causing that antagonism."

"Because nothing seems to be right when he does get home. I wait for him to criticize something I've done or not done. And when he does talk about something he sounds so angry much of the time. Or he's sarcastic. I never know when I ask a question if I'll get a straightforward or sarcastic answer. He makes me feel stupid for asking it. And it seems as if every time I say something or make a suggestion, he disagrees—on even the most minor, unimportant matters. If I say it feels like it's getting warmer, he'll say no, it's supposed to turn cool. I stay tense, waiting to see what his opinions are so that I can agree with him. If he's angry about something, and I indicate I feel he's angry with me, he says not to take everything so personally, or not to be so defensive. That only makes it worse, because I feel he is constantly putting me on the defensive."

"And there are no pleasant times? Times when you feel at ease with him?"

"Yes, I didn't mean to sound as if he's always that way. Days can go by when everything seems perfect, and we get along beautifully. But you see, I never know. So I'm very

524

conscious of those good times. 'What a nice time we're having,' I'll think, as if I were with a stranger I'd just met and want to please."

"Lisette, I hesitate to ask this, but—do you think there's someone else in his life?" So much of what Lisette was saying about Gerald—and about herself—reminded Leah of the misery she'd experienced during the Celeste and Simone episodes. And how relieved she'd been to learn there'd actually been nothing between Baptiste and Simone. More important, after Aix-les-Bains, Simone had vanished from their lives for good.

"No, Mama, I honestly don't think so. He's at the vineyards or the winery all day and with me in the evening. He never comes to Paris unless I'm with him. No, I don't think there's anyone else."

"Then do you think maybe it's you? Are you becoming more and more disturbed because you can't be married to him? Or maybe you're both going through some kind of period of adjustment. Did you ever think that maybe you've gotten too sensitive about—about the way he's always been? You're letting things bother you that never did before?"

"I don't know," Lisette said. "I just know I can't take it much longer."

"I think you should try. Live for the pleasant times and ignore the others. No marriage is going to go smoothly all the time."

"If I felt indifferent toward him, or merely liked him, perhaps I could. But I'm fond—I love him, and that's what hurts, what makes it so hard. You know how his opinion of me has been important right from the beginning, so when he's critical, it tears me apart."

"And he loves you?"

"I'm certain of it. He can be so loving and gentle at times. If I thought he didn't, well, that might make it easier to understand."

"People are often most critical of those they love," Leah said gently. "More so than of people they care nothing about."

"All that is easy to say, Mama, but words don't help right now. I know that as soon as I walk into the apartment tomorrow evening, I'll brace myself for him to say something to start me churning inside. It's always worse when we've been apart a while."

Leah sat back in her chair and thought for a long time. "How about a change of scene?" she suggested. "A real

525

change of scene. I'd like to go back to England for another visit, and I'd need you with me."

"It sounds wonderful," and Lisette realized it was exactly what she'd been wanting to do. "Papa wouldn't mind?"

"We'll persuade him to go with us. And we'll go up to Scotland. I've longed to see Scotland."

When approached a few days later with the idea, Baptiste agreed heartily they should go, but said he couldn't be away for too long. "Stay a month, at least," he said, "and then I'll come over and meet you in London for a week. This time I promise I'll be there."

Gerald was less enthusiastic about the plan. "I know your mother needs you with her, but I don't see how I can get along without you all those weeks."

"You'll do fine," Lisette assured him. "There's so much to do with the vineyards right now, you could stay with Jean and let Céline take care of you. *And I'll have time*, she thought, *to think about which would be worse, living with you or without you.*

When Gerald saw them off on the boat train to London, the last thing Lisette said to him was, "Take care of the garden for me."

After Lisette left, Gerald found himself spending more and more time in Paris. The vineyards were going well under Jean's able care, and Gerald was occupied much of the time with the exporting end of the business. Since coming to France, he'd also transferred the handling of his other investment interests to Paris and put a good manager in charge of the Cornwall estates. He missed Lisette dreadfully and wondered why he had the feeling she'd wanted to get away from him. He'd sensed a real tension between them at the train, and she'd said good-bye as formally as if she'd been bidding farewell to a casual friend—or as if she didn't intend to return. There was more to the trip, he thought, than a need to accompany her mother.

Maybe it was because of the dinner party at Emily Berthold's. He'd noticed how bright her cheeks were while they were dressing and asked if she were wearing rouge; then she'd turned on him in a fury and announced she never wore make-up. When he'd suggested that maybe her dress was cut a little too low in front and she should wear a light scarf, she'd stormed out of the bedroom. At the dinner she'd devoted all her attention to young Monsieur Jimeaux, who was not her partner, instead of Monsieur Berthold, who was.

During a brief intermission in the musicale that followed, Gerald had said in a bantering tone that since Lisette had been spending so much time in the village, she was turning into a real little peasant. At that, she'd whispered something to Monsieur Jimeaux, and they'd left together. Not until well after midnight had she returned to the apartment. When he asked her where she'd been, she said she preferred not to talk about it, and he'd said nothing more. As much as he wished she were his wife, she was not, and so he couldn't very well play the stern, demanding husband.

A few days later, he learned from Monsieur Berthold that Monsieur Jimeaux had left suddenly for England. "I understand Lisette is over there," Monsieur Berthold remarked casually.

"Yes, she's traveling with her mother," Gerald said.

"It should be very pleasant in England right now. A pity you couldn't be with them, too."

I could, Gerald thought. He could leave immediately and join them. He could use the excuse of having to see how the manager was handling the Cornwall estate. But the trip would look exactly like what it was—a spy mission to see what Lisette was doing and whom she was with. No, he'd stay in Paris and hope she'd return. If only he knew what had gone wrong, what had caused her to turn to Monsieur Jimeaux—or want to go to England in the first place.

Walking along the banks of the Seine one afternoon, Gerald saw a young woman standing beside a group of paintings. In paint-splattered skirt and blouse and wearing only sabots on her feet, she was strikingly beautiful. Her glossy, straight black hair fell to below her waist, and her thin face was dominated by an immense pair of ebony eyes. He wished he could see her full, generous lips open into a smile.

"Are these your paintings?" he asked.

"Yes." Nicole heard the faint trace of an English accent and assumed he was a tourist. "These are the most popular views of the city."

Gerald looked at them and thought they were some of the most hideous pictures he'd ever seen. They were nothing more than garish, enlarged postcard scenes. But the young woman fascinated him. He had to know her better.

"I think I'd like this one of Notre Dame." Only heaven knew where he'd put it once he got it back to the apartment, but maybe the concierge would like it.

Nicole named a higher than usual price. It was the only

527

one she'd sold that day, and she needed the money. The man looked as if he could afford it.

"Here you are, Michele," he said, handing over the notes. She looked startled at the use of the name. "Your name is Michele, isn't it? That's the signature on the painting."

"Yes, yes, that's my name. I was surprised you noticed it."

"I'm alone in the city," he said tentatively. "I wonder if you'd care to have dinner with me, Michele."

"I wouldn't mind." A free dinner would be welcome right now.

Sitting across from her in the restaurant, Gerald was tantalized by how familiar she looked. He knew he'd never seen her before, and yet there was something about her face, especially her eyes, that taunted him.

"You have family here in Paris?" he asked, hoping to elicit a clue.

"No, I have no family. And I prefer it that way. There are no ties or responsibilities. I can live my life as I wish."

"But aren't you lonely at times?"

"I'm always lonely," Nicole said, "whether with people or by myself. I was born lonely. I'm the odd man out."

"I feel that way myself, right now. But not from choice. Someone I love very much has left me."

"She's dead?"

"No, it might be easier if she were," he answered. "She simply left me for a reason I haven't yet discovered." He saw no point in mentioning Lisette's name. Michele wouldn't know or care whom he was talking about.

"It's very painful to lose someone you love." She thought about Jerome who, in spite of his cruelty, was never far from her thoughts. And about her precious Mary.

"Yes, the apartment will seem very empty when I go back there tonight, especially after enjoying this dinner with you."

"Are you asking me to sleep with you?" Nicole asked. "If so, just say it. Don't couch it in pretty euphemistic words."

"Yes, but I don't know what to offer you."

"Nothing!" She glared at him. "I'm not a prostitute. I'll do it because I want to, because I like you."

"Thank you, Michele. Do you want to go to my apartment or to yours?"

"Apartment?" Nicole started laughing. "I have one room and it's a mess. I'd prefer to go to your place."

"Agreed." He signaled to the *maître d'*. "Will you order a cab for us, please?"

They were driving along the boulevard when Gerald

528

asked, "What about your paintings? Shouldn't we return to the quay and pick them up?"

"Raoul will take them to my room."

Gerald looked at the young woman in the darkened cab. She'd said she wasn't a prostitute, and she didn't look like one. Nor was she a simple country girl in spite of her clothes. The peasant skirt and blouse belied the subtle sophistication he saw in her face and the cultured tone of her voice. She'd been reared in a fine home and given a better than average education. As horrible as they were, her paintings showed training and talent. She was an enigma that fascinated him more the longer he talked to her. And she reminded him more and more of someone he knew, and knew quite well. If she would, he hoped she'd stay with him for a while. *God knows,* he thought, *there's no point in wondering if Lisette will return.*

At the apartment, Nicole walked through the hall and into the drawing room as if she'd lived there all her life. In a way she had. The place was almost identical to her family's, a few blocks away. She looked around the large room.

"This place is lovely," she said, "but your taste in art is atrocious."

"Worse than yours?" He held up the painting he'd bought.

"Oh, that junk. That's just for money. When I have time and don't need to be earning a living, I paint quite differently."

"I'd like to see your other things sometime."

"No reason you can't. Some are hanging in Monsieur Ébert's café, in Montmartre. They don't sell on the quay." She laughed. "They don't sell in the café either, but I haven't any more room for them at my place."

"If you had the room," he asked, "and you didn't need to worry about making a living . . . ?"

"I'd turn out the finest paintings you've ever seen. I'm really a great artist, except that no one has discovered me yet."

She slipped out of her sabots and began to unfasten her blouse.

"What are you doing?" Gerald asked.

"You brought me here to sleep with you, didn't you?" If she were lucky, she'd spend the night and he'd buy her breakfast, too.

"Not entirely. I'd like to talk, too. The bed is not the only cure for loneliness." He left her for a moment and returned with wine and fruit. "Sit down and tell me about yourself."

"I don't know yet," she said. "I can't see into the future."

"I mean your life, your past life." He found her response strange and mystifying.

"Oh, I never talk about the past. Yesterday is gone. It has no meaning."

"You can at least tell me your last name." If she had something to hide, he had no intention of probing. It was enough to have her here with him now.

"I have no last name. I'm just"—she hesitated—"just Michele."

He wondered if there were any way to break through that defensive shell. "Why are you so different, Michele?"

"Because I'm me and no one else. Everyone is different. Only most people don't realize that."

"Yes, you're right. We—or they—are. I think I need you, Michele, need you very much. Will you stay here with me? Not just for tonight, but longer."

"I'll let you know in the morning. I never plan ahead or dwell on what's past. There is no past and no future."

"Would you like to see the rest of the apartment? It might help you make up your mind."

"Yes, but it will be you and not the rooms you live in that will determine my answer." She followed him from room to room, noting the luxurious bedroom and bath and the efficient kitchen. Nothing moved her, however, until they arrived at a many-windowed sunroom overlooking the back garden. This was the kind of studio she'd dreamed about since she left home. She'd been wrong. The place did make a difference, and she knew she'd stay. But she wouldn't tell Gerald until morning.

Gerald was a comfortable lover. It was, perhaps, a strange adjective to use, but that was exactly how she felt with him. Yes, it would be easy to live with him.

"I'll stay," she told him while they were still in bed.

"I'm glad, Michele. I think you're going to make me very happy. And I hope you will be, too."

"You'll know soon enough if I'm not." Beyond that she would not commit herself.

"Shall I send for your paints and—and whatever other things you need?"

"No, I'll start all over with new ones. This will be a whole new life, and there should be nothing of the old about it."

"Your clothes?" Surely there must be something she needed from her room.

"I wear only one skirt and blouse at a time. This will suffice for a while. Then you can buy me new ones."

Yes, indeed, she certainly was different, Gerald thought, and not averse to asking for what she wanted. He admired her spunk. Life in the apartment would be anything but dull with Michele there.

"If you like," he said, "you can wear these." He walked to the huge wardrobe on one side of the bedroom and opened the doors. "These belonged to—to someone who used to live here. But I don't think she'll be wearing them again."

Nicole examined the abundant display of dresses, created by the finest couturiers in Paris. "They're a bit extravagant and fussy for my taste, but they'll do to wear around here."

Gerald could only shudder at the thought of the outburst Lisette would have at Michele's opinion of her vast and very expensive wardrobe.

"I may have to leave for most of the day from time to time," she said later over breakfast. "And I won't be questioned about where I've been."

"You'll be free to go whenever and wherever you wish. I'll understand. I hope you'll return, though."

"I make no promises," she said. "Then I don't have to break them."

"I admire your independence, Michele, even if I could never be like you."

"You must know something, Gerald. I'm the center of my own world. I'm the stone dropped into the water. The circles around me are the people I meet. They surround me, but they never touch me. I let no one touch me; then I don't get hurt."

"I won't hurt you, Michele. I promise you that. Nor will I try to get too close to you. I'm very fond of you, and I'm pleased you want to stay here, at least for a little while, but I won't ask for more than you can give."

Nicole settled as easily into Gerald's apartment as a kitten on a soft pillow. He'd been almost prodigal in buying everything she said she needed for her work: an armload of canvases, the largest tubes of paint, the most expensive brushes in all sizes, and sturdy, adjustable easels. Her days were her own, to stay in the sunroom and paint or to go wherever she wanted, to sketch. Once during the second week, she left for an entire day and didn't return until after dark.

"I'm glad to see you," was all Gerald said when she came in.

"It took me longer than I thought." She walked into the

531

bedroom to change into a velvet robe. She'd begun wearing some of the clothes in the wardrobe, and she especially liked the touch of velvet against her skin. It was comfortable for lounging in during the evening. At least Gerald had kept his promise and not asked where she'd been or why she was late. All he said later was that he'd been worried about her being out after dark.

"Never worry about me," she said. "I've long since learned to take care of myself."

Gerald agreed that the fancy furbelows and lace trimmings of Lisette's clothes did not become Nicole. Her beauty was perfect by itself, and she made the gowns look tawdry and cheap. Except for the velvet robe. In that, she looked like something out of a medieval painting.

She had been with him nearly four weeks when he received a letter from Lisette. She thought she'd extend her stay in England. As long as they couldn't be married, she said, she felt it better for her not to return. There were some problems that simply could not be resolved in the present situation. Gerald sighed. He loved Lisette, and he'd miss her terribly. He'd known something was wrong when she left, and it helped a little bit, although not much, to learn what had been troubling her. If he had to rearrange his life without her, he could do it, although it wouldn't be easy. At least Michele showed no inclination toward wanting to leave, so he'd enjoy her presence as long as she was willing to stay.

* * *

Baptiste looked out the window of the train taking him to Lyons. This was a journey he never thought he'd make. Simone's brief note had not insisted he come, but he could sense she really wanted him to. For her to ask him to travel there instead of Paris—or even to write after this length of time—indicated a great urgency. He was apprehensive about seeing her in her home. After the rather unfortunate picnic, he had worried for a while that she might be feeling some rancor about the way he'd summarily ended their up-until-then idyllic interlude. Since then, however, he'd seen her twice in Paris. For dinner only. No rides in the park, no all-day excursions into the country. They were easy, sociable evenings such as one might have with a very good friend. Memory had not intruded noticeably.

But going to her home was different. The invitation implied that Charles, her husband, would not be there. The distance required an overnight stay and that raised other possibilities.

Baptiste felt both apprehension and anticipation, both disaffection and desire about spending several hours alone with Simone. His first view of her would determine which he would succumb to.

A maid answered the door, and Baptiste followed her through a long hall toward a rear room overlooking the garden. He thought at first it was a sunroom, and then realized it had been converted to a first-floor bedroom. When he saw Simone lying on the chaise longue, he had to steel himself to keep from revealing his shock at how painfully thin and pale she was. She didn't have the dry, emaciated look that so often accompanied severe loss of weight, but her skin was almost transparent.

She rose slightly to a sitting position. "Baptiste, I am so very happy to see you. Come here and let me look at you."

"No happier than I am to see you." He went over to a chair already placed next to the chaise longue, as if in anticipation of his coming. "You're looking very beautiful." And she was, in spite of the obvious state of her health.

"I thank you, but I know you're merely flattering me."

"No, I'm not. You'll never be anything but beautiful to me." He'd been right. With the first glance, desire and anticipation had won out. No, they had been the reasons he'd accepted her invitation in the first place.

"I had to see you," she said. "One more time." She made it sound as if they'd never meet again.

"I was pleased, and a little surprised, to get your note." He could see the tears forming in her eyes. "Tell me, what's wrong?"

"Oh, something about my blood. Not making enough red cells or some such nonsense."

It wasn't nonsense, and he knew she was being flippant to keep from crying in front of him. Pernicious anemia, he thought. She must have had it quite a while, and it was obvious she didn't have much longer to live.

"What are the doctors doing for it?" He reached for her hand.

"Nothing can be done. Rest, they say. As if I had the strength to do anything else." The long, thin fingers of her other hand played restlessly with the lace ruffle around the neck of her robe. "So I lie here waiting for it to do what it will."

"Where's Charles?" Baptiste had to change the subject. If

533

they talked any more about her illness, he'd be the one to weep.

"In South America. Some new venture he thinks will bring in millions and millions of francs. Don't frown. He's been very good to me, and he'll be back next week."

"So you called on me because you're lonesome. I'm glad you did. I'm lonesome, too. Lisette and Leah are gallivanting around England."

"I wrote for another reason. There was something I had to tell you before—before it was too late. I hope you won't misinterpret it." She gripped his hand in hers. "I needed you to know you're the only man I've ever really loved. My first marriage was on parental order. Then, while it's true I once loved Jacques, it was an adolescent crush. I married him for the simple reason I couldn't have you. And the same with Charles. If that shocks you, I hope you'll forgive me."

"It doesn't shock me, Simone. It touches me very deeply. As long as we're being honest, I'll tell you something, too. If I hadn't thought I was falling in love with you, I would never have stopped—have stopped seeing you." He started to say "stopped making love to you that day in the country," but he thought it better not to invoke that memory. "But I knew where it was leading us, and I couldn't see anything but tragedy for all of us."

"Well, you're safe here today." She smiled impishly. "I won't try to seduce you this time." She, too, was remembering how close, how very close, they'd come to beginning a long-term affair. "I haven't the strength for it."

"You didn't seduce me either time. You didn't make me do anything I didn't want to do."

"And they meant something to you? The afternoon at my house? Or in the hotel at Aix-les-Bains?" She looked at him as if the answer were all-important to her.

"They meant very much to me. Why do you think I didn't dare stay another minute in the country? The failure was only momentary. Before we reached the carriage, I was— Never mind, it's all past history now."

He moved from the chair to sit beside her on the chaise longue. "If you were stronger, I'd have you tell your maid you weren't to be disturbed for the rest of the afternoon."

She leaned toward him. "Take me in your arms and hold me very tight." Her tears wet his cheek. When he kissed her, he could feel her gradually responding to him. "Having you here has made me feel much stronger."

She picked up a silver bell from her table, and in a minute the maid came in with wine and biscuits.

"Just leave them here, Nina. And I don't wish to be disturbed for the rest of the afternoon. Please tell Sophie there will be two of us for dinner."

"Shall I pour you some?" Baptiste reached for the wine.

"Yes, the doctors say it will help keep my strength up. I rather think I'll need quite a bit this afternoon."

"We'll probably finish the whole bottle," Baptiste joked.

Simone moved over slightly so Baptiste could lie beside her. "I'm glad now I had this chaise made wider than usual. I don't sleep well at night, so I nap a good bit during the day. This is more comfortable than the bed, but I wanted it big enough so I wouldn't feel confined. It makes a very nice place for a tête-à-tête, doesn't it?"

"It's perfect." He turned on his side and gathered her into his arms. He knew for certain now that he'd never see her again. Before, there'd always been a nagging, aching desire to see her one more time. After today that ache would be dispelled, and memory would be enough for him.

During the moments that followed, Baptiste realized he'd almost forgotten how warm and tender and passionate she could be. He worried lest making love would exhaust too much of her strength, but she was, if anything, more responsive than he'd remembered. The other encounters had been brief, hurried affairs. Now they took as much time as they wanted to enjoy each other, to kiss and caress before being caught up in the need to seek the ultimate moment of satisfaction.

When it was over, Simone fainted and went limp in his arms. Trying to revive her with wine, Baptiste was frantic at the thought he'd allowed her to become overwrought, that their being together had harmed her in some way. Soon she was breathing normally, and he saw she'd fallen asleep. After more than half an hour, his arm she was lying on grew numb, but he didn't want to move her. As long as she was resting, there wouldn't be any pain, and he knew there could be considerable pain with her condition.

"I'm sorry," she said, opening her eyes and coming wide awake in an instant. "It was pretty rude of me to fall asleep."

"I'm not sure what that says about me as a lover," he teased, "but I dozed a bit myself."

"I took it for granted you'd stay for dinner," she said. "Will you stay the night, too?"

"I'm surprised you'd ask. Would you expect a man who has spent one of the most pleasant afternoons in his life to leave immediately afterward? As long as," he added, "we don't have to move from this chaise."

"No easier said than done. Nina will serve dinner in here, and we can watch the moon come up over those trees. It should be full tonight, and there is no more beautiful sight around here."

"Yes, there is. You. With your flushed cheeks and hair all in disarray. Will Nina be shocked?"

"No. She mailed the note for me. She knows most of my secrets."

While he ate, Baptiste sat in the chair, but as soon as he was finished, he returned to the chaise longue, and they sat up to watch the moon. They talked about all the things they'd done in their lives and all the things they wished they had done.

"Is being faithful to Leah one of the things you wished you'd done?" Simone asked.

"I'd be lying if I said no. But I wouldn't have missed knowing you for the world. That's quite a dilemma, isn't it?"

"But one you've solved quite nicely, I think," she said. "It isn't always to one's credit to be totally honest."

"You're right. Not if it means hurting someone you love. I feel, though, that I've hurt you."

"You have, but being here with me now makes up for all of it, because I know you have loved me a little bit, too."

"That's why I came. I wouldn't have otherwise."

This time the lovemaking was briefer but no less passionate or tender or satisfying. Then they slept, without waking, until morning.

"I haven't slept like that for months," Simone said while they breakfasted. "You're far better medicine than the drugs and wine the doctors prescribe."

Baptiste looked at Simone. She appeared rested and yet more wan than ever. His visit had been good for her in one way, but in another, he was sure, it had had a dangerously debilitating effect.

"If you want to catch the mid-morning train," she said finally, "you'd better leave now."

"I don't really want to go."

"I know, and I don't want you to. But it has to come sometime, and postponing it will only increase the agony."

She didn't need to tell him she was extremely tired and in

real pain. It wouldn't do either of them any good for him to stay.

"Take care of yourself." He leaned over to kiss her good-bye. Her lips had far less color than the afternoon before, and he saw it was a real effort for her to raise her arms to put them around his neck.

"I will. I promise."

Baptiste was grateful he had the compartment to himself on the way back to Paris. He hadn't cried while he was with Simone, but now he let the tears flow freely until they reached the outskirts of the city.

Chapter Forty-four

SEÑOR QUINSARRO learned about the aborted duel between Robert and Émile, and the reason for it, while drinking his morning coffee at the Café du Monde. He hurried home at once and strode into his wife's dressing room. Within ten minutes Isabella was sent for.

"Do you know," her father demanded, "who this Robert Fontaine is you've been seeing?"

"Yes, Papa." She was immediately on the defensive. "His father is from one of New Orleans' finest families."

"And do you know who his mother is?"

"The cousin of Marcel Bonvivier," she said. "Why?"

Señora Quinsarro broke in. "It's not so much who he is but *what* he is." She was so overwrought she could hardly speak. "A nigra!"

"No, Mama! You don't know what you're saying." She looked frantically from one parent to the other.

"Yes, Isabella," her father said, "his mother is a Negro—actually an octoroon, but there's no difference."

"I don't believe you." Isabella was on the verge of tears. "I've seen pictures of Madame Fontaine, and she's well respected in France."

"*Madame* Fontaine, indeed," the señora said. "Over here she wouldn't be honored with that title. She was Baptiste Fontaine's mistress, and I don't know who else's. A whore!"

Her last exclamation was directed as much at her husband as at Isabella. Señor Quinsarro made no secret of his many extramarital affairs.

"That's enough, my dear," he said. "I think Isabella understands what we're saying."

Throughout this unbelievable conversation, Isabella lost all power to think. She loved Robert, but she was horrified at what she was hearing. Not so much that he was one-sixteenth Negro, but that if they married they couldn't remain in Louisiana. She couldn't live at her beloved Casa Verde. She remembered something she'd heard.

"I love Robert, and I want to marry him, in spite of what you're saying. Ambrose Delisle says plenty who call themselves Creoles have dark blood. No one would dare interfere if you agreed, Papa," she begged. "You're the most powerful of the Spanish Creoles in the *Vieux Carré*."

"And who is Ambrose Delisle to talk," her mother said. "A bastard!"

"If I want to marry Robert, you can't stop me." She no longer tried to control her tears.

"You don't know what you're saying." Her father spoke more gently. He adored his oldest daughter and would have given her anything she wanted. "You'd be made to feel the shame for the rest of your life, because everyone in the *Vieux Carré* knows now who Robert is. And you couldn't be married here. It is the law, and I cannot change it, not even for you."

"Our whole family will be shamed—is shamed now," Señora Quinsarro moaned. "I'll never be able to hold my head up again. I think it's time, Marcos, you told her what we decided."

"Yes, yes, of course." He turned to Isabella. "It goes without saying that you're forbidden to see Robert again."

"Not—not even to explain? To tell him good-bye?" She had to see him, to tell him she still loved him. As much as he loved her, he'd find a way for them to marry and stay in Louisiana. They could hide at Casa Verde, lock themselves in, away from the world and its horrid laws.

"No," her father said sternly. "I've already sent him word to that effect. If he's a gentleman, he will honor my wishes. And I expect you to do the same."

"And," her mother interrupted, "your father and I think it best if you spend the next few weeks in the country, away from prying eyes and embarrassing questions. I can't be

538

away from here, but Tia will go with you. You will leave this afternoon."

Isabella bowed her head as if loath to agree, but she wasn't sorry about having to leave the city. She loved the plantation so much, she'd spend the rest of her life there if she could.

"It's rather ironic," Señor Quinsarro added casually, "that you should be living in a home that once belonged to Baptiste Fontaine."

"What? This house?" Isabella was stunned.

"No, the plantation. I recall now that my father bought it from Monsieur Fontaine's cousin; he was only the agent, though, or at least no more than part owner. It had been in their family for several generations."

No wonder Robert loves it as much as I do, Isabella thought. *Yet he never mentioned it. Or is that why he asked me to marry him? No, he merely said he had strange feelings about it. He must never have been told that it once belonged to his father.* She had a second reason to be willing to go to the country, and she set about writing a note.

Robert would have been completely disheartened at receiving Señor Quinarro's stern command not to see Isabella again if he hadn't received a terse, rather cryptic note from her soon afterward. It contained only four words: "Next week. Wharf. Nap." But it was as clear as if she'd written pages. She was being sent to the plantation, and she wanted him to meet her next week at the wharf while Tia Martina was taking her usual afternoon nap.

He knew why Isabella had not suggested coming out immediately. She needed time to lull Tia Martina into believing that Señor Quinsarro's orders would be obeyed. Robert would use that same time to do some steady, rational thinking. Isabelle still loved him, or she wouldn't have sent the note. If learning about his heritage truly had turned her against him, she wouldn't send for him merely to say goodbye. She would have been more than willing never to see him again. He had to hope she still wanted to marry him.

They would have to leave Louisiana, of course, and go to France. As much as the plantation meant to her, that would be the real test of her love. It had been his dream as well as hers to settle at Casa Verde, to make it bloom like the beautiful place it must have been at one time. And to fill it with children. Coming from a large family, he could think of nothing more satisfying than having his own—and Isabella's—brood around him.

During the days that followed, Robert involved himself in the business of the office and prepared to take over Marcel's position. He was grateful to have something to keep his hands busy and his mind occupied. There were shipments to be opened, checked, and ticketed for the various establishments—both large wholesale firms and small, independent shops—all over the States, from the Mississippi to the East Coast.

In the evenings, he frequently met Ambrose for drinks and dinner, but he discouraged any attempts of his friend to lure him to a place like Madame Eugénie's. In his heart he was already pledged to Isabella, and he'd remain true to her.

"Then for God's sake," Ambrose said one evening, "let's go to the theatre. We've got to do something to dispel this gloom. You sit at this table much longer and you're going to develop cobwebs."

"I don't think I'd enjoy it much in the mood I'm in."

"Well, I would. But I don't want to leave you."

"Don't worry, Ambrose, I'm not going to put a pistol to my head if that's what you're thinking."

"I agree. No woman is worth it."

"Isabella is. But she sent a note asking me to meet her near the plantation next week. I'm hoping to persuade her to go to France with me where we can be married."

"Good for her," Ambrose said. "I didn't know she had that much spunk."

"No congratulations yet. I'm not only asking her to marry me, but to exile herself in France. You forget about the laws against miscegenation."

"I'll wager those laws will be changed before you've been two years in France. At least for anyone with one-eighth or less Negro blood. After all, don't forget that Virginia and some other Southern states had mixed-blood laws that allowed anyone with one-eighth or less to marry a white."

"That was before the war, a long time before," Robert sighed.

"What about the fifteenth amendment, right of equal suffrage? It won't be long before that extends to aspects of life other than voting."

"Don't be an idealist, Ambrose. That was passed over thirty years ago. What makes you think there'll be any changes in the next two years?"

540

"Well, dammit, it's not right," Ambrose said angrily. "If you and Isabella love each other, there shouldn't be a law that says you can't be married." Ambrose poured himself another drink. "I think I'll run for some office and get the law changed."

Robert leaned back in his chair and roared with laughter. "Oh, Ambrose, you are a dreamer. If you were elected, you'd probably be a minority of one. And you might not get elected."

"I know, because I'm a bastard. Here." He passed the bottle to Robert. "At least we outcasts can stick together."

"Funny," Robert said, "I never felt like an outcast in France, nor over here either, until this question of marriage came up. I never could understand Henri's feeling that he had tainted blood. I'm proud of my mother, and proud that I'm part of her. I'm proud of my father, too, for not letting foolish myths destroy their love."

"I know you are," Ambrose said. "You don't have to defend them to me."

"It's more than that, Ambrose. I want to be just like them. I want to know I have the same kind of strength and courage they showed through all the difficult years. I couldn't call myself their son if I didn't act on my convictions."

"But you're not the one who has to make the important decision. It's Isabella."

"I know that," Robert said. "That's what makes me uneasy."

The sun was setting over the river when Isabella rode back to the house. It was a relief to be on the plantation, away from her mother's tantrums and her father's fierce scowls. From their behavior, one would think she'd been caught in bed with one of the foreign sailors who frequented the levees near Jackson Square. So what if Robert's great-great-grandfather had been a Southern planter who "jumped the fence," as the saying went among thoroughbred horse breeders? That had to have been a hundred years ago, and times were different now. Anyway, she loved him. Papa had never denied her anything before, and once he realized she was determined to marry Robert, he'd find a way to circumvent the law or have it changed. Everything life had brought her, including being loved by Robert, Isabella considered her due. To her, marriage meant an elaborate wedding and a "happily-ever-after" idyll on the plantation with an adoring Robert. It did not include sacrifice.

After sending the note, she never doubted that Robert would come. He would know exactly the right thing to do to solve their predicament. For all the goods and attentions showered on her, Isabella was neither spoiled nor willful; she merely charmed everyone she knew into acquiescing to her wishes. She then appeared so grateful that the giver felt like the one being gifted. She had learned early to despise her mother's habit of whining or crying to get what she wanted. It was not only disgusting but stupid, Isabella thought, since her mother was usually disappointed with the outcome.

Each afternoon, as soon as Tia Martina retired to her room for her nap, Isabella waited until she was quite certain her aunt was asleep and then saddled her horse for the ride to the deserted wharf. For five days she was disappointed. Surely Robert had gotten her message; and if he truly loved her, he'd come to see her. Each day, her disappointment was intense, and she found it hard continuing to be civil to her aunt. Tia Martina mentioned Robert's name only once, and then with a reproving click of her tongue against her teeth.

"If you don't mind, Tia, I don't ever want to hear his name again. He has humilated me and the family beyond redemption." There, she thought, that should put her aunt off guard.

On the sixth day, Isabella wasn't feeling well and went to her own room to nap. There seemed no point in going to the wharf again. Robert wasn't coming. He was following her father's warning not to see her. She wouldn't believe it was because he no longer loved her.

By Thursday of the week following the fracas with Émile, Robert could wait no longer. He couldn't go another day without seeing Isabella. He would take the chance that she had worked out a way to elude her aunt.

He saddled his horse and rode out along the Natchez Trace. This was the very same route, he thought as he cantered along, that his mother had taken when she first tried to flee North and had been kidnapped by men intending to sell her into prostitution in Natchez. And somewhere along here, his father had rescued her. It sounded very romantic, and yet, Robert thought, it must have been a frightening time for her. He smiled to himself and wondered how Isabella would react if he kidnapped her and whisked her off to France.

Tying his horse among the trees so it couldn't be seen

from either the road or the bridle path, Robert walked to the wharf. It was, as always, completely deserted. His heart sank. He supposed he'd been imagining Isabella sitting there waiting for him. It was an ungentlemanly thought; he should be the one waiting for her. For a while he paced the length of the rotting boards before sitting down and leaning against one of the pilings. He waited for more than an hour and had about decided she'd either changed her mind or been unable to get away. When he heard the sound of hooves and looked up to see Isabella galloping toward him, he was once more confident she loved him enough to marry him, no matter what the future might hold for them.

Before Robert could help her dismount, Isabella began crying. She'd been so afraid of being disappointed again, she couldn't control her relief.

"I thought you weren't coming," she sobbed. "Every afternoon—and you never came."

"There, there, it's all right now. I'm here. I wanted to come. I would have been here the day after I got your note if I were sure you could get away."

"Hold me close and tell me you love me. That's all that's sustained me these past few days."

"I love you and I'll always love you." It felt so right to have her in his arms; no one could tell him it was wrong for them to love each other, to want to be married.

"I almost didn't come today," she said, after they'd sat down and were looking out across the water. "I was so tired of being disappointed. I didn't think I could stand it one more time."

"It wouldn't have mattered." Robert turned so she could rest her head against his shoulder. "I would have come every afternoon from now on. I would have gone to the house if I had to. There's no way anyone is going to keep me from seeing you."

"For how long? Until someone finds us? I want us to be together, Robert, not meeting like this."

"We will be. I have it all worked out. There's a company ship leaving for France the first of next week. We'll sail on it, and we can be married when we get to Paris. Or, if you like, when it stops in Martinique."

"France?" Isabella had never thought about leaving Louisiana. She'd been so certain something could be worked out so they could marry and remain here. "But I don't want to live in France."

543

"You'll love it over there, darling. We'll be happy, I promise."

"I don't know." She eased out of his arms. Things were not going at all as she'd hoped. "I'd always dreamed of living here at Casa Verde. I don't see how I can leave it."

"It won't be for always," Robert tried to assure her. "We'll return and live here. Someday the laws will be changed and we can come back. We'll live at Casa Verde just as we planned. I love the plantation as much as you do. I don't know why, but I feel I belong here. And not because I love you. It's very strange. I've felt that way from the first day I came out here."

"Then your family never told you," she said. "Casa Verde was once Belle Fontaine. It was your father's home."

She waited for some exclamation of surprise, some look of disbelief. Instead, he turned away and gazed across the river.

"I should have known," he said quietly. "I told you once I felt as if I were coming home. I knew he'd had a plantation on the river, but I don't think I ever heard the name or any description of it."

"So we will return, won't we?" Isabella asked. "If I decide to go to France with you?"

"I can't make any promises, darling. It wouldn't be fair to you. I wish I could, but all we can do is hope."

Isabella settled back into his arms. "I love you, Robert. But I need a little time. To leave this—and my family—for maybe years and years. Please understand. I can't answer you right now."

"I do understand." Holding her close, he felt the rapid beating of her heart, and understood well her turmoil of indecision. He was asking her to leave everything that was familiar and dear to her, not only the life she had known until then but also the future she had dreamed of. "I'll come out every afternoon, so you won't be disappointed again. Meanwhile, I'll make the arrangements for us to sail next week if—if you say we are to go to France."

Isabella reached up and held his face in her hands. "Kiss me and tell me our love will be strong enough to keep me from looking back, from any regrets if I marry you."

"It is and it will be." He kissed her and then, seeing the tears on her cheeks, he kissed her again and again until the tears vanished and she was smiling.

"I have to get back," she said. "I don't want to, but if Tia wakes up and becomes suspicious, I won't be able to ride out here again without her."

Robert helped her onto her horse, and then wondered why he felt such sadness when she looked back while riding away.

Knowing now just when Tia Martina retired for her nap, Robert timed his arrival the next day so he wouldn't have quite so long to wait for Isabella. Even so, she wasn't at the wharf when he arrived. Less impatient than the day before, he lounged against a piling and watched a school of fish circling close to shore.

"Monsieur Fontaine!"

Robert jumped at the sound of the all-too-familiar voice.

"Señor Quinsarro!" Robert's hand shook as he threw his cigar into the water. Damn! He should have known their trysting place would be discovered sooner or later. Tia Martina's eyes had seen more than he realized. They should have thought of a different place to meet.

"I'm sorry you chose to ignore my orders not to see Isabella again," Señor Quinsarro said. "Not for your sake, I assure you, but for hers. I do not enjoy having to punish my daughter."

"Punish?" Robert felt his scalp tingling and his face turning red. He had to keep his temper even though nothing would give him more satisfaction than wringing the man's neck. "What are you planning to do to her?"

"What we are doing is for her own happiness. Which she would never find with you. She has been given the choice of going to Spain and entering a convent or remaining here to marry a man we choose for her and live at Casa Verde. I don't think I need tell you which she has chosen."

"I understand, sir. I know how much she loves the plantation."

"And," Señor Quinsarro's voice deepened and became more stern, "do not think about contacting her and making plans for an elopement. She will be well guarded. Should she try anything so foolish and be caught, she will not be given the option a second time. She *will* be sent to Spain."

"You have my word, sir. I will not try to see her. Nor will I communicate with her. I have only one request to ask of you in return. Will you please tell her I love her and I always will?"

"I think not. It would only upset her too much. You are presumptuous to make such a request. She has been deeply

545

hurt by all of this, and I will do nothing to intensify that hurt. If you wish to assign blame for all this, Monsieur Fontaine, place it on yourself, not on me. And now I bid you good day."

Robert stayed on the wharf a long time after Señor Quinsarro left. What the man said at the last was true. He had to bear the guilt for hurting her, for letting her fall in love with him. He should have known from the beginning that nothing could come of their love for each other. But that didn't ease the hurt in his own heart.

From time to time, Robert saw Émile, who made it a point to turn away and avoid conversation. That would never do, Robert thought, if he were to carry out the revenge he had in mind. At first he'd meant to avenge the insults against his mother. Now he had a dual reason for wishing to make Émile suffer. He had lost Isabella. He knew Émile thought him both a coward and a fool, and that was exactly the impression he wanted to establish. He would not let Émile ignore him.

He spoke whether Émile answered or not. He invited him to his table for a drink, and he suggested they go to the steeplechase and trotting races together. His first overtures were met with silence. Then, obviously curious as to why Robert was courting his friendship, Émile warily accepted the invitations.

Robert could endure Émile's superior attitude and the sarcastic comments of those who wondered why he would choose friendship with the man whose slanderous remarks against his mother had so aroused his fury. After a few weeks, in fact, it began to seem as if there'd never been a disagreement between the two, let alone a situation volatile enough to bring them to gunpoint. That, too, was what Robert wanted. He could afford to bide his time and let all the gossip die down. He was simply waiting for the right time and place to get the revenge he hungered for.

Meanwhile, he thought about returning to France for a visit. He had to get away from New Orleans with its constant reminders of Isabella. And the plantation that had been his father's and had nearly become his. While in France, he'd talk to his father about the possibility of opening an office in San Francisco. It would be an exciting new venture, one he'd been thinking about before he met Isabella.

Chapter Forty-five

NICOLE HAD NO IDEA when she moved in with Gerald Boswick that she'd stay longer than a few weeks. It was now a little more than two months. They were not always together. He frequently had to spend several days at a time at the winery or in the vineyards, but he insisted the apartment was her home for as long as she wanted to stay there. He gave her a generous allowance as well as paying for everything she needed, so she was able to spend one day a week in the country. She liked the arrangement. Gerald allowed her privacy and demanded very little except her company. She had the large bedroom all to herself most nights, and she found his reluctance to ask to sleep with her both amusing and touching.

For Gerald, the situation was ideal. Nicole was a delightful companion. He was surprised, after the serious mien she displayed the first few days, to find she had a keen sense of humor and enjoyed making him laugh. More than once he caught an expression on her face that teased him unmercifully, taunting him into trying to remember who she reminded him of. All his memory told him was that it was a woman, but older than Michele. Then he tried to pass it off by thinking it must be someone he'd merely seen in passing.

When Nicole was in the mood to make him laugh uproariously, she'd put on something of Lisette's and prance around in a burlesque of a fine lady, or she'd become a grotesque clown with a painted face. Once she lifted up the frilly skirts of a dress and startled him by dancing the can-can. Then she threw the skirt over her head and revealed she wore nothing underneath. She was like an impish child in so many ways, and then in other ways, like a woman who'd suffered a great tragedy. When she felt troubled, she let him take her in his arms and hold her all night, as if needing desperately to forego all her independent airs.

Nicole was in the sunroom, painting as usual, when she

heard someone opening the door to the apartment. Since it was always kept locked, she assumed Gerald had returned early from the country. He'd said he might be back today, but probably late in the evening. She started to wipe her brush on the silk hostess robe she was wearing before going to meet him. Then she saw one more spot on the canvas that needed touching up.

That was the scene Lisette walked into: Nicole, in one of her own favorite hostess gowns, standing at the easel. "Nicole! What are you doing here?" Her first impulse was to run over and throw her arms around her sister. She couldn't believe that after all these years, she'd finally found her. Then an expression on Nicole's face stopped her.

Nicole turned her head and dropped the brush she was holding. "Lisette?" In contrast to Lisette's startled, high-pitched scream, Nicole's voice was amazingly calm and self-controlled. "I might ask you the same thing. Why are you here?"

"Why? This is my home, that's why." She was too dumbfounded to say anything more even when she saw Nicole wipe her palette knife on her already paint-smeared skirt.

"Oh." So Lisette, her own sister, was the woman Gerald had loved and who'd left him. It was ironic but no less amusing that Gerald had chosen her to take Lisette's place. "I was under the impression you'd be gone for good." It had been so long since she'd seen Lisette, and so much had happened during the intervening years, she felt she was talking to a stranger instead of her own sister.

"Well, I'm not. I'm here." Nicole's cool, impervious demeanor surprised and hurt her. It also put the quietus to any notion that this might be a tender sisterly reunion. For the moment, the sight of Nicole wiping her brush on her best hostess gown made her more furious than the obvious fact that Nicole was living with Gerald. Then the implication of that dawned on her, and she became livid.

Lisette had spent the last several weeks vacillating between her choices: a new life without Gerald or continuing with him and learning to endure the difficult times. She'd finally chosen the latter. She had returned because she loved Gerald, loved him more than she thought when she left him. She could not see herself living without him.

Nicole was no longer her sister. She was now an interloper—a rival—and a threat to any reconciliation with Gerald. She looked again at the figure in the paint-splattered gown, and Nicole suddenly became the embodiment of Lisette's alter ego. She was what Lisette felt Gerald never allowed her to be: her own self with her own needs and weaknesses. She didn't care about the gown; it had not really been one of her favorites. But if she'd soiled it the way Nicole had, Gerald would have been outraged. Nicole had a self-assurance and freedom of spirit—and of action —that Lisette lacked, because, she thought, Gerald had forced her to subordinate herself to him. Not consciously, perhaps, but because his good opinion of her and her need for his approval controlled everything she said or did.

Lisette's chest was heaving, and she was having difficulty breathing. She was torn between sitting down to keep her legs from giving way and turning and running out of the apartment. She decided instead to remain standing, and she gripped the back of a chair. "I'm here and back to stay," she said. "You still haven't answered my question. What are you doing here?"

"I'm living with Gerald. He bought one of my paintings and asked me to move in."

"Well, you can damn well get out right now. Take your things and go."

"Oh, no," Nicole said, "not until Gerald gets here and tells me to. Don't think you can push me around, or do as you please with me. You did when I was younger, but you're not going to do it any longer."

Lisette moved around the chair until she was standing within two feet of Nicole. "I love Gerald. That's why I came back. I think he still loves me. I want you gone from here by the time he comes home."

"I don't think so. Gerald wouldn't like that very well. He adores me. I keep him amused, and it's obvious no one has done that for a long time." She spoke more in pity than with scorn, but the effect on Lisette was the same.

"You little bitch," she said under her breath.

Gerald chose that moment to walk in. At first, neither of the women saw him.

He was stupified at the scene before him. He looked at Lisette first, who appeared as poised and beautiful as usual; she was, however, gripping the back of a chair as if to steady herself and her eyes were blazing with fury. Then at Nicole, who stood calmly in the middle of the room, flicking her paintbrush back and forth across the skirt of the gown. At that moment neither woman was saying a word.

Good God! he thought. *Why did Lisette have to walk in on this? Why didn't she let me know she was coming home?*

It was too late now for wishing away what had already happened. Nor could he think of any explanation acceptable to Lisette. If he lost her again, it would probably be for good and it was his own damn fault.

A change of expression on Nicole's face made Lisette turn around. She was furious and she was hurt. At the sight of Gerald she became too numb to cry and too proud to raise her voice. "I came home at a rather awkward time, didn't I?"

"I—I was about to say the same thing," he stammered.

"I suppose you found it rather piquant to take up with my sister as soon as I was out of the way. But the irony of it doesn't amuse me."

Gerald looked again from Lisette to Nicole. He saw absolutely no similiarity between them. Yet he should have known. Nicole was the image of Leah; it was Leah's face that had haunted him when he tried to think who it was Nicole resembled.

"Your sister? Good God, I didn't know. You never told me you had a sister named Michele. Please believe me, I—"

"Michele?" Lisette interrupted and then started laughing hysterically. "Is that what she calls herself now? This is Nicole, the black sheep of the family. Keeps everyone worried sick most of the time wondering where and how she is." *What a stupid, inane conversation this is,* Lisette thought. *I come home to find Gerald has taken a mistress. The mistress is my sister. And all we're doing is standing around talking like actors in a farce.*

"I—I saw the name Michele on her paintings, and she never told me differently."

"Why should I?" Nicole chimed in. "What difference does a name make? How was I supposed to know Gerald was your cast-off lover? Nor," she added, staring straight at Lisette, "would it have made any difference."

Lisette decided it was time for someone to act. She turned on Gerald. "Aren't you going to tell her to leave?" If he didn't, she'd know she'd lost. It was a gamble but she had to take it.

"No. I'm going to get some brandy. I think we all need it." He hurried out of the room as if seeking a momentary reprieve from the feminine wrath he knew would explode before long. He wanted to take Lisette in his arms, tell her he'd do anything to make up for this lapse if she'd stay. But he didn't want to hurt Michele—Nicole. She'd come to him when he desperately needed to ease the pain of losing Lisette. He would have to find some way to make it up to her for ending their affair so abruptly. Even if Lisette chose not to stay, he could no longer continue with Nicole.

"Don't worry," Nicole said after Gerald left, "he doesn't have to tell me to leave. I hadn't planned to stay here much longer anyway."

Lisette watched, fascinated and horrified, while Nicole unfastened the hostess gown, let it fall to the floor, and walked stark naked across the room. What if Gerald walked in!

"For God's sake, Nicole," Lisette shouted, "put some clothes on."

"I will. And don't worry, they'll be my own." She began looking through a pile of things in one corner. "I'll never touch anything that belongs to you again." She found the old skirt and blouse she wanted.

Lisette looked at Nicole standing barefoot in the middle of the room. She seemed more like a pitiful waif than a dangerous rival for Gerald's affections. She supposed her fury and hurt came not so much from the fact it was Nicole who had supplanted her, but that Gerald had turned to someone else so soon after she left.

"I'm sorry, Nicole," she said, "I shouldn't have shouted at you or said the things I did. I couldn't help it. Maybe you can understand how I felt when I walked in and saw you. I should have said how wonderful it was to see you again." Lisette hesitated. "Are you in love with Gerald?"

"No, but he's been kind to me, the first kindness I've known in a long time."

"Yes, he's a very kind and gentle man. We're not married. He has a wife in England. That's why I left him. I thought I couldn't live with him any longer without being married to him. But I came back because I love him. I would have fought to get him back from you."

"You'd never have to do that," Nicole said. "I made up my mind a long time ago that no one would ever get so close to me, mean so much to me, that I couldn't live without them."

Lisette knew very well what Nicole was saying, and it saddened her to think their own family had made her so bitter. Nicole had run away the first time soon after Robert was born; now she was still running away—and trying to hide—from the hurts of the world.

"Will we see you again?" Lisette asked. "Mama and

Papa have been so terribly worried about you all these years."

"I don't think so." Nicole shook her head. "Best not to."

"But I can tell them where you are?"

"How I am, but not where I am." All the while she talked, she gathered up paints and brushes and placed them neatly on a table. "I'll return to my studio. I have everything I need there and someone waiting for me. He's not always kind, but he loves me, and he's a damn good artist. He's what I'm used to and better for me—for my painting—than this. I was getting lazy and too well fed. I need to be hungry to do my best work." She saw the pained look on Lisette's face. "Don't worry, I didn't mean it literally. I don't starve. Just ask Gerald. He'll tell you about the paintings I sell."

"Well, at least sit down and wait for him to bring the brandy. Then we'll go out for dinner. We ought to celebrate this–this reunion in some way." There had to be some way to reach her, to bring her back into the family.

"No, I'm going to leave." She bent down to put on her sabots. "Tell Gerald good-bye for me and that I thank him for everything. These few weeks have been very happy ones, but even the best has to come to an end sometime." She gathered up her canvas bag and started toward the door. Then she turned around. "Gerald loves you, but being alone frightens him. He has never learned to live with loneliness."

She made no move to embrace Lisette or to kiss her good-bye, and Lisette watched her leave as casually as if they'd been having a friendly chat. Lisette wanted to run after her, beg her to stay a while longer, but she knew it would do no good.

Gerald came in carrying a tray with brandy bottle and glasses. "Where's Nicole? In the bedroom? I never will truly comprehend the fact that she's the sister I heard you speak of so often."

"She's gone."

"I should have known who she was," he said, as if he hadn't heard what Lisette said. "The whole time we were together I tried to think who she reminded me of. She looks just like Leah, doesn't she?"

"The image of her. I'm really surprised you didn't realize who she was." She saw him looking around. "I said she was gone, Gerald. She's left. For good. She said to tell you good-bye and thank you for everything."

He walked over to put his arms around her, then stopped. "Do I dare ask if you're going to stay? If you forgive me? It was just that I missed you so desperately and was so damned lonely for you. And then you wrote that you weren't coming back."

Lisette reached for his arms and put them around her waist. "If you forgive me for running away."

"Why did you? What went wrong?"

"Too many petty reasons to bother you with. I was more upset than I realized that we can't be married, and so a lot of foolish reasons grew into one gigantic one."

He kissed her for a long time. "I'm glad you're back. I won't ask why."

"The most important reason of all—I love you very much. I was miserable the whole time I was away from you. Married or not, I want to spend the rest of my life with you."

"I couldn't have gone much longer without you. I was already planning to—to end things with Nicole. I was going to England and ask you to come back with me. I can't live without you, either."

Their joyful and passionate reconciliation was made the more intense by Lisette's realization she had very nearly failed to see where and with whom her true happiness lay.

"Tell me," she said later, sitting up in bed. "Did Nicole wear all my clothes?"

"Oh, no," Gerald laughed. "I don't believe it. I think that bothers you more than the thought I slept with her."

"Well, not really, but it's the second most bothersome thing." She wasn't going to ask, she didn't want to know, why he had brought Nicole here to live with him. Nicole had given her the answer when she said she amused him. Lisette couldn't remember the last time she and Gerald had had fun together, had laughed uproariously, or teased each other. Their life had become too sedate and settled. They'd both taken everything too seriously. It was time to resurrect the sense of humor that had amused him when they first met.

"No," he said, "she didn't wear them all. She usually preferred her skirt and blouse—when she wasn't naked."

"Naked!"

"Yes, she said it made her feel freer. 'Unemcumbered' was the word I think she used."

"And, my Lord, I don't suppose you minded," Lisette said in a bantering tone.

553

"No, I rather enjoyed it." He grinned. "After I got over the first shock."

Without reaching for her nightgown, Lisette slipped out of bed, walked over to her dressing table, and began brushing her hair.

"Lisette! What are you doing?" Gerald sat straight up in the bed.

"I'm finding out what it's like to feel free. And I think I like it."

"Do put on a robe, or—" he looked at her long, lithe body, still very youthful and seductive "—or come back to bed."

"Which do you prefer?" She gave him an adoring, bewitching smile. "The choice is yours."

"Come back to bed," he said gently.

She'd been right to return, Lisette thought as she lay cradled in Gerald's arms. They might never be able to marry, and she'd never become Duchess of Highcastle, but as long as they continued to love each other, she had something more important than a wedding ring or a title.

Leah put the receiver down on the telephone stand. She'd long since got over her awe of the telephone.

"It's for you, Baptiste." She waited until he was settled in his chair, phone in hand, and then returned to her sewing room. A few minutes later he wheeled in.

"Who was that?" she asked when he didn't say anything. He looked unusually pale, and she worried lest it was bad news from the office. When he didn't answer, she asked again, "Anyone I know?"

"Simone is dead." His head fell forward into his cupped hands. He'd known it was coming, but it was still a shock: with her death something beautiful and precious went out of his life. More tangible than memory if less than reality.

"Simone!" It had been years since Leah'd thought of Simone, years during which the past had been forgotten by her but evidently not by Baptiste.

"How?" she asked. "And who was that?"

"Her brother in Lyons. She died after a lingering illness. Just two days ago."

Strange he should be so moved, Leah thought. Simone had, thankfully, died for her a long time ago.

"I wonder why he called you," she said, "and how he knew you'd want to know." Had there been letters between them all these years? Or clandestine meetings in Paris when she assumed he was staying overnight because of pressing business at the office? Was she ever to have the pain eased completely—or, better yet, destroyed?

"Simone asked him to—to let us know if she should die," Baptiste said sorrowfully. "It was one of her last requests. All these years, and one of her last thoughts was of us."

Or of you? Leah thought. *The brother didn't tell me on the phone. He asked for Baptiste.*

"Have you—have you seen Simone since we were at Aix-les-Bains?" she asked fearfully.

"I went to see her in Lyons while you were in England with Lisette. She was very ill then, and I knew she was dying."

"How did you know?" She knew she was probing for answers that would be better left unknown.

"She wrote to me—to us—asking us to come for a visit. I could tell from her tone if not her words that it was an urgent request. Even though you were in England, I felt I should go."

"And—?"

"She wanted to tell us how much our friendship had meant to her. She was very ill. Pernicious anemia, I think. She wasn't very specific, but she was too weak to move from her couch."

"Strange, though," Leah said, "that she should write after all these years." If Simone had been that weak, she thought, at least nothing could have taken place between them.

"I suppose she simply had a tremendous desire—need—to see old friends one more time."

"I suppose so." But it wasn't enough. If it had been nothing more than seeing a long-forgotten friend when she was ill and then hearing of her death, Baptiste would not be as dispirited and mournful as he was now. "You saw her before that, didn't you?"

"A few times, yes. In Paris." There no longer seemed any reason to hide the truth from Leah.

"I see." Her hands were clammy, and her whole body was covered with cold sweat. Her heart began fluttering, and she thought she was going to be sick. After all these years, the pain she thought dead had been revived by a phone call.

"We met again—after Aix-les-Bains—by accident," he said, "in a restaurant. She saw me across the room and came over. She seldom traveled to Paris; when she did, we

555

saw each other briefly. An hour or two for dinner, or a glass of wine if she had other plans."

"Yet you kept it from me." His words sounded innocent enough, but he would have told her about those meetings if they, indeed, had been innocent.

"Not intentionally," he said. "It was just that—well, it had nothing to do with us."

"I'm sorry if I fail to understand," she said tersely, "but I thought anything involving you or me had to do with us."

"It should, and I was wrong. But those few hours with her were like moments out of time, not part of my day-to-day world. I never loved her, Leah. I've never loved anyone but you. I enjoyed being with Simone the way one enjoys the song of a beautiful bird or the sight of a fragile flower. A moment's joy, nothing more. I'm sorry if I hurt you. I never meant for you to be hurt."

Leah looked at the handkerchief she'd shredded in her hand. "I'm not so much hurt as angry. Angry that I've never been someone's beautiful songbird or fragile flower. I've been denied something I should have had. I've missed part of life, and now it's too late. I can't live my life over and be either of those things. I'm too old. That's why I feel like crying."

"It's not enough to have my love?" he asked. "And the children's?"

"Were they enough for you?" she spat out.

Baptiste winced. "I deserve that, but I can't answer it. She gave me a brief taste of the youth I thought gone forever. Nothing more. I wasn't looking for love—I had that here. But I was looking for something no one ever finds. You said it yourself—you can't live your life over."

Leah wanted to scream, to curse, to shout words at Baptiste that she blushed just to think about. He didn't say he hadn't been unfaithful in his desire to live his life over, in his search for his lost youth. *Living life over. Life over.* The words became jumbled in her mind and took on new meaning. One chapter of their life had ended with Simone's death. Did it also write *finis* to the whole book?

"Is your life over, Baptiste? Is ours? Will you find it unbearable to go on without her?"

"Until I went to Lyons, Leah, I had not seen her since right after young Edouard was born." He thought it best not to mention the two dinners in Paris; this would be an added complication and make it more difficult for Leah to

556

understand. If it were not already too late for her understanding.

"Oh, yes. The time you came rushing back to Denise's from Paris. I remember how very amorous you were. Was it guilt or a rebuff that brought you back?" If only she could hurt him as he'd hurt her.

Baptiste ignored the barb; Leah had a right to her bitterness. "Neither. It was love for you. And my need for you. We were having a picnic—"

"A picnic. How quaintly bucolic." She choked back a sob. "I'm sorry I'm not young enough to restore your youthful vigor or to tumble in the grass on a picnic."

"Dammit! We didn't tumble in the grass. And all I could think about was how much I wished you were with me."

"Please don't swear, Baptiste. I want to believe you, more than I can ever express. You said you never meant to hurt me, but you have. It will take time. You'll have to give me a great deal of time."

"As much as you want, chérie. Just don't leave or ask me to leave. If you want me to sleep in my office—"

"I don't know yet. As for the office, whatever else, I am still your obedient wife." *And I love you so much I can't think about anything else.*

He winced at her last remark. "I'm not your master, Leah. I'm your husband who loves you more than life itself." Never in all their years together had he exerted his husband's prerogative to take her against her wishes. He was hurt to think she believed he might make such a demand now, but he knew that in her own hurt she was lashing out in every way to save her pride.

"I'll need time, a great deal of time," she kept repeating. She stared out the window, unmoving, almost as if in a cataleptic trance. "I can't think right now." Truly, she had begun to feel numb all over. Her arms were too weak to raise and her legs too weak to walk across the room.

"Would it help to go and spend some time with one of the children? A few days with the grandchildren might do you good. You—you wouldn't be forced to see me. It would give you time to decide how you feel about—about us."

"No, that wouldn't solve anything. 'Twould do me no good to leave. One carries one's burdens in the heart, not on the shoulders." She spoke as if she were reciting a text from memory.

"What did you say?" Baptiste was puzzled by her words and her tone of voice.

"I was quoting something a very wise woman once said. Sarah, the Quaker I knew in Indiana. She and her family had been unmercifully harassed because of their religious beliefs. She'd lost a husband and son in tragic accidents. Her home had been burned. Yet when I asked her why she didn't go to live with another son out west, that was what she told me. Sarah was a woman of quiet fortitude and I determined then to live by those same words. But there are times when even quiet fortitude is not enough."

"If only," Baptiste said desperately, "there was something more I could do or say to help."

"There isn't. This is something I must resolve for myself."

She turned from the window when Blanchette appeared to ask about dinner. "I'm not feeling very well, Blanchette. I think I'd like a light dinner on a tray in my room. Monsieur Fontaine, however, will be eating in either the dining room or the library. You can ask him which he prefers. I'll be in the garden if you want me for anything." Without another glance at Baptiste, she walked out.

In her cutting garden, Leah tried to pull some weeds that were choking the flowers and to pick a few roses, but one vision, huge and obscene, crowded everything else out of her mind: Baptiste and Simone in each other's arms. She was certain now it was Baptiste she'd seen with Simone in their room in Aix-les-Bains. He'd told her it was Charles, and she'd wanted so badly to believe him, she had. But a woman knows her own husband, and she'd shut her eyes to the truth of what they showed her. She had to force herself to accept the fact that Baptiste had been unfaithful. One time or a hundred times, it made no difference. And after she accepted it? Then what?

She didn't know which she resented most: his seeing Simone throughout the years or his keeping their meetings from her. In all the years they'd been married, she'd never kept anything from him except Lisette's secret about Philippe. And that had been Lisette's secret, not hers.

The early-evening breeze had transformed the crisp, shimmering leaves of the oleander into an Aeolian harp, and the sweet, plaintive notes made Leah's heartache all the more poignant.

Time. She had asked for time, and Baptiste would give it to her. She loved him, and she believed him when he said he loved her. If love were strong enough, it might, in the long run, be the answer to everything.

She'd think about visiting the children. Or spending some time in Paris if the strain between her and Baptiste became intolerable.

She knew why she was hesitating about leaving for any length of time. Baptiste had betrayed her, but her departure would be a betrayal of the whole family. She would be relinquishing not only her place as Baptiste's wife but as mother of their children. If she left, the break would be complete. She could never bring herself to return. She had to weigh her pride and hurt against her needs. As distraught as she was, it was not the time—nor was she emotionally stable enough—to make that decision.

Chapter Forty-six

LYING ON THE COUCH IN HER LIVING ROOM, Lisette only half heard what Gerald was saying. With his first words, she'd fainted and then revived to find him bathing her forehead with a cool cloth. Now he was trying to give her some of the details, but they didn't interest her. She choked back a sob, and then found herself in Gerald's arms as he insisted she should go ahead and cry.

"I can't believe it, Gerald. I never thought such a tragedy would happen in our family."

"It has, and we have to face it. I think we should leave as soon as you think you're able. Your mother and father both need us."

"I know. I'll be all right in a few minutes. We can take the early-afternoon train. Does Jean know?"

"I called him immediately after I spoke to your father. He said he would drive over and tell Denise. He thought it would be easier for her if it came from him in person. I've also wired Robert and Henri. Robert, I'm sure, will want to come home. Henri may be separated from the family all these years, but I felt he would want to know."

"I don't know what we'd all do without you, Gerald. You have such a calm way of handling situations like this."

"Only on the outside, darling. I'm as distressed and sorrowing as you are. This has become my family, too."

Lisette wiped her eyes and forced herself to go to the bedroom and pack. She'd done it many times before, but never for a reason like this. Separated or together, they had been a family, whole and complete. She couldn't believe it would no longer be that way.

Robert took the cable the messenger handed him. He hoped it was the one he'd been waiting for, saying the long-delayed shipment had finally left Marseilles. He glanced at it almost casually. He read it again, and before he could help himself, dropped his head onto his arm and began to cry uncontrollably.

"What is it?" Marcel came running over from his desk. For a moment all Robert could do was shake his head and clutch the wire in his hands. He couldn't believe what he'd read. He didn't want to believe it.

"Your father?" Marcel questioned him gently. "Your mother?"

Robert still couldn't bring himself to answer, not until he'd got his feelings under control and was able to speak without sobbing. Finally he sat up.

"I need to leave for France on tomorrow's ship. I'm sorry, Marcel. I know you were looking forward to returning to Martinique. I'll be back as soon as I can. But I have to go. My sister Nicole is dead. She was murdered."

Leah lay on the bed in her darkened bedroom. Baptiste sat quietly beside her, staring out the window. Except for an occasional moan, there had been no sound from her in all the hours since Gerald called. He'd taken the call from Jean saying that he and Céline, with Denise and Edouard, would be there that evening, probably on the same train with Lisette and Gerald. The wire had come from Robert with word that he would be arriving on the next ship to Le Havre. Baptiste expected there would be a wire of some kind from Henri before long. When it came a few hours later, he was not surprised to read that Henri couldn't get away right now, but his thoughts were with them.

Blanchette brought in dinner. "I couldn't possibly eat, not tonight," Leah said. "Have something ready for the children, though. They should be arriving before long."

Baptiste wheeled into his office and came back with a bottle and two glasses. "I won't insist you eat, Leah, but drink this. You'll be in no condition to see the others when they get here if you don't. And you know you want to."

Leah sat up and then fell back into the pillows. "How did it happen, Baptiste? How could something so terrible happen?"

"I don't know, but Gerald does. He'll tell us when he gets here."

"I don't mean her death. I mean letting her get so far away from us, so lost from all of us, that she'd end up where she could be killed like that."

"Leah, you cannot let yourself be destroyed by remorse. All of us, in one way or another, played some part in Nicole's decision to leave and make her own life in Paris. What you have to remember is that Nicole herself played just as important a part."

In three other houses, much the same words were being spoken.

"I should never have let her leave the apartment the way I did," Lisette was saying. "I should have insisted, held on to her bodily if necessary, to make certain we knew where she was going. We were the ones who finally had the chance to bring her back into the family, and we failed."

"She would not have stayed, Lisette," Gerald tried to comfort her. "I got to know her very well, I guess as well as any of the family could, during those few weeks. She was the most independent spirit I've ever known. You couldn't have held her any more than you could a butterfly, unless you trapped her. And then she would have been miserable. Several times she left for an entire day, and I was never certain she'd return. She never told me where she went, and I never asked. I was merely grateful to see her again. She lived the life she wanted. That is what we must always remember."

Denise cried the entire time she packed the suitcases for herself and Edouard. Thank heavens for a good neighbor who was coming to stay with the children. No one could convince Denise that the responsibility for Nicole's death shouldn't be placed directly on her shoulders. If she hadn't turned from Nicole to Robert when he was born, Nicole wouldn't have felt deserted and neglected. The first time she ran away and hid in the tunnel should have been a clue for all of them that she needed special attention.

Denise's sorrow was intensified by the fact she was the

only one of those remaining in France who had not seen Nicole in recent years. Jean said he'd seen her and then lost her one time in Montmartre. Mama and Papa had seen her the one time she'd returned to the château. And Lisette and Gerald had seen her not long before she died. Each would probably be thinking they carried the greatest guilt for not having brought her back into the family, but Denise was certain the original fault lay with her.

Jean didn't cry, but he raged and stormed around the house until Céline thought he'd start breaking things if he didn't calm down.

"I don't see how you can think it's your fault," she said. "You haven't seen her since that one time you thought she saw you and ran away."

"But I knew where she was. I knew she was in Montmartre, and I should never have stopped looking for her. I think I could have talked to her, at least persuaded her that the family wasn't all against her."

"Your parents couldn't do it. Lisette and Gerald couldn't do it. Nicole was her own person. You have to believe she lived the life she did because she wanted to."

"I'll try." He slumped in the chair and reached for his pipe. "Are you packed?"

"Just about. Although I'm not at all sure I've put in the right things."

Céline had never known Nicole the way she'd got to know Lisette and Denise. Nicole had been little more than a delightful, if somewhat precocious, child when she was thirteen and had spent three weeks with them in Paris. At that time Céline had been unsure of her place in the family, and she'd hesitated to try to become close to any of them. But she'd loved Nicole and knew full well the burden of anxiety all the family had borne throughout the past years.

While Robert prepared to sail, he shared the same feeling that somehow, some way the tragedy might have been averted. No one had ever told him in so many words that his birth had precipitated Nicole's first flight, but he'd heard enough through the years to know that her ultimate break with the family dated from that time. He'd never been particularly close to Nicole, although he could remember times when she would unexpectedly start playing with him or offer to take care of him for a few days. Then, just as suddenly, she'd ignore him again. The Nicole he remembered had devoted most of her time to painting. Unlike Henri, who'd let him come into the workroom and help with all his strange gadgets, Nicole had strictly forbidden him to enter her studio. The few times he had been allowed in, he'd stood in awe of all her paints and canvases, although the pictures themselves meant little to him. Then Mama had locked the studio, and he'd never felt any desire to re-enter it. He was not sorrowing so much over the death of Nicole, as he was over the way the tragedy must be affecting his mother and father. They were the ones who needed him now.

With the arrival of the children, Leah insisted on getting up and dressing so she could join them in the library.

"There's no need, chérie, if you feel like staying in here and waiting until morning to see them."

"We are a family, Baptiste, and at a time like this we all need each other. They need me as much as I need them. And you, too. I know how much you're crying inside, even if you try to hide it from me. You've lost a daughter, too, and they've lost a sister. I can't be selfish and think I'm the only one who is suffering."

"Then I'll go and tell them you'll join us in a few minutes."

"And—please—tell Gerald to wait until I get there to—to tell us how it happened. I couldn't rest if I didn't know."

Although all six of them had come on the same train from Rheims to St. Denis, they had spoken very little. All were too engrossed in their own quiet thoughts. They had embraced and cried at the station, and then sat dry-eyed, deeply lost in memory for the rest of the trip.

When Leah and Baptiste joined them in the library, there were more tears and embraces, until finally Baptiste said that the best thing for all of them would be to talk about Nicole's death, to learn as much as possible about how it happened.

"I don't know all the details," Gerald said. "I'm not even certain why the police finally got in touch with me."

"I do," Lisette interrupted. "I had forgotten until just now. But I gave Nicole our address in the country, in case she needed—or wanted—to get in touch with us. She must have had it in her pocket."

563

"Or more likely in her room somewhere," Gerald said. "Otherwise we would have known sooner."

"How—how long ago did it happen?" Baptiste asked. Gerald had said nothing about that on the phone.

"About ten days ago."

"You mean—" Leah started up from her chair, then fell back, reaching for Baptiste's hand.

"Yes. She'd already been buried in a small cemetery on Montmartre. It's the last resting place for many artists, so she's among those with whom she always felt most comfortable. There was a funeral, if that's what you're wondering. I understand she had a great many friends, and they took care of everything."

Knowing the family would be too caught up in the tragedy to think very far ahead, Gerald and Edouard had simply taken over the task of making decisions. "Gerald and I thought you would want to have a memorial mass after Robert gets here," Edouard said.

"Yes, thank you for thinking of it," Leah said.

"How did she die?" Baptiste asked.

"That is the hardest part for me to tell you," Gerald said. At least he didn't have to tell them about Nicole's having been with him for several weeks. They knew about that incident already and had been kind enough to keep whatever thoughts they had about it to themselves. "Some days after she returned to her room, Raoul, the young man she'd been living with, stabbed her in a fit of jealousy. The concierge heard her screams, but by the time he got up there, she was already dead. Raoul fled, but he was captured a few days later. It seems that everyone in the colony knew about his fits of temper and helped the police to hunt him down. Nicole was very much loved by her friends in Montmartre. That is what I think we should all remember."

She would try to, Leah thought, but she knew her nights would be haunted by the screams she'd never heard.

"I think there's something else we should consider, too," Gerald said. "Every one of us is feeling that Nicole would be alive today if we'd done something or acted in some way other than we did. We can spend the rest of our lives berating ourselves for failing to save her, which will not bring Nicole back, or we can console ourselves with the knowledge she was happy with the life she'd chosen for herself. And she did choose it. We did not force it on her."

"Gerald's right," Edouard said. "Nor are we being callous because Nicole was not our own flesh and blood. We couldn't love her as you did, but we do love you; it is you we're thinking about now."

"Thank you, Edouard," Leah said. "You are quite right, of course. I don't know about the others, but I've made my life—and Baptiste's—miserable by believing her various flights were all my fault. I felt it was particularly true because she was so much like me that I, of all people, should know how to reach her. I think it's time I asked your forgiveness for very selfishly thinking I was the only one who really loved her." She turned to Gerald. "Gerald, if you and Edouard will make all the arrangements for the memorial service after Robert gets here, we will be most grateful."

She looked a long time at Gerald. At first she'd wanted to condemn him and speak her piece about his having had an affair with Nicole. Strange as it might seem, she was now thankful he had. It was Lisette's return to him, in spite of having found Nicole in the apartment, that made Leah realize how wrong she would be to leave Baptiste. Lisette had shown her that love could be strong enough to overcome pride and hurt. It was not always the older who was the wiser.

The service in the village church was crowded with the friends Nicole had made during her short lifetime at the château: Messieurs Villemont, Boileau, Beaumont, and Jacquard, who had helped search for her the first time she ran away; the men from the village who had joined that search and later ones; Monsieur Balaine, the tutor, and Monsieur LaBorde, the village schoolmaster; Madame Schumann, the baker's wife, and all her family; all of Nicole's schoolmates, many of them now married and with children of their own. And a stranger who sat in the back of the church and who tried to leave before any of the family could approach him.

"Pardon me, sir," Jean said, catching up with the man. "I'm Jean Fontaine, Nicole's oldest brother. I don't believe we've ever met."

"No, I think not. I'm Jerome Trowbridge. I knew Nicole in Paris. I was a friend of hers, but I didn't know about her death until some time after the funeral. That's why I'm here today."

"It was kind of you to come," Jean said. "My mother is having a light repast served at the château. She would be pleased if you'd join us."

"Thank you, but I have to return to the city. Please give her my deepest sympathy. Nicole was someone very special."

"Yes, yes she was," Jean said and walked back to the family.

"Mama, I don't think you should go to Nicole's room and sort through her things," Lisette said. Leah was sitting with Lisette, Denise, and Céline in the sunroom, while the men were talking business in the library.

"Indeed not, Mama," Denise insisted. "Edouard can return home, and I'll go into Paris with Lisette and Gerald. There's no reason to force yourself to do something that will be very difficult for you. You've been through enough already with the memorial service and having everyone back here afterward."

"I'm not being stubborn just to be stubborn," Leah said. "I need to do it. I need to see where she lived, to sit in her room and try to understand what her life was like. Only then will I be able to find peace. Come with me if you like, but I am going in there tomorrow." They would think her really foolish if she tried to explain that going to Nicole's room would be like making a pilgrimage to a shrine. It would be her last motherly act for a dearly loved daughter.

"All right," Denise said. "I can see now what Papa means when he says there's no point in arguing with you once your mind is made up."

"I heard Papa," Leah said, "telling Robert he wanted to go to the office tomorrow, so I expect we'll be quite a congregation getting on the train in the morning."

Céline had remained quiet during the conversation. There was very little she could say at a time like this.

"I want you to come, too, Céline." Leah held out her hand to her. "We've been through this together before. You most of all can understand the feelings of a mother. Denise, you and Edouard can stay with Lisette and Gerald in their apartment. Céline, I want you and Jean and Robert to stay with us. Then, I think, once we've taken care of everything in Nicole's room, we should all go out to dinner. I'm quite sure that each of us will continue to mourn in our own way, but I think a little festivity will not be amiss right now. Robert is home, and I think we need to show him we are as glad to have him with us as we are sorrowful over the loss of Nicole."

Denise and Lisette looked at their mother, wondering again at the great strength she displayed during the most difficult times. It was no wonder that they all, including Papa, depended on her so completely. Although they knew, too, that she would be the first to insist it was their father who provided her with that strength.

While the young women went through Nicole's few personal things, Leah stared in awe at the paintings on the easels and leaning against the wall.

"I had no idea she was capable of such beautiful work," she said finally.

"There are a few in Monsieur Ébert's café," Lisette said. "The concierge told us about them." She laughed self-consciously. "There are also several in our apartment. In a frenzy of passion, Gerald bought all that Monsieur Ébert had at the time."

Leah looked at Lisette in amazement. There had not been a trace of bitterness in her voice, merely an indulgent good humor. Denise raised an eyebrow, but said nothing.

"Then we must be sure to get all of them," Leah said. "Except for those already purchased, of course." She smiled at Lisette.

"To take back to the château?" Denise asked. "I'd like to choose one or two if I may."

"Most certainly," Leah said. "We'll divide them, choosing the ones we want. But first, we have to do something else. For a moment I thought it might be too late, but I don't think so now."

"Did you see this one, Mama, of the little girl?" Lisette asked.

"Yes, she seems to have used her often as a model. She is in some of the Madonna paintings Nicole loved doing."

"She must have been very fond of the child," Céline said. "There are two more over here. The little girl is younger, but I'm sure she's the same one."

"I'd like one of them," Lisette said. "Especially this one that seems to be the oldest one of the child. It's really very tender and beautiful."

"But first," Leah said, "we're going to have a showing of all her works. Papa and I planned one for her a long time ago, but—but it never took place."

Leah had thought that such a showing would be in one of the better galleries down in the city, but after talking to

567

some of Nicole's artist friends, she was persuaded to have it in an empty building in Montmartre.

"She was one of us, Madame Fontaine," one of the artists had told her. "You would do us a great honor by having it here. We have the contacts to make certain the critics and the buyers attend."

"I wasn't thinking so much of them as I was of finally having the showing we'd once planned. I don't think we'll sell any of Nicole's work. It's all very precious to us now."

Leah was surprised at the number who did come to the old store, turned into a gallery by Nicole's friends. There were many who wanted to buy, but Leah and Baptiste refused to sell any of Nicole's work. They gave one painting to Monsieur Ébert to hang in his café, and told the others who'd been so helpful to choose what they wanted from among her sketches.

Every day they were in Paris, Leah walked to the small cemetery where Nicole was buried. *If she is at peace,* Leah thought, *then I can be, too.*

A sculptor friend offered to carve a headstone. "I would donate the stone as well," he said, "but I—"

"I understand," Baptiste said. "We'll provide the marble, and are most grateful for your wanting to do this for us."

They had assumed he would carve only her name and the appropriate dates on the stone. Instead, when they returned a few weeks later, they saw he had carved a sublime, reclining figure of a young woman. It was certainly not a traditional cemetery monument, but it seemed so very appropriate for Nicole.

Before their final decision as to where to have the showing, Leah and Baptiste had visited a number of galleries. In one of them they saw a strikingly beautiful oil painting of a nude "Venus in the Garden." Leah clutched Baptiste's hand and forced back the tears filling her eyes. It was a magnificent, full-figure portrait of Nicole. Her long black hair fell over her shoulders and outlined her small, firm breasts. The genius of the artist had given her skin an opalescent radiance that glowed like a fine pearl. There was a hint of teasing laughter in her half smile, and the deep purple highlights in the eyes matched the clusters of wisteria on the vine that trailed across the palm of one hand.

"Baptiste, I have to have that painting."

"I don't think so, Leah. You could never look at it without weeping or being tormented by memory. We have her paintings. I think that's enough."

568

"Please, I couldn't bear the thought of it hanging in any-one else's home, of people looking at her with anything but love."

"You're upset because she posed in the nude. If that's so, I definitely don't think you should have it."

"It's not her nudity that bothers me; it's what might be in people's minds when they look at it. It seems almost blas-phemous. But that's not the real reason I want it. It's a very beautiful painting of Nicole at a moment when I think she was happy. It would help me if I could remember her that way."

"We'll see," Baptiste said. "Gerald and Lisette will be wondering where we are. We promised to meet them at the apartment half an hour ago."

Leah never mentioned the painting again. Perhaps Baptiste was right, she thought; it would be the wrong kind of re-minder of her loss.

When their time in Paris was over and the others had returned to their homes, Leah welcomed the quiet of the château. Robert would be staying on for another week or so, and it would be good to have him all to themselves. Leah found she was more exhausted than she'd realized, and all her plans for keeping busy around the house and in the garden had to be temporarily put aside. She had prepared herself for sleepless nights and restless days; instead she slept easily and had none of the nightmares she'd dreaded. Not a day went by without its memory of Nicole, but they were pleasant memories now, ones she could cherish.

"Madame Fontaine!" Blanchette, now much too old to run, plodded breathlessly into her room. "There's a delivery man out here with a very large package he says is for you."

"He must be mistaken. I haven't ordered anything."

"He insists. He said Monsieur Fontaine bought it a few days ago."

"And of course Monsieur Fontaine is in the city," Leah said indignantly, "so I can't ask where he wants to put what-ever it is he bought. Well, we'll leave it in the hall until he gets back tonight."

When Leah walked into the hall and saw the shape of the large package, she began at once to tear off the wrappings.

"Look, Blanchette, isn't it magnificent?"

"Why, madame, it looks like Madamoiselle Nicole." Blanchette threw her hands over her face, horrified at the nudity.

"It is Nicole." Leah smiled to herself. Baptiste knew how

569

badly she wanted the picture, and he'd gotten it for her. "Isn't she beautiful?"

"Yes, madame, if you say so. Where do you plan to hide it?"

"I do not plan to hide it at all. It will hang right here where everyone who comes in will see it. And don't look so embarrassed, Blanchette. Think of it as a very fine painting."

"I'll try, madame," Blanchette replied, all the while wondering if she would learn to walk through the hall with her eyes closed so as not to see the picture.

"Why did you do it?" Leah asked Baptiste when he came home.

"Because you wanted it and never said another word after we left the gallery. I've learned that's your way when there is something you want very, very much. I couldn't deprive you of it."

"She was really beautiful." Robert looked at the picture as if trying to remember the girl who had posed for it. He'd thought Isabella beautiful—and he thought about her often since coming back to France alone—but Nicole's beauty had a purity about it that set her apart. Her beauty was as unique as she herself had been, and that was what he'd remember when he returned to New Orleans.

Chapter Forty-seven

IN THE SPRING OF 1905, Gerald received word that his wife had been thrown from her horse during a hunt. She was seriously injured and was not expected to live. It was at Lisette's insistence that Gerald went to the bedside of his legal spouse, to be with her and her family during her last days.

After the funeral he returned to France, and within a month he and Lisette were married in a quiet ceremony at the château.

"Does this mean we have to bow to you now that you're the Duchess of Highcastle?" Denise asked.

"If you do, I'll never forgive you. But there is one thing

I'm thrilled about. I'm to be presented to their majesties at a garden party. Imagine! Being presented to the King."

"As if you didn't know him very well already," Leah said, but under her breath so only Lisette could hear.

"But not as the King, Mama, nor as Gerald's wife," Lisette answered just as softly. Raising her voice, she said, "Look, isn't it beautiful?" She held out her hand to show the wide gold wedding band.

"It is and I'm happy for you." Leah was remembering the beautiful golden morning on the lawn of Belle Fontaine when Baptiste told her of his plans for them to live in France and then showed her the wedding ring he'd bought. There had been a magnificent diamond engagement ring, too, but it was the simple gold band that had brought tears to her eyes.

"How about Cornwall?" Baptiste asked Gerald. "Will you be spending much time there?"

"We'll probably spend a few months a year there," Gerald said, "as well as the season in London. But," he smiled, "with my interest in the vineyards, we'll stay over here as much as possible."

"But now we're off to Italy," Lisette said. "The long-postponed trip Gerald promised me—how many years ago, darling?"

"Please, don't remind me. Far too long."

"Yes, but now it's our honeymoon."

Leah watched Lisette smile at her husband and knew this marriage was the one she had wished for her those many years earlier when she married Philippe.

"I don't need to tell you to be happy," Leah said as Lisette embraced her just before they left. "You've waited a long time for this moment."

"It was worth the wait, Mama."

Leah sighed with contentment after they left. She had waited a long time herself, to see Lisette happily settled as the wife of someone she loved and who loved her. Jean, Denise, and now Lisette. Henri, too, she supposed, although she knew in her heart she would never meet Louise or see any of their children. It was painful to think of having grandchildren she'd never get to know and love as she did Jean's and Denise's. She also wondered if she would ever see Henri again. He was almost as lost to her as Nicole.

She thought about Robert. He hadn't said anything to them when he came home at the time of Nicole's death, but Pierre DeLisle had indicated in a letter to Baptiste that

Robert had suffered through an unhappy love affair in New Orleans. Pierre hadn't come right out and said he'd fallen in love with a girl he was forbidden to marry, but Leah had surmised as much. It was what she'd feared when he went there to live. She wanted happiness for him, too. If he planned to stay in New Orleans, she could only hope he would fall in love with a young woman who was right for him.

Robert had been extremely disappointed when his father put the quietus to any plans for a San Francisco office in the near future.

"Perhaps after the Panama Canal is finished," Baptiste had said, "we can talk about it again. Right now I don't see how such an office would be feasible."

The canal was now being built by the United States, and although many of the same problems that had destroyed the hopes of the DeLesseps company still had to be faced, there was every indication the project would be completed.

Having committed himself to the New Orleans office, and not wishing to tell his father why he wanted to leave, Robert returned to the United States after Nicole's death and worked hard to prove himself a good manager. Except for seeing Ambrose often, he kept his social life to a minimum. He bought a fine horse; then, when he found himself thinking desperately about leaving Louisiana, he went for long rides by himself. As tempted as he was to see Isabella again, he avoided riding near the plantation.

Then he was startled to receive a note from Isabella, asking him to meet her at the small house, now deserted, where a plantation manager had once lived.

Robert hesitated, unsure whether he wanted to see her again. He'd heard she was engaged to be married, and he could foresee only pain and frustration resulting from such a meeting. For a brief moment he wondered if she'd finally found the courage to defy her parents and flee with him to France. Then he realized that this was a forlorn hope, and if he thought about it, he'd fall right back into the same despondent mood he'd suffered when she'd been taken from him.

Yet she must have an urgent reason for wanting to see him. He couldn't bear the idea of her waiting—hopefully, expectantly—and being disappointed when he didn't appear.

Robert rode slowly along the river road. He had plenty of

time. He would see her, learn why she'd asked him to meet with her, and leave immediately.

Isabella was waiting just inside the door when he walked onto the small porch after tethering his horse among some trees.

"Thank you for coming, Robert." She took his hand and led him into what appeared to be a parlor. Their shoes left deep footprints in the dusty carpet. The few pieces of furniture were covered with dust sheets, and the draperies were overlaid with cobwebs.

"I don't think I should have." The desire to take her in his arms was straining his self-control to the limit.

"I know. We should be in France together. I should have found a way to be with you. But I couldn't help myself; I hadn't the strength to defy my parents."

"And there was Casa Verde."

"Yes, that and other reasons. I was too much of a coward to leave everything I've always known."

In spite of his resolve to keep a distance between them, he took her in his arms and held her tenderly. "Don't cry, Isabella. I understand. But why did you want to see me tonight?"

"I need you. If ever you loved me, please help me."

"In what way? I'll do whatever I can." He was puzzled and, at the same time, fearful. What could he do—what did she want him to do—that someone closer to the family could not?

"I'm to be married in a month, to a man my family chose for me. I don't love him, but he's a good man and wealthy enough to restore Casa Verde to what it should be."

"You are going to marry him? You're not asking me to pirate you away in secret?" Robert felt himself being slowly torn apart with each word he spoke.

"No, nothing like that. I'm going to marry him. But I'm frightened. I—I don't want the first time to be with someone I don't love."

"My God, Isabella, what are you saying?" The almost unbelievably monstrous duplicity of what she was suggesting smote him, while at the same time he felt an overpowering desire to possess her right then and there.

"I want you to make love to me. I want this to be the night I remember—I want it to be your face I see when—"

"No! It's all wrong. I can't take from your husband what is rightfully his, what he has every right to expect."

"Please, Robert, please," she begged. She took his hand

573

and slipped it inside her bodice. Beneath her warm breast, he felt her heart pounding.

"Dear God, Isabella, I can't let you go. Not now. Not ever. You can't leave me now."

"I have to, but we can have this one time together."

Closing his mind to any thought of losing her again, thinking only that once she was his, she'd never belong to anyone else, he picked her up and carried her to a couch. Frantically, he pulled off the dust cover before laying her down. Like a child—eager, expectant, timid—she looked up at him trustingly.

"I love you, Robert. Please, please be gentle. I'm frightened."

At the thought of her belonging to another man after today, he'd been in no mood to be anything but brutal and forceful—until he heard the pleading in her voice and saw the fear in her eyes. "I'll be gentle. I promise."

Later, Isabella sat up on the couch. "I have to go now."

"It's good-bye then, isn't it?" Robert followed her to the door. In spite of his determination not to let her marry anyone else, he knew he had no choice.

"Yes." She stood on tiptoe to kiss him good-bye. "But I'll never forget this day. Ever."

Robert stayed only a short while longer, then rode slowly back into the city.

"How about trying our luck on the new gambling ship moored north of the city?" Ambrose asked while they were eating dinner.

"I don't think so. I don't feel much like it."

"Better than brooding by yourself."

"Do I look as miserable at that?" Robert asked, forcing a grin.

"No, but I know what you're thinking about."

"Thank you for the offer, but I think I'll go for a ride. I don't feel like staying inside."

"As you wish, but if you want a nightcap when you get back, I'll be in the apartment."

Ambrose was a good friend, Robert thought, but there were times when even the best of friends got in the way of one's need to be alone.

He saddled up his horse and rode out along the river with his destination firmly in mind. This time he would not avoid Casa Verde. There would be no one there, and he could walk through the grounds without being disturbed.

He took the route along the river bank, dismounted at the gazebo, and tied his horse to the latticework of the small white building.

If things had been different, he thought, looking across the wide expanse of lawn to the house, all of this would have been mine—mine and Isabella's. After tonight, she'd be living there with the man she had married that morning, the man her parents had chosen for her. He had long since decided that their interlude in the deserted house should best be forgotten. He had done what she'd asked: prepared her for her wedding night and all the nights to follow. It must not mean anything more to him than that.

He sat for a while on the bank and watched the boats plying the river, the brilliant lights on the pleasure craft, the kerosene lanterns and pine-knot torches on the flatboats. There was something soothing about the steady movement, the deep sounds of the horns to signal passing, and the gentle but inexorable rhythm of the waves, like a heartbeat.

Like his father before him, Robert had had dreams. The war had not been able to destroy Baptiste's dream of regaining his land and restoring it to its original greatness. It was ironic, Robert thought, that his mother, who had found the means to help his father regain the plantation, was the very one who had bequeathed him the blood that now denied it to him. Damn! If only his father hadn't sold it, he could be the owner of it right now and to hell with who or what he was.

He sifted some of the soft earth through his fingers, then washed them off and went to lie down in the gazebo. For a long time he lay there and looked through the latticework at the full moon and the galaxy of stars. He would spend the night. For a few brief hours it would all belong to him.

Sophia Belmar considered herself among the more fortunate of the *gens du couleur* in New Orleans. Like many octoroons, she grew up with her quadroon mother in the heart of the *Vieux Carré,* in a small house provided by her white father. More than that, he had enveloped her with love and provided her with a convent education. Unfortunately, he died during the Civil War when she was still a child—too young to understand why he was killed but old enough to remember him well. Except for missing him dreadfully, his death had brought no change in her life. He had left her mother a generous bequest in a trust fund, the principal of which eventually came to Sophia. Other than a brief hiatus during the Federal occupation, when the convent was closed and her mother taught her at home, Sophia was able to continue with her formal education and graduate from the convent.

Although Sophia's mother had met her father at one of the famous—or infamous—quadroon balls and become his *placée*, that was not the future she had wanted for herself. She wanted marriage with one of her own people. Until she met the right man, she had seen nothing wrong with being a seamstress and then designer at Cecile's, New Orleans' foremost *modiste*. Her mother had been horrified when Sophia announced she was in love with and planning to marry Alan Belmar, the octoroon brother of her best friend at the convent. He had been sent to France to receive a legal education, but he'd found his attention caught by the many exquisite jewels designed by the famous Parisian house of Cartier. After an apprenticeship, he had returned to New Orleans, becoming first an associate and then a partner in Thibedeau and Sons.

In spite of her mother's foreboding, Sophia was comfortably settled in the social milieu proscribed by her birth and marriage. Two of her sons had become master craftsmen like their father and were working in the back room of the jewelry shop, and her oldest daughter had gone North to be educated as a teacher. Her youngest, Felicité, was without question her favorite and, like Sophia before her marriage, was working for Cecile as a designer.

On his numerous visits to Cecile's with Ambrose, Robert had noticed Felicité in the shop, but paid little attention to her. He would glimpse her in the back room, if she were sewing or designing, or if he saw her in the front room, she would nod quickly to Ambrose and scurry away. When Robert's whole world had revolved around Isabella, he gave no thought to Cecile's pretty little assistant.

After his final night at Casa Verde, Robert found himself becoming reconciled to his loss. Gradually his bitterness ebbed, and he began to feel that New Orleans was not such an intolerable place to live after all. Although he was ready to discard his self-pity, he was not quite ready to become again the flamboyant *bon vivant* he had once been. His rashness in falling in love with Isabella had taught him a sobering lesson.

"There's only one answer," Ambrose offered once, when he and Robert were discussing the situation. "Remain a bachelor like me."

Ambrose had suffered his own disappointment in love. The parents of the young woman he was courting had refused to allow them to marry because he was a bastard.

"We're two pariahs together," Ambrose said, "so let's make the most of it and have a good time. It's a carefree life, with no responsibilities."

"I'm with you," Robert said. "Falling in love is too painful."

But the role of a debonair, freedom-loving, slightly arrogant man-about-town soon palled. Robert was not a man who enjoyed the solitary life; and while he sought pleasure in occasional nights at some of the more exclusive bordellos, he found nothing more than a brief physical release. His need for a deeper, more meaningful relationship was in no way satisfied. He would not have considered himself any more promiscuous than Ambrose or any of the other friends he cavorted with, but such nights usually left him with a bitter aftertaste, as if he'd got drunk on cheap wine rather than taken time to savor the taste of a fine champagne.

With Isabella he had known what it was to love and be loved, to feel that he was the most important person in her life just as she was in his. He longed to know again the emotional comfort and security, as well as the tender passion, he'd shared with her.

On a subsequent visit to Cecile's, Robert found himself looking at Felicité with eyes no longer clouded by love for someone else. He had heard Cecile mention her name, but he'd never been introduced to her. While Ambrose chatted with his mother, Robert watched Felicité, bent over the sewing table in the back room. Her eyes focused intently on her work; she didn't glance up the entire time he stared at her. With her petite figure, she looked more like a child than a young woman. Her long black hair was coiled into an intricate bun on the back of her head. In profile, her delicate bone structure, small upturned nose, and firm mouth were accentuated by her long, dark eyelashes. He thought her a pretty little thing, but his thoughts went no further than that.

More and more, however, when he went into the shop, Robert found himself hoping to see Felicité. Her quiet gentle ways appealed to him, and he was moved by her soft voice when she spoke to Cecile. Always she did no more than nod to Ambrose, as if from a sense of deference to her employer's son. She had never so much as smiled at Robert, and yet he knew she must have a very beautiful smile.

If he'd been in Paris, Robert simply would have asked

Cecile to introduce him to Felicité; this was not Paris, however, it was New Orleans. He would not make the same mistake with Felicité he'd made with Isabella. He had no reason to believe Felicité was a young woman of color. With her black hair, large, dark brown eyes, and brunette coloring, she was as typically French as his father, or as Spanish as Señora Quinsarro. Yet there was something about her, some subtle nuance that made him feel she was, perhaps, an octoroon.

Robert thought first of talking to Cecile, then hesitated. She might be hesitant to discuss such a touchy subject with him. If Felicité had Negro blood, she might very well have revealed it only in confidence to Cecile. If she did not, Cecile might find it difficult to tell Robert why she could not introduce him to Felicité.

But he had to meet her. He found himself thinking about her when he should have been checking invoices, approving requests for credit, writing mollifying letters in response to complaints, or making certain that shipments were going out on time. At night he was unable to sleep for seeing her face in front of him and thinking about her placid, almost diffident, manner. He'd never seen her in anything but the simple tan smock she wore while working; she reminded him of the little brown birds that fed in the courtyard of his apartment only after the larger, more colorful birds had eaten. For several days he remained in a quandary over how and whom to ask about Felicité. Ambrose was the obvious one to ask, but Ambrose was a tease. After their decision to remain bachelors and enjoy the fruits of the *Vieux Carré*, Robert was loathe to admit that he thought of Felicité in more than a casual way. There was no help for it, however; he had to meet her and Ambrose seemed the only way.

"Are you sure that's wise, Robert?" Ambrose asked. "You don't want to find yourself involved with someone like her, as attractive as she is."

"Why? Is there something about her I wouldn't approve of of?" He couldn't bring himself to ask frankly about her life outside the shop.

"No, no, not what you're thinking. Felicité is as pure and innocent as the day she was born. She comes from a strict, upstanding family. I didn't mean that."

"Then because she's a designer?" After all, Ambrose's mother, whom he adored, did essentially the same work even though she was now a *modiste* with her own exclusive shop. Robert found himself bristling at the implication. "I never thought I gave the impression of being a snob."

"Believe me, Robert, I didn't mean that. I know you're not. But I think you should know that both her parents are octoroons. Well educated and much admired in the *Vieux Carré*, but, nevertheless—"

Robert's hopes rose. He had been sure of it, and yet it was a relief to hear it spoken. Yet he wondered why Ambrose should think her color a deterrent.

"Then I should think you'd feel it highly proper for me to meet Felicité. God knows, there wouldn't be the barrier there was between me and Isabella."

"No, but should you begin to escort her around the city, you would be putting up a barrier between you and many of the people you've been associating with. And should you, by any chance, fall in love with her and marry her—well, the barrier would be too high and wide for you to cross ever again."

"With you, Ambrose?"

"Never. I'm not a sometime friend. Nor, in all fairness is everyone you've met. I think, though, it's something you should consider."

Robert had been considering it. Associating openly with Felicité in any way other than a casual, illicit liaison would be to move away from the stratum of the *Vieux Carré*'s acknowledged first families into that social limbo of educated and prosperous people of color, who were well above the servant class but equally far below the Creoles and other whites. Position for its own sake meant little to Robert. A gregarious young man who made friends easily with everyone he met, he felt as much at ease in the homes of the men who worked under him as he did in the elaborate drawing rooms of the largest mansions in New Orleans.

More important to Robert was being accepted for himself, for who and what he was. If he had allowed Isabella to fall in love with him under false pretences, it had not been intentional. In his naïveté and in the pleasure of being welcomed to the city by both his father's friends and Ambrose's, he had not even thought of his racial heritage. Now that it had become an issue, he felt as if he'd been thrust into a limbo of his own. He felt the need to belong somewhere, if not among his father's people, then perhaps among his mother's.

"And if I still want to meet Felicité?" Robert asked.

"I'll introduce you, but don't be surprised if she is less

than enthralled by your attentions. She's had many men with less than honorable intentions seek to know her. For some husbands who come into the shop with their wives, her modesty and shyness have made her look like easy prey, to be used and then tossed aside. Thanks to my mother's sharp tongue and no-nonsense manner, most of them have been sent packing with their ears burning. A few, however, who came when Mama wasn't there, were more than vulgar; they were downright uncouth in their approach. One even tried to seduce her in the sewing room. Only a sharp pair of scissors discouraged him. Fortunately she didn't have to use them."

"Poor child," Robert murmured.

"She's no child," Ambrose said, "and she knows enough of the world's evils not to fall for any flattery or blandishments. I've known her all her life, and I happen to be very fond of her. If you promise you'll do nothing to hurt her, I'll introduce you."

"Fair enough. Right now all I want to do is meet her. I find her attractive, and I think I'd enjoy her company. But I promise I will not lead her on. And I hope you know me well enough to realize I'd never behave like those men you were talking about."

When Ambrose said it would be several days before he'd be able to meet him at the shop, Robert knew he couldn't wait that long. He'd go in and introduce himself. Having no desire to go through the same dialogue with Cecile as he had with Ambrose, he waited until she left the shop. There were other seamstresses in the back room, and he hoped it would be Félicité who came forward when the little bell over the entrance jingled.

Robert's frequent presence in the shop with Ambrose had not gone unnoticed by Félicité. She thought him very handsome, and while she sewed, she had listened to him talking to Cecile. He had a low, pleasant voice, and she loved to hear him laugh, honestly and unself-consciously. As a friend of Ambrose, he was no one she could ever hope to know. Like her mother, she planned someday to marry a man of her own kind, but unconsciously she began to measure the young men she knew against Robert. Although the *plaçage* system as such had gone out of existence years earlier, there were still back-street liaisons between white men and women of color. The difference now was that there were few permanent relationships, and the women were thought of more as prostitutes than acknowledged mistresses. Nor was it expected that the men would provide for them and for their children for the rest of their lives, as had been the custom under *plaçage*. No, as attracted as she was to Robert Fontaine, she would never consent to see him outside the store, in spite of her rapid heartbeat when he walked into the shop or her blushes when she knew he was watching her.

When the bell rang, she put down her sewing and walked through the curtains to attend to the customer. She felt her heart begin to pound when she saw Robert alone.

"Good afternoon," she said shyly. "Neither Madame Cecile nor Monsieur Ambrose is here right now. Perhaps if you would care to return in about an hour's time?"

Robert heard the questioning lilt in her voice and was enchanted by it.

"I didn't come to see them," he said. "I came to see you."

His words were not those she expected to hear, and she didn't know how to respond. "I don't understand."

"I wanted to meet you and to ask you to have dinner with me tonight."

"Oh, no, monsieur, that would be quite impossible. I am forbidden to associate with the customers." It wasn't exactly true, but it was what Cecile had suggested she say if any of her patrons' husbands made unwelcome overtures.

"But I am not a customer," Robert said, and tried a reassuring smile.

"No, that's true. But you are a friend of Ambrose, and I'm sure Madame Cecile would not approve of my taking time away from my work to—to talk to someone who is not a customer."

"I won't stay here any longer than it takes for you to say yes and tell me where I may call for you and at what time."

"Monsieur Fontaine, I know you are a gentleman or you would not be Ambrose's friend or be made so very welcome by Madame Cecile. So perhaps you will understand when I say it would be better for me not to accept your invitation."

"I'll say nothing more about it and will never mention seeing you again if you tell me you are refusing because you don't want to go out with me. If there's another reason—"

"There is, and if you ask Ambrose, he will tell you what it is."

Her refusal to say simply that she was a woman of color puzzled Robert at first. Then he realized that was not the reason she was referring to. It was the way she'd been approached by some of the other men of having to fight off the ones who thought any young woman of color was eager to have a white lover. Felicité had no way of knowing he wasn't like them.

"Felicité, look at me. What do you see?"

She blushed under his steady gaze but looked directly into his eyes. "A very nice-looking young man whom I would be pleased to have dinner with if—if certain things were different."

"And would you consider them different if I told you my mother is an octoroon and was my father's *placée* for many years here in New Orleans? That they are now living in France because they could not be married here?"

Robert watched Felicité's timorous smile become a bewitching grin of sheer delight. It was the first time he'd seen the dimples in her cheeks.

"I would be pleased to have dinner with you tonight," she said shyly. She reached into the drawer of a finely carved Louis Quatorze desk and wrote something on a sheet of paper. "My address," she said. "I will be ready at eight o'clock."

"Until then," Robert said, bowing slightly, less out of courtesy than to keep from reaching across the counter and taking her hand.

For the remainder of the day, Robert found it impossible to concentrate on work. It was a beautiful afternoon—the sun was shining for the first time after several miserable, rainy days—and he felt as light-headed as if he'd drunk a magnum of champagne. He ordered his horse brought from the stable and rode south along the river. Once away from the city, he threw his hat into the air and galloped along shouting and whooping like a schoolboy on a holiday. Finally drained of all his excess energy, he slowed the horse to an easy amble. The land was beautiful along here. If the former Belle Fontaine could never belong to him, he might consider finding out if one of these plantations were for sale. He wanted to own land, acres and acres of land. Then he'd feel he truly belonged somewhere.

Robert knew that Felicité had been as strictly brought up as any of the Creole daughters, but he was nevertheless surprised when it was her father, and not she, who answered the door. And her mother sat waiting for him in the parlor.

"Good evening, Monsieur Fontaine," Sophia Belmar said. "Won't you please come in and sit down? Felicité will be with us in a few moments. Meanwhile I thought we could talk a bit."

Robert soon discovered that this bit of talking was a stern catechism about his family, his background, and his upbringing in France. Rather than immediately divulging his right to be calling on Felicité, he answered each of her questions as they were put to him. There would soon be an opportunity to tell them what they really wanted to know, although he felt quite certain Felicité had already apprised them about his mother.

"And your mother's name?" Sophia asked.

"She was Leah Bonvivier—that is, Bonvivier was her father's name. She was, of course, his natural daughter."

"Leah. Leah." Sophia mulled over the name. "She is about my age? I should know her if she lived here in the *Vieux Carré*."

"No, madame," Robert grinned. "I came somewhat late in her life." This was getting to be a rather tiresome subject, and Robert wondered just how pleased his mother would be to keep hearing him tell how old she'd been when he was born.

"Then she was not a student in the convent just before or after the war?"

"No, in fact my father was seriouuly wounded and she was a nurse in the hospital. She had been his mistress for some years before that. She did attend the convent, though, and I think she also taught there for a while when my father first went away to war."

"Ah," Sophia nodded. "Your mama is the famous heroine of the occupation. How often I heard the story from Sister Angelique at the convent! Did your mama never tell you how she rescued your father and several other officers when they were about to be taken as prisoners of war by the Federal troops entering the city?"

"No, madame, I don't believe she did. I don't recall her ever mentioning it."

"Then you should know. The first northern troops had already occupied New Orleans. Under orders, our soldiers and officers had fled, leaving us helpless. But that is another story. The wounded enlisted men in the hospital were to be released on their word that they would return home and no longer fight. With the officers, however, it was quite a different story. They were to be taken as prisoners of war. It would mean sure death for most of them, since they were to be sent to camps with no facilities to care for them. Several city officials, who had surrendered with the promise of house arrest in one of the hotels, had been sent instead to Ship Island and forced to work at hard labor.

"Anyway, your mother came up with a brilliant plan which, with the help of Sister Angelique and others at the convent, as well as a strong slave named Étienne, was carried out. Four at a time, in a rickety old wagon and covered with bloody sheets and blankets, the men were spirited out of the hospital and brought to the convent. When stopped by Yankee patrols, Étienne informed them the men had died of yellow fever and were being taken to be buried. They took a different route each time."

"Very clever," Robert said.

"Clever but extremely dangerous. By the time the last load was being driven to the convent, the Yankees had become suspicious. Étienne and your mother were shot at, but they managed to get past a roadblock by running the wagon through the line of soldiers. Étienne fled to the swamps immediately afterward. He didn't dare get caught in the city."

"And Mama? And the sisters at the convent?"

"Fortunately there was no investigation there until the next day. By that time, the rooms at the convent had been turned back from hospital wards into schoolrooms and all the patients had been taken into the swamps. They stayed with free people of color until it was safe—and they were recovered enough—for them to make their way to their own homes. A few Yankee soldiers tried to follow them into the swamps, but the quicksand and muddy waters and water moccasins sent them scurrying back."

"What if they'd been found?" Robert asked. "What about the people who hid them?"

"They would have been in serious trouble, but they didn't worry about that. Your mama was a voodoo princess, you know. She would have been a Mamaloi, a voodoo queen, if she'd stayed in New Orleans. Her mother was. And the people who hid the officers loved both of them. There wasn't anything they wouldn't do for Leah."

"She's a wonder," Robert said.

"Yes, she was. I didn't know about all this at the time. I remember her as my teacher. For only a few months, but how I loved her." Now she looked lovingly at Robert. "And you are her son. To think I've met a child of hers. I can't think of anyone I would rather have calling on Felicité."

"Then I have your permission to take her to dinner and to continue seeing her?"

"Indeed you have." Alan Belmar spoke up for the first time. "And you'll always be welcome in our home."

"Now go along, you two, and have a good time," Sophia said as Felicité came into the room and walked over to kiss her good night.

Sitting at dinner a few weeks later, Robert reached for Felicité's hand. Until now, although he'd seen her every day since their first evening together, he'd never done more than hold her hand for a brief moment when he bid her good-night.

"I'm falling in love with you, you know," he said.

"Not yet, please." She lowered her eyes and Robert was startled to see tears.

"Why not, if it's true?"

"I'm—I'm not ready to cope with that."

"Are you afraid of me?" He was puzzled. He couldn't think of anything he'd done to hurt her.

"No, nothing like that. I'm very fond of you. It's something I can't really explain."

Robert pulled his hand away and sat back in his chair. Surely Felicité had known from the beginning that he thought of her as more than a friend. If she didn't want him courting her seriously, she should have put a stop to his visits sooner. He could only suspect that, like Henri, she might have dreams of going north and passing as white. Lord knows, she was beautiful and light-skinned enough. If that were what she wanted, he wouldn't stand in her way.

"You don't want to stay in New Orleans?" he asked.

"Oh, I'd never want to leave here," she said breathlessly. "I couldn't possibly live anywhere else. I love everything about the city. No, it's just that I've felt you were going to say you love me, and I'm afraid of what is coming next. There's only one kind of commitment I would be willing to make, and if—if you want something else I'd find it hard to refuse."

"Because you love me, too?"

"Please, don't ask me that."

"Felicité, I love you very, very much. I don't know what you think I have in mind when I say that, but I would never do or say anything to hurt you. I want to marry you. I want you to be my wife. I want to spend the rest of my life loving you. If there's someone else or you don't love me, say so, and I won't ask you again."

"If you don't mind missing dessert," she said, "I think I'd

585

like to leave." She was trying very hard to keep from crying.

"Of course. I'm sorry I upset you. I shouldn't have spoken so soon."

He followed her small, hurrying figure out the door of the restaurant and to the carriage parked next to the banquette. By the time he climbed in, she was sitting stiffly upright and as far to the other side of the seat as she could get.

"Do you want to go right home?" he asked.

"Yes, I think so," she sniffled.

"You're quite certain? If not, we could go for a drive. It's still early." He slid over and tentatively put one arm around her shoulders.

In another moment she had her face buried against his chest. "I never thought you'd want to marry me." Robert barely heard her muffled whisper.

"Yet you agreed to see me, and to continue going out with me."

"I couldn't help myself. I waited each time for you to suggest we go to your apartment or—or someplace else. I was so afraid, and I knew I wouldn't know what to say when you did."

"Why did you think that, love? Did you think I was like other men who come into the shop?"

"No, you were always so soft-spoken, and then so thoughtful when we went out. But what could I think, with you being the son of a Fontaine who once owned a river plantation and now owns a great import house? I'm only a seamstress."

"Do you think that matters to me? Are you forgetting my great-grandmother was born to a slave?"

"No, but—"

"And I love you." He turned her head so she had to look at him. "Will you marry me, Felicité?"

Again she hid her face in his shirtfront, and he couldn't tell whether she was nodding or shaking her head. When he finally managed to lift her head enough to kiss her and she kissed him in return, he knew he had his answer.

"Imagine!" Leah exclaimed when she read Robert's letter. "He's to be married, and to the daughter of one of my former students."

"Do you remember Sophia Belmar?" Baptiste asked.

"Yes, though of course she wasn't a Belmar then. But she was a little minx. Always getting into scrapes. How well I remember the time she climbed onto the roof of the convent to ring the bell from up there just to see if it would sound different."

"And did it?"

"I don't know. I stood beneath the eaves and prayed I could catch her if she fell. She was a very pretty little thing. I wonder if Felicité looks anything like her."

"It's too bad we can't be there for the wedding. I know how much it would mean to you."

"I just won't think about it. I'm happy enough he's found the right young woman to love and marry. And he says they'll come over to see us as soon as possible. We need to think of something very special for a wedding present." She already had that something in mind, and she was quite certain Baptiste would approve. It would take no more than a letter to Pierre, who had been acting as her attorney all these years, to transfer the title of her house in the *Vieux Carré* to Robert and Felicité. They should have a place of their own from the beginning, as she'd had when she went to live with Baptiste.

With the wedding set for early in June, Robert knew there was one more thing he must do to finally erase all memory of Isabella from his life. The time had finally come to satisfy his lust for revenge against Émile. Throughout the nearly two years since the contretemps, he had plotted and schemed and waited. He had lured Émile into complacency by remaining his friend.

At the weekly poker games, Robert was as affable as if they'd always been friends, with no bad blood between them. Émile and Robert drank together, whored together at Madame Eugénie's, raced their horses against each other. Robert had even asked Émile to be a groomsman at his wedding, but he doubted Émile would attend after their next meeting. He had no intention of killing him; that he could have done a long time ago. Instead, he planned to leave scars that everyone who looked at him would see, unlike the invisible stigmata Émile had inflicted on him. It would be a sweet revenge, made all the sweeter by the waiting and the anticipating. In a way Robert would be sorry when it was all over, but he wanted no loose ends left in his life when he married Felicité.

"Émile," Robert said casually one afternoon, "are you going to be busy tomorrow?" Robert was having an aperitif with Émile and Ambrose before going to meet Felicité at the shop.

"Nothing I can't put off until the next day. What did you have in mind?"

"There's a piece of property between here and Chalmette I've been looking at. You know more about that part of the country than I do. How about riding out with me and taking a look at it and telling me what you think of it?"

Robert was appealing to Émile's self-importance; as a land broker, Émile prided himself on negotiating some of the most lucrative deals since the Yankees had come down and grabbed whatever they wanted.

"Be glad to," Émile said. "You thinking of buying?" He was already figuring on the commission he'd ask.

"I might, if the price is right and the land is good enough for cane. Or rice."

Émile knew very well why Robert was interested in owning land. Losing Isabella had also meant losing the plantation that had once been the pride of the Fontaines, one of the finest pieces of property along the entire Mississippi.

"You want to borrow my carriage?" Ambrose asked.

"Thank you, but it's not that far. We can ride out. Anyway, I want Émile to ride over the property with me, and we couldn't do that in a carriage." Everything was working out perfectly, just as he'd planned.

In early afternoon, Émile and Robert rode south-southeast, roughly paralleling the river.

"How much farther?" Émile asked. He was beginning to sweat under the hot sun.

You'll sweat a lot more, Robert thought, *before this day is over.*

"Not much. We'll turn off in about a mile."

As soon as they reached the spot Robert had scouted earlier, he guided his horse off the road. "We can walk the rest of the way. Get down and tie up your horse."

"I'd rather not," Émile said. "No sense in not riding. The place is full of moccasins, and I didn't bring a gun."

Robert had to force himself not to smile. "But I did, so you're safe from snakes." He pulled his gun out and held it easily in his palm. "I think you'd better get down. I want us to walk over all the land."

Émile looked at the gun and knew he had ridden, un-thinking, into a trap. "My God, Robert! Are you planning to kill me?"

Robert had to admire Émile's cool way of standing his ground while he spoke it.

"No, but you might wish I had before I'm through with you. Now start moving."

Just as Robert had said, they walked for miles across the land, along the river, and to the edge of the swamp. When a moccasin slithered near the black water a few feet away, Robert moved the gun ever so slightly in his hand and, without even appearing to aim, shot the snake in the head. Émile shuddered. He had no idea Robert was such an expert shot. Nor did he know Robert had made it a point to become one.

"I think we've gone far enough," Robert said. Except for the soft patch of ground they were standing on, they were surrounded on all sides by swamp. "Now strip."

"What?" Émile envisioned himself being forced to run through the swamp while Robert shot all around him. Strangely, he believed that Robert would not kill him. But the swamp might.

Slowly, while Émile undressed and laid his clothes on the ground, Robert removed only his jacket and vest. Then he put the gun on top of them and pulled out a long strip of cowhide he'd hidden under his belt.

Émile knew he had two choices: make a run for it through the swamp and be shot at, or try to get the leather whip away from Robert. Opting for the latter, he crouched near the ground, waiting for the first sting of the lash against his skin. If he planned his moves carefully, he could grab hold of the leather and pull it out of Robert's hand.

Instead of flailing the whip around his head and snapping it across Émile's body, Robert wrapped it around his fist. Émile was taken completely off guard when Robert pulled him up to a standing position and began beating him with both fists.

"Fight, you bastard! Fight!" Robert screamed.

It took a second for Émile to grasp what Robert was saying. By that time his nose was already bloodied and one eye had taken a smashing blow. But Émile was a fighter, and now he went into it with all the strength he could muster.

For over an hour they fought, two bare-knuckled opponents battling it out toward a finish, which Émile now knew meant the death of one of them.

Both of them fell more times than either could count, but each time they got up. Robert was beginning to tire, and he wanted it over with. The next time Émile fell, Robert leaped

589

on his back and pushed his face into the murky water. But he didn't want him dead. He wanted him alive, so that every time he looked at Émile, he'd be reminded of how he'd finally gotten his revenge. He pulled Émile's head out of the water, hit him one final blow across the face, and left him lying unconscious. He reached into his pocket and pulled out a knife. Carefully, so as not to spill too much more blood, he drew the point of the knife slowly the length of each cheek. The bloody nose would heal; the black eyes would return to normal, and the bruises would fade. But the knife scars would remain forever.

Robert put on his jacket, picked up all of Émile's clothes, and walked back to the horses. He untied them, climbed wearily on his own, and led Émile's back to town.

Robert didn't see Émile again for over two weeks. When they did meet in one of the bars, Émile didn't turn and walk away as Robert expected him to do. The scars were still ugly, swollen, inflamed streaks coursing down both sides of his face. He looked Robert straight in the eye. "Someday I'm going to kill you," he said. Only then did he turn and walk out the door.

Chapter Forty-eight

THE GREAT SORROW OF JEAN AND CÉLINE was that Céline had miscarried twice after the death of Fleur. Céline considered the failure to bear Jean another child her fault, a punishment for the wanton life she'd led before she met him. She couldn't tell Jean about being attacked by the miller, seduced by his assistant, and then giving herself to others she found attractive. Jean had such implicit faith that she'd been a virgin when he became her lover. Always loving, he had become increasingly sweet and considerate with each miscarriage, assuring her that all that mattered to him was her recovery. He acted at times as if the loss of the babies were somehow his fault.

And indeed, he was certain that Céline's inability to carry the two children to full term and her failure to become pregnant again was retribution for the affair he'd had with Josette while Fleur was dying in Paris.

While each of them bore their secret shame in silence, they rejoiced together over the way Armand, now twenty-two, and Roland, twenty, had developed into strong, good-looking young men who continued to take an avid interest in the vineyards. From the time their sturdy legs could keep up with Jean's, they'd followed him around the fields. At harvest time, their greatest delight was being allowed to pick the grapes. Then they would watch, fascinated, as the grapes were pressed and the rich juice flowed into the vats.

Armand was now manager of several acres and in charge of the underground cellars where the champagne was stored and matured. During harvest time he supervised a number of *vendangeoirs,* the small buildings where the grapepickers lived and where the grapes were pressed as soon as possible. Steady and dependable, Armand was already being groomed to assume management of all the fields while Jean concentrated on the winery.

Although Roland was a hard worker under someone else's direction, as soon as the day was over he was ready to take off for the nearest village that promised an evening of festivity and a night with whatever pretty wench flipped her skirts at him. Roland fully intended to take his place in the winery, but he figured there was plenty of time to settle down and become serious about the business. Meanwhile he was going to enjoy himself.

Celia Metterine, a pretty but shy girl of sixteen, caught Roland's eye when she came to Villedommange from vineyards in Vaux-en-Beaujolais to live with her grandmother; however, she turned aside every suggestion that he'd like to see more of her. When it came time to harvest the grapes, she joined a number of other villagers whom Jean hired as temporary field workers. She was assigned to the section managed by Armand.

"Think I'll come work under you, big brother," Roland said when he saw her walking beside one of the wagons.

"I thought Papa wanted you in the office, to help pack the boxes for shipping."

"No rush. He and Uncle Gerald are busy with something else right now." He sauntered across the field to where Celia was examining the grapes before picking them. The wagon had left, taking a full load to the press. For the moment, Celia was alone and hidden from the other workers by rows of thickly clustered vines.

Sweaty from the hot sun, her back hurting, she thought she was going to faint. Nearby was an empty *vendangeoir*, unused since the press had broken down and been removed. She thought no one would see her if she stopped for a little while and sat just inside the door. Finding some relief in the cool darkness, she leaned her head against the doorjamb and closed her eyes. She didn't see Roland until he grabbed her by the shoulders, pulled her farther inside, and shut the door.

Celia had time to scream just once before Roland clamped his hand over her mouth and began pushing her legs apart with his knees. With his other hand he was already frantically pulling up her skirt and trying to rip off her underpants. His fingernails clawed at her skin, like an animal wounding its prey before the kill. Celia tried pushing him off her, but he was too strong for her. When she went for his eyes with her fingers, he buried his face between her chin and shoulder and began biting her neck. She could feel his body touching her bare skin, and she gritted her teeth against what would follow.

Armand heard the scream, and his first thought was a worker had cut himself severely on one of the long, sharp knives used to cut the heavy clusters off the vines. He thought it had come from the row where the young woman was working, and he cursed his father for assigning an inexperienced girl to his section. He thought at the time he'd have to keep an eye on her; but he'd had so many other things to do, though, between watching the pickers and checking the press that he'd forgotten all about her.

He'd never have thought to look inside the *vendangeoir* if the door hadn't swung partly open on its loose hinges and a narrow shaft of light coming through a window hadn't reflected off Roland's white shirt. One look told Armand what was going on, but his only thought at the time was to give his brother hell for luring a worker off the job when every hour counted in getting the grapes picked at exactly the right time.

Celia was still braced for the violence she knew was coming when she suddenly felt Roland being lifted off her as easily and quickly as one picked a flea off a dog. She opened her eyes in time to see Armand strike him hard across the face and knock him to the floor. In a moment, Roland picked himself up and ran out the door.

"I'm sorry," Armand said quietly. "I apologize for my brother. I hope he didn't hurt you."

"Not too much. At least you got here in time before—before—" She tried to stand but would have fallen if Armand hadn't got her over to a bench.

"You are hurt," he said. "What did he do to you?"

"Scratched me some, but mostly I'm weak from fright. I'll be all right now. Give me a few minutes, and I'll be back in the field."

"No, you won't," Armand said. "You're going home. You live nearby?"

"In Villedommange, with my grandmother."

"Then you go straight to her. I'll take care of Roland."

"Please," Celia begged, "don't—don't say anything to anyone else, or do anything to cause trouble."

"I'd like to kill him," Armand swore, "but for your sake and the sake of the family, I won't. But I promise you this: he'll never bother you again. I'll see to that."

Because Celia had said she wanted no one to know about the incident, Armand said nothing to his father; from then on, though, he kept an eye on Roland to make certain he didn't go near her. Nor was Roland about to stir up his brother's wrath again after the beating he'd taken at his hands. Instead, he stayed close to the winery and helped in the office. When Jean inquired about Roland's bruises, he laughed them off and said he'd run into a little trouble in a bar in Rheims. Jean shook his head and wondered why Roland couldn't be more like Armand.

Roland wasn't the only young man hovering around Celia, and Armand found himself watching her whenever he was in the fields. Before long he realized he was falling in love with her. When the church bells rang out at noon to signal the midday meal, Armand finally got up enough nerve to ask if he could sit beside her under the tree she was leaning against.

Celia found herself attracted to this quieter older brother, not just because he had saved her from Roland but because he was so much like herself. Conversation didn't come easily to him, and sometimes they sat through most of the meal without saying anything. When he did speak, it was to tell her about his love for the land and how much the vineyards meant to him.

"I hope I'll never have to leave this place," he said one day. "I can't think of any greater happiness than working these fields, tending the vines, and watching the grapes grow

593

into plump, rich fruit. Sometimes I can almost see them growing, swelling until they're ready to burst their skins. Their sweetness in my mouth is like—like nothing I can describe. I only know it must be the sweetest taste in the world."

"I grew up in the vineyards," Celia said, "so I know what you mean. My first memory is of crawling between the rows of vines and reaching up for a grape hanging just beyond my grasp. Mama says I was too young to remember, that what seems like a memory is her telling me about it. But she's wrong. I can still feel the warmth of the ground when I crawled along and the frustration I felt when my arm wasn't long enough to reach the cluster over my head. I remember crying and Mama lifting me up. Then she picked a grape and popped it out of its skin and into my mouth."

The harvest was nearly complete. The best grapes had been picked and the vats were filled with their juice. Most of the pickers had left to attend a festival in Villedommange. Armand and Celia stood in the fields, watching the setting sun paint the sky pink and gold and brilliant red.

"I'll be returning home soon," Celia said. "Grandmama is better and Mama wants me back."

"I don't want you to go." Armand turned so he could put his arms around her.

"I don't want to go either, but it's time." She let her head fall against his shoulder.

"I love you," he said softly. "I want to marry you. If I let you go, will you come back to me?"

"I promise." She stood on tiptoe so he wouldn't have to bend down to kiss her. "But I won't be leaving for a few days."

"I wish I could tell you how much I love you," Armand said earnestly, "but I don't know the right words."

"Yes, you do." Celia had taken off her shoes and was carrying them in one hand. Armand pulled her tighter against him, and she dropped the shoes to the ground. When she wriggled her toes in the soft, dry earth, it felt like fingers caressing her skin. The air was redolent with the heavy, rich aroma of grapes lying crushed on the ground, and Celia felt drunk with their odor, with the sweet taste of Armand's lips, and the pressure of his body. She offered no resistance when he settled her gently on the ground beside him. This time she was not frightened.

"This has been a good year, the best so far," Jean said as he lit up his after-dinner pipe and settled into his chair.

594

"You about ready for me to take over management of all the fields?" Armand asked.

"I don't see why not, after we check which vines have to be uprooted. Shouldn't be too many, maybe only that one oldest acre in your section. I'll be glad to turn them over to you."

"Good." Armand sighed with relief. He'd need more money if he were going to marry Celia and rent a place of their own. "I'm—I'm planning to be married."

"Oh!" Jean sat up straight in his chair. He hadn't even known Armand was seeing anyone. "Is she from Villedommange? Do we know her?"

"I don't know whether you do or not. Her grandmother lives in the village, but she lives with her parents in Vaux-en-Beaujolais. She's been working with me in the vineyards. Loves them as much as I do."

"Who is her grandmother?"

"Madame Rouger. She's been ill and Celia came to help her this summer and fall."

Jean was jolted when he heard the name, but then he relaxed. It might or might not mean anything. Madame Rouger had a large family. "How old is the young woman—Celia?"

"Only sixteen, Papa, but much more mature than her years."

Jean flinched when he heard her age. It corresponded too well with what had been an unhappy year for all of them. "Who did you say her parents were?"

"I didn't, but her last name is Metterine, and I think I heard her refer to her mother as Josette. I don't remember her father's name."

Jean slumped back in the chair. He knew who her father most likely was. Himself. It was a real possibility that she was a child born from his hurried, sordid affair with Josette. He started to panic, then thought it best to adopt a calm approach, to convince Armand she was too young or they hadn't known each other long enough.

"Summer romances aren't unusual," he said. "You say she's returning home in a week. You'll probably forget about each other in a month's time. After all, you haven't known each other very long."

"Long enough to know I love her," Armand said.

Jean felt himself turning cold all over. This was going to be harder than he thought. He and his sons had worked side by side in the vineyards for years, yet now he couldn't remember really talking with them. He was not a dour man, and he loved his family, but, like Armand, his quiet nature didn't lend itself to casual chatter. He'd always found it embarrassing to talk about personal matters.

"You're still young, Armand. There will be many you think you love before you're ready to marry. Maybe you'd like to go into Paris and work with your grandfather in the office there. You might like it better than the winery."

"I don't think so, Papa. This is where I've always wanted to stay. And I do love Celia and want to marry her. I'm older than you were when you fell in love with Mama, and you've had a good marriage."

True, Jean thought, *except for that one lapse into unfaithfulness, and now look at the result.*

"I—I trust nothing has happened yet that shouldn't," Jean said.

Armand wanted to smile at his father's shy attempts at asking the difficult question. He hadn't realized how really very modest his father was.

"If you're trying to ask me if we've become lovers, yes, we have. But that isn't the reason I want to marry Celia. I mean, not because it's the proper thing to do. I really love her and want her for my wife. We—we didn't become lovers until after I asked her to marry me."

Armand's words were an echo in Jean's memory; they were the same ones he'd spoken to his father over twenty-three years ago. He'd been in love, so madly in love with Céline, he couldn't think beyond being with her. Now their son, the grown-up Armand, stood in front of him and pleaded that he was in love with Celia. The words "I love her and want to marry her" were no longer simply the words of a boy in love; they were demons come to haunt Jean for his infidelity. How could he tell his son, for whom, so many years ago, he'd slaved and humiliated himself, that the girl he wanted to marry was undoubtedly his sister? He tried to say something, but his mouth was dry and the words would not come.

"We haven't been hasty, Papa," Armand continued. "We can turn the attic into a parlor-bedroom until we can afford a small place to live. You can still pay me laborer's wages until I prove worthy to manage more of the land."

"No, Armand. When you do marry, you will become a partner in the winery." Why this hesitation? He couldn't keep postponing the truth. But he knew that Armand would hate him, and he'd surely lose him. Armand might stay with the vineyards, but the rift would be as deep as the one between himself and his father when he fled from the château. And he doubted this one could ever be healed. "You say you've become lovers. Is there—is there going to be a child?" The horror he felt at the thought was overwhelming.

"I—we don't know yet. We didn't—we didn't do anything until I asked her to marry me a little more than a week ago."

"Then we must pray there is not." Jean paused. Should he ask Armand to get them some wine to ease the pain of what was coming? No, there was only one place he felt completely at ease. "Let's go walk in the fields. I want to tell you a story—a true story."

While they walked out into the autumn night, Jean pulled his heavy sweater more tightly around him. The first hint of winter's chill was in the air. They walked silently for a while, commenting now and then on the beauty of the moon coming up over the fields and the brilliance of the stars. All the while Jean was remembering how he had said, "Thank goodness for one piece of luck," the day Josette had appeared at the house to help them while Céline was in Paris. Now those words would haunt him for the rest of his life, and they would become the silent spectre haunting Armand as well.

"You said you had a story to tell me, Papa." They had arrived at the fields and Jean immediately began busying himself checking some of the vines, but he didn't see them. All he saw was Josette lying on the couch in the parlor.

"Yes, so I did." He cleared his throat, hit the bowl of his pipe against his heel to empty it, then took time to refill and light it. "I don't suppose you remember when Fleur died."

"I remember very well. She was so tiny and frail. Mama took her to Paris. You were distraught but you tried to keep things cheerful for Roland and me."

"And you both came down with colds and chills and fever. Do you remember that?"

Armand laughed, and Jean felt his bones grow cold. Would it be the last time the boy would laugh like that? "I remember you thought you were supposed to put the hot stones on our chests instead of using them to make the flannel hot. Then someone came to help, and we had proper meals again and she took care of us."

"Do you remember her very well?"

"I remember she was good to us, although she was also very strict about our washing our hands before we ate. I seem to remember she told us some funny stories. I knew things were easier for you after she came."

597

"Yes, yes, they were. They were better and they were worse." It was getting harder and harder. "You're a man now, Armand. You're not wild like your brother, but you know what it is to be tempted by a woman. Not the woman you love, not the woman you want to marry, but one who will satisfy a momentary craving. Perhaps to fulfill a need that shouldn't be there in the first place, but is anyway."

Armand was confused at the turn the conversation was taking. "If all this is to ask me if I feel worthy of Celia, I suppose I'll have to admit she was not the first. But I never thought of loving them, and I'll certainly not be unfaithful to her after we're married."

How different from me, Jean thought. He had been a virgin when he seduced Céline; it was only afterward that he was unfaithful. "You think you won't be, Armand, and you really mean it when you say you won't be. But there are always temptations, and few men are strong enough to resist them. Especially not at a time when they are particularly vulnerable because of worry—or loneliness."

Armand found himself gripped by a strange premonition, and he was frightened. Was his father merely going to reveal some indiscretion, to warn him perhaps about the dangers of disease or fathering a bastard? If he was trying to dishonor Celia in any way by these hints—! Armand clenched his fists. He'd let his father talk a bit more, and then he'd have something to say.

"Celia is not just a temptation," Armand said in as calm a voice as he could muster.

"No, I'm sure she's not. But Josette—Madame Metterine—was." There, he'd finally said it.

"I don't understand," Armand said.

"I had a brief affair with Josette. I make no excuses. I was unfaithful to your mother, and I was wrong. I've hated myself ever since. I've lived with the guilt all my life and cursed myself for being so weak that I couldn't keep from seeking comfort with someone else, while she was bearing up alone in Paris all the while Fleur was dying."

"Enough, Papa. Don't try to relieve your so-called burden of guilt by telling me about your sufferings. What is it you're really trying to say?"

"I'm saying that Celia could be your half-sister."

"I don't believe it!" Armand had been prepared to hear almost anything but this. That Celia was illegitimate, perhaps, or that, sweet and innocent as she seemed, she'd had other lovers or even borne an illegitimate child. But not this.

598

He was too bewildered to think. Then he became furious. "It's not true. I won't believe it." He put his hands over his ears and turned away from Jean.

"It's not a question of *don't* or *won't* believe, Armand." Jean longed to go over and put his arm around his son, to comfort him and ease him over the pain, but he knew that Armand hated him now as he'd never hated anyone in his life. "It's a matter of truth. She's the right age. Josette easily could have been pregnant when she left our house. She married soon after, but there is no way—no way—she could know which of us was the father. There is too great a risk that Celia is your sister."

"Then we'll run away and get married where no one will know who we are," Armand shouted defiantly. "I'll just tell Celia you don't approve, and we'll leave this damned place forever."

"And you could be committing a mortal sin."

"I don't care. I love her too much to lose her." The world was spinning around him, and then he was spinning with it, whirling and whirling into the bottom of a vortex.

"You love her so much," Jean said, "that you're willing to take the chance to let her commit the sin of incest without knowing it? Maybe your soul can bear the burden of your own sin—but can you carry hers, too? Knowing there is a strong chance she will have no hope of salvation?"

"It's not fair!" Armand swung around and went for his father as if to strike him. Then he lowered his head and leaned against the vines. There was no way to stop the tears. "Why didn't you tell me sooner?"

"I'd heard there'd been a child, but I didn't find out whether a son or daughter; I wanted to hear nothing that would remind me of what I'd done. I certainly didn't know when Celia came to me to work in the fields that she was Josette's daughter. Nor did I know you were seeing her. What was there for me to tell you?"

"You could have mentioned the affair."

"Would it have meant anything if I had? I've never referred to it since then. It was my shame, but over and done with. Or so I thought." *But is anything we do ever really over? No, our actions remain part of us, emerging and re-emerging to affect us, for good or for evil.*

"It's not fair, not fair at all!" Armand raged. "Two people fall honestly and deeply in love and then—then to be told their love might be sinful! I don't believe our love is wrong.

599

I hope you are damned to hell! And I never want to see you again."

Armand ripped off part of the vine he was clinging to. Holding it in his hand, he ran, crying and stumbling, through the fields toward the village.

He's gone, Jean thought, *and I'll never see him again. I have cursed him as surely as he damned me. Whether there is a heaven or hell after death, we've already entered hell now.*

Armand walked for hours, until he was so exhausted he fell to the ground and lay with his face buried in the earth. He had to believe what his father had told him; he would never make up a lie as cruel as that. He had to give Celia up, tell her he couldn't marry her, but without revealing the true reason. They had sinned in loving each other before they were married, but she must never know they might have committed the deadliest of mortal sins, the one spoken about only in whispers. She had trusted him, and he had hurt her, the person he loved more than anything in his life. And now he'd have to hurt her more deeply still by saying he couldn't marry her—and without telling her why. For a brief moment he thought of running away and leaving a note, but then he'd be doubly damned for being a coward.

It was too late to see her tonight. The moon had already begun its westerly descent. He couldn't return home, but he'd sleep where he lay, on the soft ground between the vines. He'd thought he'd spend the rest of his life here in the vine-yards with Celia. Soon he'd be leaving both of them behind and seeking a place where he could try to forget them. Here in the vineyards he'd gorged himself on the rich, pulpy fruit, and here on this very ground he'd tasted the sweetness of her lips and known the joy of loving and being loved. Now, because of his father's one moment of weakness, he was to be denied both. He hated his father, a hate intensified by the love he'd had for him until a few hours ago. No son ever loved his father more than he had. In experiencing the death of love, he was suffering an agony as great as any he would ever endure.

Armand slept until nearly noon, exhausted from the walk-ing, the crying, and the confusion in his mind. When he awoke he brushed the dirt off his clothes, and walked to a nearby spring to slake his thirst and wash the grime from his face and hands. The thought of food made him physically ill. He'd wait for Celia near the abandoned *vendangeoir*

600

where they'd been meeting every day. In spite of having been attacked there by Roland, the place held no terrors for her. To her it was both the place where Armand had first been attracted to her and a sanctuary for their love.

Shortly after noon, he watched her walk across the vineyard, one hand shielding her eyes, her head turning in search of him. Tiny though she was, she walked like a goddess of the fields, all beauty and joy. How could he possibly destroy the happiness he knew she was feeling at the thought of being with him?

When she saw Armand, Celia held out her arms in the sure faith that he wanted to come into them, that he wanted to embrace her as much as she wanted to feel his arms around her. Armand could not resist her touch or the expectant face tipped back for his kiss. He held her close and wished to God something would strike him dead at that very moment. It would be easier to die than to tell her they couldn't be married.

They began walking toward the small building. Armand knew he couldn't postpone telling her. Once they were in the *vendangeoir,* she would be in his arms and it would be too late.

"Wait, Celia, there's something I have to tell you."

"Your father wants us to wait, doesn't he?" If only she weren't smiling at him, her eyes all aglow, assuring him it didn't matter.

Yes, Armand thought, he could use that as an excuse, say they had to postpone the wedding. But would that keep them from meeting like this and loving as though their love were still innocent and pure?

"No, Celia, that's not it. I—I can't marry you. I lied when I said I loved you." If only she'd accept that, hate him for it, but run, run as fast as she could away from him.

Instead he had to watch while her eyes grew bigger, her face drained slowly of all color, and her lips began to quiver. "Because I let you love me, isn't it? You think I'm a harlot, and yet no one ever touched me before you. I was foolish to give you my innocence and think you'd treasure that gift. I should have known." She turned away and leaned against the door-jamb.

"No, Celia, I swear it. That's not the reason. My God, I loved you for your innocence, but—"

"For my innocence, perhaps, but not for myself. Isn't that what every man wants? To be the first. I loved you too much to deny you, or to deny that I wanted you, too." Sobbing and choking, she turned to enter the building. She tripped on the step and would have fallen if Armand hadn't caught her. With his arms around her, she clung to him, crying like a lost child.

"Oh God, Celia, I lied. I love you and I can't bear to let you go. But I have to."

"Whatever the reason," she begged, "hold me close and love me one more time. Then tell me and—and I won't see you again."

We mustn't, we mustn't, Armand thought over and over, but all the while he was untying the string of her blouse and she was unbuttoning his shirt. The touch of her warm, soft body drove him nearly crazy. He couldn't leave without making love to her. Quickly, before reason could take hold and force him to stop, he slipped out of his trousers and lay beside her on the wooden bench. He knew a few brief moments of pleasure before he released her and rolled over on his side, crying and beating his fists on the rough wood. Everything he loved was lost to him now.

"What is it, Armand?" Celia was terrified at seeing him cry and not knowing what caused it. "You said you had a reason we couldn't marry. I can't bear not knowing what it is."

He turned over on his back and flung his arm across his eyes to keep from looking at her. "I wanted to tell you I didn't love you. I hoped you'd believe it. I knew it would hurt, but —but far less than the truth."

"There's someone else, isn't there? Are you already married?"

"If only it were as simple as that." As much as he dreaded it, there was no way to keep from telling her the truth. Making love to her again, after he knew there was a chance she was his sister, gave him no hope of salvation. He was beyond redemption, but she could still be saved. That was the one thing he could do for her. "My father and your mother—she worked for us for a few days—had an affair. Your mother might have been pregnant when she left. There's no way to know for certain, but—"

Armand waited in the darkness behind his closed eyes for her to say something. He couldn't bring himself to look at her face, to see the horror that must be etched on it. He waited for her screams, her cries of disbelief, but he heard nothing.

"I see," Celia said finally. She had cried when she thought Armand didn't love her, but there were no tears now to ease this pain. Weeping and tearing her hair would avail her nothing. In a single, small fraction of time she'd had revealed what she had to do, what her life would be from that moment on. "I'll always love you, Armand, and I'll pray for you as I'll pray for myself." Quickly, she donned her skirt and blouse; then, without looking back, she left the dark building.

When Armand sat up, she was gone. He lay back down. He couldn't bear the thought of seeing her running across the fields. If there'd been any way to atone for the pain he'd caused her, he would have followed her; like him, though, she would have to find her way out of the depths alone.

Chapter Forty-nine

BAPTISTE STUDIED THE REPORTS from his New Orleans, Martinique, and Marseilles offices. Robert was doing very well in New Orleans. In the three years since his marriage and the five years since he took over the office, he had more than tripled the tonnage being carried from the States to Europe on Bonvivier-Fontaine ships. Martinique had been weaker until Marcel investigated the South American trade, and now the tonnage had picked up considerably—in both directions. The handsome ladies of Argentina, Brazil, and Colombia, in particular, were still clamoring for Parisian styles and Belgian laces. Claud Bonvivier, the son of Leah's half-brother, did a consistently good business through the Charleston, South Carolina, office. Marseilles was considerably smaller than any of the other offices, being primarily a loading center, but the manager was doing well.

Turning from these reports to the latest ones on the ships themselves, Baptiste's brow furrowed. Over the past few years the firm's fleet of sailing ships had been considerably reduced through age, necessary repairs being considered too expensive, and a few shipwrecks. Baptiste shook his head. He knew why those had not been properly cared for. The money that should have gone for repairs and refurbishing had been swallowed up by the Panama Canal fiasco and problems with the vineyards. It was his fault, no one else's, that they were now having to ship a large percentage of their goods on British and American steamship lines.

Baptiste tapped the end of a pencil against his teeth. For some time he'd been mulling the feasibility of investing in enough ships to form their own steamship line; then they could carry profitable cargo from other firms and various wineries as well as their own. There was a real possibility that there could be greater profit in hauling than in importing.

Although Baptiste, as the oldest member of the firm, was general manager of the entire enterprise, Marcel, as a direct descendant of the original founder, had now assumed the presidency from his father. No transaction as immense and important as investing in steamships could be undertaken without the approval of him and of Claud in Charleston. Out of deference to the splendid work he'd done since moving to New Orleans, Robert had also earned the right to be consulted.

Within two weeks, word to proceed came back from all concerned. Baptiste now had to consider whether to order the building of new ships or try to find old ones in good condition. As if in answer to his question, he received word that an American steamship company was selling six ships, less than ten years old, in order to expand their railroad holdings. Baptiste immediately cabled both Robert and Claud, suggesting they go to New York to check the freighters. Robert's return wire, a week later, was enthusiastic. Claud's was more staid but said essentially the same thing. The ships were in excellent condition. Baptiste sent in the bid that Claud recommended and waited.

Baptiste knew all too well that the success of the enterprise depended on getting enough cargo from other firms to fill the holds. To this end, he suggested to the managers of the various offices that they turn over the routine work to assistants and devote their time to contacting firms in their areas with goods to ship. Marcel, for his part, went to New York to meet with the former captains and officers of the ships to see if they would now work for Bonvivier-Fontaine. When word came that Baptiste's bid had been accepted, the ships were ready to sail with a full cargo manifest.

For some months following his marriage to Felicité, Robert genuinely feared for his life. He knew he could defend himself in a direct confrontation with Émile, but after his own underhanded attack, he couldn't expect to be warned. What concerned him more was Felicité, since Émile might think to get his revenge through her. Robert dared not tell her about the threat, and without her knowing it, hired a guard to watch the house during the day and to follow her whenever she left it. Then suddenly, to no one's surprise, Émile left New Orleans. Word sifted back that he'd headed west, and Robert found himself breathing easier than he had in a long time.

Robert was absentmindedly skimming through the mail on his desk. Felicité was expecting their first child in two months, and his mind was on her plans for decorating the nursery. Strange to think that Jean had slept in that nursery when their mother first returned from Indiana. And that René, an older brother, had died there from yellow fever before the Civil War. How many memories this house must hold for his mother and father. Robert was still considering buying land along the Mississippi; however, since they'd been given the house as a wedding present, neither he nor Felicité was in any hurry to move. He knew they'd always keep it, just as their mother had kept it all the years after she left.

One envelope caught his eye, and he ripped it open quickly. It was from a firm he'd contacted more than a dozen times over the past year in an attempt to get a shipping contract for at least some of their goods. The firm was one of the largest manufacturers in the States, and to have its business would guarantee that the Bonvivier-Fontaine shipping lines stayed in the black.

"Whoopee!" Robert shouted, jumping up from the desk. He might project the image of a conservative businessman, but there were times when his boyish enthusiasms overrode his usually subdued demeanor. Like a well-rehearsed chorus line, his three assistants looked up from their desks.

"This is it!" he shouted. "If we can be successful in this, we'll have it made."

"What is it?" John Alderman, his assistant manager, walked over.

"The Bestcraft Corporation—and they must have nearly fifty subsidiaries—will sign a contract to ship all their goods —all of them!—with the shipping line that can make the fastest run across the Atlantic. Do you know what that would mean, John?"

"It means we'd need a hell of a lot of luck if you think we could compete with what we've got. There are at least six other lines that could beat us without even trying."

"Not if we augment the steam engines with those new engines I was telling you about."

John shook his head. "You say they run on fuel oil instead of coal? I don't know. Coal's a lot more dependable."

"Come off it, John. You've been driving a motor car for two years now."

"Yes, and I never know when it's going to stall on me. What the hell do you think we'd do if the ship stalled in the middle of the ocean? Call back for a new engine?"

"No, because we'll still have the steam engines, too. More important, we'll take mechanics along that can make the repairs."

"Well," John said, "we're not going to make the decision anyway. Your father or Marcel will do that."

Robert sat right down and wrote two letters, one to his father, detailing the terms of the race, and the other to the manufacturer of the petroleum-fueled engines. If the second letter brought the answer he wanted—a guarantee of a faster speed and the use of one of their mechanics on the run—he'd fight with everything he had to put Bonvivier-Fontaine into the contest. And, by damn, they'd win!

By the time Marcel came over from Martinique to discuss the idea with Robert, the letter from the Detroit firm arrived. Robert read it with mounting excitement. Running at full speed, the petroleum-fuel engine, in conjunction with the steam engines, could far outdistance anything fueled by coal. A certain amount of remodeling of the ship would be required to accommodate the two additional engines, but that could be done under the supervision of a senior member of the Detroit firm. "In fact," the letter went on, "I would be more than delighted to do it myself as I feel I have a personal interest in this enterprise." The letter was signed "Cordially, Henry Fontaine."

"By God, it's Henri!" Robert exclaimed. He went on to read a more personal note attached as a postscript, asking about the family and hoping to hear from Robert soon.

From then on, cables passed rapidly between New Orleans and Paris, until the final one from Baptiste to Robert: "It's your baby, you take it from here. Good luck."

Within a week the two brothers met in New York.

"I can't believe it," Henri said. "Look at you. The last time I saw you—"

"I know," Robert said, slapping his knee with his hand, "I was only this tall."

"And now you're going to head up this venture. Well, I'm damned glad we're in it together. And we'll win, Robert, make no mistake about that. I don't take on anything that won't be successful."

Robert looked at his older brother and was inclined to agree with him. Henri was the quintessence of the successful executive and internationally recognized inventor. When they weren't looking at charts, engine diagrams, and ratios of such things as thrust and fuel usage, which Robert found as confusing as Egyptian hieroglyphics, they were talking about their families and the family back in France.

"Tragic about Nicole," Henri said. "And what about Jean's Armand? Any word about him yet?"

"None. Some unhappy love affair that sent him running God knows where. Jean thinks he might be in the army, and government officials have agreed to try to find him; if he's using an assumed name, though, he could disappear for years. Be killed even, and we'd never know. Such a pity after they lost Fleur as a baby. One good thing came out of it. Roland has harnessed his wildness and proved to be a real comfort and support for Jean and Céline."

"Do you get home often?" Henri asked.

"Not as often as I'd like. Wish you'd come with me sometime. Or go on your own. Mama and Papa aren't getting any younger." He wanted to say "you owe it to them," but Henri was still the older, somewhat intimidating brother he'd been when Robert toddled beside him in the workshop.

"I'll think about it." He saw the frown on Robert's face. "Seriously, I mean."

"Maybe on this run across the Atlantic? We're landing in Southampton, but—"

"Maybe I will. At least there'd be a logical reason for leaving Louise and the children behind this time. She'd never consider letting me take a pleasure trip to Europe without her."

He didn't say any more, but Robert knew what he was implying. There was no way Henri would let Louise meet their parents, especially their mother. Robert still loved Henri, but he felt ashamed for him.

Robert read over the rules for the race across the Atlantic. All ships were to start from the ports of Baltimore, Norfolk, Charleston, or New Orleans. Those whose home ports were elsewhere would be accommodated at one of the four ports prior to the race. The discrepancy in distance between the various American ports and Southampton would be taken into consideration. Because the manufacturing firm had plants in several locations in the East and Southeast, it would be necessary for whichever line received the contract to make a number of stops before heading across the Atlantic. Thus, all ships would be required to begin the race partially loaded and stop in New York to take on additional cargo.

Over and over again, Robert studied the pages of figures in front of him. So much of the firm's money had been invested in the new engines, the remodeling of the ship, and some additional crew, that now they had to win or face the threat of bankruptcy. Sometimes he wished his father and Marcel hadn't had such complete faith in his judgment. It would make things a lot easier if there were someone with whom to share the responsibility. Both Baptiste and Leah had been elated that Henri had actually been the inventor of the engines they were using and that he would be sailing on the ship with Robert. They were eagerly looking forward to seeing him in Paris.

Five days before the start of the race, Henri was to arrive in New Orleans, and for weeks Felicité had been all atremble at the thought of entertaining Robert's older, affluent brother in their home.

"I'm sure he must live in a tremendous mansion in Detroit, she said, "with numerous servants. What is he going to think of our little place here?"

"He is going to think it is absolutely as charming as you have made it, and I will bet you he asks for seconds of everything you cook."

Robert took the baby from Felicité's arms. "You finish with supper and I'll put her to bed. She all ready?"

"All but changing her if she's wet."

"Come then, Leah Angelique, Papa will get you nice and dry and tuck you in."

Five-month-old Leah was lying on the bed, gurgling, kicking her legs, and trying desperately to turn over, while Robert tried just as desperately to get a diaper pinned around her. "I think I'll change your middle name," he laughed at her as she wiggled off the diaper for the fourth time. "You're no angel, you're a little imp." He was just getting the second pin fastened when he heard the front-door knocker.

"Can you get that, darling?" Felicité called from the kitchen. "My hands are covered with biscuit dough."

Robert picked up Leah, tucked her against his shoulder,

and went to the door. Somehow he wasn't surprised when the messenger handed him a wire from Henri.

"It's from Henri," he said, walking into the kitchen. "He won't be going on the run with us. Louise is ill."

"You don't seem too upset," Felicité said. She took Leah, who was trying to grab the telegram from Robert's hand.

"I am, but I was half prepared for it, especially after I suggested he go on to Paris with me to see the family. I don't know whether it's because Louise would be upset at the idea of his going alone to the Continent, or whether he can't face Mama and Papa after all these years of passing as white in the North."

"It doesn't worry you that you won't have him along in case anything goes wrong with the engines?"

"He's sending down his best mechanic. We'll be all right on that score. I'm disappointed, though. I was really looking forward to our being in this together. After all these years it was really great seeing him again. It brought back a lot of good memories."

"Well, put Leah down. Dinner's about ready."

Throughout dinner and the rest of the evening, Felicité found herself listening quietly to the stories Robert told about all the various contraptions Henri had designed. He talked about the ones that worked and the ones that failed, as he had watched, fascinated, or been allowed to help.

"You really miss him, don't you?" Felicité said at last.

"Yes, but there's no point in dwelling on it. I don't think I'll ever see him again. I'd better accept it the same way I've learned to accept Nicole's death. And I'd better be concentrating on the race. Right now, winning that is the most important thing in my life." Yet he was bitterly disappointed that now he'd never be able to re-establish the old bond he'd once had with his favorite brother. He'd almost forgotten how much he'd loved Henri until he saw him again in New York. Then the old admiration and hero worship returned. No matter how much he disliked Henri for turning his back on their parents, no matter how much he despised his renunciation of his heritage, he couldn't hate him.

Although now living in Texas, Émile LeRogue had inherited a major share of stock in a New Orleans-based shipping line. Among the various reports sent to him from the home office was the news about the Bestcraft proposition. He'd had no intention of entering the race, until one of those reports included a preliminary listing of companies competing for the contract with the corporation. He saw Robert's name and grinned to himself while he re-read the rules of the competition. This would be the perfect way to get his revenge for the beating he'd taken at Robert's hands. Until now the humiliation of being left naked in the swamp, of having to make his way back to New Orleans, and finally of having to realize his face was scarred for life had festered like an incurable, painful boil. Now, perhaps, it could be excised. Émile was not concerned about whether the ship he chose for the run would be faster than Robert's. He had already plotted what he considered a foolproof scheme for outmaneuvering his and all the other ships. It was merely a matter of contacting the right people and paying what they demanded. On one hand the cost would be exorbitant; on the other, it was negligible considering the satisfaction he'd get from defeating Robert. Besides, he'd get every bit of it back when he won the contract with Bestcraft.

By the time he reached New York, loaded the cargo waiting for him there, and started across the Atlantic, Robert was certain he was well ahead of the other three ships making the run from New Orleans. So far, he'd spent nearly all his time staring at charts, keeping his own log of the run, and comparing his entries to those of the captain. He was assured by Captain MacIvor that they were keeping to the schedule they'd worked out before leaving New Orleans. The ships from Charleston, Norfolk, and Baltimore would, of course, reach Southampton ahead of them; after time and distance had been computed, however, Robert's *Sealady* should be well ahead of the others. The run across the Atlantic was smooth and uneventful. Not once did the mechanic from Henri's firm have to do more than check the engines daily and make a few minor adjustments.

When they entered the English Channel, Robert opened the locker in his cabin, took out the bottles of champagne, and put them on ice. They'd be in Southampton before long; then, as soon as their winning time was substantiated, he'd open them and every man on the crew would celebrate. The additional engines had cut so many hours off the normal run, there was no way they could lose.

He was not the least bit dismayed when he saw nearly a dozen ships berthed in the port. These would be the ones from along the eastern seaboard. He bounded ashore and walked jauntily toward the temporary office set up in a warehouse by the Bestcraft company. A representative on the docks had already clocked the *Sealady's* time of arrival. Just as he was introducing himself to the man behind the desk, he felt a heavy hand clap him on the shoulder.

"Sorry, old man," Robert heard, "but I'm afraid you've been outdistanced this time."

Robert didn't have to turn around to identify the voice. He recognized it after the first word.

"What are you doing here, Émile?" Did he work for Bestcraft? Robert wondered. If he did, could he, in some way, deny the contract to Bonvivier-Fontaine?

"Winning the Bestcraft contract." His satisfied grin made the scars on each side of his face stand out menacingly.

Robert's heart sank, but he'd be damned if he'd give Émile the satisfaction of gloating. "Congratulations. Where did you sail from?"

"New Orleans. Same as you. In a faster ship than yours."

I don't believe it, Robert thought. Captain MacIvor had assured him there wasn't a ship built that could beat the *Sealady*. Yet there Émile stood. Robert had seen all the ships pull away from the wharves in New Orleans just five minutes apart, and none had passed him in the Gulf. The fastest shipping-lane route between New York and England had long been established, but was it possible that Émile had found a faster one? He certainly hadn't passed the *Sealady* in the channel. There'd been a lookout posted the entire time to report on such an eventuality.

"Well, as the saying goes," Émile said, "to the fastest goes the reward. Buy you a drink?"

"No, thank you. Captain MacIvor is waiting for me." He dreaded seeing the expression on the burly Scotsman's face when he told him they'd lost. Well, if they couldn't celebrate with the champagne, they could drown their disappointment in it.

Robert had more to worry about, however, than MacIvor's rage. He had to go to Paris and tell his father they'd lost the race, and with it all the money he'd invested in the new engines and the best crew Captain MacIvor could hire. Right now he was too despondent to think about the future. As soon as he told MacIvor and listened to the captain calling down the wrath of the heavens on whoever beat them, Robert retired to his cabin and opened a bottle of Kentucky bourbon. He could take defeat when he expected it, but not when he'd been certain he would win.

After the fourth, or fifth, glass—he stopped counting at

three—there was a knock on the cabin door and his third mate entered.

"What is it, Jordan?" Robert asked. He hoped the likable young man hadn't come to offer his condolences.

"I have a note for you, sir."

"Who from?" Robert managed to rise to a partial sitting position in his bunk.

"I'm not exactly sure, sir. Captain MacIvor gave some of us shore leave. We were sitting in one of the pubs—the Fox and the Grapes—when a sailor from one of the other ships came over and handed me this note. Something funny about it, sir. I saw him watching us a long time before he approached us. In fact, he waited until the other sailors with him left. Anyway, here it is."

"Thank you, Jordan. Let's find out what it says." In an almost illegible pencilled scrawl, Robert was requested to meet the writer at another pub, the Unicorn, just after eleven that night.

"Why the hell does he think I'd be interested in meeting him?" Robert asked.

"He said to tell you he thought you'd be interested in what he had to confide. And, oh yes, the information will cost you."

"The hell it will! What he wants is for me to go there with my pockets loaded so he can waylay and rob me. He must think me some kind of damned fool. You don't know what ship he was from?"

"No, sir. He wants to see you alone, but there's no reason why Captain MacIvor and another of our crew can't be in the pub at the same time. He'd recognize me, but not someone who wasn't with me earlier."

"All right," Robert said. "The way things have gone to-day, a little excitement might take my mind off my other troubles. Ask Captain—no, I'll talk to him myself. Thank you for bringing the note."

Sometime before eleven, Robert, followed closely by Captain MacIvor and second mate Albright, made his way through the dark back streets of Southampton. He didn't know when he might be jumped by professional muggers or ragged street urchins who made their living by rolling sailors who came ashore with full pockets. Robert was too intent on finding the Unicorn to care that he'd insulted a number of tawdry prostitutes by ignoring their invitations to " 'ave a bit o' fun, mite."

Finally he located the Unicorn, a small, stinking pub wedged between two soot-blackened tenements. The narrow, shrunken building sagged in the middle, and its door hung askew on its hinges. It looked as if at any minute it would be crushed by the tenements that tilted at perilous angles toward each other above its roof. A sign announcing rooms to rent by the hour partially covered a broken window on the first of the pub's two floors.

A jolly place we have here, he thought, wondering why he'd let his curiosity tempt him. He glanced over his shoulder. MacIvor and Albright, singing and weaving along the sidewalk like sailors too drunk to care what was going on around them, were no more than fifty feet behind him. At least they'd be following him into the pub. Robert entered and looked around the dusky interior, which smelled of gin and cheap perfume. Only two men stood at the bar. On one bench a prostitute was encouraging a sailor to run his hand up her thigh. On another, a sailor sat alone. Robert hoped that was the one he'd come to see. He didn't relish waiting long. Ordering a glass of stout and casually seating himself near, but not too close, to the sailor, Robert was relieved when MacIvor and Albright came stumbling through the door two or three minutes later.

Robert nodded but kept on drinking his stout when the man on his bench mumbled something that sounded like, "You're a stranger here, ain'tcha?"

"Me, too," the man said a little more clearly. "Just come ashore offen a ship from New Orleans." Robert choked and nearly spilled his drink. Was this the man who sent the note or just a sailor who happened to be sitting in the Unicorn? There was only one way to find out.

"Arrived on the *Sealady,*" Robert said under his breath.

"Thought so," and the stranger slid a few inches closer on the bench. "If you brought what I asked, I've something I think you'd like."

"Such as?"

"A bit of information. But I want more than money." The sailor was still speaking too low for anyone else in the room to hear, but his words were quite clear enough for Robert to understand. "I need a guarantee you'll never reveal who told you. I ain't going back to the States. I know how to get lost over here, but it wouldn't help to have my name mentioned."

"I'll guarantee that," Robert said. He opened his jacket wide enough so the sailor could see the money in his inside pocket. "What's the information? It better be worth what I brought."

Quickly, in a few clipped sentences, the sailor explained

613

the ruse by which Émile's ship had beaten Robert's to South-ampton. Instead of sailing into New York to pick up the cargo there, he'd had a supply boat pick up the goods and meet his ship farther out at sea. Émile had saved hours by this fraud.

Robert was stunned. It hadn't occurred to him that any-one would fail to abide by the rules. The question now was how to prove the accusation if he challenged Émile and pre-sented the information to the Bestcraft officials.

"Why should I believe you?" Robert asked. "What's in it for you?" This man could be no more than a disgruntled sailor wanting to cause trouble all around or a con man with a new trick for getting his money and disappearing.

"The money you're going to give me. It'll be enough to open a pub of my own in Wales. I'm sick of the sea, and I had something of a run-in with Mr. Émile LeRoque."

"How do I prove what you're telling me? They're not go-ing to take my word against the official record."

"I'll give you names. Names of others on the crew who'll testify—they already got berths on other ships so they ain't desperate like me—and names of those in New York who loaded and ran the supply boat. Some of us thought the whole thing stank, but we was promised a bonus. When we got here and asked about it, Mr. LeRoque just laughed and gave us enough for a pint of ale. That ain't no way to treat a crew what worked extra shifts."

"You have the names?" Robert asked.

The sailor pulled a sheet of paper from his pocket, opened it to show what was written on it, and traded it for the money Robert turned over. "Three of us is gonna split the money you brought. This here one will be waiting for you at the Bestcraft office in the warehouse tomorrow morning at eight. He ain't afraid of the Devil himself, but he had something else to do tonight. He'll tell 'em. Derrick over there," he nodded to the sailor seemingly captivated by the prostitute, who now had her skirt pulled up to her hips, "will vouch for what I told ya. He's been watching to make sure you didn't snaffle one over on me."

But not too intently, Robert thought. He'd had a hard time keeping his eyes off the activities on the second bench while his informant was talking to him. Now the man disen-gaged himself from the woman's clutches and came over to them. "Everything he said," nodding at the man beside Rob-ert, "is true. I'll be there in the morning with Simpson." With that he wasted no time returning to the prostitute, who had remained sprawled with her legs apart on one end of the bench. Robert watched them walk through the dingy gloom to the stairs at the rear of the pub.

In another few minutes, Robert left by the front door, followed soon by MacIvor and Albright.

"What do you think?" Robert asked after the two caught up with him.

"I think we have to believe them," Captain MacIvor said. "At least until we get to the offices in the morning and see if Derrick and Simpson are there. If they're not, you just paid several hundred dollars for a single glass of stout and a tour of what must be the God-awfullest, most rat-infested section of Southampton."

Robert agreed when a four-legged rat scurried across his foot and a two-legged one slunk into an alley after MacIvor nonchalantly opened his jacket to reveal a pistol tucked in his belt.

In the morning, a vice-president and another officer of Bestcraft listened with mounting interest to what Derrick and Simpson had to tell them. Robert, Captain MacIvor, and second mate Albright stood to one side during the intensive questioning.

"We'll have to get in touch with New York, of course," the vice-president said. "Meanwhile we'll call on Mr. LeRoque and apprise him of what we've learned. The issue of a contract will have to wait until we can investigate the facts and verify what these men have told us. I think it's safe to say, however, that Bonvivier-Fontaine will be awarded the contract. It shouldn't take more than a few weeks, and you'll be hearing directly from me."

Robert waited until they were outside the office to throw his arms around Captain MacIvor. "We did it! We beat every one of those others. And we beat that bastard Émile. Damn his sorry hide."

After telling MacIvor he'd see him in New Orleans within a month, Robert headed for the channel ferry to France. How he would love to clap his hand on Émile's shoulder, tell him, "Sorry, old boy," and then beat him up again for being such a pain in the ass. Better yet, though, was the assurance he'd never see his miserable, ugly face again.

Chapter Fifty

NEARLY TWO YEARS had gone by with no word from or about Armand. Céline had been inconsolable when Jean told her their son had left because of an unhappy love affair.

"He'll be back," Jean kept reassuring her, "once he realizes how foolish he's being." He had to lie, to her and to himself, to keep on living. He knew in his heart Armand would never return unless somewhere, somehow, he came to learn that every man has committed acts he is ashamed of and for which he must suffer the consequences. And that one could only hope to be forgiven by those he'd harmed or betrayed even though he might never be able to forgive himself. If there were a peace that passeth all understanding, there must also be a forgiveness that passeth all understanding. A forgiveness issuing from faith rather than from knowledge.

When Baptiste and Leah heard about Armand's flight, Leah wept for Jean and Céline's sorrow. She knew what it was like to lose a child: René and Nicole to death and Henri to flight. More than ever she depended on Baptiste's strength.

"As long as he's still in France, we'll find him," Baptiste said. "As far as that goes, if he's crossed a border, there's a good possibility he's had to register someplace. We'll simply alert the police and let them take it from there."

And so the search had begun, a search that still continued. It had led them down avenues neither Jean nor Baptiste had dreamed they would have to take: from back alleys, where sleazy, underground informants hung out, to wide boulevards and imposing foreign embassies.

If it had been impossible, Jean thought, to find Nicole in the labyrinth of Montmartre, why should they believe they'd ever locate Armand in the vast expanse of the Continent? Or of the world, if he'd chosen to follow Henri's lead and gone to the States or gone to seek his fortune in England? And yet he'd never given up hope that one lead, one word from someone, would bring them to Armand.

"He's probably changed his name," Baptiste said, shaking

his head over a negative report from the Italian authorities. By then, Armand had been gone for nearly a year and a half. "I wonder, Jean, if we should continue looking for him. Every time someone shakes his head, it makes it that much harder."

"No, I need to know where he is. If he's dead, I'll accept that, but if he's still alive I want to know where and how he is."

"Then it would be easier if you and Céline would think of him as dead. I don't mean to be cruel, Jean, but he could have been killed in—oh, someplace like Marseilles, and no one would know. If he's alive, he'll come back once he's gotten over thinking he's the only man jilted by someone he loves." Like Céline, Baptiste and the others were under the impression that Armand had left in a fit of pique after a disastrous love affair.

Lisette was also mourning the loss of someone very dear to her. King Edward VII had died in early May of 1910. To the world he was Edward or Bertie, the scapegrace son of Queen Victoria, who after finally ascending to the throne had proved to be a most estimable monarch. To Lisette he was her beloved Eddie, the man she loved only when he was no longer her lover but her friend. From masquerading as Henry VIII to her Anne Boleyn, he had gone on to become her advisor and confidant when she could see nothing in her future but bleak despair. Without his encouragement, she would have faltered several times along her way toward becoming Gerald's wife and Duchess of Highcastle. Multitudes wept the day of his funeral, but few with greater sorrow than she.

Almost two years to the day after Armand fled, Jean finally received the message he'd waited for throughout the tedious, despairing months. But he found it hard to rejoice when he read the words in the official letter. Armand had, indeed, changed his name and enlisted in the French Army. For most of the time he'd been stationed in Algiers and fought in minor desert skirmishes. A few weeks earlier, while reconnoitering a Bedouin stronghold, his small force had been captured. As of now, the Army didn't know whether the men were being held prisoner or been executed.

The letter went on to say that Armand Fontaine had enlisted under the name Jean Duvall and had indicated he was an orphan with no family to notify in case of death. It was only when one of his comrades was going through his things that he found a small book of devotions. Under the words "To Armand from Mama, Christmas 1893" was his full name "Armand Claud Fontaine" written in a childish scrawl. The book could have been given to him by a friend named Armand, but since he'd been captured and if he did have a family who should be notified, they had begun an investigation.

Jean balled the letter up in his fist and went to tell Céline. He knew only too well the habits of the desert tribesmen. They would torture and then kill. If Armand had been captured by them several weeks earlier, it was doubtful he was still alive. They would not begin a second period of waiting.

To everyone's surprise, it was Roland who kept their small family from falling apart. As if he knew that in some way he had to take Armand's place, he assumed a greater responsibility around the vineyeards and in the winery. He gave up gallivanting around the countryside and spending every night in a different bed, and he was now engaged to the daughter of a vintner in Sillery. Jean had been able to put all of the vineyards under his management, and Roland seemed to have an intuitive knowledge of exactly when each bunch of grapes should be picked and which were going to make the finest wine.

"A good harvest this year, Papa," he said while they strolled home through the fields after determining which ones could be replanted after lying fallow for two years.

"I think so, too. We've been lucky these past few years. Good vintage years, every one of them."

"I saw something in Monsieur Havré's store the other day you might want to get Mama for Christmas. A gold filigree cross with a diamond in the center. I think she'd like it."

With a feeling of remorse, Jean realized it had been a long time since he'd thought of getting something special for Céline. She'd always loved pretty things, but somehow it hadn't occurred to him to buy them for her. He'd do what Roland suggested and get the cross tomorrow. He might save it for Christmas, and then again he might not. That was still a month and a half away. Perhaps he'd find another pretty trinket for her then.

Jean walked along the narrow street. While he looked in some of the other store windows, he patted the gaily wrapped package in his pocket. Céline would be surprised and pleased.

She'd scold him a bit about spending the money, and she might tease him about trying to lure her into bed with jewelry —she still knew how to keep their marriage exciting by sometimes flirting with him and at other times sliding quietly into his arms—but she would love the gift.

"Monsieur Fontaine."

Jean slowed his steps and turned around. He looked quizzically at the woman hurrying to catch up with him. There was something familiar about her, but he couldn't place her.

"You don't remember me, do you? I'm Josette Metterine. Madame Rouger is my mother. I worked for you while your wife was in Paris."

Josette! The last person in the world he wanted to see right now. He looked around, expecting to see his own shock reflected on other people's faces. But she'd only said she'd worked for him. She hadn't said she'd slept with him.

"Of course I remember you," he said and managed to draw up a friendly smile to indicate he was pleased to see her again. "I was just thinking about having some coffee and pastry. Won't you join me?" He didn't know why he'd asked her. He should have said he was expected home and asked her pardon for hurrying away.

"Thank you. I have a little time. My mother is not well, that's why I'm here."

Jean ordered the coffee, and they selected pastries from the glassed-in counter.

"I'm sorry your mother is ill," he said. "I hope not seriously." He cut the rich torte apart, then laid the fork across his plate. He didn't know why he'd selected it. He'd never be able to eat any of it.

"More age than anything. I'm thinking of taking her back to Vaux-en-Beaujolais with me." She sipped her coffee. "How are the boys, Armand and Roland? I grew very fond of them while I was with you. It was only a short time, but they seemed so much like my own."

Jean winced at her words. "Roland is fine. He works very hard in the vineyards and will probably be managing the whole thing in a few years. I can't tell you much about Armand. His is a tragic story." How much should he tell Josette? How much might she have learned from Celia? "He's in the Army, stationed in Algiers. That is, he was until he was captured by Bedouins and now is either a prisoner or dead."

"I'm so sorry," Josette said. "I know how you must be suffering. It's very hard to lose a child."

The import of her last words was lost on Jean for the moment. "Yes. In a way we've lost him twice. He left home two years ago, and then when we finally learned where he was, we also learned about his capture."

"He left home?" She gave him a sympathetic smile. "A family quarrel?"

"In a way." He suddenly wanted to change the subject. "Do you have children?" He was waiting for her to say something about Celia. To give him a hint of what she knew.

"Four, two sons and two daughters."

"Are they all at home?" More indirect questions. Why couldn't he come right out and ask?

"All but Celia, the eldest." Josette shook her head. "She's in a convent. I never thought she'd be the one to enter a cloistered life. Vivacious, pretty, a bit shy, but she loved life. Unfortunately there was a tragic love affair. She never told me much, only that she could never love anyone else."

"Celia, yes," he said as if reaching back into his memory. "Very pretty, and a very sweet girl."

"You knew her?" Josette looked puzzled. "Oh, yes, the summer she was here with her grandmother. In fact that was just before she entered the convent. Perhaps you know the young man who broke her heart."

"All too well," Jean said. "She was the reason Armand ran away from home, but he didn't jilt her. They were very much in love and wanted to marry. But, of course, I couldn't let them."

"Why not?" she exclaimed defiantly.

Jean was taken aback by the fury in her voice.

"You thought a daughter of mine not good enough to marry your son? I might have worked in your house, but my family have owned vineyards around here for generations. Not until my father died and there were no sons to carry on did my mother have to sell them."

"No, no." Jean was amazed and disbelieving at her question and his apparent insult to her family. Didn't she realize what he'd been saying? "I had to tell him that Celia could be my—our daughter."

"Our daughter!" Josette dropped her cup, spilling coffee all over the table and herself. In a flurry of embarrassment and exasperation, Jean tried to wipe off the table with their napkins, while Josette dabbed frantically at the front of her dress. Then they were very quiet while the waitress brought second cups for each of them.

"Oh no, Monsieur Fontaine!" Josette wailed after the girl

had returned to the counter. "Whatever made you think— I knew I was pregnant before I came to work for you. But Auguste didn't want to marry me. So I stayed with you, in your house, to make him jealous. And after I left, we were married."

"Oh, my God!" Jean moaned. He put his hands over his face and clutched at his hair. "And Armand might be dead because— He'd be here today if—" He found it impossible to finish what he was saying.

"That's right," she said coldly. "Weep for Armand, but weep for Celia, too. She might as well be dead. You destroyed her as well. Secluded in a convent. Spending all her life praying for her sins—for sins she never committed." Josette began laughing hysterically.

"Is she ill, Monsieur Fontaine?" the waitress asked solicitously.

"No, she's heard some unfortunate news. She'll be all right in a few minutes." How easy it was to say that. If only it were true.

"Never allows me to see her," Josette sobbed. "Won't speak to me. I knew—I knew when she insisted on going into the convent that they'd been lovers. But, oh God, for her to be thinking all this time she might have been guilty of incest. And no way I can tell her. No way."

"Through another nun?" Jean was trying desperately to assuage her pain, to end her agony. At least Celia could now return to life. If only the same were true for Armand. "Surely you can write to her. Ease her mind."

"She belongs to a cloistered order. They've all taken a vow of silence. She lives in a private world within a small cell; it is a world of praying and fasting except for one meal a day pushed through a slot in her door. Not unless she becomes seriously ill would I be allowed to see her and then only if she permits it. No, Monsieur Fontaine, she has already died, and she is serving out her penance in Purgatory."

"I'm sorry, Josette, sorrier than I can say. If only there were something I could do."

"There is nothing you can do. Through your own stupidity you ruined two young lives. And mine as well. I hope you can live with it."

Quietly, and as if she'd been having a pleasant afternoon coffee with a friend, she rose from the table, nodded to the proprietor, and walked out.

Jean sat for a long time. As if in a trance he stared at his coffee cup and the untouched pastry on his plate. Josette was right. He'd acted in haste. He'd sinned in having the affair with Josette, but he'd committed a far more grievous error when he assumed that Celia was his child and had not taken the time to write to Josette about Armand and Celia wanting to marry.

This, he thought, *this is the hell Armand damned me to.*

Chapter Fifty-one

LEAH LOOKED AROUND THE TABLE, which was heaped with flowers and multi-colored ribbon streamers. On the sideboard, the birthday packages, all opened and exclaimed over, were now piled haphazardly in their nests of crumpled tissue and gaudy bows. Because the dining-room table was no longer large enough to seat the whole family, the work table from Baptiste's office and the cutting table from her sewing room had been placed at right angles to the ends of the dining table. Leah smiled, remembering how Baptiste had fussed at having his accumulation of papers disturbed.

"I'll never find what I'm looking for," he mumbled while Colette, the young housemaid, carefully removed the assorted conglomeration of magazines, reports, letters, newspapers, and notes and stacked them in neat piles on the floor.

"Nonsense," Leah said. "You know you simply toss every letter and every report up there and say you'll look at them when you feel like it. I'll bet you haven't sorted through them in years."

"Maybe not, but I know what's there."

"And after the dinner everything will all be right back where it was," she assured him.

In the midst of noisy chatter, spurts of hilarious laughter, the clatter of forks against plates, and occasional exclamations over the dish Colette was passing, she became reflective. She was suddenly remembering the birthday dinner when she was pregnant with Robert. While she'd tried to keep her spirits up for the children, she hadn't known for certain whether she was pregnant or whether she had a malignant tumor. It had been a fearful time—a time for confronting the awareness that she might not have long to live, that her fortieth birthday might be her last. Now she could look back and appreciate how much had been granted to her in the thirty years since then.

Thirty years. She could hardly believe it. There had been seven around the table that night. Now there were twenty-one. In spite of those who were absent, the number in the room had tripled in thirty years. In being able to celebrate her seventieth birthday with most of her family she had been granted a special benison.

Leah's eyes come to rest on Jean. He and Céline had endured a trying three years since Armand left and joined the Army. An unhappy love affair, Jean had said through tight lips. The letter with the news that Armand was alive but had been captured by Beduoins had been a mixed blessing. It had eased their minds to learn where he had been during those years, while bringing the new fear that he had been killed by his captors.

Jean was smiling now, though. The desert outpost had finally been retaken by the French Army. During the skirmish, Armand had been wounded, but he was now recovering in an Algerian hospital. He'd written his parents to tell them he'd be home as soon as his wounds healed enough for him to travel. Whatever the rift between him and his father, it would soon be healed.

Across from him sat Lisette. She and Gerald had arrived only a few minutes before they were scheduled to come in to dinner. Blanchette, no less obstreperous despite her age and the able assistance of Colette, was about to begin a harangue on the possibility of an overcooked roast. With Lisette and Gerald appeared a little girl of about ten walking between them and holding tightly onto their hands. Her long, glossy, dark brown hair, tied with a blue bow, hung below her waist, and her dark, almost black, almond-shaped eyes were opened wide in either fear or amazement. She was a beautiful child, and Leah couldn't take her eyes off her.

"Who—who is she?" Leah reached out her hand, and the little girl moved to hide behind Lisette.

"We'll tell you when we're inside," Lisette said, "with both you and Papa."

They went into the library where Jean had opened the first bottle of their 1906 vintage champagne.

"Welcome, welcome," Baptiste said when Lisette ran over to embrace him and Gerald shook his hand. "Blanchette was about to have a fit, but then she usually does."

623

"I'm sorry we're late," Lisette said, "but we had a little trouble with the car." She was well aware that everyone's eyes were focused on the little girl. "Now, I want all of you to meet Mary—not Marie—but Mary. And be prepared for a real surprise. She is Nicole's daughter."

Leah made no attempt to hold back her tears, and she saw Baptiste reach in his pocket for a handkerchief and wipe his eyes.

"Nicole had a child?" Leah's voice was somewhere between a whisper and a sob. "No wonder she is so beautiful. And, oh, I can see the resemblance. I should have known when I first saw her."

Leah held out her arms, but Mary would come no farther than the side of her chair.

"This is your grandmother, Mary," Lisette said gently.

"How do you do," Mary said, very rigidly polite for a girl of ten.

"Give her a little time," Leah suggested. "There are so many of us here and all strangers." She looked up at Lisette. "How did you know? And how did you find her?"

"It's a long story. Will dinner wait?"

"Indeed it will. Céline, will you please go and ask Blanchette to put the hot food in the warming oven. And keep the other things chilled. I have no idea how soon we'll be sitting down to eat."

"You probably remember, Mama," Lisette began, "that I once made the rash statement I didn't want any children. To my sorrow, the gods must have heard me and decided to grant my wish. Gerald and I have been thinking for some time of adopting a child. I do a bit of volunteer work for the Sisters of Charity, especially in connection with the orphanages. Bazaars, that sort of thing. Anyway, one day I mentioned our idea to the Mother Superior of the home near Paris. For some reason I also happened to mention Nicole's name on one of my visits, and told the Mother Superior a little about Nicole's life in Paris and her death. I wondered for a few minutes why she began asking me for more details about the years Nicole had been in Paris and the year she died.

"You can imagine my shock when she said she thought Nicole's daughter, now ten years old, was with them. She began telling me about Mary. Her mother had brought her to them as an infant, maybe six months old, saying she could no longer provide for her. They knew only her given name. Nicole had refused to reveal either her last name or that of

624

the father, so they had presumed the baby was illegitimate. Her mother, however, did visit her, once a month, until Mary was three or four years old. That, of course, corresponds with the time Nicole was killed. They assumed the mother had moved away and was no longer able to come out there. They did not know she was dead.

"I wanted to believe that Mary was Nicole's daughter, but I knew I would not be satisfied until I had some proof. By this time, though, I had seen her and was determined to adopt her whether or not she was Nicole's. The Mother Superior was as anxious as I to determine who Mary was. She brought out a locket and asked if I might know what was engraved on the back. I thought a moment, and then I said, 'The initials N.A.F. and the date June 3, 1892.' I remembered that you gave each of the girls a locket on her sixteenth birthday. A locket for the girls and a watchfob for the boys. The date and the initials were there. Then she brought out the rag doll that Nicole cherished. Remember? Nicole took it with her the first time she ran away."

"Nissi," Leah whispered.

"And Mary has kept it all these years," Lisette said.

Leah could not resist holding out her arms again, and this time Mary came into them. She put her arms around Leah's neck and snuggled against her as if knowing that here she could find the love and the family she'd missed all these years. Leah held her close, unable to say anything. Mary was not Nicole, but at least Nicole was not completely lost to them. She had left them something as beautiful and precious as herself. When Mary was a little older, she could be given the full-length portrait of Nicole, so she'd know how very beautiful her mother was and how much she resembled her.

"And so, Mama," Lisette continued, "we've adopted her. She's the child Gerald and I could never have, and she's so very precious to us."

Leah looked at Mary, sitting between Denise and Denise's nine-year-old daughter, Jeannine. The two little girls were giggling over some secret joke. *She already feels a part of the family,* Leah thought. She'd been with Gerald and Lisette for nearly a month, and how wise they'd been to postpone bringing her to the château until cousins her own age would be present. Children have such a wonderfully ingenuous way of putting each other at ease. Leah noticed she wasn't the only one who couldn't look away from Mary. Baptiste was finding it hard to concentrate on his food, and he'd already won Mary over by telling her that he was going to take her on a personal tour of the house after dinner and show her all her mother's paintings.

Mary, however, was not the only surprise to make Leah's seventieth birthday something special.

Earlier that week, when Colette had come out to the garden to say there was a caller waiting in the hall to see her, Leah gathered up the flowers she'd been picking and hurried into the sunroom.

"Here, Colette, put these in water. I'll arrange them later."

"Yes, ma'am. I would have told Monsieur Fontaine—the man asked for both of you—but he's still in his dressing room."

"That's all right, Colette. I'll see the visitor myself."

Who in the world, Leah wondered, would come out to the château to see them without sending word first? Or for that matter, ask to see her without giving Colette his name?

She walked into the hall and held out her hand to greet the man. There was something familiar about the face behind the large, graying mustache and neatly trimmed beard, but she couldn't place it.

"Don't tell me you've forgotten me after all these years, Mama."

"Henri! My God, is it really you?" If his arms hadn't already grabbed her into a bear hug, she might have collapsed onto the floor.

"It is, Mama. Nothing was going to keep me away from your birthday this year."

"Let me look at you. I can't really believe you're here." His hair was turning gray and receding slightly from his forehead, but otherwise, she realized now, he hadn't changed very much. In his neatly tailored, conservative suit, he looked very much the successful executive. "Why didn't you let us know?"

Leah's eyes began watering and she wiped them on her sleeve.

"Here, Mama." He handed her a handkerchief. "I haven't forgotten you never have one when you need it."

"You should have sent word," she said, chiding and hugging him at the same time.

"I wanted to see the expression on your face when I walked in. And," he laughed and hugged her tighter, "it was worth the wait. For a minute there I thought you were going to faint."

"And if I had, I would never have forgiven you. Now, for goodness sake, I'd better go tell Papa. We don't want him falling out of his wheel chair."

"Does he walk much anymore?" Henri asked more seriously.

"Almost never. The prostheses are very uncomfortable, so he's really given up using them, even when he goes to the city. His office staff gave a dinner in his honor a few months ago, and I think that was the last time he wore them. But he gets around amazingly well in the chair."

Henri followed Leah into the bedroom.

"Baptiste," she called through the dressing-room door, "come see who's out here. Don't worry if you're not finished dressing. And be prepared for a shock."

"Henri!" Baptiste said the minute he wheeled through the door. "Damn, but it's good to see you!"

"There," Henri said with a grin. "He knew me right away. I'm ashamed of you, Mama, not even recognizing your own child."

"And I'm sure you'll never let me forget it, either. Now, tell us all about everything—Louise and the children and your business."

"Louise and the children are fine. I've brought pictures, of course. I knew you'd want to see what your American grandchildren look like. They wanted to come with me, but we're building a new home in the hills north of Detroit, and Louise is very busy with decorators and selecting new furniture."

"I understand," Leah said.

"Papa," Henri said, changing the subject abruptly, "you'll be fascinated with what our company is producing. But I'll talk to you about that later. Mama wouldn't be interested in all the mechanical details." He took the cigar Baptiste offered and lit up. "By the way, how's the firm doing with the Bestcraft contract?"

"Filling up our ships. Robert was sorry you missed the race. It had a rather spectacular ending."

"So he wrote me," Henri said.

"If you'll excuse me," Baptiste said, "stay here and talk to Mama while I finish dressing." He wheeled his chair around and rolled into the dressing room.

"How long will you be here?" Leah asked.

"I'll stay at least a week." He pulled on the cigar and looked out the window toward the garden. "You know, of course, why I didn't bring Louise."

627

"I think so. How did you manage to get away without her?"

"I told her it was a business trip," Henri said. "No time for sightseeing and she'd be bored to death. It is true we're building; and she's so involved with the house, she didn't insist. Can you understand, Mama, why I did what I did?"

"I'd be the last one not to understand, Henri. After all, I fled North, too, out of a desperate desire to 'pass' and to live in a society that had been denied me all my life. I would probably have stayed if James had lived and if I hadn't loved your father so much. Yet, there was always that unspoken fear."

"I know; I live with it, too. And it's kept me an exile from all of you. I didn't dare invite Robert up for a visit. I knew he was hurt, but he never said a word while we were together those few days in New York."

"Well, Robert doesn't exactly agree with you, but he realizes that you and he see things differently."

Henri stood up and walked to the window. "He thinks I'm ashamed of you, Mama, and I'm not. You have to believe that."

"I never thought you were," Leah said. "Come, sit back down." She waited until he was seated on the couch next to her, and she took his hand. "I've had six children, seven counting Lisette, who has been like my own since she was a few months old. One of the hardest, but one of the most important things for a mother to learn is that her children are not all alike. You are as different from Jean as Robert is from you. And, God knows, no two girls could have been more unalike than Denise and Nicole. There's no point in trying to explain it, since you all have the same parents and the same rearing. It can't be done. Oh, we might come up with little, insignificant reasons, but the truth is, everyone is an individual."

Leah paused for a moment and then continued. "Strangely enough, Nicole said that very thing to Gerald once when he asked her why she was so different. She said everyone was different but most people didn't realize it. I think, maybe, when he told me that, I was able to understand for the first time why she'd left home. I guess what I'm trying to say is that all a parent can do is love her children for who and what they are. And I'm also trying to say that you've never stopped being my son, and I've never stopped loving you."

"Thank you, Mama. I'm only sorry I waited so long and had to travel so many miles to hear you say that."

Leah watched him unbutton his suit coat and heard his deep sigh. Henri had been fearful about coming home, she knew, perhaps dreading a hostile reception and unwanted questions. She knew that his desire to escape from his maternal heritage was only a very small part of the drive that had sent him to the States. In his own way, he was as independent as Nicole. From the time he was a child, he had striven to be the best student, to invent things no one else had thought about, and, as an adult, to rise to the top of his profession. Second best was never good enough for him.

He'd been right about not staying in France, she now believed. Here he would always have been his father's son, the heir apparent. Henri wanted to found his own dynasty, and she couldn't fault him for that. He'd inherited his pride from both her and Baptiste. The fact that he'd wanted to come home and to have him here now was far more important than why he'd left in the first place.

Leah reached over and patted Henri's hand, which was resting on the table to her right. Without turning his head, he squeezed her hand and kept on talking to Gilles, Denise and Edouard's sixteen-year-old son. Gilles, another of the family fascinated by motors and gasoline engines, had already taken apart Leah's car twice, under dire threats that it had better work properly when he was finished or his grandfather would skin him alive. Henri was explaining the workings of the gasoline-driven dumbwaiter he'd invented when he was no older than Gilles—and which was still working—and Gilles was just as intently trying to explain the ways he thought it could be improved.

"All right," Henri said. "You show me after dinner, and we'll see what we can do while I'm here."

Leah's glance automatically sought out Mary, who was now smiling up at Denise and answering some question her aunt had put to her. Plump, matronly Denise. Of all of them, Leah supposed her life had turned out to be exactly what she'd wanted from the time she was a little girl. She was happily married to the man she loved. If she didn't have the hundred children she used to talk about, she had six she could be very proud of. Jeannine's birth in 1902 indeed had been the beginning of a second family, with Josianne arriving in 1908 and the baby, Robbie, just a year ago. Robbie was sitting in a highchair beside Edouard, and no one could be a more doting father than he was. Young Edouard, though only eighteen, had already taken over the management of most of their winery. He was as much in love with the vineyards as Gilles was with engines, so Denise and Edouard had no worry about who would carry on the family business.

Laughter from her left made Leah turn her head to where Éliane, Denise's oldest daughter, was helping with Robert's two little ones, Leah Angelique and Pierre.

What a wonderful reunion it had been when Robert, Felicité, and the two children arrived the day after Henri.

"Here we are," Robert had said. He leaned down to kiss Baptiste and then picked his mother up and swung her around. "All four of us."

"Gracious, Robert, put me down. Felicité will think you have no respect for your old mother."

"Felicité," Robert said, putting his arm around his wife, "these are my wonderful parents. My mother who, as you have just witnessed, claims she's old, though she's not, and my father, who is still almost as handsome as I am."

"Welcome, welcome to our family, Felicité," Leah said. "You don't know how much it means to me to see you at last."

"I don't know where you found someone as pretty as this," Baptiste said, after Felicité, too, went over and kissed him. "If she ever gets tired of your nonsense, there's a place for her right here."

Making an obvious point of ignoring his father's last remark, Robert said, "And this is Leah Angelique." Leah could not repress a smile when the little girl dropped into an awkward curtsy. "And this is Pierre." Pierre came out from behind his mother's skirts, then stuck his thumb in his mouth and retreated behind them again.

"What a wonderful family," Leah said. "My, I can't believe that almost our whole family will be here for Thursday night. Did you know that Henri arrived yesterday?"

"So the old bastard finally decided to come," Robert declared.

"Robert!" Baptiste said. "What a thing to call your brother."

"All in fun, Papa. It'll be good to see him again."

Felicité finally gave in to Pierre's pleadings and picked him up. "Mama said to give you her very best."

"Yes, you'll have to tell me all about her. It's hard to believe that you're the daughter of Sophia, one of my students. But come, I'm forgetting my manners. I know you'll want to get settled in your rooms."

"Splendid, Mama," Robert said, "we'll be down as soon as we've cleaned up a bit."

Leah watched while Robert led his family up the stairs. "What do you think, Baptiste?"

"I think the boy has done very well for himself. She's a lovely girl. He didn't make a mistake when he fell in love with her."

No, he didn't, Leah thought, *especially since he plans to stay in New Orleans, at least for a few years.* She'd never gotten over the feeling that there had been an earlier romance with someone he couldn't marry. Now that she'd met Felicité, she would cease wondering if he'd married her on the rebound; obviously, he was deeply in love with her.

After the arrival of Jean and Denise and their families, the house was filled with chatter and laughter that had Leah almost bursting with happiness. In one room, Denise and Céline were comparing household notes with Felicité, as if they'd known her all their lives. In another, Baptiste and his sons and sons-in-law were listening to Henri describe his work in America, and then in turn explaining to him how to make champagne. And the grandchildren were everywhere! Leah went from one room to another and then joined the children playing in the garden. She had a perpetual smile on her face the entire time.

Leah came out of her reverie to find Baptiste looking across at her with a twinkle in his eye and the smile that could still melt her heart. With his head of wavy white hair and white mustache, he was still as handsome as the evening she met him at the quadroon ball. He winked at her, and she could feel herself blushing. If the children could see into her mind now!

While they were undressing for bed the night before, she'd been sitting at her dressing table and taking down her hair. Unexpectedly, Baptiste called to her.

"Come sit next to me and let me brush it for you." He patted the bed invitingly.

She went to him and handed him the brush, and he began running it through her long, still thick and glossy white hair. "Umm, that feels good," she said.

With laughter in his eyes, he said, "Don't let me forget to put the brush on the table. I wouldn't want to leave it on the bed and roll over on it again."

Leah knew all too well he was referring to the night, years and years earlier, when he'd stopped in the middle of brushing her hair to pull her down on the bed and make love to her. He'd rolled over on the brush and jumped up screaming that he'd been stabbed. From then on, when he brushed her hair, it was an unspoken invitation.

"Why, Baptiste Fontaine, it's been a long day and you should be exhausted. Can't you ever remember how old you are?"

"No, because all that matters is how old I feel." He put his arms around her and bit her gently on the back of her neck. "I'll never be too old to make love to my beautiful wife."

"Nor I to want you," she said.

Leah loved to be loved by Baptiste. She still found intense pleasure and gratification in their intimate moments. After all this time, their lovemaking had never become hurried or routine or mundane, or just something to do before going to sleep. They had been lovers for more than fifty years, yet some nuance, some small act, some touch made each time unique. Sometimes Baptiste made her laugh. Sometimes he shocked her, but the result had been to keep their love new, their passion intense.

Leah had long since come to realize that their lovemaking was a ritual in the truest, deepest meaning of the word. It was an outward and visible expression of an inward and spiritual devotion.

When later, relaxed and filled with love, Leah lay beside Baptiste, she thought she'd never known such happiness and contentment.

"What are you thinking about," Baptiste asked, "lying there and smiling to yourself in the dark?"

"How do you know I'm smiling?"

"Because I've seen you when it isn't dark, and you always smile right afterward. That's about the finest boost there is to a man's ego."

"I was thinking about the first night you made love to me. I'll never forget it. I was so terribly frightened."

"Of me? Of making love?"

"No, of relinquishing so much of myself. And of becoming something I'd sworn I never would. I think I knew then that when I gave myself to you, I could never really belong to anyone else."

"Any regrets?"

"None," Leah said. "Believe me, darling, there are no regrets. I used to plan what I wanted my life to be." She laughed. "But now I think I prefer letting things happen as they will."

Baptiste slid one arm under her head and the other around her waist. "Love me?"

"No, I've been living with you all these years only because you have such a terrific sense of humor."

"You wound me!" He moved his hand from her waist and slapped his chest. "Not because I'm a great lover?"

"If you're hinting that you'd like me to enumerate all the reasons I love you, we'll be awake until morning. Will this suffice instead?" She leaned over and kissed him.

"It will do for a start." He reached across and pulled her toward him again.

No, Leah thought as she winked back across the table at Baptiste, there are no regrets. There had been soul-rending tragedies: the deaths of René, Nicole, and Fleur. There had been lesser ones like Henri's decision to live in America, Lisette's first marriage and her life in England, and Armand's disappearance. But there had been a multiplicity of joys: the happy marriages for Jean, Denise, Henri, Robert, and, finally, for Lisette. Her life had not been without its sorrow, true, but each sorrow had engendered new hope, new promises, and new life. With Baptiste still beside her and surrounded by her children and grandchildren, she knew she had been more blessed than deprived throughout her long, rich life. She and Baptiste had seen their love flower with their children, and now they could rejoice in the bountiful harvest that love had produced.